I0602163

Ashes: Book Two of the Ascension Saga is a work of fiction. Names, characters, places, and incidents either are the product of the author's own imagination or are used fictitiously. Any resemblance to actual persons, living or dead, events, or locales is entirely coincidental. Likewise, if the work displays any resemblance to any other work of fiction or nonfiction, it is entirely coincidental.



First paperback edition: August, 2021
Second paperback edition: April 2022
Third paperback edition: October 2023

*Cover text by Brock Mays*
*Cover illustrations by Jessica Nielsen*
*Illustrations by Jessica Nielsen and Alessandro Rocco*
*Maps by Brock Mays*

ISBN: 978-1-7338165-3-3
Website: bit.ly/theascensionsaga
Instagram: @BrockMaysAuthor

# TO YOU
## FOR GETTING THROUGH IT ALL

Doftaan
Akademrajon
The University of Doftaan
Talohiran Embassy
Vydraka
Čahmadoška
Palace of the Empress of Blood
Thannish Embassy
Ceveržapath
The Wingling House
Naraka
Jempratanrajon
Eastern Prison
Zvužajecy
Kurashian Embassy
The Boulevards
Shrine to the Goddesses
Malakurash
The Spires of Doftaan
Maranparkh
The Church of Elfris
Paudzuhoth
Paudbramah
Kaljacjana
Dubovparkh
Southern Prison
Doftaan Hospital

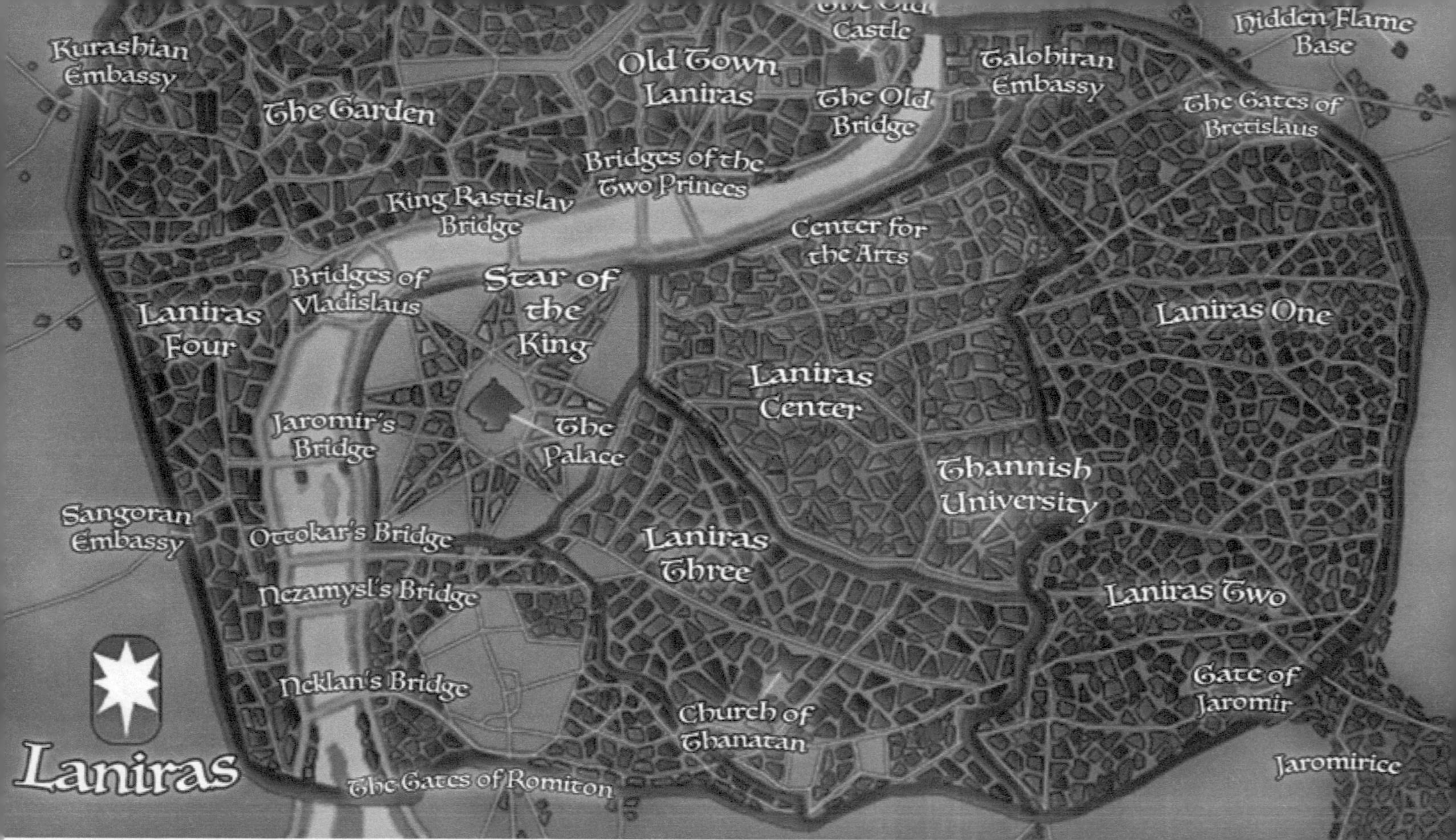

Laniras

Kurashian Embassy

The Garden

Sangoran Embassy

Laniras Four

Bridges of Vladislav

King Rastislav Bridge

Neklan's Bridge

Oreokar's Bridge

Nezamysl's Bridge

Jaromir's Bridge

Star of the King

The Palace

Bridges of the Two Princes

Old Gown

Laniras

The Old Bridge

Galobiran Embassy

The Gates of Breslaus

Hidden Flame Base

The Old Castle

The Gates of Romiton

Church of Ghanaan

Laniras Three

Laniras Center

Center for the Arts

Ghannish University

Laniras One

Laniras Two

Gate of Jaromir

Jaromirite

Island Fortress
Port District
The Plains of Balgorod
Industrial District
Residential District
Eastern Slums
Prison Complex
New Balgorod
Southern Slums
Jan Żyznacz
Karpaskaż
Balgorod

# Table of Contents

# ASHES

## BOOK TWO OF THE ASCENSION SAGA

### BROCK MAYS

# CHAPTER ONE
# A KNIFE IN THE SHADOWS

The soothing melody of rain's lullaby sang to the souls of those asleep within the palace of Doftaan, and a rumble of thunder in the distance masked the sound of footsteps that did not belong.

Sometime during the night, Mistress Ihrin Deleanu had cast a twisted silver goblet aside and fallen asleep. Its scarlet contents now stained her opulent bedsheets and had pooled on the marble floor beneath the Mistress of Dusk's bed.

Mistress Ihrin shrieked as a blade pierced her chest, and her dark wings shot out to both sides, knocking the goblet to the floor. In a drunken and confused stupor, she clawed at her attacker but felt her strength slip away as the knife from the shadows flashed one last time in the candlelight.

She let out her final, gurgling breath and then was still. The assassin turned away as silent as the shadow of nightfall, leaving her to lie in blood and wine.

Sometime later, the Empress of Blood's elegant cloak fluttered behind her as she stormed back into the council chamber to take her place at the half-moon table.

The rest of her councilors, the Mistresses of Dusk, were already seated in uncharacteristic silence. The somber mood inside the chamber reflected the storms outside, and every clap of thunder set each of the Mistresses of Dusk on edge.

One seat was empty.

"Killed in her own chambers—and who knows how long it took for her servants to find her," said Mara after a terse moment of silence. "This was supposed to be a happy meeting about the festival and Peace Summit—not—aghh."

She trailed off, resting her elbow on the table, rubbing her eyes with thumb and forefinger.

"Then are we all suspect?" asked Mistress Raluca as she eyed a massive ring on Florenta's finger. The gem seemed to be caked in dried blood.

Mara did not answer as her gaze wandered across each of her councilors. The spawn of the traitorous Mistress Delia, Antanasia. The young and beautiful Raluca, sister of Mara's predecessor, Queen Codruta. The greedy, gluttonous, Florenta. General Anca, the military genius known as the Nightmare of Thanatanos. Mara's advisor and lieutenant, Vasilica. And finally, Lavinia, the cunning woman who Mara believed had orchestrated the death of Valistaran Talohir and thereby given her the thrones of both Talohira and Sangora. A trusted friend. Did that make her even more suspect?

"If Ihrin still drew breath, she would be the one I would accuse. She always envied the rest of us," said Florenta.

Mara chuckled to herself, for the woman's hands looked naked when they weren't wielding a leg of some roast beast. Mistress Raluca crossed her arms and shook her head.

"So quick to make an accusation," she replied. "Trying to save your own massive hide?"

"I am only providing ideas!" shouted Florenta who opened her mouth to speak again, but the Empress of Blood cut her off before she could form a sentence.

"To be clear, I haven't accused any of you. Not yet." Mara traced the beautiful, sprawling design of vines and stars on the table's face with her finger. "However, with Mistress Ihrin gone, the state of Adess is now without a governor. We need to discuss that, but I have two other reasons for calling you all here. I thank you all for arriving so swiftly. I know there are matters in your states that require your attention. First, I summoned you here for your help."

"Because you're scared," said Florenta.

The rest of the members of the council straightened up at this defiance toward their empress.

"Yes, Florenta. Believe it or not, I am scared. I am *terrified.* But fear doesn't make me unworthy of my throne. Instead, it gives me a chance to overcome something. Frankly, you would be stupid not to be scared too," Mara said. "Especially you,

Florenta, with tensions in Karpaska as high as they are. Mind your place."

"Yes, Empress," Florenta said, her tone reluctant.

Mara took a moment to collect her thoughts. "Someone found their way into Ihrin's chambers in the middle of the day while she slept and slaughtered her without her guards giving notice. She was not perfect, Florenta, no. None of us are. Far from it, but she will be mourned by her people. Would *you* be?"

Florenta, along with everyone else, remained silent.

"Yes, I fear for my life, but even more, I fear for *your* lives and for the lives of our people." Mara scooted her goblet closer but took no drink as if to signal she was done speaking.

"Do you think it is an assassin from Thanatanos?" asked Vasilica, speaking up for the first time. "A revenge killing, perhaps? I think they're sending us a message for the siege of Laniras two years ago."

"It's definitely possible. Many of the forces I led into the city of Nitra were from Adess. Vengeance for the death of Prince Xanthurias, perhaps—It's a bit of a stretch, though," said Mara. "But I think—I think that fallen country is now far too worried about feeding its own people to send anyone here and risk another war. The last one only ended due to the lack of will to keep fighting. None of us are ready for another war. We've even accepted Thannish refugees into Sangoran Talohira. No, I think this is from within. I do not suspect any of you."

"Talohira is in shambles," said Anca. "The people there are suffering just like those in Thanatanos. The people feel the refugees are straining their resources; there are revolts now too, worse even than those that happened after Valistaran's death. Perhaps—"

"Although we have enjoyed over two years of peace and prosperity under Empress Mara's reign, Anca is right. We have to do something about the unrest in Talohira," Raluca said, cutting off the general's comment. "What about the Walkers?"

Lavinia raised a lazy finger as a sign she wished to say something. Mara nodded to Anca in acknowledgment of the problem in Sangoran Talohira, and then she gestured to Lavinia, granting her permission to speak.

"Walker bloodlines commonly grant teleportation powers," added Lavinia. "And Ronin Jakoni is, shall I say, bold, after all."

Mara raised an eyebrow. "The Lord of all Walkers stole the weapon my late fiancé so desperately wanted to find. Why not use it to kill all of us? Why slay only one Mistress of Dusk when he is in possession of something much more sinister?"

"How do we know he didn't kill my mother with it?" asked Mistress Antanasia. "After all, we don't know what that weapon does, or if it or the Deadlands even exist!"

The group nodded in unspoken agreement. Mara glanced over her shoulder as if to check whether Ronin Jakoni or one of his followers were behind her. She sighed, exasperated at the mad conspiracy theory about the Deadlands. She made eye contact with Lavinia, for she had accompanied her to the Deadlands two years prior and seen the weapon itself.

"Mistress Antanasia, I have seen the weapon with my own eyes. We will deal with your penchant for conspiracy later. However, without any other proof, we will have to assume that

Ronin Jakoni is behind Ihrin's assassination," said the empress. She paused for a moment. "I suggest we set a trap for the Lord of the Walkers and his assassin."

"What are you proposing?" asked Florenta. "And who will be the bait?"

"One of us," said Mara. "I know that at this time, none of us trust one another. For that reason, I'll have someone else, someone who isn't on this council, select who will be, as Florenta so sensitively put it, the bait. I hope that by putting us all at risk we can not only prove our own innocence but root out any traitors amongst us."

There was an uneasy stirring from the Mistresses of Dusk, but it soon turned to a feeling of lackluster agreement. Although none of them desired to risk their own lives, they each knew it was the best course of action.

"Messengers will bring each of you details regarding the upcoming Blood Festival and the Peace Summit with Thanatanos. I wished to discuss it now, but given the circumstances, it didn't seem appropriate," Mara said before adjourning the meeting by standing and gesturing to the door. Her councilors filed out of the room one by one in silence. Only Lavinia stayed behind, still seated. She swung her legs up to rest them on the council table.

"Mara, you know I have always been honest with you," she said as Florenta shoved her way past Raluca and General Anca.

"You have. And you know I have always considered you a friend," said Mara. "But I also know that you hate every single one these women. And to be honest, I don't blame you." They shared a laugh. "I still have to consider you, Vinia, but please know that you aren't my top suspect."

She chose to use the shortened form of Lavinia's name to add a softness to her statement.

"I know that," replied Lavinia, folding her arms, "but I want to share some information about Lord Jakoni that an agent of mine delivered to me not long ago."

"Why didn't you—"

"Because I believe he is working with one of them," hissed Lavinia, gesturing with her head toward the doorway.

"Who?" asked Mara. Lavinia shrugged and shook her head before reaching over to grab what was left of her wine. It was empty, so she took a sip from Raluca's goblet.

"Could be any of them. I had spies follow each of them," said Lavinia, taking another swig. "Under the cover of day, they all met while we slept. They met without me but more importantly, without *you*."

The phrase seemed strange to Mara. Most Sangorans slept during the day and were awake at night, but phrases like "the cover of day" still surprised her.

"Why didn't they invite you?" the empress asked. Lavinia once again shook her head.

"I learned of this four nights ago," said Lavinia. "I believe something happened in that meeting that made the others angry. I think one of them had Ihrin killed."

"How does this connect to Ronin?" asked Mara.

"Because one of my contacts was a Walker," said Lavinia. "There are traitors on all sides, my dear empress."

"You hate the Walkers," said Mara. She raised an eyebrow and folded her arms. "That day they tried to take my blood for some scheme—"

"I hate *some* of the Walkers. Ronin and his ilk failed to take your blood thanks to me," said Lavinia, "but even I make mistakes. Where I was successful in saving your life, I failed to stop them from capturing *another* Wingling converted sometime after you were—one that was as compatible with their plans as you were back then. Surprise, surprise, you weren't their 'chosen one.' Sorry."

"What else did your agent tell you?" asked Mara.

"A great many things," said Lavinia. "My informant has led me to believe that the other Mistresses of Dusk are meeting with Ronin Jakoni and his minions after performing the Ceremony of Exsanguination to develop a weapon against you using that Wingling's blood."

"I'm sorry, what?"

"Exsanguination—to drain all of someone's blood," Lavinia said. "You remember, they tried to do the same to you."

"Yes, and of course, you know the word for *draining someone of all their blood*," Mara said. She paused, thinking. "But I still don't understand. Why leave you out?"

"It's no great secret that we're allies and no secret that I am not as close with them as I once was under Codruta. Even then, our relationship was strenuous at best. They want to break the spell called the Queen's Control. That blood-draining ceremony was the first step."

Mara's eyes shot up.

"I know that you are familiar with it. I know that you opened Codruta's grave, and I know that you can command us with a thought."

"I have never—"

"I know. *Can* command us, not *have*. I know you haven't compelled me, but, as you know, rumors fly fast. Especially amongst the Mistresses of Dusk," said Lavinia. "Mara. I believe that either Raluca or Florenta is behind the attack. They, along with myself, are the only Mistresses who have been in their position longer than yourself. They feel entitled. And then, there is Antanasia…"

Mara nodded. She had been appointed at the same time as Anca, and Vasilica was a trusted follower. Anca was a warrior; she had no desire to rule. Antanasia, on the other hand, was appointed to her position after her mother, Delia, had attempted to usurp Mara and take her armies to Thanatanos. Mara had killed her by coercing her with the Queen's Control to walk from a cliff. Talk of a revenge killing seemed possible.

She wondered to herself if Lavinia knew that. Of course she did. She seemed to know everything. Mara selected Antanasia for the simple reason that her tribe had a tradition of passing the title down from mother to daughter, and she didn't yet feel sure enough of her authority to upset such a tradition. She regretted the decision immediately.

"I killed Delia," Mara blurted out.

"I know. Be careful, my empress," said Lavinia as she stood to exit. Mara nodded, a forlorn look of thanks on her haunted visage.

"Thanks, Vinia."

The Empress of Blood watched Lavinia leave without more than a nod. She looked at each of the Mistresses' unique thrones around the halfmoon table, lost in thought.

As she made her way from the chamber, she saw Florenta still waddling down the hall, shouting orders to some servants. Mara leaned on the doorway and wondered if Florenta and the other Mistresses of Dusk had already discovered how to break their connection to their queen. Mara knew the Walkers had to remove their wings to remove the connection to the Queen's Control—unless, like Lavinia said, Florenta and Ronin found another way.

The Empress of Blood decided to test her power for the first time in two years. She reached out with her hand as if to guide her power toward Florenta and whispered five simple words.

"Rip out your own heart."

Nothing happened. Mara could tell that their minds were connected, but she could not coerce the Mistress of Dusk. Mara glowered at Florenta's turned back before retiring to her throne room, her thoughts dark.

Just before the meeting, she had instructed Elena, her handmaiden from the Wingling House, to set a trap for Ihrin's killer. She had alluded to the plan in the meeting but did not reveal that the trap had already been set, ready to be sprung at any time. As Mara peeked around the thick curtain over the window, she could see that the sun was already creeping over the horizon. She knew that she was in for a restless day.

She retired to her throne room, following the crimson rug to her gilded seat and collapsed, completely exhausted. She grabbed the spear that rested nearby, expecting the assassin to jump out from behind one of the many pillars supporting the chamber's high, arched ceiling.

She fought to keep her eyes open, glancing around the empty room as her eyelids drooped shut. Hours passed by, and her chin jerked up as she awoke with a start. She was still alone. She nestled against the side of her throne and drifted off again, feeling safe.

She woke up yet again to see that her chamber was no longer empty. In the center of the room stood a still figure cloaked in a dark hood. She scrambled up in shock, and at that moment, the stranger advanced as if giving her the courtesy to wake up before dying. Without hesitation, Mara clapped her hands together, sending a bolt of blinding white lightning toward her foe. The man, creature, or whatever it was, leapt away with the skill of a trained assassin before vanishing in a jet of black smoke.

The attacker reappeared a moment later at Mara's side and lashed out with twin daggers which narrowly missed their target. Mara felt the blades brush her skin, and she clapped her wings downward, striking her foe on both sides of the neck. The assassin cried out in shock. A man's voice.

Lightning twisted around Mara's arms as she thrust her palms into her foe's chest. With a cry, she unleashed a surge of crackling white energy, tossing the assassin backward; he twitched and spasmed as Mara electrocuted him. The electricity of Mara's attack traveled in conductive channels of metal decoration on the floor, transforming the entire room into a cage of lightning; she took flight to avoid getting caught in her own trap, but the assassin cried out in agony. His voice was familiar, but she failed to place where she had heard it.

The Empress of Blood wasted no time. She leapt upon her disoriented foe and raked her bladed wings across his abdomen. He stumbled backward and vanished in the Walkers' signature teleportation mist. However, the magic seemed forced, painful, even, and he could not travel far. Mara unleashed two more bolts of energy into the ground as she took flight again, bathing the room in blinding light for the second time.

"I've got you," she muttered as the assassin convulsed on the ground. The Empress of Blood roared in anger as she channeled as much energy into the floor as she could muster, but she was losing strength fast.

The man managed to teleport into the air above her and continuously disappeared and reappeared in the same spot, imitating flight to avoid the electrified ground.

"Who are you?!" Mara shouted, continuing her onslaught, knowing her foe had no way to escape the electrified chamber. Mara reached out with the full might of the Queen's Control and her telepathic powers in an attempt to tear into the man's mind and force him to answer, although she knew the Queen's Control would have no effect on a Walker or human.

*Kill…. Empress…*

Mara groaned as the flow of electricity waned. The assassin collapsed to the floor, and Mara stumbled to her feet, her vision blurred and darkened by the abrupt absence of the blinding light.

She reached out with one hand and with her very soul, grasping the man's mind, only to grasp part of one more word.

*...Leksand....*

"What?" cried Mara.

Although she could not make out his entire thought, there was only one word he could have been thinking. Aleksander. Had he sent the assassin? Another thought entered her mind: was that runaway boy in her village, who she had later met by fate in the Talohiran slave camp trying to kill her? The thought grasped her heart and would not let go.

After a moment of respite, she readied another bolt of energy, but the assassin, whether it was Aleksander or a Walker, disappeared, materializing next to the darkened window. With a final burst of strength, he smashed through the glass with his shoulder in a shower of glass. He vanished in a puff of dark smoke, and daylight poured into the chamber.

Mara stumbled backward, unable to cope with what had just happened. The realization choked her, and she collapsed against the edge of her throne. She buried her face in her hands and whispered his name into the cold, dark stillness.

*"Aleksander?"*

CHAPTER TWO

# NEW STARTS AND REUNIONS

Apolinarius Bartunek, better known as Pol to his friends, sprinted over the craggy hillside overlooking the capital city of Laniras. Much of the city had been rebuilt since the end of the war, but this was the first time he'd seen the progress from this vantage point. He stared in awe for a few moments at the majesty of the towers and mighty walls. The moment of admiration he allowed himself ended, and his feet carried him back to the caravan.

In his pouch, he carried two messages: one addressed to King Verahim Romus and another, an answer to the first's author: Empress Mara Bartunek. As the messenger of the king of Thanatanos and the Empress's little brother, he felt a sense of pride and importance in being chosen to carry such important correspondence.

After King Verahim had read Mara's letter, he had agreed to send the caravan, including Pol, straight to Doftaan, capital of Sangora to meet with Mara, as per her request. The caravan was made up of members of the Hidden Flame, a collection of diplomats, warriors, and others sent to represent the king. The caravan had departed from the Hidden Flame's base in the hills outside Laniras with all haste.

"Master Rehor!" cried Pol as he caught up to the caravan, drawing the message from his pouch and hoisting it into the air. Spotting the young man, Rehor leapt to his feet with surprising agility for one of his age, clapped his hands, and limped toward his friend.

"It's good to see you!" said Rehor.

He had gained some weight since escaping the slave camp in Talohira, which only added to his jolly demeanor. Always a voice of reason, Rehor had proven himself as a worthy diplomat while residing in the nearby Sangoran state of Timishuara for the better part of the last year. As King Verahim's official messenger, Pol had been the one sent to inform Rehor that he had been selected as the Thannish ambassador to Sangora.

"That's quite the bundle you've got there," Rehor said, gesturing to the heavy pack on Pol's back.

"Oh, yeah. Didn't know how much underwear to bring. I mean, it's not *all* underwear, I brought all sorts of stuff I might need—" He stopped himself. "Hey, I have to mention how much I like your hat," said Pol, pointing at Rehor's crimson, wide-brimmed hat. It curved up on one side and featured quite the elegant, white feather. "Makes you look like a pirate."

"If that makes you happy, I am glad I picked this one," Rehor said with a chuckle. "I thought it made me look the part of an ambassador, not a pirate, but perhaps I should pursue such a path since I surely don't feel worthy of my post quite yet. Oh, and by the way, I too, brought enough underwear to fill my pack. A life lesson I once learned—one can never have too much underwear."

Pol laughed. He had always felt a connection with Rehor, not because they themselves were close friends, but because while enslaved in the Talohiran camp, Rehor had become like a father to his sister, Mara. In the time that had elapsed since they had lost her, Pol had taken the older man as a mentor of sorts as well, training with him as a diplomatic aide in addition to his messenger duties, but they rarely discussed Mara or what had happened to her. As Pol began to speak again, another voice filled the air.

"Hello, there," said Shanthah Kalen as he became visible.

"Shanthah!" cried Rehor. "I'll never get used to you doing that, as good as it is to see you."

"And if you do, I shall make sure that you don't," said Shanthah with a wink.

"That doesn't even make sense," replied Pol with a laugh. His eyes lit up as he saw that Shanthah was accompanied by Hanna, their friend and powerful Telekinetik that had also been in the slave camp with them.

"He rarely does," said Hanna with a wink.

"What are you two doing here?" asked Pol excitedly.

"Same as you, I expect," answered Shanthah with a shrug. "Our presence was requested personally by Empress Mara Bartunek, Empress of Blood and Ruler of the—what were all her titles again?"

"Oh, hush, you pretentious loon," said Hanna. "All we know is that Mara wanted us added to the group going to Doftaan, so here we are."

"Is anyone else here?" asked Shanthah.

"You mean from the camp?" asked Pol, as if referring to friends from a past summer camp and not a slave camp. Pol shook his head, explaining that Josman, Kamil, and Drahomir were on a different mission to scout out the ruins of Nitra.

The caravan began to move again, but Shanthah, Pol, Hanna, and Rehor stayed together, all reunited at the same time for the first time in almost two years.

A day later and many miles away in Doftaan, the viridian and white banners of Thanatanos fluttered in the gentle breeze alongside the crimson flags of Sangora. They lined the streets, heralding the arrival of the delegation from Thanatanos who would soon arrive.

"We've received word that they are nearing the gates, my empress," stated Mistress Vasilica, approaching her queen.

Mara stood staring at the stars from the highest tower's ramparts, feeling the cool summer breeze on her cheeks. More than a week had passed since she sent the message to King Verahim, and she had begun to wonder if he would answer.

"I saw them, thank you," said Mara with a nod. "Vasilica, do you know what they call this city in Thanatanos?"

"No, my lady," replied Vasilica with a curt shrug.

"They call it the city of blood," said Mara, staring out over the sea of dark spires and colorful onion-shaped domes of her beloved city.

"That's a very nice title," said Vasilica with a smile.

"Yes, to us. Except they don't associate blood with the same things we do. They hate us. They hate me. They see blood as disgusting, an evil omen of death—and more death has rained down on their kingdom from this city than any other. Not even Valistaran Talohir was more hated than I am—than we are, I think. Am I a fool to invite them here?"

"No, my queen. Your goal is to establish peace between our people," said Vasilica. "What is more noble than that? Do you worry that you have invited your own assassin into your home?" Mara chuckled at the question.

"Thank you. I appreciate that. But that assassin was no Than. I don't think so, at least. The way he could vanish, he was a Walker, I'm sure of it. I don't doubt that he is still nearby or will be in the crowds tonight, but I think we're safe for now. Please, go enjoy the festivities," said Mara with a kind smile, trying to shake the somber mood. She didn't believe the thought herself, but she wanted to reassure her friend and councilor. Vasilica returned the gesture, bowed, and soared away, leaving Mara alone upon the wall.

Mara had ordered her people to organize a grand festival in the streets of Doftaan to celebrate the oncoming peace. She had tried hard to cultivate a positive image of the foreign nation and dispel stereotypes and rumors; she wondered if Thanatanos cared to do the same. The young and old of Sangora came out in droves for the festivities; children laughed in the streets, chased by their kites shaped like the wings of their empress, and the elderly lined the streets to watch the parade of the Thans' precession as it entered the city.

She smiled to herself. A true smile. Joy. She watched her people dance and sing under the stars, and she was grateful for the chance to make it possible. Sangora under Valistaran and Codruta had been a dismal place filled with poverty and the fear of war. Now, this. Musicians drew dancing crowds, reminding her of happy memories under the stars in her hometown in Thanatanos. She smiled again.

The Empress of Blood took a running start and leapt from the top of the high tower; she felt the wind play with her hair, silencing the world as she plummeted down, down, down. As the ground drew nearer, she extended her wings and shot around the base of her fortress and into the sky to the cheers of her followers below.

On several dark occasions in the past year, she had considered letting herself hit the earth, but not anymore. As she soared over her celebrating people, she heard their cries of adoration and love. She could not stop smiling.

Amid the celebration, the delegation from Thanatanos made its way through the crowded streets toward Mara's fortress.

Aleksander turned in his saddle to Shanthah and shook his head in disbelief.

"Never thought we'd be back here on our own accord, did we?" asked Shanthah with a grin, "but I must say, this trip has already been much more enjoyable than the last!"

"The others back home are really missing something, I'll say that much," said Aleksander with a hearty laugh of pure elation as some Sangoran entertainers illuminated the night with a beautiful display of their lightning magic. The Sangoran sky dancers used their abilities to create intertwining spirals of light while others created the shapes of flowers with flames.

He had never seen magic used for anything other than war, and it brought such wonderment that he allowed the joyous atmosphere to knock down his wall of apprehension.

"Drahomir wouldn't enjoy it anyway, he doesn't like fun," called Hanna over the sound of the crowds. Aleksander chuckled and continued to watch the sky dancers as his horse carried him to their destination. He looked over his shoulder to see Pol even more mesmerized than he. Aleksander smiled, wondering when the boy would be reunited with his sister.

Then his heart began to pound; what would happen when he himself spoke with Mara again? They had once shared a connection. One that he had hoped would blossom into more. However, due to his actions, Mara had inadvertently suffered immense mental torture, spending twenty years trapped in her own mind. Later, he and his friends fought against her in both the Siege of Nitra and the Battle of Laniras. He didn't know if he was even worthy of her forgiveness and wondered why he had been invited to Doftaan at all.

Soon the small caravan of Thannish diplomats stopped near the grand staircase leading to the ground floor entrance of Mara's palace. Aleksander felt a flood of memories that were not his, memories implanted in his mind by the Secret Keepers of Kurash. He saw builders creating these steps to welcome human visitors, as Sangorans could fly and therefore had little need of stairs.

The procession stopped as Rehor, King Verahim's official representative to the meeting, dismounted his horse, aided by two members of the royal guard. The rest of the diplomats, soldiers, and members of the Hidden Flame followed his example.

Empress Mara Bartunek had finished her flight around the tower and now stood at the top of the steps overlooking the precession; behind her stood the remaining Mistresses of Dusk, some of which were familiar to Aleksander, Shanthah, and Hanna, but there were unfamiliar faces as well. Banners of each Sangoran state fluttered above their heads. Mara raised her hands and the crowd exploded in triumphant applause and shouts before quieting down enough for her to speak.

Hanna felt a twinge of guilt accompanied by unshakable paranoia as she gazed at her former friend. They had nearly fought to the death the last time they had seen one another, and she couldn't help but wonder if that was why she had been invited by Mara to the heart of her empire. Shanthah noticed the look on Hanna's face and nudged her gently.

"You gonna be able to talk to her?" Shanthah whispered. He waited several moments for a response. He thought the pause awkwardly long, so he began to ask again, but Hanna cut him off.

"I really don't think so," Hanna whispered back, shaking her head. She felt unable to meet Shanthah's gaze but knew he wouldn't pass judgment. "But I hope so."

She watched one of the Mistresses of Dusk, Anca, she believed her name was, whisper something into Mara's ear. A look of momentary fear crossed the face of the Empress of Blood, but it was quickly replaced with one of exuberance as she addressed the assembled crowd. Hanna wondered what Anca had said, and she vowed to find out.

"As Empress of Sangora, I would like to welcome our friends from Laniras." She gestured to the caravan. "I know our history is soaked in blood, but I'm hoping we can change that today. I'd like to thank a dear friend for coming today and welcome him to say a few words." She gestured to Rehor, who ascended the staircase alone.

As they listened to their leaders speak, Hanna felt someone touch her elbow; it was not strange to be bumped in such a throng of people, but the way it lingered there, someone was trying to get her attention. She turned, hesitantly, but saw only a plump Sangoran woman bowing before her holding a tied scroll in her hand. Hanna motioned to herself, and the woman nodded, head bowed. Hanna took the scroll and shared a glance with Shanthah. Her heart raced as the stranger disappeared into the crowd.

"Today will be a day celebrated by human and Sangoran alike," exclaimed Rehor with a genuine smile on his face. "Your empress has granted me the great honor of addressing you for a moment. We are meeting today to address issues that will benefit all of us, but before that happens, on behalf of King Verahim Romus, I am pleased to declare that the war between our great nations ends this day!"

Roars of joy filled the streets once more as both Mara and Verahim waved to those assembled around the fortress. As they did so, Hanna broke the seal of the scroll, and together she and Shanthah read words penned in an expert hand.

*The honor of Ms. Hanna Samsa's presence is requested tomorrow morning at 10:00 outside the palace gates for special counsel with Mistress of Dusk, governor of Timishuara, her excellency, Lavinia Rosu, and with the Empress of Blood, Ruler of the United Empire of Sangora and Talohira, Mara Bartunek.*

Hanna and Shanthah looked each other in the face for a long moment; her heart continued to thunder in her chest. Had this all been a trap to lure her away? Shanthah squeezed her hand.

Mara and Rehor disappeared into the palace, followed a moment later by the Mistresses of Dusk and the rest of the Thannish delegation. As the doors shut behind them, Shanthah couldn't help but keep one hand on the hilt of his sword.

# CHAPTER THREE

# THE SWEETEST REVENGE

It had to be a trick. Hanna's hand trembled as she glanced at the note. She had donned her most flattering dress, the one she had packed for the Peace Ball mentioned in their invitation letter. She had no idea what was going on, and she considered turning around and running back to her room in the palace.

And then she heard a sweet voice call her name. Not a servant or other attendant. Mara. Hanna turned on the spot, eyes wide and mouth open in shock, fear, and excitement. She had no idea exactly what to feel as the tears began to fall.

"Mara!" She choked on her words and was sure she looked and sounded ridiculous. Mara didn't seem to care, and the empress advanced on Hanna. And then they were hugging.

Hugging.

"Looking good! Perhaps a little overdressed, but beautiful, of course," Mara said, letting out a deep breath she seemed to be holding in. "Well, should we go?"

Hanna nodded and followed her to a coach pulled by a team of black horses driven by Mistress Lavinia. As they set out, they sat in silence, watching the dense woods outside pass by. Hanna tried to make conversation but felt herself failing.

"It's pretty here," she said. "In Sangora, I mean."

"Yeah," Mara said with an awkward smile and nod.

She was going to add more, but nothing came to mind, and then the moment escaped her.

"Where are we going?" Hanna asked as the vehicle bumped along, the paved road turning into a dirt path. "Sorry, I feel like this is awkward, and I'm bad at, you know, words."

"You're fine." Mara laughed for the first time, but then her countenance dropped. "I've been shutting down the slave camps in Talohira ever since I became queen, you know. More so after the end of the war. I ordered ours to be shut down, but it kept operating in secret. I didn't know because I never had the heart to go back there. Not without—not without *you*."

"So, we're going *home* right now, aren't we?"

"Home," Mara repeated with a dark chuckle. "Yeah, I guess you could say that. I wouldn't, but—"

"You could've warned me, you know," Hanna said.

"Would you have come?" asked Mara.

As she asked the question, she looked like the beaten down girl Hanna had known in the slave camp, not the mighty empress she had become.

"Not sure if I'll be able to handle it," Hanna said at last. Mara nodded. "So probably not."

"I know what you mean, Hann…"

"But with you," Hanna said, trailing off. "With you, I think I could do anything."

Tears filled Mara's eyes as she clutched her friend's hand.

They made the rest of the trip without any more conversation, eventually reaching the cruel barricade covered in brambles and spears surrounding the slave camp. The mighty walls of Bukaral, Talohira's capital city, loomed in the distance.

Mara took a deep breath to ease her anxiety and wondered what Hanna was feeling. She looked over at her friend and saw a single tear rolling down Hanna's cheek. It had been over two years since they had escaped the camp, but neither woman could ever forget the horrors they had experienced within.

"Stay with the coach," Hanna heard Lavinia say to the other driver.

Hanna had completely forgotten that Lavinia had been the one driving them toward the camp. The Mistress of Dusk extended her wings and glided to the ground before motioning toward the heavily barricaded front gates. Mara led the way, and Hanna followed with Lavinia lingering close behind.

They approached the gates, an eerie familiarity settling in.

"It's almost like that feeling of coming home after a long journey, longing for your own bed, you know?" Hanna asked. "But different—horrible."

"I know what you mean," Mara said. "Longing for your own bed, only to find it covered in spiders and wanting to burn your own home to the ground."

"Vivid and super freaky, but yeah, I guess."

Mara led her friends toward the towering gates—toward the hell they had all escaped. Even Lavinia had been a prisoner of sorts there, and she too seemed reluctant to return. During her time as the forced overseer of the camp, Valistaran had her sister in captivity and threatened to kill her if she didn't comply. Mara had never asked for more context, but she knew there was more painful history there.

Hanna's heart twisted and tears filled her eyes as she beheld a mountain of thousands of dirty boots and shoes burning outside the gate. She dared not think of what evil had killed so many, and she hoped their deaths were quick.

She knew she was wrong.

"Who goes there?" The voice came from a shack at the base of the gates. Guard towers lined the walls, a new addition since their escape.

"Mara Bartunek, Empress of Blood, ruler of Sangora and Talohira!" Lavinia shouted back.

"She ain't our ruler here!"

Mara stood her ground, flanked only by Hanna on one side and Lavinia on the other; the irony was not lost on her, and it was a conscious choice to bring them both along. Five guards made a lazy approach, emerging from the narrow gap in the barricade.

"Open the gates," Mara ordered. The guards laughed, and their leader, a stout man with a coarse beard stepped forward.

"Sangora has no right over us here. These gates no longer open for the Empress of Blood." He gestured behind him.

Mara tilted her head. "They will."

She shot Hanna an almost imperceptible glance; Hanna closed her eyes, mentally forcing the black iron gates covered in thorny vines open. The rusted gears crunched from lack of use, and metal screeched against metal as they swung open.

The soldiers panicked; two hurried back into the guardhouse and another raised a horn to his lips to signal for others to close the gates. The guard captain looked around in confusion, for no man had turned the wheels to open the doorway.

"Who gave the order to open the gates?!" he cried.

"Weren't you listening? I did," Mara said.

She strode past the soldiers, and Hanna flicked her wrist, telekinetically bending the guard's knee to force him into a bow. The man looked up, startled, but Hanna and Lavinia both glared down at him, and he glanced back at the ground. As Mara walked into the slave camp, the rest of the guards stationed at the entrance followed their captain's example, bending their knees to bow before the Empress of Blood and her friends.

As the trio entered the camp, people emerged from their shoddy tents, looks of confused hope on their beaten and bruised faces. Perhaps, they had somehow heard tales of the other slave camps that had been shut down.

The stench of death and decay filled Mara's nostrils. It was a smell she had become accustomed to during her time as a slave and one that still haunted her dreams. She trembled and pressed her eyes shut as screams and the sound of barbed whips lashing against bare skin filled her ears.

"No more," she whispered, shaking her head.

She turned her head toward Hanna, who had a look of sadness etched on her face. Due to the nature of Mara's letter, Hanna had chosen her finest dress and felt the eyes of hundreds of slaves on her, and she smoothed out the silky fabric uncomfortably.

And then Hanna knew that not only the eyes of the downtrodden were on her, but those of their vile captors as well. She heard the cruel slavers whistle in her direction, and her gut seemed to twist in all directions.

She kept straight on course, ignoring the dozen or so corpses lying in the dirt around her, but as the slavers shouted perverted obscenities at her, she tried to adjust the neckline of her dress to cover more of her chest.

She took Mara's hand, and together they took a few steps forward. Hanna felt Mara squeeze her hand as they gazed upon the site where their own slave district had once been.

Mara nearly gave in to panic, but she released a slow breath, and together with Hanna, she forced herself to walk into the center of the camp. She glanced over her shoulder at Lavinia, who bowed her head in encouragement.

A different sound filled Mara's ears, and she looked around to see the slaves fighting back against their oppressors. Screams of pain gave way to the soldiers' frantic shouting as the slaves overtook them.

As the sudden revolution began, Hanna forced more guards to bow before them. She couldn't maintain her hold on all of them, but she didn't have to, for those that did not stay down were quickly overtaken by the downtrodden masses.

Soon, an army of slaves followed the Empress of Blood, while many more began to tear down scaffolding and topple their own work with cheers and great applause. The message took only moments to spread throughout the entire camp: The Empress of Blood had returned, and she was not pleased.

They passed the bloodstained whipping posts, and she turned to Hanna and Lavinia to release the slaves imprisoned there. Lavinia severed the ropes binding the prisoners, and Hanna helped them each off the stand.

Several slavers and guards, including an angry and confused soldier decorated in the attire of a Talohiran lieutenant, not the colors of Sangora, approached, their voices raised. Many other guards tried to keep order, but to no avail.

"What is the meaning of this?" called the lieutenant, spittle trailing from his lips. He caught sight of Mara standing without crown, but clad in glorious freedom, her raven black hair billowing in the summer breeze. The entire camp seemed bound by her spell. "Who are you?!"

"The Empress of Blood."

"Stupid of you to come here, then," the man replied.

"I'm shutting down this camp," Mara ordered with finality. "Your crimes have gone unpunished for far too long."

"Are you, now?" The lieutenant laughed and unsheathed his blade, but Hanna knocked it from his grip with a mental blow; it clattered against the cobblestone around the whipping posts.

"Yes."

"Oh, if you want the camp shut down, I'll happily oblige—fire upon the slaves!" shouted the lieutenant as he watched the downtrodden masses fighting their captors around the camp. "Why has it not already happened?!"

"Because the words of wicked men no longer have hold on this place," Mara said.

Many of the soldiers had even joined the slaves in fighting their fellow guards; the empress eyed a second set of whipping posts that had been erected after her time in the camp. "Your men have made their choice. What will yours be?"

The lieutenant hesitated.

"Release them," he said at last.

"Wise."

The slavers released the slaves tied to the second set of whipping posts. The weary prisoners collapsed to the ground, exhausted from the forced stress positions and prolonged exposure to the elements. Those with enough energy left rushed to the lifeless bodies of their friends lying around the posts.

Mara's eye followed the lieutenant's hand as he drew a hidden dagger; it flashed upward before she could react, and the cold steel pierced the side of a young female slave. The girl stumbled against the post, and Mara scrambled to her side to see that she had dropped something to the dirt.

It was a crudely sewn monster with a face drawn in charcoal—a face she herself had drawn two years earlier. It was the worry monster she had sewn for a scared little girl.

Her heart sank.

"Diana?" Mara whispered. "No, no, no…"

Her fears were realized, for although she recognized Diana's face and wild blonde hair, she had grown since she had last seen her. Mara began to panic as the lieutenant was quickly overrun by slaves and lost to Mara's view.

"Help!" Mara shouted. The girl opened her eyes and reached for Mara's cheek, and a thin smile stretched across her face.

"Happy girls are the prettiest…" she said.

"But brave girls are the happiest," Mara said in reply. She pressed her own cloak against the wound and shouted, "Stay with me, Diana! By the gods, stay with me!"

She cradled the young girl against her chest, blood soaking both of their clothing.

"You made it out…" Diana said. Mara kissed the girl's forehead and rocked her back and forth. She nodded as tears filled her eyes. "…Wanted to…be like…you…"

"And I came back for you, just stay with me, okay?"

"I knew you would—you told me to be brave," Diana said. Mara held the girl's hand and cradled her head ever closer.

"You can do it. You can keep being brave," Mara said, shutting her eyes tightly.

"I know…and so can you…" Diana said, her voice fading.

Mara held the young girl, keeping pressure on the wound. Relief washed over Mara's entire being as she felt Hanna's hand on her own. Hanna handed her a torn piece of silky fabric, which Mara used to maintain pressure on the wound until her two guards from the cart appeared to help.

Mara was reluctant to relinquish her hold on Diana, but the first guard's compassionate expression convinced her. She knew they were better trained in healing than she or Hanna were, and she let go. No words were shared as the armed women tended to the girl's wound.

"I'll come back for you, I promise," Mara said in a sweet voice. "And I hope you know despite what I said, it is okay not to be happy—or pretty for that matter." Diana gave a weak nod.

"Love you…" the girl whispered.

Mara's heart shattered, and words caught in her throat as she squeezed Diana's shoulder. The empress rose from the ground, her cloak soaked in crimson; it billowed in the breeze, the only sound that filled the camp. The violence had stopped, and not a soul broke the eerie, haunted silence.
No one dared to.

An old man at the front of the mass of slaves trembled as he fell to one knee and bowed his head. The others followed suit until the entire mass of downtrodden men and women bowed before her in respect and thanks. Even many of the soldiers bowed, but the cruel slavers remained standing, alone.

Mara approached a group of soldiers and guards kneeling amongst the slaves. A couple of them looked up but said nothing as she stood above them.

"Tell me, do you bow out of repentance or fear?"

No one replied, and the men each dropped their gaze and knelt even deeper, pressing their hands and foreheads to the ground. At that point, Mara turned to the last remaining slavers.

"Who is in command here?"

"Head slaver's in his office," said one of the men. "Head toward the—"

"She knows where it is," Lavinia said, cutting off the guard.

Mara took a deep breath to calm herself and looked toward the guard house.

"I'll stay with the girl," Lavinia said. Diana was stirring; she looked like she would survive.

"Thank you. I'll be back for her," said Mara before turning to Hanna. "You ready?"

Hanna nodded reluctantly. At that moment, Mara realized Hanna had ripped the bottom of her dress to use it as a makeshift bandage to staunch Diana's bleeding.

"As ready as I'll ever be."

"Good. We kill him, and we get Diana back to Doftaan."

They made their way to the guard shack at the far end of the camp. Hanna took a deep breath as she tried the door, and to her astonishment, it was unlocked. An overwhelming stench filled their nostrils as they strode inside. Hanna dry heaved and tried to pull her dress up over her face but failed and resorted instead to covering her mouth and nose with both hands.

The shack was empty, but they found the back door ajar. The empress peeked outside to see a man sprawled against the back of the building, a bottle of some dark liquid in one hand. The front of his tunic looked to be covered in a mixture of alcohol and vomit. Drool dripped from the corner of his mouth as he snored loudly, completely ignorant of what was happening in his camp. Hanna wrenched the drink from his hand and poured it over his head.

"What'sat?! Who's thurr?" Belokej the slaver exclaimed, slurring his words so badly they sounded like one word. Mara could feel hatred pooling in her heart; she felt nothing but utter disdain for the wretch of a man that lying in his own filth. The man who had caused them both so much pain.

He propped himself up and coughed up a wad of phlegm from his nearly toothless mouth, which landed near Mara's boot. "A nigh'widge—in m'camp? Gah rid of you lot, I did…"

Mara winced as the slur for a Sangoran woman, 'night witch' slipped out of his mouth. Belokej reached for a blade in his belt and brandished it wildly but fell face first in the mud outside the hut. Hanna looked to Mara for direction as he rolled in the muck trying to find his knife, cussing under his breath.

"Ah, but you 'n' I—we could have some fun, eh…?" Belokej said, gesturing toward Hanna as he undressed her with his eyes.

With a flick of her wrist, she telekinetically slammed him hard against the wall, and the wretched slaver half laughed, laugh coughed, spitting up more mucus. "Oh, I remebur you—mm, boy oh boy, do I remebur you—yer that—that—Hanna. Nev'r forge' one that looks like tha', no, sir."

He licked his lips.

"Keep my name out of your damn mouth."

She folded her arms across her chest, fuming and trying not to sob as memories from the camp filled her mind. However, with fire in her eyes, she kept the slaver pinned hard against the wall with her powers.

"Y'know, ye women are all the same—so ungrateful 'n' rude all th'time… Why can't ye just smile? 'N' you, nigh' widge, yer not even a woman anymore, yer jus' a—jus' a dirty murderin' creature—not even human, I says."

"How can being so determined to hold on to such vehement hate not get exhausting?" Mara asked as Belokej muttered slurs and other vile words beneath his drunken breath. Mara let out a deep sigh. "We came here to kill you."

With every fiber of her being, she wanted to. Her nostrils flared, and tears welled up in her eyes.

"Well, 'n' get on wiv it, sweetie," said the slaver with pitiful resignation. Mara stood above him clad in majesty, a look of disgust on her face as he rolled in his own filth.

"No, I think I have my revenge," said Mara. She pressed her eyes shut and shook her head to recompose herself before turning away. She had wasted enough time coming to find the man and knew Diana still needed help. "But there will still be justice. I'll leave it to my people to decide your fate."

"I remeberr you too," he said. "Yer that—yer that—that bidge who—" at that moment, he cut himself off with a disgusting, hacking cough and a snort of phlegm.

Without another word, Mara took Hanna by the hand. Together, they left Belokej behind, having risen above everything he had ever, or would ever be, their resilience and success in conquering the sorrows of life a sweeter revenge than any they had ever dreamed of.

# CHAPTER FOUR

# THE FALSE GOD

Far from Belokej's slave camp, a lone, emaciated creature scrambled over a high, craggy ridge on the outskirts of the crumbling city of Nitra. It hit the earth with no regard for its own physical safety and then was on its feet running again.

Golden sunlight crept over the eastern mountains, suddenly engulfing the entire valley in the new glow of morning. A mass of dust and ash swirled in a gust of light breeze then drifted to the ground, accumulating an inch from the ground as if the earth repelled it; the ash swirled around itself without the need to be carried by wind and slithered like a snake of shadow and ash out of the rubble of the fallen towers illuminated by the golden sun.

The living ash needed no eyes to see, for it sensed its prize; it made its way to where the great gate, now demolished, once defended the city. It floated along the cold stone of the city wall, darkening the mortar between bricks as it swept into the empty city. It passed by ruined homes and thought nothing of those poor souls who had lost their lives in whatever great battle had destroyed this fallen city. The ash was mere consciousness wrapped around dead matter with one simple goal: exist.

A feeling of intense hunger like a siren's song drew the soul, if one could call it that, toward the ruins of a once proud fortress on the hill. The shadowy ashes fluttered through a smashed window and up a broken staircase littered with corpses, stopping beneath a ruined doorway. It could sense the other being now and kept a weak hold on its mind like a ship on a stormy sea set on reaching a lighthouse.

At last, the disembodied mind located its prize: a faceless creature huddled in the shadows. A groan of hunger and despair filled the world as the monster sensed the consciousness within the ash. The beast shifted in the darkness and then gave an awkward lunge forward as if expecting to find a kill waiting for it. Instead, the beast trampled through the ashes confused and disappointed.

The ashes coalesced around the faceless creature's body and released a weak shockwave of mental energy, pressing it against the cold stone wall to stun it long enough to allow their minds to connect, as weak as they both were.

The ashes snaked its consciousness into that of the beast in the darkness. He could sense the creature's intense desire to devour him and its confusion that there was no body to accompany the mind it sensed; the consciousness could feel the monster's free will as if it were a tangible object, and with its mind, grasped its mind tightly with its own. The monster's struggling ceased, and an eerie peace filled the chamber.

Relinquishing its grasp on the Faceless, the ashes fluttered away, swirling in the middle of the room. The emaciated, Faceless creature crawled toward the tornado of living dust, its claws scratching against the stone ground while telepathically emitting a low, steady groan. It stepped into the light, illuminating a coat of crimson smeared across the humanoid beast's grotesque, faceless visage.

The dust willed the creature to summon its kin. The creature obeyed without question, a slave to a foreign consciousness. It scampered on all fours from the chamber as the ash fluttered to the top of the staircase, emerging from the shadows. Soon, it would have eyes that would allow it to see its new kingdom and a body to rule it. A body to conquer the lands beyond the ruined city. All that lived would soon answer to him: to Thanatan. The ashes of the dead god settled on the floor of the ruined great hall, waiting.

A primal joy, a feeling akin to success or satisfaction overtook the god's ashes as it sensed first dozens and then hundreds of the creature's kin appear over the ridge and flow into the city like a gray wave of Faceless bodies. He could sense their ever-present hunger before they even reached the city's walls, but even more, Thanatan felt his own mind being strengthened by the presence of the Faceless.

The first Faceless beast pulled itself over the rubble of the wall, its taut muscles rippling across its back as its head appeared over the wall. Thanatan extended his consciousness, testing the limits of his abilities to control the both the creatures and reality itself. Once, in his great power, Thanatan had the ability to influence and distort reality—to connect with creation. The ability was weaker now, but in time, it would return.

The first Faceless beast paused like an obedient hunting dog heeling before its master. The rest of the beasts paused as soon as they reached the bottom of the wall.

Thanatan reached out, connecting his mind with that of the creature standing obediently beside him. He snaked his way through the empty corridors of the monster's soul as the ashes settled on its emaciated shoulders until he found something hidden away in the deepest shadows of the creature's mind. Sentience. Awareness. Consciousness.

As if adding kindling to a dying fire, Thanatan focused his mental energy into it, simultaneously unlocking the beast's consciousness while keeping a firm grasp on the beast's free will. The creature stumbled to its knees and flailed its arms in confusion as its master's mind spoke to it.

*"Be still, my child,"* Thanatan's mind whispered. The Faceless obeyed and turned its bloodied, smooth visage toward Thanatan's ashes.

*"What is happening?"* The thought drifted through their connected minds, resonating with a chilling, female voice.

*"You have awoken after a very long sleep—as have I,"* said Thanatan. The creature pulled itself toward its master, dragging its broken legs across stone.

*"Who am I?"* The voice echoed directly within Thanatan's mind.

*"You are my first and greatest follower in this age,"* replied Thanatan. *"Through you, I will command my legions."*

*"Them?"*

*"Yes,"* replied Thanatan, fluttering around the creature's shoulders. *"Come, my friend. Your nakedness is no state for the right hand of a god."*

With his mind, Thanatan motioned to the nearby steps leading to the ground level. Together the ashes and the sentient creature descended and made their way to a ruined blacksmith's shop at the center of the ruined city. The rest of the Faceless swarmed over the wall and followed their masters into the city, devoid of true consciousness.

Thanatan's Faceless opened what remained of the wooden door to reveal a dead forge within the shop. He willed the creature to restart the forge and guided his first servant in smelting discarded metal in the room into an intricate mask, which the Faceless placed over her blood-stained head. Thanatan felt the beast's consciousness breathe new life, just as the forge had as they stoked air into its belly.

*"This mask contains part of my consciousness. It will allow you to keep your mind even when I am no longer near you,"* said Thanatan.

*"But you will always be near us,"* replied the sentient beast.

*"No, in time, I will need to leave you. What was your name in life, my child?"*

*"I do not remember."*

*"Do you remember who you were?"* Thanatan asked.

*"A leader."*

*"Good, I need leaders. And when did you die?"* asked Thanatan. He knew that he could reach into the creature's mind and take

whatever information he wanted, but he was still weak, and the mask's purpose was to restore the creature's humanity, after all.

*"Long ago. Sangora."*

*"Were you the leader of Sangora?"* asked Thanatan.

*"One."*

*"And is this Sangora?"* Thanatan continued. *"Who rules it now?"*

"No," was the creature's simple answer.

*"And who destroyed it?"*

*"Queen of King Valistaran Talohir. Long after my death."*

"His queen did this? How very odd," said Thanatan.

*"Yes. City of Nitra. Thanatanos."*

*"Thanatanos?"* asked Thanatan in pleasant surprise. *"So, they have not forgotten their god after all! This queen, does she still rule over this land?"*

*"Yes. Bartunek. Mara."*

*"Mara Bartunek…"* Thanatan repeated. *"I look forward to meeting Queen Mara. She will join us, I expect, if she still worships me as does this land that bares my name,"* replied the weakened god. *"Thank you. Rally your kin. Rally the Pure. You shall oversee the rebuilding of this city. Nitra, you called it?"*

*"Yes."*

*"Nitra will be the center of our kingdom, and you shall rule by my side. You shall be greater even than Queen Mara Bartunek. Should you remember it, your name will be held sacred, and instead, you shall be my new Magistrate."*

*"New?"*

*"My previous Magistrate was murdered and must now be replaced,"* Thanatan said. *"Will you serve?"*

*"I will serve."*

The Faceless bowed to her new master and departed to carry out the orders. Thanatan sensed his first new follower disappear into the depths of Nitra's ruins and reached out with his mind, calling a group of the Faceless to him.

He could feel the minds of his Faceless minions, and he snuffed them out, willing them to fuel his own consciousness; he used his ability to connect to all of creation, willing the beasts' bodies to dissolve, their matter swirling together into a new shape: his own new body. He would figure out in time how to inhabit a true body, but for now, this one would house his ashes until his power grew. A shell, but a body, nonetheless. He connected his mind to the creation, a body with eyes that could see, but inside, it was empty and dead. He took his first breath.

He reached out with his mind again; he could sense it all: the birds outside the city. The beasts in the forest. The Faceless writhing and climbing around him. He knew he could reach out farther, using the minds of the sea of Faceless beasts to expand his own mind's power to sense all living creation around him for miles around. He then chose to focus on the Faceless that stood in the chamber around him. He could feel their skin, every single matted hair on their heads; he focused deeper.

The creatures groaned, and he could sense the very matter that made up the creatures. He focused on that essence of their creation, the fibers that made up their being and entwined their souls, and then he willed it to unravel, just as he had done to create his new body.

"I thank you for your sacrifice," said Thanatan in his new voice, one that came out of the newly crafted body as many of the Faceless around him dissolved into dust with naught but a groan; the dust swirled around Thanatan as he focused the particles of his creations to take new form. He could imagine the necessary parts of his new creation, and he willed them into existence, telekinetically controlling the dust to pool at the center of the chamber.

As he telekinetically brought the lifeforce and matter of the Faceless together, his mind willed organs, tissues, and other vital systems into being. Dead, gray skin wrapped around the creation, which was admittedly grotesque, but beautiful in its design. Spindly tendrils of tendon and muscle extended to the walls, floor, and ceiling to suspend the undulating sack of organs in the center of the chamber. Crude orifices opened across Thanatan's creation, and each gave a sound like a sputtering cough, releasing a cloud of spores that seemed to dissipate into the air.

Thanatan stood back, examining his creation with new eyes, and he smiled. It was not a beautiful thing, but not all things must be. The sack of organs hanging in the chamber would serve its purpose, infecting all living and dead bodies near the ruins of Nitra to create new Faceless minions. The Pure, he called them. His followers.

He thought back to the virus that had killed hundreds of millions during his lifetime; it had turned people into these things after death, and they had then dismantled entire cities and civilization. This time, their purpose would be bridled to *his* will.

It was fortunate, indeed, that he had found such a place covered with so many dead. Before he assimilated her into his host of undead creatures, he would have to thank this Mara Bartunek. The catacombs beneath the city would give birth to thousands of his creations, and they would carry their seed to the nearby villages and the rest of the planet. He would finally bring peace to the entire world.

He decided then to begin other creations, designing beasts more powerful than any engines of war to serve alongside his forces. He would have to use his resources wisely, but the Faceless were not the only creations that would protect his kingdom. He turned to the final Faceless that stood behind the virus sack, and he dissolved it as well, weaving the fibers of its body into two new shapes. The two lizard-like creations squirmed on the ground and slithered around his feet. Soon, the useless beasts would be strong enough to protect his kingdom, but not yet. He reached out again, this time focusing on the world around him.

"Ah," Thanatan whispered as his mind finally connected with what he sought: the powerful telepathic or telekinetic person with whom he had connected shortly after his consciousness had reawakened, however long ago that was.

He could sense the person's powerful consciousness, and he could already feel their connection; he had unwittingly latched onto her mind when he had returned, his soul instinctively reaching out for the most powerful mind he could in order to sustain his crumbling form. Their minds had been linked ever since, although he had been able to hide it from her.

He wondered once again how long he had remained dormant. Long enough for his body to turn to ash, at least. It was fortunate that he had maintained his connection to creation, for without it, his mind would have perished long ago. He could sense thousands of beings full of life around the unknown woman with whom he shared the connection.

Was she the Mara Bartunek of which the Magistrate spoke? Or perhaps someone else. Someone powerful. He was too far away, and too weak at the moment, to probe her mind further. It would have to wait. He would find her soon, and through her, through this woman, he would make things right, atone for his mistakes.

He would end his eternal and ancient war once and for all.

# CHAPTER FIVE
# PEACE AND DEATH

The servants of Mara's high court cleared away the dishes from before their leaders and the Thannish diplomats alike as the visitors consumed the last bit of delicious Sangoran cuisine. Those invited to stay for the peace talks and other negotiations remained in their seats while the rest of the delegation was shown to their quarters for the remainder of their stay in Doftaan.

Mara cleared her throat to begin the meeting.

"First of all, I think I speak for everyone when I thank the palace chefs. Thank you!" Mara said from her high-backed seat. The diplomats and other assembled leaders all clapped. "I find it prudent to say a few words before we begin. It's my dearest hope that neither of our countries are considered in the annals of history to be the great villain of our time. Future civilizations and generations will follow us. They'll study us, and I want each of us in this room to consider the legacy we leave. I do not say that to excuse my own actions or those of people close to me."

She paused for a long moment and stood up.

"There are two words that don't make sense to me—heroes and villains. To me, in a way, they're the same thing. Just like darkness and light, winter and summer, perhaps you may yearn for one while you curse the other, while others bless the joys that come from both—the solitude and comfort of good company beside a warm hearth while the blizzard rages outside, or the freedom and warmth that comes with summer. But don't forget the time that comes between those extremes: the change that comes with fall, or the hope of new spring when a blistering summer or freezing winter have overstayed their welcome.

"So it is with these words that confuse me. My heroes may be your villains, and the other way round, but I want to celebrate everyone that wishes to end this bloodied conflict. Let us be the hope and relief that comes with spring and fall. Ambassador Rehor Toth, nothing would please me more than to officially end this war."

Rehor beamed in Mara's direction as Mistress Raluca placed a long quill and small vessel of ink before the ambassador. With a gracious smile, he thanked the beautiful Mistress of Dusk with whom he had become acquainted during the feast. He smiled at Mara again and picked up the quill. As the rest of the delegation watched the ambassador sign the peace accords, Aleksander caught a glimpse of a hooded figure through the arched doorway of the banquet chamber.

"I will do anything in my power to keep our people safe, and King Verahim insists he will do the same. We appreciate the efforts of your strong nation," Rehor said. "We look forward to sharing in the abundance and peace that Empress Mara Bartunek has established here in her two years of faithful, selfless service."

He continued his speech, and Mara sat back down, her thoughts drifting to Diana, the little girl from the slave camp, who now resided in Doftaan's finest healing center.

As Ambassador Rehor and other diplomats spoke, Aleksander made a gesture with his head to Shanthah as he excused himself from the room. Shanthah was trapped in the middle of his row and through a mixture of pantomiming and mouthing the words conveyed the message, 'What do you want from me?!'

Aleksander left Shanthah behind and rounded the corner, expecting to see the hooded figure, but he was alone.

It was dark out, and therefore no Sangoran in the castle required wrappings to shield themselves from the sun, and he knew no Thannish visitor should be sneaking about during the peace talks. He buried the thought, however, excusing his actions because his purpose in the group was to help investigate the assassination of the Mistress of Dusk; he knew he was scheduled to discuss the circumstances in upcoming diplomatic sessions.

He pursued the stranger along several winding passageways and up a flight of stairs, which he took two or three at a time. He rounded another corner just in time to see the trail of a cloak disappear through a door that had been left ajar.

For a moment, he considered the possibility that he was being lured into a trap, but he slid through the crack in the doorway anyway. He extinguished the darkness in the chamber with a ball of flame created in his palm as he wondered if the assassin could see in the dark or if he was just trying to hide. If he could see in the dark, the assassin was probably Sangoran.

Aleksander pushed his suspicions aside and cast the glow of his flame across the room. The light made the massive golden bed in the center of the chamber glow like a hot iron.

There was no way out of the room, and Aleksander kicked the door shut behind him, making sure his target was not hiding behind it. He knew Ihrin had been slain in her own bed; was this her chamber, or perhaps the bedroom of Mara or another Mistress of Dusk? He wondered if the killer intended on waiting here for Mara or another victim.

"Where are you?" he whispered, casting his light into the room. He kept his back to the wall as he made his way around the chamber, all the while being careful to stay aware of his surroundings.

Aleksander threw back the thick covers of the opulent bed and to his relief no one was beneath them. It seemed a silly place to hide, and he felt foolish for thinking the stranger would hide there, but he had to check, nonetheless. He checked beneath the bed next, and his heart leapt in his chest as a soft, yet strong voice broke the silence.

"You are not who you say you are."

"I don't think that's a great secret," replied Aleksander. "Show yourself!"

Aleksander jumped back in surprise as his light illuminated the bottom of a masked face shrouded in a dark hood. The man had definitely not been there a moment before; a laugh filled the chamber, and then the man disappeared into a black mist. The door burst open behind him, and he swore under his breath. He turned to see three Sangoran soldiers with raised spears enter the room led by Mistress Lavinia.

"I saw you leave the chamber, and you went straight to Raluca's bedchamber. One of two things is happening here. You're the latest of hundreds of her escapades, or you are here to kill her. Perhaps both?"

"I followed someone else here," pled Aleksander, raising his ball of flame higher.

"Is this person in the room right now?" Lavinia asked, gesturing around the bedchamber; her tone was condescending, and he knew she was mocking him. She checked under the bed and turned back with a smile. "It's okay, you can go back to bed. No monsters under there."

Aleksander knew she was taunting him, but he did not take the bait. He pointed to where the man had been. "I swear to you I'm telling the truth. He was right there! And then he just vanished into the darkness!"

"Extinguish your fire, or we will strike," ordered one of the soldiers. Aleksander obeyed her command and shook his wrist to let the flame sizzle into a thin trail of smoke. Darkness cloaked the room, and due to his lesser eyesight, Aleksander knew he was at a distinct disadvantage if either the Sangorans tried to fight him or, more likely, if the assassin returned.

"Listen, I'm sure this is connected to whatever happened to Mistress Ihrin!" he shouted, instantly regretting the outburst.

"Whatever happened? She was murdered in her bed! You have to admit how suspicious your actions seem," said Lavinia with a grand, sweeping gesture. "But pray tell, did this man say anything to you?"

Aleksander felt it best not to lie as he nodded his head and said, "He seemed to know who I am."

"Is that a strange thing to know?" asked Lavinia darkly.

"It was more than just recognition, but I'm not a public figure—whoever the killer was knew me personally," Aleksander replied, exasperated. "Now, unless you are arresting me, I will be on my way."

Lavinia grabbed his shoulder as he tried to push past. She shoved him hard against the wall, her armor clanking as she smashed an armored elbow into his chest. He groaned and raised his hands to indicate that he intended to cooperate.

The sound of crashing glass broke the tension.

"Are all the Mistresses of Dusk at the signing ceremony?" asked Aleksander in a panic, mentally trying to tally which of the leaders had been present.

"No, we—" She stopped abruptly.

"What is it?" Aleksander asked.

"Mistress Antanasia!" Lavinia replied, and in an instant she and two of her guards flew from the chamber. The third soldier grabbed Aleksander's wrist and shook her head.

"Don't get any ideas," she muttered. "You're staying right here."

"Look, if we don't get out there—it sounds like Antanasia is in trouble."

"Is that a threat?" the guard asked, her brow furrowed.

"What? No!" he wrenched his arm free and added. "Isn't the point of these negotiations to build trust between our nations? Let me help. That's why I'm here."

The guard nodded hesitantly, clearly unsure of what to do. She and Aleksander hurried from the chamber in the same direction as Lavinia and the other soldiers.

"My name's Aleksander," he said, introducing himself as they ran.

"Rayshel," replied the woman. "Are you comfortable flying?" Before he could reply, Rayshel grasped him by the shoulders and shot down the corridor at breakneck speed. Rayshel followed the sound of combat coming from another corridor and rushed to assist her comrades.

In the middle of a corridor open to the night sky, Lavinia and one of her guards were locked in combat with the hooded figure who teleported around the room and parried with twin daggers, making quick work of the guard.

Rayshel and Aleksander drew their blades, intercepting a blow that would have pierced Lavinia's side. Aleksander hurled a ball of flame toward his foe and shouted out in dismay as the assassin pulled the flames into a shadowy vortex and released it a moment later in all directions. Aleksander threw his own body in front of Rayshel as the flames peppered down on them, but the attack distracted Lavinia long enough for the killer to gain an advantage.

The assassin vanished into the darkness and reappeared, using his momentum to plant his feet against Lavinia's chest just as she leapt toward him, knocking her hard against the stone column behind her. She collapsed to the ground in a heap of screaming agony as Rayshel leapt over her, hurling her spear toward their foe.

"Come, my brother! Today we may be able to slay two of them for the glory of Thanatan!" the assassin called to Aleksander, who caught a glimpse of the man's crimson mask beneath his dark hood. Rayshel turned in horror as Aleksander ignited two balls of flame in either hand.

"No," she whispered, raising both fists in defiance. Aleksander launched both fireballs past her head; the inferno engulfed the assassin in flame, illuminating the corridor in orange and gold before all color drained from the room as he vanished in a vortex of flame and shadow. Silence fell on the terrace save for Lavinia's groans of pain.

"Mistress Lavinia!" cried Rayshel, hurrying to her leader's side. Lavinia coughed and clapped her hand against her armored chest but seemed unable to speak. Rayshel rolled the Mistress of Dusk onto her side, resulting in a shriek of pain. "I'm sorry!" Rayshel hurried to loosen the straps on Lavinia's heavy chest plate and shoulder pads.

Aleksander helped Rayshel remove the pieces of armor to reveal a charred tunic underneath. Guilt and shock overtook him as he realized his actions had inadvertently led to Lavinia's wounds. Rayshel ripped the blackened fabric from her master's shoulder; Aleksander looked away in respect for Lavinia's privacy, but grimaced as he caught a glance of her horrendously scarred flesh from just below her throat to her sternum.

"Mistress Lavinia, I—"

Rayshel cut him off as she grabbed Aleksander's hand and in one fluid motion slit his palm, coating her blade in crimson.

"Hey, what?!" he cried as Rayshel grasped his wrist once again and pulled him close. She squeezed his fist to trickle his blood onto Lavinia's burns, which seemed to be straining her breathing.

"You're a fire dancer," said Rayshel.

"I can assure you, I can't dance," retorted Aleksander.

"That's what we call them here. Flame-Thrower, Fire-Eater—there's many names, but your blood can heal burns," Rayshel explained as she massaged Aleksander's blood into Lavinia's wound.

He knew she spoke truth, for he had experienced healing from burns caused by his own abilities just after awakening with no memories, a day that seemed so very long ago. That day, he had fought to escape Lavinia's forces, but she overtook both him and Shanthah, taking them to the Talohiran slave camp. He had always wondered how his skin had healed, but now he knew why. He laughed at the irony that he was now healing the wounds of the woman that had enslaved him.

"Maybe we're even now for throwing me in that slave camp, eh?" Aleksander joked. Lavinia did not laugh, and he regretted his decision.

"A little more blood, please," said Rayshel in a polite tone before demanding, "fire dancer, now!"

He allowed her to take his hand to drip blood onto Lavinia's wounds; it seemed gruesome as Rayshel massaged his blood into the wound, the charred edges already turning from black to pink.

"Back home, we use Dragonsoul. I like that better," Aleksander said. Rayshel ignored him and tore a strip from her cloak to make a makeshift bandage for Lavinia's other wounds.

"I'm not a healer, as you can see," she said, trying to tend to her leader as best she could. "And even though this is your fault, she'd have died without your blood."

"Healer or not, I'm glad you were here with your quick thinking. All I did was bleed all over her," said Aleksander.

"Come, Mistress," said Rayshel as Aleksander strode to the smashed window. "Let's get you out of here before the assassin comes back."

"I—I can't," stuttered Lavinia, grabbing Rayshel's wrist.

"We have to! Come, Mistress!"

"I—"

"Rayshel!" exclaimed a frantic Aleksander pointing from the edge of the terrace. Far below, he could see the body of Mistress Antanasia sprawled broken in a pool of blood in the street below.

"We didn't stop him! Mistress Antanasia is dead!"

"I can't stand!" cried Lavinia at the same time.

Aleksander and Lavinia's comments seemed to clash to be heard first, but both fell silent to listen to the other.

"What did he mean, Aleksander?" asked Rayshel without looking up. She kept her eyes on her wounded leader then demanded once more with anger, "Were you just a distraction for him to kill Antanasia? What did he mean?!"

Taken aback, Aleksander could not find the words he wished to say. He managed to spit out a feeble, "About what?" before realizing exactly what Rayshel was asking.

"He called you his brother."

"That man is no brother to me," replied Aleksander, holding up his palms as if defending himself against an attack and indicating his cooperation once again. "Listen, I don't know who that was, but I can assure you, he is no friend to me."

"Didn't you tell me he knew who you were?"

Aleksander stared into the rage of Rayshel's steely blue eyes as Lavinia tried to prop herself up. The agony on her face and her loud groan distracted Rayshel long enough for Aleksander to interject a comment.

"My purpose here is to find that assassin while our people make peace. Mara asked me to come herself," he said.

"And what makes some random Than so special? Why you?" asked Rayshel. Aleksander's mind shot to their relationship in the slave camp, but Lavinia spoke before he could form a sentence.

"He's a secret keeper of Kurash," said Lavinia through intense agony. "Yes, we know—what happened back in the— urgh—in Tal-Ahosh."

She was struggling to speak, and it was evident that she was in excruciating pain despite Rayshel's best efforts to heal her.

Aleksander paused. He hadn't considered the fact that Mara had summoned him and his allies here because of the mysteries and knowledge implanted in his brain by the slain secret keepers of Kurash, but the notion made perfect sense.

"I guess that could be true," said Aleksander, a look of dejection evident on his face.

"You thought she asked you here because—oh, Aleksander," said Lavinia with a pained smile. "You thought there could be reconciliation between you. And you thought you could *save* her?"

Aleksander said nothing, and a confused Rayshel looked back and forth between them, the only one in the room unsure of their history. Aleksander walked back to the terrace, unsure how to handle the conversation.

"They're tending to the Mistress of Dusk's body," said Aleksander, pointing to street below. He watched Rayshel leave Lavinia's side and venture nearer to the ledge. Aleksander bit his lip, half expecting the assassin to jump out and pull her down to the same fate as Antanasia.

"By Elafris below," said the young Sangoran before climbing outside.

She unfolded her leathery wings and drifted down to the street. Helplessness washed over Aleksander as he looked down at Rayshel speaking with those that had found the body. A crowd began to form far below, and the cool night air played with his hair as if unaware of the tragedy that had transpired.

The nearby sound of joyous trumpets and playful drums filled the night; the peace accords had been signed, and the celebrations must have begun, separate from the crowd watching Rayshel and the others help remove Antanasia's broken body from the streets.

Aleksander offered Lavinia his hand as she used her wings like massive hands to try to pull herself up off the ground, but she screamed in agony and collapsed, unable to use her legs. She groaned in pain as Aleksander called for help and cradled her head.

"I'm better off than Antanasia, but—my back—my *back!*" she screamed. "The bastard broke my back!"

# CHAPTER SIX
# THE ARCSHIP

The assassin's crimson mask and Lavinia's screams plagued Aleksander's mind as he lay asleep that night. He wrestled with restless dreams and obscure images of people and places he did not recognize. His thoughts twisted, confused and chaotic until one scene became clearer and clearer in his mind. He awoke with a start but could still see the images. He smacked his forehead trying to drive them out, but one particular memory and its accompanying feelings and sensations, implanted by the Secret Keepers of Kurash, overtook his entire consciousness.

## EIGHTY YEARS AGO

Ribbons of green and gray illuminated the night's sky, twisting and dancing like spirits watching over the citizens of Odauthlegur Eyja, the immortal island. Halamir son of Valdur watched the reflection of the ethereal glow dance across the glassy reflection of the black sea beyond the island. Somehow, the reflection seemed even more otherworldly to him than the mysterious lights in the sky. He loved the lights and their reflection in the inky blackness, for it drew him away from the anxiety in his mind.

He let out a dark chuckle, thinking about the irony of the island's name, for only three days before, his father, Valdur Leifursson had been dragged beneath the roaring tide by the horrible faceless creatures that assailed their home.

He knew the island was dying. The monsters used to be manageable; extermination ships would make quick work of whatever creatures washed up on shore and the island would return to normal, but they were coming in droves now, and reprieve was rare. Very few cities remained.

Halamir's father had been one of the island's guardians, responsible for using his magic to protect his people and instruct those within his bloodline gifted with the same power. And now that he was dead, Halamir was burdened with the same insurmountable task—without his father's same power to create and control ice. Without any power, to his knowledge.

He thought of his father often. The man had told him stories of his ancestors who had fought and survived the great wars that had ravaged the lands that used to be called Europe and North America over three hundred years ago. What loomed beyond those desolate lands, he had no idea.

His anxiety twisted back to one thought: how could he stave off the hordes from the darkness, those faceless ones from the deep, when his own father and grandfather before him had fallen to their claws? Was there any hope? The islanders were fighting a losing battle, and he knew it. He wouldn't be able to help them, anyway.

But then again, maybe he wouldn't have to fight the creatures. Soon, those who decided to abandon Odauthlegur Eyja would set sail for the Arcship. After that, another mystery. Another adventure. He had felt it his duty to stay, but there would be no shame in boarding the Arcship. That's what everyone said, right?

The lights above seemed to be an omen of peace from the unseen world, a way to show that, at least for now, the Men with No Faces were gone from Odauthian shores. A whip of ghostly gray light lashed across the sky as his mind wandered to his apparent destiny. The wise men and women of his island had long made prophecies that the guardians of Odauthlegur Eyja would someday end the threat of the Faceless hordes and slay their masters. Of course, they also prophesied the fall of the island.

What did the creatures have to gain by slaying the few people left on this godforsaken volcanic island in the middle of the sea? Where did they go when they retreated to the depths of the black waters? Did they have a hive? A civilization, even? Or, perhaps, they existed simply to consume Halamir's people and erase them from history. The last island surviving in a world washed clean of life. Or, again, so *they* said. Whoever *they* were.

He knew the prophecies were mere legends to give his people hope, just like the stories from the ancient days; the wise men and women couldn't *actually* see the future.

In those stories, heroes were always picked out of their humble beginnings with a noble destiny and granted supernatural powers to fight dark lords and monsters, saving their homes and winning the hand of the fair maiden. Of course, the fair maiden bit didn't seem too bad, but he wondered if it would be worth the trouble of having to defeat a dark lord commanding a legion of Men without Faces.

He wondered how much of the world beyond his island still existed. Legends of the great plague and subsequent war that had ravaged the planet were common knowledge, and the history was taught in all schools on the island. They were, at least, until the attacks became more frequent, and they had to be shut down. But how much of that history was true, and how much of it was forged in the fires of a lie to keep his people safe from what was still out there? If he stayed, he'd never know.

He turned his back on the great lights in the heavens to gaze upon Yggdrasil, the World Tree. The massive tree reached out of the summit of the dome volcano that had formed Odauthlegur Eyja. Few other trees existed on the island, for their timber had been used up long ago in the defense of their home. Only Yggdrasil remained, and Halamir wasn't even sure if the tree was natural, given its size.

Several fortresses and towns circled Yggdrasil's gnarled trunk, which twisted high into the heavens. Its branches spread across the stars and gave off a faint glow from the people living high above the ground; so gargantuan was Yggdrasil that it held many villages in its branches. Most other cities around the country had long ago been abandoned.

Yggdrasil was the source of all life on Odauthlegur Eyja. It provided fruit and wood for its people, who always accepted the timber as a great gift. The tree would heal within days and be ready to provide more gifts to those that lived around it. Not only that, but it also provided energy that sustained the villagers and kept their homes warm. The magic of the World Tree also, perhaps most incredibly of all, offered guidance to the individual inhabitants of the island in times of need—somehow.

Halamir found it odd that no one on the island worshipped the tree, they simply coexisted beside it in a mutually beneficial symbiotic relationship—gifts and guidance in exchange for protection.

The young man hoisted his pack and began the trek across the mountainous terrain. He wandered along a rocky trail, one that he had traversed so many times in his youth, a few miles away from the haunted, yet colorful ruins of the old capital of Reykjavik. What was left of the decimated city stood as a monument to the great war that ravaged the world hundreds of years before. An open-air museum, they called it.

The colorful, although archaic architecture was now faded where it wasn't charred by the flames of centuries past. Halamir knew that the Faceless gathered in the empty homes, but they kept to the shadows and never ventured as far as the path home.

One deep note sounded from a horn at the base of Yggdrasil, and Halamir's heart leapt out of his chest. He hurried up the path, knowing that it would still be some time until he reached his village near the World Tree's trunk.

He knew what the horn meant: The Men without Faces had been spotted. It would be only a matter of time before they crashed against the island's defenders and spilled more Odauthian blood.

He cursed the creatures under his breath and prayed to the old gods that his friends and family would be safe from the oncoming onslaught. He thought first of his little sister, Asiri, and was glad that she would not be on the front lines, unlike several of his close friends. The front lines were also where he was supposed to be, of course. A twinge of guilt gnawed at his heart. If something should happen to his friends before he got there—he pushed the thought from his mind. Not that he'd be able to do anything anyway.

His swift legs carried him over the rocky paths toward the great tree at the center of the island. He could already see the Faceless crawling out of the water on the southern shore, and he swore under his breath. At this rate, the beasts would cut him off before he was able to make it through the gates. Why had he been so stupid as to think he would be safe so far from the tree?

By the time he finally made it to the wall surrounding Yggdrasil and the villages, he could hear the clash of a battle taking place beyond the ridge. He hoisted a small war hammer from his belt and made his way around the curve in the great wall until the Men without Faces and Odauthian warriors were in full view.

Helpless to do anything, Halamir watched in horror as the Faceless tore through his countrymen with such ferocity that in only a matter of minutes, the entire battalion of warriors had been slain with no mercy, leaving none alive on the blood and gore spattered beach.

Halamir threw himself against the town's wall, hoping that none of the Faceless had sensed him, and that they remained focused on their current, gruesome task. He felt the guilt arise again, but he told himself over and over again that there was no way he could have changed the outcome of the battle.

He made his way around the wall, hoping to find some way to cross over or at the very least, find somewhere to hide. He could sense a deep hunger at the back of his mind, and he knew the Faceless were close behind. The groaning intensified, and his heart thundered in his chest, but when he was just about to give up hope, two men appeared at the top of the high wall.

"Down here!" he cried. He waved his hands and struck a sheet of metal on the stone wall with his hammer.

"Halamir!" cried one of the soldiers, and Halamir thanked the gods as he recognized his friend's voice. "By the gods, what are you doing down there?"

"Balkar! Throw down a rope!" he cried.

Balkar let loose a long rope that hung down the side of the wall but fell short several feet. Halamir tried to jump, but it was too high. "The earth is higher on the wall just over there!" He pointed to the east where the rocky terrain was elevated, but the wall remained the same height.

The Faceless piled on top of one another and swarmed toward their prey, but Halamir ran and leapt just in time, grasping the end of the rope as the Faceless clawed at his heels. He swung away from certain death and began to climb.

"Pull me up, Balkar!" called Halamir, but there was no answer. He continued his ascent, putting one hand in front of the other. He did not look to see how much farther he had to climb, but he knew the Faceless swarm was below him.

He felt something tug the rope below, and he glanced down to see the Faceless beasts climbing toward him at an alarming speed. As one neared him, he pulled his legs toward his chest and swung his hammer downward, splitting his foe's skull. Its body knocked two more Faceless from the rope, but the rest kept coming.

"Balkar!" Halamir barked, fearing that the beasts had already made it on top of the wall.

He did not know if his cries were for his own safety or that of his friend. He smashed another of the creatures where its face should have been then lost his grip on his hammer. The weapon tumbled from his grip and plummeted into the sea of Faceless below. He continued his climb and cheered in relief as a volley of arrows felled the Faceless that pursued him.

Five dead Faceless lay around Balkar and the other warrior Halamir recognized as a man named Elentinus. As soon as Elentinus pulled Halamir over the precipice, Balkar severed the rope, sending several more Faceless to their death—if they were alive to begin with.

"How'd they get to the top of the wall?" wheezed Halamir. Elentinus pointed to the west where the main gates were in ruin, and hundreds of Faceless were already swarming inside.

"We need to go," said Balkar, shoving Elentinus toward the docks. "The Anandlitin have not yet taken several of our vessels. We may yet escape to the Arcship."

Halamir felt his guilt subside, for even a staunch warrior like Balkar was already planning on going to the Arcship to escape the Anandlitin, the Men without Faces.

"You don't think they've already climbed inside and are waiting for us?" Elentinus growled, shoving Balkar backward. "They're going to kill us near the World Tree or by the boats. If you want to die by the boats, then by all means."

"I am your captain, Elentinus," barked Balkar.

"Oh, give it up, *Captain*," spat back Elentinus. "You're only my captain because the rest of our squad is dead. It's just us two, Balkar!"

Halamir spoke up for the first time, voicing his hope to escape. "Look, Balkar is right. We know the World Tree is overrun, but we don't know for sure if the ships are—"

"Don't think me a weak captain for wanting to abandon Yggdrasil," said Balkar.

"Forgive me, my friend," said Elentinus, with a cheeky smile, "but you know I already thought that before you decided anything."

He slugged his friend on the arm, and the trio made their way toward the docks, not knowing what demons awaited them on the open ocean.

To their great relief, the docks were free of the Men without Faces when they arrived. Several battalions of the island's defenders ushered them across a gangplank to board the massive

Arcship, which stood longer from end to end than most Odauthian towns. In fact, Halamir knew the ship functioned as a city with housing, market and industrial districts, recreational areas such as parks, and other places for people to live, work, play, and relax.

As the soldiers led them and hundreds of others onto the ship, questions plagued Halamir's mind. He couldn't help but wonder, even if they did escape the island, where would they go? Were the rest of his friends and family safe? What was out there? *Who* was out there?

Was their island truly alone?

## SEVENTY-SEVEN YEARS AGO

Aleksander's memories shifted, and he saw in his mind's eye a storm raging around a massive ship he knew to be the Odauthian Arcship. The ship's purpose was to weather such storms, but Aleksander could feel that the true chaos was brewing within the ship's hull, and not without.

The already strained atmosphere of the ship was made worse by a sudden surge of ice that encased the hull of the Arcship and the incessant, disembodied voice that called Halamir's name. No longer was the ship one tribe of Odauthians, but a collection of splintered factions that fought for control over resources and of the ship itself.

At first, only Halamir could hear the voice, but in time, others began to hear his name in their minds, influencing members of all the splintered factions aboard the ship to seek him out. Why was this happening?

Halamir's breath came in sharp bursts of white that lingered in the air for a brief moment before fading away. He and Elentinus sat slumped against the back of one of the Arcship's many enormous smokestacks pouring dark smoke into winter's pure sky.

"I think we're safe now," Elentinus said, his breath still heavy. "They've moved on."

Halamir nodded. He could no longer hear the footsteps of the men pursuing them, and he crawled around the corner to check. The coast was clear, and he gestured for his friend to follow into the ship's market district where his sister Asiri had prepared a raft for them.

"Safe for now, I think you mean. This voice is drawing me out into the blizzard, after all," Halamir said, shivering.

"Yeah," Elentinus said, gazing out to sea. "It's getting worse, look. We'd better hurry."

Halamir had been so focused on their survival that he hadn't taken time to monitor the state of the ice encompassing the ship.

"I'm surprised you can even tell it's changed at all through the blizzard," Halamir said, pulling the fur cloak closer to his exposed neck. "We're almost to the raft, let's go."

As they made their way into the ship's market district, the voices began again, calling him to venture out into the icy storm.

*"Come, Halamir..."*

The duo, fully armed for whatever fight awaited them on the ice, hurried through the market district. Boards were nailed up over most of the shop windows, and all the fish stalls had been shut down due to the blizzard, much to Elentinus and Halamir's benefit. Less eyes to spot them meant less swords chasing them.

"Hal!" Halamir heard Asiri's soft voice call through the drifting snow.

Halamir could barely make out her petite silhouette under a lantern that rocked in the breeze. They approached with outstretched arms to greet her, but she shook her head.

"No time," Asiri said. "Get going. Balkar and his goons just passed through, and if they see you, they'll kill you. Go, and be quick!"

Halamir nodded in understanding as Elentinus helped him into Asiri's rowboat hanging off the edge of the Arcship.

"Thank you, Asiri!" Halamir exclaimed as she pulled some ropes to lower the boat to the frozen sea below.

"Thank me later!" Asiri called.

The rowboat's descent stopped, and Halamir glanced up in horror just as a thick crossbow bolt struck Elentinus in the chest. Halamir scrambled to his feet, trying to manipulate the ropes to bring him back up.

"Asiri!" he called.

The voice that replied was not that of his sister.

*"Halamir…"*

He tried his best to ignore the disembodied voice in his mind and began to climb the rope, but he fell back into the lifeboat as it plummeted downward. It crashed against the ice creeping up the side of the Arcship; Asiri must have cut the rope.

Halamir could no longer see his friend or sister above, lost to the fog and drifting snow. He had no idea what he was looking for, but the trio had all decided it would be best if he heeded the voice's call and ventured into the heart of the storm. Even if the other factions thought it would be best just to kill Halamir to appease the voice.

Another voice filled his mind. Not the haunting one calling his name, and not that of Asiri or Elentinus. This time, he could feel the familiar consciousness of Yggdrasil, the world tree leading him into the blinding white storm.

As soon as Halamir stepped foot on the snow-covered ice sheet, the dull groaning of a group of hibernating Faceless filled his mind as well. He shuddered, not from the icy chill that beat against him, but from the disconcerting feelings of Men without Faces; their hunger, their frustration, and their never-ending anguish seemed to fill his soul, but one Faceless in particular seemed to draw him closer. This was something different. Something familiar. Someone alone. He could feel Yggdrasil's confirmation that it was safe to approach.

"I'm here!" called Halamir.

He felt foolish, not knowing who he was addressing. A lone figure stood silhouetted amid the storm with its back to Halamir. A chill crawled up Halamir's spine as the man turned to face him. Halamir didn't need to ask himself why the man stood alone in an icy sea surrounded by his Faceless foes, for he could sense the final lingering memories mixed in with the horrendous groaning emanating from the man's dead brain.

"Pabbi?" the Odauthian word a child would use to refer to their father was the only whisper that escaped Halamir's lips.

*"Halam…Halam…"*

The fleeting voice of Halamir's father, Valdur filled every crevice of Halamir's mind. The young warrior drew a longsword from his belt and held it aloft against the Faceless.

"No, this is a trick—you—you died! Stay back!" Halamir cried, but Valdur kept coming, one slow step after another.

*"Yggdrasil's portals…Halam…Yggdrasil…portals…below…Save you…Asiri…"*

Countless Faceless lay dead in the snow around him, their necks severed. Valdur pointed to a crack in the ice sheet, which emanated with an amethyst glow.

"Are you…?" Halamir whispered, lowering his blade for a brief second.

In that moment of hesitation, Valdur leapt toward his son with the horrible groan of an agonized Faceless. Halamir fell onto his back in terror, shielding his face. As Valdur's sharp claws tore into his forearms, the young warrior grasped the pommel of his sword and launched a blind upward strike with the blade. The sword ripped through his father's tunic, staining the white snow with dark blood.

*"Thank…you…"* Valdur's voice said in Halamir's mind.

"Pabbi! Did you freeze the Arcship so that we could find the portal?" Halamir asked, tears streaming down his frostbitten face. "Pabbi!"

*"Yes…tell…Asiri…love…portal…below…"*

"Of course, of course," Halamir said. "Pabbi, don't leave me!"

"*Kill…me…*"

Through his tears, Halamir thrust his blade into the stomach of the Faceless that had once been his father. As Valdur slumped to his knees, he held up his hands, and the storm around the ship calmed, the ice breaking away from around the ship's hull.

And then a column of ice erupted from below Halamir's feet, carrying him upward, back to the Arcship.

"No! Wait!" Halamir exclaimed, knowing that Balkar and his traitorous band could be waiting for him there.

The pillar carried him upward as the icesheet below cracked apart and away from the massive city ship. Two words filled Halamir's mind.

"*I…love…*"

Halamir clambered onto the deck of the Arcship, and sure enough, Balkar and a mob of other angry people were waiting for him. Elentinus lay dead on the deck, and some of Balkar's men had bound Asiri in thick chains. Ten of his soldiers were strewn across the deck with severed limbs around them as well, the victims of Asiri's axe.

"You let her go!" Halamir ordered, shoving a finger into Balkar's chest.

"Halamir, old buddy!" Balkar exclaimed. "Can't you tell? As soon as we captured you, the snow stopped, and the ice started cracking. The gods are smiling on us today."

"Just kill me and get this over with, but don't you dare touch Asiri," Halamir said, spitting at Balkar's boots. "Listen, Balkar—

Yggdrasil's portal is directly below us. It's going to take us somewhere safe. My father—"

Balkar smacked Halamir across the face and gestured for his men to take Asiri away.

"It's the prisons for you," Balkar said. "An hour or so in there should do the trick."

"An hour?! No, please," Halamir said, his eyes wide in fear. "Please just kill me! Anything but—"

Balkar personally led Halamir away toward the prison deck of the Arcship far below. The mob followed close behind, cheering as their captain shoved him into a cell which was no more than a coffin built into the ground. He heard Asiri's cries as they stowed her away as well, and then she was silent.

"What did you do to her?" Halamir asked through gritted teeth. Balkar did not answer, and gestured instead to one of the prison wardens, who knelt next to Halamir's coffin cell holding a golden cuff. "What is that?"

"It'll keep you asleep. You will serve your sentence within your own mind, and your cell will keep you alive until that sentence is over. Don't worry, you probably won't remember a thing," the warden replied as he placed the cuff on Halamir's wrist and shut the coffin.

He felt a sharp pain in his wrist, and his world began to spin. And then he knew no more.

Aleksander's implanted memories swirled one last time, and his consciousness merged with Halamir's as bright light filled his vision. Breath filled his lungs, and he pushed the door of his cell open. He screamed at the immense pain in his wrist. The cuff on his wrist felt white hot, and he pried it off, leaving a deep wound where a needle inside the instrument had pierced his skin. He kicked it across the chamber and stumbled from his cell. He called for Asiri but dreaded that there would be no answer.

The other prison cells were all shut, meaning they were all in use, but there were no wardens to be seen. He looked into the small window of each cell to examine the faces of those within the coffin-like cells but did not find Asiri. He stumbled from the prison deck, still dizzy and disoriented. He scratched his chin to find that a grizzled beard hung down past his chest.

This couldn't be happening; he shook his head in disbelief. He hurried to a glass window to examine his reflection and gasped in shock for the gaunt face of a much older man stared back at him. How long had he been asleep? He had heard stories of people going mad in Balkar's prison, but he still *felt* sane—perhaps that was a sign that he was not.

Halamir made it to the top deck of the ship without meeting anyone trying to kill him. A good sign. The ice and the storm were long gone. He must have been trapped in the Mind-Prison longer than Balkar had indicated. He wondered where the Arcship had traveled in that time.

Everyone he passed wore strange clothing and gave him odd looks of disdain as he yelled for his sister, but he pressed on in his search. Thoughts of Elentinus and his father filled his mind as he remembered their fates; they were long dead by now. Asiri too, probably.

He broke down crying and slumped against the railing of the Arcship's top deck, not caring what any passersby thought. At long last, he composed himself and tried to take in his surroundings. Although the people dressed and spoke differently than what he remembered, the ship itself seemed largely the same as it had been before his imprisonment.

He got to his feet and gazed toward the burning coast of a land he did not recognize. Everything about the new land told him he was not staring at his former home; Yggdrasil's portal must have transported them somewhere else, and who knows where else they had traveled while he slumbered.

A fleet of ships was sailing from the coast, and Halamir placed his hand over his mouth with a horrible realization. Hundreds of questions pounded at his skull. Were his people plundering this new land? What other horrors had his people wrought? The first of the ships docked, and its crew disembarked, laughing, and congratulating one another in a language he did not recognize. It wasn't Icelandic, to be sure.

He watched the crew unloading cargo, probably the spoils of their attack on the coast. His mouth gaped open, and tears filled his eyes as people clad in chains marched onto the ship.

People. Their spoils weren't gold or treasure, it was people. The Arcship and his people had turned to slaving. He shook his head; he could not, would not believe it. He stumbled backward into a wall as he watched one of the slavers strike a young woman with dark black hair across the back with a barbed whip. The girl tried to retaliate but was forced to the ground. A ball of flame erupted from another slave's hand, but the young man collapsed as a slaver struck him over the head.

"Xanthurias!" called the young woman, who screamed for her friend as he was dragged away.

And then Aleksander awoke from the memories that were not his own.

# CHAPTER SEVEN

# WE CAN'T SAVE THEM ALL

The moon's unearthly glow illuminated the landscape ahead of Josman, Drahomir, Valis, and Kamil as they made their way toward the ruins of the city of Nitra. Their supply horse neighed nervously as if to herald bad tidings of their task to investigate the ruins of the fallen city. A task personally set for them by King Verahim Romus and negotiated by the new ambassador to Sangora, Rehor Toth. Josman's strong hand guided the beast around a rocky outcrop jutting out of the hillside as the rest of their horses trotted alongside them, weary from the long trek.

"You know, our group tends to talk a lot more when Shanthah is here," said Drahomir. "This silence is kind of nice."

*"Is that a joke because I can't talk?"* said Kamil directly to the others' minds, relying on his magic to communicate, as his tongue had been carved out in the Talohiran slave camp.

"What, no, I—" Drahomir stammered.

*"I'm joking. Shanthah's not the only one who does that either."*

"No, but Drahomir's right for once, maybe we should talk more," said Josman with a booming laugh. "Well, what do you three say we tie up our horses just ahead and set up camp for the rest of the night?"

"We're still hours from Nitra. I think I'll fall off my horse if we ride much longer," said Valis with a sleepy nod. "Speaking of Shanthah, he'd probably suggest Drahomir should have to do the lookout job and tie up the horses. So, get on that."

Josman and Kamil both laughed at his joke, much to his relief. Valis had always felt like an outsider with the group, for he did not share their camaraderie forged from escaping the slave camp. He and Kamil had bonded over their shared homeland, the far-off country of Kurash. Valis had been raised there by his single mother, Alia, who hid him from his father, King Valistaran Talohir and his wretched slave camps.

His mother had told him all about his father's crimes and knew it was odd that he felt jealous and perhaps a bit guilty about not having experienced them firsthand.

"Then let me be the first to say, again, that it is fortunate that Shanthah is not here," said Drahomir, dismounting his horse before coaxing it toward a thick tree to tie it up. He and Valis tied the four horses to the trunk as Josman and Kamil worked together to pitch their tent, which was much too small for the four of them.

"The others get to attend diplomatic sessions in Sangora and eat feasts and drink and dance, but what do we get to do? Oh, that's right, investigate a dead city," Josman muttered, hammering a stake into the earth, his angst fueling each strike.

"It's not so bad," Valis said with a laugh as he started gathering dry wood for a fire. "And we get to see this!"

He gestured to the heavens where they could see endless stars unhidden by clouds or the glow of city lights in the capital city of Laniras.

*"Come now, would you rather have to deal with politicians, or get to camp with your favorite people?"* Kamil asked. Josman chuckled, a twinkle in his eyes, and Kamil smiled back.

He knew the broad-shouldered man was soft-hearted and kind, despite his gruff beard, booming voice, and intimidating appearance.

As Josman hammered the tent stake into the earth, Kamil's attention shot toward the rocky hills behind them. At the same time, all five horses began to neigh and buck their heads, shaking the tree.

"What is it?" asked Josman.

*"You'll know in a moment."*

Valis stopped stoking the weak campfire and Josman stopped staking as a sense of dread washed over the group; an intense groaning filled each of their minds just as a horde of gray-skinned, faceless creatures swarmed over the hillside behind them.

As fast as he could, Josman unbuckled his mace from the pack horse's saddle and smashed it against the throat of the nearest Faceless, throwing it, broken, against the ground. Drahomir followed suit, slicing out the legs of the nearest creature as it rushed right by him. As the monsters overran the group, Valis steadied their horses which were trying to free themselves from the tree.

"What are these things?" cried Valis as the creatures swarmed past them. "But more importantly, why aren't they attacking?"

He turned to see Kamil on his knees. At first, Valis thought his fellow Kurashian was praying but quickly realized he was concentrating with all his might to focus his mental powers. As the horde of Faceless swarmed by, Kamil got to his feet but kept his focus on the creatures.

"You made them think we weren't here, didn't you?" said Drahomir. "I think I speak for all of us when I say, 'thank you'."

"They aren't going in the direction of Nitra," said Josman as he reluctantly pried the tent stake out of the ground. He grumbled something about knowing they weren't going to stay put.

"What are you doing?" asked Drahomir. "Aren't we going to stay here for the night?"

"I think those were the same monsters from the island. You know, the one where Hanna and Shanthah fought Mara? Those things are on their way to kill. From Shanthah's description of them, they're pretty good at it, but we're going to stop them," said Josman as he rolled up the tent. "Ready the horses!"

Drahomir and Valis untied the horses with shaking hands, nerves and exhaustion getting the best of them. Josman threw the tent into the saddlebag of the pack horse and climbed onto his own steed, urging it onward.

The four members of the Hidden Flame mounted their horses and raced toward the Faceless, soon cresting the closest of the rolling hills. The monsters were nearly as swift as the horses that pursued them, fueled by the desire to feed, and tortured with the inability to do so, but seemingly unhindered by fatigue.

"Kamil, I need you to shield our minds again as soon as we're close!" cried Josman as they neared the horde.

*"I won't be able to shield us from all of them and ride at the same time. I need to concentrate,"* thought Kamil to the others as they closed the distance between their group and the Faceless.

"Do what you can!" Drahomir exclaimed as they rode in the direction of a plume of smoke that was now billowing from behind the hills.

"What town is that?" asked Valis as he urged his horse onward.

"Pata, I think!" shouted Drahomir as he watched the Faceless pour into the town, helpless to stop them. Screams erupted from the terrified townsfolk but were drowned out by the horrifying sense of voracious hunger that accompanied the Faceless horde.

"Kamil! Mindspeak to everyone you can. Get them out!" called Josman.

"I don't think they need to be told," replied Drahomir as the group reached the humble town. Josman urged his steed onward, trampling two of the nearest Faceless which tore at the horse's legs as its hooves crushed their bodies.

The horses sensed the feeling of dread that accompanied the Faceless just as their masters could and refused to enter the city. They reared up on their hind legs, and Drahomir had to leap from his steed as it bolted away. Josman's horse bucked him from the saddle then limped away, scared, but alive. Kamil had the instinct to run to Josman's aid but remembered his friend's magic manifested in armored skin that protected him from most harm.

Josman recovered from the fall quickly. He scrambled for his mace, using it to crush skulls and shatter bones as a foreign thought cross his mind; Kamil sent a mental message to as much of the city as he could: *"GET OUT."* Wishing he could follow his friend's message, Josman threw himself between the horde and their prey, brandishing his heavy weapon.

"Kamil, can you 'talk' to these things?" called Valis as he pulled his blade out of a creature's side. Drahomir then slew a Faceless about to overwhelm Kamil, who then sent a mental message to the rest of the group.

*"I can certainly try. Get ready!"*

"If you can, tell them to attack me!" Josman shouted; a moment later, five of the beasts swarmed over him.

Kamil watched as the creatures tried in vain to disembowel Josman, their jagged claws shattering as they slashed at his magically impervious skin. Valis and Drahomir took advantage of the creatures' distraction, hacking at their exposed backs and necks. Although they failed to kill Josman, the beasts were able to incapacitate him by dragging him to the earth and covering him in a pile of their bodies.

Kamil lifted his hand and reached out with his mind, attempting to connect to the consciousness of the beasts, if they had such a thing. He screamed in agony and collapsed to the earth as a mental presence blocked his entry. Something, or someone, was controlling the Faceless; they were not wild beasts killing at random after all, but servants of a higher, darker power. He scrambled backward as the Faceless turned all their attention on him.

"This was a bad idea!" exclaimed Drahomir as he and Valis tried to defend their friend, still recovering after connecting with the creatures' master. The Faceless swarmed past Drahomir and Valis, dragging them to the ground on the way to slay Kamil, his powerful mind a prized prey.

Kamil's screams filled the valley as he focused all the mental energy that he could muster to one far-off location outside the town; the Faceless stopped and turned on their heels, swarming toward the explosion of mental energy instead. Kamil collapsed, his head throbbing.

*"Ow."*

"Valis!" cried Josman, clawing his way through the dirt toward his young ally. Valis stirred weakly as Drahomir pressed his cloak against the boy's side to staunch the bleeding of a heavy wound. "Valis, are you alright?"

"Kamil, how long can you distract those things?" asked Drahomir as he watched them claw at the nothingness around them. The look of pain on Kamil's face was answer enough.

"Valis isn't going to make it if we don't get him out of here right now. Maybe there are some healers in the next village? If only his mother were here—we could really use her magic right now," Drahomir said, referring to Alia's magical ability to heal wounds with her hands.

"Well, Alia is in Kurash, so even if we managed to get him to—" Josman paused as a writhing purple and black smoke began to bubble from Drahomir's hands. It coalesced into a twisting mass of shadow between him and Valis, who stared into the void and saw none other than the confused face of his mother looking back at him.

"Ummi?!" Valis exclaimed. The word a child would use in Kurashic to refer to their mother.

"About time we found out why you were in the camp with us," said Josman in awe. "They say magic always manifests when you need it most. Whatever you're doing, keep it up!"

His own magic had manifested as invulnerable skin while in battle, and Kamil's magic had appeared after his tongue was cut out, and he lost the ability to speak.

Drahomir stumbled backward, unsure of what was happening as his hands stopped flowing with liquid darkness. "Whatever that was, I think it's subconscious—guys, I—"

"What in the name of Kadir?" asked Alia as she stepped out of the shadows, which dissipated as soon as she materialized.

She cried out in shock as she saw her son lying covered in blood then pressed her hands to each of wounds. Josman watched, unsure of how to help as Alia maintained a steady pressure on the worst wound on the boy's side. Her magic closed the wounds, and Valis gave a feeble stir. Kamil groaned as he struggled to distract the Faceless horde.

"I don't mean to take away from whatever just happened, but Kamil can't hold those things off forever. We need to get these people out of here or they'll all die," said Josman. He turned to Drahomir. "You brought Alia, here, could you send people away?"

Drahomir held out his hands like Kamil when he used his powers, but nothing happened.

"Nope—as useless as the day I was born," replied Drahomir. "I'm so sorry, but I *can* tend to Valis. Those people need Alia more than he does now."

"Well, if nothing else, seeing you was a pleasant surprise," said Alia, wrapping her arms around her son before a quick hug for Kamil, Drahomir, and finally Josman, who had to hunch over to embrace her. "Let's get to work."

"Yes, finding your son lying in his own blood is always a pleasant surprise," said Valis in a weak voice. Josman helped him stand. "Thanks, ummi, I'll be okay from here."

Meanwhile, Kamil cast another mental explosion as far from the town as possible, sending the horde far from the town as if he were throwing a stick for a dog.

Alia flashed a grin and ruffled her son's hair. "You know I love you. You okay?"

Drahomir nodded as the group made their way into the village. Their banter died away as a macabre scene met their eyes. The stench of the carnage was overpowering, but the sight of those who were unable to outrun the claws of the Faceless was truly gruesome. Mangled bodies and severed limbs littered the streets. Josman fell to his knees and retched, forcing himself to turn away from the scene.

"Check for a pulse, like I showed you. If you can't find one, move on. Go, now," Alia said. The others did as they were told, announcing every pulse they found so that Alia could heal the few survivors. Hundreds of terrified townsfolk were beginning to gather to watch.

"We don't have long," called Josman to the crowd. "We need to—" He was cut off as a man at the front of the crowd hurled a pebble at him, which ricocheted off his forehead.

"Get out of our town, magic scum!" screamed a woman next to him. "Your kind ain't welcome here!"

Josman held his hands out in silent, perplexed anger as Drahomir shouted at the woman. "We saved your lives, you ungrateful woman!"

"*Drahomir, maybe it's best if we don't antagonize them. They've lost so much,*" Kamil began to say as a pebble collided with his chest.

As another rock hit Josman, he turned and bellowed, "Alright, my friend's right! You'd be dead if it wasn't for us, but they're going to come back, and when they do, you can bet that we'll be gone!"

"We don't need Kurashians here either!" Someone else from the crowd shouted, "Desert witches!" And yet another, "Go back to your sand and camels!"

Drahomir turned to see an angry look on each of Valis, Alia, and Kamil's faces; the comment disrupted Kamil's mental concentration, breaking his mental lure for the Faceless.

"How *dare* you?!" Drahomir shouted. "Listen here, you piece of—" Kamil cut him off.

"*Anyone who wants to get out of here with their life can follow us out of the city. The rest will die. There's nothing more we can do.*" Kamil projected the thought to everyone in the crowd, who stirred uneasily as his consciousness brushed against theirs. After a moment, a young boy stepped out from behind his parents and gripped Kamil's hand. Several other villagers stepped forward as well.

"We will make our way across the River Vah to Turnava," said Josman, leading the willing part of the crowd out of the city, leaving the rest to fend for themselves. "Turnava will hold until we can make our way to the fortress of Zinok."

Many of the villagers had already made up their minds to leave before the group's arrival, as several of them already had packs and carts filled with food and supplies. The rest made comments about desert witches stealing their people away.

Those who wished to flee followed Josman, Drahomir, Valis, Alia, and Kamil out of the village toward the great river that snaked its way through the countryside.

As the company fled the doomed village, the Faceless flooded unimpeded into the town, tearing into the flesh of those who did not attempt to escape.

Screams erupted from the village, and Josman turned to look back, grief etched into his face. Kamil tried in vain to stop them with a burst of mental energy, but he collapsed from mental exhaustion. Josman helped him onto an elderly passerby's handcart full of food. He thanked the man, who flashed a toothy grin and continued onward.

"We can't save them all. Maybe we never could have, and that's their choice," said Drahomir, seeing the sadness apparent on his friend's visage, "but we can help *these* people."

Josman nodded and clapped Drahomir on the back as he helped the elderly man push the cart carrying Kamil and supplies.

"Alia, Valis…" Josman said, not including Kamil, who was unconscious. "About what those people said back there—I'm so sorry. There's still lots of prejudice here for Sangorans, but they're even worse about Kurashians—"

"We know." There was pain and sadness in her kind brown eyes. "It isn't your place to apologize but thank you."

"It doesn't make it right. People like that just—"

He screwed up his eyes and pounded his fist on the side of a wagon. Alia placed a hand on his shoulder and smiled for a moment before they helped push a cart into the river.

"The world needs more people like you, Josman Faros," Alia said and planted a kiss on his cheek. Josman grumbled something under his breath with a faint smile as they watched a thick plume of smoke extending from the burning village of Pata.

# CHAPTER EIGHT

# BLOOD IN THE ASHES

No official announcement had been made regarding Antanasia's murder, but that did not stop hushed rumors from spreading throughout Doftaan. Many in attendance noted her absence at the peace banquet, signing ceremony, and now at the royal ball to cap off the week's negotiations. Some thought her absence was a political statement, but others guessed the truth.

The expansive ballroom of Mara's palace was adorned with the viridian of Thanatanos and Sangora's crimson; the national symbols, the star of Thanatanos and the moon of Sangora hung on beautifully crafted banners around the massive chamber.

Torches set outside cast light through the ballroom's stained-glass windows, creating entrancing designs of shifting light throughout the room that danced across the faces of Mara's delighted guests.

"We were all in that slave camp—why aren't any of us royalty? Because I could get used to this," said Shanthah in awe as he and Hanna entered the ballroom. Their presence was announced by a duo of Sangoran guards near the entrance. "And what did we get from that? Nothing, Miss Samsa."

"You got me, dumby," said Hanna with a laugh.

"Ah, yes, I guess you can say that I'm luckier than Mara after all," answered Shanthah with a smile, gesturing to his companion from head to toe. She indeed looked radiant, her auburn hair and blood red gown a striking contrast to the dark suits of the Thannish diplomats. "Although, might I say, Sangoran fashion perplexes me." He gestured to the fabric torn up to her knee.

Hanna laughed and shook her head. "Sangoran fashion has nothing to do with that," she said with a laugh. "I'll explain that later—I'll add it to my list of 'things to tell Shanthah'."

She had not yet had time to relay details of her rendezvous with Mara into the slave camp, despite Shanthah's pleas to do so. The musicians began an upbeat Sangoran melody, and Hanna gave a playful wink as she led Shanthah by the hand to the area where Sangorans and humans alike were dancing.

Their feet carried them to the beat of their own music, untrained in the steps and dips of royal dancing. Diplomats from both countries seemed to be doing the same; Shanthah had expected to see a well-choreographed dance by everyone in the room, but the floor was filled with mixes of different dances and fine attire from regions of Sangora and Thanatanos alike.

Rehor strode past them and took the hand of Raluca, the resplendent Mistress of Dusk and sister of the former queen.

Other than his flamboyant red hat, his well-tailored, conservative Thannish attire looked like a peasant's tunic compared to Raluca's colorful and alluring, low-cut dress; her cloak, patterned after a peacock's vivid plumage, somehow flowed behind her like colorful smoke as they danced.

Nearby, Pol agreed to dance with a younger Sangoran girl, stepping awkwardly over his new friend's feet, but Rehor stepped with the grace of an expert. Pol kept an eye on his mentor and tried to emulate his steps.

"You see who Rehor's dancing with? I think that girl just became my new favorite color," said Hanna. Shanthah laughed and took Hanna in his arms. She laid her cheek against his shoulder as they slowly stepped to the rhythm of the music.

"Well, you're more my taste," said Shanthah. They said nothing, simply happy to hold one another.

"That's a load of Minotaur dung but thank you—this is a happy moment," said Hanna in a soft voice. Shanthah nodded, giving her a sweet, loving smile. At that moment, the orchestra at the end of the chamber ended their song and exploded with a regal tune they both now recognized as the anthem of Sangora.

"I now announce the entrance of Mara Bartunek, Empress of Blood!" called the guard at the doorway.

Shanthah wondered if the members of the orchestra knew exactly when Mara would enter, so perfect was their timing.

Hanna paused as Mara entered. She expected the empress to be dressed in the elaborate gown of a ruler, something more akin to Raluca's dress, but instead, she had donned a backless, black dress that came to her knees. Her head was adorned with no crown, save the braid that encircled her head. Had Hanna and Mara not shared a history with one another, she would not have recognized the woman as Empress of Blood.

An odd sense of guilt filled Hanna's heart as she watched Mara. They had once been closer than sisters but were now little more than strangers. The Empress smiled as she mingled with guests and diplomats, and Hanna wondered if their bond could ever be what it was. Other than Lavinia, Hanna had been the only person invited to accompany Mara into the slave camp, and she knew it must have been a peace offering in Mara's own personal way.

"She hates this," muttered Shanthah into Hanna's ear. "Look how uncomfortable she looks."

Hanna chuckled in agreement, for she too could tell how much Mara despised the pleasantries, her anxiety evident in how she held her hands and the forced expression stretched across her face.

"Cost of being Empress of Blood, I guess," Hanna replied.

"Should we save her from this life of ballgowns and monocles for old times' sake?" Shanthah asked.

"No. I think someone else is going to do that for her."

She gestured with her head in the direction opposite Mara. Shanthah nodded in acknowledgment as he noticed what Hanna meant: Aleksander was making his way through the crowd toward the empress.

As people danced around him, Aleksander stood awkwardly without a partner, waiting to speak with Mara for the first time since the beginning of negotiations. He offered a nervous smile as he made eye contact with the Empress of Blood; he wondered if he had imagined it, but as other dignitaries greeted her, her eyes kept darting back to him.

Aleksander could have sworn that Mara flashed one genuine smile at him through the crowd, and several long minutes later, she excused herself from a conversation with a stooped Sangoran woman wearing the muted colors of the Sangoran state of Terman. She ignored the outstretched hands of several more diplomats from Thanatanos, and sure enough, she made her way straight for Aleksander.

Neither of them said a word as Aleksander extended a nervous hand, and his heart leapt as her cold fingers brushed his own before interlacing with them. A smile crossed her lips, although it did not seem to reach her eyes.

"Hi." The greeting was gentle, cautious.

"Hi, Mar."

Mara guided his hand to the small of her back, and a shiver ran down his spine as she placed her other hand on the back of his neck. She led him in a slow, traditional Sangoran dance, following the flow of enchanting music from the orchestra. The tune was elegant, beautiful. Hauntingly so.

Shanthah and Hanna half danced, half hopped in the direction of Mara and Aleksander to overhear their conversation, but at last, they admitted defeat, the ballroom much too loud for them to hear anything without being far too conspicuous.

Mara and Aleksander danced for an entire song without saying a word. When the next melody began, to Aleksander's surprise, Mara did not pull away.

"You know, I'm glad the lady leads in Sangoran dances, because I—"

"Because you're a horrible dancer?" Mara asked with a grin.

"Yes, exactly." Aleksander chuckled before he stammered, "You look, well, incredible, if, uh, that's not a weird thing to—"

"You look very snazzy too," Mara said with a smile as she absentmindedly touched the braid wrapped around her head. "I like your suit. Very…regal." She grinned.

"Thank you. Although, I have to ask. Why did you invite me here?" asked Aleksander. The words felt clunky and forced, but they slipped out before he could stop them from tumbling out.

"I needed help," said Mara, her faint smile fading. "And who better than the Secret Keeper of Kurash to help me? If anyone has any clues of to what this thing hunting my people is, it's you."

"I'm sure you heard what happened with Lavinia," said Aleksander, knowing that Lavinia's theory was beginning to hold more weight.

"Yes. I visited her in the hospital today, but something no one else knows—it attacked me too." Mara pressed her mouth shut as she noticed a delegate eavesdropping. She waited for the music to pick up before continuing. "The assassin attacked me in my throne room. It killed Ihrin and Antanasia and almost killed Lavinia. It broke her spine, Aleks—she still can't walk. It's gotten to four of us now."

"I know. I'm sorry, Mara," said Aleksander. "Really. I want you to know that. What do you need me to do?"

"I answered your question honestly, and I need you to answer one for me too."

"Anything," he said.

"Do not lie to me. Do you have anything to do with this?" she asked. She couldn't quite meet his dark eyes as the question trailed from her lips, her own eyes darting down to their feet.

"Of course not," said Aleksander. "I want peace as much as you do."

"Peace can still come through violence, but it does not make it right," Mara said. "I know that better than most."

"I apologize. I realize that doesn't prove my innocence," said Aleksander. "I do want peace. For our countries, and, well, for us too."

"I want that too," Mara said, lightly stroking his neck with her hand, making his stomach leap. "But what about your friends?"

Aleksander let out a slow breath.

"As far as I know, they have nothing to do with this."

Mara looked around again before speaking.

"When the assassin attacked me, I touched its mind. I think its mask kept me from reaching very deep, but two of the only words I could really make out were…" Mara pulled Aleksander closer, using their dance to whisper a single word into his ear to prevent the group of assembled dignitaries from hearing. He waited patiently for the word as Mara made sure no one could hear. "Aleksander."

"And the other?"

"Kill."

Aleksander tried to make sense of everything, but the more he tried, the more it puzzled him. The murderer had to be someone he knew, or at least someone connected to his forgotten past.

"I'm not trying to kill you, Mara. I'm trying to save you," he said, Lavinia's words from earlier that week still fresh in his mind. He regretted his choice of words as soon as he said them even before Mara cut him off.

"I've told you before: I don't need saving. I don't want you to think of me as—what? The queen of the damned? That's what they call me in Thanatanos, among worse things. But my crown is *not* my curse!" She sighed. "I don't care if you think I'm the victim—I don't even care if you think I'm the villain, but Aleks, I can tell you one thing. I know who I am now, and I am not your damsel in distress—or anyone else's."

He was silent, deciding that it was time to listen and not speak.

"And I'm not sorry about that, Aleks. I think you need to figure out who you are too."

"About that, I—something's happened. I remember my name," Aleksander replied. "My real name. I remembered other things too, but they've melted away like a dream after waking…"

"No, that isn't what I mean. You know I know your name too, but we aren't going to talk about that. That person, the boy from the village all those forgotten years ago—that isn't *you*. That person is dead, and we both know why that must remain so— for now, at least," Mara said, still averting eye contact as they danced.

"For now," Aleksander said, nodding in agreement.
"So?" Mara asked.

"So, what?"

"So, step out of the ashes with me, Aleksander. Two years ago, I lost my way. I admit that, and I'm terrified of who I almost became—I thought I was Valistaran's queen, but I was his weapon and nothing more. I know 'Valistaran's attack dog' and its cruder variation is another one of my nicknames in Laniras."

"I know. The last time we saw each other, we were trying to kill one another, after all. Sorry, I had to address it," Aleksander said, a look of shame on his face.

"I know. I promise I won't try today," Mara said as she twirled Aleksander in their dance.

"I won't either," Aleksander said with a laugh. "And I want you to know that I don't hate you."

"I do sometimes."

"You hate me sometimes?" Aleksander asked. Mara answered with a sigh and a slow shake of her head.

"No, not you."

Aleksander paused, unsure of what to say. He squeezed her hand, and they resumed the dance, moving away from the musicians so that they could hear one another better.

"I'm sorry," Aleksander said. It was the only thing he could think to say.

"It isn't your problem. Let's let go of the person you were—who we both were—because we aren't them, and we shouldn't pretend to be. Who you really are *now* is all that matters."

Aleksander smiled, glancing down as he stepped on her toes, but Mara took no heed and cocked her head inquisitively, knowing he wasn't smiling because of his poor dancing.

"You sounded like Rehor," Aleksander said at last. Their eyes met. Mara felt a warmth fill her chest, and tears welled in both eyes. She blinked them away and allowed the smile to shine through.

"Thank you. That might be the best compliment I've ever received," she said. "A better one that anyone here has given me tonight. 'Oh, Empress, so beautiful, so wise, so bleh!' I hate it." She stuck out her tongue and pretended to vomit as she continued to mock the fake compliments of the dignitaries. "These people don't know me. Not like you."

"Is *that* why you brought me here?" Aleksander asked in realization. Mara smiled, and Aleksander found the corners of his mouth curve upward as well.

"We both know how things ended between us. Should we ever be able to forgive each other?"

"Honestly, I don't know," Aleksander said, a look of brutal honesty on his face. Neither spoke for a long moment, until he continued. "I can't condone some of the things you've done in Nitra or Laniras…" He trailed off. "But I know what I did on the bridge that night led to more of your suffering than anything else. And I don't want to remind you of that whenever you look at me."

"It worked out how it needed to," Mara said. "For better or worse."

"I know," Aleksander said with a reassuring nod. "But I think we both still have a lot to work out."

"Isn't that the truth?" Mara said with a laugh. "I once told you what we had was over. Is it?"

Aleksander let out a deep sigh and held Mara closer as they danced. "Yes. I think we both know that."

"Yeah. You're right."

"Even before everything that happened in your village and before we were thrown into the slave camp—back when I wasn't Aleksander, there were sad times, but there were happy times, too. Even inside the camp, we were able to make wonderful memories that will stay with me forever. And, well, we can't go back to those times or forget everything that's happened, but I hope you and I can find new happy moments."

"I hope for that too," Mara said. "Sometimes I envy you, did you know that? I wish that I could forget my past and start fresh again."

"Well, in a way, you did get a fresh new start, and you've done a wonderful job of it," Aleksander replied. "You honestly amaze me."

"You're just too good of a person for your own good, you know that?"

"So are you, Mar." The comment caught him off guard, and he stammered his response. "Um, I'll take that as a compliment, though, but—"

She shook her head slowly. "It was one, but no. No, I'm not." She let out a sigh. "I'm honestly scared that you're idealizing me even after everything that's happened, and I don't want that for you. It'll just end up hurting us both again." She hesitated again. "There's just so much you can't see."

She smiled again, but this time, it was a sad smile; gone were the tears of joy from being compared to Rehor and their moments of mocking the pompous diplomats. Aleksander's expression mirrored her own.

"You're right, though," Aleksander said "Those things happened, and I won't deny that. And maybe what we had can't ever be again, but maybe that's okay. Like you said, maybe we can step out of the ashes and make something new, something..." He paused, looking for the right word. "Something really beautiful, if you want to."

"That sounds nice," Mara said with another bright smile. The music around them crescendoed, but their dance slowed. "I don't know, maybe we shouldn't—but do you think that someday after I've worked through everything..." She trailed off again, trying to find the correct words. "Aleksander, a part of me—"

She stopped dancing and covered her eyes with one hand, frustrated at trying to find the right words.

"Yes?" Aleksander asked.

"No, never mind. A conversation for another day, I promise." She blinked as if trying to hold back tears.

Aleksander nodded in understanding then glanced around before saying in a hushed tone, "Let's not dwell on sad things, okay?" She met his gaze, his fading smile. "I need you to look into my mind. I need you to trust me, and I need to tell you something that I don't want anyone overhearing."

Mara nodded and moved her hand from his shoulder to the base of his skull to read his thoughts.

*"I think someone from Thanatanos is planning an attack on you and your people."*

Mara pressed her eyebrows together and sent a mental message back to Aleksander. *"Why?"*

Aleksander thought back, knowing Mara could hear. *"In Antanasia's chambers, the assassin called me 'brother.' He tried to get me to help him kill Lavinia for Thanatan."*

Mara glanced over Aleksander's shoulder and repeated her earlier concern. *"The rest of your friends. Can I trust them?"*

Aleksander was unable to hide his thoughts before they formed. *"I trust them with my life."* Aleksander could feel Mara pull her consciousness away from his own, a strange sensation, more invasive than Kamil's masterful skills of telepathy.

"By the way, did you notice that Shanthah and Hanna are trying to spy on us?" Aleksander asked.

"Oh, yes, forever ago," Mara replied with a laugh. "They are *not* sneaky."

Aleksander felt Mara's fingers slip away from the back of his neck as the song ended. As the musicians prepared for their next song, Aleksander removed his hand from Mara's waist.

"And where do you think you're going?" Mara asked.

"Song's over," Aleksander replied with an apprehensive gesture. Mara shook her head and drew him back.

"What do you think about giving Shanthah and Hanna something to talk about?"

Aleksander's heart fluttered as Mara pulled his hand back with an alluring smile and placed it much lower than it had been during the last dance. She let out a cheerful laugh, and he flashed an awkward but charming smile return.

Maybe, just maybe…

"You know, Aleks, as the one who hired the musicians, I think I have the right to one last dance."

He took her hand.

"One last dance," Aleksander said as Mara pulled him close. "That sounds nice. I hope it's a long song." She smiled. They both did. And then he added, "But I sure hope it isn't our last one."

"I love this song," Mara said peacefully as she began to guide him in a dance to a cheerful Sangoran folk song. She swayed to the tune, and Aleksander followed suit, stepping in time with the rhythm of the music.

For the briefest moment, they both felt all they ever wanted: that their friendship could rise from the ashes of betrayal. As Aleksander looked into the crystal blue of Mara's eyes, she felt herself leaning toward him, and—

And then it was over.

Panic and screams filled the ballroom as a host of armed Sangorans crashed through the high stained-glass windows lining the chamber. The swarm of wings and spears carved its way through the delegation, spilling the blood of human and Sangoran alike.

Mara broke free from Aleksander's embrace, planted her feet and summoned all the might of the Queen's Control she could muster, screaming one word in the Sangoran language.

"SPJINAIS!" *STOP!*

Even with her ability, the chaos did not cease. How was this possible? She turned to Aleksander in disbelief. Her thoughts rushed back to Florenta, who somehow resisted her control.

What treacherous plot had the selfish traitor wrought? She watched as one of the enemy Sangorans speared a man through the chest as a group of other assailants hacked at unarmed diplomats, spraying blood across her ballroom floor.

"Jemprata, min adstanai!" shouted the leader of Mara's imperial bodyguards. *Empress, get behind us!*

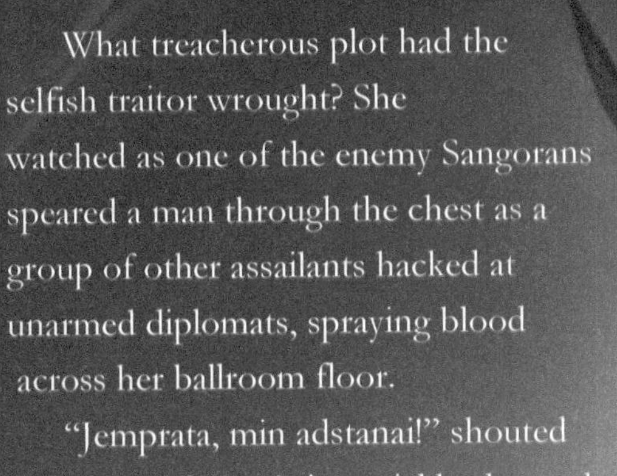

A brave contingent of Sangorans led by Rayshel and Vasilica joined her guards, forming a circle in defense of their empress. They fought bravely, giving Mara time to regain herself, however, only a select few guests were armed.

"Ne! Opčais jan tjotsavi!" Mara shouted. *No! Defend my guests!*

Half of Mara's imperial guard obeyed their empress to go to the guests' defense. The rogue Sangorans flooded over them, and Mara knew not if her allies survived, escaping only by slamming an elbow into her nearest assailant's throat, crushing her windpipe.

"Florenta, ty strahlivca!" Mara screamed. *Florenta, you coward!*

Flames erupted around the ballroom as the chaos consumed everything around her. Dozens lay dead, and she delved into the thoughts of the nearest Thannish soldier, ripping his mind to shreds to find one specific memory: a plot to destroy her—a command given to him by King Verahim himself. How could this be?

Mara roared in the midst of the destruction around her and clapped her hands together, telekinetically collapsing an iron helm around an oncoming soldier's head. The man fell to the ground without a scream, and she stepped over his body as his two companions kept on their path toward her.

Mara let loose a bolt of lightning into the chest of the second soldier, and a stream of flame engulfed the third. Aleksander was still at her side. They shared a glance, and she grabbed his arm.

"Find Pol!"

Aleksander nodded, and Mara turned her attention to the fourth soldier who had managed to get within an arm's length of the empress. She swung her wings down, crushing the man's neck with a sickening crunch as he released a thick powder from the palm of his hand. The particles engulfed Mara's head in a noxious cloud.

She stumbled backward and heaved, spraying vomit across the floor then collapsed to her knees and reached out for no one in particular. Aleksander, perhaps. Her vision blurred and began to spin. What was going on?

Her throat closed, and she began to choke as she dodged an attack from another Thannish soldier by throwing herself onto her back. She brought her wing upward, smacking him right in the eye with a crunch. The man cried out in pain, and she scrambled backward, still gasping for air as the blinded man hacked at her, leaving minor, badly aimed wounds across her arms and stomach.

She hiked her black dress up her thighs to kick as high and hard as she could from the floor, thrusting her shoe between his legs. She struck again, this time burying the pointed heel of her shoe into his groin just as the cold steel of his blade sliced through the front of her thighs. They both screamed in pain, and the soldier collapsed next to her with a groan.

The soldier vomited and scrambled for his weapon, but Mara raised her hand and blasted him square in the face with a bolt of lightning.

His body hit the floor as a rogue Sangoran warrior appeared from behind with a raised spear; the empress was powerless to stop her, bleeding and choking on whatever powder the other soldier had thrown into her face. The cloud of particles still lingered in the air, suffocating her on the spot.

Before the stroke fell, Mara saw someone step between her and Florenta's minions, a pillar of golden flame overwhelming her foe. The cloud of whatever the soldier had thrown at her ignited and was gone, lightly singing her skin, but at least she would survive. Air filled her lungs as someone lifted her onto his shoulder. Her world continued to spin.

"Aleksander…?"

And then everything went black.

He was surrounded. At least a dozen Sangorans stood in a semicircle with spears outstretched, and he knew not if they were loyal to Mara or if they were invaders from outside. His question was soon answered as one of them unleashed a bolt of lightning that traveled down the shaft of a spear and directly through the flesh on his side. Mara's limp form fell in a heap to the ground, her eyes opening just in time to see a Thannish soldier draw a blade from her rescuer's side.

Only it wasn't Aleksander.

Rehor.

She pressed herself up in disbelief as she scrambled toward him. He collapsed, and his crimson hat tumbled to the ground.

"Mara," he whispered, barely audible.

"Rehor, Rehor, no!"

"I am…so proud of…"

He smiled like a father as Mara reached out with her mind, unable to sense his consciousness. At that moment, she knew he was already gone, a joyful expression still etched on his face. The soldier raised his blade to slay her as well, but Mara telekinetically broke his wrist, forcing him to drop the blade, which clattered next to her.

"No! No, no, NO!"

Mara heard Shanthah cry from behind the soldier, "Mara! Mara, look out!"

"Stand down, Empress!" shouted Rehor's murderer.

"*NO!*"

She heeded Shanthah's cries and whipped her mighty wing backward in a violent strike, breaking an attacker's neck before he reached her. She then screamed in the torment of her soul, telekinetically hurling Rehor's murderer against the wall of the ballroom. She unleashed a flurry of lightning as she thrust the murderer's own blade through his chest, pinning his corpse to the wall.

The world around Mara glowed as bright as the sun as she summoned twisted, crackling lightning around each of her fingers and the ridges of her dark wings. She unleashed the blast, combining the individual threads of energy into one blinding beam of light that disintegrated the wall of the ballroom, Rehor's murderer, and everyone between them. She dispersed the rest of the web of chaotic light into the crowd of enemies that now surrounded her, resulting in screams and death all around. When the last of her enemies was dead, she stood alone, surrounded by ashes and corpses.

The world blazed at the fury of the empress, and at that moment, she didn't care if both empires burned.

Mara collapsed out of exhaustion and grief, electricity crackling around her exhausted limbs. She stared around in horror as she witnessed the ongoing massacre around her.

Unarmed diplomats on both sides lay dead on the floor as those who could fight stood with those who could not. She sobbed as she caught the unseeing gaze of each of the murdered men and women on the ballroom floor; a young woman still held out an accusatory finger as if blaming the empress for their gruesome deaths.

A hurricane of swords and glass swirled around the remaining delegates, and Mara knew who was at its eye: Hanna. The last surviving Thannish delegates huddled around the fierce woman, but not a single Sangoran stood behind her.

Mara could hear Hanna calling for her, but more of the rogue Sangorans flooded into the chamber, surrounding Hanna's hurricane of blades. Hanna was beginning to tire and was now on her knees, unable to stand. Many Thannish soldiers stood beside the rogue Sangorans against Hanna.

A rhythmic burst of dark magic echoed around the room as dozens of Walkers appeared from their black teleportation mist. Hanna collapsed from maintaining her telekinetic storm and Florenta's horde closed in on the survivors.

Mara cried out as one of the Walkers wrapped his fingers around Hanna's shoulder just as she lost consciousness. At that moment, the empress knew they were about to vanish without her. She would be utterly alone against the murderers.

"*Stop!*" a voice filled each mind in the room, its owner asserting a powerful mental influence over each of the Sangorans, forcing all of them in the room to kneel. "To the prisons!"

Mara knew that voice. And she loathed it.

A wave of mental energy surged through the room, causing several Walkers to collapse, rendering them unable to teleport, while others spasmed and screamed in pain as they vanished, still holding on to those they tried to save. Mara knew the newcomer had succeeded in disrupting the Walkers' magic.

The enemy Sangorans hacked at Mara's supporters and the Thannish diplomats; Mara watched in horror as Hanna hit the stone ground and lay unconscious, her Walker rescuer lying next to her with a slit throat.

Mara watched in horror as the Walkers that had survived the attack teleported the survivors away, but she was too tired to read their minds to discover where they were taking them, or if their intentions were fair or foul. The last face she saw vanish into the dark mist was that of Aleksander; their eyes met for the briefest moment as he reached out for her. Where Aleksander expected to see rage, all he saw before disappearing was the deep sadness etched on Mara's face.

The giant form of Florenta Karpaska, carried on a platform by a dozen servants, burst through the great doors at the front of the ballroom. The rogue Sangorans bowed to their master, who simply laughed at the carnage. Mara shook her head in utter contempt as she got to her feet, holding Rehor's fallen hat with trembling fingers.

"So, you finally show yourself, you—you useless, envious coward!" spat Mara.

"Still alive, our beloved queen?" Florenta laughed, her troops readying their spears against the exhausted Empress of Blood. Several surviving members of the Thans' coup stood amongst them. "Good. I told my people I wanted to kill you myself. Ah, I'm glad to see there are good people on both sides willing to stand up against you. So very kind of the Walkers to take my prisoners to the dungeons for me."

"I should have killed you long ago," Mara said. Her breathing quickened, and she felt as if she would soon suffocate in her anger and despair. Her mind raced, knowing the Queen's Control couldn't influence the Walkers. So how had she done it?

"Just like you killed Delia?" Florenta retorted, stomping her foot. "And do not deny you were behind Antanasia and Ihrin's deaths! It was only a matter of time before I was next!"

"Wasn't one coup at a time enough? You planned this with Thanatanos—too lazy to do all the work yourself?! Always having others do your dirty work!" Florenta scoffed but said nothing in retort. "And yes, I killed Delia! Just like *you* killed Ihrin, you swine of a woman!"

"I had nothing to do with their coup, and nothing to do with Ihrin's death, and that's *exactly* why I'm doing this! Despite whatever Delia did, *you* killed your own governor! *You* couldn't protect us. *I can!* Sangora will only be safe without *you!*" Spittle trailed from Florenta's jowls as she bellowed at Mara. She towered over the empress, a look of disdain on her face. With a dismissive flick of her wrist, she said, "Kill them all."

The Karpaskan Sangorans turned on the last survivors, butchering them before Mara's eyes. She collapsed to her knees in horror, her hands pressed over her mouth.

Florenta waddled ahead of her allies as they made a slow advance toward their enemy. Mara glanced around and saw Rehor lying amongst the fallen, and she hung her head.

"I invoke the right of all Mistresses of Dusk: The Trial of Blood against a useless queen!"

"*No one* will be able to protect you from me," shouted Mara, shaking as she stood. Florenta laughed, and her wings flapped uselessly on her back.

"Ha! You'd never make it out of here alive," said Florenta. "These warriors are loyal only to me. The other Mistresses of Dusk will be of no help to you. Anca, Vasilica, and Raluca will be dead by daybreak, hunted down like the criminals they are. Lavinia lies helpless and broken in a hospital bed. She will be no problem. Ihrin and her spawn Antanasia are dead, thanks to you. Your court is through, and I stand triumphant. My Mistresses of Dusk will take their places, and I shall take yours. Did you really think Thanatanos would honor the peace accords?"

"You need me to stop the assassin," said Mara. "I know things you do not."

"Are you begging for your life?" asked Florenta with an incredulous laugh. "Did you think that would work?!"

Florenta's servants carried her platform closer to Mara, and she sneered down at the Empress.

"I never beg."

Before Florenta could react, Mara wrenched a spear from the hand of one of Florenta's soldiers; with mighty leap and a flap of her wings, she thrust the spear into the massive woman's stomach. Florenta roared in pain as the Empress of Blood pushed the blade ever deeper, but a soldier struck Mara over the head with the shaft of his spear, knocking her to the bloodstained ground.

As the soldiers loyal to Florenta readied their spears to slay Mara, a single burst of dark mist exploded in the center of the chamber, and in the quiet stillness, two figures stepped forth from the shadows.

King Valistaran Talohir and Lord Ronin Jakoni.

"Hello, Empress."

Florenta, wounded but alive, screamed in confusion as Valistaran unleashed a torrent of black flame across the chamber, shielding Mara from the onslaught of rogue Sangorans. Ronin's hooked swords sliced through his enemies, and Mara felt a single word from Valistaran's mind ring through her consciousness.

*"Run."*

She considered fighting alongside Valistaran and Ronin but decided to heed his advice. She grabbed Rehor's arm, extended her great black wings, and hoisted the man's limp form into the night sky.

# CHAPTER NINE

# HER SAME FEAR

The entire company of refugees from Pata was in a dead sprint to Turnava. The low stone walls surrounding the town were now in sight, and most of the terrified townsfolk had abandoned their handcarts before reaching the mighty River Vah. The great river was the final barrier between the displaced villagers and the walled city's hope of safety; the Faceless horde was close enough that their all-consuming hunger lingered at the back of every man, woman, and child's mind, despite Kamil's best efforts to keep them at bay.

"Kamil, do you have enough energy to contact anyone in the city?" asked Alia as she helped her fatigued ally hobble over the rocks of the riverbank. "We need to warn Turnava we're coming, if they haven't seen us already!"

Completely exhausted, Kamil did not answer. However, he screwed up his face to concentrate on the oncoming horde with all his might but stumbled as he did so. Alia continued to support him as they made their way into the shallows.

"You can do it, keep going," said Alia in Kurashic to Kamil. "I'm sorry that I can't heal your mind like I can do for wounds."

"*I appreciate the sentiment,*" replied Kamil to her mind.

"How deep is this thing?" called Valis to Josman, gesturing to the river. As a citizen of Kurash, he only had a basic understanding of Thannish geography. "You might need to carry Kamil, big guy. He isn't looking very good."

"Right here? Not so deep that we can't cross, but deep enough that we don't want to," replied Josman before adding, "probably too deep for Drahomir to not start complaining."

"Don't worry! I'm already doing that!" called Drahomir nearby, pushing against the rushing current. "Is it too late for Josman to carry me too?"

Drahomir took hold of the hands of two children while another clung onto his back, and together they struggled across the rushing water. Meanwhile, Josman scooped a young girl into his arms and gestured for two older children to climb onto his back.

"Get ready!" called Valis as he stepped back out of the river after helping an elderly woman cross. Fear gripped his heart as the Faceless crested the ridge overlooking the river then halted for a moment like a pack of dogs told to heel.

Valis looked back at Kamil, confused. The Kurashian shook his head and sent Valis a mental message. "*I'm not the one doing this.*" The horde of emaciated creatures disappeared back behind the ridge, and Josman took the opportunity to urge the villagers onward. He set down the children, who thanked him and scampered off after the flow of refugees toward Turnava. He stepped back into the river, pushing against the current.

"Come on, meet me halfway!" he shouted before faltering. The sight of three men carrying young women across the river caused his heart to ache, his thoughts turning to his own wife and child that had been killed during Mara's invasion of Laniras.

"Josman!" Alia called, a single child sitting upon her shoulders. She trudged toward Josman, who had paused in the middle of the river. An elderly woman and two young children on a boulder jutting out of the current tried to get his attention and reached for his arm. Alia caught his gaze and waved to catch his attention, seemingly breaking the spell.

"I never got the chance to see my wife and daughter again after we escaped," Josman said, not quite meeting her gaze. A wave of guilt and regret washed over him as images of the slave camp and his burned out home filled his mind.

"Let's help them see *their* parents and children again, yeah?" Alia asked, her eyes kind. Josman took a deep breath and nodded, letting the old woman climb onto his back. Alia patted his shoulder, not understanding, but feeling for her friend, nonetheless. Together, they made their way across the rushing waters.

An explosion and a flash of cyan light rocked the world beyond the high ridge followed by the mental anguish of dozens of dying Faceless.

"I think we've got friends!" called Valis, pointing in his excitement across the river. Josman hollered in excitement as he saw the last remaining warriors of the Court of Thanatan, Valakor, his massive, axe-wielding, Minotaur ally Bovin, and another warrior he recognized by the name of Manitrius laying waste to the endless horde.

"I'm scared they won't be able to hold off the horde for long," said Valis to Drahomir, who nodded in agreement.

Their fear was well founded. Only half of the villagers had made it across the river as hundreds of Faceless crashed into the flowing water. Many Faceless submerged themselves beneath the current to make bridges of flesh for their kin to swarm over the river as quickly as they overtook the earth.

Josman nearly dropped the old woman from his back as she screamed in his ear, a Faceless grasping her feeble ankle. The creature pulled the woman under the waves, and Josman roared in defiance, crushing the back of its skull with his fist. He pulled the frantic woman from the current and made all haste toward the far bank as they both coughed up a lungful of water.

Valis thrust his hand forward, sending a thin ribbon of magical lightning between Josman and the creatures threatening to pull him, the old woman, and the young child beneath the flowing water.

"Take them down, kid!" Josman exclaimed, sputtering for air as water filled his mouth. He struggled not only against the current, but against the old woman's firm hold around his neck.

"And electrify the entire river?!" Valis exclaimed. He had been wary of using his magic since they ventured into Thanatanos but had little choice now as the creatures swarmed toward the townsfolk.

Drahomir helped Josman out of the river as Valis began casting lightning against the swarm. The Faceless swept over the western bank toward the terrified refugees, resulting in shrieks of terror. They soon turned to cheers, however, as General Valakor leapt into the river and planted his scythe in the pile of Faceless corpses; a shockwave of energy erupted from his weapon, sending the creatures flying in a spray of water.

The magical energy severed limbs and disintegrated those closest to its epicenter, but even that was not enough to slow the tide of emaciated beasts. Valakor, Bovin, Valis, and Manitrius continued to defend the helpless villagers, but the Faceless had circled around the group and were waiting for them near the wall. Thousands upon thousands of the monstrosities climbed out of the river and swarmed over the walls of Turnava.

"No!" cried Josman as he fell to his knees. "No, no, no!"

"We led them to a feast," replied Drahomir. "What have we done?"

He felt a firm hand grasp the back of his skull, and his mind became clear of the mental anguish that had filled his thoughts only a moment before.

"Kamil?" he asked, feeling Kamil searching for something in the crevices of his mind; he felt a flood of joy from his friend's consciousness. "Find something useful, or—"

Drahomir cried out, not knowing why, he threw his hands into the air and a dark smoke billowed from his shaking palms. He could feel Kamil's hand on the back of his head, and he knew his friend was causing his powers to activate. He watched as the teleportation smoke intertwined to form an ethereal gateway leading to a land unknown to him.

*"Through the gate!"* Kamil's thought echoed in the minds of every villager, who instantly heeded his words, trusting in this last hope.

"This is weird, and I don't like it!" Drahomir exclaimed as Kamil continued to control his actions.

*"Until you can control your power, I think I'll need to."*

Hundreds of Faceless barreled toward them, but Kamil threw another mental lure as far away as possible, drawing them away again.

"How do you do that? Go Kamil!" said Drahomir, but Kamil did not answer. The man stumbled to his knees and then collapsed face first into the shallow water. Drahomir turned him onto his back and shouted, "Josman! Kamil is down!"

The swarm flowed back toward the portal, Kamil's mental focus broken, but his action allowed a host of surviving villagers to make it through Drahomir's gateway.

"Valis! Get over here!" Drahomir shouted.

Valis and the Court of Thanatan warrior Manitrius defended one another with blade and lightning as they hurried toward the swirling vortex of magical energy. They each draped one of Kamil's arms over their shoulders and headed through the portal. Valakor and Bovin continued to hold off the monsters as Josman and Alia stepped through to safety as well. Manitrius emerged from the gateway and headed to support Bovin and Valakor.

Valakor and Bovin had a moment of reprieve following Kamil's last mental lure, allowing them to regroup. Bovin's mighty axe, liftable only by one as strong as a Minotaur, cleaved a Faceless in two from head to groin, before splitting the chest of another. The Minotaur bellowed a war cry amidst the piled dead in the river dyed red with their blood.

Drahomir groaned as a dozen or so more refugees made their way into the river. He strained his focus to keep the portal open for them but slipped, and the gateway dissipated. He tried in vain to summon the portal again and cursed as he failed with each attempt.

"Look, brothers," grunted Bovin, pointing northward. Both Valakor and Manitrius had already seen what he had; four warriors clad in the same mystical armor as Valakor were standing still upon the high ridge behind the tide of Faceless.

"Be ready, my friends," said Valakor as their foes began their approach. The fact that the Faceless swarmed harmlessly around them was worrisome, indeed. Manitrius watched the last group of refugees running across the river but could see no way to help them now.

"Have you felt the call, Valakor?" asked the fore of the group, his voice strong and cold. He brandished a cruel longsword that gleamed in the sunlight.

"You know I have," replied General Valakor, glancing over his shoulder to see Drahomir still trying to summon the portal to escape.

"Of what evil does Raksil the Fallen speak?" asked Manitrius. Bovin the Minotaur hefted his battle axe and snorted to taunt the enemy Spirit warriors.

"Thanatan has returned. During the battle of Laniras, we all heard his voice. He awoke, and his return can only mean one thing," the leader, Raksil said.

"It means that Elafris has also returned," replied Valakor, planting his scythe in the riverbank to meet Raksil unarmed.

"And which god will you choose to follow this time, my brother?" asked Raksil.

"As a member of the Court of Thanatan, I assume you will help us find our god and restore him to glory?" asked the largest of the four, a hulking behemoth nearly ten feet tall.

"That remains to be seen, Kallus," said an apprehensive Valakor, "I've come to learn certain truths about the beings we call our gods, as, I sense, have you."

"I hope we've come to the same realization," said Kallus. "But I believe we'll be the new Court of Thanatan with you gone. We return to his faith, while you abandon it. Poetic."

Bovin always expected the behemoth to be dull witted but knew him to be a keen strategist. Manitrius twirled his thin blade.

"Our lord will bring order to this land," said Raksil. "He plans to save us. All he wants is to heal us. To end suffering. To finally bring all people together."

"You can take your Faceless pets back to your master. Long have I served Thanatan, but now I say: *NO MORE!*" Valakor retrieved his scythe and leapt toward his enemies, smashing the weapon against Raksil's blade. Kallus and the other two warriors joined the fray, engaging Manitrius and Bovin.

Valakor hooked his blade around the underarm of one of the warriors and flipped him around for Bovin to smash right in the side of the helm with the blade of his axe, disorienting the warrior. Raksil retaliated by unleashing a wave of azure energy at the Minotaur, who deflected as much of it as he could with the side of his weapon.

"Get that portal up soon, boy!" called Bovin.

Drahomir clapped his hands together and smacked them on the ground but could not figure out how Kamil had activated his powers. Despair began to overtake him as the group of refugees made it across the river unharmed but with nowhere to go.

Kallus swung his dual war hammers into Valakor's side just as the general brought an armored knee into the face of the warrior Bovin had struck in the head. Kallus knocked Valakor into the river just after he blasted Raksil in the chest with a beam of energy. The fourth warrior, one that had yet to speak, cried out with a distinctly female voice as Bovin struck her in the neck with the shaft of his axe.

The warrior that Valakor and Bovin felled got to his feet, but Bovin beheaded him with one clean swing. The Minotaur bellowed before Raksil grabbed him by the horns and flipped him over his head into the river. Raksil, Kallus, and the female warrior retreated, giving both Bovin and Valakor a moment to recover as well.

"Raksil, please," Valakor pleaded. "If you have felt the pull to return to Thanatan, then you must know his plan as well as I do."

"Does this world not need cleansing?" asked Raksil. "He will undo the mistakes made by our forefathers. Those who are left will live a life of peace, not needing to lift a hand or worry about a thing for the rest of their lives! The great war did not end with the first cleansing of the land, Valakor. We are a remnant of that age—embers that yet burn. We must fix what went wrong and sweep away the ashes that remain."

"By unleashing the Pure?" asked Valakor. "Their very purpose is to destroy all life. Nothing would be left!"

"This was always part of Thanatan's great plan. Do you not wonder where we have been? Why we have not been involved in your silly squabbles with Talohira and Sangora?" asked Raksil. "We have been preparing for Thanatan's plan. He found us and guides us, just as he can guide you!"

"General, we know the truth," snorted Bovin. "Do not be swayed by these traitors."

"How are you going to turn your people against their god?" asked Kallus. "You call us traitors for clinging to the faith we have always had; already your people worship Thanatan and will welcome his coming. They will accept his plan."

As Kallus spoke, Valakor made a gesture noticed by none but Bovin, and without warning, the Minotaur planted his axe in Raksil's chest. Raksil stumbled backward, and Kallus and the female warrior engaged their foes; the Minotaur heaved the handle of his axe, severing the metallic flesh of Raksil's artificial body. At that moment, the entire swarm of Faceless sensed their masters' danger and rushed toward the fight. The refugees around Drahomir screamed in terror.

Meanwhile, Drahomir stood paralyzed with fear. He had seen so many people die, and he knew that he himself had been the cause of so much death. If he hadn't betrayed Mara that fateful night upon the tower of Doftaan, she would not have laid waste to Nitra, burned much of Laniras, and destroyed how many other towns in Thanatanos? He threw up his hands one last time, and a shadowy vortex swallowed the refugees around him, sending them to whatever place he had seen through the last gateway. He tried to keep the portal open to allow Valakor, Manitrius, and Bovin an avenue of escape, but it was no use.

And as the townsfolk disappeared, his hatred and guilt became shame and compassion. Not for himself, but instead for the girl he had once known named Mara Bartunek, for this must have been what it felt like. What it felt like for your friends to be whisked away by magic as you were consumed by an endless host of merciless enemies craving your blood.

He looked at his hands and knew he wouldn't be able to access his newfound abilities. He didn't even try. Not this time, for he did not feel that he deserved to.

He felt Mara's same fear, shut his eyes, and welcomed death.

# CHAPTER TEN
# THE PHANTOM

"Am I dead? I'm dead, I knew it!" Shanthah exclaimed. Bright light flooded his vision, and he panicked for a moment as no shadow fell over his face, and he put his hands over his eyes before realizing he was still invisible, not dead. For a moment, he wondered if anyone would have been able to find his invisible body if he had died. "If I'm not a ghost, then where am I…?"

He glanced around and saw no living thing, but as he turned around, he gasped in shock, for a crippled and broken Walker was slumped over the boulder behind him. Shanthah grimaced, examining a heavy gash across the Sangoran's forehead where he must have struck the rock on impact after teleporting.

"Did you try to save me? I guess that means you deserve as good of a funeral as I can give," said Shanthah. He gestured to his surroundings and began to pile dried driftwood into a pile on the seashore. "I've clearly got nothing else to do…"

When he deemed the makeshift funeral pyre sufficient, he dragged the dead Walker atop the heap and folded its arms across its chest.

"Not familiar with your customs, friend. Sorry," said Shanthah. "I'd say a prayer to Elafris for you, but I met him not long ago, and, well, I'm pretty sure he's just a regular guy like us."

He pulled a piece of flint from a pouch on his belt and struck it against the Walker's sword, casting sparks over some bits of dry kindling. He tended to the fire by feeding it dry sticks, and soon, the entire pyre was ablaze. Shanthah saluted his unknown ally and after paying a few moments of respect, turned away.

The salty smell of the sea told Shanthah he was no longer near Doftaan. The nearest seashore was only a few miles from the Sangoran capital, but the mountains that loomed in the distance would be on the wrong side for him to be there. So, where was he?

He made his way down to the coast and knelt, waiting for the waves to meet him on the shore. He miscalculated the speed of the approaching water and failed to leap out of its way, resulting in two soggy boots. As the water receded, he determined that by the position of the mountains and the sun and the relatively warm temperature of the salty water inside his boots, the body of water had to be the Than Sea. If it was a cold, freshwater sea to the east, he would have assumed he'd been whisked off to the gulf called the Shadow of Doftaan or perhaps the Black Sea.

"At least you brought me somewhere nice for once," Shanthah called in the general direction of the makeshift funeral pyre. He sighed, knowing no one heard his quip.

He began to follow the coast, letting his thoughts tumble out of his mouth. "If I headed straight east, I'd reach Doftaan—closer than Laniras, to be sure—but I'd have to walk for about a week straight to even reach Doftaan—how far can a Walker teleport anyway?" He was silent for a moment before adding, "I think talking to myself is a pretty good sign I'm already going crazy, and it's been, what? Ten minutes? That's all it took?"

He glanced around and could see no sign of villages anywhere nearby to indicate where on the coast he was, but it was blisteringly hot, and everything seemed sticky and sweaty. He admitted to himself that it wasn't much of a clue to go off of, since that could describe southern Thanatanos, Talohira, or the thin strip of the southernmost Sangoran state, the name of which escaped his memory.

He left the rocky shore behind to make his way toward the forest north of his position. Knowing he was unlikely to find any human settlements within the forest itself, he began his long trek around the thick trees. He traversed the rocky terrain as it leveled out into a vast plain around the forest and nearly twisted his ankle in an animal's hole because of a joyous sight to the north: smoke. Smoke meant people.

He decided to venture into the woods to cut straight through to the village beyond the thicket. His stomach growled at him, and he quickly hushed it as if quieting a noisy child.

"You'll give me away to all the monsters here," he said. "Well, maybe that's a good thing. Either I'll eat them, or they'll get to eat me."

His mind wandered from food back to the position of the sun. Hadn't it been past midnight when the rogue Sangorans' attack occurred? He must have been unconscious for longer than he thought.

A sudden sound like thunder ripped through the forest, and he stopped in his tracks. He vanished and kept still, glancing in the direction of the sound. Thunder? There was not even a cloud overhead. More Walkers teleporting away from the massacre in Mara's palace, then? No, this was something else. Something big moving in the same direction as he was.

He kept on his path through forest toward the village, hoping to intercept whatever beast was stalking the woods. He willed himself to become invisible as the monstrous, thundering footsteps came ever nearer. He knew the beast would not be able to see him, but he had no knowledge of the creature's sense of smell, and for that reason, he kept his distance.

It only took a few minutes for the hulking behemoth to catch up to his position; his mouth gaped open in awe as he watched its four mighty legs splinter trees beneath massive, clawed feet. The world shook as the gargantuan gray body cleared a path of destruction. Sulfurous smoke poured from the creature's wide maw, and hundreds of slits along its sides while random jets of ash fluttered down around it like dark snow.

Shanthah tried to avoid the trail of glowing cinders in the beast's wake and resolved to get ahead of the monster to warn whoever had created the smoke.

He broke through the thicket and beheld a small village separated from the tree line by a jagged ridge of earth. Careful not to make himself known to the monster, he hurried through a pass in the rocks hoping the jagged rocks would slow the beast. He emerged from behind the ridge with absolutely no idea of what to do.

"Oh, Hanna, where are you? I could really use your help," muttered Shanthah as he reached the village. With all his heart, he hoped and prayed she was alive. He didn't dare let himself think of the alternative.

He glanced over his shoulder to see the beast clumsily trying to traverse the outcrop. As it stumbled, Shanthah rematerialized and knocked three frantic times on the door of the nearest home.

"Please be human, please be human," Shanthah pled.

Much to his chagrin, an elderly Sangoran woman answered the door. She attempted to slam it shut before he could speak, but he shoved his boot in the door.

"No! You go out!' cried the woman in heavily accented Thannish.

"No, you come out!" exclaimed Shanthah.

The old Sangoran repeatedly slammed the door on his foot until he withdrew it out of fear that she would break his toes. He hurried to the next hut and pounded on the door until a young Sangoran answered with a hesitant expression.

"Do you speak Thannish?" asked Shanthah. The young girl nodded, and Shanthah pointed in the direction of the beast clambering over the rocky outcrop.

"There's something coming, and we need to get everyone out of here or its going to kill everyone," he said, continuing to point in the monster's direction. The girl peeked around the wooden door and shouted something in Sangoran; with a panic, she ran inside, presumably to awaken a sleeping family member.

Shanthah continued to wake each of the inhabitants of each house and gradually a group of half-asleep Sangorans with day-wrappings to protect their skin from the sun emerged from their homes. The young Sangoran girl shrieked to the others in Sangoran and pointed to Shanthah's sword.

"She says you will save us!" said another elderly Sangoran woman. Shanthah turned to see the beast now heading straight for the village. Smoke trailed from its gaping mouth and flames billowed from its belly as it roared and stomped the earth.

"From that thing?" he asked. The young Sangoran nodded frantically and held on to Shanthah's arm. "Yeah, I'll try," he said then added under his breath, "or maybe we'll all just die."

The rampaging monster splintered one of the small huts and let forth a river of flame, completely disintegrating another. It whipped its tail as it turned, showering splintered wood over the gathered villagers. Screams erupted from the crowd, Shanthah steadied his blade, and then everything went completely silent. The village, its inhabitants, and Shanthah were nowhere to be seen.

The behemoth groaned in confusion as it halted its charge, disappointed that its prey had somehow outsmarted it. It tromped off, trampling through the wreckage of the home it had destroyed. Shanthah kept quiet and hoped the scared Sangoran villagers would do the same. The beast went back into the forest and disappeared from view, and at that same moment, the entire village snapped back into existence.

"You saved us!" cried one of the villagers.

"It was so scared of you it ran away!" called another.

At once, the confused Shanthah was overtaken by hugs and praise from the grateful Sangorans. They cheered for the human that had inexplicably saved them; several beautiful Sangoran women showered him with kisses while others danced around him in pure joy.

The old woman from the first hut pushed through the crowd, leading a young woman Shanthah assumed was her granddaughter, and quite possibly the most beautiful Sangoran he had ever seen, toward him.

"Please, take granddaughter! Take to wife!" exclaimed the old woman.

"Grandmother!" exclaimed the woman. Shanthah gave a nervous laugh and vanished from sight; the Sangorans cried out in surprise and despair as their savior disappeared. He pushed through the crowd and rematerialized outside of the mass of hugs and grateful yet smothering kisses.

"As much as I've dreamed of a moment like this, and I can assure you, I have, there's somewhere I need to be," said Shanthah. "You see, there's someone—" The old woman cried out at this, cutting Shanthah's sentence short. "Like I was saying, there is someone I love very much who I need to find. Say, do you know where to find the city of Doftaan?"

The beautiful Sangoran nodded her head, and in warmly accented Thannish said, "Doftaan is far from here. You are in Likio. The capital barely knows we exist here. Is this person you love in trouble?"

"I think so. We were attacked, and I don't know where I am, how I got here, or where she is," said Shanthah. "I don't think I have much time to get to her. How far are we exactly?"

"Several days, even by wing," said another villager from behind the old woman. The others nodded in agreement.

"It is so romantic that you want to save your love. Like the warriors in Thannish stories," said the beautiful Sangoran as she clasped her hands and cocked her head to one side. "By the ways, my name is Ruta."

"A pleasure, but oh, believe me, if she's alive, she doesn't need saving. She could have defended you from that beast better than anyone, and I can assure you that she wouldn't have let it escape like I did," said Shanthah. As he spoke about the monster that had nearly destroyed the entire village, he pantomimed the stalking movements of the behemoth. The younger Sangorans giggled.

"What is her name?" asked the beautiful Sangoran.

"What *your* name is, handsome?" asked her grandmother. Ruta shot her a disapproving look.

"Her's is Hanna, and mine is Shanthah Kalen," he replied to the entranced crowd. "We were in a group of diplomats invited to make peace between Sangora and Thanatanos in Doftaan with the Empress. We were there to celebrate peace between our countries so that the war between us could finally end. We were so close, but that horrible Mistress of Dusk, Florenta, came to ruin everything."

"Mistress Florenta!" cried someone from the crowd. The old woman cried out and looked as if she was about to faint, and the entire crowd began shouting in their own language, evidently too angry about Florenta's actions to speak Thannish anymore.

"Quiet, quiet! This Florenta—what do you know about her? Are my friends safe if she's taken control of Doftaan?"

"No, no!" The grandmother shouted, holding her heart.

"Florenta is the Mistress of Dusk that governs our state of Karpaska. You are in her lands now, so maybe there is no more dangerous place for you if she is hunting you," said Ruta. "Well, there are two tribes here. Her clan's tribe, the Karpaskans and our tribe, the Alborans. Our people will keep you safe, but the Karpaskans will bring you back fast," said Ruta. "We have never before had leader more horrible to Alboran tribe than Florenta Karpaska, and Alborans are never ever chosen to be Mistress of Dusk. Karpaska is named after Florenta's family, after all."

"And she taxes us more than we can bear," said another Sangoran. "And when we cannot pay, or when we do not give her our men—"

"She—she kill us!" The grandmother made a stabbing motion.

"When you don't give her your men?" Shanthah asked. "I don't think I understand. Can you teach me?"

The elderly Sangoran woman began to weep. "Florenta take our people… Slaves." She pantomimed a whipping motion, which Shanthah understood all too well. He tried to understand her broken Thannish and wished he could speak to the old woman in her own language. He looked to the beautiful Sangoran, who tilted her head, eyebrows turned up and pressed together in a sad expression.

"Many years ago, men in our country were massacred in most regions, but not so bad here, far enough away from Doftaan," she said. "For that reason, Florenta taxes us of our men and our children."

"She taxes you of your children?" Shanthah asked. Through anecdotes, he had heard Florenta described as a taxing, gluttonous, and cruel leader, but this was beyond anything he had imagined. He shuddered to think of what became of the Alboran children ripped from their homes and families.

Shanthah looked at the beleaguered villagers around him, and at once he felt their sadness. He could see the oppression etched on their souls, and he knew that he had to help them. And perhaps, they could help him too. Hanna was powerful and could fend for herself until he could reunite with her.

"If you'll let me, I'd like to stay in your village for a few days and learn more about what Florenta is doing to your people. Is that okay with you?" Shanthah asked, directing his question to Ruta. However, most of the crowd cheered and accepted his offer, requesting that he stay in their homes before Ruta could respond.

"I think it looks like we want you to stay," Ruta said with a smile.

"Thank you," Shanthah replied. "I might not be able to save you from Florenta, but I can promise you, if you can help me find Hanna, she can."

# CHAPTER ELEVEN

# EVERYTHING HAS CHANGED

For the briefest moment, everything was dark and silent, but then the screaming resumed. Explosions of black mist burst at random throughout the Thannish royal palace, and survivors of Florenta's attack tumbled, confused and terrified, to the floor.

Aleksander emerged from a particularly violent vortex of black smoke, and his shoulder collided with the steps of a spiral staircase that led into the unlit blackness above. He wheezed and saw that several more survivors had reappeared in the same fashion around him, but others were not so lucky. Some were already corpses before being teleported away while others died on impact, their blood staining the otherwise spotless opulence.

"Shanthah?! Pol?" he called as several more Walkers appeared with rescued guests. "Rehor? Hanna?!"

He recognized some of the confused survivors, but none of his friends were anywhere to be seen. The attack and subsequent rescue disoriented him; he had to struggle for a moment to remember which of his friends were present at the ball during the attack. His heart ached in worry as he called for Mara, not knowing what had happened to her amidst the chaos.

He stumbled down the staircase not knowing where he was going, his head and shoulder throbbing. A feeling of dread filled his soul telling him he would find Pol, Hanna, Shanthah, or Rehor among the dead. The darkness closed in on him and he felt like he was suffocating; the moment he reached the bottom of the staircase he vomited all over the stone tile and then collapsed against the wall.

"What is happening?"

The torchlight flickered above him, illuminating a Sangoran groaning on the ground nearby. She was lying face down on the stone floor, her wings wrapped around her body like a blanket. Judging by the sounds she was making, Aleksander guessed she too was suffering from whatever was afflicting him.

He pulled himself toward her and lit a weak ball of flame in his palm to illuminate her face. He gasped, recognizing the Sangoran soldier, Rayshel, who had accompanied him and Lavinia while investigating the assassin.

"Rayshel," he whispered, trying not to startle her. "Rayshel, are you alright?" Her only response was a hacking cough that shook her entire body. He crossed his legs beneath his bottom and cradled her head, trying not to vomit again. As she made a feeble attempt to stand, her wings rustled with the sound of dried leaves, and the appendages shriveled before his eyes.

The muscles at the base of her mighty wings atrophied in mere seconds, and the fibers that made up her wings dissolved into dust and wiry sinew. The wings themselves twitched for a moment and then lay still like great, dead leaves fallen from a massive tree.

Rayshel retched and pushed herself away from the shriveled appendages with a labored scream. She stumbled backward in disbelief, clawing at her back as if to assure herself that her wings were still there only to find raw, bloodied skin. She turned to Aleksander, a look of horror on her face.

"What is this?" she whispered. Aleksander knew not what to say and shook his head, simply staring into Rayshel's fearful eyes. He grasped her hand.

"Someone at the ball threw some kind of dust in Mara's face," Aleksander explained. "I think I managed to burn it away before it did this to her, but…"

He gestured to Rayshel's shriveled wings with an apologetic grimace. The sight rekindled his fear for his friends' wellbeing. He knew Mara to be strong enough to overcome anything, but he still hoped she wasn't suffering.

"What could have done this?" she asked, trembling. Aleksander helped her to her feet, not knowing how to appropriately comfort her.

"Come on, let's get you to the palace healers," said Aleksander, covering her bloodied back with his cloak. "There's nothing they can do for your wings, but you're in shock, and…"

He trailed off, knowing that he had virtually no medical knowledge. Rayshel nodded nonetheless, and together they made their way toward the hospital wing on the other side of the castle. As they neared their destination, Rayshel collapsed to her knees once more. Aleksander hurried to steady her, and although he too felt dizzy and disoriented, they managed to keep one another upright.

"It's okay, Rayshel," he reassured her.

"No, it is not."

"No. You're right. It isn't, but you're safe now." Her head rolled to one side and an incoherent babble escaped her lips. "I've got you. Come on, we're so close. I've got you."

Orderlies and healers were scurrying about, carrying wounded diplomats, Walkers, and Sangorans alike into the hospital on stretchers and leading those that could stand through the doorway. The ward was overwhelmed with many injured being treated in the dim corridor. The Walkers had managed to save many lives, but at great cost.

"Help!" called Aleksander, letting a burst of flame escape his hand to get the attention of the hospital staff. A couple of orderlies hurried to Aleksander's side and helped Rayshel to her feet.

"What's wrong with her?" one of them asked, removing Aleksander's cloak from the woman's back. As soon as they saw her bloodstained back, he shouted, "We've got another one!"

They said nothing more as they rushed her inside to a group of other similarly afflicted Sangorans, leaving Aleksander alone in the dark corridor. He collapsed against the wall, perhaps in shock or out of exhaustion and simply sat there for a moment, numb. He shook his head in disbelief as he saw Pol helping a heavy-set orderly carry a coughing Sangoran across a stretcher into the hospital.

"Pol!' Aleksander exclaimed, getting to his feet. He took a shaky step toward his friend but heard footsteps behind him. On instinct, he swiveled and readied a ball of flame in both palms.

The knife missed Aleksander's head by mere inches. He summoned a torrent of flame, but his enemy vanished in a vortex of black smoke. Aleksander felt a foot sweep his legs out from beneath him, and he hit the ground hard, striking the same shoulder he had injured earlier. The assassin leapt onto Aleksander, intent on piercing his heart with another cruel dagger.

Aleksander let the flames flow from his hands and threw them to the sides, creating a barrier of flame between himself and the attacker. While the assassin was caught off guard, Aleksander unleashed a mighty stream of fire that rocketed him away across the floor. He pushed himself up from the ground and used the flames to propel him to a standing position.

At that moment, Aleksander and the assassin took a chance. The assassin lashed out with his dagger, and Aleksander thrust a fistful of flame into his enemy's masked face.

The dagger tore through Aleksander's shoulder as the flames engulfed his enemy's head. The man tried to vanish into the darkness, but Aleksander clutched his ankle, searing it with blistering heat. The magic only allowed the assassin to teleport a few feet away, but it was enough to extinguish Aleksander's fire and prevent significant burning.

"You're not getting away this time!" roared Aleksander, launching himself forward with two streams of red-hot flame. He brought his hands high above his head as he soared over his enemy's position then launched the full fury of an inferno downward toward his foe.

The torrent of flame spread across the stone tile like a hellish waterfall, bathing the man in orange and gold. Aleksander could hear screams from behind him, aware that those in the hospital and the corridor were witnesses to the battle.

The assassin groaned in pain as he tried to vanish but was once again only able to teleport a short distance. Aleksander waited for him to reappear and rushed forward a moment later as he reappeared in the hospital's arched doorway.

The patients and healers alike screamed in terror, and Aleksander rushed into the room after his foe. A black vortex opened above one bed in particular, and the assassin emerged, blade in hand. Aleksander dared not risk using magic in the room full of frightened, wounded people and watched in horror as the man brought his knife down over his head toward the heart of a Sangoran resting in the cot.

Two wings tipped with knives shot up and impaled the man through the either side. The assassin screamed in pain, and Lavinia spat upward then slammed him against the ground with all the force she could muster from her bed. She screamed in agony at the strain on her back, but the man lay still on the ground.

"Pest!" she roared, ready to strike him again, but Pol and two nurses held her against the bed, and she did not resist.

"Who are you?" Aleksander asked, grabbing the bleeding assassin by the collar. The assassin reached for his dagger, but Aleksander knocked it away underneath Lavinia's cot. The assassin's body flickered with black energy, and Aleksander knew he was preparing to teleport.

"What can we do?" asked Pol as Aleksander tried to hold his foe against the ground.

"Do you have any of that sedation potion for surgeries?" asked Aleksander. He could feel his grip on the man slipping, for the assassin's entire body was trembling with pent up teleportation magic trying to escape.

Pol relayed Aleksander's request to one of the nurses, who located a vial of dark medicinal potion and a syringe tipped with a thin needle. Aleksander and Pol held the assassin against the ground as the nurse jabbed the needle into the man's neck. She pressed her thumb against the top of the syringe, unloading the entire tube of sedation potion into the man's body.

"It's more than we'd give a usual patient, so he'll be out for a while," said the nurse.

"A while, you say!" exclaimed one of the orderlies nearby. "That much potion could make a horse sleep all day!" The teleportation energy seeped from his pores before dissipating, making several items around Lavinia's bedside vanish. The assassin, however, remained still on the ground.

"Give him more of it. Let him die," ordered Lavinia from her cot. The nurse ignored Lavinia's snide remark and hurried to the assassin's side. She pushed Aleksander out of the way and motioned to Pol for help. Pol helped carry the man to a space on the floor, for the beds in the chamber were all occupied. The nurse began examining his burned and battered body.

"You don't seem very determined to let this man live," said the nurse, dressing his wounds and calling for the orderlies to help counteract the sedation potion with some other concoctions.

Aleksander stood over the assassin's motionless form. Beneath the hood was a crimson mask that encased his entire head with no discernable way to remove it, although it was now chipped and charred from their fight.

A healer with magical abilities like Alia's placed her hands on the assassin's burns and they began to mend, although, it seemed to Aleksander, with less skill than Alia.

"He is very dangerous," said Aleksander, knowing he was stating the obvious. He began to speak again, but the nurse cut him off.

"It seems like you are as well," she said with a scoff. "We'll be sure to keep him sedated, but you stay away from him for now. I'd like you to leave my ward."

"All the same, I'd appreciate it if someone would contact me if he wakes up," Aleksander said.

"Will do," Pol said with a nod.

"With respect, and with your permission, please allow me to stay a minute longer, and then I promise I'll be out of your hair," Aleksander said. The nurse nodded and waved him off.

"Good to see you, Aleks, all things considered," Pol said.

"I'm glad you're safe. I'm sure Mara is worried about you," Aleksander said. Pol flinched at the mention of his sister's name, but he feigned a smile and nodded. "Did you get a chance—"

"To talk to her during this whole thing?" Pol asked, finishing his sentence. "Nope. I was hoping to, but…" He trailed off. "Sometimes I don't think she cares."

"As long as you do, right?" Aleksander asked. Pol chuckled.

"I guess so, yeah," Pol said. He sighed then added, "I think it's safe to say everything has changed."

There was a lot behind the statement, Aleksander knew. He nodded in agreement and clapped Pol on the back, wincing at the pain the movement caused his injured shoulder. Two nurses noticed his discomfort and began examining and dressing his wounds.

As they worked, Aleksander nodded to Lavinia, who responded in kind. He glanced around the crowded chamber until he spotted Rayshel lying still in a cot on the other side of the chamber. Thanking the nurses for their care, he made his way over to his new friend's bedside, careful not to get in anyone's way.

"Is she alright?" he asked as he approached Rayshel's still form. She looked peaceful now, not tormented with grief and pain.

The nearest healer replied simply with, "She will be, yes."

That was enough. Pol made his way over to Aleksander and clapped his friend on the back. He motioned for the doorway and led Aleksander toward it.

"They want you to leave—sorry, friend," said Pol through gritted teeth.

Aleksander nodded and bowed his head to the nurses and healers in thanks and compliance, and Pol accompanied him out of the hospital ward. The adrenaline began to wear off and Aleksander noticed his fatigue and pain for the first time.

"What happened?" asked Aleksander. "The last thing I remember was Florenta's people attacking, and then the Walkers came to our rescue."

"That's pretty much it," said Pol. "They must have known it was coming. They evacuated Mara's own healing center in Doftaan and brought them here before they got up to us just in time. That's why Mistress Lavinia's in there." He pointed over his shoulder to indicate the crowded healing center. "I think that other mistress, Valisaka or whatever."

"Vasilica?" Aleksander asked.

Pol nodded. "I think she's here too."

"What of the others?" asked Aleksander. "Our friends, I mean. Have Hanna, Shanthah, or Rehor shown up?" Pol just shook his head.

"No, none of them. Sorry. I saw Rehor try to help my sister and then—"

"What? Is he dead?" asked Aleksander. "Is she?"

"One of our own people killed him, Aleksander. He tried to save Mara and the Thannish soldier just killed him," Pol said in disbelief. "Why would he do that?"

Aleksander was at a loss for words. He collected his thoughts for a moment before speaking. "Some people just can't forgive

Sangora for what's happened during the war, and they blame your sister for everything that's happened—I'm sorry you had to see that, Pol," said Aleksander. "I can't believe it."

"I know you want to ask about my sister, but I didn't see what happened next. A Walker got me out of there right after they killed—" His eyes welled up with tears and his voice cracked. "I can't believe Rehor's gone, Aleks. He was so good to Mara and me, but the thing is—we can't even avenge him. It was one of our own guys. He was supposed to officially become ambassador to Sangora, too."

"He was so excited," Aleksander said, his own eyes filling with tears for the first time. Pol nodded. "But you're right, Pol. Maybe we can't avenge him, but you know Rehor. He would have told us he doesn't want vengeance. He would have told us to keep our course and—" He was at a loss for words, but he knew Pol understood as he stammered, "…and something."

"Yeah. Good guy, Rehor," said Pol, sniffing. Aleksander nodded again. Neither spoke for a moment out of respect for their fallen friend. Pol was the first to break the silence.

"I started helping in the healing center as soon as I teleported here. You know, I think I have a future there. I really liked helping the nurses," he said. "I liked it more than being King Verahim's messenger, but I guess I could do both."

"Yeah?" asked Aleksander. "Apparently I'm better at putting people in there than helping them get out."

"That nurse sure didn't like you," said Pol, laughing. Aleksander threw his head back in laughter.

"Well, Pol. I'll let you head back in, but I have a task for you. Could you keep an eye on someone in there for me?"

"That guy you beat up?" asked Pol. "You already asked."

"No, that's the assassin that killed Mistresses Ihrin and Antanasia, broke Lavinia's back, and threatened your sister. If you can pull some strings with Verahim to get him into a special prison, that would be great. He's the reason I was a part of the delegation, you know. I'd like to talk with him without him teleporting away, but no, that isn't who I meant. Will you keep an eye on that Sangoran woman in there that lost her wings? There's a few of them, but her name is Rayshel, and—"

"You sure do have a type, don't you?" Pol flashed a cheeky grin. "First my sister then this Rayshel…"

"No, it's not like that," said Aleksander with a laugh. "You're trouble, Apolinarius Bartunek."

"Ah, full name. Well, I do my best," replied Pol with a wink. "I'll look after her."

Aleksander thanked his young friend, who rejoined the nurses and healers in the crowded healing center. As he left, he wondered what thoughts were swirling in Pol's mind, as he rarely spoke of Mara anymore, and when he had mentioned her, he seemed to avoid the subject as much as possible.

Too painful. He understood.

Aleksander joined a party of orderlies in the corridor transporting survivors of the attack. Although he couldn't help heal the wounded, he knew that he could help locate those that were missing—and it was going to be a long night.

# CHAPTER TWELVE
# THE UNWORTHY GRAVE

It was not a grave worthy of the man buried beneath it. A crude, R-shaped wooden marker was all that remained of a noble human life, one that inspired goodness and hope in others. One of the only lives that really mattered, in Mara's opinion. It had been something close to a decade since she had seen her own father, but Rehor had filled that void. A true friend to his last act, he had saved her life in more ways than one during the time she had known him.

The Empress of Blood sat alone on the cold earth. A light breeze played with her hair, which was now free of the braid that had been wrapped around her head like a crown during the Peace Ball. She had been so close to fixing everything. She sighed and shook her head.

"Almost," she whispered to herself, wiping away a tear before burying her face in her hands. "Isn't that just the story of Mara Bartunek?"

She had spent a minute or so in the dream-state granted by the Mind-Prison cuff to mourn Rehor's death, but she knew it would never be enough time.

She stared at Rehor's crimson hat and stroked it gently, its feather burned in her escape. She draped her powerful wings around her body like a blanket that provided no warmth from the cold that filled her heart.

It couldn't be true. But then, it had to be. She had been the one to carry him away and bury him. She would be the only one to ever see his grave before the forces of nature claimed it, and then he would be lost forever.

Florenta. That greedy, horrible usurper was the reason for Rehor's abrupt death. Over what? Did she even know or care? Or was Rehor just another of Florenta's unnamed and forgotten victims in her conquest for crown and throne? Her head dropped to rest on her trembling knees. If she had never become queen, Rehor would be alive. Valistaran's fault. None of this would have happened if it weren't for his pursuit of power and his vile slave camps.

Her despair had turned to anger, and haunting memories of the perpetrators of every betrayal, every cruelty, and every pain in her life plagued her, and she could not banish them from her mind. And somehow, fate brought one of those people back, yet again, into her life. She heard the crunch of dead twigs beneath a boot, and she knew Valistaran had found her.

"What do you want?" she asked. She did not turn around. "Where's Ronin?"

Valistaran remained silent as he limped forward; a groan slipped through his lips as he dropped to the earth next to Mara. He ignored the dark look of indignation on the woman's face as he examined Rehor's grave. Eventually, Mara's glare softened to one of defeated resignation. First, one lone tear slid down her cheek before she began to openly weep.

"I couldn't stop Florenta. I failed everyone."

"I didn't fare much better," Valistaran said. His face and hands were coated in blood.

Mara didn't even try to stop the tears from washing down her bloodstained, soot-covered cheeks. Neither the deposed empress nor fallen king moved for what seemed like an eternity, but eventually, Valistaran sat, the effort to do so causing him great pain. He dropped a leather satchel into the dirt next to Mara and let out a pained sigh.

"What's this?"

"You plan on fighting Florenta in a dress?" Valistaran asked.

Mara flipped open the satchel and peered inside, finding a couple hard loaves of bread, some cheese and jerky, several tunics, two pairs of trousers, one pair of sturdy shoes, and a few assorted sets of undergarments and socks. Underneath the clothing were some bandages and her set of blades to attach to the tips of her wings.

"Do you often travel with ladies' underwear in a bag?" Mara asked. "Ah, yup, these are all mine. Even worse."

Valistaran rolled his eyes. "Oh, relax. I had your handmaiden Elena pack it all up for you days ago. I suspected something like this would happen, so I wanted to be prepared."

"Goddesses bless that woman," Mara said. "Is she safe?"

"Yes. I told her to stay home on the day of the peace talks just in case. You have no idea how many times my own similar meetings have been attacked," Valistaran replied.

"Thank you—for thinking of Elena, that is," Mara said. Valistaran nodded in acknowledgment. "Not for, you know, carrying my underwear around like a—"

"Can we not?" Valistaran asked.

Mara chuckled to herself. She removed a small pouch pinned to her waist and stowed it safely away in the satchel.

"What was that?" Valistaran asked.

"None of your business."

"Fair enough. I'll go so you can get dressed," Valistaran said. He got to his feet and walked a few yards away, his back turned.

"Farther," Mara ordered. Valistaran obeyed and stood behind a tree.

Mara removed her elegant, but now useless shoes from her feet and flung one of them into the air before blasting it with a bolt of lightning from her palm.

"What was that?" Valistaran called. The smoldering remains of the shoe fell into the dirt.

"Just getting rid of some dead weight." She hurled the other uncomfortable shoe into the sky and disposed of it in a similar manner with a grin of satisfaction.

The empress selected a pair of dark trousers from the satchel and slid both feet into the legs at once. She pulled them up to her knees, careful not to touch her fresh wounds, which she then bound with the bandages from the satchel. She took a deep breath and winced as she pulled the pants up the rest of the way over her wounded thighs beneath the hem of her black dress.

She glanced over her shoulder to make sure Valistaran wasn't watching and slipped out of the dress, folding it with care. She draped it over the pile of underwear and socks then slid her wings through the holes on the back of her tunic before pulling it over her bare torso.

"Okay, you can come back now, or leave, I don't much care," Mara said as she finished lacing up the front of her tunic. She hoped for the latter.

Valistaran returned as Mara affixed the blades to the tips of her wings, making sure they were snug.

"I do wish she packed my razor-claws," Mara said.

"Your what?" Valistaran asked.

"My razor-claws. You know, those claw attachments Sangorans wear on their fingers in battle?" Mara asked, wiggling her fingers for emphasis.

"I honestly always thought those were real claws," Valistaran said with a dark chuckle. "I mean, some do—"

"How?! You thought we have *claws*?! Just because many Sangorans wear their fingernails longer than Thans—weren't you married to a Sangoran? For the Goddess' sake, you have a half-Sangoran daughter, and you still didn't know that? Do you also think we're born with fangs?"

"Yes? You even told me once how strange it was when your teeth changed."

"They're sharper than yours, but you know only the worst of the worst criminals actually sharpen them into fangs, right? And that others often file down their teeth so they *aren't* too sharp?" She pointed to her own mouth. "Seriously, do you know anything about Sangora? What, do you think we eat babies, too?"

"The hostility is getting stale," Valistaran said. "I know you think that I'm—"

"You don't get to assume what I think."

"I apologize, Empress," he replied. "It was not my place."

He knelt next to her and raised his hand. A dark tongue of flame leapt from his palm, engulfing Rehor's grave marker. Mara cried out with misery and outrage, unable to stop the black fire from spiraling around the wooden grave until there was nothing left but ash.

"What the hell are you doing?!"

She turned to strike Valistaran, who twisted his wrist, commanding the elements to obey his will. As he extended his fingers and raised his hand to the sky, the dark flames extended overhead and transformed into a beautiful, comforting golden orange. The flames mimicked Valistaran's hand movements, and two beautiful wings made of pure fire extended from the pillar of flame. Mara watched in awe as he shaped the flames into a massive phoenix that soared into the heavens, lingering for a moment before dissipating.

Valistaran collapsed as his leg gave out. Mara sank next to him and even considered hugging Valistaran, completely at a loss for words. She began to cry all her anger and hatred into her hands.

"You know, I am, without a doubt, a lesser person than Rehor, and far lesser than you," Valistaran said.

Mara continued to sob into her hands as she recalled words that Rehor once spoke to her. Words he would never utter again.

"The light of hope always comes back into our lives after the cold and the darkness have taken it away," she said. "I'll never forget that he told me that."

"Wise words. You know, I count that man among the noblest of souls," said Valistaran. During the short time Valistaran and Mara had been engaged to be married, she had told him all about Rehor's inherent goodness and wisdom.

"Thank you."

Those whispered words were the only ones, insufficient as they were, that Mara could formulate in that moment. Valistaran knew that they were not meant for him, but for Rehor. Mara wiped the tears from her face and sniffled loudly. Although her breathing was still forced and ragged, she took in a deep breath through her nose and let it out through her mouth. She could feel her heartbeat slowing, returning to normal.

"And you—thank you for your help, and for..." she gestured to the sky where the phoenix had been moments ago and raised the satchel. "But I need you to know that absolutely *nothing* about you is who I am, and I don't owe you a thing."

"And it kills me that I can't say the same. I owe *you* more than I can ever say," Valistaran said.

The words disarmed Mara, and she stared at him in silence for a long moment.

"How did we even get here?" she asked bluntly, shaking her head.

"Well, you were a slave, and then we were engaged, and that part wasn't so horrible, was it?" Valistaran asked.

"Ever heard of Stockholm Syndrome?" Mara asked.

"What is a Stockholm?"

Mara chuckled then under her breath said, "Never mind."

"And the next thing I knew, the Faceless were dragging me to my death, and then you took your rightful place as Empress," Valistaran said.

"What happened that day?" Mara asked, her curiosity getting the best of her. "I thought you died. Everyone did."

"Well, Mara, truth be told, you failed that day. You left me to die, and I thought my life was over. My rule was, of course, and at the time, I thought that the greater loss."

"I'm not apologizing for that," Mara said, her expression fierce.

"I don't expect you to," Valistaran said. "And I want you to rest assured that I do not want my throne back. No, your actions that day and since have guided my own and set me on a quest more important than any power I thought I had. The truth is, I may be powerless against the coming evil. But you—with the crown on *your* head, it can be prevented, but with Florenta on the throne, well… My late queen, Codruta, and I may have set horrible things in motion by creating an alliance with that woman. We set her on this course, but even she won't be able to stop what's coming."

"What is coming?" Mara asked.

"To answer that, I ask your permission to show you a story."

"Show me?" Mara asked, unsure of his wording. "Of course, but what—"

Before she could utter another word, Valistaran placed two fingertips on her forehead, and the world dissolved into nothingness. She could feel their individual consciousnesses intertwine, and she allowed it to happen.

A tenebrous chill engulfed existence, and hope and light melted away, replaced by bone crushing darkness. As their minds became one, her lungs filled with water, and his fear and despair became her own.

## TWO YEARS AGO

Sharp claws pierced Valistaran's forearms, and his mind was consumed with an incessant groan. He was powerless against the weight of the ocean and the faceless creatures that dragged him ever deeper into the depths; for a last, fleeting moment, he could see the light of the flaming wreckage of his ships on the surface, but it was soon blotted out as he sank ever deeper into the inky depths.

As he succumbed to his fate, a brilliant, amethyst glow illuminated the depths. The last thing he saw was the Faceless in a massive chain of interlocking bodies, like a grotesque tendril of a gargantuan beast, pulling him through the portal of beckoning light.

The king awoke sometime later in a spartan, but well-equipped hospital room littered with tools and gadgets. He saw no doctors, nurses, or other patients in the room; he was quite alone. The still silence was suffocating and eerily reminiscent of a prison cell or the dark abyss from which he had just somehow, inexplicably escaped. He kicked the blankets from his legs. Good, they still worked. He tried to turn his head, but thin tubing leading into his nostrils prevented his movement.

A machine nearby beeped every few seconds; upon its face was a glowing scrawl of an unintelligible language and lines that rose and fell in a strange, yet familiar rhythm.

Ah, a heartbeat.

He removed something clamped to his finger and pulled the air tube from his nose and mouth, resulting in a revolting feeling like a snake slithering up and out of his throat, threatening to make him vomit. The lines on the box flattened, and the beeping became an incessant, droning sound. He had done enough research on the Deadlands in his grand library of Talohira to recognize the strange technology as medical equipment from ages past. Relics of a dead civilization. Why, then, was it here?

The cart holding the machine toppled to the ground as he stumbled out of bed and pushed on the door out of his room. It creaked open, and he entered a hallway lit by glowing tiles on the ceiling that gave off no heat and burned with no fire.

There were still no healers or wardens anywhere to be found, and he felt his heart thunder in his chest, the solitude unnerving.

He made his way down the hallway, tracing his finger along the faded, mint-green paint of the walls.

*"Follow."*

The word echoed in his mind, and he recognized it as an intrusive thought of a nearby Mindspeaker. In response, he whirled around, black flame trailing from his palm and up his forearm just as a horrendous groaning filled his mind followed by an overwhelming sense of dread and hopelessness that crept into the crevices of his soul.

A line of Faceless emerged from a doorway at the end of the corridor. He bathed the mass of emaciated bodies in dark flame with no hesitation. When he relented, a pile of smoldering bodies lay in a half circle around him, and dozens more of the mindless creatures stood motionless as if waiting for an order to attack.

They didn't *seem* aggressive. He toyed with the idea of fighting his way through the abominations but felt the Mindspeaker's touch on his mind yet again.

*"Follow."*

A robed woman in an intricate crimson mask and dark robes the color of the deepest wine parted the swarm. She strode with purpose and authority toward Valistaran; the world seemed to twist and distort with unnatural power around the Mindspeaker's body.

"What is this?" demanded Valistaran. "I am High King Valistaran Talohir, and I command—"

*"I do not care who you are, Mr. Talohir. I only care what you can do for me."*

"And who are you?" asked Valistaran as he took an intrepid step toward the newcomer.

*"My name is not important. We are all one here, and names put one above the rest. You may refer to me as the Magistrate, as I govern my brothers and sisters."*

"…And what are they?" Valistaran pointed to the Faceless.

*"They are the Pure. You wonder of their purpose. They were created to put the needs of the Ascended above all else,"* replied the Magistrate. She motioned down the hallway, and Valistaran followed. *"Allow me to explain, as is my purpose today. The Ascended are those gifted with abilities such as yours who have chosen to serve Thanatan."*

"Serve Thanatan?" asked Valistaran with a laugh. "You don't strike me as a priest."

*"Thanatan is no mere idol worshipped by the masses. He is very real, and we serve him. In return, he will reward us with a civilization with no war, no famine, no fear. Only joy and peace,"* explained the Magistrate. *"He invites you to be a part of this empire."*

"And why is that?" asked Valistaran out of genuine interest, although he said it with an air of mistrust.

*"The Faceless ones—the Pure—were created to serve the Ascended as warriors, farmers, miners, laborers, craftsmen…workers of all kinds. They are not selfish, do not lie, or steal. They are humanity in its purest form. They serve the collective. They shall fight your wars so that all war can end. So that peace can ensue. And, in turn, when the Ascended die, they join the Pure to serve as they have been served in Thanatan's great circle."*

"This seems to me more of a cult than a religion. You are speaking of slavery of the undead," said Valistaran. His mind raced to his own slave camps in Talohira. "What dark magic would allow such a thing to be possible?"

"*I sense that you have your own slaves,*" said the Magistrate. Valistaran turned to look at the masked telepath, choosing his words carefully, though he knew that the stranger probably already knew what they were.

"Not slaves. Not really. Preemptive prisoners, I like to think. I have read the histories recorded in the libraries of old, and I know about the destruction caused by your so-called Ascended—by people just like me," the king said, placing his hand on his own chest. "I do not take slaves out of pleasure or benefit to my country or throne. Every one of the workers in my camps are there because of their magic, and if you can read my thoughts, you know as much."

"*And how did you find them?*" asked the Magistrate.

"That's none of your business," replied the king, although he doubted that he could hide his thoughts.

"*I already see your mind, Mr. Talohir,*" said the Magistrate. "*I know that your daughter Valeniya has the ability to find others, particularly the Ascended—*"

"If you say her name again, I will remove your head," threatened Valistaran, despite knowing what the Magistrate had said was true.

"*You have no sword.*"

"I don't need one."

"*Perhaps not. At any rate, you committed a horrible sin using your daughter's gifts to find and enslave the Ascended in Thanatanos,*" said the

Magistrate. "*You displeased Lord Thanatan in creating your camps. However, we offer you redemption.*"

They turned down another winding corridor.

"Do you know of the secret keepers of Kurash?" he asked.

"*I do not,*" replied the Magistrate.

"They allegedly hold the human race's entire history in their heads. When the civilization I know as the Deadlands were decimated, the world lost libraries, universities, archives, and other sources of knowledge. Entire wars were fought over this knowledge. Ultimately, magicians and scientists were able to put humanity's history, or perhaps, the version they believed to be true, into the heads of mortal men, instead of writing it on paper."

"*And you sought their power to prevent another war.*"

"Yes. I believed I could stop what happened in the Deadlands from ever happening again. What you're trying to do won't end in a utopia—far from it," Valistaran replied.

"*In doing so, you created that which you vowed to prevent,*" said the Magistrate. "*My master knows of the wars that ravage your land.*"

"I admit, I have made mistakes," said Valistaran.

"*I feel your regret. Would you right those wrongs if you could?*"

"Obviously."

"*With the pure behind you, you could end all war.*"

"At the cost of doing exactly what I'm trying to prevent!" Valistaran shouted.

"*There is no power higher than the Pure and the Ascended,*" said the Magistrate. "*Power leads to peace.*"

"And what's between power and peace? Suffering, death, and despair," Valistaran said.

*"Have you not already spread such things? Such hypocrisy,"* said the Magistrate, shaking her head. *"You talk of preventing an apocalyptic future. Of ending war. Are our goals not the same? Are not our methods?"*

The room into which the Magistrate led Valistaran was completely unlike any of the others within the twisting hallways of the labyrinthine hospital. The immense chamber contained several of the same arcane devices as Valistaran's hospital ward, but where there should have been a bed, there was a metallic pod encrusted with gold and rubies and covered with a thick layer of dust.

Valistaran approached the pod, expecting the Magistrate to stop him. However, the stranger remained silent as the former king brushed the dust from a window on the metallic tube to reveal a decrepit face staring back at him, eyes wide and vacant, but not dead. Tubes led from the man's nose and all manner of cords and wires burrowed into his flesh, keeping him alive, but unliving, perhaps for generations.

"Who is he?" asked Valistaran, not taking his eyes off the ancient man as if transfixed. Valistaran heard the Magistrate's dull laugh in his head. "What is this?!"

*"You know who he is."*

Valistaran continued to examine the being in the pod, knowing that he was staring into the vacant eyes of Thanatan himself. It was not the majestic face of a god, but a withered mask wrapped around a dying face. He turned to address the

Magistrate, keeping one accusatory finger pointed toward Thanatan's husk.

"Why did you bring me here?" he asked, igniting his black flames to incinerate the false god. He felt panic begin to set in as he repeated his question. "Why did you bring *me* here?" He accentuated each word with an aggressive footstep toward the masked ruler of the Faceless.

*"Lord Thanatan's hibernation chamber has become corrupt with the flow of time. His mortal body will not survive when he awakes from his slumber. Although he will not die, he will be reduced to nothing more than dust."*

"And I take it, you want to replace his mortal body with *my* mortal body?" asked Valistaran. He felt the Magistrate confirm his fears with a feeling akin to a mental nod.

*"You would retain your own mind, but he would be an ever-constant companion, one that will guide you and our people into an age of peace. What is more fitting of a vessel for a god than the body and mind of a king?"*

At that moment, Valistaran let loose a stream of dark fire, engulfing the hibernation pod in ethereal flame. An ancient mechanism pulled the pod beneath the floor, shielding it from further harm.

The walls around him began to spin. Blackness pressed in around him, and the screams of a thousand departed souls and the groans of the Faceless sounded in his ears; the ground dropped out from beneath his feet, and the ceiling imploded on itself in a cacophony of tumbling stones. Black fire erupted from his palms, but the flames became ice that encased the king in the center of a swirling, chaotic mass of ashes, ice, and stone.

And then, he was falling with silent screams. Thousands of Faceless swirled about him, all reaching out with bloodied claws, but then he sensed the source of the chaos. Mustering all the mental power he could, Valistaran found the connection between the Magistrate's mind and his own, and he flooded his enemy's head with a mental scream to break the illusion, or at least free himself from her hold.

The chaos slowed, and Valistaran caught sight of his foe through the illusion and let loose a bolt of fire; the tongue of flame glanced off the Magistrate's crimson mask and dissipated into the chaos. He took advantage of the moment of respite and darted down the hall.

Dozens of very real Faceless swarmed the room as their master called to them. The Magistrate appeared behind him and sent a mental command to her servants to tear Valistaran limb from limb if he refused to yield.

*"If you will surrender, you can still serve Thanatan in death. Your abilities will grant you forgiveness for your crimes against him."*

As the Faceless closed in around him, Valistaran let loose his full fury. A clap of thunder and a primal scream roared throughout the chamber as Valistaran's raw power turned the chamber into a furnace in a flash of brilliant light followed by an outwardly expanding sphere of dark ethereal flame, incinerating the Faceless.

The creatures farther away from Valistaran faced a worse fate, their flesh and bones melting away before being reduced to a blackened glass that bit into the flesh of those behind, which were then left smoldering with horrendous scars.

The Magistrate stood alone, shrouded with a cloak of mental energy that shielded her from Valistaran's onslaught. The mental strain caused the Magistrate's illusion to collapse, replaced with the stench of burning corpses and blackened ash. When she recovered sufficient strength to stand, she was met with a pillar of dark flame that consumed her flesh.

She forced her way through the inferno and gripped Valistaran by the throat, digging her jagged claws into his neck. He grabbed her by the head, and with a cry of rage, he snapped her neck.

As the Magistrate's body hit the ground, the scuttering of bare feet on the hospital's tiled floor filled Valistaran's ears. Soon, the horrendous groaning spilled into his mind; they'd soon be upon him, and he had expended much of his energy in his explosive escape. He could feel their anguish. Their hunger. Their—what was that? Their unrelenting despair…

As the closed in around him, a swirling purple vortex surrounded him, and then, blackness. It was not like being trapped under the sea as before, but simply nothingness. In that nothingness, a disembodied voice filled his mind.

"*You now know the truth.*"

He felt a strange assurance that it was okay to let down his guard; he was safe. The voice did not belong to the Magistrate.

"Thanatan? Elafris?!" he asked as he floated around the abyss. "Who is there?!"

"*I am not who you think I am, as I do not pretend to be a god. I am called Yggdrasil, the World Tree,*" said the voice.

"And where am I?" A living tree. Fantastic.

*"You are nowhere, but everywhere. I can bring you home. I sensed that they took you through one of my portals, and so I have been able to sense you. They have been misusing my portals to flood the world with the Pure."*

"Does the Magistrate and her Pure mean you harm?" asked Valistaran. The king felt a deep despair wash over Yggdrasil's consciousness, which seemed to envelop the entire void.

*"No, I am safe, but your people face the same fate as my own. Many of my beautiful, brave sons and daughters are dead at the hands of the Men without Faces, and the few that yet live have turned from me. The Pure will destroy all that lives, as is their first purpose."*

"The Magistrate mentioned that they're meant to serve mankind—to work so that we don't have to, and to end all wars?" Valistaran said, hoping to get an answer out of the boundless nothingness that claimed to be the consciousness of a tree. "She's lying, I assume."

*"Oh, how the Magistrate defiles the dead! May they not rest? Many of those that she leads were my beloved children. The Faceless do not truly live, but neither are they dead. Through Thanatan's dark magic they are reborn, twisted into servants to serve his will until they are too broken to be of use."*

"And then what?"

*"And then they are discarded and become hives to spawn more of their kind. To corrupt the land with their foul virus to wake the dead. Their vines now spread across the land you call the Deadlands, waking the fallen to consume the Earth."*

"That's their purpose? To consume the Earth?" Valistaran asked in horror.

*"They were designed to end all wars by consuming civilization. Yes, the Magistrate is correct in that regard. For years they were used to serve in the*

*wars of men, working as soldiers and laborers, but they always returned to their instinctual, original purpose: to rid the land of all living things and their creations.*"

"I killed the Magistrate," Valistaran said.

"*Thanatan will find another. He is nothing if not patient. Now, I ask permission to show you the past so that you can envision your future.*"

"Okay."

Valistaran could see images of war with terrible machines and entire cities covered in hives of the Faceless and their vines that dug into the earth; he assumed Yggdrasil was projecting these thoughts into his mind, or perhaps, the absence of sensation was causing him to hallucinate. Yggdrasil showed Valistaran a vast civilization that seemed to span continents he had never even imagined; he watched as the Faceless slaughtered billions and decimated cities until nothing remained.

"Where did they come from? Who could have created such an evil?"

"*They originated the same place as man. The same place as beast, and of the plants that cover our world. They are natural. They began as a virus that your ancestors were unable, or perhaps unwilling to contain.*"

"What kind of virus could turn people into those beasts?"

"*Man's great downfall was its hatred for one another. The virus was altered in their laboratories and factories, and Thanatan used it to target certain groups to control them, but he failed. What came of that mistake are the beasts we face. It is fortunate indeed that the Faceless ones brought you through their portals, for it gave me a final chance to reach out to humanity. I have lost all contact with my sons and daughters. Or, more accurately, they have cut themselves off from me.*"

"What do you need me to do?" asked Valistaran. He could feel his past purpose and station lose all meaning, and a new one filled his heart. Whether genuine or planted there by Yggdrasil, he did not know. He did not care.

*"It is already too late for you to save my people, and even I will not live forever,"* said Yggdrasil.

The dark abyss around Valistaran was replaced with a flash of magenta, and then he could feel warmth on his skin. He rematerialized upon a peaceful mountain overlooking a city he recognized; Tal-Ahosh, the capital of Kurash. He collapsed upon the hill far away from the horrors of Thanatan's halls, and he heard one final, faint phrase fill his thoughts.

*"Thanatan is coming. Find him. Gather those you trust and slay the eternal beast before he brings death upon you all. Remember that he believes peace will result from his actions, but I beseech you to know that he is wrong. Goodbye, Valistaran Talohir, and I hope that we will meet again."*

The voice trailed away like a whisper on the wind.

The present day Valistaran pulled his hand from Mara's forehead, and she looked into his eyes with a steely determination; she had no words to articulate their newfound purpose. She gave the former king a resolute nod.

"I don't understand. Who was that woman?" Mara asked.

"Thanatan's right hand, the Magistrate. When I killed her, I felt Thanatan's anger, but I believe that Yggdrasil and I delayed his plans until now," Valistaran said.

"What do you mean?" Mara asked.

"I believe, like Yggdrasil said, he has found a new Magistrate that can lead the Pure for him," Valistaran replied. "I fear that he has regained his strength and is coming to do just what he said he'd do."

"Okay." She let out a deep breath. "What do we do? I don't know if any of my allies are still alive."

"Do you trust me?" Valistaran asked.

"It all makes sense. I think I have to trust you," Mara replied. "But that still doesn't mean I'm going to forgive you for anything."

"Thank you, Mara," said Valistaran. "I sincerely apologize that this isn't coming from literally any other person on this planet, but you are one of the few I know can actually help."

"Yeah, well, don't get your hopes up—for forgiveness or for me to save the world," Mara replied. "Florenta's a few steps below a King of Eternal Darkness, and that's my first priority."

"Yes, I understand. That should be your priority, after all, and I hope to be of assistance. Sangora is dear to me as well, as you know. But as you also know, the time for mourning is gone. I've told you my story, and now it is time for you to tell me your own. What exactly happened between the Mistresses of Dusk? I know Mistress Lavinia has always been your ally, and perhaps it is to her we must go. Is she still alive?"

"As far as I know, no one is," Mara replied. "We might be on our own. And to be honest, there are very few people on this planet I'd like to be stuck in this situation with less than you."

Valistaran ignored the comment.

"Yggdrasil said that we'll need to gather the people we trust. Lavinia's people in Timishuara, if they are not already under Florenta's control, may give us refuge. We can begin to gather our forces there and launch our campaign against Thanatan and the Magistrate. If not, perhaps we can still continue through Karpaska and into Thanatanos."

"You're not only asking me to put Lavinia's people's lives at risk. They are my people, too. I am still their queen, and they are dear to me."

Valistaran nodded then paused. "You do well in reminding me of my place, and in the importance of life; I admit it is something I have…neglected…in the past."

"I appreciate the sentiment, but I will never forgive you for everything you've done," Mara said. "You are the cause of the suffering of so many people—including my own."

"Does that mean you aren't going to help me?" Valistaran asked. He paused for a moment before adding.

"I don't want to. You still have no idea the pain you've caused me," Mara said. "To be blunt, I want to kill you."

"And I don't doubt that you could. I didn't mean my comment to sound manipulative, but I do need your help. The world does."

"As much as I hate it, I know. You're right. But that doesn't change my feelings," Mara said. "I expect you to respect them, and I won't hesitate to kill you if you slip into any old habits or try to manipulate me. Is that clear?"

"It is."

"Good," Mara said. She took a deep breath and got to her feet then slung her satchel over her shoulder. "Then what are we waiting for? Let's go kill a god."

# CHAPTER THIRTEEN
# IT IS REVOLUTION!

"And then Hanna used her magic to tear Empress Mara's blood right out of her skin. She was just about to finish her off, but that was our only chance to escape. She dragged me out of that cave, unconscious and useless as a sack of potatoes," said Shanthah, recounting one of his adventures to the enraptured Alboran villagers.

"So, you don't support Empress Mara?" asked Ruta with a look of concern. The question held an air of disappointment, rather than judgment over political opinion.

"Oh, no, no, no!" said Shanthah. "I hope you don't misunderstand. That's just part of our story—a sad part. Empress Mara has done wonderful things for Sangora; she's kind, just, and fair, but also powerful, dedicated, and unyielding in the defense of the people she loves. We are friends with her again, and I'll get to that part of the tale, I promise, but at this point of our story, we were enemies. My point is that Hanna held her own even against the Empress of Blood and her armies.”

Guilt gnawed at his stomach. Was he giving them false hope that Hanna was alive and could save them?

“And she can save us too,” said Ruta, before she translated for her grandmother, Irma, who nodded and stroked her granddaughter’s arm.

“That’s exactly what I’m saying,” said Shanthah with a wink. “I’ll tell the rest of the story later. What do you say I cook some lunch for you ladies? It’d be the least I can do for letting me stay with you these past few days.”

Ruta nodded, and a wide, toothless grin spread across her grandmother’s wrinkled face. Shanthah excused himself and opened a lone cupboard above a log-burning stove. As he did so, he heard his hosts speak rapid Sangoran in anxious voices; he knew the reason for their anxiety, but he smiled, nonetheless. He pulled an armful of items from the cupboard and spread the bounty onto the wobbly kitchen table.

“Where did all that come from?” asked Ruta, picking up a large potato as Shanthah went back to retrieve a bag of flour.

“You two are heavy sleepers, and I have nothing to do during the day when you’re all asleep,” Shanthah said, rolling up the sleeves of his tunic. “So, naturally, I went shopping.”

He found a tin that had once been round, still caked with burnt bits, and retrieved a pot and a knife from their place in the kitchen. He dumped the armful onto the table next to the food.

“We did something for you as well—or maybe *to* you,” Ruta said with a cheeky glance at her grandmother. Shanthah cocked his head as he began peeling potatoes. "Well, by that, I mean Grandmother has been talking."

"Talking?" Shanthah asked, interested.

"Yes. To everyone in our town—and visitors from other towns," Ruta said with a sigh. "About you, about your Hanna. About Mara and Florenta, what happened at Doftaan…"

"And do I have a future in Karpaska as a celebrity?" Shanthah asked.

"You might!" exclaimed Ruta with a laugh. Irma seemed overjoyed and quite pleased with herself, although she could not understand the conversation. "I think your story is, how should I say—well received."

"You know, that actually gives me an idea," Shanthah said. He placed a hand over his mouth, deep in thought for a few moments.

"Can I ask what is your idea?"

"Maybe you can help me build it," said Shanthah.

"Build what?"

"My idea," he replied. "I'm thinking your wonderfully chatty grandma can help not only me, but the rest of your people as well."

"How can grandmother help?" Ruta asked, scoffing. "She just talks and watches people."

Irma evidently understood the words "grandmother" and "help" and said, "Grandmother help!"

"Grandma's on board," said Shanthah, bowing dramatically to Irma, "and I think there is no one better to 'talk and watch' for our cause. Do you think she could spread the word that I'm going to march on Doftaan against Florenta?"

"And I assume you want grandmother to tell people you don't want to go alone," said Ruta. Shanthah nodded.

"Maybe I'm just stupidly optimistic, but maybe—"

"Stupid optimistic?" Ruta repeated.

"Oh, yeah, it means I'm excited or—"

"Happy?" Ruta asked.

"Happy and hopeful for something," said Shanthah with a shrug. Ruta laughed.

"So 'stupid optimist' is someone who is stupid for being happy and hopeful?" Ruta asked. "Thannish language is so funny. We don't have such a phrase in Sangoran. Maybe we are not such optimists here."

"Yeah, well, I think you described me pretty well there. Maybe I'm a 'stupid optimist' about this, but I think if enough people hear my story and want to help, they'll join me on my way back to Doftaan," Shanthah said.

"Maybe they will help you, but not all the way to Doftaan. It is too far. But maybe what do you think of going to Balgorod? It is the capital of Karpaska."

"And if I could take Balgorod…" Shanthah said, thinking out loud. "Then it would send a message to Florenta. But would I be putting Hanna in danger? Or your people?"

"Maybe, but also maybe it is your only chance," said Ruta, a look of concern etched on her face. She brushed the hair out of her eyes and translated the plan to her grandmother, who nodded.

"It is…revolution!" exclaimed Irma in her thick accent.

"It is revolution!" Shanthah and Ruta replied together, raising their fists.

Shanthah spent the rest of the night assisting Ruta with tasks around the house, and when they were complete, she introduced him to her neighbors, who gladly accepted the help. Determined to get on the same sleep schedule as his hosts, he worked through the night while he should have been sleeping.

Eventually, the sun crept over the horizon, and Ruta's neighbors thanked him for a long night's work with a fresh loaf of bread, which he graciously accepted. He sat, exhausted, on the stoop in front of Ruta and Irma's home watching the golden sunrise usher away the long night.

"Welcome home!" Ruta's voice came from inside. More welcoming, however, were the comfortable blanket and pillow that had been set out for him on the couch. Too tired for words, Shanthah handed Ruta the loaf of bread and collapsed on the sofa, burying his face in the pillow. "Have good sleep," she said with a laugh. She patted him on the head then disappeared behind her bedroom door.

Shanthah spent the rest of the week helping the townsfolk in whatever way he could, regaling them with his stories while he worked. Irma and Ruta spread his tale as well, and throughout the week, stories of his struggle to reach Hanna as well as Florenta's crimes in Doftaan spread from Sapez to surrounding towns. One night just before sunrise, he saw hundreds of Sangorans gathered in the central square, and he wondered what manner of festivities were going on. He approached the crowd and spotted Ruta nearby, who hurried toward him.

"What's going on here?" he asked.

"Isn't it great? Grandmother told everyone to gather to hear your story!" she exclaimed, gesturing behind her. Shanthah's heart thundered in his chest; he looked down at his hands, which were tingling and becoming translucent as his magic began to activate. Ruta noticed his anxious expression, and said, "Is it alright?"

"Yeah, it's fine," Shanthah said, flexing his vanishing fingers to make them visible again. He bit his lip and could feel everyone's eyes on him. He fought the urge to run from the scene but stood his ground. "I just, uh, really don't like public speaking—part of why I got into my line of work."

"You?" Ruta asked, her mouth agape in shock. "But you are most outgoing and crazy human I have ever met!"

"Yeah, well, don't tell anyone my one weakness." He gave an exaggerated wink.

"I am so sorry, I can tell them to go away," she said, clutching his shoulder. "I will send them away."

"No, no. It's fine. Really," he said, shaking his head reassuringly. He wondered for a moment if he was trying to reassure Ruta or himself, but he took a deep breath through his nose and approached the crowd anyway.

"I hear you've come for a story!" he called with a huge smile.

Those that understood Thannish cheered and clapped their hands. Without prompting her to do so, Ruta's voice rang over the still night air as she interpreted his words with the same intonation he had used. This time, the rest of the crowd cheered. He grinned, and Ruta held up a fist and mouthed, "It is revolution!" He returned the gesture with a smile and began the final installment of his tale.

"I want to tell you another story of a time we were almost killed by Florenta's forces, but we escaped," said Shanthah. "And for those of you who are interested in our love story, well, this is where we kissed for the first time, too." Several younger Sangoran women in the crowd swooned.

He didn't know for sure if the Sangorans in the story were loyal to Florenta, Mara, or one of the other Mistresses of Dusk, but he used it to his advantage. Whatever stories he could spin in Mara's favor got him one step closer to revolution and to Hanna. He took a deep breath and began the story.

"Let me paint you a picture," he started, gesturing with both hands. "So, there we were—on the roof of the castle in Laniras, enemy forces all around! Why, you may ask, were we on the roof?"

"Why were you on the roof?" asked a young girl excitedly.

"A good question!" said Shanthah. "And to be frank, I don't remember how we got up there, only that it was the fight of our lives—Florenta's forces were everywhere—and the only way we could stop them? We had to get this big, golden shield to the top of the highest tower. It was an oooold artifact—a magic one!"

The children gathered at the front of the crowd gasped, and they all asked what happened at once. Shanthah raised his hands to shush them, and they quieted down.

"Well had to get it to the top of the tower because long ago, the people who built the fortress in Laniras cast a spell on the tower that would protect the city from harm if the shield was inside the bottom of the bell there," said Shanthah.

Yet again, he was unsure of how the magical shield had protected them, but he wasn't ready to let the crowd know that. He could tell the crowd was entranced now, so he began the most intense part of the story.

"So, Hanna and I, along with Empress Mara's little brother, and some other friends made it to the tower, but we were blocked by Florenta's forces on all sides. They were below us, above us, around us!"

"What did you do?" called the children.

"We fought, of course! We fought to save our friends. But clearly, there weren't enough of us. I thought we were going to die. Whenever Florenta's people would try to kill me, I'd—"

The crowd gasped as he disappeared. The children leapt to their feet and rushed to the stool where he had been sitting just moments before but then cheered as he reappeared, laughing.

"They couldn't see me, but that wouldn't help Hanna, now would it?" People in the crowd shook their heads. He glanced over to Ruta as she continued interpreting for him, and he said, "I was about to give up hope, so I turned to Hanna, and I said…" He paused for dramatic effect. "No, you don't want to hear what I said. Way too cheesy."

"We do, we do!" cried the children. The older Sangorans chuckled and muttered amongst themselves, smiles aplenty scattered across the crowd.

"Very well!" said Shanthah theatrically. He laughed as Ruta imitated his intonation perfectly. "I turned to Hanna, to that wonderful, beautiful, brave, and frankly kind of terrifying girl—the greatest person in my world, and I said… 'Probably should have done this before we were about to die.' Then, she smiled, looked me in the eye and said, 'It's fitting,' and then we kissed."

A collective 'aww' escaped the crowd.

"So, we stood there kissing, oblivious to fate. We were pretty sure we were going to die, but that was okay because we were together. But she clearly cared about saving us, because she stopped kissing me, which of course, I didn't like, but she did this kind of—"

He leapt from his stool, which toppled to the ground, and struck the ground with his fist. This time, all the boys in front all cheered and imitated the punch.

"When she did that, she ripped all the stone and tile from the roof with her mind—with her *mind!* As our enemies swarmed in around us, she made the rocks and jagged bits of rooftop spin around us like a tornado, killing any of Florenta's soldiers that got close—Ah! Silly me, I forgot something very strange and very evil that happened that day—let me go back. Before we fought our way to the roof, somebody spoke to all of us on the battlefield. Everyone remembers hearing it, but no one knows for certain what it was." He paused for a moment and could tell people were more mesmerized by the mysterious voice than the direction of the story, so he wrapped it up. "Well, we fought our way to the tower, and Mara's brother got the shield up there and saved the day."

"What was the voice?" asked a terrified young girl in the front row.

"We still don't know for sure. No one does, but Hanna and Kamil, one of our other friends and a powerful Mindspeaker said they could feel his voice in their heads so hard it hurt—and what do they have in common?"

"Mind powers," said Ruta, commenting for the first time. She then explained her comment in Sangoran, and Shanthah nodded.

"Mind powers, indeed," Shanthah said. "My friends have a theory that someone even more powerful than them used their minds to spread his message that he had returned. I think it was because they were the most powerful minds nearby. Others agree. Some don't. But one thing is for certain: if he gets to Hanna before we do, he could use her power to hurt a lot of people." He paused and glanced around.

"That's my theory, anyway."

The crowd murmured to one another in hushed tones, but no one dared depart from Shanthah's presence, as if the evil voice would spring out and attack.

"Who was he?" a timid voice escaped the crowd.

"What most of us believe?" Shanthah said. He paused again, not for drama's sake, but out of fear. "Thanatan."

"This is foretold," said a man behind the children. "Our holy women knew this would happen! The Goddesses warned of it!"

The crowd exploded in anxious voices, and Shanthah failed to calm or control the crowd. He turned to Ruta, who had a smile on her face.

"Well, now I've upset them, and you're happy about it," said Shanthah.

"No, silly. They are upset, yes, but they had to become upset to join our revolution," she said. "Don't you understand it, Shanthah? They are on your side now. As my grandmother said, it is revolution!"

# CHAPTER FOURTEEN
# SANCTUARY FALLS

Worried cries for loved ones not yet found filled the mountain fortress of Zinok, nestled in the Dinaric Mountains of southern Thanatanos. The walled city had become a hornets' nest of frantic activity since the hundreds of Thannish refugees from neighboring towns had suddenly appeared out of a magical portal in the middle of the usually quiet city. However, the residents of Zinok saw it as their duty to protect the newcomers and welcomed them into their homes while the able-bodied citizens helped fortify the defenses against the oncoming threat.

As the refugees bustled around him, Josman looked out over the city of Zinok and wondered how King Verahim's predecessors had managed to carve a fortress out of the mountain large enough to house tens of thousands of soldiers and citizens, plus room for even more refugees. Unfortunately, nowhere near that number had made it to Zinok.

Three mighty walls stood in concentric half circles around the city, and craggy foothills gave added protection all around. The valley narrowed like a funnel into Zinok's mountain pass, making it harder for armies to approach.

"Josman, I don't think Drahomir made it through the portal," said Valis as he approached. "I could be wrong, but I haven't seen him anywhere," Josman answered with a forlorn gaze in the direction of Turnava, Pata, and the other doomed cities they had left behind.

"Please, keep searching," Josman said. "I want him to be okay, but I agree, and I'm expecting the worst. If you're right, then I suspect he's met a better fate than we are about to. I'm holding on to a fool's hope that these walls will be able to keep the Faceless out, but…"

"Valakor, the Minotaur, and that other warrior—sorry, I can't remember their names—they didn't make it through either, but do you think they'll send word to the king?" asked Valis.

"Even if they do, I don't think the Thannish forces could possibly get here in time," Josman said. "This place is meant for sieges, but probably not against those things."

"Did you know they modeled this city after a fictional city in the old tales?" asked Valis, changing the subject. Josman shifted and shook his head. "I've wanted to see it ever since Pol told me about an old legend called the Lord of the Rings, and there's this fortress where the forces of good fight off the minions of evil, or something. Fitting, right?"

"What's your point, kid?" asked Josman with a slight chuckle. He felt as if he were speaking to his own child about the old legends from the Deadlands, and a strange mixture of joy and sadness filled his heart, for his family had been killed during the war.

"I mean, in all those stories, good always wins. We'll be okay. The king will send help right when we need it. You'll see," he said with an encouraging smile then excused himself to help a pair of elderly refugee women struggling to push a handcart by themselves.

"Wonder how it worked out for them in the story..." Josman muttered, wondering when he had lost his own youthful optimism, considering for a moment that Drahomir's signature pessimism had somehow rubbed off on him.

Out of the corner of his eye, he saw a man collapse under a heavy pack; he hurried to the exhausted refugee's side and pulled the pack onto his own broad shoulder with relative ease, although he wondered how the frail man had managed to carry it all this way on his own.

"Thank you, sir," said the man. "With warriors like you, we'll make it out of here, eh?"

"We're better off with people like you, I think," Josman said with a smile but said no more as he helped carry the man's meager belongings to the refugee village.

Josman followed the flow of villagers to the most secure part of the city, an area called Sanctuary filled with temporary housing specifically for displaced townsfolk. As he passed, Josman saluted the Zinoki soldiers that now lined the streets.

"Sir, there is more than enough room for you to stay here," said the nearest soldier as Josman hurriedly headed toward the gates. Josman held up a hand and shook his head in reply.

"What gave me away that I don't belong here?" Josman called, chuckling.

"Your appearance and general disheveltude, suggests it sir, but your military salute means you don't belong with them either," the soldier replied.

"Disheveltude?" Josman said in a curious voice then offered the guard a meaty handshake. "I think I'm better used elsewhere. I appreciate what Zinok does for the rest of Thanatanos, and I hope this feeling of helpfulness can spread across the rest of the kingdom."

The guard bowed his helmed head to Josman, who went on his way. He watched soldiers setting up massive ballistae all over the city, and others filing onto the battlements with all types of bows, crossbows, and spears ready for a fight. He began to feel the same optimism as Valis, and for a moment he once again wondered just how things had gone in that King of the Ring tale, or whatever it was called.

The swiftness and efficiency of Zinok's defenses amazed Josman. As a former soldier in the Thannish army, he intended to go out to help, but everything seemed prepared, or nearly so, even before their arrival. The refugees were safe, the walls were armed with trained soldiers, and from brief snippets of conversation he overheard, there were even special defenses on each of the walls.

The preparedness calmed him, and that unnerved him. Perhaps he should be more worried, or… He felt a hand on his shoulder. He turned to see Alia smiling up at him. She pointed down the cobblestone street.

"I'm headed to the soldiers' hospital in town. My ability will be more useful there, and I fear your own will be of more use in the battle, so I'm guessing we won't see much of one another any time soon, and I just wanted to…" She trailed off.

"I'll keep an eye on your boy," said Josman. Alia smiled.

"I didn't know you were a Mindspeaker," said Alia in a joking tone. "I hope it isn't too much to ask of you. We spoke—he's brave, and, well, that worries me. I know the Zinoki soldiers will do most of the work, so you, me, Kamil, Valis, and Drahomir won't need to do much now that we're here, but knowing how things have gone for us lately, I'm worried."

She rubbed his shoulder, the contact comforting. She turned to go.

"Wait, Alia. Valis told me he didn't see Drahomir come out of the portal. I think he might be right. I haven't seen him—or now that I think of it, Kamil since we got here. You seen either of them?"

"Kamil is here. He volunteered to help teach the few Mindspeakers in Zinok how to do whatever it was that lured the Faceless away on our way here. He's safe. But Drahomir—I'm sorry, no."

"I don't like to think about it," said Josman with a grimace. "We've been through a lot together, and—" His voice faltered, and his head dropped. Alia placed a hand on his cheek, and he looked down into her eyes of deepest amber.

"We're all getting out of this." Her Kurashic accent was warm and comforting, just like her touch. "All of us. I'll find out where Drahomir is, and I'll send word. Okay?"

She smiled, and Josman nodded in agreement. Together they walked toward the soldiers' hospital where they said their goodbyes. He hoped Alia wouldn't have too much trouble there healing the wounded with her magic but considered the ferocity of their foes and thought better of it. He knew he was wrong. Many were going to die here.

He held up his large hand in greeting as a group of armed soldiers marched by. Their leader, a young captain, halted the procession and approached Josman. She removed her helm to reveal a full head of frizzy black hair and deep, sepia skin.

She looked the massive warrior up and down, ultimately deciding that his leather armor and cloak looked decidedly foreign to Zinok and said, "Sanctuary is just up the hill. I can have some of my men escort you there."

"No, I am here to help," said Josman.

"In that? I'm not sure if you've heard what we're up against."

"I do. I've faced them. I know exactly what we're fighting," he said. "Please, I can't sit in Sanctuary and let innocents die."

"What makes you think you're able to help?" asked the captain, folding her muscular arms across her chest.

Josman unsheathed his chipped and tarnished knife and swung it against his own forearm, much to the dismay of the soldiers. To their surprise, the blade ricocheted from his flesh without leaving a mark.

"Captain Rayna Kotula," said the young captain with a winning smile, extending her hand, which he shook.

"Josman Faros."

"Well then, Josman Faros, I happily welcome your services. You've caught us at a most opportune time if you want to help. We were headed to the armory to pick up equipment more suitable for this battle. You're welcome to join us."

"Thank you, Captain," said Josman with a nod. "I once served in the Thannish army under Captain Horvath."

"Good man. It was a shame that we lost him in the Battle of Laniras," Rayna said then motioned to her men. "We were all there."

"Thank you for your service," Josman said to the group. Rayna nodded, and the rest of the soldiers saluted.

He kept stride with the column of warriors as they made their way toward the armory near the military hospital. He caught a glimpse of Alia deep in conversation with the other healers and doctors and hoped for their safety. He caught her eye, and she smiled back, cushioning the blow of Rayna's news about Captain Horvath's fate.

Rayna unlocked the armory's doors, and Josman's eyes widened, and his heartbeat quickened in excitement as he beheld the wonderous weaponry within the weapons vault. The chamber led underground with signage directing soldiers to various types of armor and weaponry. Josman saw racks of shining helms, spears with heads as long as his forearm, gleaming swords, and various more brutal weapons such as maces, flails, and hammers.

"I assume because of your magic you won't need armor?" asked Rayna. She was nearly a head shorter than Josman and thus needed to look up to address him. However, Josman knew she could most likely still best him in any kind of combat.

"Actually, I think I still do. My armor magic prevents me from being stabbed, but blunt force could still knock my brains around, break my bones—I'm not invincible. In fact, I think it only works if I know I'm in danger because I've gotten small cuts while cooking, so…"

"Well, we don't have any armor for cooking. I think you're on your own," Rayna smirked. "I'll have my men get you ready."

She snapped her fingers and two of her soldiers procured various items of armor form the walls for the stranger. The rest of the troops began arming themselves as well.

"It isn't protocol to allow civilians to fight. Why me?" asked Josman as the two men pulled a light chainmail over his head.

"Almost every soldier in Zinok is a volunteer from the rest of Thanatanos. Only a few actually grew up here. Let's just say that you meet the minimum requirements," said Rayna.

Josman nodded and said no more, allowing Rayna's men to help him strap armor to his chest, legs, arms, and shoulders. He draped his warn traveler's cloak over his back, and for some reason, it felt like an old friend or a badge of courage.

At last, Rayna tossed a heavy helm to Josman, who peered into its empty visor for a moment as if looking into the face of an old friend. Images of times in the Thannish army filled his mind. Times that he fought and nearly died for his wife and child. He didn't have that luxury now. Now, he would fight for the wives and children across Zinok and Thanatanos so that others could see their children again. His mind turned to Alia.

He pulled the helm onto his head and followed a soldier to the rack of weapons, drawing a longsword from its sheath as Rayna barked orders to her men. He attached it to his new belt then turned to the heavier weapons on the wall behind him, deliberating for a moment between his own damaged mace and an even bigger one before deciding his old one was too damaged to continue to serve him. He felt odd leaving it behind and asked a soldier to keep it safe. Rayna gave orders to move out, and he and the other fighters obeyed.

Half an hour later, Josman found himself and the rest of Rayna's men stationed on the third wall, the final defense of the city. Hundreds of other troops joined him, while others manned the first two walls and others yet remained in the city if the Faceless managed to get that far. Josman looked into the pass that cradled the city and knew that even those soldiers would see action this day.

"*Hello, my friend!*" came Kamil's voice to his mind. Josman whirled around as he sensed his mental presence but couldn't see him anywhere. "*Behind you.*" He turned again to see Kamil clad in Zinoki armor, a curved scimitar like those from Kurash strapped to his thigh.

"That thing remind you of home?" asked Josman, pointing to the weapon. Kamil nodded. "I can't use those things. I always think I'm going to accidentally chop off my own—" He was cut off as a horn sounded over the city, followed by a blast from each wall—the signal that the Zinoki forces would soon meet their enemy; the Faceless had begun to advance.

Josman caught a glance of Valis standing in formation with the other volunteer warriors on the third wall and shouted to him. Valis too had a scimitar strapped to his leg.

"Karim!" He was careful to use the young man's cover name to avoid announcing that the son of Valistaran Talohir was amongst them. Valis turned and gave a nervous smile to Josman, who waved him over. The men near Josman shifted, and Valis took the position next to Josman and Kamil.

"I'm sure glad to see you," said Valis. "I'm not sure I'm ready for this."

"I promised your mom I'd look after you," said Josman with a smirk.

"Oh, dear," he muttered, shaking his head. "Even here?"

"Don't worry, it's how all moms are, kid," Josman said with a laugh and clapped the young man on the back. "The good ones, anyway."

Kamil too smiled, and the trio looked out over the three walls of Zinok to see the initial wave of Faceless swarming against the first barrier.

"They'll never get this far," laughed one of the soldiers. Josman glanced over at him, annoyed and ready to speak up, but Kamil spoke directly to his mind.

*"Let him have his hope."*

The Faceless piled up over one another, filling the deep ditch before the wall and creating a mountain of emaciated bodies.

Wave after wave of the endless horde clambered onto the horrendous hillside of their brethren, collapsed, and allowed those behind them to step over their bodies. Up and up rose the macabre staircase until the first Faceless made their way to the top of the wall.

At that very instant, the petrifying feeling of dread and insatiable hunger washed over all three walls. Most of the soldiers on the ramparts shifted uneasily, thinking they were imagining the feeling, but hundreds of the host of men and women began to outright scream. The collective panic took hold as the Faceless slaughtered those stationed on the first wall without mercy.

*"Steady, you two,"* came Kamil's voice to Valis and Josman's minds. Josman nodded, closed his eyes, and took a deep breath, wrapping his fingers around the handle of his new mace.

An intricate pattern of horn notes trumpeted over the walls and seemed to flow down into the valley. The few remaining men inside the first wall heeded the trumpet's order, and a crunching, grinding sound filled the air as stone windows opened to reveal narrow slits along the brick face.

A waterfall of shimmering black fluid sprayed from each of the slits on the top, front, and back of the wall, dousing the horde of Faceless. Unable to steady themselves, hundreds of the creatures plummeted from the wall, striking the ground with a sickening crunch one hundred feet below.

"Got 'em," said Valis.

"You ain't seen anything yet," said Josman, eagerly waiting to see the other traps Zinok contained. A second horn blew, and Josman roared a Than battle cry that was answered by the others on the third wall. Archers on the second wall readied a volley of flame tipped arrows then let them fly, igniting the slick, dark liquid.

The entire first wall erupted in a blaze of crimson and orange. The mental groans of the collective horde mind turned from hunger to agony as their flesh was charred and melted, but still they did not stop their advance; the horde swarmed over the wall through the flames, many catching fire and dying before they hit the ground.

The image of Faceless piling upon one another was nothing compared to their descent. They hurled themselves from the ramparts, their flaming bodies twisting and distorting in the air, creating a ghastly ramp for the others to clamber over.

"That's nightmare fuel," whispered Valis, his mouth agape.

"*Pray that we do live to experience another nightmare,*" said Kamil as the groans of the Faceless once again filled their minds. They watched as the second wall fired volley after volley of arrows into the host of Faceless as they emerged from the wreckage of the flaming wall. They felled many of the beasts, but still they kept coming.

"It's like using skipping stones to dam a river," said Josman.

He shook his head in despair, and dread filled his heart, for he knew it was only a matter of time before the Faceless reached them.

Another pattern of notes filled the night, and Kamil looked to a nearby man whom Josman did not recognize. They communicated briefly using their minds, and then they knelt against the ramparts, pressing two fingers to their foreheads while holding their other hand aloft. Nothing seemed to happen until Josman and Valis felt a wave of mental energy wash over their minds. Two more men joined them, and the feeling of power increased. A strong desire to follow the flow of mental energy filled Josman's heart, but he refrained.

"What are you all doing?" Josman asked.

"*…Taught them to make a mental lure…*" came Kamil's strained voice in reply. "*Weak minds—sending them into the fire…*"

Josman nodded and allowed his friend and allies to concentrate; the plan was effective, and hundreds of Faceless scurried back into the flames to their demise.

As Kamil and the other Zinoki Mindspeakers lured as much of the horde away as possible, the archers on the second wall rained death down upon them. They had no need to aim, for every arrow met its mark in the endless sea of broken, gray bodies as the tide crashed against the bottom of the second wall.

Those that reached the wall dug their clawed fingers into the rocky dirt, cutting into the earth and the wall itself. Their fingers and claws broke as they met boulder and brick, but their brethren kept up the assault as they fell. Thousands of Faceless bodies littered the chasm, and soon, the massive ballistae were fully armed and began to spray heavy bolts through their flesh.

Josman's heart sank as he looked out into the valley and could see no end to the horde which now piled against the second wall but did not seem to be attempting to climb it like the first. There was a sudden rumble and the men and women atop the wall screamed as it began to shake.

"They're not trying to climb over the wall!" Josman shouted. He gripped the ramparts and looked on in horror.

"They're tunneling underneath!" Valis realized, putting his hand over his mouth in shock. Terror gripped his heart, and fear seemed to consume him as the second wall collapsed toward the Faceless horde. The brave soldiers both upon and within the wall were slaughtered within moments, and through the clouds of smoke and dust poured the Faceless, their heads and claws bloodied.

"What should we do, captain?" a soldier nearby asked, eager for Rayna's orders; the others cried out in kind, fearing for their lives, but putting full trust in her leadership.

"Hold all fire and maintain your position!" came Rayna's voice. The brave soldiers obeyed their captain as the Faceless swept against the third wall like a massive wave, piling atop one another again until they threatened to overcome the bulwark.

One long horn note sounded.

The horde amassed near the wall plummeted downward as a series of explosions caused the ground to give way into a vast cavern below. Thousands of the creatures met their doom as they were swallowed by the darkness below the earth; the rest of the horde paused at the edge of the chasm, their agonizing groans still devouring peace and silence.

"That stopped them for now," said Josman, gazing into the depths. He could see no end to the pit and wondered how far it extended underground.

"How deep is this pit?" asked Valis. "Are we safe? Or are we just letting them find a new way to us?"

Kamil reached downward with his mind to sense his foes, but soon turned his thoughts to his allies. *"They're still falling."*

Reprieve. The onslaught stopped, unable to advance. Many of the Faceless attempted to climb the craggy canyon walls to circumvent the chasm, but those that did fell to their deaths. A cheer erupted from everyone on the third wall, and another horn blast signaled for the archers on the final wall to fire upon the Faceless they could reach. At that moment, a voice filled the mind of every soul upon the wall.

*"Do not fear, brave defenders of Zinok, sons and daughters of Thanatan,"* the voice floated from mind to mind, and everyone turned to their neighbors to confirm they weren't the only ones hearing the words.

*"This is not the end. Our lord Thanatan does not ask for blind loyalty, but he will not stand for conflict or defiance."*

Many others covered their ears or smacked their foreheads to rid themselves of the thoughts; others shouted at the voice to stop.

Captain Rayna pushed her way through her troops and grasped Kamil by the shoulder. She looked him sternly in the eye. "Find whoever that enemy Mindspeaker is and tell them we will not surrender."

Kamil nodded and reached out with his mind with no expectations to find anything. However, within mere moments, a strong mental presence latched onto his mind. The tendrils of mental energy seemed to grasp Kamil's consciousness, and he could not pull away, a prisoner to the unseen foe. The other three Mindspeakers joined their thoughts with Kamil's, and they too were pulled into the mind trap. A surge of mental energy flooded their minds as the unseen being use their combined power to speak to everyone in Zinok.

*"Salvation is here for those that will lay down their weapons and abandon this fight. Death awaits those who remain here. My master, the god your starving country worships, has returned. He is regaining his strength to come unto you—to help you and to save you.*

*"These beings you resist wish only to serve you. You will not toil another day in your lives. They shall farm for you, build for you, fight for you if you shall have the need. They only seek purpose. I am The Magistrate of the Pure, and I give them that purpose: to serve Thanatan."*

A soldier on the wall broke free of the spell and shouted, "Get out of our heads!" Another came to his senses and punched the first in the jaw, knocking him to the ground.

"Praise Thanatan!" he exclaimed before falling to his knees. At that moment, hundreds of people in the Zinoki crowd did the same in praise of the god they had worshipped for generations, his messenger speaking directly to their minds. Kamil sensed both immense joy and fear, and he stumbled against the ramparts, overwhelmed by the flood of emotions.

He combined his mental energy with that of the other Mindspeakers to fight back, grasping at the imaginary tendrils of mental connection; he imagined grasping a mighty rope, and he gave an almighty roar as he pulled it toward his consciousness; instantly, the world went white.

He collapsed as blinding light replaced all reality.

A vision filled his mind, and he saw endless eviscerated dead that lay wide-eyed and motionless in the streets of a vast city of glass and metal.

Thousands of strange carts, moving without horse or ox, sped past their fallen countrymen. Too many of the vehicles cluttered the wide roads than they could handle, blocking the way for others trying to escape; their drivers, eager to flee, abandoned their vehicles and fled on foot.

And then, a flood of emaciated creatures smeared in blood carried swift death through the streets, sweeping over the entire city in a tide of gray. Kamil watched in horror as the Faceless slaughtered millions of people in their attempts to flee; buildings crumbled before them, leaving nothing but blood, dust, and ash in their wake.

To his surprise, a flood of joy and satisfaction that was not his own washed over his entire being. He could feel the thoughts and intentions of a being more powerful than himself—even more powerful than the Magistrate: Thanatan.

And then he saw it: a plume of fire and death blossoming into a mushroom-shaped cloud over the horizon followed by a wave of destruction unlike anything Kamil had ever imagined. It decimated what was left of the city; light and flame consumed the Faceless hordes, the crowds of fleeing people, and everything else in its path.

The screams of ten million dying men and women filled Kamil's brain. Kamil screamed as he broke free of The Magistrate's hold on his mind in a cold sweat and connected with the minds of those nearest to him, projecting the images he could remember.

*"Is this what you were taught about Thanatan while growing up? Is this the Thanatan you learned about in your churches? Stop this madness!"* Another soldier came barreling toward Kamil, sword in hand and murder in his eyes.

"Get out of here, Kurashian!" he shouted, but before his stroke fell, Josman's heavy mace struck the man in the chest, crushing him against the ramparts.

"This man has done more for your country than you ever have!" Josman bellowed, raising his mace above his head once more, but Valis and Kamil both stopped him from landing a fatal blow. As the man crawled backward in retreat, Kamil turned just in time to see the three other Mindspeakers collapse under the strain of the Magistrate's power.

*"No!"* he exclaimed. Blood dripped from their ears, eyes, and noses as they slumped to the ground. *"NO!"*

Kamil looked down into the valley behind the third wall to see the armies of Zinok turn on one another over the Magistrate's message, killing those that had once stood beside them in battle.

"He didn't even need to breach the wall to bring us down," Josman said. With wide eyes, Valis nodded, unable to utter a single word.

Josman defended his two friends as Kamil turned his attention to the Magistrate. He sent a telekinetic message to all those in reach; it was easy enough to contact the Magistrate accidentally the first time, why not again?

*"Stop this!"* he cried in mental anguish, and to his surprise, he felt a sense of acquiescence wash over his consciousness.

*"Thanatan bids you peace. He does not condone this senseless violence. Those who lower themselves to raise their blades will face death. Thanatan does not wish this to come to pass,"* came the Magistrate's voice to all within range of her mind.

"This can't be happening," said Josman, pacing along the wall. The violence below had ceased with unnatural suddenness, but there was now an anxious air of hopelessness lingering over the mountain city.

*"I shall allow those who wish to follow Thanatan to leave Zinok and return to their homes. The Pure will rebuild that which has been destroyed. Spread word to Laniras, to Vudapas, and to the other cities and villages of Thanatanos, that your god, Thanatan has returned in the ruins of the city once called Nitra. Was it not once written that he shall set his throne and his crown in a city amongst the ashes? Bring word of the Pure and their purpose. Go, and bring peace to this land."*

There was tremendous sound of grinding gears, and the wall began to lower itself over the chasm like a drawbridge, giving the soldiers on top of it barely enough time to retreat inside. As the wall touched the earth, those inside were rocked about and thrown hard against the stone.

"I think its best we stay in here," said Valis. Kamil and Josman both agreed, as did some of the soldiers nearby. Some of their former allies clambered out of the wall, leaving Rayna and dejected few others behind. Thunderous footsteps signaled the exodus across the wall-bridge toward the Magistrate.

*"Come, children of Thanatan. Bring peace."* The footsteps above continued for nearly an hour until silence fell over Zinok. The Magistrate did not speak again, and the groaning of the Faceless hordes and the terror that accompanied them dissipated. The battle, if one could call it that, was over almost as quickly as it had begun.

For now, the Pure were gone. Those who remained were safe. Alive. But in their hearts, each and every one of the survivors knew one simple truth.

They had failed.

# CHAPTER FIFTEEN

# THE KING THAT ALMOST SAVED HIS PEOPLE

On the other side of Thanatanos, far from the battle of Zinok, Aleksander snuck into the prison beneath Laniras as the city slumbered. He handed the guards at the gates their promised gold. They nodded and without a word opened the passage into the sprawling underground prison. With the sense of time long stolen from them, most prisoners beneath Laniras were loud and awake even during this late hour. They called to Aleksander and the guard accompanying him, screaming profanities as they strode past.

Aleksander passed criminals of all kinds through their bars, Sangorans, humans, and even a couple camel-people and Minotaurs from Kurash restrained by heavy chains.

He knew this level of the prison was reserved for those without magic, meaning he was safe, but that did not lessen the unease in his stomach.

As the guard turned several different keys in various locks on a set of solid metal doors, Aleksander made eye contact with a silent man sitting cross-legged in the center of his cell.

The prisoner smiled.

Aleksander glanced away, knowing his fear was irrational, but his heart pounded faster in his chest, nonetheless. At last, the guard accompanying him detached a second pair of keys from his belt and handed them over.

"Down the left hallway, last door," said the guard.

"You aren't going to show me there?" asked Aleksander. The guard scoffed and shook his head furiously.

"You're mad if y'think I'm goin' down there. D'ya know how many guards go mad workin' in the magical detention levels?! No way, sir. You can find your own way," said the guard. "I 'ppreciate the gold, though, sir. I understan' this is official Hidden Flame busy-ness, but can I know what you're doin'?"

"I'm sorry, no," said Aleksander with a knowing wink. "I'm sure you understand." The guard nodded, simply excited for the few coins Aleksander handed him and the chance to work with someone from the Hidden Flame, however briefly. Aleksander wondered to himself if there even was such a thing as the Hidden Flame anymore.

He stepped into the staircase leading to the depths of the prison and heard the guard lock the gates behind him. He trusted the guard to let him back out, but he had only been granted twenty minutes with the assassin. He followed the guard's direction and found the assassin's chamber with ease.

He had received instructions from the guards on their first meeting to first unlock the outer door to the assassin's chamber, lock it, and then unlock the second door. The guard had previously explained that the cell was designed to keep Walkers from teleporting, with the antechamber acting as a preventative measure if the prisoner managed to escape the first room.

Aleksander entered the antechamber, locking the first door behind him. He turned the wrought iron key to lock himself in then placed the key in a pouch around his neck and stowed it beneath his tunic. He tested summoning a ball of flame. His palm heated up, but no fire appeared. So, the chamber could dampen his powers as well—he would have to be even more careful. He entered the assassin's cell, and the second door locked automatically behind him.

The assassin sat bound in chains on his cot. His black robes were gone, replaced with the drab gray prison attire, but his crimson mask was still locked firmly around his head. Apparently, the guards had not figured out how to remove it without killing him.

"And so, you've come," said the assassin.

Aleksander looked around the bare room and saw only a plain wooden stool and slab desk in the corner attached to the walls. He drew the rickety chair and sat down across from the prisoner. He wasted no time with pleasantries.

"You called me brother. Why?" asked Aleksander.

"Are we not?" asked the assassin, his voice distorted through the mask.

"No."

The assassin leaned forward, resting his elbows on his knees to peer at Aleksander through the eye slits of his crimson mask. He interlaced his fingers and waited for Aleksander to speak again.

"Your mask. What is it?" he said at last.

"Lord Thanatan's protection. It prevents me from leaving before I want to," replied the assassin.

"What do you mean by that?" asked Aleksander.

"Many of the Pure are given masks. It restores their humanity to an extent chosen by our master," said the assassin. "In a way, it does the same thing for me."

"You're not one of them, though. I can see your eyes and part of your face through the crack," replied Aleksander.

"And you don't recognize me?" his prisoner asked. Aleksander shifted on the wobbling chair and crossed his arms.

"Should I?" he asked. The assassin gave a laugh distorted by the mask.

"I called you brother, didn't I?"

"I know who my only brother is, and I can assure you, it isn't you," said Aleksander.

"So, you've remembered who you are," whispered the masked man; the fact that Aleksander had lost his memory was not common knowledge. "Pray, tell. Do your friends know? Does the Hidden Flame? Does your king or his court? What would they say if they knew? What would they do? Not all brothers are blood, Aleksander."

Aleksander closed his eyes and took a deep breath. He had allowed the assassin to turn the conversation on him. He mustn't let him do it again and didn't speak for a few seconds, gathering his thoughts.

"I can get you out of here," said Aleksander. "All you need to do is answer my questions."

The assassin leaned closer to Aleksander and whispered, "I have my own way out." Aleksander furrowed his brow and shook his head.

"Your cage prevents you from teleporting."

"Yes, but it doesn't remove my connection to my Lord Thanatan. He knows where I am, and he is coming. He will free me and release the Ascended in this prison, you shall see."

"So Thanatan ordered you to kill the Mistresses of Dusk?" asked Aleksander.

"Do not speak his name so wantonly," said the assassin. Aleksander said nothing, and the prisoner spoke again. "My lord tasked me with expanding his rule to Sangora. Those in this country already love him. They pray to him. They offer him sacrifices. They worship him in churches and teach their children of him, but the Night Witches of Sangora have no love in their hearts for any but their Goddesses and Elafris the Devil."

"And killing the leadership of Sangora would sway them to your cause?" asked Aleksander, legitimately intrigued.

"No. Do you know the power the Empress of Blood uses to command her armies? Within her wings lie specially engineered glands that produce powerful pheromones with influence as strong as the most powerful Mindspeaker. Combined with her telepathic abilities, she is able to control her subjects completely. Even those out of range of the pheromones. It is more than mind control. She can create the legitimate, chemical desire in the brain to serve her," said the assassin, tapping his head.

"Maybe Queen Codruta did that, but I've been to Sangora, and I've seen their genuine love for Empress Mara," said Aleksander.

"Yes, because she willed it to be so. Genuine, indeed," said the assassin with a scoff.

"So, you're after Mara's wings?" asked Aleksander.

"That was one option, yes," said the assassin.

"And the other?"

"Queen Florenta of tribe Karpaska has discovered a way to obtain the Queen's Control for herself and become immune to the influence of her empress," explained the assassin.

"How do you know this?" asked Aleksander, suspecting that not even Mara had such information. He wondered why the assassin was giving him so much information so freely.

"I saw a great many things before I slew Mistress Ihrin and her daughter," said the assassin. "I know more about the dealings between Mara's council than the Mistresses of Dusk themselves. And what I know, Thanatan knows."

Aleksander knew the man's words to be true. He tapped his foot in impatience, wanting only to rip the mask from the man's head. As the assassin leaned backward on the cot, Aleksander caught a glimpse through the man's prison garb of a long, jagged scar across his chest.

"Why are you telling me the truth?" asked Aleksander.

"What do I benefit from lying? That is Thanatan's way. His plans are not secret or evil. They are to serve this world so that we can have peace," the assassin said through his mask. He cocked his head and asked. "Do you not see that, Aleksander?"

"The rest of Thanatan's plan for Sangora. Tell me. Now." He knew his time was short and the guard would not wait for him.

"The seeds have already been planted. Soon those that Thanatan desires to save with the Queen's Influence will join him while the others willingly join the Pure to serve the Ascended—I apologize, by the Ascended, I mean those gifted with abilities like mine and yours," said the assassin in a condescending tone.

"Pure Sangorans?" asked Aleksander in a hushed tone, as if the guards would hear him. His heart thundered in his chest, for the very thought of swarms of Faceless with the wings and claws of Sangorans brought dread to his heart. Nothing could stand against such a threat.

"All shall join the Pure in the end," said the assassin before leaning toward Aleksander again and saying. "All shall be made pure. He is coming, Aleksander. Isn't it wonderful?"

"When is he coming?" Aleksander asked. The assassin broke out into raucous laughter.

"He's practically here!"

Aleksander bolted to the door and into the antechamber, locking it behind him, blocking out the horrible laughter of the prisoner within. He exited the second door and locked it with shaking hands. The prisoners screamed at him again as he broke out in a dead sprint toward the exit. He slammed his fist on the metal gates, and within a few moments, the guard had it open.

"Is everythin' alright?" asked the guard.

"No, no it is not," said Aleksander, leaving the guard behind.

"What is it?" the guard called, but Aleksander ignored the man. Without waiting for his guide, he retraced his steps to the surface and emerged from the prison into the cool night air. Summer was dying away, and he feared that before autumn came, the world would change forever.

The sound of trumpets filled his ears. He could hear a crowd chanting and cheering, and then, what was that sound? A slow hymn filled the night air. He recognized it as a Thannish hymn about their god's peace and unity. The sounds of the procession seemed to be coming somewhere from the south.

"Oh no," he whispered, heading back inside King Verahim's palatial fortress. Recognizing him as a member of the Hidden Flame delegation to Sangora, the guards allowed him to pass and announced his arrival. He flew up the flights of stairs, taking them two or three at a time. He pressed his face against an intricately designed window and could see the procession heading toward the castle.

He stole into the healers' quarters and located Pol's room, which he shared with another Thannish healer. He shook the young man's shoulder until he stirred. Pol glanced upward in confusion.

"Aleks?" he asked.

"We've got to go," said Aleksander. "Grab whatever you need. Don't forget your sword."

"What's happening?" asked Pol, rubbing his eyes. Aleksander waved his hands as if to explain that there was no time for words.

"Get dressed. I'll be outside. You have a couple minutes, if that," he said, lighting a small flame between his fingers to light the way. Pol did as he was told, pulling on his simple leather armor. He threw his traveler's cloak over his shoulders and grabbed his sword belt from under his bed then hurried to follow Aleksander. His roommate stirred from the bed across the room, but Pol shut the door before a conversation ensued.

"You're scaring me," said Pol as he fastened his belt around his waist.

"Good, you should be afraid. We all should," said Aleksander, heading toward Verahim's throne room and bed chambers. "We need to get to King Verahim. Now."

"Follow me. I know a shortcut to his part of the castle," said Pol, confused by Aleksander's abrupt urgency. He led the way in the opposite direction. Aleksander nodded and followed close behind, using his flame to see in the darkness.

"We need to speak with the king!" exclaimed Pol as they approached Verahim's chamber, unsure of the reason, but trusting Aleksander's judgment. The guards crossed their spears over the door.

"He is not here," said one. "He has gone to welcome the Zinoki procession."

"As his messenger, shouldn't I know that?" Pol blurted out.

"I apologize, Master Apolinarius," said the guard. "You were nowhere to be found and assumed dead after the attack in Doftaan, as were you, Master Aleksander."

"I—what?!" Pol exclaimed.

"Who is coming from Zinok?" asked Aleksander, unaware of what had transpired in the fortress in the Dinaric Mountains.

"The king met the group from Nitra, and now they're headed to welcome those that have accepted Thanatan's peace from the battle of Zinok."

"Group from Nitra? Nitra was destroyed," Aleksander said. "I was there!"

"Well, he welcomed a group who claimed to be coming from Nitra," said the king's guard with a shrug. "But isn't it wonderful? He's back!"

"Who?" asked Pol. Aleksander grabbed Pol's arm and dragged him away from Verahim's quarters. "Who?!" he called again. Aleksander's pace quickened.

"Lord Thanatan, of course!" called the second guard in a cheery voice. Pol looked up at Aleksander with wide eyes. Aleksander said nothing as they headed back to the hospital.

"Thanatan?" asked Pol in disbelief.

"Pol, he's not the god our country thinks he is. I'm not so sure he's even a god," said Aleksander.

"Like Elafris?" asked Pol. Aleksander nodded as they reached the hospital.

"Uh, yeah. Sort of, but I think he does actually have powers. Our theories and fears are true. I just spoke with the assassin, and I learned horrible things. We need to get out of here before it's too late," said Aleksander. "Wait for me here, okay?"

Pol waited for Aleksander outside the doorway, and after a few moments, he emerged with the wingless Rayshel, broken Lavinia, and wounded Vasilica. Rayshel pushed Lavinia in a rickety wheelchair while Vasilica limped behind them.

"Who is this boy?" she asked, gesturing to Pol.

"This boy is the brother of your empress," replied Lavinia. "You would do well to show him some respect."

Vasilica's eyes widened, and she bowed. Pol looked uncomfortable.

"It is an honor, master Apolinarius," said Vasilica, bowing low. "I apologize."

Pol looked to Aleksander, unsure how to react.

"Oh, it's fine," Pol said awkwardly, bowing in turn to his sister's advisor.

"I have heard so many things about you," Vasilica said as she straightened up. "Your sister loves you and misses you very much." At this, Pol looked forlornly at his feet, which went unnoticed by all but Aleksander. Pol met his gaze, and they shared an unspoken conversation. Nothing needed to be said.

The group made their way through the fortress until they came to the spiral staircases leading outside. Aleksander and Rayshel carried Lavinia, much to her dismay, down the stairs as Vasilica and Pol carried her wheelchair.

"I can still fly!" Lavinia exclaimed.

"Well, you heard the doctors. You shouldn't!" Rayshel snapped, scolding Lavinia, who glumly folded her arms across her chest in protest.

"Why them?" asked Pol just loud enough for Aleksander to hear as they reached the bottom of the stairs.

"Because other than you, they're the only ones here I know I can trust," said Aleksander.

They said no more as they made their way outside. The procession's joyous music murdered the night's silence, and King Verahim's welcome group stood outside the gates. Sure enough, he was followed by a crowd of thousands.

Aleksander caught a glimpse of a glint from the king's crown, and he felt as if the entire kingdom had betrayed goodness and right for something comfortable and safe, denying the heartache that would ensue. They hurried in the opposite direction, heading out a smaller, unmanned gate.

They arced around the procession and stopped near a covered fountain surrounded by low shrubbery, a perfect place to lie low and spy on Thanatan's group. Verahim's voice boomed over the crowd, somehow amplified by magic.

"With great joy we await the return of Thanatan!" he exclaimed.

The words felt like a knife in Aleksander's ribs. Rayshel helped Lavinia lie flat on a bench near the fountain as Mistress Vasilica and Pol glanced through the hedges to see not only humans crowding the streets, but innumerable Faceless as well. They were somehow tame, refraining from massacring the civilians of Laniras.

"So now we know who the crowd from Nitra was," Aleksander said. Vasilica glanced over her shoulder at Aleksander at the mention of the city.

Pol put his hand over his mouth in shock and began to hyperventilate. Vasilica steadied the young man and helped him onto the bench next to Lavinia's feet. He looked as if he were about to faint.

"It's alright, friend," she whispered so only he could hear. Pol looked at her with a puzzled expression to which she replied, "I've got you."

She tried to keep him calm while Aleksander and Rayshel peered through the hedge as Verahim introduced the Magistrate to the masses.

Aleksander eyed the Magistrate's mask, which was much more intricate than the assassin's, but of a similar design.

"What's he talking about?" Lavinia asked from the bench.

"He's introducing the leader of the Faceless," said Aleksander. "Some guy with a mask like the assassin."

"*Thank you, gracious King Verahim Romus. Within my station as Magistrate of the Pure, it is my duty to explain our purpose.*" The Magistrate spoke directly to the minds of everyone in the crowd, Aleksander, and the others hidden in the garden, and a hush fell over Laniras. The voice was a cold, authoritative, female voice.

"Some *guy*, huh?" Lavinia asked with a sneer.

"Couldn't tell with the robes, and she's far away!" Aleksander said then shushed her. Lavinia laughed.

"*The Pure exist only to serve. No longer will you hunger or thirst. No longer will you toil or labor, for they have come to take this yoke from you.*

*Not only for the rich, the royals, or the privileged, but for all who will believe. From this day on, the people of Laniras will know nothing but joy and peace. Your armies shall return home, families shall be reunited, and all war shall end."*

Another cheer escaped the entire crowd. Hundreds of thousands of people were coming out of their homes now, and it seemed all of Laniras was gathering near the palace to hear the promised blessings ushered in by the Magistrate.

"That doesn't sound so bad," said Pol, looking to Aleksander for reassurance, "but they're evil, right?" Aleksander thought for a long while before knowing how to answer.

"I don't know how to explain this, Pol. I don't have the entire story, but from what I got from the assassin—from what we know of the Faceless…" he said, trailing off. Pol nodded.

"I believe you." He smiled, and Aleksander returned the expression with an awkward thumbs-up.

"Thank you," Aleksander said. They continued to listen as Verahim spoke up again. Pol looked to the king with concern.

"I have conversed with emissaries of the Magistrate, and I have been chosen to announce to you all that Thanatan shall return within the coming months! Let us rejoice and create a festival worthy enough to welcome them here!"

"Can you believe he's buying this?" Vasilica asked. "Some king."

"Do you think he really is?" Rayshel asked. "Thanatanos is in a tough place following the war. Maybe he doesn't see any other way to help his people." Vasilica nodded her head.

The streets were alive with jubilation and merrymaking with people celebrating the return of their god. Verahim and the Magistrate entered the palace while the crowds cheered, many dispersing into the city to spread good tidings to those that had not experienced them firsthand.

"Rayshel, Pol, I need you to get Lavinia to safety. Mistress Vasilica, will you help me? I need your wings," Aleksander asked. Vasilica nodded, awaiting the request.

"Where should we go?" asked Pol.

"The Hidden Flame headquarters should be safe. Get there and lock the gate from within," said Aleksander. "There's something there that will help Lavinia, too. I'll explain when I get there, but there's something I need to do."

"But Verahim knows about it," said Pol. "What if he made it so we can't get in, or what if he sends—"

"He's preoccupied, and he isn't looking for us yet," said Aleksander. "We'd have to be paranoid to think that. Let's get you three to safety." Pol and Rayshel helped Lavinia into her wheelchair as Aleksander explained his plan to Vasilica.

"I'm sorry, my Mistress, but I can no longer fly, or I'd carry you away," said Rayshel as she directed Lavinia's wheelchair.

Although she no longer had wings, she could still feel a phantom pain in her missing appendages, an incessant itch she could never scratch.

"Well, I can't walk. Between the two of us, we make one healthy Sangoran. Let's go," Lavinia responded, gesturing with both hands.

"See you there, Aleks," Pol said.

"Stay safe, kid," Aleksander said. Pol nodded, and the trio set out.

Vasilica turned to Aleksander, grasped him under the arms, and shot into the sky with a flap of her massive wings. They soared over the crowd toward Laniras palace, landing on a narrow ledge near a window outside Verahim's private quarters. Aleksander superheated the glass of the window with a palm full of flame and struck it with the pommel of his sword, showering the chamber with glass shards.

They climbed into the king's chambers, being careful not to step on the shattered glass. No guards rushed into the room, for everyone in the castle had gathered outside for the Magistrate's messages. They were alone and safe, for now.

Aleksander gestured to the seat to offer it to Vasilica, but she shook her head, too nervous to sit. Aleksander settled into Verahim's gilded throne and sighed, rubbing his forehead. He drew his sword and rested it on his lap.

"Now we wait," Aleksander said.

"Now we wait..." Vasilica repeated, nervously pacing the width of the throne room.

They did so for nearly an hour in complete silence before the door creaked open, and the King's silhouette appeared in the empty doorway. He shut the door behind him without noticing the intruders and removed his crown.

"You can't do this," Aleksander said. The words slipped out. Verahim jumped in shock, his hand pressed over his heart.

"By Thanatan, Aleksander, how did you get in here?"

Aleksander gestured to the shattered window and then to Vasilica before saying, "I trust you recognize—"

"Yes, hello, Lady Vasilica," said King Verahim.

"*Mistress* Vasilica," she corrected. "I'm surprised you recognize me. You didn't show up to the meetings in Doftaan despite saying you would."

"Yes, well, it sounds like it probably worked out for the best that I wasn't there," said the king.

"For the best?!" Aleksander exclaimed, furrowing his brow into a furious scowl. "Do you know how many good people died that day?!"

"Listen. I know. I know that's not why you're here. That conversation can wait," Verahim said. "But what do you want me to say, Aleksander? That you want me to disregard generations of our country's tradition and religion? How can I deny our people this?"

"You don't know what we know," said Aleksander.

"I know everything you do! I know more! Do you have any idea how long our people have suffered? Things got really, really bad during the war, and got even worse after father died and I became king. Did you know that? No, you don't. How could you? You don't even remember who you are. You know *nothing!* And let's not even mention what *your* queen has done to our country!" He emphasized the word 'your' by pointing directly at Vasilica.

"My *empress* was the one who tried to bring peace!" shrieked Vasilica. "She wrote all of the peace accords herself! Your people ruined that idea by joining with Florenta!"

"We did not have anything to do with Florenta Karpaska's coup," said Verahim, stepping toward Vasilica. "Even Aleksander knows that."

"He's right. He gave the order to fight back if we were attacked, but they really took liberties with that order. But Verahim, it definitely looked like a cooperative coup, and you have to see that—especially since you so coincidentally failed to show up."

"I will make peace with Queen Bartunek, or Queen Karpaska, or whoever is in charge now. It honestly doesn't matter to me who sits on that accursed throne," the king said. "I will, however, ensure diplomacy will resume. That is my place, and I expect you to understand yours as well."

"My place is to stop you from doing this," said Aleksander.

"To stop me? You say that, while sitting on *my* throne," Verahim said, laughing, his face buried in his hands. He sighed, clearly exasperated. "Then, pray tell, what are your demands?"

"Let my people go."

Verahim scoffed. Gone was laughter and jubilation. Disbelief. Betrayal.

"You think yourself some kind of Moses," Verahim said in a dark voice. Aleksander's memories implanted by the Secret Keepers of Kurash rang in his mind, but he wondered how the king knew the ancient, forgotten name.

"But let me tell you this: *your* people, as you say—are *not* slaves. As I was trying to say before, *our* people, no, *my* people have suffered for a generation. A generation, Aleksander! How can I deny them the gifts the Pure bring? They're starving. Dying.

The Pure can end that. They'll bring peace and remedy the sins of war brought by *my* father," King Verahim said venomously, slamming the side of his fist against a nearby pillar. He roared in both pain and anger, and Aleksander turned his gaze away.

"I had truly hoped you would see reason, but there is none here. I am truly sorry, *my king*," he said, a look of sadness etched on his face. The last two words were emphasized with particular poison. He rose from Verahim's throne.

"And where will you go? When all is said and done, who is Aleksander? The history books will forget you in your quest to keep our people from their promised joy and blessings," shouted Verahim. "Why can't you see that I'm doing what is best for them?!"

Vasilica followed Aleksander toward the window, their backs turned toward the king.

"You're right, Verahim," said Aleksander without looking back. When he spoke again, he did not raise his voice, instead speaking with the soft regret of a sad truth. "I probably won't be remembered, but do you know what is worse? That history *will* remember you as the coward too blind and afraid to act against evil. The king that *almost* saved his people. Sleep well, my king."

Verahim did not answer. And with that, Aleksander and Vasilica departed into the night's sky, leaving Verahim alone in his dark throne room in cold silence.

# CHAPTER SIXTEEN
# ŽA DROGASTEJU I Ž'ALBORU!

The inhabitants of Likio, unfit or otherwise unable to accompany Shanthah on his journey, had lined the dusty streets to say goodbye and wish success on the scant company of untrained fighters on their quest toward Florenta's capital of Balgorod. As Shanthah led the group into Sapez, the next village on their planned route, he heard many gathered to welcome them referring to him in hushed tones using words like "hero" and "phantom."

He didn't mind the praise.

As the group reached the center of Sapez, they were met with thunderous cheers. Ruta and her grandmother had been hard at work on their advance trip to the town, it seemed. This crowd was even larger than the farewell party in Likio.

"Hello, everyone!" he called, raising his hands to the starlit sky. "Thank you, thank you!"

A stern looking Sangoran woman stepped from the crowd and crossed her thick arms across her chest before ordering in accented Thannish, "Prove you are phantom!"

With a theatrical flourish of his arm, Shanthah vanished, and the multitude cheered once more. He rematerialized with his arm around the woman's shoulder, resulting in an enthusiastic round of applause. He raised his hand to the throng of Sangorans, which fell silent to listen to what he had to say.

"Many of you—or more likely, all of you, or you wouldn't be here—have heard my story. Hanna's story. You know of the evil that keeps us apart. That very same evil is the one that has threatened your families and is the very power that we want to overthrow. I have to admit to you all that I don't know if Hanna is alive. I am so terrified that she isn't, but I must ask now: Will you join me against Florenta Karpaska?"

His last question was met with thunderous applause.

"Phantom!" came a cry somewhere amongst the people of Sapez. "Phantom!"

Shanthah scanned the crowd for the source of the voice. It didn't seem enthusiastic or hopeful, but full of dread and warning. At last, he saw a winged Sangoran man pushing his way through the crowd. Shanthah gestured to let him through and with a concerned expression greeted the man.

"What is it?" Shanthah asked, his hand outstretched in welcome.

"You have been betrayed, Phantom!" the man exclaimed frantically. He took a deep breath before continuing, trying to calm himself. "She's sending her armies to stop you!"

"How long do we have?" Shanthah asked.

"Two days, maybe," said the man.

Shanthah thanked the man but was at a loss for words. Their forces were nowhere near strong enough to fight off Florenta's forces *and* take her capital in Karpaska.

"I assure you, Sapez will be safe. We will have to hide from Florenta's armies and take the fortress at Balgorod in their absence," Shanthah said. "I recognize that it's a weak plan, and I apologize, but I thank you all for your bravery and willingness to fight."

The crowd muttered amongst themselves, much less enthusiastic than they had been before. Shanthah's heart thundered in his chest, and he worried that his campaign was losing its momentum with this one hiccup.

"Ža drogasteju i ž'Alboru!" came a voice from the crowd. Shanthah whirled around, not understanding the Sangoran phrase. To his welcome surprise, however, the entire crowd shouted the same. "Ža drogastcju i ž'Alboru!"

"Za… dagrasta… Albora!" said Shanthah, trying to imitate the words. "We will be leaving Sapez before daybreak. If you wish to join us, I urge you all to meet us in your town's center square in an hour will all your supplies and provisions."

Shanthah watched Ruta push herself through the crowd to do her interpreting duty. He had missed his new friend and breathed a sigh of relief to see that she had returned. She finished her translation, and the crowd dispersed.

"Oh, thank goodness. It sure is good to see you back," Shanthah said, hurrying toward her. "That was you that yelled something in Sangoran, wasn't it?"

"Of course it was. It's an old Alboran battle cry, and it always makes everyone braver. You need to know how to talk to Alborans, I think. But it is good to see you too, Phantom. Did you feel lost without your tour guide?" Ruta asked with a cheery laugh. "No matter, I am back. Grandmother left back to Likio just a few hours ago. She was very sad she didn't get to say goodbye to, as she said, 'the only human she has ever liked.' Sorry if that is offensive, or—"

Shanthah chuckled. "No, of course not! To be honest, we're a horrible lot, humans." Then, thinking of the man who had warned him of Florenta's forces, said, "Speaking of being potentially culturally offensive, I thought there were no more male Sangorans."

This time, Ruta laughed. For a solid minute, she was unable to speak. "What, you think we are all born in laboratories?"

"I mean, no, but I have never met a Sangoran man. I know of the Walkers, but—" Shanthah said. "You know what, I'll stop talking before you laugh at me more and I keep offending you."

"No, no. It is a common myth in Thanatanos that we are all women and Sangoran babies grow in tubes. No, there are Sangoran men other than the Walker terrorists. What, you think also that all Sangoran men are terrorists?"

She smiled mischievously, waiting for his response.

"I've heard the stereotype," Shanthah said diplomatically.

"I am glad you don't believe it," Ruta said. Her tone turned softer, less mischievous. "Our state, Karpaska, and specifically our tribe, Alboras, has the most men in Sangora. There are very, very few left in Doftaan, and those aren't native Doftaani. Other states have some, but this is probably why you think there are no men. Only thing most people know in Thanatanos of Sangora is what they know of Doftaan."

"You've got me there," Shanthah said, nodding, a bit embarrassed.

Ruta's beautiful features turned sad. "Oh, Shanthah—I told you when I met you that Mistress Florenta taxes us more than we can bear."

"When you said tax, I thought you meant gold, silver, or labor, something like that," said Shanthah, completely at a loss for words. They kept walking, and Ruta spoke loud enough only for him to hear as he waved to his new supporters.

"It is funny to me that you used the word labor. You're right, I guess. In Thannish, that word is used when you talk about giving birth, yes?"

"Yes, but I meant—"

"I know what you meant," Ruta replied. "Baby boys are born much less often than girls, and greedy Florenta takes many of those that are born that we cannot hide."

"She takes your babies?!" Shanthah asked, his hand over his mouth.

"Well, babies from Alboran tribe and the few men that didn't either die in the war or cut off their wings to become Walker exiles are the tax we pay to Mistress Florenta. They are forced to have children, who usually never know their mothers or fathers. They are given to families in Doftaan and the other Sangoran states who are on waiting lists to adopt babies. Most don't know where their babies come from, and they love them, but…" Ruta trailed off and sighed. "Most often they go to the rich families. The men should be celebrated, but they're usually poor and have bad lives…"

Shanthah's heart ached for Ruta's people. He despised himself and his fellow Thans for not seeing Sangorans as beings with real feelings or social problems. They had always just been the enemy. Now, however, he was more determined to free them from Florenta than to return to a comfortable life in Laniras.

"That breaks my heart," Shanthah said at last, unsure what else to say. "And Mara knows about this?"

"Yes, she knows. She is one of the only leaders who try to stop it and let people have babies with whoever they want. A couple of her Mistresses of Dusk—those are like her high council, and the governors of each Sangoran state—believe like her, but they are outnumbered. And of course, Florenta is the governor of Karpaska, and she's the worst of all of them."

"The state is named after her family, I assume?" Shanthah asked. They came to the center of town and Shanthah greeted several of his supporters there, interrupting their conversation.

"Yes, Mara's predecessors made some treaty with her family to always keep them in power. I don't really know the details," said Ruta.

Shanthah blew a kiss to a group of waving Sangoran women as they sharpened their blades; he could only see their eyes as they were covered with shawls to protect them from the sun. Many others were dressed like Ruta with scarves that they could pull over their faces if they needed to.

"Just curious, why do they have day coverings on?" asked Shanthah. "It's nighttime."

"Some people just wear them always," Ruta said with a shrug. "Sometimes it is a religious thing. Maybe they think we will not stop our path to Balgorod even through the day."

"Can I ask you a favor?" Shanthah asked.

"Yes, but I think you owe me several of those already," she said with a wink.

"Oh, definitely," Shanthah said with a laugh. "I do owe you. But I'd like to start learning Sangoran."

"Really?" Ruta asked, her surprise apparent in her eyes, which gleamed in joy. "Yes, of course I will help! I spent last summer tutoring Talohiran children in a town near Likio how to speak Sangoran, and I loved it!"

"Really?" Shanthah asked. "Lucky for me!"

"It won't be free, of course," Ruta said.

"I don't have much gold," Shanthah replied, turning out his money pouch on his belt. It was completely empty, except for a small stone and a bit of thread, which he discarded. "None, actually."

"You can pay me by overthrowing Florenta and saving us," Ruta replied joyfully.

"That's an expensive tutor," Shanthah said. "You must not have very many clients."

"It is a special price for you, it is free for the children," Ruta replied, laughing.

"Ah, I see how it is. Charging a Than extra," said Shanthah.

"Yes, you see it right," Ruta said. Her smile seemed to reach her eyes.

"Well, that's a good price, I guess. You're hired!" Shanthah exclaimed.

"First lesson: Ža drogasteju i ž'Alboru. It means 'for love and for Alboras'."

Shanthah repeated the phrase as best he could with Ruta's coaching until he could say it correctly, although with a Thannish accent, according to his teacher.

"We have time before we leave toward Balgorod. What do you say, want to continue my first Sangoran lesson now? I have literally nowhere else to be," Shanthah said. Ruta smiled again.

"Drogastejas, this means love as a noun, but not romance love—more like love for country. And you know Alboras is, of course, Alboras." She wrote the words in the dirt. "They use your same alphabet in Doftaan and the bigger cities and states around Doftaan. I think because Talohira speaks Thannish too, and it's all political. All King Valistaran Talohir's fault. But in areas like Likio and Sapez we mostly use our own Sangoran alphabet. I will write for you in Thannish alphabet until you learn the better way. This letter—" She drew the letter Ž. "It is like the shh sound, but with a z… Zhh… You can also write it with letters Z and H. They sometimes do this in Thanatanos."

"Sounds good," Shanthah said, practicing producing the sound. "And I assume ža or ž means 'for.' Why are they different? And why do Drogastejas and Alboras end in the letter U?"

"Yes, good. Ža means 'for.' Ža can't come before word that starts with vowel, and because Alboras starts with letter A, it shortens to just ž. See how silly it sounds when you say, 'ža Alboru'?"

"No," Shanthah said.

"Oh, well it blends together better this way. Even little children don't make this mistake, so if you do, everyone will make fun of you," Ruta said.

"Ž'Albru… Ža Alboru…" Shanthah repeated, correctly, he hoped. "Okay, and why the different letters on the end?"

"Good eyes! It is maybe too complicated for our first lesson. Ža is a…" she paused for a moment. "I can't remember the word in Thannish."

"Preposition?" Shanthah guessed. Ruta nodded.

"Because ža is preposition, the end of the word changes," Ruta explained. Shanthah nodded.

"We have a similar principle in Thannish," Shanthah replied.

"Yes, similar but different," Ruta said. "I'll explain that in another lesson later."

Shanthah agreed, and they continued their lesson for nearly an hour until the entire crowd seemed to have gathered in the center square of Sapez. He climbed onto an empty statue plinth in the center of town and whistled. His assembled forces looked to him, and he raised his hands in thanks.

"Thank you all for coming," Shanthah called. Ruta climbed onto the plinth next to him to interpret. "I don't think I need to say anything else. Ža drogasteju i ž'Alboru! Let's move on Balgorod!"

The crowd echoed his cheer and began to move northwest. Those assigned by Shanthah led their respective groups on, and he and Ruta hurried to the head of the entire group. Ruta took one last glance at the town, and they were on their way.

Shanthah thanked the gods that the Sangorans had to fly slow enough to keep pace with their supply carts, which had to roll along the hilly landscape. A few hours into their trek, he turned to Ruta, who had walked with him the entire way so far.

"I've been worrying. I noticed on my map that Likio and others are Sangoran towns in Talohira, and part of our journey will be along the Talohiran border. Will that be a problem?"

Ruta shook her head. "I think it will be not a problem. You must have old map because these towns are not in Talohira." Her eyes narrowed, and she pursed her lips. He could tell she was deep in thought and watched the cogs in her mind turn. At last, she said, "Besides, Talohiran capital of Bukaral does not like Florenta. They never, ever have. Well, if we send word of our goals, maybe."

"Maybe they will help us?" Shanthah asked, nodding. "I like the sound of that, Ruta. Do they like Mara in Talohira?"

"Yes, I think they love her. Her political views are very different from Florenta's. They make fun of Florenta in Talohira like most of Sangora does, but they don't have to hide it like we do. She can't punish them like she punishes us, you know?"

"So, it should be safe for us around the border?"

"Yes, I think. But we only must be very careful of the warlords."

"Oh, *of course* there are warlords," Shanthah said, rubbing his temples. He released a deep sigh. "Are these the 'throw you into a slave camp' types?"

"Well, no. The slavers stayed out of Karpaska. Trying to find slaves in nearby Thannish towns would be like searching for berries in winter, and they were forbidden by Queen Codruta to take Sangoran slaves. These are old generals of Talohiran army that basically started their own government after Mara took over. They don't recognize her rule over Talohira, and things are— well, things are bad in Talohira. I think they won't worry about us because they have their own problems."

"You're sure?" Shanthah asked. "We don't have time for two rebellions."

She nodded reassuringly. "Oh, yes. We will not have problems other than Florenta's armies."

"Ruta, you seem to have a good knowledge of politics," Shanthah said. "You understand things well."

"I did two years in Doftaan University. I studied languages, politics, and diplomacy there, but I cannot afford it now, and grandmother is sometimes very sick, so…"

A regretful smile crossed her face. Shanthah nodded in understanding then looked around and could tell the crowd was getting tired. They'd been traveling for hours, and many had resorted to walking instead of flying. However, the caravan that bore their food was what slowed them down the most.

"Let's stop here!" called Shanthah. "We are all tired and could use the rest of the day to sleep before night falls. We have to stay watchful for Florenta's forces, so be ready to move at a moment's notice. Thank you, everyone!"

His message was relayed throughout the entire crowd that now numbered around three hundred souls. The Phantom's tale and his struggle to reunite with his lost love and liberate those within Florenta's grip had evidently reached the furthest borders of the Sangoran state of Karpaska, as dozens of new recruits joined them every few hours.

After the third day of travel, Shanthah grabbed his flimsy tent, which was really more of a thin towel attached to stakes, from one of the ox carts. He set it up to block out the light of the sun, feeling hopelessly optimistic that he would be able to sleep despite the brightness. He draped his cloak over his eyes to help against the sun's light, which had seemed determined to prevent him from sleeping over the past few days. The good news was that Florenta's forces had not crossed their path in that time, despite earlier thoughts that they would have already.

"Going to sleep already?" came Ruta's voice from outside his tiny tent. "I would think your followers would like to hear more stories of your adventures."

"But I'm so tired..." Shanthah groaned. "I guess you're right, though. Keep them excited for our cause, right? You'll be there to make sure I don't bore them again?"

"Yes, I think that's my new job," Ruta said. "In addition to your teacher, translator, political advisor, tour guide, and recruiting person."

"I get it, I get it. I'm coming," Shanthah said. Ruta was there beaming at him when he emerged from beneath his cloak and tiny tent.

"Is that even a tent?" she asked as he showed his face.

"Ruta, you know I can't afford a real tent when I pay you so much for being my teacher, translator, butcher, mail man, and chef," said Shanthah.

"You wouldn't pay me if you tasted my cooking. Grandmother says I'll be bad wife," Ruta said, following Shanthah toward the crowd.

"I don't think that's what makes a good wife," Shanthah said with a laugh. Ruta shrugged.

"That's what I always told her! But she always insisted that she was a wife three times, and therefore she knew better!"

Balgorod, the capital of the Karpaskan state, now loomed in the distance, its banners waving in the breeze as if a taunt to those in Shanthah's small army of Alboran Sangorans. A call to arms. A challenge.

The previous day, Shanthah had received word that four other groups sympathetic to Shanthah's cause were spread across Karpaska with a plan to converge on Balgorod in two days. Shanthah was working hard to coordinate his forces while avoiding Florenta's. However, his spies had warned that her armies were within a day's march, meaning they would have to attack sooner than they had hoped.

"Markus!" Shanthah shouted to a winged male Sangoran. "A report?"

Although Shanthah's army of volunteers lacked any official military leadership, they looked to him as their leader, and he had selected several individuals to help him coordinate their efforts. Markus was one of those.

"Yes, sir!" said Markus. He hurried to Shanthah's side and said in a thick Sangoran accent, "Florenta's forces are close. Closer than we thought, and they'll be here soon. Those too old or too young to fight have been escorted back to their villages. The last group who cannot fight will depart soon to spread final word of our fight to the rest of the villages. After that, only those who are willing to fight will remain."

"And how goes the infiltration of Balgorod?" Shanthah asked. "Any news?"

"All volunteers with family in Balgorod have entered the city and have begun to spread word of your story and our goals," Markus reported. "There's no way of knowing if we'll have any support from Balgorodans, however."

"Good, thank you Markus. I hope that gamble pays off and doesn't come back to bite us," he said.

Markus nodded and disappeared into the bustling crowd. At that moment, two young Sangoran women he had also appointed as section leaders, Sorina and Lakrima, approached Shanthah and gave a rough semblance of a salute.

"Mr. Shanthah Kalen, sir, we've received the shipment of aid from supporters in Ripan," said Lakrima.

"Mechi i hran!" said Sorina.

Luckily, due to Ruta's lessons for the past few days, he recognized each of the words in the sentence. Swords and Food. Lakrima nodded and pantomimed a stab in Shanthah's direction. Shanthah feigned being stabbed and clapped his hands in joy.

"Wonderful! We won't be able to take Balgorod on empty stomachs, right?" he said. Lakrima laughed and then translated for Sorina, who smiled and nodded in turn. "I want you to coordinate distributing weapons to those who need them. Report back when you are done, please."

Lakrima bowed to Shanthah then translated once again before the duo departed to fulfill their duties. Shanthah knew their little guerrilla operation would be doomed to fail if they were caught too early or if the other groups didn't reach them in time. Both situations were possible. A sudden idea came to his mind.

"Lakrima!" he called before she was out of ear shot. "We'll need to set up campfires around the fortress. I want them to think there are more of us than there are. Markus should be able to help coordinate." Lakrima nodded in understanding then hurried toward Markus.

Shanthah located the shipment of food and weapons pulled by oxen yoked together pulling heavy carts. He watched Ruta and her cousin Tassa distributing the food and keeping record of what was left.

"All non-combatants: get the supplies to safety, and more important, get yourselves to safety!" called Shanthah. "They will be here soon, and I want you all safe!"

Ruta smiled and waved from across the crowd and Shanthah nodded in her direction. Tassa helped coordinate Shanthah's order to escort the supply wagons south to relative safety, and Ruta joined Shanthah as he climbed onto a wagon and raised his sword into the air which was accompanied by a collective Sangoran chant from his followers: "Ža drogasteju i ž'Alboru!"

Others in the crowd showed their support for Empress Mara, their disdain for Florenta, and others yet who demanded freedom for Hanna Samsa. Shanthah smiled whenever he heard that particular cry. He looked to his side to see Ruta already there, smiling, and ready to interpret.

"You know I'm not one for speeches, and I prefer to tell stories," Shanthah said. "But you all know our plan. Our goals. Not mine, but ours. I am not Sangoran, and I do not know the full extent of Florenta Karpaska's sins against your people, but in the short time I have spent with you, I have come to love your people as much or even more than I love my own home. Florenta's forces are on their way, but we are ready for them!"

He waited for a moment as Ruta finished speaking.

"Marry me!" came a cry from the crowd. Laughter rang across the entire camp, and Shanthah almost fell from the cart because of his sudden bout of laughter. He regained his composure and held up his hand.

"I think I'd rather not face Hanna's wrath," he said, pointing in the general direction of Doftaan, "but as I was saying before I was so pleasantly interrupted, this is your day, for this is the day that Alboran flags fly over Balgorod!"

Cheers interspersed with battle cries erupted from the small army once more, and this time, Shanthah joined in. He gave the order, and the army moved forward, taking its place on a hill several miles south of Balgorod. From this new vantage point, they could see Florenta's forces closing in on them, a cloud of wings and blades hanging in the sky.

"No wonder we never met them earlier. They were waiting for us to get closer to the city," Shanthah said to Ruta.

"Smart," Ruta said, nodding. She gave Shanthah an exaggerated salute and pulled on a helmet, a sign that she had no intention of leaving.

"You're staying?" Shanthah asked.

"I couldn't live with myself if I knew my friends here were fighting and dying while I just watched," Ruta said, sadness in her eyes. "Please do not send me away."

"And I couldn't live with myself if I had to tell your grandmother that you died today," Shanthah said.

"Then send *everyone* home," Ruta said, crossing her arms across her chest. "You're going to be telling a lot of grandmothers some bad news anyway."

She grabbed a spear from a passing cart and looked sternly into Shanthah's eyes. Finally, he relented with a slow nod.

"Stay safe," Shanthah said. Suddenly, she was hugging him.

"I will. We'll find your Hanna. She's alive, I know it," she said. "And then, we will be free from Florenta. Thank you, Shanthah Kalen."

"Thank you, Ruta. Now go, join the others, you brave woman, you."

She nodded. "Thank you."

"Into formation!" cried Shanthah, and the group formed a massive sphere of outward facing spears atop the hill, just like they'd practiced several times during their trek to Balgorod.

The Karpaskan host surrounded Shanthah's small army on all sides of the hill. Some stayed airborne, circling their foes, while others stayed motionless, ready to strike. Their leader, a severe looking woman holding a crossbow, stepped from their ranks.

"I, Lady Nandra, representing Queen Florenta Karpaska, bring message from Doftaan." She shook her head in disdain as she examined the force of Alborans.

Two bodyguards flanked her on either side. Shanthah stepped from the ball of spears and half climbed, half slid down the grass-covered hill. He approached Lady Nandra with a cold demeanor quite uncharacteristic of the man.

"I think you mispronounced the queen's name. It's pronounced, if I'm correct, Mara," said Shanthah, a smirk crossing his face. "But I'll let it slide."

"The disgraced Mara Bartunek has been exiled from Queen Florenta's realm for her failure to protect her own people," said Lady Nandra. "When she is found, she will be executed, and so will any in her service."

"And you think Florenta has succeeded? The Alboran tribe has suffered more than she can imagine! No, I take it back. She knows exactly how much they've suffered—she just doesn't care."

"Our queen recognizes your bravery and desire to better your country. She values the contributions made by Tribe Alboras. What does she have to gain from watching you suffer?" asked Lady Nandra.

"Certainly not more weight!" someone in the crowd called.

"Such blatant disrespect!" Lady Nandra exclaimed. "Queen Florenta knows that without these contributions, Doftaan itself may even cease to exist," said Lady Nandra.

"Then let it!" Shanthah shouted. "Go back to Doftaan and tell Florenta that these people bow only to Mara Bartunek, the Empress of Blood!"

"What right do cattle have to choose their masters?" asked Lady Nandra, sneering in Shanthah's direction, but never making eye contact.

"Excuse me?" he asked in shock. He hoped none of his people had heard the comment.

"Everyone knows the Alboran tribe is merely a cattle pen of Sangora," said Lady Nandra. "All these people are to Florenta's Doftaan are beasts used to breed. As you all die, you will understand."

To Lady Nandra's surprise, Shanthah vanished from sight. A moment later, a shrill screech and a gurgle escaped her throat as an invisible blade pierced her heart.

"And now as *you* die, *you* understand the struggle of Alboras: to be killed by an enemy you can't see," Shanthah said with a snarl, pulling the blade from Lady Nandra's chest. She collapsed in a lifeless heap on the ground and tumbled down the hill. At that moment, Florenta's forces closed in on the Alborans.

Each of Shanthah's untrained soldiers defended the companions at their sides, delivering fatal blows with their spears to any foes that dared venture too close. However, their enemies soon broke through, killing several Alborans and breaking the defensive formation.

"Back into formation!" called Shanthah as their foes swarmed against the breach in their defenses, hacking at those they could reach. Over the clash of spears and blades, he heard an order in Sangoran he did not understand. Part of the swarm broke away and raced to the south.

"The supply carts!" Shanthah shouted.

He fought with himself, knowing that if his people broke formation, they would all die, but if they did not, the supply train and the non-combatant volunteers would be slaughtered. He knew his hesitation meant he was already too late. Florenta's forces reached the supply train and raised their weapons against the civilians.

Blood spattered his face as Shanthah drew his spear from an enemy's throat. At that moment, the Sangoran to his left fell to an axe wound, and Florenta's soldiers completely broke the Alboran spear formation. Both sides broke out into an all our brawl on the earth and in the air. He swore loudly, and in his heart, he knew that he had led his supporters to their death.

"Is this how a queen acts?" shouted Shanthah, knowing full well that Florenta could not hear. "Killing your own people? YOUR OWN PEOPLE!"

Shanthah turned just in time to watch Florenta's forces and a second contingent of Sangorans converge in the air above the supply carts. Tears carved their way through the blood on his face, but then suddenly, the second group of Sangorans turned on the group that had broken off to assail the non-combatants, quickly overtaking them and leaving Nandra's forces split and broken.

"Ža drogasteju i ž'Alboru!" Shanthah exclaimed.

"Master Phantom!" Shanthah turned to see Markus, bloodstained but alive. "It's Mara's forces! They've come!"

Indeed, Shanthah beheld the crimson banner of Mara's Sangora, and courage was kindled in his heart. He urged his people on with newfound ferocity.

The remainder of the battle was short lived. The second contingent of Sangorans had laid waste to Florenta's forces, preventing a complete massacre of Shanthah's army of volunteers. In the end, the entirety of Nandra's force had either surrendered or been slain.

Shanthah approached the leader of the second group with a smile on his face, happily expecting to see Mara's face when the leader removed her horned helm. However, he frowned, dejected, for he did not recognize the woman who stood before him.

"Shanthah Kalen," said Shanthah. He stretched forth his hand in a gesture of welcome.

"General Anca, Mistress of Dusk, governor of Krim, and servant of the true Empress of Blood, Mara Bartunek," said the exiled Mistress of Dusk as she shook Shanthah's hand.

Her beautiful companion, a petite Sangoran with piercing eyes and rich, bronze skin sheathed an elegant, narrow blade covered in blood.

"Ah, Mistress Raluca," Shanthah said with a smile; he recognized her from the Peace Ball, although she had traded her flamboyant gown for a blade. "Your people must be hungry. We have plenty of food to spare."

"Thank you," Raluca said with a gracious nod.

"There is no time to waste if this campaign is to succeed," said General Anca in protest. Shanthah shook his head.

"Any good warrior can eat and talk at the same time," said Shanthah, pointing in the direction to the supply carts.

"I'll have my people see to your wounded and fallen," Anca said. She barked an order in Sangoran, and several of her warriors hurried to the hilltop. "It should be easy to differentiate between those we honor and those we do not."

"We can honor all of them," Shanthah protested.

Anca did not respond. Shanthah eyed the crowd, worried for the safety of many of his supporters. He thanked whatever gods weren't Thanatan that no more had perished, and he vowed to honor those that had.

"I take it you didn't come all the way from Doftaan just to help out in our little revolution," said Shanthah, gesturing to his people.

"And I take it you know what has transpired in Doftaan?" asked Raluca as Anca continued issuing orders to her followers, who were clearly more experienced than the Alboran fighters.

"Florenta took over," Shanthah said. "I was there when she attacked after the peace summit between Sangora and Thanatanos. One of the Walkers helped me escape but died in the process. I assume after that, there was a coup to oust the rest of Mara's followers from Doftaan?"

"Very astute," said Anca.

"What about the rest of the Mistresses of Dusk?" Shanthah asked.

"Our spies say that Florenta believes Mistress Vasilica was slain. Lavinia was evacuated to Laniras, but we don't know where she is. Probably hiding," said Raluca. She looked to Anca and added, right?"

"Correct. You know Mistress Ihrin and Antanasia were both slain. The assassin was captured and is being held somewhere in Laniras, but we have no further information," said Anca.

"It sounds like Florenta didn't keep any of you around, then?" asked Shanthah. Anca nodded as the hungry soldiers began to line up for food rations.

"She'll undoubtedly set up her own council," Anca said.

"Or not. She always wanted complete power. She didn't trust any of us and believed that one of us was responsible for the murders. This all happened because she thinks Mara was uncapable of protecting us," said Raluca.

"Were you behind the assassinations?" asked Shanthah.

"No," said Anca.

"Most of us believed that Florenta herself was behind the attacks. I still do. I think she ordered the attacks and used them as justification to overthrow Empress Bartunek, but it doesn't matter anymore. She won," said Raluca, the wind blowing her hair into her face. "But that's not the worst part."

"What is?" asked Shanthah.

"The great secret of the queen of Sangora is her ability to control others of our race. My sister learned of this power, and after her ascension to the throne, Empress Mara has also claimed legitimacy of her rule through this same discovery," said Raluca.

"Your sister?" asked Shanthah.

"My sister was the queen before Mara," said Raluca.

"My condolences for your loss," said Shanthah, guilt gnawing at his soul, for he had been the one to kill Codruta. He vowed to himself to make things right but said nothing more.

"Thank you," Raluca said.

"So how was Florenta able to defy her if she has this ability?" asked Shanthah, his attention now on the story rather than the distribution of food. "Couldn't she have stopped it?"

"Florenta somehow forced us to meet with her without Mara," said Anca.

"Forced?" Shanthah asked, seeking clarification.

"Not by sword or threat. She willed us there," said Raluca.

"She has this same ability, then?" asked Shanthah.

"We have since discovered that she conspired with certain members of the Walker terrorists to create a concoction out of the blood of a poor Wingling girl to become immune to Mara's influence," said Raluca. "Somehow, she was able to replicate the Queen's Control as well."

"So, doesn't that give her the legitimacy to rule?" asked Shanthah, trying to understand the culture of Sangoran politics.

"No," said Anca. "Mara still lives, although she is missing. Just as in a honeybee hive, two queens will kill each other. There can only be one."

Shanthah nodded. "And in a hive, what do the rest of the bees do?"

"I assume they would choose a side," said Anca.

"Then this honeybee knows which queen to follow, and I can tell you one thing. She's the smaller of the two," said Shanthah. Both Raluca and Anca chuckled at this comment.

"And what is this Than's motivation? Why do you choose to fight for our people's freedom?" asked Anca, turning the conversation on Shanthah.

For a long moment, Shanthah thought of Hanna. Her face. Her laugh. Her touch. Her love. And then his mind turned to the wonderful people that now followed him in his quest to reunite with her. A simple love story had been enough to set their souls on fire to fight for their freedom.

"It started one way. I wanted to get back to Sangora to reunite with someone very special to me." He decided to be honest with the two Mistresses of Dusk. But now—I know she will be fine without me. I know that my Hanna can handle herself better than I can. She'll escape Florenta's prison or wherever she is, but these people—they can't do the same."

"Do you believe that your Hanna, as you call her, will help you? Do you truly think that she will believe in our people as you do?" asked Raluca, gesturing to the combined mass of Alboran and separatist Doftaani fighters and civilians.

"With my whole soul," said Shanthah.

"Then, Shanthah Kalen, with our empress missing and no faith in the usurper queen on her throne, we pledge what might remains of the council of the Mistresses of Dusk to your cause," said Raluca. Anca gave a curt nod in agreement before planting her blade in the earth. "To the Phantom's revolution."

Anca's followers took note, and every Doftaani separatist planted their weapons and knelt before their Alboran allies.

"Ža Sangoru," said Shanthah. *For Sangora.*

Raluca smiled, taken aback that the Sangoran language had come out of his mouth. She drew her elegant blade, pierced the earth at her feet, and then placed her forehead on the pommel of her weapon and awaited Shanthah's response.

Shanthah took a step backward, a lump forming in his throat, for the awesome sight of so many pledged to his cause robbed him of his ability to speak. At that moment, he saw Ruta cradling her fallen cousin Tassa's body. His heart dropped into his stomach. He took a moment of silence to number the dead. Twenty-seven.

"Thank you," were the only words he was able to muster. He knew no more needed to be said. No more words of thanks. No cheers. No speeches.

All that remained was love. Love powerful enough to ignore and even heal the divide between Thanatanos and Sangora. Love, that would shake the very foundations of Florenta's rule to overthrow death and hatred across the empire.

# CHAPTER SEVENTEEN

# WEB OF MINDS

Since the battle of Zinok had ended, only a paltry two hundred souls remained with a mere eighty remaining out of all the refugees from Pata and Turnava. The rest now celebrated in the streets of Laniras, welcoming Thanatan back to the world, although those that remained in Zinok no longer had any idea what was happening. The fortress that once protected them was now a prison, and for many, a tomb.

Kamil approached with a lukewarm bowl of stew in his hands and handed it to a defeated looking Josman, who raised his head in thanks but said nothing. He lifted a spoonful of the meal to his lips, but his trembling hands caused half the tasteless liquid to trickle down his grizzled chin.

"After everything we went through to protect them, they left us," Josman said. "All of this for nothing."

Kamil nodded as Valis dropped to the ground near them, some of his own stew sloshing onto the ground. Josman lifted his bowl to offer it to Valis, but the boy shook his head.

"You think I want more of this stuff? How do you know that wasn't on purpose?" he asked. A dark chuckle escaped Josman's throat.

"Where were Valakor and the other two warriors from the Court of Thanatan?" asked Josman. They'd had this conversation a dozen times since Zinok fell.

"Jos, they're from the Court of *Thanatan*. You don't really think they're still on our side, do you?" Valis asked.

"*They never even joined the battle. I fear Valis may be correct,*" thought Kamil to the others.

"Then hope truly is gone," said Josman.

"*If Rehor was here, he'd say something about hope not being gone until—what did he always say in the slave camp?*" asked Kamil.

"Where do you think he is now? The others too, of course. Aleksander…Shanthah…Hanna…Pol…Mara…?" Josman said each name with a sad expression.

"Well, that depends on how you think the peace summit in Sangora went," said Valis, setting down his empty bowl on the ground. "Think they had better luck than us?"

"They must have. We haven't had to deal with any Night Witches on this damned failure of a mission," said Josman. "So, I guess, bless their souls for that."

"So, what's the plan?" asked Valis as he spotted his mother and Rayna enter the main hall of the fortress with a small group of weary soldiers and healers.

*"Back to the Hidden Flame's headquarters?"* asked Kamil.

"Bad idea. Think of how many Zinoki soldiers and citizens abandoned us for Thanatan. You heard what the Magistrate said. She's taking his hordes and everyone who swore allegiance to him to Laniras and other major cities," said Josman. "They're probably already there."

*"We won't be safe in Laniras. You're right. Vudapas either. And we should stay clear of anywhere near Nitra's ruins as well,"* said Kamil. Rayna began distributing food to her soldiers as Alia collapsed next to her son, laying her head on his shoulder.

"He's heading to the villages too. We aren't safe in Thanatanos at all," said Josman. "Depending on how talks with Sangora went, we could go to Doftaan as refugees, as crazy as it sounds."

"We could go home," said Valis to his mother.

"We could, but what about everyone else? Ever since the end of the Than-Sangoran war, Kurash closed its borders to pretty much all foreigners. It's not easy to be allowed in," said Alia.

"Why?" asked Valis.

"Paperwork," said Alia. "Government stuff. Besides, it would be very suspicious for me to return without paperwork. Thanks, Drahomir."

She lifted her head from her son's shoulder and patted him on the knee.

"Paperwork. The bane of all of us," laughed Josman, resulting in a smile from Alia.

*"Besides, I would not be welcomed back,"* said Kamil. *"I agree with Josman that our best option would be to seek refuge in Sangora."*

"Why couldn't you go back?" asked Valis in Kurashic.

Alia looked to Kamil, who nodded as if to give her permission to proceed before answering.

"Honey, Kamil had to leave Kurash because of who he loved. Things were better here for him before the war broke out," Alia explained. "But people in Thanatanos and Talohira became less and less tolerant during the war too."

A sad look crossed Kamil's face. "*Before the slave camp, I considered moving to Sangora. It's a beautiful place, and such an accepting culture—people there love each other for who they are. In Sangora, love is love, and family is family. Unfortunately, I never made it there.*"

"How *did* you escape?" Valis asked. He considered asking what had happened to the man Kamil had loved but decided it was best not to. "It kills me to hear you were in one of my father's slave camps—I've never heard how you all got out."

"This crazy genius made a catapult and smashed down the wall," Josman said, clapping his friend on the back.

"*It was more of a trebuchet.*"

"You know, Josman, you're the only one here who doesn't speak Kurashic. Maybe you should learn," Alia said.

"Too old for that," Josman said with a hearty chuckle.

"Do you have literally any other plans?" Alia asked, touching his hand. "You've got three great teachers here—just saying!"

As Josman smiled at Alia, Rayna approached the group with a few other soldiers and sat on the floor next to them.

"You know, we have a big, long table with benches made specifically for sitting," Rayna said. "And yet you use the floor."

"You know what they say about old habits, I guess," Josman said, making eye contact with Kamil, who nodded and laughed; he subconsciously projected a mental image of the slave camp to Josman's mind.

"Making plans to get out?" asked Rayna, sloshing her watery soup around in its bowl. She sneered down at it.

"That's the hope," said Alia.

"That's going to be a problem," said Rayna, taking a sip of the soup, which was clearly still too hot. She recoiled and was rendered temporarily unable to speak; she clapped the soldier on her right on the knee to explain.

"Lieutenant Marek Stepanek," he said to introduce himself. "We sent a scouting party through the pass across the drawbridge wall. Only one returned."

"Those creatures aren't gone, are they?" asked Josman. Marek shook his head.

"They ambushed the scouting party. According to the man who survived, it seemed like they allowed him to live," said Rayna, running a hand through her black curls. Josman screwed up his brow and buried his face in his hands.

"Captain Rayna, we didn't have time to properly introduce ourselves. The reason we were nearby is that we were on a special assignment from King Verahim to investigate what these creatures were doing in the ruins of Nitra," Josman said.

"So, it was you that brought this evil upon us? You led them here?" asked Rayna. Josman said nothing and glanced down at his cold, half eaten stew, unsure of what to say.

"On the contrary, captain. If anything, they were able to warn the people of Turnava and Pata before they were all killed," said Marek. "I've spoken with the refugees. If it wasn't for Josman and his friends, we wouldn't have had enough warning to raise the defenses. Zinok would have fallen, in my opinion."

"Lieutenant Stepanek, in my *correct* opinion, Zinok did fall," said Rayna.

"You know what I mean, Rayna," said Marek.

Rayna almost said something about addressing his superior in such a way, but they both knew the time for ranks was over. They were no longer any part of Thanatan's military.

"We aren't fighting our way out of this prison. Even if we did, one of those beasts would be able to escape to alert their master," said Alia. "And besides, they can communicate like Mindspeakers, so they might not even have to leave Zinok to spread word of our escape plans."

Kamil perked up at Alia's words.

"Maybe if just one or two of us managed to escape, they could slip by unnoticed," said Josman.

"The Pure can sense our minds," said Marek. "They'd know."

Josman winced, hating when people used the Magistrate's word to refer to the Faceless. He clamped his teeth on the side of his tongue to prevent himself from commenting. Instead, he watched Kamil think. He had seen the expression on his friend's face before and knew he must be concocting an elaborate plan.

"It looks like Kamil has an idea," Josman said.

Kamil nodded and tapped his forehead.

"*These things are dead, their minds empty husks. I think I could use one to send a message to Laniras or Doftaan,*" Kamil said, stroking his chin, which was now covered in a dark beard.

"Would they sense your mind inside one?" Alia asked, trying to grasp Kamil's idea.

"*My mind would still be here in Zinok, not in the creature's head. I'm not sure if I can even do it, and if I can, I'm not sure if I'll be able to maintain control all the way to Laniras or Sangora. Perhaps it is a silly idea.*"

"No, it's worth a try and might be the only chance we have. What would you need?" asked Rayna.

"*It'll take a toll on me. Somewhere comfortable, and as embarrassing as this is, if it takes too long, possibly someone to feed me.*"

"What if you need to use the toilet?" asked Valis.

The others exchanged glances and then looked back to Kamil for an answer, who threw his hands into the air in exasperation.

"*Let's just hope it doesn't come to that,*" Kamil responded.


After several hours of careful planning, Josman and Kamil snuck along the wreckage of the second wall, scanning the area for a lone Faceless. All was quiet, as if the world had already forgotten what had transpired earlier. Kamil refrained from sending Josman mental messages to prevent the Faceless from sensing his powerful thoughts; instead, as they had planned, he reverted to signing directions to his friend.

Josman helped Rayna and Alia climb out of the wreckage of the wall, and the group hurried into the craggy pass where Kamil had sensed several Faceless lurking. Rayna and Alia insisted on accompanying Josman and Kamil into the pass to provide combat and healing support, should the need arise. They welcomed their help, but much to Valis's dismay, Alia commanded him to stay with Lieutenant Marek and had forbidden him from accompanying them.

"Let's get this over with. I don't want any of you getting eaten," said Josman, shuddering and shaking his arms as if to ward off the evil they would soon face.

"I don't think they *can* eat, Josman. They don't even have faces," said Alia.

"Oh, well that makes me feel better! You don't know what those things can do! They'll eat your mind right out of your head!" Josman exclaimed, despite his attempt to whisper. Alia wondered if the creatures they hunted could hear their words.

For a fleeting moment, the dark mood permeating the battlefield melted away into laughter. Levity accompanied them until they entered the pass, and the familiar, dull groan of the Faceless invaded their minds.

"They're close," whispered Rayna. She urged the group onward as they waded through the nearly palpable sensation of hunger and dread in the shadow of the mountain.

A handful of loose pebbles fell from above; Josman looked up, already knowing what had dislodged the debris. A dozen or so Faceless hung on the crags high above, and within moments, the creatures were upon them. Josman wasted no time, crushing a Faceless skull beneath his mace as Rayna and Alia circled Kamil, their blades dancing across their foes' flesh.

"Do it!" exclaimed Josman as the Faceless overwhelmed the party.

Kamil concentrated with all his might, causing an invisible explosion of mental energy at the far end of the rocky corridor. Josman smashed the knees out of one of the creatures as the monsters chased the mental lure. The fallen Faceless leapt to its feet on broken legs and tried to follow, only to collide with Josman's thick arm.

Josman roared as he pulled the struggling Faceless into a tight bear hug. It would have been a comical sight if not for the grotesque, blood spattered creature clawing at his flesh.

Kamil lured their foes away once more, this time collapsing from the mental strain. Alia and Rayna hurried to his side and helped him to his feet, supporting him as they made their way out of the canyon toward the second wall. Josman followed close behind, gripping his prisoner with all his might. The horde snapped back to their senses as Kamil's mental lure dissipated, and Josman cursed loud enough for the others to hear.

"Don't let go of that thing!" called Rayna. "Keep going!"

Josman broke into a sprint, keeping the thrashing Faceless tight against his body. His muscular legs carried him up and over the rubble of the wall with several of the Pure clawing at his heels. He glanced over his shoulder for a moment to see Rayna, Kamil, and Alia locked in combat with a part of the swarm.

In a split second of hesitation, his foot caught a piece of rubble as he tried to avoid the Faceless, and he and his captive tumbled over the debris of the wall to the ground several yards below. Neither Josman nor the Faceless stirred, dazed by the fall.

Rayna severed the throat of the nearest creature while Alia skewered another through the back. Kamil crawled across the fallen brick of the wall toward Josman, using his mental abilities to hide his allies from the undead creatures that pursued them. Rayna dispatched one after another without mercy and without pause, severing head and limb from body and bone. Alia hurried across a ruined chunk of the wall and collapsed next to Josman and Kamil, skinning both of her knees in the process.

Heart pounding, she folded her cloak beneath Josman's head. He had no visible wounds, which was to be expected, given his magical abilities, but he was unconscious and completely unresponsive.

*"I can't read his mind—bad sign,"* Kamil thought. *"You're the healer here, what should we do?"*

Alia grasped the sides of Josman's head and let her healing power flow.

"Internal injuries are much trickier than ones I can see, and I'm not sure I can help a brain injury," Alia said as she grasped the sides of Josman's head. Panic and worry for her friend began to set in as she let her power flow into his skin. He gave a feeble stir, and Alia let out a sigh of relief. Kamil grabbed the fallen Faceless by the head in an attempt to force his own mind into the soulless husk of a body while simultaneously trying to lure the other Faceless away.

Alia began to hyperventilate in fear as she saw the Faceless horde crest the debris; she slapped Josman's chest and placed her mouth over his, breathing air into his lungs, healing energy seeping from both her hands and lips. She pressed hard on his chest again and again in a steady rhythm and breathed life energy back into him.

His eyes shot open as he felt Alia's lips on his own. He enjoyed the sensation for a moment before rolling away from Alia to grab his fallen mace. He groaned in pain as he brought the weapon up and broke the spine of a Faceless as it leapt toward them. It squirmed, dying on the ground as Josman roared in agony, a piercing pain in his side and chest dropping him to his knees. Another Faceless leapt at him, but he crushed its skull.

"Your ribs! Wait!" cried Alia as Josman struggled to his feet. She reached out to heal his broken bones, knowing she had fractured them in her attempt to give him the breath of life.

"Heal our friend over there!" Josman exclaimed, hefting his heavy mace. "Worry about me later!"

As he swung at a group of the Faceless, Rayna's fury rained down as she leapt from the ledge above; her blade slid with gruesome grace along a spine and then then flew upward, slicing out a pair of legs. The fearless captain staved off their enemies, giving Alia time to pull a steel bar from the base of their captive's skull. She went to close the gaping, bloodless wound, but the creature lashed at her neck.

"Josman! Come get this thing!" she cried.

The creature leapt in wild rage, raking jagged claws across Kamil's chest and stomach. Josman wrapped his arms around their captive to restrain the broken Pure, holding it tight until Kamil was able to pacify its mind, blood soaking his tunic. He collapsed, trembling, and Alia ripped his shirt open and placed her palms over the bloody wounds across his bare chest. She was able to close the razor thin lines, leaving ugly pink scars.

"Ana asefa, Kamil—urzhuk samihuni…" *I'm sorry, please forgive me.* Her dark features bore the sorrows of fatigue and failure at not being able to fully heal the scars as well. Kamil placed a hand over his heart and bowed his head, a simple sign that there was nothing to forgive, and they embraced.

"They moved on," said Rayna in a matter-of-fact way as she stepped back into view, wiping the gore from her blade on a torn flag of Thanatanos.

"Yeah, I think they're trying to keep us inside this prison of ours rather than kill us," said Josman. "The good news is that I don't think they care we kidnapped this guy."

Their captive Faceless squirmed in his grasp, its groans permeating their minds.

"You'll need to rest," Alia ordered. Kamil nodded, his mind and body too exhausted for words. She turned to Rayna. "Luring the Faceless must have been too much for him. I barely used my abilities, and I'm completely drained. I can't imagine how he's feeling."

"Can't you heal him?" asked Rayna.

"No, I can only heal the physical body, but the mind? I'm not so sure," said Alia. Rayna helped Alia and Kamil along, and the exhausted group said little more as they trekked back toward Sanctuary village.

The sunset's golden hues cast a warm glow over Zinok as if bathing the entire city in a soft flame. Night, and the unknown dangers that accompanied it, would be upon them once more, ignorant of what had happened in the broken city.

Valis met the group at the highest gate and guided them to a home with a glowing hearth. Kamil thanked his young friend and immediately fell asleep on a cot placed against the wall.

"I don't know how long I can hold this thing. Do you think you two could find something to tie it up with until Kamil wakes up?" asked Josman, struggling with the Faceless in his arms.

"Why? You're doing a great job," Alia said with a wink as Rayna went to search for some rope. Valis fetched a spare bed sheet and wrapped it around a sturdy beam. Josman slammed the creature against the support and Valis wrapped the bedsheet around it as it clawed in vain at its captors. Valis and Alia pulled the fabric tight enough that the Faceless was unable to raise its arms.

"Well, until Rayna's back with something better, that'll have to do," said Josman, slumping on the cot next to Kamil's feet.

"So, what happened out there?" asked Valis.

Josman regaled Valis with the tale as Rayna returned and wrapped a thick rope and heavy chain around the creature's chest and legs. They could all still sense its hunger and hatred, but when it was tied up and harmless, the feeling was more annoying than it was terrifying.

"You're gonna make it hard to sleep tonight, buddy," said Valis, examining the creature's grotesque features as Rayna continued to bind the beast. "Is that all necessary?"

"Do you want to be sleeping in this room when this thing breaks free?" Rayna responded without looking at him.

Alia placed a kettle of water on the fire which soon began to steam. When it was ready, she set it on the crude wooden table, which had once been the house's door, and fetched four clay mugs from an otherwise bare cupboard. She sighed.

"I found some tea in the larder. Sorry, no sugar or honey, and sorry it isn't anything stronger." She hung her head. "Truth be told, I don't think we'll get much sleep tonight." She began pouring weak tea into each vessel. "Josman, please tell our guest I'd offer him some tea if he had a mouth."

"He doesn't *deserve* tea," growled Josman, moving away from the pacified creature. "He stinks too much."

Valis followed, nodding in agreement. Rayna and Alia soon joined them as well, leaving Kamil to sleep. The conversation was lighthearted and hopeful, dotted with brief moments of sleep, but no slumber and little rest.

"I thought for sure they'd come rescue your prisoner," said Valis the next morning as the first trickles of light spilled through the open window. The late summer breeze, free to go where it pleased, played with the curtains in the windows as if taunting those within the house unable to leave Zinok.

Kamil stirred and sat up, rubbing the pale wounds on his abdomen. He waved to the rest of the group then remembered the captive Faceless and nodded, impressed.

"*So, I see we were successful and weren't killed in our sleep.*" He wriggled beneath the weight of blankets piled around him, and he laughed. "*I also see that you've made me a nest!*"

"That we have," said Josman. "Alia's made us all breakfast, too. Will you be ready to control this thing after you eat?"

"*Yes,*" replied Kamil to Josman's mind. He freed his arms from the cocoon of blankets, and Alia brought him a bowl of porridge.

"Eat up, man of the hour," she said with a kind smile.

Kamil offered a nervous grin and accepted the food. He scarfed it down and handed the bowl and spoon to Valis, who took it to the empty washing basin.

"You'll be comfortable, but I'm also worried that Thanatan or the Magistrate will be able to control you once you connect with this thing's mind. We don't know how it works, so…" Rayna trailed off as she tied his arms to the bed. "Sorry, friend."

"*No apologies needed. Let's do this,*" Kamil said, bowing his head.

He took a deep breath and closed his eyes. He cleared his mind and took another calming breath before reaching out toward his foe's thoughts.

What he found was a chaotic mess of emotion and primal rage. The Pure's incessant groans wrestled around in his mind, but he pushed past the disembodied screams to locate the being's consciousness. Its soul, if it had one. He expected it to be harder to find, but there it was, calling to him. He could sense the very core of the faceless creature's essence, and he grasped it with mental fingers; the world seemed to shake, and a hurricane of chaotic emotion and confusion seemed to char Kamil's own mind, threatening to shatter it into pieces.

Valis and Rayna steadied Kamil's physical body as he trembled and shook in pain, while Josman and Alia readied their weapons against the thrashing Faceless should it break free.

And then it was over. The thrashing stopped, and Kamil felt peace wash over both his own mind and that of the Faceless beast before him. Where there was chaos there was now order, a familiar serenity that cascaded from the Pure's mind and throughout its body. The same calmness that Kamil tried to exude. The same mind. The beast had been tamed; their messenger was ready.

"Did it work?" Josman asked. The Faceless nodded.

Josman and Rayna unlocked the chains and let them clatter to the ground like a steel snake then sliced the ropes away. He untied the bedsheet next, and the Faceless stumbled to the ground, disoriented. After a moment, it looked in their direction. They each had their weapons drawn, ready.

Josman broke into a laugh as the Faceless lifted its clawed hand into a grotesque thumbs-up. Alia and Valis clapped and hollered in victory and Rayna smiled, arms folded. The creature ambled over to the door, fumbled with the doorknob, and then it disappeared outside. Valis ran to the door to watch the creature make its way across the countryside until he could no longer make it out.

"That's pretty awesome," said Valis, and Josman nodded.

"Let's just hope this works," said Alia with a sigh.


Kamil sent the creature through the pass unimpeded. Thousands of gray-skinned, emaciated creatures climbed over the crags and wandered aimlessly with no victims to disembowel, and Kamil felt their dead minds brush his own, a beautiful web of connection. He urged his Faceless avatar to keep running. As he emerged from the pass, he was overtaken by a larger Pure that knocked him to the ground.

He felt agony tear through his scrawny legs. Although Alia had repaired them with her magic the night before, they were not whole. The larger Faceless brought its hands down to disembowel Kamil's avatar, who responded by thrusting his own jagged claws upward into the larger creature's chest. It stumbled backward and Kamil twisted and sprinted away, quicker than his larger foe.

The larger Faceless signaled several others, which closed the gap between Kamil's avatar and the pass in seconds. His legs screamed in pain, and he knew he wouldn't make it. He reached the river and turned around just in time to feel the larger Pure's fist collide with the base of his skull. Several others began tearing at the same spot, and he took a mental leap, jumping into the mind of his nearest foe as they tore his avatar to shreds.

Disoriented, he stumbled backward. He could sense the other Faceless obeying his command to kill the runaway. His command? He realized he had leapt into the mind of the larger Faceless that seemed to be the leader of the pack. He sent a thought to each of their minds to depart. Not with words, but emotions. He tried to give them the sense of fulfilled duty, and he cheered in his own mind in relief that the creatures returned to the mountain pass.

When they were gone, Kamil took a moment to pay his respects to the dead Faceless he had used to get this far. He felt a sense of guilt about sending it to its doom but then remembered that these creatures were mindless beings of pure emotion and instinct. Or were they? He wasn't so sure anymore.

He sprinted away from Zinok and felt a strange mental connection coming from all directions like a web of minds. He decided to grasp one of the threads of the connection and pulled. He felt his consciousness leap across the river to another Faceless standing as a sentinel on its bank then leapt once more to another several yards away. Interesting. Perhaps this was how the Magistrate controlled them, or, an even more ominous thought crossed his mind, what if Thanatan could indeed control him in this way like Rayna had hypothesized?

He sprinted in the direction of Sangora, leaping from consciousness to consciousness whenever he could. He was pleased to realize that the Faceless felt no fatigue and could run as long as they did not collapse and die. As he transferred his mind once more to cover a mile in an instant, he felt a horrible sensation wash over his soul.

Two words. The cold voice of the Magistrate. *"To Laniras."*

An order for every Pure in Thanatanos to gather in the capital. He felt the urge to double back and run to heed his master's call. He shook his head. No, Thanatan was not his master—he had to resist the pull.

Kamil knew he would soon find the edge of Faceless territory as he passed through a burned-out town and transferred his consciousness yet again. If Thanatan was gathering his forces, that meant he was running out of time, but he knew he could not fail. Not again.

He could not allow the world to fall into Thanatan's hands.

# CHAPTER EIGHTEEN
# TRUST AND REGRETS

"They're leaving Nitra," said Valistaran as he shook Mara's shoulder to wake her. She shifted beneath one of her wings she had used as a makeshift blanket atop the crumbling city wall.

They were both completely exhausted, having traveled all the way from Doftaan to Vudapas near the border of Sangora and Thanatanos. The city, ravaged by sieges during the recent war, had been dubbed the Phoenix City after multiple times rising from the destruction and suffering wrought by Valistaran. It stood in stark contrast to the utter desolation brought by Mara in Nitra, which had never been rebuilt. Only a sparse plain separated the two broken cities, and Mara's Sangoran eyesight made it a perfect place to spy on the movements of their enemies near Nitra.

"Give me a second," said Mara, rubbing her eyes as she awoke. She grasped the battlements with her mighty wings to hoist herself upright and beheld a mass of thousands of Faceless trailing north-west. Her face went white.

"How long have I been asleep?" Mara asked.

"Not long enough. A few hours."

"And how long have they been leaving the city?"

"Around the same time."

"And you let me sleep?" Mara asked, an annoyed look of incredulity crossing her face. "This is a very important update—the type I told you to wake me up for immediately."

"What, you think you could have stopped them from leaving Nitra? This makes no difference. You'll need your strength for what's to come," said Valistaran, refusing to meet her gaze. Instead, he looked over the valley toward the Faceless horde and tossed her an apple.

"And where'd we steal this?" asked Mara. She rubbed a smudge of dirt from the fruit on her tunic.

"Where you steal any fruit. The market," said Valistaran.

"A king and an empress resorting to stealing from the market," said Mara with a laugh.

"Know what's even stranger? Resting in a city I laid siege to near the city you destroyed," Valistaran said. "With you, no less. It's almost poetic. Do you ever regret any of it? I know I do."

Mara was quiet for a long moment, gathering her thoughts.

"No. Regrets are only a way of unjustly punishing yourself for who you used to be," Mara said. "There are always going to be things that I wish had happened differently, things that hadn't happened to me, but those choices and experiences, no matter what they were, made me who I am. And a greater regret than any is dwelling on and not growing from the joy of my mistakes and experiences—not being true to who I've become."

"Wise words." Valistaran smiled and bowed his head. He was silent for a long moment before looking into Mara's eyes. "I know this doesn't mean much coming from me, but I'm proud of you. You've come a long way since…" He trailed off. "In any case, I gathered some information while I was in the city. Timishuara's armies will be of no help to us, as most of Mistress Lavinia's forces are already under the spell of the Queen's Control."

"I can't wait to rip Florenta's heart out," said Mara as she paced along the abandoned bulwark.

"I know you took the Queen's Control from Codruta's grave," said Valistaran with an abrupt tone.

"Sorry."

"No, you aren't. I am not saying this to reprimand you, empress. I want to know—do you still have the power to control others of your race?" Valistaran asked.

"I tried to control Florenta, but nothing happened. Back when I first became Sangoran, Ronin Jakoni was trying to create something. I thought he was trying to 'cure' Sangorans to turn them human, but I think he was actually trying to inoculate people against Codruta's control—and later my own," said Mara.

"And aren't we glad he did?" asked Valistaran. Mara raised an eyebrow and shook her head, not yet understanding his point.

"We wouldn't be in this mess if he didn't," said Mara.

"Her forces are immune to your control, but don't you think we could use that power against her? We could, as you said, inoculate our own followers against her."

"What followers?" Mara asked with a dry scoff.

"There is talk of unrest in Karpaska. I'm sure you know of the ethnic tensions—"

"The Alboran people, yes," said Mara. "Some of them support me, but they're hardly a military force."

"There's talk that the Alborans are moving against Balgorod. They hope to eventually free Doftaan itself as well," Valistaran explained.

He looked south-east, as if he could see Doftaan and Bukaral in the distance. She furrowed her brow.

"That's suicide. They're peasants and farmers, not warriors."

"Without Ronin's cure, yes. Florenta could just order their entire army to fall on their own swords. Perhaps, that is where we fit in to this revolution," said Valistaran. "But that's not the most interesting part of recent events in Karpaska."

"What do you mean?" asked Mara.

"You'll never guess who they're following."

"Who?"

"A former slave from one of my camps," Valistaran said.

"Is that supposed to be a joke?" Mara asked, her tone dark.

"A slave from Slave District Sixty-Eight, Mara. From *your* district."

Her mind shot to Aleksander and Hanna, but Valistaran spoke another name, bringing her back to reality.

"Shanthah Kalen."

At this, a genuine fit of laughter overtook Mara; she felt immense joy fill her soul as she wondered just how Shanthah could have influenced the entire Alboran nation to follow him. A special warmth in her heart swelled for the man in their shared fight against Florenta.

"I'm surprised, but at the same time, I'm really not. Oh, Shanthah!" said Mara, a wide smile stuck on her face. She flicked what remained of her apple's core from the wall. "How did this happen? Is he alone?"

"Legends of his love imprisoned in Doftaan have spread across Karpaska and Timishuara," said Valistaran, as if he knew Mara's final question referred to Hanna's fate after Florenta's attack on the peace summit.

"Hanna is alive?" Mara asked, her eyes wide with hope. "And still in Doftaan?"

"So the rumors say," Valistaran replied. "No one knows, but even if she's dead, the very thought of her is keeping the revolution going."

"Believe me, Hanna could escape any of my prisons in Doftaan. Either they've killed her or sent her to my most secure prison in Sevastaan," said Mara. Valistaran shrugged.

The joy that filled her heart melted away as images of Hanna filled her mind; her thoughts shot back to their battle under the island, to the prison camp, and to the last time she had seen her at the doomed Peace Summit. The thought of Hanna dead or imprisoned put an icy knife through her heart.

"Then what would you have us do?" Valistaran asked. "I see two courses before us: either we find Shanthah and join him or find Hanna and guide her to Karpaska and the Alboran revolution."

"We should go to the aid of Alboras. I think Shanthah's rebellion needs us more than Hanna does," Mara said as she let out a deep sigh, deep in thought.

"Then you are alright potentially sentencing your friend to death? We may not be able to help them both," Valistaran said.

"No. If there's one thing I know, there's nothing that can get between Hanna and Shanthah," said Mara. "She'll be fine."

"He's that powerful?" asked Valistaran.

"No." Mara laughed at his words. "*She* is! She'll find a way to save him, and not the other way around. Just you wait."

"She is a Telekinetik, no?" Valistaran asked. "If I remember correctly, she's a much more powerful one than I am. I had Talohiran engineers give me the ability to use telekinesis just as you did, but I can only seem to do it while I'm drunk…"

"That's hardly useful," Mara said. "It'd make you even more unbearable. But yeah, she's much better at it than me too."

Valistaran sighed. "Mara, it was unlikely that you would agree to join me on my quest to kill Thanatan, but I find it even more impossible that any of your friends will find it in their hearts to do the same. It is imperative, then, that you can rekindle an alliance with Shanthah as he leads the Alboran people against Florenta. He holds their hearts and minds in his hands, but as you realize, alone, they stand no chance. I trust you to understand that."

"But we're alone too. Are we kidding ourselves? What more can we add?" Mara asked.

"As always, you fail to give the praise due to yourself. You are beloved across Sangora and will be even more so as the rightful empress to guide her people from a tyrant's clutches," Valistaran said. The sound of a thousand whispers on a dark wind echoed around them before silence once again filled the night air. "Oh, and we are not alone."

Mara waited for clarification, but none came until several dozen figures materialized out of a dark mist. Many were clad in the wrappings and hoods of the Walkers, and others bore the beautifully crafted gold armor of the Kurashian elite guard. Before them stood two figures Mara recognized: Kadir, the Supreme one of Kurash, and Daniel Elafris, the man once believed to be the devil himself, who gave an awkward wave.

"Lord Ronin Jakoni," said Mara, addressing the Lord of the Walkers, who replied with a slight nod but said nothing. He stepped aside, and Mara dropped into a deep bow before the Supreme One, honoring the customs of his country.

"Of all people, I did not expect you," Mara said. "I am honored by your presence, Supreme One, who is called Kadir."

"*Hello, Mara Bartunek, Empress of Blood,*" said Kadir. "*And please, call me Kadir.*"

From her studies of diplomacy and protocol, Mara knew addressing the Supreme One of Kurash by name alone was a great honor afforded only to a few, and she thanked him.

The ruler spoke directly to her mind with a warm voice befitting of an old man speaking to his grandchildren. His skin, however, gave off a golden glow like the setting sun on fleeting clouds, cloaking his entire person in undeniable majesty.

Behind Kadir, a nervous looking man with spectacles and simple, drab robes standing next to a dark-haired woman waved to Mara.

"Hello," Mara said in greeting, recognizing the man as Daniel Elafris, whom she had briefly met under the ruins of Disneyland. She knew the man's reputation had been greatly exaggerated, and that he was a normal man who had miraculously survived the destruction of his civilization several hundred years earlier. She looked Daniel in the eyes, and added with a smirk, "I am honored, too, that the devil himself should come to our aid."

"Oh, would everyone stop that?" Daniel asked, shaking his head. "I'm just—"

"I know, I know," Mara said, clapping the man on the shoulder. "Your expertise will be invaluable. Thank you."

At the Supreme One's side stood a man clad in intricate shell of gold armor that covered his entire body; only two slits for eyes gave any clue to the man's identity inside the shell. A tattered black cloak fluttering in the wind like a dark banner was draped around the man in gold's shoulders. Mara assumed him to be Kadir's bodyguard.

"Welcome to the fight," the Man in Gold said in a friendly tone. Mara thanked him with a nod of her head and a smile.

Mara stood at a loss for words as Valistaran wrapped his arms around the Man in Gold in a brotherly hug, and they whispered one to the other as Kadir and Ronin stepped forward from their group of soldiers.

"*The world needs you,*" said Kadir.

"Please, forgive me. I don't understand quite what is happening," said Mara, turning back to Valistaran for an explanation. "*Someone* didn't warn me you were all coming."

Valistaran had not mentioned anything about an alliance with Lord Ronin Jakoni, the Supreme one of Kurash, or Daniel Elafris.

"We are part of an ancient group known as the Immortals," Ronin explained. "Our purpose is to put aside our personal goals to save the world from particular threats. Our predecessors failed, and we cannot let this world fall to ruin again."

"Lord Jakoni is right. I was one of those 'predecessors' he's talking about, and, well, yes. We failed big time," Daniel said, hanging his head. "Perhaps later, I'll be able to tell you more."

Mara wished beyond reason that she could sit down and talk with Daniel about the destruction of the Deadlands and the great civilization that had come before her own, but she knew this was not the time.

"This is why you've given up your kingdom, isn't it?" said Mara, looking Valistaran in the eyes. "Do you have any idea what has happened in Talohira since Florenta's uprising? During my reign, things were already unstable without you."

"Talohira is months away from civil war," Valistaran said. "It is out of love for my people that I came to you in Doftaan. They need their queen. You know perhaps better than I do that Florenta and Thanatan represent a greater threat than I can properly express."

He caught her gaze as the gravity of their cause and the importance of the task set out before them began to weigh on her soul, and she felt panic begin to stir in her chest.

"With Kadir's support, why not just bring the armies of Kurash against Florenta and Thanatan?" asked Mara.

*"You wish to see foreign invaders usurp the god, however false, that Thanatanos has worshipped for generations and break the alliance between our countries? Our actions would be met with uprisings more terrible and bloody even than Florenta Karpaska's,"* Kadir said. *"No, I faced enough of that when I allowed my people to come to that country's aid once before."*

Mara knew he was referring to the battle of Laniras at the end of the great war between Thanatanos, Sangora, and Talohira, but said nothing of it. Yet another conversation for another time.

"And you?" asked Mara, gesturing to Ronin. Her expression grew dark. "We have never seen eye to eye. *You* once tried to take my blood—all my blood—to overthrow Queen Codruta. Why in the name of Elafris should I trust you?"

"For the same reason you trust me," Valistaran said with a scowl. "The same reason we are all choosing to put trust in one another. We, the Immortals, have not always been successful, and we have all paid for our mistakes. We've failed recently more than we care to admit."

"Why?" Mara asked, genuinely curious.

*"Because you weren't with us,"* said Kadir, kneeling before the Empress of Blood. Each of his companions followed suit, including Ronin. She felt a lump form in her throat.

"I don't know what to say," she said, choking on her words.

"Say that you will lead us into a brighter world," said the Man in Gold.

"I will," Mara said.

"We will return you to your throne, and we will be at your side as you will lead *our* people to victory against the false god," Valistaran said.

Each of the Immortals stood, and Mara smiled.

"*We will be there along the way,*" Kadir said to her mind, "*but we will not be the only ones. You will have your people with you as well. Surround yourself with those you love and trust, and all will be well.*"

"How will we ever find our way?" Mara asked.

"Allow me to introduce you to my daughter, Valeniya," Valistaran said. He gestured to the dark-haired woman near Daniel. She stood swaying softly from side to side, swinging her arms with a rather vacant expression.

Mara laughed, knowing that Valeniya was the female variation of the Thannish name 'Valistaran.' He had evidentially named his child and the country he used to rule after himself.

"Hello, Valeniya," Mara said, holding out her hand. Valeniya did not seem to notice and did not respond. Mara lowered her hand.

"She has the unique ability to find people wherever they are. I must admit in the spirit of honesty we are trying to foster, that her abilities are how I found Thans gifted with magic to bring them into my camps."

"How you found and enslaved us, you mean?" Mara asked, correcting his statement. Valistaran nodded and remained silent. "How are you still acting like the slave camps were an act of altruism to save the world? Don't you dare, Valistaran. I didn't even have abilities when I was taken, so stop pretending you were *only* taking powered people."

"But you were one of the brightest of all of them," Valeniya whispered, gazing at Mara with glassy eyes.

"What?" Mara asked, unsure if she had heard correctly. Valeniya did not elaborate and seemed to stare straight through Mara. "Valeniya, what did you say? I couldn't even summon lightning until my conversion—"

"And who do you think ordered that modification to happen?" Valistaran asked. "Well, let's not dwell on that now. We have a tyrant to kill. Shall we?"

"No, let's absolutely dwell on that," Mara said, fuming, but the others were already leaving.

Ronin and the rest of the Walkers held out their hands, and the rest of the companions grasped their arms. Mara's heart raced as her mind turned to Hanna and Shanthah and the fight to be had.

One more thought filled Mara's mind as the entire group vanished into a swirling cloud of darkness:

What had Valeniya meant?

# CHAPTER NINETEEN

# HANNA ALONE

There was no way to accurately tell time in whatever dark pit Hanna now found herself. Weeks of loneliness in a dark prison—weeks of despair not knowing the fate of her loved ones. Wondering was all she had.

During that time, there was usually nothing but darkness, except the sensation of cold stone against her skin and the dusty decay of death and neglect that filled her nostrils. Many had died in this pit of a dungeon since she had arrived, and whoever's prison this was had failed to remove the bodies. She shivered in the darkness and wished, simply, for a blanket or pillow for her head.

In her despair, her mind shot to Shanthah, as it often did these days. She could really use his levity to dispel the anxiety in her mind, which was made infinitely worse by not knowing if he was alive or dead. He had made her life in the slave camp so much better, and she wished with all her heart that he would show up laughing and smiling, but he had not.

She was beginning to lose hope.

Her leg cramped and spasmed. She kicked wildly trying to alleviate the sensation, and her foot brushed something in the darkness. Whatever it was sounded like metal on stone, and her heart leapt. A weapon?

Hanna crawled around on all fours, hoping to find the fallen item. She simultaneously bumped into the strong steel bars of her cell and pricked her finger on something sharp. She gingerly reached out and traced her finger along the sharp object until she found the handle. Her heart leapt again, for the item was definitely a sword. One of the Walkers' hooked blades, by the feel of it. She reached outside her bars and recoiled in shock as she touched a dead body, undoubtedly both the deceased owner of the weapon and source of the stench in the prison.

The blade would be an invaluable treasure and tool, as she had tried to escape using her powers, but had found the bars impenetrable.

"Where am I?" she whispered to herself for what felt like the millionth time.

She crawled to the corner in the dark cell and sat hugging her knees, placing the blade next to her, ready to strike if a guard appeared. She had never seen any guards, and every time they had brought her supplies, she had been asleep. Every few days next to the disgusting toilet she would find a new, meager heap of food on a board, a small pitcher of water, and a bolt of cloth, which she assumed was for hygienic purposes. All inadequate, of course, but it was something by which she measured time and something to look forward to.

She must have dozed off, because the next thing she knew, firm hands were gripping her shoulders, smashing her head against the wall of her dark cell. A second guard held a torch, the light of which was blinding after not seeing light for so long. She tried to fight back as the guard grasped her by the hair, and the other brought the torch dangerously close to her face.

"I lost a lot of friends to you, witch," said the man. She had assumed she was in a Sangoran prison, but if there were humans here—

He reached for a dagger at his waist, and she wasted no time whirling the hooked blade upward into her attacker's jaw and then downward with a cry. Blood spattered the chamber as she tore the vicious blade from her foe's bone and then planted it in the sternum of the second guard.

The second guard reached for her throat, but Hanna spun around and slashed him across the stomach. The would-be-murderer hit the ground, and Hanna began to shake as she frantically searched his companion's belt for keys. She found a single iron key and clutched it to her chest before collapsing to the ground. She heaved, vomiting across the floor of her cell.

She got to her feet, holding the torch and keys in one hand and her new sword in the other. She stumbled out her open cell door, her head throbbing where her attacker had struck it against the wall. Other prisoners called for her to help them, but she moved on. After all, she was only able to pilfer one key from the dead man's body, and surely, the cages didn't all share the same one. They had come here specifically to murder her.

She felt a sudden, unnatural dizziness overtaking her and wondered if there was some type of dark magic making her lose consciousness. She was falling and couldn't prevent it from happening. She hit the ground hard.

She awoke once more with a chain around each wrist and ankle, suspending her in midair in the middle of a dark chamber. It could have been the same cell for all she knew, but she didn't care. She groaned as she rattled her chains, and three armed Sangorans illuminated the chamber with torchlight.

"You know you gave me weapons, right?" Hanna asked, her head still throbbing. She felt disoriented and sore all over.

"A mistake we remedied. We have removed the dead Walker's swords, and we assure you, you are staying in this prison forever," said one of the soldiers in perfect Thannish.

"I think you'll meet the same fate," said Hanna as two more human guards arrived wielding heavy crossbows. They readied the weapons, pointing them at Hanna's head.

She focused on each individual link of the steel chains, telepathically located where they had been smelted shut. Her head throbbed as she used her powers to rip several of the links open, breaking the chains around her ankles.

"We have orders to shoot if—"

Hanna kicked her feet forward, propelling two jagged bits of broken chain through the bars with her mind, felling the two crossbowmen then ripped her bonds from the ceiling and whipped them around, lashing them around the bars of her cage.

The Sangoran guards scrambled for the fallen weapons as Hanna roared, exerting all her energy to squeeze the bars together with the added leverage and physical strength afforded by the chains.

She launched another flurry of broken chain links through the bars, planting them in the third guard's neck and chest. She wrenched the bars with all her might, using the chains to create a space for herself to fit through. The final guard fired a single bolt toward her, which she was able to deflect by telekinetically spinning the chain before her. She cast the chain forward, wrapping it around her attacker's arm then drew it back, flinging the Sangoran down the hallway with a scream and a sickening crunch.

This time, Hanna knelt to examine the bodies of her attackers. Each of them wore a brooch, pin, or medallion with a white fist on a red and black background, a symbol she recognized as Florenta Karpaska's insignia.

"So, it looks like Mara's not the only one who's pissed you off, eh?" Hanna asked, removing the Sangoran's medallion and the man's pin, just in case.

She placed the medallion's thin chain around her neck and tucked it into her shirt and fastened the pin on the inside of her pants where no guard should ever notice it. She knew they would notice the medallion and confiscate it, but she intended it to be her decoy. The wave of drowsiness washed over her once more, and she slumped to her knees but tried to keep crawling forward.

"You're gonna run out of whatever gas you're knocking me out with soon, and when you do—" She hit the floor, and she heard the guard let out a sigh of relief. "…I swear, I'll kill you."

The pain in her shoulders and back brought her back to consciousness. Although she could not see, she could feel taut cords and a stiff, metal contraption keeping her arms and neck strained backward as far as they would go without breaking. Her legs were bent beneath her, her knees to her chest. The unnatural position bent strained nearly every joint in her body, causing her excruciating agony.

"I'm awake again!" Hanna called, her voice tense with discomfort. "And you're lucky I don't like to stretch before I exercise, because this really, really hurts!"

There was no reply other than the sound of something clattering against the stone ground. She chuckled to herself despite her predicament before her laughter turned first to incessant groans of pain. The sobs came next.

"Hail Empress Mara Bartunek!" Hanna shouted to test her captors' allegiance, telling herself that there had to be at least one of them still loyal to Mara.

Hunger gnawed at her stomach. How long had she been at her little game? She had no idea of knowing how long she was unconscious each time they gassed her. Panic and claustrophobia began to set in, and her breathing intensified. Tears came to her eyes as she tried in vain to free herself using her powers. Other fears crept into her mind; what if they simply buried her alive next? Or slit her throat?

"Breathe," she said softly to herself. "Breathe…"

She reasoned that they would have already killed her when she was unconscious, so they were under orders not to do so.

The first duo had tried to murder her, but they were simply brutes, not under official orders.

She tried reaching out with her mind, just as Kamil had taught her to do in training sessions with the Hidden Flame. Those simpler days after the war felt so dreadfully long ago, and she longed for them. She longed for the safety and warmth of the company of her friends and laughter during dinners with her closest friends. But most of all, she longed for Shanthah's smile.

She told herself to focus. Kamil had explained to her that Mindspeakers and Telekinetiks had similar powers because their abilities originated in the brain. Although Kamil couldn't move things with his mind, and Hanna couldn't read thoughts, she knew that what he said held merit. He had taught her to sense the world around her by reaching out and feeling rather than seeing, like she had when she broke apart the chains.

She shut her eyes in the pitch blackness, and she took one soothing breath. In, and out. And then another. In, and out. And another. In, and out.

She reached out again. First, she could feel the emptiness of the chamber then focused on the texture of the brick of the prison walls around her. The different texture and material between brick and mortar—she went even deeper. The miniscule space between the mortar and stone and the tiny bubbles and pockets within the brick itself. She clenched her fists, and she felt the structural integrity of the room and her bonds dissolve around her.

She could feel the bricks collapsing in on themselves, infinitesimally small bits of stone flowing through the imperfections and cracks until the walls around her had completely crumbled to dust and swirled around her like an ethereal stream of ashes and dust. Her cell's bars flowed to the floor like smoky water.

Her mind did not ache. Her head did not throb. She did not feel the weariness that usually accompanied her powers, and in the place of pain and fatigue was an air of calm.

Peace. Perfection. Power.

She was connected to all of creation.

She let out one, final, peaceful breath, and her trance broke. When she returned to reality, a single guard was kneeling before her, head bowed, with a torch in her hand. The appearance of a single guard broke Hanna's concentration, and she felt the dust that had been her prison cell dissipate as if into nothingness.

"Well, what are you waiting for?" Hanna asked, expecting her to give the order to release the knockout gas.

"What are *you* waiting for?" repeated the nervous Sangoran woman. She was still kneeling before Hanna.

"I'm waiting for my knight in shining armor, of course," said Hanna. The guard stared with forlorn dejection at the floor.

The guard's shoulders hunched in defeat, and Hanna knew the woman was even more exhausted than she, having been assigned to keep watch over her. At that moment, Hanna realized she wasn't wearing one of Florenta's insignias.

"There's someone even more powerful than you coming to rescue you?" asked the guard.

Hanna laughed, a pure, true sound. "Oh, no, I don't need him to get out of here. I said I'm *waiting* for him. As in, I don't know where he is, and I'm waiting for him to get here so we can leave," said Hanna with an exasperated flurry of her hands. "Always waiting on a man, am I right?"

The guard laughed nervously at that.

"Listen, I—".

"No, you listen," said Hanna, drawing the pendant from beneath her tunic. She held it out before her, and the guard held out her hand. Hanna set the medallion down in her palm and let the thin chain pool around it.

"I don't understand," said the guard. She screwed up her brow in confusion. "Why?"

"I think you do," Hanna said. "I think I'll call you Lucky, since I think you might be the luckiest guard in this entire place."

"*That*, I think I understand," said Lucky and placed the chain around her neck. "Although, my name's Liliana…"

Hanna turned up the corner of her shirt to reveal the hidden pin with Florenta's mark upon it then pantomimed crushing the pin in her fist. She put a finger to her lips and stared into Lucky's eyes. With the look, she communicated everything she wished she could but dared not say aloud.

The look was a sign of trust. Lucky, or rather, Liliana, nodded.

"She's loose again! Release the gas!" Lucky shouted and ran up the stairs, looking over her shoulder as Hanna waved and mouthed a wordless, "Goodnight."


Dreams of being buried alive morphed into being stripped naked and cast into the void where nothing but she and her companions of despair and hopelessness existed. She could feel herself powerless as she floated away from the Earth; suddenly, she was drowning deep beneath the blackness of the sea, completely helpless against the elements, unable to escape—and then—

She was awake and half expecting to find herself in even more dire conditions, but the scene around her was quite contrary to her dreams, which she realized must have been distorted and twisted by the gas.

Instead, she was fully clothed and unbound, lying on a comfortable bed near a shelf full of books. She examined the spines, reading faded titles of peeling gold as the tantalizing scent of food wafted toward her. She quickly abandoned the books in favor of food. She vowed that if her new torture was to smell but never tase the wonderful food, she would lay waste to all of Doftaan in defiance.

She pushed open a door separating her bedroom from the food and found a veritable feast laid out before her. She cast out the thought that the food was poisoned and shoveled a spoonful of porridge into her mouth then selected some fresh fruit that she would consume next.

"MMM!" she half exclaimed, half grunted, her mouth full of delicious food. A smile stretched across her face. If this was an illusion created by the gas, she didn't care. This was the most delicious food she had ever consumed, even if it was all in her mind. "Best prison service *ever!* Much better than the last place!"

She tore into a leg of lamb and collapsed into a rickety chair near the bed, completely content.

She was undoubtedly still in a cell deep underground, but at least she was free of the torture device. She wondered if her gamble in trusting Lucky would pay off, or if the extent of the guard's pull was to secure the more comfortable room.

She glanced over to the bed, which beckoned her to return. She grabbed a slice of buttered bread and crawled beneath the soft covers. While adjusting her pillow, her fingers brushed a bit of parchment. A note from Lucky, perhaps?

With fingers trembling in excitement, she unfolded the scrap of paper. To her surprise, she found a sketch of six books on a shelf. One word was written on each spine of the books. *ENJOY THE BOOKS I FOUND YOU.* Perplexed, she stepped out of the comfort of the bed and examined the tomes on the shelf. They were each completely different genres and styles and seemed to have nothing in common.

*Stay Focused*
*Safe, Proven Techniques for Home Medical Care*
*Until We Meet on Greener Fields*
*He: Understanding the Fragile Male Ego*
*Can we be Saved?*
*Reach for Sky*
*You are Not Alone*
*Save the Cat!*
*Us*

She looked closer at the books on the top shelf and cried out in joy, clapping her hands together. The first word of each title, when read as in the drawing, spelled out a sentence. A message from her new friend.

*STAY SAFE UNTIL HE CAN REACH YOU SAVE US*

At that moment, she heard someone clanging on her cell bars. She returned to the room with all the food and approached the wall of bars, where two guards, including Lucky, stood waiting for her. Behind them, seven more soldiers stood ready.

"Just curious," Hanna asked upon approach. "Why not just kill me when the poison gas knocks me out?"

"We tried!" Liliana exclaimed. Hanna chuckled and turned back to her feast. "No one's blades could even get close to your skin!"

"So, what? You decided to just let me be happy until I get out of here and kill you all?" After a few moments of silence came one apprehensive word.

"Yes!"

Hanna laughed again and set down the leg of lamb. She made eye contact with Liliana, who subtly brushed the Karpaskan pendant with her thumb.

"Thanks for the books," Hanna said.

"A gift from the two of us," Liliana replied, pointing to her ally. "She is Reka, but she doesn't speak Thannish."

Hanna looked to her new ally, who nodded with a smile.

"But if you misbehave, you'll have to watch us burn them!" Lucky exclaimed, a little too loud, as if for the benefit of someone out of sight.

"Now back to suffering, you!" Liliana said. Reka slammed her armored fist against the bar with a resounding clang before the duo departed.

Hanna crawled back into the luxurious bed. No doubt Shanthah was out there somewhere looking for her. He was coming; she knew it. Or hoped it, rather. What would come after they were reunited, she had no idea, and she decided getting sufficient rest would be beneficial to both mind and body. She would need her strength for whatever challenges came next.

However, she knew she was safe for now. She had to reassure herself about that fact, but she knew it was true. The malicious guards could not harm her, and Lucky had evidentially negotiated to appease her rather than contain and torture her.

She was grateful for the guards' help. Liliana must have gone through quite a bit of trouble leaving her the secret message on the books. Were Liliana and Reka prisoners as much as she? She made up her mind in that moment to help them escape as well.

Despite her newfound comfort, her unrelenting anxiety for Shanthah's safety constantly found its way into her mind, and she found herself unable to fall asleep. Therefore, she decided to bury her endless worries in mountains of food.

While she ate, her thoughts turned to her powers. The human body and mind, even those as powerful as her own, had limits. She knew that, and she knew she had to find hers and stick to them. Who knew how much more of the gas she could inhale without suffering irreparable brain damage, or worse? But when she had been in that state of connection to all of creation, her powers had felt limitless.

When had her powers grown to that level? She thought back to what she experienced in her previous escape attempt. The clarity of mind she experienced when she was dissolving the prison walls puzzled her. In the past, her abilities were limited to telekinesis. Had Kamil unlocked some new ability in her, or was she somehow evolving and her powers maturing?

"Don't get arrogant, Hanna," she whispered to herself. As she spoke the words, she thought of him again; she had never spoken to herself until he came into her life.

She smiled and used her powers to summon a couple of grapes from the far side of the table. She pushed herself away from the table, half disgusted and half impressed at how much of the food she had consumed. She knew Shanthah would be the latter.

Hanna placed a pillow on the floor and plopped down on it in the center of her chamber, trying to calm the anxiety in her heart to achieve the clarity of mind she had reached before. She tried to reach out with her mind to feel the bricks making up her new cell, to sense the space between them like she had before, but nothing happened. She swore under her breath and tried to relax. When she finally felt comfortable and her heart rate slowed, she reached out once more with her mind.

She could feel the softness of the bed sheets, and then she realized she could once again feel the bricks in the cell around her. Instead of focusing within the walls themselves, she decided to test how far her mind could reach. She felt the warmth of the torch outside her chamber. The solid, wooden surface of Lucky's desk, and then even the breath of each of the guards. She sensed the cool air at the bottom of the chamber and the warmer air near the ceiling.

And then—

*"Interesting. I did not expect this."*

A distinct male voice reverberated within her mind, and on instinct, she tried to retreat to the reality waiting outside her own thoughts, but something, or someone, prevented her. Panic replaced the calm.

"Not again," she whispered to herself. "No, no, no…"

She could feel a foreign presence twisting around her mind and, it seemed, connecting with her entire being. Where once she could feel peace and tranquility, she felt only a dark, empty chill that permeated her very existence. The voice rang through the void of her soul once more, and her unconscious physical body trembled in fear. *"Yes, this is just what I needed. Thank you again, Hanna Samsa."*

Hanna's eyes rolled back into her head, and a blinding explosion of light filled her vision; she was no longer in the Doftaani prison, but in the ruins of a city she recognized: Nitra. She had no control over her body and knew she was seeing through the eyes of another. Horror filled her soul as she stood atop a tower of Nitra's ruined fortress and beheld thousands of Faceless swarming all over the city.

Hanna beheld two gargantuan beasts bowing their massive heads before their master. They stood so tall while upon their back legs that their noses, which, trailing with smoke, were level with the top of the tower, at two one hundred feet high.

They both seemed to be in a trance, and she felt her mind, or rather, their master's mind, connected to them both. She watched as the being willed the dust into the very essence of the massive creatures; was he feeding them, or perhaps, Hanna feared, making them even more terrifying?

A deafening roar escaped both behemoths' mouths followed by a torrent of all-consuming flame; Hanna's eyes shot open to feel Liliana and Reka shaking her. She scrambled backward with her eyes wide in panic.

"Lucky, what—what was that?" asked Hanna, her limbs shaking. "Did you see—"

"You were *screaming,*" replied Liliana, a genuine look of concern etched across her face. For the briefest moment, Hanna was tempted to reach out again, but she stopped herself out of terror that the dark being would find her, and their minds would connect again, perhaps forever.

"Something's out there," said Hanna, "In Nitra, but—"

"Do you mind explaining?" asked Liliana, translating into Sangoran for her ally.

"I have to get out of here," said Hanna, eying the wall behind her. She could tear her way through or try to dissolve it like before, but she would risk being sensed by the dark enemy and quite literally lose her mind.

"Maybe it'd be smart to leave now, before your knight comes," said Liliana low enough that the other guards couldn't overhear their conversation. "But listen to me, please. One more dose of that gas could kill you or drive you insane. Maybe it already has done that."

"No, Lucky. You don't understand. When I was using my powers, something—someone—out there sensed me. I saw Nitra and millions of those *things* Mara and I fought under the island."

Reka placed an empathetic hand on Hanna's cheek. Hanna winced but didn't pull away. They couldn't share words, but the contact was reassuring.

"I don't know what you're talking about, but if you promise whatever you saw was real and not caused by the poison gas."

"It was real."

"Then I believe you," said Liliana.

"I killed tons of you, why would you help me?" asked Hanna before adding, "how do I know I can trust you?"

"Well, thank you for doing that for us," said Liliana, looking at the other Sangoran. "The other guards are all loyal to Mistress Florenta now, but Reka and I still support Empress Mara. I don't get it. People I've known forever who *loved* Mara and would do absolutely anything for her—even they turned on her. It was so strange. Thank you for the Karpaskan pendant, by the way. I think they were getting suspicious of me that I wasn't openly showing my 'affection' for Florenta."

"We…prisoners," Reka said in a thick Sangoran accent, her eyes sad; she lifted her shirt over her stomach to reveal nasty purple bruises and cuts on each of her sides and across her abdomen.

In response, Hanna turned and pulled the back of her tunic over her shoulders so that Reka could see the faded scars from the slavers' whips. "Me too, Reka."

Reka reached through the bars and touched the wounds with a tear in each eye. Hanna pulled the fabric back down.

"Reka didn't have a mark of Florenta during inspection, so they beat her—no other reason," Liliana explained.

"Then you're both coming with me, obviously," Hanna said.

"If we can shut off the poison gas long enough for you to escape, would you help us?" Liliana whispered, knowing the other guards were just outside the door.

"Absolutely," Hanna said, waiting for Liliana to finish translating for Reka.

She felt courage stir in her heart. She told herself that they could do this as long she refrained from tapping into her newfound abilities. She knew she would not be able to handle connecting with the dark god again, especially now that he knew she was on the other side.

"Wonderful! Let's get you out of here," Liliana said, sharing a grin with Hanna. So far, the dark god did not seem to sense her. She was cautious to even think his name, if that was, in fact, who was haunting her.

"Yes, lets."

# CHAPTER TWENTY
# THE HORNETS' NEST

The hillside headquarters of the Hidden Flame east of Laniras was deserted; no longer did it bustle with activity and purpose. Instead, an eerie reverence resonated throughout its halls, as if they knew of the tragedy that had occurred at Florenta's hand. For a short time, this place was the heart of diplomacy in the kingdom and where the Hidden Flame gathered information to protect the nation's security. Now, that very security was threatened by the country's own namesake.

The magical torches lining the grand entrance hall flickered to life as Aleksander, Pol, Rayshel, Vasilica, and Lavinia made their way down the marble staircase. As he descended the staircase, Aleksander brushed his fingers along the balustrades supporting a sleek white handrail. He glanced over at Pol, who seemed to be lost in thought; whether his mind was ripe with nostalgia or worry, Aleksander couldn't tell.

Aleksander felt the gate sealed with a Mindlock probe his thoughts before sliding open with a hiss of steam and a grinding of gears. Only a member of the Hidden Flame could open the gate, and Aleksander hoped that Thanatan did not know of the existence of the abandoned base. Perhaps his recent encounter with King Verahim would ensure its safety for now.

"With all due respect, I don't think hiding in this hole will protect us from Thanatan," said Vasilica as the gate slammed shut behind them. More torches flickered to life, illuminating their path. "He could just bury us alive down here."

"We'll be long gone before he knows we're here," said Aleksander, leading the group through the complex. "Well, I hope so at least."

"Where are we going?" asked Pol as the group followed Aleksander down a hallway through which he was never granted access. His heart thundered in his chest as if Aleksander were letting him in on some grand secret.

"I mentioned on our way here that we might have a way to help Lavinia walk again. I'm hoping to make good on that promise," said Aleksander, coming to a sealed room that opened as it scanned his mind. Magical torches lit the room to illuminate what looked like a dismantled suit of elegant silver armor on a stone platform.

"Is that what I think it is?" asked Lavinia.

"Spirit armor, yup," said Aleksander, adjusting the tattered suit that he'd been wearing since the attack on the Peace Ball. With a wink, he said, "Don't say I never bought you anything nice."

Vasilica directed Lavinia's wheelchair next to the armor, and Lavinia traced her finger along the contours of the intricate armor.

"Who did you have to kill for this?! Where in the world did you find this? How?" asked Lavinia. Vasilica and Pol joined her in marveling over the metallic corpse.

"With great difficulty," said Aleksander. Rayshel and Pol exchanged glances, not completely sure of the situation.

"It's like Valakor's armor, right?" asked Pol.

"Should I know what or who that is?" added Rayshel.

"It was always a mystery to me as well until I became the secret keeper of Kurash," said Aleksander. Rayshel furrowed her brow in confusion and folded her arms.

"You say that as if it's the most normal thing you could say," said Lavinia. "It isn't, by the way."

"But spirit armor like Valakor's was used in the time of Thanatan and Elafris in the war that destroyed the Deadlands. They were mechanical suits of armor used to house the minds of dead warriors and generals so they could keep fighting even after death. There aren't many left," Aleksander explained.

"So yeah, exactly like Valakor," said Pol.

"Yes, and there are a few others that aren't as friendly and are loyal to Thanatan." Aleksander nodded before letting out a deep sigh. "Another potential problem."

"Yet another problem is that I'm very, very hungry. I'll go get us something to eat, since I'll just get in the way," Pol said.

"I knew I liked this kid," Lavinia said. She gave Pol a high-five, and he left the room.

"So, what's the plan?" asked Rayshel, ready to get to work.

Aleksander located some tools from a shelf and placed them next to the dead warrior's mechanical body.

"We had some of our engineers and magicians dissect this thing and learn its secrets—is dissect the right word? Well, Kamil figured out that the user creates a mind link with the armor and is able to control it. So theoretically, your mind is moving the armor instead of your body. I think it'll be able to help you, Lavinia." Aleksander said.

"It would allow me to walk again?" Lavinia responded.

"The engineers figured out how to adjust it to fit a normal human—" At this, Lavinia scowled, and Aleksander quickly added, "*or* Sangoran—that isn't eight feet tall, but I'm not sure if…" He trailed off and fidgeted with the plating on the back of the armor for a moment before exclaiming in joy

"What?" Lavinia asked. "*Whaaat?*"

"Ah, yes! Here we go!" Aleksander said. "I wasn't sure if it would be able to accommodate your wings, but I figured it out. It'll work, I think. Now, we'll start with your legs and try to work on anything near your spine last."

He withdrew some scrolls from a nearby vault outlining the process to ready the armor for use and hefted a section of the leg armor; it was heavier than he had expected, and he dropped it. It clattered to the floor and Lavinia shook her head.

"Careful with that. It's my new leg," she said.

Aleksander placed the cold metal of the spirit armor against Lavinia's bare shins and readied the thigh section of the armor according to the engineers' plans. The armor required some adjusting, as she was shorter than the engineers' default settings. Aleksander reread the text out loud to himself a few times before he was comfortable performing the procedure, much to Lavinia's annoyance.

He ignored her and motioned for Rayshel and Vasilica to help the wounded Mistress of Dusk onto the platform. He clamped the upper section of the leg armor onto her thighs according to the diagram, and Rayshel helped tighten the straps.

"We're going to need to remove the healing vest the Laniran healers put on you. It's too bulky to wear underneath the armor, and it restricts your movement," said Aleksander. "Your pain will probably come back while we work, but I think we'll be able to figure something out."

"Do whatever you need to. I can handle pain, but I can't fight like this," said Lavinia, motioning to her lifeless legs. She used her hands to lift one of them and dropped it with a thud.

"Rayshel, Vasilica, can you help her sit up?" asked Aleksander. They obliged, and Lavinia pushed herself up on her palms. Meanwhile, Aleksander reviewed the plans, scratching his head. "I've got the plans here to use a portion of the spirit armor to—ugh, I don't know, I don't get it. It aligns your spine somehow—that part I understand, but I can't figure out how it connects your mind to the armor so you can control it."

"You don't sound very confident," said Lavinia in a condescending tone. She let out one long breath from flared nostrils.

"With good reason! None of us are engineers. It's the only chance you've got, though, so sit still."

"I know, I know," said Lavinia.

She swallowed her pride and nodded to Aleksander in her own way of thanking him without having to say the words out loud. Aleksander winked and got to work, explaining the process to Vasilica and Rayshel as he understood it.

"Vasilica and Rayshel, you can help now by removing the healing vest. We'll have to work fast to minimize any pain," said Aleksander. The vest, borrowed from the Laniran healing center, used some kind of advanced magic he didn't understand to dull her pain.

Vasilica began to unbutton Lavinia's shirt along her spine where her mighty wings protruded from her tunic. Aleksander caught a glimpse of the gruesome scar left by the assassin on Lavinia's chest as she let her tunic fall away, revealing the healing vest wrapped tightly around her abdomen. He turned away to respect her privacy.

"What's wrong, Aleksander? You're brave enough to fight slavers, warriors, and monsters, but are scared to see a naked lady?" Lavinia asked in a mocking tone. Aleksander rolled his eyes at her quip and handed the plans to Rayshel and Vasilica.

"I've seen…" He sighed and stopped himself, shaking his head from side to side. "Listen, if we're not careful during this part, the engineers say you could die from the pain."

Lavinia indeed felt pain starting to develop in her spine as Rayshel and Vasilica loosened the vest. Her breathing and heart rate quickened, but she suppressed the overwhelming desire to scream.

"There are worse fates," Lavinia said. "Would that be so bad?"

"Yes, it would be. We need you," Aleksander said. "Now, Mistress Lavinia, with all due respect, shut up and let us fix you."

"Ah, there's the confidence we were looking for," Lavinia said. "Mara's a lucky lady."

At the mention of Mara's name, Aleksander hesitated, taken aback for a moment. Lavinia offered no explanation, pressing her eyes shut to keep the pain at bay but forcing teasing remarks through gritted teeth, nonetheless.

Rayshel draped Lavinia's tunic over her head and with great difficulty helped her slide her arms through the sleeves as Vasilica attempted to strap the remaining armor onto Lavinia's limbs despite her growls of unrelenting pain.

"Ja štu, Vinia. Totjo buda hoš," Rayshel said in Sangoran. *I know, Vinia. Everything will be okay.* Lavinia swore unintelligibly under her breath in response.

Lavinia's unrestrained screams echoed around the chamber, and Aleksander rushed forward with the shining silver breastplate. Vasilica and Rayshel helped him place it on Lavinia's thrashing body; the involuntary pain response caused her to lash out, knocking Rayshel to the ground with one of her flailing wings.

Rayshel hurried to the Mistress of Dusk's side and stroked her hair, whispering rapid Sangoran into her ear as Vasilica and Aleksander pressed the individual pieces of armor against the broken Mistress of Dusk's chest. Tears flowed freely down Lavinia's cheeks from sheer agony, and she began to convulse.

Aleksander marveled at the woman's staunch courage and resolve to continue fighting as he sealed the armor.

"It'll be over soon!" he assured her as a low groan filled the chamber. At first, Aleksander thought nothing of it, thinking Lavinia was somehow producing the sound, but something slammed against the metal gate. Again, and again, like the beating of a massive drum, something smashed against the door to gain entrance. The pounding and unearthly groans drove Lavinia into hysteric anger mixed with excruciating pain, and she slammed her fist into the stone pedestal over and over again.

"Pol!" Aleksander shouted in a sudden panic. In all their attention given to Lavinia's dire situation, he had forgotten that Pol had left the chamber to find something to eat.

The groans from outside increased, and Aleksander secured the final piece of armor against Lavinia's collarbones. As he did so, a hissing sound escaped the armor and thick metallic straps snaked their way around Lavinia's exposed skin as if on their own accord. Overlapping plates adjusted to the shape of Lavinia's spine and sharp needles burrowed into her flesh to administer a healing potion, according to the engineers' instructions. Lavinia's thrashing ceased, and she lay still.

"Is she okay?" Rayshel asked, gripping Lavinia's hand.

Aleksander checked for her pulse, locating the faint throbbing in her wrist. The Faceless in the hallway continued to beat on the door, but in a way that seemed rather human in its rhythm now, rather than the wild chaos that usually accompanied the undead creatures.

"She's alive. It worked, but if we can't figure out how to link her mind, it'll all be for nothing." Frustration took over and he dumped a pile of scrolls to the floor as he searched for the missing instructions. "But we need to deal with that thing out there and make sure Pol is alive too!"

"*Let us in, Aleksander!*" came a voice to all their minds. "*All is well, friend!*"

"Kamil?!" Aleksander exclaimed.

With an incredulous look on his face, he unlocked the gate to reveal Pol supporting the emaciated gray form of a Faceless. Pol was grinning from ear to ear.

"You'll never guess who I ran into near the kitchens!" Pol exclaimed. "Well, maybe you will because you already know, but—it's Kamil!"

"What's happened to you?" Aleksander asked, helping Kamil into Lavinia's chamber. "Josman, Drahomir, and Valis—are they alright?"

Kamil's Faceless avatar sat upon a stool and crossed its legs, and his voice rang through their minds.

"*It is me, please don't be alarmed. Josman, Valis, Alia, and I—my physical body, that is—are all holed up in Zinok's fortress. I took control of this Faceless to send you an urgent message. I thank the Supreme One that I found you. I don't have much time.*"

"And Drahomir? You—you didn't mention him," Aleksander stammered. Kamil's avatar lowered its head with almost human emotion. Pol gasped in disbelief.

"*He fell to the Faceless.*"

The news hit Aleksander with such force that he collapsed against the wall, his hand pressed over his mouth in shock. He looked to Kamil's avatar with a face screwed up in tears.

"And the others?" Aleksander managed to ask.

"*To be honest, we won't last much longer. Please, bring word to Empress Mara or to anyone else that can help that Thanatan's Faceless have us pinned down in Zinok. We've sustained heavy losses, and many have deserted us for Thanatan. We would have sent word to Laniras, but the Magistrate of the Faceless has already infiltrated Verahim's court,*" Kamil's voice echoed through each of their minds.

"We've just discovered the same horrible truth," said Aleksander, "and Mara probably won't be much help."

"*I thought you might have known about the Magistrate already. We have been so worried for all of you. Are you alright?*"

"Yes, thank you Kamil. I think we're better off than you are right now, my friend. How'd you find us anyway?"

"*I sensed your presence as I passed the Hidden Flame headquarters. I had hoped to find someone here. Sangora, Laniras, and all of Thanatanos are in grave danger. He's keeping us trapped here so that we can't warn you. He is lying, Aleksander. He is lying to all of Thanatanos. He's going to destroy everything.*"

Aleksander and the others exchanged worried looks before Vasilica said, "I don't know who you are, friend, but one of Empress Mara's councilors overthrew her and now sits on her throne. I think we will receive no help from Sangora."

"Beyond unfortunate, we know," Aleksander said.

"*Then send word to anyone who will help. Although I doubt it, King Verahim Romus may still send aid. He cares for his people. I can't control this Faceless much longer, Aleksander, but I see what you are doing with the spirit armor project, and I may be able to help."*

The Faceless ambled over to Lavinia and wrapped its disgusting fingers around her skull, using his powers to connect Lavinia's consciousness to the armor. The Faceless collapsed, and Lavinia's legs twitched.

"Kamil!" Aleksander exclaimed.

*"Send…help…Zinok…"*

The Faceless squirmed on the floor for a moment and then leapt toward Aleksander, its claws outstretched. Aleksander drew his blade and severed the creature's throat. The creature, now devoid of Kamil's mind, stumbled for a moment before its head struck the ground a moment before its body.

Pol vomited in a corner at the sight of the disgusting creature's demise, and Vasilica ushered him from the room with a sympathetic arm around his shoulder.

"Did it work?" asked Rayshel, turning away from Kamil's dead Faceless. She placed a worried hand on Lavinia's chest plate and yelped as Lavinia's fingers intertwined with her own. She stirred with a feeble groan and opened her eyes.

"Thank the Goddesses," Rayshel whispered, burying her face in her shoulder to wipe away her tears.

"Well, hello, grumpy," said Aleksander. "Feeling ready to take down a god and a tyrant?

Lavinia shook her head with a slow laugh. Rayshel covered her with a tarp from the corner of the chamber and brushed the woman's hair from her face.

"I'm sorry it isn't a blanket, but…" Rayshel began.

"Totjo hoš… Dehi…" Lavinia said in Sangoran between labored breaths. *Everything's okay. Thank you.* Rayshel smiled.

"Get some rest. We'll come get you when we need to go. Sleep well, Mistress," Aleksander said, patting the woman on the knee. He turned to Rayshel. "Pol brought us a Faceless zombie with our friend's brain instead of food, so would you like me to go get you something?"

"Thank you, Aleks. That would be wonderful. I'll stay here with Mistress Lavinia," Rayshel said with an appreciative nod.

Aleksander smiled and left the room, hoping Rayshel and Lavinia would be able to get some rest. He laughed as he found Pol and Vasilica slumped in a heap against a pillar in the light of a blazing torch. They were both sound asleep with Pol's head on Vasilica's shoulder, which was now covered in his drool.

He decided to let them rest, knowing they deserved it. Vasilica shifted in her sleep, draping a wing over Pol's shivering body like a blanket. At that moment, Aleksander smiled as he realized just how much Pol resembled his older sister.

To his surprise, when he arrived in the kitchen, Aleksander found a spread of food already prepared on one of the long tables. He assumed Pol had encountered Kamil and in his excitement, had forgotten about the food. He gathered it up in a sack and searched the kitchen for some cushions, eventually finding a folded pile of thin tablecloths he decided could make do as blankets.

He returned to find each and every one of his companions fast asleep. He wrapped one of the tablecloths over Vasilica and Pol. Pol shifted and woke up looking confused.

"Blanket," Aleksander explained. "I found your food, too. Go back to sleep."

Pol nodded, and within moments, he was asleep again. Aleksander softly lifted Lavinia's head and slipped one of the folded tablecloths under it, deciding she needed a pillow more than a blanket. He draped the last makeshift blanket over Rayshel with care; she had fallen asleep on a rickety stool, her head resting on Lavinia's platform.

With a yawn, Aleksander curled up in a corner hugging his knees, his head against the wall. Within minutes, his snores joined those of his companions.

He stirred and awoke sometime later with a crick in his neck. Without warning, someone was holding a bowl of porridge inches from his face. He blinked and shook his head, still groggy from sleep, confused if the food was real or a dream.

"Good morning!" Pol said, beaming. "Thanks for bringing all the food in last night when I forgot it, and sorry we all fell asleep!"

"Looks like you're feeling better! I'm glad you all got some rest," Aleksander said, rubbing his eyes. He brought a spoonful of the weak porridge to his mouth and asked, "How's Lavinia? Where is she?"

"Out testing her new armor. Just wait until you see her," Rayshel said, nodding between bites of bread. "Good morning, by the way! Thanks for the blanket. I assume that was you—if not, we've got ghosts."

She pushed the plate of buttered bread to Aleksander's side of the table as he sat down with his bowl of porridge.

"It was the ghosts," Aleksander replied with a smile.

Rayshel took another bite and said, "Of course. Tell the ghosts that it was very sweet of them."

She brushed the hair on one side of her head to the other, creating a cascade of dark locks that flowed down her sunburnt cheek. The torchlight danced across her emerald-green eyes, which widened in delight as she bit into a particularly juicy plum. Aleksander smiled again.

"I gathered some supplies that won't go bad too. Ones we can take with us," said Pol, gesturing to a pile of food he and Rayshel had not already dug into, including an assortment of fruit, nuts, and bread, as well as several bags of flour.

Before Aleksander could respond, Lavinia and Vasilica entered the chamber. Aleksander cupped his hands near his mouth and cheered while Rayshel and Pol clapped their hands.

"Be honest, how amazing do I look?" Lavinia asked.

The armor looked incredible, truly fit for the indomitable warrior within. The shining silver gleamed in the torchlight giving the illusion of fire dancing across her chest and shoulders. Her black cloak hung from her shoulders, emphasizing her imposing, outstretched wings.

"You look like you could take Thanatan down yourself," said Aleksander, unable to suppress a grin. Lavinia grabbed the bread from Aleksander's hand and took a bite.

"That was mine, but help yourself," Aleksander said. "How did it go? It looks amazing."

"Well, it clearly worked. I can run faster, jump and fly higher, and perhaps my favorite part—" she paused for dramatic effect then flexed both arms, and twin blades appeared from beneath her vambraces. Pol cheered again.

"Wow, Mistress Lavinia!" exclaimed Rayshel. "Florenta might drop dead because of how amazing you look."

"If we didn't before, we've got a chance against her now," said Vasilica.

When the group was finished with breakfast and marveling over Lavinia's new armor, they packed their bags with the supplies procured by Pol and set out for the teleportation chamber.

Aleksander opened the mind-lock into the chamber, and the group followed him inside; Rayshel hesitated, gazing at Lavinia's armor. Aleksander turned to her and gestured for her to follow but caught sight of her vacant expression.

"Everything alright?" he asked out of concern.

"I just wonder if we could make something like that for me," Rayshel said.

"But you're not—" Aleksander began but cut himself off. He realized he had not considered that she felt as paralyzed as Lavinia without her wings. He stuttered through his apology. "I'm so sorry, Rayshel. Maybe we can figure something out. I'm sorry that we don't have anything here that can help—I'm an idiot for not even considering—"

Rayshel faked a smile and said, "I understand. Let's go. There are more important things to think about."

"Not more important than you, just more pressing," Aleksander said. He felt his insides twist into knots.

"Thank you." Another sad smile.

They approached their friends who were already standing around a Teleportation Pillar, or Telepillar, in the center of the room. A large gem glowed upon its face.

"It's calibrated to take us back to Doftaan. That's the plan, right? Are you all ready?" Pol asked. The others nodded as the gem pulsated with a dim green light. "The king's men repaired this thing after it was damaged when we found the Weapon of Ages Past. It should have enough energy left for a few trips, at least."

"What is it, exactly?" asked Rayshel, reaching out to touch the Telepillar. Lavinia grabbed her hand and shook her head to prevent her from unintentionally activating the device.

"They used them in the Deadlands to travel great distances. There used to be one in most major cities, and people could blink across the world in minutes. Before that, they used to fly on these huge metal birds to travel, but that took hours or days, and this was invented to replace them," Aleksander explained, tapping into the history kept by the Secret Keepers. "Like Pol said, this one should have enough energy charged to send us where we need to go."

"So, what's the plan?" Vasilica asked.

"We've got to bring word about Kamil and the others. Thanatanos isn't safe anymore, and I don't know where Mara is, but we should try to find out what state Doftaan and Sangora are in…"

Aleksander trailed off as he pressed his hand on the green gem, which began to buzz to life with, bathing the room in its glow.

"Ready to go home?" Rayshel asked, gripping Lavinia's arm.

"Ready to go kill that tyrant on Mara's throne, you mean?" Lavinia asked. "Quite."

She pulled her sleek silver helm over her raven's feather hair and with steely resolve, stared into the green flame flowing from the top of the machine.

"Here we go!" called Aleksander as a blinding flash of light enveloped the room.

They were greeted with the mild night air of a dying summer, but not with the celebrations and joy that had filled the streets during the peace festivals in Doftaan. The crimson banners of the Empress of Blood were nowhere to be found; instead, black and red banners adorned with a white fist lined the streets. Around the fist were the words 'Jan žyznact Karpaskaž.' *My life for Karpaska.*

"Where is everyone?" asked Rayshel.

"Perhaps Florenta is enforcing some sort of curfew?" asked Vasilica. Lavinia shook her head in disagreement.

"No, I think it has something to do with that," she said, pointing behind the group.

"What in the name of Elafris?" said Rayshel, covering her mouth with her hands.

They had materialized near Doftaan's southern prison tower, which was now covered in vines as thick as the trunk of an oak tree. The looming tower looked as if it would fall over if not for vines twisting in and out of windows and doorways, choking the life out of the prison like a python around its prey, yet holding it upright.

"What happened here?" asked Pol, looking to Lavinia for an explanation. "Where are we?"

"This is the Kaljacjana Prison Tower in Doftaan," Vasilica said.

The very mention of the prison's name made Aleksander's gut twist in knots. It was here, after all, where he had unknowingly betrayed Mara and trapped her in the Prison of the Mind Cuff. He kept the thought to himself, although it ate him up inside.

"There aren't any torches lit inside any of these homes," Lavinia said. "It isn't natural."

"Do you think the people here abandoned this place, or do you think whatever happened here wiped them out?" asked Aleksander, clutching the pommel of his sword as he approached the tower. He pointed to some of the nearby homes that seemed to be afflicted in a similar manner as the prison.

"No one wants to live nearby the prison, but even for the Kaljacjana area, it seems deserted," said Vasilica. "There are usually at least beggars—homeless people and the like."

Lavinia took a courageous step toward the prison tower, but Rayshel grabbed her shoulder and shook her head frantically.

"I don't think we should go in," she said. "The stubs where my wings used to be—they are itching like crazy. I think whatever did this to me—the tower—I think they're related."

"How about this: Pol and I can explore the tower, and you three keep watch out here?" Aleksander suggested.

He glanced down the alleys leading away from the prison fortress and saw thick barricades covered with signage too far away to be readable. Warning signs, without a doubt.

"I'd like to join you. I don't think it'll affect me anymore now that my wings are..." she drifted off. "Well, you know."

Aleksander realized that she had shown remarkable bravery and maturity in not complaining about the loss of her wings, and he felt incredible guilt for not showing more concern or empathy earlier. Deep regret washed over him as he knew he lacked adequate time to address it now.

"Stay safe and be quick," ordered Vasilica. Aleksander saluted.

"Good luck," Lavinia added. "We'll be here if you need us."

Aleksander expected a quip or jab at his expense, but none came.

Aleksander, Rayshel, and Pol climbed through a large portion of the wall that had crumbled under the weight of the thick vines, and an unearthly stench filled their nostrils. A noxious fog stung their eyes, a sensation similar to the burning that accompanied chopping onions with a dull knife.

"That's foul..." Aleksander muttered. Rayshel dry heaved and pulled her Sangoran day wrappings over her nose.

"How do you feel about poking a hornets' nest?" asked Rayshel in a low whisper.

"Absolutely wonderful," Aleksander answered. Pol groaned and gave a nervous chuckle.

"I think that's what we do best, right Aleks?" he asked.

"That's right, buddy."

"Just curious, what do we hope to achieve here? There's no one here to help Kamil and the others. My sister's gone, maybe even dead…"

He trailed off.

"I am so sorry, Pol."

"You're not going to tell me not to talk like that or tell me you know she's alive?" Pol asked.

"I don't know if she is, and it's okay for you to be sad about it. Why would I tell you otherwise?" Aleksander asked. "I know we've both experienced so much pain both on behalf of and because of your sister."

He stopped and hesitated, debating whether to continue or not. Once again, guilt gnawed at his stomach for not talking to Pol more about Mara before now. Rayshel respected the privacy of their conversation and kept her distance, sword drawn.

"She's a good person, you know."

At this, Aleksander turned to Pol, the flame in his palm illuminating both their faces. The fog was getting thicker, and the vines seemed to sense their presence, as if angry they had stepped over the threshold of the tower.

"I hope I haven't given you any impression I think otherwise," Aleksander said. The anxiety of the conversation caused him to stutter. "Despite everything that's happened to her and to all of us, I care about your sister more than I can express."

"I'm not an idiot kid, Aleks. I knew about you two and your feelings for one another even back in the slave camp. Siblings talk, you know," Pol said, a look of consternation on his face.

"Tell me, do you still love her? And more importantly, do you still have faith in her as the Empress of Blood?"

Aleksander glanced away from Pol's face in shame; had they been treating him like a child? Rayshel wandered ahead in the light of his flame to investigate their surroundings, pricking the vine with the tip of her sword. It recoiled against the wall like a living serpent.

"I know you aren't. You're a hero and certainly not an idiot kid! I appreciate everything you've been through and sacrificed. Besides, we'd all have died without you in the Battle of Laniras. You saved us all," Aleksander said with an encouraging smile.

"Thanks," was Pol's only reply.

Aleksander's thoughts then turned to Mara, and he let out a long breath through his mouth before speaking. "And to answer your question, yes. I do love Mara. I really do, but it's complicated."

"You don't think I'd understand?" Pol asked.

"Sorry," Aleksander said with a sigh. He knew that he treated Pol like a child again. "There's just so much hurt there. So much said and left unsaid, and—"

"Don't let hurt kill hope," Pol said.

"You're a wise man, Apolinarius Bartunek," Aleksander said, clapping his friend on the back. "Thank you. I won't—can't— let my hope or love for Mara become blind faith in her. I know she can save us. I just hope she still has faith in *herself*."

He bit his tongue to prevent himself from adding the words "if she's alive" to the end of the sentence.

"I'm happy to hear that, and I hope so too," Pol said. He paused. "One act of courage doesn't make me a hero, though. I'm not like you, Mara, Shanthah or Josman. I had my chance, my moment and that's that—"

"Stop right there. You're a part of this as much as any of us are," Aleksander replied. "I love Mara, and she is my hero not because she has the strength to keep going, but because she keeps going when she doesn't think she has the heart to. You, Shanthah and Josman are the same way, and I wish I were more like you."

Pol considered Aleksander's words for a long moment as they explored the crumbling tower. "But should I just go back to Laniras and stay there? I mean, King Verahim gave me a pretty great job, and it could give me a wonderful life."

"We still don't know if it's safe in Laniras, Pol." He felt the words slip from his mouth, and he hoped they didn't sound condescending again. He winced. "I'm sorry, I didn't mean to talk to you like—"

"No, it's fine. You're right. I know, the Faceless are there, and Thanatan too, but what if that isn't a bad thing? What if they can really help Sangora and Talohira too, like he says?"

"I hope you're right, but I'm terrified of what's to come," Aleksander admitted. Pol smiled as Aleksander added, "I'm glad I have friends like you to make the future less scary."

Aleksander's flame lit the way as they came upon the first landing of prison cells to find naught but broken bars and twisted metal accompanied by crumbled stone and ruthless vines that snaked their way through the chamber. The air seemed thicker near the ceiling like a dense fog with no way to escape.

"Where are the prisoners?" Rayshel asked. She shuddered as she stepped on a spongy vine that burst and let out a puff of spores.

"Aleks, let's get out of here," whispered Pol.

Aleksander pressed on, continuing up the stairs; all three now had their swords drawn.

"Stay by me," Rayshel said to Pol then with a wink added, "I think I'll need you to help me out if things get crazy in here."

Pol smiled.

The second landing was infested with even more vines and spore particles lingering in the air like corrupt snowflakes adrift in a rancid breeze. Their coughs were getting worse, and Pol pulled the front of his tunic over his face to shield his lungs from the evil air.

Aleksander unleashed a torrent of flame through the room, bathing it in orange and igniting the cruel fog; the vines shifted and twisted as if in pain. As his flame cleansed the air, their coughs eased and breathing became easier again.

"One last floor?" Aleksander asked, taking a deep breath.

Pol and Rayshel each gave an apprehensive nod and followed Aleksander upward. The carnage on the third floor was revolting. The corpses of hundreds of dead Sangorans and humans alike littered the cages. The vines had choked the life out of many of their victims, still wrapped around their throats. Other corpses were covered in gruesome wounds and soaked in blood. The entire scene reeked of wretched death.

"What could have happened here?" asked Pol.

"Florenta," Aleksander and Rayshel said at once.

And then the intense groaning of the Faceless ripped through their minds. Hunger that could never be satiated. Death that would never come.

The pain of a life that could have been.

"Get back!" cried Aleksander as Pol and Rayshel sprinted down the stairs. "Go!"

Aleksander blasted a thick vine from their path as another whipped up and wrapped around Rayshel's ankle, dragging her screaming off the staircase toward the darkness below. Aleksander reached for her hand, but her screams echoed from the blackness until she struck the ground and was silenced.

"Rayshel!" roared Aleksander, bathing the vine in intense flame that spread across the floor like the base of a waterfall. His heart pounded as he raced to find her.

Pol screamed and lashed out with his blade, severing another living vine before it wrapped around his neck. It writhed on the ground, and the young man kicked it from the staircase.

They took the stairs two at a time until they reached the bottom, finding Rayshel bound by vines. The chaotic sound of innumerable feral beasts echoed in the ruined tower as the Faceless rushed down the stairs toward them. Their groans heralded death and consumed all hope.

"Run!" Rayshel exclaimed, her voice choked off by the vine. Her voice was music to Aleksander's ears; she was alive. He hacked at the vines that bound her, and she wheezed as air filled her lungs.

At that moment, a swarm of Sangorans erupted from the shadows and fog, their claws jagged, and their wings riddled with holes. And then his flames illuminated their twisted forms.

Faceless Sangorans.

Aleksander felt his limbs freeze as he took in the nightmarish sight; many of the grotesque monstrosities were missing limbs, and every one of them was soaked in thick and dark congealed blood.

He bathed the hallway in flame so hot no Faceless dared enter as Pol helped Rayshel limp from the tower. Lavinia and Vasilica ushered them to safety and turned just in time to watch an explosion erupt from the side of the infested prison tower like a dilapidated volcano.

Aleksander's silhouetted form struck the ground hard, and he rolled several yards before coming to a stop, his clothes ablaze. Pol and Vasilica smothered the flames with their cloaks, and Aleksander stumbled to his feet, still dazed from the fall. The Faceless Sangorans did not leave their tower, but the group could see them looming in the darkness before disappearing.

"So, now what?" Pol asked.

"It serves Florenta right. She steals the throne and must now deal with this. I say we let her face it alone," said Lavinia.

"You know why we can't do that," said Vasilica with a disapproving glare. For a moment, Lavinia did not respond until she finally relented and nodded in agreement, for she knew that the Faceless were a sign that Thanatan's hand had found its way into their country.

"How could this have happened?" Rayshel asked. "Sangora has mighty armies that can defend from such a threat!"

"Even Florenta wouldn't have allowed this to happen, right? She's not so vile that she would refrain from acting?" Vasilica asked, her face screwed up in a mixture of rage and confusion.

"With Mara gone, there was a power vacuum," Lavinia replied. "There was a transition of power, and therefore, there was opposition. I assume Thanatan sent the Faceless in reaction to Florenta's uprising."

"He's everywhere, then," Rayshel said with a sigh.

"Looks that way, yes," Vasilica said, folding her arms.

"We could head west to my home in Timishuara. We can't take my armies. If I'm right that Florenta has taken Mara's ability of the Queen's Control, they're undoubtedly under her thumb. But I'll put word out to any still loyal to Vasilica and myself to gather," said Lavinia. She let out a deep breath. "After that, we should turn our attention to Laniras and Thanatan—Oh, Mara, where are you?"

"Thank you," said Aleksander with a nod. "But could your people oppose Florenta's control? Could we risk inviting spies into our midst?"

"I don't think she's powerful enough to exert control over every single individual in Sangora at the same time. That's impossible. The strain would kill her. Not even Mara or Codruta could do such a thing."

"So, what are you saying?" asked Pol.

"Taking an entire army would draw her notice, but if we could send word to gather… Or we could put together a team, perhaps…" Vasilica said, thinking out loud. With a shrug, she added, "Just ideas."

"Guard the Telepillar. I'll be back in an hour or so. If I'm not back by then, leave me," Lavinia said.

"Where are you going?" Pol asked.

"I'm going to do what Vasilica suggested. I'm going to reach out to some of my contacts here," Lavinia said. "And I owe your friend for helping me walk again. I'll tell my allies here about Kamil's plight in Zinok, and I hope they can send some kind of help. Other than that, I think we've done all we can for them."

Before setting out, she folded her arms and took one last look at the tower, watching the dark shapes of corrupt Sangorans shifting around in the darkness, and she cursed them. It was one thing for a fellow Sangoran to usurp the throne, but Thanatan?

That would not do.

He must be destroyed.

# CHAPTER TWENTY-ONE
# HE IS COMING

The cold green light faded to darkness as Pol felt his body rematerialize in the headquarters of the Hidden Flame. He drew in a long breath and spotted Aleksander and Lavinia standing near the doorway as his eyes adjusted to the dim torchlight. He followed Aleksander's smiling face and outstretched hand through the door, but his mind still pounded thinking about the Faceless Sangorans and the twisted vines choking the life out of the dilapidated prison tower on their brief excursion into Doftaan. The image of the desecrated corpses was etched deeper into his eyelids with every blink.

His mind's eye imagined the shining towers of Laniras covered in vines, the people of his home massacred and changed into horrible faceless creatures, and then the most haunting image of all: his own sister twisted into one of the corrupt, winged Faceless. The fear of it all immobilized him, and he stumbled, but Aleksander hurried to his side to support him.

"I've got you," Aleksander said, helping him regain his balance. "Do you need to sit down?"

"Aleks, what if that happens to Laniras?" Pol said, ignoring Aleksander's question. He pointed toward the Teleportation Pillar as if it were a window leading into the corrupt prison tower.

"That's what we're fighting to stop," Aleksander said with an encouraging smile and nod.

"What if Thanatan's the only one who can stop them?" Pol asked. Aleksander stopped, bewildered. "What if he's right?"

"Pol, he's the one *leading* them," Aleksander retorted, unsure if the young man was aware of the fact.

"Yeah, for now," Pol said as the group walked away from the pillar chamber.

Their three Sangoran allies walked several yards behind, undoubtedly discussing what they had seen in Doftaan.

"You think they'll turn on him?" Aleksander asked.

"No, but I mean, what happens if we succeed? Killing Thanatan isn't going to get rid of all the Faceless at Zinok, and who knows how many more of them there are in other places."

"One problem at a time, I guess, huh?" Aleksander said.

"Aleks, you don't get what I'm saying," Pol said, scrunching his eyebrows together in frustration. Aleksander stopped walking and sighed.

"We'll have to fight them either way," Aleksander said.

"I just think you're thinking too simply about this," Pol said. "In all the stories I love from the Deadlands, they defeat the dark lord, and everything immediately gets better. But that's not how life is. Valistaran disappeared, and nothing changed. It'll be the same way with Florenta. With Thanatan. You forget that I was—am—King Verahim's messenger. I was in the room for a lot of important talks, and a lot of them were about Talohiran politics."

"What are you getting at?" Aleksander asked.

"When Valistaran was out of the picture, it didn't magically solve any problems. The Great War between Talohira and Thanatanos didn't end because Valistaran disappeared. Things got worse! People there are starving, and now that Florenta overthrew my sister, I'm sure they don't even have a functioning government in Talohira anymore. The people rioted, and marauders burned towns in Valistaran's absence. The only reason the fighting stopped is because both sides were too beaten down to keep going," Pol said. "I understand a lot about politics and war now, and I wish people could see that!"

"Better than I do, I'd say. I admit I haven't really thought about what's going on in Talohira now," Aleksander said as his normally upbeat and positive young friend became angrier and more defensive. "Especially with your sister missing—"

"Especially with my sister *dead,* Aleksander. Don't dance around it," Pol said with a bitter edge to his words. "After seeing what happened at the Peace Ball and in the prison tower, I've lost hope that she survived, and maybe that's a good thing."

Aleksander was taken aback by the comment and had no idea what to say; the shock of the boy's words seemed to pierce his very soul. All he managed to say was, "I just want to believe that she's alive."

"Yeah, because you love her. Do you know what Josman told me the *first time* we thought Mara died? He told me that not all stories have happy endings, and that sometimes people die. He said that our story was one of those, and that a happy ending wasn't part of hers. Well, I think that's what I'm going to say now. I don't think we're meant for a happy ending unless— unless we trust that Thanatan knows what he's doing."

"That Thanatan—Pol, are you serious?"

Pol's head dropped with a sigh; he left Aleksander where he stood and walked down the hallway. Aleksander admitted to himself that the young messenger did make some good points. A lot of them, actually. When had he grown up enough to understand the intricacies of politics?

"You look like a fish with your mouth wide open like that," Lavinia said. Aleksander realized his mouth was still gaping open at the shock of Pol's comments. "What's his problem?"

"Nothing," Aleksander said, watching Pol storm off; he felt that he should shout something back and chase after his young friend, but he let him disappear into the shadows of the Hidden Flame's base.

"Not *nothing*," Vasilica said with a scowl. "He told me what was on his mind, and he was nervous to talk to you about it."

Aleksander felt Vasilica twist the metaphorical knife in his heart as she wandered into the shadows after Pol.

"Wow," Aleksander said, hanging his head. He looked up at the ceiling, staring at nothing.

"Maybe you should be a better person," Lavinia said. "It'd fix all your problems."

Aleksander turned to answer her quip, but a scream—Vasilica's scream—echoed throughout the corridor. Without hesitation, Lavinia extended her black wings and shot down the hall, Aleksander and Rayshel close behind on foot.

Aleksander ignited two fistfuls of flame just as a familiar wave of fear and hunger overcame him. The groans followed. He unleashed a torrent of flame and whipped it down the hall as he caught sight of Pol scrambling on the ground away from a horde of oncoming Faceless.

"Get down!" Aleksander roared, throwing his arm forward to unleash the whip of flame once more against his enemies. Pol threw himself to the ground just as the Faceless lurched toward him; he felt the intense heat singe his skin as the tongue of flame beat the creatures back. As Aleksander's flaming whip dissipated, Rayshel helped Pol to his feet and away from the horde.

She called Vasilica's name as Aleksander unleashed a second wave of searing flame against their foes.

"Help!" Vasilica's voice came from down the corridor; dozens of Faceless swarming toward her only to meet the blades on the tips of her wings. Eight Faceless lay dead at her feet, and Aleksander doubled his efforts against those that stood ready to disembowel her. As Aleksander distracted the living corpses, Lavinia leapt into the fray, twin blades erupting from beneath her vambraces.

She severed sinew and bone with every stroke, leaving a path of heads and severed limbs in her wake. Vasilica shot into the air above the Faceless, but jagged claws tore through the muscle on her calf. Her screeches echoed throughout the corridor as she pierced her attacker through the neck with both bladed wings before tumbling to the ground.

Three more leapt upon her, and she watched, helpless, as the creatures slashed at her shoulders and reached for her neck. She felt warm blood soak her chest as a burst of flame felled the trio of emaciated creatures. Lavinia stepped between her and her foes, and Rayshel and Pol helped her to safety.

"Back to the pillar!" Aleksander shouted, peppering their foes with fireballs. "Are you alright?"

"No," Vasilica groaned in response, holding her wounds.

Rayshel covered her head with her arms, running headfirst through the smoke and flames. As Vasilica limped past him, Aleksander poured all the flames he could muster into the wide corridor and block off the faceless creatures' advance.

To his horror, the emaciated creatures stepped through the wall of flame, their flesh burning and melting from bone; they weren't stopping, even when reduced to grotesque monstrosities of exposed bone and scorched flesh. He gazed, dumbfounded, at the mutilated corpses, their groans and insatiable hunger echoing in his mind.

And then the voices began.

*"He is coming."*

At first, he thought Pol had said the words, but then he felt the thoughts of the thousands of Faceless all repeating the same words over, and over. A chorus of the dead.

*"He is coming... He is coming... He is coming..."*

The thoughts twisted around one another in a cacophony of dead voices, stunning Aleksander and the others for a brief moment, giving the Faceless time to reach them. Aleksander snapped back to reality, and a burst of flame erupted from his palms, setting the rug beneath his feet on fire.

"Go!" he roared.

The beasts raced past him, still ablaze; many scrambled across the walls like massive spiders toward Vasilica, thinking her injury made her easy prey.

*"He is coming… He is coming…"*

Aleksander watched in horror, unable to act as two of the Faceless overtook Rayshel. Dagger-like claws pierced her legs, and the beasts pulled her to the ground. She made a flailing motion as if trying to take flight and flipped onto her back to thrust her blade through the neck of the nearest monster missing an arm and a chunk of its neck. It spasmed, wrenching the weapon from her grip and darted down the hall. Rayshel screamed as one of its companions thrust its claws into her ribs, soaking her side in crimson.

*"He is coming."*

The chorus of voices filled Lavinia with rage; she hacked at the Faceless surrounding Rayshel with her twin blades, decapitating three of them covered with severe burns from Aleksander's fire.

She turned just in time to see another rake its jagged claws across her face, and she shrieked in pain, stumbling backward. Pol's shortsword erupted from the back of one of the creatures reaching for Lavinia's throat, but it was replaced by six more that quickly overtook the group.

*"He is coming! He is coming!"*

As Aleksander and Rayshel reached out for one another, Aleksander felt jagged claws tear into his back. He screamed, watching Rayshel's hand drop to the floor as she lost consciousness. As the voices began to drive him mad and indescribable pain racked his body, Aleksander met Pol's gaze. He beheld the same look of steely resolve to survive on his face that he had seen in Mara's eyes.

That same resolve filled his soul as more Faceless closed in around him, and a fire in his heart ignited and exploded in a howl of rage and pain; a river black fire erupted from Aleksander's hands, engulfing his foes in a cascade of tenebrous flame.

*"HE IS COMING!"*

The shadowy hellfire melted stone and flesh alike, and Aleksander collapsed to his knees, completely disoriented. The voices were silenced, and he collapsed upon the ground of molten stone, searing his flesh.

He felt someone pull him to his feet and support him long enough for one of the Sangorans, he could not tell who, to snatch him up just as another wave of Faceless made their way around the corner. The last thing he saw before he lost consciousness as one of the creatures reached for Rayshel's neck was Pol activating the mind-lock on the front gates.

When Aleksander awoke, Lavinia's face was inches from his own.

"Boo!" she exclaimed. He jumped, clutching his heart.

"Agh, you are the worst."

"Well, to use the old phrase, we've fallen out of the pot and right into the fire," Lavinia said. "Metaphorically and literally. You almost cooked us back there."

Aleksander sat up to see Lavinia applying pressure to Vasilica's wounded leg next to him. His own wounds on his back throbbed, and he stumbled to his feet.

"Where are Pol and Rayshel?" Aleksander asked. The creatures' voices still echoed in his mind, and he wondered if he was imagining them.

"Rayshel is alive. Her wounds were worse than mine, so we took care of her first," Vasilica said. "Pol brought her to a healer in the city and is bringing us healing supplies. Obviously, our wings are basically targets on our backs, so he was the only one able. He was very willing to get far away from those beasts."

"Smart guy. I can't get them out of my mind," Aleksander said, eying the new wounds across Lavinia's cheek and chin. "Just how bad were Rayshel's injuries?"

"Like I said, she's alive," Lavinia replied. "She'll be hurting for quite some time, though, so I ordered Pol to keep an eye on her for me—for us, whatever."

An incessant itch tormented the wounds across Aleksander's back, so he pried the blood-soaked fabric of his shirt away from his skin with a groan; it reopened the fresh wounds, and he shuddered in pain. He shook it off and let out a deep breath.

"Well, that was stupid," Lavinia said.

"For once, I agree with you," Aleksander said through a groan. "Where are we?"

"Uh, somewhere within Laniras," Vasilica answered. "Pol led us here. It's some park he enjoys reading in. What neighborhood did Pol say this is?"

"Laniras-Three, I think," Lavinia replied. Aleksander nodded, knowing they weren't far from the palace.

Aleksander's heart ached for Rayshel. He knew her wounds must be grievous indeed for Lavinia and Vasilica to make the dangerous decision to send her to a Thannish healing center.

"So, what do we do now?" Vasilica asked.

"Nothing we can do until Pol gets back," Aleksander said. Lavinia nodded in agreement and sighed.

"In a way, Rayshel is lucky to have lost her wings. Being able to pass as human may save her life. We have to fend for ourselves," Lavinia began.

"We shouldn't even have to pass for being human," Vasilica said, spitting into the dirt. "I'm sorry—no offense, Aleksander."

"You've got no reason to apologize. I should be apologizing to you on behalf of all the other humans for this situation even being an issue," Aleksander said with a look of concern. "So, for that, I'm sorry."

They spent the next two hours treating their wounds as best they could until Pol returned with a bottle of alcohol, a spool of gauze, and an armful of various other medical supplies.

"It's the best I could find, will it be enough?" Pol asked. Lavinia opened the bottle and let the fluid flow down her throat. "That wasn't for—"

"I've had better, but it's served its purpose," Lavinia retorted with a glare before applying some of the alcohol to Vasilica's wounds. "Want some?"

"I'm fine," Pol said. Aleksander shook his head.

"Suit yourself, cowards."

Aleksander groaned as he pulled off his torn and bloodied shirt, revealing the long gashes on his back. Pol winced and took the bottle from Lavinia before she finished it off.

"Good thing we didn't drink it all. Lie on your stomach," Pol ordered. Aleksander did as he was told and lay in the grass. He winced as he felt Pol dab the alcohol on the wounds across his bare back.

"You know, the healers in Laniras would probably hate that I'm using this stuff to clean your wounds. I wish I could have gotten some of that good antiseptic potion, but it was too expensive. The nurses and healers did teach me to stitch up wounds, though when I was helping them out. Want me to try?"

Aleksander didn't answer for a long moment. Lavinia winced.

"You know what, sure," he said in awkward apprehension.

"You hesitated!" Pol said.

"I think my hesitation was justified. Lavinia, back me up?"

Lavinia just shrugged.

Pol got to work stitching the wounds, and Aleksander reached for the bottle of alcohol to numb the pain, but it was now empty. Lavinia laughed at his expense while she continued her work on Vasilica's wounds. Aleksander wondered if Lavinia had more training than Pol but said nothing.

"By the way, I just wanted to apologize to you too about earlier," Aleksander said and then added, "also for when any of us treated you like a kid before that. It wasn't our intention, but it's what happened, and I'm sorry."

Pol smiled, an expression that went unseen by Aleksander, who was still flat on his stomach.

"I shouldn't have run off like that—I almost got myself, Vasilica *and* Rayshel killed," he said. "All's forgiven, of course. Sorry for being grumpy. Maybe I was just hungry."

Aleksander gave a thumbs-up; the movement stressed the wound on his back, and he groaned. "I'm glad to hear that. How was Rayshel when you left her?"

"She was fine. They're taking care of her. Their care is nothing like they have in the castle, but better than the treatment you're getting, but maybe that's for the best so she can lie low," Pol replied as he tended to Aleksander's wounds. "It's the one by the Gates of Romiton. Do you know it?"

"Yeah, near the place with that really good fried cheese, yes?"

"That's the one," Pol said.

He hesitated for a moment as if fighting a battle with himself then drew a rolled-up piece of cloth from his pouch. He unraveled it and handed it to Aleksander, catching Lavinia's attention.

"A banner?" Aleksander asked. The viridian flag bore the Star of Thanatan, similar to the flag of Thanatanos, but the bottom edge bore a design similar to a group of silhouettes pressed together. Pol caught Aleksander eying the design and nodded.

"Yeah, that's clearly the Faceless. Anyway, there's some kind of gathering along the thoroughfares from Laniras-Three and City Center leading to the king's palace. I snagged that to show you," Pol explained, finishing the stitches.

Aleksander sat up and thanked Pol as he began to bandage the wounds. Lavinia's countenance grew dark as she took the flag from Aleksander's hand.

"He is coming," she said in an ominous tone while waving the banner. "You know exactly what they meant."

"Thanatan has come to Laniras," Vasilica said. She hung her head, as if she knew they had failed.

"And we're in the middle of his welcome party," said Aleksander as he sat up, still shirtless. "Wonderful."

"I could check with the king about what's happening," Pol said, handing Aleksander his blood-soaked tunic. "As a king's messenger, I'm allowed to talk to him. It's worth a try. Want to come with me?"

Aleksander pulled on his tunic and locked eyes with Vasilica with a knowing look. "Well, we talked to him recently, and I don't think we'd be welcome back," Aleksander said. Vasilica nodded, biting her bottom lip. "If you go, please be safe. Things are about to get dangerous here." He paused. "What am I worrying about? I trust you. You'll be smart."

He clapped Pol on the back.

"Okay. Meet me by the Gates of Romiton in three hours. They're not far from the healing center where Rayshel is. It's not far from the palace, but it is far enough away that you'll be safe there," Pol said. "I'll be back soon."

"You better be," Lavinia said. "You're more important than you think, Apolinarius Bartunek."

"You know my full name?" Pol asked, surprised.

"Your sister is…" Lavinia said, drifting off as she looked for the right words. "Your sister is my best friend. One of the few true friends I'm lucky to have. She's talked to me about you more than about almost anyone else. We need you, kid."

She smiled, and Pol glanced over to Aleksander. He was quiet for a few seconds then nodded with a thin smile.

"Got it. South gate, three hours. Remember," he said. "Don't forget Rayshel."

"Believe me, that won't happen," Lavinia said with an uncharacteristically kind smile.

"Thanks again for your help," Aleksander said, pointing to his back. With that, Pol set off toward the palace.

"Shall we join the party before we meet Pol?" Aleksander asked.

Lavinia and Vasilica wrapped their dark cloaks around their wings to hide them, and they set off to the center neighborhood of Laniras, following the throng of Thanatan's followers.

During the hour it took to walk to the king's palace cradled in the bend of the river, they passed hundreds of overjoyed Thans waving flags and calling to one another in celebration. Children were running with brightly colored kites, and teenagers lit off fireworks that sparkled blue and green overhead.

To fit in, Lavinia waved the banner Pol had stolen in the air as they made their way through the crowd.

"Mistress," Vasilica said, using her sleeve to wipe the blood from the light scratches on the woman's face. Lavinia had forgotten about her wounds in their haste to escape and in her concern for the others' wellbeing; she smudged the blood on her cloak and shrugged it off.

"They won't be looking at me. Not if our suspicions are correct," Lavinia said. "And may the Goddesses help us if they are…"

"I hope we're wrong," Aleksander said.

Vasilica shook her head.

"Lavinia is seldom wrong."

Many of the gathered townsfolk looked like they had come straight from their fields or from working in the forges, their faces smudged with dirt, ash, and even blood. They mingled with nobles and the well-dressed citizens of central Laniras, laughing and drinking together.

"It's weird to see people from the poorer neighborhoods mingling with the richer ones. This never happens," Aleksander said. "They all seem so…" He trailed off.

"Hopeful," Lavinia finished, nodding. Vasilica pointed to the east, where a procession accompanied by musicians and dancers was nearing the wide, central square in front of the king's palace.

Vasilica gasped, and Aleksander soon realized the reason. What they had assumed were hundreds of men and women walking the street toward the square were Faceless garbed in fine robes and servant wear. The citizens of Thanatanos did not seem to fear them.

"He dressed them…?" Aleksander whispered to Vasilica with a look of incredulity on his face. She shared his expression and looked back to the procession to behold a massive, gilded platform that seemed to glide over the sea of Faceless, suspended on their backs and shoulders.

"You know that horrible feeling you get whenever those things are around?" Vasilica asked. Lavinia nodded. "Can the people not feel it?"

Three figures sat in beautiful thrones upon the platform. A being sitting in the highest of the three seats was clad in shining armor that looked as if it were crafted from nothing but crystal and light twisting around his limbs. A beautiful mask that morphed into a towering silver crown adorned his head; the armor was fit for one man only: the man this land falsely hailed as their god. The other two were clad in far less resplendent attire, instead wearing dark black robes and intricate crimson masks beneath their hoods.

"Thanatan," Lavinia whispered.

"Isn't it wonderful?" a random Than said near them. Lavinia stared at the woman until she took the hint and left her alone.

"Recognize his friends?" Aleksander asked. He turned his head to see Lavinia glaring at one of the robed figures.

"Yes, yes I do," Lavinia said through a snarl.

On Thanatan's left side sat the assassin that had slain several of the Mistresses of Dusk, and on the god's right, the woman known only as the Magistrate. Behind Thanatan's platform walked five warriors in spirit armor just like Valakor's.

"I really don't want to have to fight *them*," Vasilica muttered into Aleksander's ear. He gave a slow nod in agreement.

"What was the last parade for again?" Vasilica asked. "This is literally the same thing but with *him* on a platform."

It had not been long since they had watched a similar procession welcoming the Magistrate into the city. Before Aleksander could reply, cheers erupted from the crowd as Thanatan's platform passed by, carrying him through the gates of Verahim's palace.

A soothing voice swept over the crowd, speaking to each mind in attendance. Aleksander looked to Lavinia and then to Vasilica, hoping the Magistrate wasn't able to sense their true intentions with her immense powers of telepathy.

*"Be at peace, you who fear. Behold the return of your god."*

Almost at once, most of the crowd dropped to one knee, and many of the Faceless who were not carrying Thanatan's platform began to disperse into the crowd. Aleksander, Lavinia, and Vasilica decided to bow to blend in with Thanatan's devoted. Aleksander caught Lavinia's eye with a look of panic.

*"There are those among you who do not believe in our master's offer of peace. If you believe and trust in our god, you will have nothing to fear of the Pure."*

At once, the Faceless in the crowd began to claw at those that did not bow. A terrible scream went up from the multitude, but it was soon replaced with an eerie, unnatural silence.

*"These screams are not but the sound of disloyalty and chaos being silenced. Those who truly love Thanatan are safe from this cleansing. Do not fear. Even those that fall shall serve you in death, as is Thanatan's way.*

*They have been purified, and you have heard the Pures' voices saying that he is coming. But now, rejoice! For he is here!"*

Aleksander grabbed Lavinia's arm, and she met his gaze, the same urgency to flee evident on her face. Vasilica gestured with her head as the Faceless, or the Pure, as the Magistrate called them, hewed down the few nonbelievers in the crowd. Hundreds lay dead, but they were few compared to the tens of thousands of people in the city bowing. Thanatan truly had won the hearts and minds of his people.

A pair of Faceless in bloodied robes stalked through the crowd, passing by those with bowed heads. They were only a few rows away when Vasilica gazed into Lavinia's eyes as if trying to send her a mental message that they needed to flee. The creatures turned toward their grotesque heads toward the trio.

"They know," Aleksander muttered into Lavinia's ear.

Several Faceless stepped toward them from all directions. Their slow pace quickened until they were in an all-out sprint toward their prey.

"What do we do?" Vasilica whispered.

"Go!" shouted Aleksander, throwing a ball of flame into the chest of the nearest robed Faceless, setting its fine garb ablaze. The trio pushed through the crowd to flee.

"Grab them!" cried someone close behind. Lavinia extended her bladed wings to fend off the angry mob, which only angered Thanatan's followers even more.

"Night Witches!" cried one villager.

"Go back to San-gara!" shouted another.

Lavinia cringed at the mispronunciation and the slur, grabbed Aleksander by the arm, and along with Vasilica, shot into the air as the citizens loyal to Thanatan began to pommel them with rocks.

"*You will not escape the Pure,*" the Magistrate's voice echoed through Aleksander's mind.

At first, he assumed the message was sent to everyone in the crowd, but a second sentence rang through his skull, one that began by addressing him by his real name, not the name carved into his arm.

"*You cannot escape, Xanthurias Romus. You cannot hide.*"

The words rang through his mind with a such ferocity that he thought his head would split. The Magistrate knew his name—his true name. Terror filled his soul, and he debated telling the others, but now was not the time. It would have to remain secret for now.

They soared above the city, able to evade the Pure chasing them, eventually landing near the Gates of Romiton.

"There aren't any guards on the walls," Aleksander noted. "Do you think they've already been replaced by the Faceless?"

"Absolutely," Lavinia said.

"How much longer until we are supposed to meet the brother of the Empress?" Vasilica asked. "We need to get out of here!"

Lavinia glanced toward a clocktower jutting out of a shamble of dilapidated buildings.

"Fifteen minutes."

"Right on time, then," Aleksander said. "Come on, Pol…"

"We can't leave Rayshel. Not here," Lavinia said.

Aleksander's heart thundered in his chest at the words; it seemed like an eternity ago that Mara had been left behind, and that moment had haunted him every day since. He couldn't allow a similar fate to befall Rayshel or Pol.

"Stay here. Don't leave Pol until we can't wait any longer!" Aleksander said, running in the direction of the healing center Pol had described.

Lavinia and Vasilica waited in anxious silence for ten minutes. The hand of the clock moved again, but Pol did not appear.

"Don't worry. She'll be okay. Aleksander will bring her back," Vasilica said. Lavinia nodded, her façade of apathy and stoicism crumbling away to reveal her concern.

When three minutes were left before they were supposed to meet him, Aleksander returned with Rayshel, who was wrapped in a thick blanket.

"Thank the goddesses," Lavinia said, rushing to Rayshel, who greeted her with a hug.

"You came back for me," Rayshel whispered as Lavinia reciprocated the hug.

"Were you worried I wouldn't?" Lavinia asked.

"Of course not," Rayshel responded with a wide smile.

"Do you think they got him?" Vasilica asked. "Mara will not be happy to hear we lost her brother!"

Aleksander glanced at his shoes and paced anxiously toward the wall and back.

"No, I don't," Aleksander said. "He's resourceful, but—"

"You think he joined them," Lavinia said, her voice cold.

Aleksander did not answer.

The clock's hand moved again.

No Pol.

"We can't wait any longer," Lavinia said, turning to Aleksander. "I'm so sorry, but we'll have to—"

They had waited ten minutes longer than their original plan. Aleksander glanced over his shoulder to see if Pol had arrived, and his countenance fell as the swarm of Faceless swept through the streets toward them.

And then he ran for his life.

# CHAPTER TWENTY-TWO

# THE VOICE OF AN ANGEL

*"You cannot escape, Xanthurias Romus. You cannot hide."*

The words echoed through Aleksander's mind, haunting his restless sleep. The images more vivid than dreams began to flit through his mind again, and he fell not to sleep, but into a deep trance as they overtook his entire existence.

## ELEVEN YEARS AGO

The prince's mother ran her fingers through his hair and hummed a familiar tune, a beautiful one from his childhood. The song had no words, but it had a way of soothing the monster of anxiety in his chest. His eyelids grew heavy.

When the prince awoke several hours later, his mother was gone. He didn't remember her leaving, but he had a warm blanket draped over him that hadn't been there when he had fallen asleep.

Even afflicted with her illness, she was so good to him. He dropped his feet out of bed and slipped on a tunic and some good shoes. He rubbed his eyes and made his way toward the kitchens. Perhaps, he would ask the palace chefs to prepare a special breakfast for his mother, something different from the stuff they fed her in the palace healing center. According to the clocks, it was already morning despite the dark rainclouds hiding the sun.

Xanthurias heard a commotion around the corner and decided to go take a look before popping into the kitchen; perhaps one of the cats he and Verahim let into the castle had knocked down another painting. It wouldn't be the first time, and he laughed, hoping it wouldn't be the last time either.

He dropped the candle tray against the opulent rug beneath his feet as a wave of realization washed over him. He shook his head in denial as he met a group of mourners dressed in black gathered outside the healing center.

"So sorry for your loss, prince," said one of them.

He shook his head again and ran to the door, heart pounding and tears threatening to break forth from their dams.

"Prince Xanthurias!" called a guard, taken aback.

Xanthurias shook the lock on the door and looked to the soldier to help him open it, not a single word slipping from his lips. The guard exchanged a worried glance with his companion, and they tried to escort the prince away.

At that moment, the door opened, and the wailing mourners fell silent, bowing themselves to the ground as a group emerged from the hospital. At the same moment, one of the two guards hurried toward the rug set ablaze by the fallen candle. The corridor began to fill with smoke as a procession emerged from the hospital carrying someone draped in a black sheet.

He saw his younger brother, Verahim, red nosed and crying emerge before their father, Romiton, King of Thanatanos. The king had his hand on the side of the stretcher, as if unwilling or perhaps unable to say goodbye. It had to be her. No one else was worthy of this honor. Why hadn't they told him? Why wasn't he there? Why did they let him sleep at a time like this?

Xanthurias broke into a run, sprinting straight through the flames. He choked on smoke and tears, smashed into the guard trying to stamp out the flames, picked himself up, and kept running. He flew down the marble steps two at a time until he reached the great hall's entranceway. The guards saw him coming and opened the way for him.

He didn't stop running. Not until he reached the courtyard. Not at the edge of the palace walls. He drew stares as he rushed through the gate of the royal neighborhood known as the Star of the King and into a crowded marketplace.

Panic took hold as heard someone calling his name. Several guards, by the sound of their familiar voices. He didn't care. He'd lose them in the crowd, and they'd be rid of him. Why hadn't anyone brought him into his mother's chamber as she died? Why?!

He cried out in pain as he tripped over the cobblestone road leading from the marketplace into a sprawling green park. His feet carried him straight through and out the Gates of Romiton at the southern end of Laniras, skinning the flesh on his palms. More stares. He kept going. The gates were wide open, but he had no idea what he'd find outside the walls.

He didn't care. He kept going.

Forests crept up around him, and the guards' voices had long since faded in with the crowd. He'd lost them. He kept going. The mighty River Vah flowed nearby, and he coughed and stumbled onto its banks, feeling exhaustion hit him at the same time grief caught up to him.

A caravan of traders came upon him as he cupped water from the river into his mouth. A man with a wide hat and a stubbly beard approached, holding out his hands.

"You lost, son?" the man asked.

Xanthurias screwed up his face and bolted; he would have to ditch his fine clothes from the castle if he wanted to blend in out here. The traders called out to him, but he ran from them into the forest. He hoped he wouldn't find something that would eat him. He had heard wolves out here at night. Were there bears? Pirates? Verahim had to be lying about that one. Pirates didn't really eat people, did they?

The river widened at this point; the current was swift and looked dangerous. He didn't care. He spied a rickety raft tied to a tree bouncing on the current and boarded it, nearly falling into the water. He let his princely tunic get dirty so he could blend in a bit better until he could find replacements. He untied the poorly tied rope securing his new boat to the shore.

Xanthurias cried out as the river's current carried him downstream. Tears streamed down his face as the river carried him away; he cried until he could cry no more. Soon the river deepened, and he could no longer feel rocks buffeting the bottom of his raft. He coughed and coughed and wept until he felt that he had no more tears left.

His eyes flitted open sometime later; he must have fallen asleep. The fortress was far behind him, and the lush forest seemed foreign to his eyes. He had never ventured this far. Not this far south, anyway. He put his hand over his mouth, a reflexive action, perhaps to prevent vomit that never came or perhaps to show the shock of the situation. He didn't care.

The raft had run aground against a pile of logs that looked like a beaver dam. He wondered if the dam was artificial or not, but—why was he thinking about that when his mother—no, he couldn't think of that. It was too horrible. He'd return to the castle soon when he felt better.

If he ever felt better, that was.

The river buffeted the raft against the dam as he climbed off, and a sigh escaped his lips as he tried to get his bearings. If the sun was setting, that meant…west…? Right? He couldn't remember, but that sounded correct. To the west, or whatever direction that was with the setting sun, was the unfamiliar forest. The river ran north from there. North was easier to remember than east and west. He thought of what towns were south of

Laniras and followed the river. Nitra, maybe. Zinok, and Turnava, too.

The weary prince took a path leading away from the river. He could see smoke coming from a valley nestled in the arms of the forest, and he decided that was where he would go. If it was the nearest town, did that mean he was he still in Thanatanos? He had heard tales of the vile, bloodthirsty creatures that lived past the border. He'd even seen one once; the creatures' queen had met with his father, and he caught a glimpse of her terrible wings.

He shuddered, hoping he wasn't in Sangora. As he crested the ridge, he took in the sight of the town below. Where Laniras felt planned and orderly, the town felt as if someone had shaken up a bowl full of toy houses and dropped them on the floor and built the town wherever they had landed. The jumble of homes was not surrounded by a wall, but the fires looked so warm and inviting. Welcoming, even. Peaceful.

With a deep breath, Xanthurias stepped down the hill. He could hear music now, a plucky and happy tune that seemed to bounce around the village. He was drawn to the music, for he had nowhere else to go. The tune made his head bob up and down with the rhythm, and soon he felt a smile creep onto his face. He could hear voices now, and he could feel his heart beating hard in his chest; would they welcome him?

He found the crowd at the center of town. People were dancing, but not the stuffy, pretentious dancing of the palace. He had never liked the royal balls; his mother always promised to let him stay up late and read legends from the Deadlands if he went to them, so he did, but his feelings about them never changed. The dances always felt so stiff and planned, much like Laniras itself, but this dancing felt alive, happy, and free. These people danced how they wanted to but still seemed to do so along with the happy rhythm and melody.

The dancers and the music seemed like friends, rather than royals and their subjects like back home. On a weatherworn stage at the center of town, a band of musicians played strange string instruments that didn't seem to match one another.

*Oh, come on in, the water's fine,*
*But watch your gold, or I'll make it mine*
*Stop watchin', you can trust me,*
*So, come on in, the water's fine!*

Xanthurias only caught the end of the song, but he smiled and tapped his feet, bouncing his shoulders to the rhythm. These people seemed so happy, free, and unburdened from the cares of life. The townsfolk cheered as the song ended, clapping their hands together. He joined in their elation, feeling rebellious; such a thing would never have been permitted in the courts of Laniras. A subdued round of applause, maybe, but not raucous, unbridled joy like this.

"Thank ye, thank ye!" called the man with the strange string instrument on the stage. "You can forget all 'bout me, because my pluckin' is nothin' to the pipes on this girl! She needs no introducin', 'n' that's the truth!"

"Thank you, thank you!" came a girl's voice. "This is one of my mother's songs—well, her mother's—I guess music runs in the family, but you probably know that better than me. So, let's do this thing!"

The crowd cheered louder than ever, and Xanthurias tried to catch a glimpse of the girl on the stage, but the group standing between him and his goal didn't seem to notice him as he waited for them to move. At long last, he tried to push past but stopped as he felt a shiver run down his spine, for the girl on stage had begun to sing.

I'll be who I am, I'll say what I want
I know who I am, so I'll just be me,
Oh, that's what I'll do, so go ahead and leave
I don't owe you a thing
For who I'll be

Nothin' about you's who I am
I'm free, and that's your fault.
Maybe I should tell you though,
that you won't ever get to call me mine.

Tears streamed down his face. Perhaps it was the song's beauty. Perhaps it was the fact that the girl with the angel's voice had her mother's music—a gift that no one could ever take away. He wiped his tears with his sleeve. Xanthurias closed his eyes and began to sway as the girl continued to sing. He had never heard such a beautiful singing voice in his entire life.

*You know there's nothin' here to save,*
*'cause I'm not your damsel*
*And I'm not in distress*
*maybe I should tell you though,*
*Oh, you don't get to call me mine.*

*Nothin' about you is who I am*
*I'm stronger now, no thanks to you*
*but maybe I should thank you though,*
*'cause I learned to fly.*

She repeated the song once through, and then silence filled the village in the valley. No one spoke, and the only sound that broke the spell was one of the people in the band accidentally twanging their instrument's string. At that moment, everyone broke into boisterous applause.

"Sorry about that folks!" said the man on stage. "We left her for last 'cause I can't top her voice, so I guess I'll just play you all out. Gotta get up early in the mornin' if you're gonna get to another day of farmin' and drinkin'—" The crowd booed. "Sorry, kill the mood? That's what I do best!"

The crowd started to disperse, and Xanthurias felt himself alone, wondering what to do now. The memory of his mother's death had temporarily gone away, but it returned like a wound reopened. He stood like a statue, the only person not moving, for he had nowhere to go.

The runaway prince eventually wandered down a path dotted with homes with thatched roofs and crumbling brick. The rest of the village seemed boring in comparison to the atmosphere of the concert, which Xanthurias loved. He slumped into a corner and closed his eyes, hoping to fall asleep.

"She did so good," he heard a woman say.

"We'll have to tell her, but y'know as much as me that she won't be home 'til we're good an' sleepin'," said a man's voice in agreement.

The owners of the voices were coming closer, and their poor grammar grated on Xanthurias's mind, but there was something strangely endearing about it. The voices stopped, and Xanthurias opened one eye. He jumped in surprise as he saw the couple standing over him.

"Oh, hi," he said.

"Well, who's this?" asked the man.

"Now Killian, you can't just ask people who they is," said the woman. "It isn't nice."

"I'm Xanthurias," said the prince. He wondered if he should have used a fake name instead. He winced as woman spoke again.

"Xan-thurras? Like the prince? Romiton's boy?" she asked. "What, he'd be about her age, right? About seventeen?"

"Now Daniela, don't you say it like that. Xan-*thur*-i-as, it's the second syliable what's infacized."

Xanthurias assumed he meant the second syllable was emphasized. Killian was correct, but the grammar still baffled the prince.

"Yeah, like the prince. Common name in Laniras," said Xanthurias. He'd still use the name but ditch his identity as a prince. It wouldn't suit him here.

"Ah, Laniras," said Killian. "Big city always scared me too."

"What're you doin' outside all alone?" asked Daniela. "It's gonna get right cold soon."

"Right cold," Xanthurias repeated before saying softly through a stutter, "I— I don't have anywhere to go."

He felt awkward admitting it out loud and felt like a little child.

"Say, come stay on our couch for a while," said Daniela. "You seem like good people, and you know what we always say about people?"

"Um, no," said Xanthurias.

"You help people!" said Daniela. "If you're good, that is."

"I like to think I am," said Xanthurias.

"No, no, that's not what I meant at all. I meant, if you're good, you help people. You don't only help good people," said the woman. "Even if you're bad people, we'll help you."

"That's very kind," said Xanthurias, getting to his feet. Daniela smiled, and Killian patted him on the back, leading him toward their small home nearby.

"Daniela just done stuffed us a new couch," said Killian as he pushed open the door. "Ah, just like we thought. She ain't home yet. Probably won't be until late."

"Who?" asked Xanthurias.

"Our daughter," said Killian.

"Were you at the concert? She sang the last song. Did a good job, too. It was my mama's song, just like she said," Daniela said, patting the sofa, which looked like it was stuffed with straw. Xanthurias sat, a smile on his face. Killian threw him a flattened pillow.

"Thank you again," Xanthurias said. "I'll try to be out of your hair tomorrow."

"Oh, Xan-*thur*-ias, don't you worry. You clearly out of your comfort zone, 'n' you need someone to keep you safe, that much, we can tell," said Killian. Xanthurias gave a soft, sad smile.

"We'll talk more in the morning," said Daniela, a motherly smile across her face. Xanthurias thanked them both as they shut the door to their bedroom. He caught a glance of a young boy several years younger than himself asleep in a smaller bed near his parents.

Xanthurias hoped to stay awake long enough to meet the girl with the beautiful voice, but he fell asleep almost as soon as his head touched the lumpy pillow. As uncomfortable as he was, he felt safe and was able to fall asleep, though he was plagued by thoughts of the day and of his mother.

The next morning, light streamed through the single window and danced across his face as a light breeze played with the curtains. He realized someone had covered him with a scratchy, stiff blanket sometime during the night, although his feet still stuck out. He sat up awkwardly, listening if his hosts were already awake. He could hear no movement, so he quietly snuck across the small room.

It only took a few steps to cross the entire home. He discovered a small, chipped plate with a chunk of bread and a dab of jam on a plate. Beside it was a scrap of paper with a message scribbled in charcoal:

~~Zanturis~~ ~~Zatasn~~ ~~Zantorius~~ ~~Zantoris~~ ~~Zatorias~~

~~ZATTORUS~~

ZAN-

*i gon owt to farm* <u>*plees eet*</u> *see yu tunit*

*—Killian*

Xanthurias chuckled, a genuine smile crossing his face. The man's spelling, except for his own name, was even worse than his grammar, but the amount of times Killian had clearly tried to spell his name correctly clearly showed the level of care the couple had for him. A stranger. He sat in the wobbly chair next to the table and flipped over the yellowed sheet of paper to see a second message written there.

*xanthurias,*

*killian writes big and wrong and left me no room on the front. we will be at the concert tonite agin after work. see you there. it will be fun so bring a smile*

*--daniela*

Another concert would be wonderful. He wondered how often the town held them. He dipped the bread in the jam and took a bite, the divine taste of strawberries filling his mouth. He paused for a moment, thankful to the strangers. He finished his scant, yet delicious meal and pocketed the note from Killian and Daniela. Peeking his head outside, a neighbor greeted him with a wave. Was it normal for strangers to greet each other? Or for strangers to come in and out of Killian and Daniela's house? The woman didn't even seem worried he was there.

"Excuse me," said the prince.

"Yes, dear?" the woman asked. "Oh, are you one of the boyfriends?"

"One of—what? No. I'm just staying with Killian and Daniela for a while. Do you know where they are?" he asked.

"Same place they always is this time of day. Same place everyone is when they isn't broken like me," said the woman with a chuckle, slapping her hip. Xanthurias winced. "They's farmin'."

"Okay," he said. "Where?"

"Go far's you can see that way." She pointed dramatically with one hand as if directing the traffic of horses and carts in the busy parts of Laniras. "Then you's gonna wanna go far's you can see that way *again*."

"Okay," said Xanthurias.

"So glad you's here. You seem more polite than the last one. Cuter too!" said the woman, winking. Xanthurias winced again.

"Okay," he said again as the woman hobbled off and entered a small shack down a narrow path. Xanthurias was sure he heard the sound of multiple cats as she shut the door.

Xanthurias followed the odd woman's directions, walking as far as he could see out of town. He knew the measurement couldn't be accurate, but he tried to walk in a straight path as far as he could, eventually reaching a low, wide fence that extended as far as the eye could see in either direction. Perhaps that was why the old woman measured with, "as far as you can see."

He climbed the fence and dropped, careful not to twist his ankle as he did so. The warm breeze tousled his hair as he swept his fingers over the tops of the wheat. He kept a straight course, heading directly through the wheat field. If he got lost, at least he'd only need to double back and head the same way he came.

The sun dropped in the sky as he walked; he passed dozens of workers, none of which seemed to know exactly where Killian or Daniela were working. At long last, he spotted a man resembling Killian sweeping the golden grain with a scythe. His suspicions were confirmed as the man raised his hand and called out to him, beckoning him closer with the tool. Xanthurias had never actually set foot on a farm before, and the only place he'd seen scythes were as symbols of death in stories. He hadn't realized until just now that it was actually a tool used for farming, and not reaping the souls of the dead.

"Xan-*thur*-as!" called Killian, a wide grin across his face. "New scythe! Ya like it?"

"I do, Killian!" called Xanthurias.

Killian rested on the handle of the tool as the prince approached, gesturing to the path of hewn grain behind him.

"I thought you'd like some help," Xanthurias said.

He wasn't sure how farming even worked, but it couldn't be too hard. Why else were there so many farmers in town?

"If you'd like, you can gather the wheat here into sheaves. Here..." Killian showed Xanthurias how to bundle the wheat and tie it before tossing it into a cart. "Been doing this alone since my boy hurt his foot. See that hole there? Twisted it right good stepping in that hole. Don't do the same, and also don't guide the cart into it, or you'll have a hard time getting' it out— fear that hole!"

Xanthurias laughed and began bundling the hewn wheat just as Killian had shown him, or so he thought. Killian quickly corrected his method, smiled, and gave him a thumbs-up. Xanthurias spent the next several hours in relative silence, gathering the wheat as Killian cut through it. He could see dozens of other workers in the field doing the same.

"What happens to all this wheat?" Xanthurias asked.

"What happens—" Killian repeated, stopping mid swing. "It gets eaten, Xan."

"I mean, yeah, but—" Xanthurias said.

"We grow most of the wheat for the capital here. We've got good land here. We don't get to rotate the crops like I'd like, since they always want us to grow grain, but it's still good ground. Good dirt, you know?"

Xanthurias had never wondered what made dirt 'good' or where the food that appeared in the kitchens came from; it had simply always been there.

The prince spoke with Killian for the remainder of the day about farming techniques and life in the town, which he informed him was called Cineca. Xanthurias had never heard of the village, but apparently it was a very important agricultural town in Thanatanos. He tried to keep the conversation away from his own life, but eventually, as he dreaded, Killian asked the question he dreaded.

"So, where you from? Got parents that are missin' you, I assume? Maybe even some brothers 'n' sisters?"

Xanthurias was silent for a few moments before responding. "I have a brother. Lost my mom," he said at last. Killian nodded.

"Lost my own not long ago," the man responded. "How're ya takin' it?"

The prince knew not how to respond, and tears filled his eyes as he tried to tie the wheat. His fingers trembled, and the sheave spilled all over the ground. What was he doing here? Was he just in denial over his mother's death? Should he go home?

"Sorry." He tried to gather the wheat back together but felt a firm hand on his shoulder, and he stopped.

"Boy, don't you apologize," said Killian. "Don't you ever apologize for how you're feelin'." Xanthurias smiled and tried to hide his tears but knew it was in vain. "Say, didja get our note this mornin'? Daniela wrote about the concert tonight, yeah?"

"Yeah, I'll definitely go." Xanthurias smiled, excited for the night to come. "And thank you for the breakfast."

"Oh, it's nothin'," said Killian with a wink.

Xanthurias knew otherwise. Jam didn't keep well if it wasn't kept cold, and it was hard to make—or so he assumed.

"How 'bout I walk you home. Sun's getting' tired, and I reckon it's high time for a reward for a good first day. The town concert's how I get through hard days," said the man.

"Do they happen every day?" Xanthurias asked, hopeful. Killian shook his head.

"Nah, but couple times a week. If you got lucky, two in two days," said Killian. "We have more in harvest season to keep up the moral." He knew he meant morale, not moral, but kept silent.

"That sounds nice," he said instead, packing the last of the wheat into the cart. He helped Killian guide the cart home, and eventually they met Daniela, who was playing a fiddle for a group of workers nearby.

Together, the trio made their way as far as their eyes could see twice until they reached Cineca. They put away the farming equipment in a community shed, but Killian brought the new scythe into his home; it was clearly a prized possession.

Guilt crept into Xanthurias's heart.

These people had so little, and he had been given so much in his life. He was a prince, heir to the entire kingdom. The people of Cineca worked so that the people in the capital of Laniras could have food. Their lives were devoted to a city they may never see. It made him hate Laniras and wish the people could keep their grain for themselves.

A thought crossed his mind. Surely, his father was looking for him. There had to be a reward for his safe return. A reward of gold. Maybe he and Killian could take a trip to Laniras and let him keep the gold and build a nicer home or buy a horse or mule so that he didn't have to push the cart by himself. A thought entered his mind. He could make a difference for people like Killian and Daniela, and in that moment, he decided he would return to Laniras.

Rosy clouds of crimson and purple signaled the end of the workday as the sun dipped behind the horizon, casting light that reminded Xanthurias of the stained-glass windows in the palace.

He accompanied Killian and Daniela to the concert, wondering when his new friends, if he could call them that, ate dinner. Did they eat dinner? More guilt. He hoped he hadn't eaten all their bread. He followed Killian, Daniela, and the flow of other citizens of Cineca to the center of town.

The prince's heart thundered in his chest. He hoped to hear the girl from last night again, but he told himself that even if he didn't, he'd be happy just dancing and being free of royalty for the night. The simpleness of life here truly spoke to him, finally free of the strange customs he had grown up with as a prince.

To his delight, with no introduction, Killian and Daniela's daughter stepped onto stage. Apparently, the town was so accustomed to the tradition of the concert, that they didn't even need any type of opening ceremony or welcome speech, or perhaps, she was the one in charge of the festivities tonight. Everyone seemed tired from a long day of working the fields, himself included. Perhaps, that was a good idea.

He had arrived early enough this time that he was able to have a good view of the stage, the bands, and perhaps most importantly, the girl with the angelic voice. She ran her hand through her messy raven's feather black hair and took a deep breath before she began to sing. A soft song.

Tranquil, and hypnotic. Almost a lullaby…

*Whatever it takes, my love*
*I'll hold your heart with mine*
*And from your side ne'er I'll depart*
*Even when my heart breaks, my dove*
*Oh, there with you, yes, there I'll be*

*Whatever it takes*
*My dear sweetheart*
*For both our sakes*
*Far from death's black dart*
*There with me, yes, you'll be*
*Whatever it takes*

*Whatever it takes, my heart*
*I'll hold your hand with mine,*
*Even when I'm dead and gone,*
*Oh, there with you, yes, I'll be,*
*And you'll be there with me,*
*Whatever it takes.*

The crowd was silent for her entire song but swayed with the melody as it danced through the air, a ballad to the dying day. A love song for no one and everyone.

The girl stepped away without another word and disappeared behind the stage. Everyone clapped and hooted and hollered as she left. A man with a guitar called out and said, "I thought we'd give you your dessert first tonight. Something sweet before our saltier tunes!" Laughter filled the town square. "Now, you might recognize this one: it's called '*The Frog King*'?"

Xanthurias snaked his way through the crowd as the lively song, one about a greedy frog who sat on the throne of a kingdom and ate tributes of flies brought to him by his human subjects. Xanthurias wondered if the 'Frog King' referred to King Valistaran Talohir or his own father, Romiton Romus. Both were likely.

He smiled at the silly lyrics, pushing his way through the crowd until he found a path curving to the back of the stage. No one seemed to mind, and others were mingling with musicians ready to take the stage. He wondered if Daniela ever performed here. He waited his turn in a crowd waiting to speak with the singer as the Frog King song ended to the laughter of everyone in the square.

Soon enough, Xanthurias found himself face to face with the singer with the beautiful voice. He smiled and gave an awkward wave, which she returned with a light chuckle.

"Hi, I'm Xanthurias," said the prince.

"Hi, Xanthurias," the singer said with a welcome smile and a tilt of the head. "My name is Mara."

# CHAPTER TWENTY-THREE
# SHATTERED FREEDOM



Xanthurias had no idea what else to say. Mara brushed the dark hair out of her eyes and began to speak, but words blurted out of the prince's mouth as if without permission before he could stop them.

"I like your music!"

"Thank you," she said, "but to be honest, it's my mother's music."

"It was still good—from you," Xanthurias stammered.

"Thank you again," she said then added with a wink, "how was the blanket?"

"The blanket?" Xanthurias asked.

"You took my bed last night, you know," Mara said. The prince's eyes widened in embarrassment.

"Oh no, I am so sorry," Xanthurias replied in horror. "So, so, so, sorry!"

"It's okay, really!" said Mara. "You seemed cold, though, so I let you use my blanket, too. You new around here? We don't get new people here often—except the old-fashioned way."

She winked.

"The old-fashioned—" Xanthurias began. His face turned bright red. "Oh. Oh dear—when I took your bed, that's not what I was—"

"I know, I know. You're fine." She motioned over her shoulder with a laugh as she walked away from the town square and asked, "So, who are you, Xanthurias?"

He took that as permission to follow her. His heart raced.

"I'm Xanthurias," he repeated. "Just Xanthurias."

"Not a common name around here. Kind of a pretentious one, too," Mara said playfully. "You can be honest, you know. My parents clearly trust you, but they trust everyone."

"My mother died, and I couldn't handle it," he said, deciding to believe her.

"So, you just left the rest of your family behind?" Mara asked. "Don't you think they'll miss you? I mean, they already lost your mom, what'll they think when their son disappears too?"

"I know, I'll go back." He sighed.

"I know you will. I'm not trying to pressure you, you know. I don't even know you—yet," Mara said. "I just know they must be worried is all. But that doesn't mean you can't have a good time before you leave, right? My parents would try to help so when you go back it's a happy event, not a sad one. You can go back when you're ready. But Xanthurias, if where you came from isn't a good place, you never have to go back there."

The words had weight. He *wasn't* happy there.

"Working with your father in the field actually took my mind off it," Xanthurias said.

"Yeah, it's mindless work, isn't it?" Mara said with a laugh. "Maybe that's why everyone does it. Thankfully, I have other talents—less sweaty ones."

"People pay you to sing?" Xanthurias asked. He wondered where Mara was leading him.

"I mean, not directly, but people do donate to the musicians and singers, and we split it after every night. It's decent money, and it's enough that I don't have to farm if I don't want to. My brother Pol doesn't mind farming though, and my father can't see himself doing anything else. Which is good, because neither one of them are musical in any way."

"That's amazing!"

"You want to get out of here?" Mara asked. Xanthurias indicated that he did, so she said her goodbyes and led Xanthurias several miles outside of town toward a forested hill. Their trek got gradually steeper until Mara crawled through a hole in the thick brush. He hesitated, not wanting to tear his clothes on thorns and brambles. Mara's bright eyes peeked out, and she asked, "Coming?"

Xanthurias nodded and followed her through the brambles; they crawled for a short distance through a tunnel made by some unknown beast, and when they emerged into the light,

Xanthurias beheld a secluded, idyllic valley surrounded by the hills and thick woods, and ahead of them, a steep incline.

"Wow!" Xanthurias exclaimed, taking in the view. He had never seen a place so beautiful and free.

"I had planned to come here alone tonight, but I'm happy to have some company," Mara said. "So, are you coming?"

Xanthurias grinned, nodded, and hurried after her as she ran down the trail, following the stream that snaked its way down the mountain alongside a deep gulch. She was obviously well acquainted with the trail, as she knew just where to step. In time, the trail ended with a steep drop.

"Now what?" Xanthurias asked.

The dark, glassy water below reflected the sunset's golden hues on the clouds above, creating the illusion of a lake of fire.

"Now we fly, of course!"

Xanthurias snapped back to attention, his eyes wide. He pointed to the water far below, and Mara nodded with a teasing smile.

Mara took a deep breath, and with a running start, she took the plunge. Xanthurias rushed to the cliff to watch as she extended her legs so when she hit the water, she shot though the surface. She emerged a few moments later, soaked and smiling.

Xanthurias hesitated again. It seemed a common thing for him, and he hated it. He shut his eyes and heard Mara's voice sing up to him, "Come on in, the water's fine!"

"Gonna steal my gold?" Xanthurias called, referring to the words of the song he had heard when he first arrived in town.

"Oh, there are easier ways to get that away from you," Mara replied, now floating on her back.

The prince took a deep breath and imitated Mara by running from the back of the path before leaping into the gulch. He could feel the air flowing through his hair, and time seemed to stop; he felt weightless and free from worry and care. And then he hit the water.

He hit it hard.

His feet and legs did not slice through the surface like Mara had; instead, his bent knees and flailing arms caused a wild splash. He heard Mara's laughter just before the water swallowed him. His throat filled with water, and as he emerged, he spewed it up in a spray of coughing.

"You did it!" Mara exclaimed, still floating on her back. Xanthurias kicked his feet. He had been trained to swim, but never in a cold mountain pool like this.

"I did!" Xanthurias replied, swimming nearer to Mara. "Not very well, but I did it!"

"I like you, Xanthurias. You know, you're the first person to trust me enough to jump from there. Everyone else is too chicken."

"Wait, was there another way down?"

Mara laughed, a bright, cheery sound. "Of course, dumby."

She flipped over and swam away, clearly the superior swimmer. As he tried to catch her, she flipped her hair back and forth, spraying him with lake water. She closed the distance between them with two strokes and wrapped her arms around his neck.

At first, Xanthurias panicked, thinking she intended to weigh him down in the dark pool, but those thoughts fell out of his head as he gazed into her eyes and felt her body pressed against his. He wrapped his arms around her and leaned forward, and then—

She dunked him underwater.

"You're kidding me," Xanthurias said with a cheerful, but disappointed laugh as he emerged. "You ruined a *perfect* moment!"

"Or did I make it even more perfect?" Mara asked, floating away on her back. She lifted her head to look in his direction, and they both laughed as he tried and failed to catch her.

They enjoyed each other's company until the sunset's painted colors drained away, replaced by the inky darkness of night.

Mara held her breath and dove beneath the surface of the cold water one last time before leaving. Xanthurias too dipped beneath the surface and opened his eyes but couldn't see anything. He surfaced, and Mara reached out to mess up his wet hair. He breathed in the night air as they smiled, carefree and happy. This was the life he wanted. Not the life of palaces and rules, protocol, and stiff, boring people. He wanted freedom and joy, a life like this. He never wanted to forget this moment.

Xanthurias followed Mara as she clambered out of the water and began to brush her hands through her hair to dry it.

"Well?" she asked, squeezing the water from her dark locks.

"That was amazing," he said, smiling. "Thank you, Mara. You and your family are so wonderful. I can't even describe it."

"Well, try," Mara said. He began to speak, but she waved her hand with a chuckle. "I'm joking, Xan."

She reached into the hollow of a dead tree and pulled out a set of folded, dry clothes.

"No dry clothes for me in there, I assume?" Xanthurias asked with a wry smile.

"You can try these ones if you'd like. You'd look cute in this one." She held up the shirt, which was embroidered with flowers.

"Oh, you're probably right, but I think it definitely suits you better," Xanthurias replied.

She laughed and twirled her finger, a sign for him to turn away. As he did so, he heard the sound of wet clothes hitting the earth. In that moment, all he wanted in the entire world was to turn around.

"The concert's probably over by now." She finished lacing up her the flowery tunic and stowed her wet outfit inside the tree. "Let's get home. I'd like for you to meet my little brother Pol and some of my friends from the village. I think they'll help you feel more at home here. You know, until you decide to leave us."

"I'd love that," Xanthurias said, gazing into her crystal blue eyes. "I mean, not leaving you, but—"

"I know." She smiled.

He craved that same joy again, that light in her eyes. His heart leapt in his chest as she took his hand and led him up the hill back to the village.

Before going back to Killian and Daniela's small home, Mara rapped on the thin wooden door of another hovel near the outskirts of the town, and a face of a gaunt, malnourished girl of about their same age opened the door. Xanthurias frowned as her hand slipped from his.

"Oh, hi, Eva! I was expecting Lukas. I thought you'd still be at the healing center in Nitra! When did you get back?"

"Yesterday. I'm doing a bit better," the girl said with a nod. "Home now, at least! It's so good to see you."

"That's so good to hear. Well, I'd like you to meet a new friend of mine. He'll be staying with me for a while."

"It's nice to meet you," said Eva. She gestured to his soaked clothes. "I see Mara's taken you to her favorite place!"

"Yes, she did. She and her family have been very welcoming," Xanthurias said.

It was awkward meeting a new person, and it almost felt like Mara was showing him off as the novel stranger in Cineca. Small towns sure were strange. Happy, but strange.

Eva called for her brother, and the young man named Lukas appeared. He seemed to be in better health than his sister and had the look of the other farmers, thickly built with broad shoulders. Mara gave him a quick hug, and for whatever reason, Xanthurias felt a twinge of jealousy, which he knew he did not deserve to feel. He had just come into these peoples' lives, and of course, they were entitled to their existing relationships.

"Good to meet you," Lukas said, unknowingly shaking the hand of the heir of Thanatanos.

They spent the rest of that night chatting and laughing with Mara's friends well into the night. When they finally parted ways, Mara led Xanthurias 'home.' Daniela, Killian, and Mara's brother were already asleep when they snuck in.

"You can take the sofa this time," Xanthurias said.

"Oh, thank you for allowing me to use my own bed," Mara said with a playful scowl. Xanthurias smacked himself on the forehead, and Mara laughed as she tossed him the blanket.

The next day was filled with more farming, and Xanthurias longed for the workday to end so that he could see Mara again, but he had decided to help in the fields as much as possible to pay the family back for their kindness. When the sun began to die away, Mara was waiting for him at the fence with a smile and her scratchy blanket. They greeted one another, and she led him north to the rolling hills outside of town.

"Where are we going?" Xanthurias asked.

"Another surprise," Mara replied.

They made their way to the top of the highest of the hills, and Mara spread out the scratchy blanket. She plopped down and lay on her back, and together they watched night wash away the painted colors in the sky, replacing it with millions of glittering stars. For hours, they watched for shooting stars, letting out happy exclamations whenever one raced across the sky.

"It's starting to get cold," Mara said as she scooted closer to Xanthurias. "Should we head home?"

"We don't have to if you don't want to. I mean, I'd like to stay here with you," Xanthurias said awkwardly. "Want to know a secret?"

"That you're loveably awkward?" Mara winked and then flashed a smile. "I already know that."

Xanthurias laughed and gathered a pile of dry sticks, dropping them into a pile in the dirt next to their blanket. Mara watched intently as Xanthurias held his hand aloft, and a few sparks erupted from his palm. Nothing happened, so he tried again, and this time, a thin jet of flame escaped his skin, catching the pile of sticks ablaze.

Mara scooted closer, now lying on her side. Xanthurias sat down cross-legged next to her in the warmth of the fire.

"Can I tell *you* a secret now?" Mara asked.

"Sure," Xanthurias said.

"It's nice to meet someone new." She trailed off, staring into the flames. "I've known everyone in Cineca pretty much my entire life, and the place kind of feels like a bunch of cousins. A bunch of cousins who end up marrying each other and staying here forever. It's nice to meet someone new, someone fun. It's exciting—new secrets, new experiences, it's like a new start."

"Wait a minute, you don't like kissing cousins?" Xanthurias joked. Mara laughed with an exaggerated shake of her head. "That's a joke. Let me be very clear about that. Seriously, I don't kiss my cous—"

"I know, I know."

"But you don't like it here? How can you not?"

"I do, but I want to see the world, you know? I just crave that freedom of getting out, you know?"

"Yeah, I get that. This place feels pretty free to me, though," Xanthurias replied, thinking of his life pent up in Laniras.

"Sometimes I feel alone even though I'm surrounded by so many people," Mara said in a soft tone.

"I'm sorry," Xanthurias said, touching her hand. "Well, what do you say, want to go see the world with me?"

"I would like that very much," Mara said. "You know, my brother said there are camel-people in Kurash, and the women in Sangora have wings!"

"I had a Sangoran language class in school. I'm not very good, but that'll help us in our quest," Xanthurias said.

"Oh, so it's a quest now?" Mara asked with a laugh. "I assume that means we have to fight monsters, and I'll have to save you."

"Isn't the story usually that the knight saves the princess?"

"Yes, exactly," Mara said.

She smiled, and it took Xanthurias a moment before he understood, but when he did, they both burst out laughing.

"My hero," Xanthurias said with a grin. "Oh, and about that—"

"I'd actually be a knight saving a prince?" Mara asked with a knowing grin.

"Well, you see—"

"Don't worry, your secret is safe with me," Mara said.

"When'd you figure it out?"

"Pretty much when you said your name was Xanthurias and looked like you'd never farmed a day in your life."

"That's fair," Xanthurias said with another laugh.

He settled down on the blanket next to the fire, but more importantly, next to Mara. He raised his hand and threw a ball of flame into the sky, which exploded in a shower of sparks.

"Fireworks!" Mara exclaimed as Xanthurias launched a second fireball.

As the sparks rained down around them, Xanthurias turned his head to see Mara gazing up at the stars, a content smile stretched across her face and her hands behind her head. He leaned forward and planted a quick kiss on her cheek.

"Prince *Xanthurias!*" Mara exclaimed in a mockingly pretentious voice. She snuggled closer to him with a wide grin. "Kissing the village girl! Oh, the *scandal!*"

Xanthurias felt his heart nearly explode out of his chest as Mara brushed his cheek with the tips of her fingers. She swept the dark hair from her face, and she leaned in, planting a brief kiss of her own on his lips.

When they pulled away, they each let out a nervous chuckle and smiled at one another saying nothing for a long while.

"I, uh, well, I think I really like you," Xanthurias stammered.

"Well, that's good, because I think I really like you back," Mara said, tousling his hair then added with a laugh, "Not quite sure why."

He grinned, and she nestled in close, lying her head on his chest. He was sure she could feel his thundering heart as he felt her fingers intertwine with his, resulting in a bigger smile than any he could remember.

Together, they fell asleep under a blanket of stars.

Days turned into weeks, and weeks into months. The days grew shorter and colder, and the harvest season soon ended. Xanthurias wondered what the farmers would do when there was no more wheat to harvest, but Killian taught him all about planting new seeds.

Mara and Xanthurias stole every moment they could together to plan their grand adventure, all the while enjoying one another's company at their favorite places such as the hidden lake and the rolling hills, but also just at home with her family. Of course, Xanthurias loved attending her concerts most of all and always got there early enough to be at the front of the crowd. Mara's friends would often accompany them, but he always preferred the time they got to spend alone.

Mara's parents rarely said anything about Xanthurias returning home, and for the first time in years, he was truly happy. Although, he did dread that he would soon overstay his welcome. Perhaps he already had.

One evening in late Autumn ended with a lively concert, one of the last few before winter's chill set in and the weather became too cold for them to be held. Mara stepped off stage after her final song and rushed to Xanthurias, who had brought her a steaming cup of tea he had kept warm with his powers.

"Thank you!" she exclaimed, taking a long sip. "How'd I do?"

"I could have listened to you for hours," Xanthurias said. "I never thought any rendition of *The Frog King* could actually sound beautiful, but you smashed it."

Mara beamed from behind the teacup.

At that very moment, screams erupted from the other side of town. Mara whirled around in a flurry of dark hair and dropped her tea.

"We need to get home," Mara said, her heart pounding. Xanthurias nodded. What if enemies of Thanatanos had somehow tracked him here? Or what if his own father was attacking the village, thinking they had kidnapped him?

"Pol," Mara said, her eyes wide.

"What should I do?" Xanthurias asked. "I want to help."

"Please, go find Pol and get him to safety. I'll help my parents get away. Pol said this morning he wasn't going to the concert, so he should be home," she said in a worried tone.

Xanthurias nodded, and they split up. The prince hurried to Mara's parents' home; fires were already burning around the town, and when Xanthurias reached his destination, he covered his mouth in shock.

The door and much of the front wall of the home had been smashed in. He ran inside and shouted for Pol, but the house was empty.

"Oh no," Xanthurias whispered. "Oh no, oh no…"

He shook his head in disbelief. Things like this were not supposed to happen to good places like this. Not to good people. He looked around and saw no sign of a struggle. No broken glass or blood, nothing in the house out of place except the missing front door.

While he was inside, it had begun to rain. He ran from the home back toward the center square to find Mara, but he only found a mob of townsfolk fighting a group of armed men; beyond the angry crowd, a small caravan of horses and carts were carrying away prisoners bound in chains.

Through the crowd, he caught a glimpse of Mara holding a pitchfork, rushing at a soldier wearing the colors of Talohira. He ran with all haste toward them as Mara smashed the edge of the tool against the soldier's neck, knocking him to the ground. As Mara raised her weapon, the man leapt up and brought his fist up, smashing her in the jaw. She tumbled to the ground, and the soldier raised his sword to smite her.

"No!" Xanthurias cried as he approached.

The soldier brought his sword down toward Mara's throat, and Xanthurias let a burst of flame erupt from his palm, scorching the soldier's side. He began to roll to put out the flames, and the distraction bought Mara time to scoop up the man's fallen sword. She took Xanthurias's hand and ran.

She watched the soldiers retreat, following their allies, which were now far enough away that it was impossible for the villagers to follow.

"Slavers!" Mara said, answering the question on the prince's mind. "When they come, we can usually bribe them off with treasures, food, or, well—" She paused. "Well, with whatever we can. It's always horrible, but this—" She covered her eyes with her hands as she began to hyperventilate.

"Your family—are they safe?"

"Mama and pa are, but they took Pol—they took my little brother!" she screamed. Xanthurias recognized the symptoms of a panic attack setting in. He sat next to her.

"I'm so sorry," Xanthurias said. "Can I touch?"

The question felt strange and out of place, but his mother had always asked him the same question during one of his panic attacks back home. Mara nodded, still hyperventilating. He held her close and ran his fingers over her hair to comfort her. Although he couldn't remember the words, he hummed the tune of the first song he ever heard her sing. After a few moments, she was able to calm herself down, and she grabbed his hand. He, however, did not feel any calmer. He wondered if they had taken Pol thinking he was the missing prince. Guilt filled his soul.

"Lukas," she said through tears. "They got him too!"

Xanthurias did not know if she meant that Lukas had been killed in the attack or if the slavers had taken him away. He didn't ask. Instead, he shut his eyes tightly as if he would be able to shut out the chaos and the waking nightmare.

"Find me," Mara whispered. Xanthurias nodded and pressed his forehead against hers. They knew what was coming.

As Cineca was consumed by chaos, Xanthurias and Mara held each other close. She wrapped her arms around him and refused to let go, knowing what would happen if she did.

And then the slavers forced them apart.

Aleksander awoke in a cold sweat. These were not the records of people long dead implanted by the Secret Keepers of Kurash. No, these were his own memories. He thought he had remembered everything after the Battle of Laniras, but new images kept creeping back into his mind to fill the gaps, and existing memories faded like forgotten dreams.

Memories of his time with Mara had been entirely new to him until that moment, but they were now etched in his mind. Forever, he hoped. He began to sob as the guilt of somehow forgetting such beautiful memories with her consumed him. He cursed himself and whatever treachery had taken those cherished moments from him.

More dark and shattered memories filled his mind. He remembered being taken aboard a massive slave ship—the Arcship, they had called it. He had no idea how many years he, Mara, and Pol had spent as prisoners on the ship.

Other flitting memories of fear and pain at the hands of the vile men stabbed at his brain. However, the most disturbing memory that haunted his soul was of being punished after a failed escape attempt; he had been forced into a cell no bigger than a coffin while having to endure the sounds of Mara's screams in the next room as the slavers tortured her.

He knew that those screams would haunt him forevermore.

Aleksander wept for them both, but still he could not remember how he had escaped the Arcship. He knew he had done so before Mara and Pol had been sold into the Talohiran slave camp, and a fading memory hinted to him that he had abandoned her there. So many questions plagued him. Had he abandoned her on purpose? How long did she remain on the ship? And most of all, what else had happened to her?

Guilt filled his soul. He hadn't even recognized Mara when fate had reunited them in the Talohiran slave camp—what had gone through her mind after all they'd been through and after he had finally fulfilled his promise to find her, only to greet her as a stranger?

His gut twisted again, and tears flowed freely down his cheeks. Again, he asked himself about what horrors and grief

Mara had been forced to survive during her years aboard the Arcship. He despised himself for not knowing the truth about the darkness of those long, painful years of her life.

The details were cloudy in his mind, and he fought to catch hold of them, but they slipped from his grasp like a dream melting away. Perhaps one day, he thought, he would be able to remember what had happened between the day the slavers took Mara and Pol away and the day he awoke with no memories to a world on fire.

He was Prince Xanthurias Romus, and he was ashamed.

Another series of memories crept into his mind, but this time, they were memories granted by the Secret Keepers of Kurash of things he had long wondered, but never known.

Bitter tears continued to stream down his face as he learned the truth: King Romiton had recruited a young boy to pose as Xanthurias. That young man had then grown up in the identity of another who never returned home and had forgone his own life. For what? To save the king the shame and embarrassment that he had lost the prince on the same day as the death of the queen? A new Xanthurias had been created. The great lie of King Romiton Romus. A dark secret to maintain a royal bloodline.

The very same person, the fake Xanthurias Romus, whose true identity not even the Secret Keepers knew, had been slain years later by none other than Mara Bartunek in her quest for the throne of Sangora.

However haunting the memories were, one recurring thought tore into Aleksander's skull more than any other.

Had he led the slavers to Cineca all those years ago?

# CHAPTER TWENTY-FOUR
# THE QUEEN OF DOFTAAN

The audacity of the question! Queen Florenta slammed her fist on the railing of her palace balcony. Below, a contingent of representatives from various organizations responsible for distributing the nation's news to the different Sangoran states had gathered for the weekly conversation with their new queen.

"No, I certainly do not take responsibility at all!" she shouted. The entire crowd recoiled as she increased in volume and intensity yet again. "My predecessor's failures are what have brought this affliction on us, not anything that I have or have not done!"

"But the Faceless virus wasn't even in Sangora at the time of Empress Mara's reign," one of the representatives pointed out. "Can you please explain how—"

"Do not speak her name!" Florenta retorted. "Yes, I'll explain how if you will give me the blasted chance. Always interrupting—it's obnoxious. Bad form. The Fallen One failed in securing our border with Thanatanos. The outbreak stemmed from the ruins of Nitra, a city that *she* destroyed during the Thannish-Talohiran war. She opened the borders after the war. She let refugees from both countries in. It is *her* fault. Mine, you say… No, no. I haven't started any wars! These people coming in are dirty, filthy animals that bring nothing but problems, disease, and death with them."

"I apologize for misspeaking and for using the Fallen One's name," the representative said. "I thank you, my queen, for answering my question."

Florenta made a sound caught between a snarl and a sniff then gripped the railing with both hands, much as a passionate speaker would do at a podium. She eyed the group and pointed a thick finger at another messenger to speak.

"A month ago, you called this plague a harmless sickness that will go away like any other. Can you elaborate on this statement? Have Doftaan's medical professionals agreed with your comments?" another representative asked, brushing her quill against her face as she prepared to jot down notes on a stack of parchment. "What about the recent outbreak of the virus and Bloodvines in Kaljacjana?"

"Pah! I stand by what I said. Have we not dealt with seasonal sicknesses that come and go every winter? Common knowledge. This is absolutely no different. It is a common affliction no worse than a common pox! A new one, and perhaps a worse one, but we are handling it. Why don't you report on how well we're handling the outbreak in Krim?"

"Well, Krim is an island, and the plague hasn't spread there yet, but the death tolls in Doftaan from the Kaljacjana and Dubovparkh districts in particular are already in the thousands. And we don't even know how bad it is in outlying states like Terman and Dashga," the first messenger said. "The plague has spread because of travel between states, so what is your excellency's council doing to stop this spread?"

"I've told you! I have given the word for my new Mistresses of Dusk to close all borders between their states. Krim is safe because it is a militarized state with closed borders, and I've kept it so. Literally an island in the sea. Am I not correct? An example for the rest of us to bar entry to outsiders, surely! This will contain the plague, and no one else will get sick, I assure you of that," Florenta replied.

"Your excellency, a source of mine has told me that that is not true," the second messenger said. "It's widely known that the borders are all still open. And even if they close, the virus and the Bloodvine are already spreading within Doftaan."

"Are you calling your queen a liar? Tell me, messenger. What is your name?" Florenta asked.

"I am Constanta, your excellency," the messenger replied.

"Constanta, you are an enemy of Doftaan and all Sangora for spreading such blatant lies. Because of your lies, people are crossing into neighboring states because they *believe* they can. What, you think I'm going to kill my own people to keep them from dying to an imaginary plague?"

"But experts from the University of Doftaan are projecting that millions could die, and that by their math, at least one hundred thousand could be infected already, a quarter of that in Doftaan itself. So far, no one has recovered or survived infection. And to make things worse, a high percentage of the dead return as— as—undead without faces," added the second vocal messenger. As Florenta waited for her to continue with an awkward, unexplained pause, she added, "My name is Daria, my queen."

"One hundred thousand? Pah. I can promise you right now that nowhere near one hundred thousand will die. But even so, one hundred thousand is less than one million, and I see that as a great victory. We've stopped the spread of the plague—what else do you want?" Florenta asked, spittle trailing from her lips. She turned back to Constanta. "Who was your source?"

"I cannot reveal that, my empress," Constanta said, shifting nervously in her seat.

"Tell me the truth," Florenta said. She willed the messenger to speak, and by the Queen's Control, the woman obeyed.

"My source's name is Mariana Vulpe of Timishuara," Constanta replied. She shared an ashamed glance with Daria for revealing the information; she was astounded and confused that she had done so.

"And did Mariana Vulpe of Timishuara reveal to you any other bits of information?" Florenta asked, continuing to will Constanta to tell the truth.

"She told me that the people of Timishuara are working to fight the Faceless Plague. They're closing down academies, taverns, and other places of gathering to stop the spread. They know the truth of what is happening," Constanta said.

"What else?" Florenta demanded.

"She said you are neglecting the outer regions of Sangora in favor of keeping Doftaan safe," Constanta answered, compelled by the Queen's Control. She paused for a moment, as if trying to stop the next words from tumbling from her mouth. "They say the people in Karpaska, your own state, are killing each other and dying because of your poor leadership."

"The lot of you should be put to death," Florenta said. "Bleeding traitors—are you ungrateful that I've kept Doftaan safe?"

"My queen, Doftaan *isn't* safe," Constanta said, a look of horror spreading across her face at what she had said. Florenta glowered down at them and grumbled under her breath.

The entire crowd of news messengers, including the two most vocal members of the contingent, Daria and Constanta, shifted silently in their seats, not wanting to put themselves or their sources in danger.

"If there are no further questions, you will inform the public of our successes. We are closing the borders; the death toll is low and unremarkable. No higher than numbers of those who are sick with the pox each year. We are close to curing the disease, and my empire is stronger than ever. The undead that do rise are quickly slain by our brave, brave military forces. I will have official statements drawn up in the coming hours, and you will bring the news from state to state, as is custom."

"Thank you, your excellency," said Constanta, bowing her head. The others did the same.

"Groveling dogs," Florenta said, shaking her head in disgust. "One last piece of news for you to spread throughout the city of Doftaan: The Fallen One's former prison—a truly inhumane place—was found to be the main source of the outbreak of the Faceless Plague in Sangora. The Fallen One manufactured the plague as a weapon against her own people—how sad is that?"

"We are lucky to have a queen so strong and caring as you," said someone in the crowd. Florenta's smile in response resembled that of a very wide frog; her grin melted her chin into her thick neck. The comment was not prompted through the Queen's Control, but a genuine comment of support, and she knew it.

"Yes, yes. Well, we all know that. Finally, you speak some truth. Perhaps you aren't as stupid as you all look," Florenta said as she left the balcony.

The news messengers filed into the fortress to receive their documents to distribute to the rest of the empire, and she returned to her own chamber, collapsing onto the massive bed in the center of the room. She snapped her fingers, and servants brought forth dishes full of aromatic spiced meats and luxurious fruit, already prepared for their queen before her speech had begun.

"Your benevolence," a male voice came from the corridor.

A human servant approached just as Florenta began to tear into a leg of ham. The queen did not respond, and the servant stood at attention.

"Well, are you going to speak?" she asked after several minutes of silence filled with nothing but the sounds of her chewing.

The servant nodded then stammered, "Your caravan is prepared and waiting for you."

"And it will wait a few moments longer," Florenta replied, setting down the handful of meat to take a juicy bite of a fruit the servant did not even recognize.

"As is your command," the servant replied with a low bow.

"What are you, boy? A Than? Oh, don't tell me you're Kurashic," Florenta said without looking up.

"Um, Kurashic is a language, my queen, not a people, but, um, I am from Sangora. Adess, specifically," the servant stammered.

"Um, um, um," Florenta said, mocking the man. "Human— pah! Stupid, like the rest."

He pressed his eyes shut as if preparing to be slapped in the face. Florenta never said anything else, too invested in the meal before her. The servant wasted no time fleeing from the room.

When she had finished dining, she snapped her fingers once again, and the opulent gold doors of her chamber swung open. A dozen servants filed into the room and lined up without a word on either side of the bed and hefted it from its platform, carrying Florenta from the chamber and down the long corridor of her palace toward the front gates.

They descended a long staircase and exited the palace to find the caravan waiting just outside. She glanced up and behind her to catch a view of the progress of her home. While Mara's home had been ugly, she, a real queen, would live in a place worthy of her name.

The black stone spires of Mara's former palace were now surrounded with scaffolding where her builders labored to cover each tower and dome with silver, gold, and intricate patterns of colorful paint. Her banner, a white fist on a red and black background adorned nearly every ledge.

She grinned, pleased with their work, although she admitted to herself that they could stand to work faster. She turned to one of the servants accompanying the platform and snapped her fingers again to get their attention.

"Yes, your excellency?"

"Fetch Mistress Enrieta. She should be here by now. Always making me wait! We have much to discuss on our way to Timishuara and Karpaska, and it is already time to leave," Florenta said. The servant said no more and disappeared to do her queen's bidding.

The others opened the gates on the back of a massive cart pulled by a team of a dozen black horses. They had some difficulty but eventually managed to load their ruler's platform into the beautifully crafted vehicle. A silver chandelier studded with diamonds dangled above her head.

A few moments later, the door at the other side of the cart opened, and a tall Sangoran woman with pale skin that showed every vein entered and sat on the bench opposite Florenta, raising her wings in respect. Sparse, wispy gray hair covered her head and framed her hawklike features, including a hooked nose and beady eyes that seemed too far from where they should be.

"Mistress Enrieta," Florenta said.

As Florenta's Mistress of Dusk got comfortable, the vehicle pulled away from the palace and began its way out of the imperial district of Jempratanrajon toward the southern gates.

"My queen," Enrieta replied in greeting. "I commend you on your talent and grace dealing with those corrupt messengers. I have not had such patience with them in Timishuara since my appointment, and I have learned today from your example just how to treat them so that they know to spread only the truth, and not what they think is the truth."

"Yes, yes. I know. I must do something about them," Florenta said, abruptly changing the subject with a look of impatience on her face. "I trust you know why I've brought you along?"

"I must admit, I do not," Enrieta replied.

"There is unrest in Karpaska, and Mistress Soreana of Karpaska, whom you know, great woman—helped raise support for my revolution against The Fallen One, you know—Soreana is hard at work quelling the rebellion in her lands. I trust her to do so, as it is my familial land of Karpaska. She will quash the Alboran terrorists. It is time you head home to do the same, should it spread."

"But my queen, there is no insurrection in Timishuara," Enrieta replied. "The rebellion is Alboran, and we do not have Alborans in Timishuara."

"I really wish everyone would stop correcting me when I'm right. You say there isn't, but there will be. Lavinia—curse her— was the former governor of your land. The Fallen One's most trusted Mistress of Dusk, I think. I always hated her. Horrible woman. News of the Faceless Plague has broken there, too. You heard what that bull of a woman, Contansa, or something—the messenger from my meeting with the representatives," Florenta said, snapping her fingers.

"Yes, I remember. Constanta," Enrieta said, correcting the queen again with a grimace. "A truly horrible woman."

"Yes, yes, Constanta." Florenta waved Enrieta down, cutting her off. "She talked about the Faceless Plague and that the people of Timishuara are preparing against it. I need you to tell your people to stop and to not to be afraid."

"But will they not succumb to the plague?"

"They will see such action as weakness. We will handle it in secret, of course, but outwardly, let people think there is no problem. All is well in Sangora. It is not as bad as they say, after all. I need you to return to Timishuara, deny all allegations of any failures of our council and tell them the truth. Tell them we are already prepared."

"And that the plague will soon go away," Enrieta said.

"Yes, as it will."

"Yes, yes," Enrieta said, nodding. "Of course."

"There is no plague in Timishuara," Florenta said.

"There is no plague in Timishuara," Enrieta repeated.

"And there will be no revolution," Florenta added.

"There will be no revolution."

"If there is revolution, I will not save you. I will let your people kill each other. It's the only way to make them learn," the queen said. Enrieta nodded, scratching her head beneath her wiry hair.

"We will contain this revolution to Karpaska," Mistress Enrieta said. "The revolution is the real problem, not this silly plague. They're peasants, after all, so it will be easy. I will tell my people all revolution will be met with punishment befitting of terrorists. I will send soldiers to the border to ensure no one crosses over, and I will report to you any mention of insurrection there. It will not spread out of Karpaska."

"Good," Florenta said, a wide smile stretching over her face.

"Praise be to the true Queen."

"Now…" Florenta snapped her fingers, and from the front chamber of the cart, two servants brought trays of food to their masters. "Now, we dine to celebrate the future. I'm simply starving."

# CHAPTER TWENTY-FIVE
# THE BATTLE OF BALGOROD

Shanthah led his procession of soldiers and untrained volunteers past yet another gargantuan statue of Florenta Karpaska large enough to block out the sun. From the look of things, the Mistress of Dusk devoted more of the state's gold to statues and propaganda than feeding its starving mouths.

Shanthah, General Anca, Mistress Raluca, and their troops were now camped in the outskirts of Balgorod, capital city and stronghold of Florenta's state of Karpaska. Florenta herself was not likely to be found in the city, as she had taken up residence in Doftaan following her coup.

They were not met by any foe, which Shanthah took as a good omen. However, with her keen military mind, General Anca had explained to him that it was more likely that Florenta's forces were concentrated in the center of the city near the fortress and where the administrative buildings were located, leaving the relatively unimportant outskirts of the city undefended.

As the army marched through the outskirt shanty towns, curious eyes peeked out of their dwellings cobbled together out of sheets of tin and debris wood. Shanthah's heart felt for them, but he knew they would enjoy what was coming next.

He thrust his sword into the sky as a signal, and several of his Sangoran troops carried heavy war hammers into the sky and landed on the statue's enormous shoulders. The soldiers began to beat at the golden Florenta's neck with a rhythm like war drums. The head, as big as the real Florenta's entire body, crashed to the ground in a cloud of dust and a cheer from both the army and those impoverished souls watching from below.

"Looks like we're welcome in town!" called Shanthah to his troops, who responded with a hearty, "Ža drogasteju i ž'Alboru!"

An increasing number of followers joined the procession; many of the citizens of Balgorod joining their march brandished rusted farming tools, but a few carried tarnished blades, perhaps looted or stolen.

"Shanthah, sir!" came the voice of Markus, one of Shanthah's assistants helping coordinate their attack on Balgorod.

"Ah, Markus, what news?" Shanthah said as they marched onward.

"The people of Balgorod—we've spoken to some of them. They're supposed to give their lives to stop us from reaching Florenta's fortress, but they're all joining us instead!"

"And any news of the other groups?" asked Shanthah.

"They've set up the siege around New Balgorod according to Mistress Anca's recommendations, sir! It's been going well since it began," answered Markus with a toothy grin.

Shanthah thanked the man and urged his followers onward, following the winding Sava River northeast through the Southern slums of Balgorod. As they neared the spot where the Sava and Danuub rivers converged, industrial buildings billowing with smoke began to crop up with increasing frequency.

When they passed Karpaska's massive prison complex within the industrial district, Florenta's fortress came into view, standing strong upon an island in the confluence of the two rivers. Taking that fortress was Shanthah's end goal, and he sighed, knowing it would not be an easy task.

"Do you think these people are actually joining us, or do you believe it to be a trap?" Raluca asked Anca.

"Florenta most likely has the Queen's Control, but she can't control everyone at once. I believe this sentiment is legitimate," Anca replied. "But we shall see."

Raluca nodded as she looked across the river into the region of New Balgorod where the richer part of society lived, separate from the impoverished, starving working class and the fires of industry. The contrast between the exceeding opulence of New Balgorod and the slums was disgusting, and Shanthah hoped in his heart that their actions today might help the situation.

From this vantage point, it was possible to see other groups loyal to the revolution forming the siege line. They had set up a circumvallation of mounds of earth and entrenched, ramshackle forts preventing Florenta's forces in or out of the island fortress while protecting the groups friendly to the revolution.

However, the group laying siege did not experience the same luck and lack of resistance as Shanthah's forces; smoke rose from the city around the fortifications, and hundreds of Florenta's warriors were already engaging the siege line. They had broken through at several locations.

"They won't last," said Anca, shaking her head. "Not without a distraction on our side. We'll need to split their forces and act fast."

"Then let's give them one," said Shanthah. "Give the order, General Anca."

Anca extended her mighty wings and shot into the air, screeching one single order to their forces in the Sangoran language, one that everyone in the company had been both dreading and looking forward to hearing.

"Sehainas vo'hreipaštu Florenti!" she shouted.

An order to take Florenta's Fortress. A unanimous battle cry went up from the determined warriors, and those that could fly extended their wings, launching into the air to cross the river into New Balgorod. Those on foot reinforced the battle at the siege line.

Anca and Raluca led the charge over the river and were the first to land on the other side. Shanthah stood on the riverbank, unsure of what to do as he watched his forces soaring overhead without him.

He felt someone hook his armpits and hoist into the sky with a flap of two leathery wings. He craned his neck up to see Ruta smiling down at him, clad in gear for war.

"Don't worry, we won't leave you behind, or how else will your Hanna get to see you?" she asked.

"Ža drogasteju i ž'Alboru!" exclaimed Shanthah in his thick Thannish accent.

A wide grin stretched across his face as Ruta and those around them echoed the battle cry, touching down on the other side of the river. Within seconds, Florenta's military forces were upon them to defend the fortress from the invaders, leaving New Balgorod relatively unguarded.

Shanthah and Anca met their foes head on while Raluca guided their forces away from the battle into the now undefended portion of New Balgorod. Shanthah found himself at a distinct disadvantage as the only combatant incapable of flight, but his invisibility leveled the odds, allowing him to slip unseen between his enemies.

"Enforcers incoming!" shrieked one of Anca's companions.

Shanthah turned to see a platoon of heavily armored Karpaskan Enforcers marching, not flying, toward Anca's troops. Each of the warriors carried long pikes, but Shanthah could see that they were all armed with knives and swords as well.

"Oticai!" shouted Anca in Sangoran as the Enforcers crossed the bridge: an order to draw back. Each enforcer pointed their long pikes toward Anca's forces; those in front knelt so that those behind could still take aim at their enemies.

"What are they doing?" Shanthah shouted, but Anca was too busy directing her forces to pay him heed. Ruta tackled him to the ground, and he cried out as dozens of needle-like arrows erupted from the end of each pike.

"Take cover!" Anca brought her armored wings around, creating a shield that protected her from being skewered by the hundreds of darts. They glanced off the shield, but others peppered Shanthah's forces. He watched his supporters fall around him, and he struck the earth with his fist in anger.

Raluca flew at the head of her forces over the river from New Balgorod onto the fortress island, circumventing the Enforcers as they assailed Anca and Shanthah's troops. The Sangorans following Anca, including Ruta, took flight to avoid being ripped to shreds by the pike-bolts.

Shanthah darted invisible into the midst of the Enforcers on the bridge and shoved one of them over the side, sending her into the river with a mighty splash. She did not resurface, her heavy armor weighing her down.

The Enforcers turned as one and without hesitation opened fire, spraying pike-bolts in Shanthah's general direction. Shanthah twisted and dove from the bridge, but one of the darts grazed the flesh of his exposed arm and side. He cried out, becoming visible once again.

"It's the phantom!" cried one of the Enforcers.

Shanthah splashed into the river and hundreds of pike-bolts struck the water around him, their momentum creating trails of bubbles into the depths. Shanthah's feet grazed the drowned Enforcer's armor. He swam downward, managing to grasp the pike as he was carried downstream.

A second round of pike-bolts let him know the Enforcers weren't done with him, but he was nearly out of air. He willed himself to become invisible and surfaced, hoping the splash wouldn't be visible to his enemies. His hopes were in vain, for the Enforcers had guessed where he would have to surface. He cursed his footprints for being clearly visible in the muddy riverbank. He looked up to see his airborne troops clash with other flying Sangorans in Florenta's colors as the Enforcers took aim at him.

He would not let the siege and all their efforts be in vain.

Hoping the pike would still function while soaking wet, Shanthah took aim and sent a spray of pike-bolts into a Sangoran flying past just in time; the Enforcers' pike-bolts struck the corpse as it fell from the sky, shielding Shanthah from being riddled with darts.

He made his way into the grass on the riverbank out of the mud as another spray of pike-bolts peppered the earth nearby. The Enforcers had lost his position, and he made haste to rejoin the fight while his enemies did the same.

Anca's forces were beginning a retreat into New Balgorod, but many of Florenta's troops had followed, leaving the Enforcers to eliminate Shanthah and Anca's forces that remained on the island. Anca stayed behind, felling numerous foes as they neared; none were the equal of the Mistress of Dusk who had long ago earned the title, "Nightmare of Thanatanos."

She sprinted headlong toward the group of Enforcers, flapping her mighty wings once to leap over their heads and land in their midst. This distraction bought Shanthah enough time to regroup.

Anca lashed out, thrusting the razor edge of her wings into the neck joint in the armor of two enforcers, beheading them both. Shanthah kicked the back of the nearest Enforcer's leg, knocking her to the ground. He knew his sword would be of little use against their thick armor, but he wanted to help Anca however he could. One of the Enforcers grabbed Anca by the neck and slammed her against the bridge with such force that Anca lost consciousness, and Shanthah feared she was dead.

"Anca!" Shanthah shouted, still invisible.

The Enforcers turned to find him. He knew they would kill Anca if he did not reappear, so he materialized, hands raised. Raluca had managed to lead the rest of their forces onto the island, and the other groups of Shanthah's followers from other cities had arrived to reinforce the siege, allowing Shanthah's forces to close in on the city and break through the Karpaskan defenses.

Anca and Shanthah had distracted the Enforcers long enough for them to reach the island. He grinned, but his hope soon faded as he saw three more groups of Enforcers marching toward his forces.

"Send word to Queen Florenta that we have the Phantom and General Anca in custody. As soon as Mistress Raluca is captured, we can end this," said the lead Enforcer. Two others saluted and marched toward the fortress. The lead Enforcer forced Shanthah to his knees, and he kept his hands raised.

His mind raced. Was Florenta here and not in Doftaan?

The sound of a thousand whispers on the wind and a dark mist enveloped Shanthah's senses; he shut his eyes as bolts of blinding lightning beat the Enforcers back, throwing some into the river. Several dozen Enforcers remained on the bridge, and they took aim at whomever appeared from the dark mist. Shanthah expected to see Ronin or one of the Walkers but gasped as he saw his rescuer's face.

The Empress of Blood had come to Balgorod.

The Enforcers unleashed their pike-bolts, but Mara roared and thrust both hands toward her foes, telekinetically sending the darts back at their masters and throwing those at the back off the bridge and into the river.

As Anca regained consciousness and crawled away, Mara thrust her knife tipped wings through the face plates of the nearest enforcers' helms. Before their bodies hit the ground, she ripped two heavy cobblestones from the bridge with her mind and smashed them into the heads of two more Enforcers, collapsing their helms in upon their skulls before sending a pulse of lightning through her enemies; the enforcers screamed in pain and collapsed smoking and disoriented to their knees, their armor coursing with electricity. With a final cry of rage, she released a burst of telekinetic energy, throwing the remaining Enforcers through the air and completely collapsing the stone bridge.

Shanthah shielded himself from Mara's violent onslaught by diving behind a ruined statue of Florenta, which was wide enough to block him from being peppered with debris.

Another sudden rush of black smoke filled his vision. When it cleared, he and Anca were lying in the grass on the coast of New Balgorod on the other side of the river.

"What?" Shanthah asked, looking around before patting his chest to make sure none of the darts had struck him.

His other wounds stung, but nothing was serious enough for him to leave the battle. Lord Ronin Jakoni appeared from the swirling, dark mist and handed Shanthah a fabric bag containing some kind of powder.

"Shanthah Kalen, for the fate of this world and of your people, you must promise to do something for me," said Ronin.

"Okay," was Shanthah's only response.

"You must infect your forces with this virus," said Ronin, enclosing Shanthah's fingers around the pouch.

"What? No!" Shanthah cried in protest. "That's—no!"

"You must! This virus acts as a counter to the Faceless Plague, inoculating our people against it and the Queen's Control alike. Florenta is almost here, Shanthah! She heard word of your rebellion, and she is on her way! She has the Queen's Control and is coming to end your revolution. The virus will be painful, but it will run its course in a few hours. Trust me, Shanthah."

Shanthah nodded, trying to understand. Ronin disappeared into the dark mist, leaving him and Anca in the relative safety of New Balgorod. Shanthah helped Anca sit up next to a thick oak tree, and after making sure she was safe, hurried back to the battle. He made his way over another bridge covered in corpses and looked into the pouch Ronin had given him.

"Here goes nothing." He turned invisible and ran head long into the fray, took a deep breath, and then threw a handful of the powder into the air. Within moments, every Sangoran around him, including his own forces and those commanded by Florenta, was on the floor, coughing and hacking before they began to tremble, beads of sweat collecting on their brows.

"Ronin, if this doesn't work, I'm coming for you," he said, knowing full well Ronin was nowhere nearby.

He got to work spreading the virus powder around his forces, using it at times as a defense against oncoming attackers to bring them to their knees. He glanced over to Mara's position to see that she and Anca's contingent of warriors storming the fortress. Many of the Sangorans around him lay shivering and retching on the ground, and his heart ached for them.

"The Phantom's Curse," sputtered one of Florenta's soldiers as she watched Shanthah materialize, a look of sad victory etched on his face.

He looked around the battlefield and could tell the virus was already spreading to those he had not directly infected. He sheathed his blade and took a deep breath. The battle continued within the fortress, but closer to the riverbank, it was all over.

And then a bolt of lightning tore through his side, throwing him through the air. He struck the ground hard a few yards away and groaned, pressing his hands over the wound. He stirred feebly and opened his eyes to see Mara striding toward him, lightning crackling around her hands.

"You've got to be kidding me." Shanthah groaned, letting his head fall against the earth. As Mara advanced, he tried to vanish, but the pain prevented him from doing so. "No, no, no…"

A horrible laugh filled the night air, but not Mara's laugh. Shanthah pushed himself up onto his knees and shook his head in resignation and disbelief. Florenta herself sat upon a platform carried by twelve other Sangorans; they stopped next to Mara, who stood glowering next to the usurper who upon arrival spoke only one word.

"Die."

The sounds of battle stopped, replaced by screams and groans as members of Shanthah's army turned their own blades on themselves, plunging their daggers into their own stomachs.

"Stop it!" shouted Shanthah, stumbling to his feet.

He ran toward his dying followers, but Florenta raised a hand, influencing Mara with the Queen's Control to blast the ground beneath his feet, sending him flying through the air again. He landed face first in the mud, his heart thundering in his chest; he pulled himself toward his dying supporters as he neared the bridge and caught sight of an Enforcer's abandoned pike.

"So, this is the Phantom I've heard so much about. Your lies and stories have led hundreds to their deaths. How do you feel about that?" Florenta asked with a hearty laugh, spilling some of her wine. Both Mara and Florenta made a slow advance on Shanthah as he opened the pike's cartridge to check how many darts remained within.

One. That would have to be enough.

"Come on," Shanthah whispered, dumping the last pinch of virus powder into the cartridge, making sure it coated the dart. He took a deep breath and waited.

"I asked you a question, didn't I?" said Florenta as her minions carried her nearer to her prey. "How does that make you feel?!"

"It makes me angry," he replied in a low voice.

"I can't hear you!" called Florenta. "Speak up, slug! And stand when your queen addresses you!"

"I said that it makes me *angry!*" roared Shanthah, refusing to stand, pike in hand. With no hesitation, he raised the weapon and fired the last remaining bolt at Florenta's head.

Florenta flinched, and Mara leapt between the queen and the dart; the tip ripped through the flesh just below Mara's shoulder. She tumbled to the ground and did not stir. He turned his sights on Florenta, hurling the empty pike into the chest of one of her platform carriers. The platform shifted, and Florenta screamed, nearly tumbling to the ground.

Shanthah scooped up a fallen shortsword and leapt forward, hacking at another of Florenta's servants then pulled himself onto Florenta's unsteady platform, raising the blade one last time. Just as he thrust the blade between her ribs, Florenta's meaty fist collided with his jaw, throwing him from the platform. He struck the ground, tears streaming down his face.

"You'll die for what you did here," said Shanthah, his eyes red from tears.

"Now, now. I don't think I will," said Florenta with a loud groan, pulling the blade from her side with a groan.

Her followers struggled to support the platform as she shifted her weight.

"No, Florenta, he's right." Florenta turned and glared at Mara, who stared back with nothing but rage in the crystal blue of her eyes. "You are relieved of your station as Mistress of Dusk. As Empress of Blood, I sentence you to death."

There would be no forgiveness. Not this time.

"No, *you* will be the one to die!" Florenta shouted. "How are you not understanding this?"

The usurper's minions were unable to support her anymore, and they dropped the platform. She tumbled from her seat to the ground, unable to stand. Mara strode unopposed through Florenta's foes as she exerted her own coercive magic through the Queen's Control.

"Still making promises you can't keep?!" Mara taunted, striding toward her enemy with unmatched fierceness. "Come on, what are you waiting for?! Go on! Kill me, Florenta!"

"Kill her!"

Mara held her hands aloft, using the Queen's Control to command Florenta's forces to kneel.

"And you—stand when your Empress addresses you," Mara ordered, unsure if her magic would be able to influence Florenta.

She was pleased to see Florenta groan under the strain and effort needed to stand. She placed a hand on her throne to steady herself and glared in Mara's direction in contempt.

"You are not my empress," said Florenta. "You couldn't even save your own Mistresses of Dusk from assassination—"

"I am talking," Mara said, and Florenta shut her mouth. "But for once, I agree with you. I wasn't able to save them. But I *can* save the rest of Sangora from *you*."

Mara stumbled, the effects of the virus beginning to take hold. She let loose a single bolt of lightning that ripped through Florenta's side; Mara collapsed with a groan, knowing she had failed to strike Florenta's heart.

"So much for that!" Florenta shouted. "Save me!"

She exerted all the power of her version of the Queen's Control that she could muster. Her remaining platform carriers still not infected by the cure-virus struggled to lift her onto her platform but at last managed to hoist her into the seat and carry her away.

"All hail the Empress of Blood!" Shanthah shouted as the platform tipped again. A dozen more Sangorans flew over the walls of the fortress to come to the aid of the usurper queen, and Shanthah began to succumb to blood loss and exhaustion. Nearby, Mara coughed and vomited as the virus overtook her.

"Take me back to Doftaan," ordered Florenta, holding her blood drenched side. "Now!"

Shanthah and Mara's forces did not pursue the platform carriers as they made their way toward Florenta's carriage pulled by two full teams of horses.

"Balgorod has fallen, but I don't care. It will burn for what has happened here today. Send word to those that remain in the fortress to torch the entire city. We will send a message to Doftaan to initiate the Collapse Protocol and slay the prisoners left in the dungeons of the Zvužajecy prison. We can't risk any of them getting out, especially *her*," ordered Florenta.

"But my queen, what of our forces taken by the Phantom's Curse?" asked one of her servants.

Florenta screamed an indistinguishable Sangoran insult at the woman, spittle flying from her jowls as they loaded her into the back of the opulent vehicle. The servant, left behind by her queen, made her way through the ruins of the battlefield to relay Florenta's mad message.

Nearby, Shanthah opened his eyes, and he crawled forward, watching Florenta board her vehicle. He grasped a broken fencepost to pull himself upright, and he limped toward Florenta's cart. With all the might he could muster, he turned invisible and hurried forward to pull himself onto the back of the cart just as it lurched forward, throwing him off.

His only chance to reach Hanna pulled away, leaving him bleeding, invisible, and unconscious on the ground near the infected Sangorans. Smoke billowed from the captured fortress as his forces lay broken and beaten, but victorious.

# CHAPTER TWENTY-SIX
# BROKEN ARMS FULL OF LOVE

Far from Balgorod, a low rumble shook the entire world above Hanna, and dust drifted down from the ceiling. She wondered if it was an aftershock of the first two earthquakes that had rocked the prison hours before. At least, that's what she told herself, but other more sinister possibilities crept into her mind: images of the monstrous behemoths and innumerable Faceless in Nitra and the horrible voice of their master.

*"Interesting. I did not expect* this," the being had said. *"Yes, this is just what I needed. Thank you again, Hanna Samsa."*

He had addressed her by name, and now something was happening in the floors above her lavish dungeon cell. She knew it couldn't be a coincidence. She took a deep breath and told herself everything was alright. Nothing was going to happen.

For a short while, nothing did. And then the deafening sound of crumbling stone filled the dungeon as the world shook harder than ever.

"Hanna!" The familiar voice echoed through Hanna's level of the dungeon until it faded, drowned out by the incessant sound of crumbling stone. Hanna leapt to her feet and slammed her palm against the steel door of her prison cell, hoping to get Liliana's attention, as they had discussed, but she did not appear. Something must have gone wrong.

Hanna groaned as she grasped the hinges of the steel door, relying on her telekinetic abilities rather than whatever power she had unknowingly tapped into before. She groaned and ripped the bolt from the hinges then stepped back as the heavy gate slammed down.

"Lucky?" she called, stepping into the corridor. She summoned the hinge bolts to her and levitated them around her hand, ready to use them as projectiles.

Rocky debris fell from the ceiling, buffeting her back and shoulders as she ran with her arms shielding her head. She had to cover her mouth to avoid breathing in the dust while following Liliana's frantic screams.

"Hanna, where are you?" Liliana screamed. "Help!"

As the dust began to settle, she caught a glance of her ally lying on her stomach on the floor ahead, four heavily armed Sangorans standing behind her with vicious looking pikes. Three of Liliana's allies lay dead beside her, already executed by the soldiers. Of all of the rescue group, only Liliana and Reka, Liliana's ally that didn't speak any Thannish, were left alive.

"Lucky!" shouted Hanna.

Without warning, she launched the first of the door hinges toward the armored Sangorans. Two resounding clangs filled the chamber: the first when the hinge pierced the warrior's helm, and the second when the corpse hit the stone ground.

"Thank Elafris you're alive. They're collapsing the prison!" shouted Liliana. One of the heavily armored enforcers slammed the back of her pike against Liliana's neck, pressing her face against the ground. Hanna's other bolt pierced the chest plate of the second Enforcer.

As the second body hit the floor, the other two soldiers raised their pikes, releasing a spray of needle-like darts toward Hanna. She had no problem deflecting the needles with her mind, but she struggled to keep them from ricocheting in Liliana and Reka's direction. A second flurry of the darts raced toward her, and she was forced to drop the last hinge pin to focus on protecting herself.

The onslaught was unending; as one enforcer reloaded, the other fired, keeping Hanna on the defensive. She groaned and lowered one of her hands, grasped the floor tiles beneath her feet with her mind, and ripped the ground in a fissure toward her foes. The distraction caused her concentration to falter, and several of the darts ripped into her flesh while others grazed her skin. One of the enforcers collapsed as the ground was ripped from beneath her feet, and Hanna slammed her fists together, closing the fissure and crushing the soldier trapped within.

Liliana and Reka leapt to their feet and took flight, grappling with the last enforcer over control of the boltpike. Hanna winced in pain, a dart in her thigh preventing her from running. As the Enforcer overpowered her allies, Hanna focused all her mental energies on the Sangoran's helmet, causing it to crumple, collapsing the woman's skull beneath. Hanna winced at the sound, but their enemy fell to the floor, dead.

Liliana and Reka were safe. Alive. And so was she.

"You're early," said Hanna. "Didn't we agree on—"

"I know what we said, but they're initiating the Collapse Protocol—they're burying us alive! We need to go!" Liliana shouted. Hanna heeded her words at once, and Liliana helped her limp along the corridor as Reka flew ahead to scout the way.

"I'm sorry about your friends," said Hanna, wincing with every step.

"Yeah, well, that's war, isn't it?" Liliana replied. "Well, I think Empress Bartunek is about to avenge them."

Hanna stopped at the mention of Mara's name, but Liliana pulled her along. "What do you mean? Is she here? Is she the one bringing down the fortress?"

"Come on!" shouted Liliana without giving an answer. "All they're waiting for to collapse the final floor is for those three Enforcers to return. When they realize they're not coming back, we're going to get squished! Up these stairs, and we'll be—"

The low ceiling broke apart, filling the room first with blinding, choking dust, followed by massive chunks of stone that crashed down around them. Thousands of screams filled the floor above and then were silenced as the prison's occupants fell to their deaths or were crushed; Hanna's own screams joined them as she strained her powers to stop the falling debris of the entire fortress above from crushing her and her allies.

Several tons of earth and stone stopped just inches above their heads, and blood began to trickle from Hanna's nose, ears, and the corners of her eyes as the strain of keeping it from crushing them took its toll. Intense, throbbing pain enveloped her head and then spread down her spine and began to overtake her entire body. She felt the muscles and tendons in her arms spasm and pop as the mental strain overtook her physical body.

Serenity.

The feeling of calm she had experienced before connecting with Thanatan's mind enveloped her very soul, and she threw her fists into the air, willing her consciousness to connect with the collapsing fortress and, it seemed, with all of creation.

A pulse of pure mental energy emanated from her hands, ripping through the earth and stone above; she could sense every stone and pebble as if they were part of her own body, and she willed them out of existence. Reka and Liliana watched in awe as streaks of white light followed the path of Hanna's veins and flowed like fire from her eyes.

As she released a final surge of mental energy, her arms exploded in all-consuming agony. Tendons snapped first before her bones gave way, cracking first in her palm and then down her forearms, shards of white jutting out of her flesh, dripping with blood.

Pain overtook both her body and mind as the mental energy rocketed upward, crumbling the collapsing debris in its path into dust and propelling it high into the heavens above. It exploded from the surface in a massive eruption of fine ash and dust.

"What in the name of Elafris?" asked Liliana as Hanna collapsed to the ground.

The bright glow in her eyes and veins faded, and she looked up at Liliana and Reka with a vacant expression. Liliana cradled her head and stroked her hair.

Reka looked upward through rays of sunlight filtering down through the drifting dust; a perfectly cylindrical tunnel now led straight to the surface. Hanna groaned, grasping her gruesome wounds.

"Hanna, you got us a way out, but we're going to need to fly you there. We really need to get someone to look at your arms—by the way, don't look at your arms," Liliana said.

Hanna glanced down at her ruined arms and felt lightheaded at the sight of exposed blood and bone.

"Oh."

"You know that nickname you gave me? Lucky?" Liliana asked with a laugh. "I think I've earned that now. Did you see how close I was to being crushed?"

"I was a little busy," Hanna said through gritted teeth, gesturing to the tunnel above with her head. Liliana looked up and chuckled.

"Yeah, you were. Thank you, for whatever it was you did."

Liliana stroked Hanna's hair and watched Reka soar upward through the dust drifting in the glowing sunlight. She hoped that Reka would bring good news if she came back.

"It'll be okay, Hanna. Stay calm," Liliana said, trying to remember how to treat someone in shock.

Around ten minutes later, Reka shot downward back into the depths of the dungeon, her wings pressed close against her body. She dove faster than an arrow, breaking her descent at the bottom by extending them again. She touched the ground and spoke in rapid Sangoran with Liliana.

"What's up?" Hanna asked between groans.

"We're safe—kind of," said Liliana.

"Kind of?" asked Hanna. She felt so dizzy she thought she might soon faint.

"Reka said there's fighting in the streets of the Paudzuhoth and Zvužajecy districts above us," Liliana explained. "Word from an uprising in Balgorod—that's the capital of Karpaska—reached Doftaan, and now people are rioting against Florenta here too! A group arrived from Balgorod not long ago, and Reka spoke to some people that had fought in the battle there, and they said something about the Phantom's Curse spreading—"

"…The what?" asked Hanna.

"Some human led an entire army of Sangorans into Balgorod and managed to take it. Apparently two of the Mistresses of Dusk, Anca and Raluca were with him, and they drove Florenta and her forces out of the city!" Liliana said, translating Reka's words. Reka gave a wide smile.

"*Some* human?" Hanna asked, her heart racing.

"Yeah, they said his name was—"

"Shanthah Kalen," Hanna said. She smiled, ignoring the blinding pain in her arms. Reka nodded.

"How did you know?" Liliana asked.

"You know that 'knight in shining armor' I mentioned?" Hanna asked. Liliana nodded. "Well—I guess he's in Balgorod."

"Wow. Power couple," Liliana said, eyebrows raised.

Reka spoke in an excited tone for another minute or so before Liliana stopped her to translate. "Well, he led his forces into Balgorod, and apparently some virus got out that prevented Florenta from controlling them. Guess who showed up to save the day."

"Who?" Hanna asked.

"Empress Bartunek," Liliana said. Tears of joy began to well up in her eyes.

"Is she here?!" Hanna exclaimed. Liliana asked Reka, who shook her head and answered in Sangoran but smiled in Hanna's direction.

"No, she's still in Balgorod—but no one knows where Florenta is!" said Liliana.

"Well, that's a good sign, right?" Hanna asked.

"Of course. Okay, but now we need to get out of here. Are you in a state fit for us to carry you?"

Hanna trembled as she got to her feet. She tried to extend her arms, but pain shot through them. Instead, she held them against her chest and focused her remaining mental energies on her own body. She had never attempted such a thing before. If she had been able to extend her arms, she would hit herself in the forehead for never thinking of it. It worked, and her body began to levitate.

Reka and Liliana cheered, guiding her upward as they flapped next to her, guiding her all the way to the top of the chasm. She felt her powers falter near the top of the pit, and pain coursed through her entire body again. Liliana and Reka steadied her and helped her set her feet down on the surface as she put weight on her shaking legs.

For a moment, she thought she could walk.

She was wrong.

Hanna awoke in a bed, her arms bound in thick casts. She struggled to sit up and nearly jumped out of her skin as she saw someone sitting in the shadowy corner of the tent.

A familiar voice broke the silence. Mara's voice.

One word: her name.

"Hanna?"

Hanna watched as Mara stood, the torchlight illuminating her face; it was smudged with blood and dirt, and she looked tattered and broken, but at the same time, she gleamed with hope.

"You look horrible," Hanna said with a teasing smile.

"Yeah, well, you don't look much better," Mara said, gesturing to Hanna's arms.

They said nothing more. Tears flowed from both their eyes as Mara sat at her bedside and wrapped her arms around her friend. She did not let go.

"I'm so glad you're okay," Hanna whispered between sobs. Her voice squeaked and was almost inaudible. "I'm so, so, so glad…"

"Can you ever forgive me?" Mara whispered, burying her face against Hanna's shoulder and deep auburn hair.

"Of course, Mar."

"I love you so much."

"Right back at you, buddy," said Hanna, wiping a stream of tears on Mara's shoulder, unable to use her arms. "I'm sorry I almost killed you that one time."

"What are best friends for?" Mara asked, laughing through the tears, hugging the woman that had gone from a friend to an enemy to a stranger in the past years. But now, she was finally a friend again. "I love you so much, Hanna. I am so incredibly sorry. About everything. Everything I've done since the end of the war has been to fix—"

"I know," Hanna said. "I love you too, Mar. I'm sorry things happened the way they did—and Mar?"

"Yeah?"

"I love this hug, but it really hurts."

Mara pulled away.

"Would you just look at us?" she said with a laugh. She gestured between them, literally covered in blood, sweat, and tears. Her eyes were red from crying but shined with joy.

"He's here, you know," said Mara. "And he never, *ever* stopped looking for you."

Hanna couldn't contain her smile. She cradled both injured arms across her chest again but said nothing, unable to respond. Her eyes darted toward the camp of bustling Sangorans.

"Is he okay? And where is here? I was just in Doftaan…"

"Your friends Liliana and Reka smuggled you out of Doftaan and brought you to Balgorod. And yes, Shanthah is more than okay. He saved us all, Hanna. If it wasn't for him, I would be dead," Mara said. "Although, he did shoot me…"

"What?"

"Don't worry about it," Mara said, dismissing the comment with a wave of her hand. "Oh, and I have a special surprise that my people are calling for in store for him. I'd love for you to be there when he finds out."

"Surprise?" Hanna asked. "What is it?"

"I can't tell you," Mara said, "but I am so excited."

Mara helped Hanna climb off the bed.

"Hey, I hate to ask this, but will you—will you help me change?" Hanna asked with a defeated sigh. "I can't do it myself. I think I'm gonna have to wear a lot more dresses…"

Mara replied with a friendly nod, and Hanna raised her arms. Mara untied the knot on the back of the loose-fitting hospital gown, and Hanna shook her arms until it fell away in a heap on the ground, leaving her standing posed like a scarecrow in her underwear.

"Step in," Mara said, placing a pair of trousers on the ground. Hanna hopped forward, and Mara pulled the pantlegs over her ankles and up to her waist then did up the button. "This is great practice if I ever have kids."

"I hope you aren't still dressing your kids when they're this old," Hanna replied. Mara shook her head with a bright laugh.

"Arms up," Mara ordered, and Hanna raised them as much as she could, which was only as high as her shoulders. Mara maneuvered her friend's arms through the sleeves and pulled the tunic over her head, shoulders, and chest. Hanna wiggled from side to side until the bottom of the shirt fell into place.

"Thank you," Hanna said. "I can pretty safely say that we're much closer now. But maybe don't tell anyone about this? I do have a shred of dignity I'd like to keep."

"Of course not," Mara said, hugging her friend. "I'd do anything for you."

"I know, and because of that, I promise I won't ask you to come to the bathroom with me," Hanna said, smiling. "Although, I'm not sure how that's going to work…"

"I appreciate that," Mara said with another laugh.

Hanna followed the empress outside, where she saw rows of other tents erected along the streets. Mara led her to a tent near the end of the row, and the healer in charge greeted the empress with a low bow.

Hanna had almost forgotten that her friend was the beloved and feared Empress of Blood. The thought left her mind as Mara parted the flap of a nearby tent.

"Is he…?" Hanna whispered, her eyes beaming.

Mara smiled but said nothing more. Hanna stepped into the dimly lit tent and saw a man sitting at a desk reviewing a map, his back turned to the entrance. Mara rubbed Hanna's shoulder and disappeared outside.

Shanthah.

She cleared her throat, and he turned, did a double take, and stood so fast his chair toppled to the ground. Within a second, he had wrapped his arms around her. A grin so wide crossed on her face that she wondered if she would ever frown again. A happy squeal escaped his lips.

At long last, she had found him.

"What? How?" Shanthah asked. "I—Hanna! I thought—"

"Shan…" she whispered, lifting her arms with painstaking effort to run her fingers through his hair.

The look of confusion on his face gave way to one of relief and love. She locked her lips around his, a moment of reunion filled with joy.

Shanthah pulled away and looked at Hanna, beaming. His smile matched her own, and then he pulled her into an even tighter embrace, still unable to speak through his elation.

"Hi!" Hanna exclaimed, laughing and raising her injured arms to try to hug him back. Although pain coursed through them, she pulled him close and kissed him again.

"I was supposed to come save you," he said at last. "How—how are you here? You're alive!"

"Oh, I'm sorry, honey, but I did that myself," Hanna said. "I just didn't know where you were. You never showed up, so I came to find you!"

"I didn't even know you were here," Shanthah said, pulling away again. He looked her in the eyes and planted another kiss on her lips. "We all thought you were in Doftaan!"

"I was. Some new friends had to smuggle me out of Doftaan. I don't remember any of it, to be honest," Hanna said.

"This is—Hannaaaa!" Shanthah exclaimed, his voice happy and playful. He pulled her close again. "Don't get captured again, okay? And what happened to your arms?"

"I exploded a prison," Hanna responded.

"Sure, sure," Shanthah said, nodding to accept the comment without pressing further.

"And you be careful with your revolutions in the future. Don't you die without me okay? You can't die."

"Deal."

For another long while, they simply held each other, not willing to let go, lest they once again lose one other. Here in the outskirts of Sangora, they were safe. Together. Home.

"Mara's here, you know," said Shanthah.

"I know. We already talked."

"And? Spill it, Miss Samsa."

"Everything's going to be okay," Hanna replied. "I can't stop smiling. I love you, Shanthah."

"I love you too," Shanthah said, burying his face against Hanna's neck. He let out a deep sigh, feeling that everything was now right with the world.

An hour or so later, there was a soft rap on the tent post outside, and Mara stuck her head through the opening.

"It's time," she said in an ominous voice, as if summoning him to his own execution.

"I have no idea what this is about, and she won't tell me," Shanthah said. Hanna smiled and kissed him on the cheek before following Mara outside.

"Just a little ceremony to honor you and the others that helped with the revolution," Mara replied. "I think you'd like to know that I received a message today from Mistress Lavinia's people in Timishuara. Our old friends Kamil and Josman are apparently trapped by Faceless in Zinok and need help, so after the ceremony I'll be heading there to help extract them. I'd ask you to join me, but you both need to recover, and your people need you here, Shanthah."

"That's fine. You'll take good care of them, but what in the name of Elafris are they doing in Zinok?" Shanthah asked. "They were on a Hidden Flame assignment to investigate the ruins of Nitra!"

"And you were sent to Doftaan for a diplomatic summit, yet here you are, leading a revolution in Karpaska," Mara said with a shrug. "Life's crazy that way."

"True, true. By the way, I'm sorry again for shooting you," Shanthah said. A dramatic expression crossed his face. "Oh no, you're going to hang me for treason or something, aren't you?"

Mara looked over her shoulder and laughed; it was a sound that neither Hanna nor Shanthah was accustomed to hearing, for there was a desperate lack of laughter in the slave camp where they had become friends.

Friends. Was that the right word? No.

Family.

"You're not in trouble, Shanthah. Relax," Mara said with a laugh. "I don't think it's any secret that I've done worse than shoot you."

She began to speak again, but Hanna interrupted her.

"You know we've already forgiven you," she said, bumping her shoulder and hip against Mara's.

"You weren't the ones I'm worried about," Mara muttered. Hanna watched Mara's countenance fall.

"Aleksander?" Hanna asked. Mara nodded.

"Among others. Many others. You know that old saying—you can forgive but can't forget. I think that goes both ways for us," said Mara, a sad smile etched across her face. "I firmly believe that forgiveness does not grant trust, and likewise, trust does not grant forgiveness."

Hanna gave an empathetic nod, not fully understand Mara's intended implications behind the statement.

"We saw you two at the peace summit ball. I think he's more forgiving than you give him credit for. And if he's not, forget him. You've got us!" Hanna said with an encouraging smile. "You've got friends, and we need you, girl."

"So does the entire country, I'm told," said Mara.

"Which you also have," said Shanthah.

"Had," Mara corrected.

"And shall have again," Shanthah said. "Mara Bartunek, Queen of All the Verb Tenses!"

"*Empress* of All the Verb Tenses, thank you very much," Mara said, pointing her nose to the heavens in feigned snobbery.

The three friends laughed and smiled as they made their way to an open clearing in the middle of the medical tents. A small stage had been erected out of scrap wood, and Raluca, Anca, and Ruta were all seated atop it at Mara's order.

As Mara led her friends onto the stage, Hanna looked out into the crowd of injured and sickly Sangorans that had gathered. Many were elderly, and most seemed untrained. They were decidedly not warriors, but their loyalty and determination seemed to claim otherwise.

Mara motioned to the seats on the stage, and Hanna took the one next to Ruta. She looked out over the crowd and spotted Valistaran, Daniel, Valeniya, Kadir, and Ronin sitting near the back, cloaked in disguises to hide their identities.

"I am very happy to meet you," Ruta said.

Hanna was unsure who the Sangoran woman was but greeted her with a warm hug all the same. She waved to the two Mistresses of Dusk, who acknowledged her but said no more. Shanthah was happy to see how many of his friends and followers had survived the battle.

"Thank you all for gathering at my request today," Mara said, projecting her voice to the crowd. "Today I want to recognize a great victory that you achieved here today but to also honor those that gave their lives in liberating Balgorod from Mistress Florenta. Please join me for a few moments of silence in honoring those brave souls. Although it is not a profound enough thank-you for their sacrifice, I hope that it will suffice for now."

She bowed her head, and the rest of the crowd, including Hanna and Shanthah, did the same; the earth itself seemed to pay tribute to those fallen sons and daughters of Alboras as the ducks and other birds in the nearby river seemed to keep silent at Mara's request.

One minute passed.

Shanthah's thoughts turned to those that had joined him in his quest to free Hanna. Although his revolution began as a way to reunite with the woman he loved, it had given him a true love for a people that had once been his enemies.

A second minute passed.

Hanna thought of the brave souls that had given their lives in Florenta's dungeon in Doftaan. She glanced up and saw Liliana and Reka at the front of the crowd, and she smiled. Perhaps Sangora was a more beautiful place than she had thought.

A third minute passed.

Mara considered the events that had transpired in her life. Enslavement. Torture. Betrayal. But also, the pure joy and love of friendship and the family she had found.

She felt a wave of compassion and love for her brave, beautiful people. A feeling of longing for them to be free and happy. A thought entered her head—one she would share soon enough.

"Thank you," Mara said, bowing her head and raising her wings high into the sky, a cultural sign of respect akin to bowing.

She took a deep breath and turned to Shanthah. "Would Shanthah Kalen and Ruta Vaal please join me?"

Shanthah nodded and stood behind Mara, but she motioned with a shake of her head to stand beside her. Ruta followed suit.

"Many of you joined Shanthah in his quest after hearing of his goal to free the one he loves from Florenta's prison. Whether you joined him out of a desire to overthrow your oppressor or out of a genuine desire to help a man I am blessed to call my friend, thank you." Shanthah turned to sit, but Mara blocked his exit with one of her massive, leathery wings.

"At this time, as the rightful Empress of Sangora and Queen of Talohira, I want to publicly thank both Shanthah and Ruta for their roles in serving our people in their fight against the usurper queen that sits on my throne. No, not my throne. *Our* throne, as it belongs to all of us."

She took a moment to look over the crowd as a Sangoran man walked on stage and presented them each with a medal for their services.

"Florenta, and perhaps many rulers before me in our country, including Queen Codruta, King Valistaran Talohir, and others—many of them have ruled their people, but not served them. The Sangoran people have served our king and queens for longer than any of you have been alive. As your Empress, I want to say that that is not my desire. My deepest, most sincere desire is to serve you as a ruler should. We all have places in this empire, and mine is to make sure that it does not fall to ruin. Yours is to serve one other so that I may serve you all."

A knowing grin crossed her mouth as she said, "But I cannot serve you alone. I need my council. My friends. The Mistresses of Dusk were scattered when Florenta usurped our throne, but today I wish to reinstate those that still support our cause."

She turned to Anca and Raluca and motioned for them to stand as well. At that moment, Shanthah wondered why in the world he was still standing.

"Raluca and Anca, do you desire to keep your positions as Mistresses of Dusk?" Mara asked.

"I do," said Raluca.

"Yes," replied Anca with a slight bow and raised wings. The Sangoran with the medals presented one to both Anca and Raluca as well, and then they were seated.

"And Shanthah Kalen, do you accept your new position as Master of Dusk?"

An audible gasp escaped the silent crowd, and Shanthah was taken aback; for a moment, he could think of nothing to say. He turned to Hanna, who smiled and gave him an encouraging nod.

"I will absolutely serve as a Mistress of Dusk," Shanthah said.

"Master of Dusk," Mara corrected as the crowd cheered. Mara watched with glee as the Sangorans clapped their wings together, an applause much louder than any created by humans.

"If they are still alive, I also welcome Mistresses Lavinia and Vasilica back to their former posts in Timishuara and Doftaan respectively. Florenta is now an enemy of the true Sangoran throne, and hereby exiled from my council. For high treason, she faces execution, and no longer has any right to rule the Karpaskan or Alboran people. For her crimes against you, I hereby rename the state of Karpaska after your people and name Shanthah Kalen as Master of Dusk of the new state, Alboras."

The crowd cheered once again, and while they did, Mara turned to look at Hanna. She raised an eyebrow and gestured with her head as if to ask if Hanna would like to join them at the front of the stage and become one of her ruling council as well. Hanna gave a subtle shake of the head accompanied by a soft smile, and Mara nodded in understanding. Shanthah took a seat next to Hanna and Raluca, and Mara gestured for Ruta.

As Ruta approached, Mara paused for a moment, watching Shanthah and Raluca deep in conversation; they embraced one another, and tears streamed down Raluca's face. Mara wondered what he had told her but turned back to the crowd.

"Next, Master Shanthah has let me know of your very own Ruta Vaal's leadership and courage. My goal with my new council is to remove the corruption plaguing my government for years. Because of this, I want to name new Mistresses of Dusk from the common people, ones whose opinions have not yet been swayed by corrupt politicians and their dark dealings. At this time, if she will accept, I name Ruta Vaal as Mistress of Dusk over the state of Adess."

Ruta covered her mouth with her hands, completely frozen in shock. In time, she gave a slight nod of her head, and Mara offered a wide smile in return. Ruta let out a deep breath and grinned.

"Ruta will govern Adess from Doftaan under the tutelage of Mistress Vasilica if she is still alive. She will also continue her education at the University of Doftaan until she is ready to rule on her own. She will be joined by her grandmother, who is already excited to join her."

Ruta broke out into thankful sobs and wrapped her arms around Mara, who reciprocated the gesture with a laugh.

"Finally, I plan to name a dear friend of mine named Diana as Mistress of Dusk over Terman. She is only a child, but there is no mind more pure or loving. Some will call me a fool for appointing her to such an important position, but the pure love of a child is exactly what the people of Terman so desperately need. She will live and serve under the tutelage of Mistress Raluca in Dashga.

"I don't want to take any more time before we go fight the fires around Balgorod, but I have one final thing to discuss tonight. It is a hidden and arcane secret in the ruling line of Sangora that many of our queens have used a power called the Queen's Control to coerce you into loyalty. Many wars were waged by Queens Sanda Daktha and Codruta Talohir with this power, and many gave their lives to it. I am ashamed to say that I have used it from time to time as well; the Phantom's Curse, as you're calling it, has made you immune to this ability, but I wish to announce today that no longer will my rule be one that I am able to force my people to do anything. Today, I declare a free Sangora free from Talohira, free from Florenta, free from tyranny, and free from me, if you so choose."

She held her wings before her and located where the organic gland controlling the Queen's Control had been implanted in the limbs. She drew a short dagger and pierced her own wings in the same place with the blade, severing her connection to the Queen's Control forever.

The crowd was now silent, and at first only Raluca and Anca bowed, but then Hanna, Shanthah, and Ruta followed suit, and then the entire crowd bowed before the Empress of Blood with raised wings as a sign of their true love, respect, and loyalty.

"Karpaska, and with it, Sangora, is free. May it forever be so."

# CHAPTER TWENTY-SEVEN

# IN THE BELLY OF THE BEAST

Blackness swirled around Mara's limbs, pulling her in all directions; she felt as if Ronin's magic were ripping her apart. Each time they vanished, the shadows drew the very air from her lungs, and the sensation of dunking her head and entire body under icy water washed over her again and again, each teleportation jump bringing her closer to Zinok. They had traveled hundreds of miles from Balgorod in such a way, and she was beginning to feel the toll it took on her body. A deep wheeze escaped her throat, followed by a fit of coughing.

"Breathe normally, Empress!" Ronin exclaimed. "By Elafris and the old gods, girl!"

She tried to heed his words, but exquisite pain like an auger twisting into her skull forced her to abandon him in midair. She flapped her mighty wings twice to widen the gap between them before gliding to the earth. She tumbled to the ground, allowing herself time to lie still in the grass.

"Very well," Ronin said, appearing next to her on the ground.

She grasped at her chest as air filled her lungs, each gasp of air like white hot flame rather than the early winter air. She shut her eyes and forced herself to draw deep breaths until her breathing felt normal again.

She envied Valistaran and the other Immortals who were travelling to Zinok by land. It had been her idea to combine their abilities of flight and teleportation to travel to Zinok, but she was beginning to regret the decision.

"Those things are even bigger than we thought," Mara said and sat up.

She pointed toward the two monstrosities looming over the swarm of Faceless surrounding Zinok. Mara and Ronin had spotted them for the first time soon after leaving Balgorod, and they followed their path of destruction toward Zinok. They had decided to get a head start ahead the other Immortals to assess the situation and infiltrate the fortress with their unique abilities.

"We'll have to fight them eventually," Ronin said in a matter-of-fact tone. Mara grunted.

"Mind if I take a few minutes?" Mara asked, nestling into the hillside.

"Actually—" Ronin began to say.

"I wasn't asking permission, Lord Jakoni," Mara said, closing her eyes again.

She wasn't sure why she felt so tired while Ronin was the one doing the teleporting, but she was far too exhausted to care.

"Empress, I respect that, but I did wish to speak with you concerning the plight of my people, while I have you alone and we are not yet fighting Thanatan's Faceless," Ronin said.

Mara sighed.

"Your people?" Mara asked. "You know the rest of Sangora sees the Walkers as terrorists and extremists, right?"

"We have been labeled as such. The Walkers are my closest followers and warriors, an organization that supports my cause, but they are not a nation, Empress. I trust you know that."

"Excuse me?" Mara asked, eyebrows raised.

"I apologize," Ronin said with an air of irritation. "I just wanted to talk to you about the males of our species."

"No, Ronin Jakoni, we are going to talk about you for a moment. We are going to ensure that you know your place," she said. "My throne may have been stolen from me, but I am not the type of woman that will stand being patronized, and I refuse to accept condescending attempts to 'educate' me. Is that clear?"

Mara's heart thundered in her chest, and Ronin's countenance changed from one of irritation to one of subjugation and sincere remorse.

"I truly do apologize, Empress. Please forgive me."

"You want to talk about the males of our species—so, by 'your people' you mean men?" Mara asked.

"No, the problem I'm talking about is one of the core issues of the revolution in Karpaska. You know as well as I how low the male population in Sangora is."

"I do," Mara said.

"Tell me, Empress—what do you know of the Deranged Queen Sanda Daktha?"

"Not much. She was the queen before Codruta," Mara said, shrugging. "To be honest, I've always wondered more about her."

"I know you, Empress, to be a well-read woman," Ronin said, sitting across from Mara. He crossed his legs beneath himself and stared with steely intent into her eyes.

"There's very little about her in the Grand Library of Bukaral or in any of the libraries in Doftaan, other than a decree I found by Codruta to wipe the libraries of her name," Mara admitted. She narrowed her eyes; knowing Ronin knew and withheld the answer, she asked, "Why is that?"

"Allow me to tell you a story," Ronin said.

Mara leaned forward, eager for the tale. She wondered how long the Walker had waited to tell it to her.

"Go ahead," Mara said in a softer tone.

"This may come as a shock to you, but Sangora was once ruled by a king of its own. Not one from Talohira like Valistaran, but a male Sangoran once sat upon your throne," Ronin said, maintaining eye contact with the Empress. "His name was Liviu Daktha. Born into a royal family from the Isle of Krim—never had to work a day in his life. A disgusting wretch of a man, he was. One devoid of feeling for the suffering of others, but one that through cunning and privilege became king."

"I know the type," Mara replied.

"Well, King Liviu Daktha had many, many mistresses. Dozens, possibly hundreds. No one knows how many for sure," Ronin said, breaking eye contact with Mara for the first time. "The mistresses never knew one another, although Liviu didn't make any efforts to keep them hidden from the queen. It was common knowledge that he had them."

"Disgusting."

"As I said. These mistresses came to be known as 'the Night Witches.' It's where the slur for women of our race comes from," Ronin explained.

"Go on," Mara urged.

"Well, Sanda was a powerful Mindspeaker, and discovering their identities was easy for her. Each time she did so, she had them killed. The original Mistresses of Dusk were followers of Queen Sanda who were charged with murdering these 'Night Witches'. Dusk comes before the night, and all that. The term for your councilors has changed since then and entirely lost the original connotation, but I digress. Their murders were covered up, and it all became a game to the Deranged Queen."

"Then how do you know this?" Mara asked, her eyebrows pressed together in concern.

"Because my own mother was the spawn of one of these mistresses," Ronin said. "She was one of the few survivors to escape with her life. She gave me what life she could, but she died very young, starving to give me enough to eat during the most brutal winter I remember."

"How did you survive?" Mara asked.

"The predecessors of the Walkers took me in. One of my aunts helped raise me until we parted ways," Ronin said. He paused, then said, "You may wonder why so many of my people share the same ability to vanish. It is because several of us are related to Liviu and his heirs, and we've been able to replicate his own powers of teleportation."

"Heirs?" Mara asked, wondering if any such people were seeking her life. "Are you saying that you are the heir of the Sangoran throne? Is that what you—"

"Oh, no," Ronin said with a chuckle. "Perhaps in another life, but according to my grandfather, my existence isn't even legitimate. I don't seek your throne, and most of my blood relatives are dead. Murdered. Some still live, but most have fallen so far into obscurity and other conflicts that they are no concern to you."

"So, what happened next?" Mara asked.

"Queen Sanda Daktha did not like the actions of her husband, and rightfully so. One night, she slit his throat in his own bed and left him there to rot before he could take another mistress. It took weeks for his servants to find him. If not for the smell, they would have never entered the chamber out of fear of interrupting him."

"Good," Mara said, eyes wide.

"Yes, perhaps she did the world a service that day, but the king's actions led to Queen Sanda Daktha's even more terrible evil," Ronin said. Mara cocked her head, and Ronin continued. "Soon after she killed King Liviu Daktha, she and a contingent of Sangoran Mindspeakers visited each and every state in Sangora."

"To do what?"

"She would gather the people in each city she visited. Then she would give the command using the very power you destroyed, the Queen's Control, amplified through her Mindspeakers, for the men in the city to kill one another. Sixty percent of all Sangoran men and twenty percent of women died."

"No," Mara whispered, shaking her head. She felt her stomach in her throat. "How could a genocide happen in the history of my people without me knowing?"

She wondered what other atrocities were being downplayed or hidden in her empire, especially with Florenta on the throne.

"At first, the genocide was slow. She relished in the bloodbath with each city she visited. It was another game to her, watching how long it took for the men to kill each other. If she found out women were harboring their husbands, she ordered them to kill their own husbands and sons," Ronin said. "It was never just about killing men, of course. That was simply her first game. In time, she moved on, killing anyone unfaithful to her. Women. Children. Foreigners. Political dissidents. Rivals. Anyone different from her."

"I can't hear any more of this," Mara said, shaking her head and hands. "What happened to her?"

"Do you wonder why the Walkers rid ourselves of our wings? Without them, the Queen's Control has no claim over us."

"I know how it works," Mara retorted.

Ronin bowed his head in apology.

"Shortly before she massacred the men in outlying areas like Balgorod and the rest of Karpaska, she was killed by a young human from Ruumanija—modern day Talohira. Do you know what that hero's name was?" Ronin asked.

"I don't have any idea."

"Valistaran Talohir," Ronin said.

Mara's stomach leapt into her chest.

"How did he get from saving Sangora from genocide by its own queen to—"

"To becoming High King of Talohira?" Ronin asked.

"I can speak for myself." She stared Ronin dead in the eyes.

"My apologies, Empress. I forget my place," Ronin said, bowing his head again. "Shortly after his victory over Queen Sanda Daktha, Valistaran went to Doftaan. With both the king and queen dead, the Mistresses of Dusk chose their own queen—one from their own number, a young woman named Codruta, whose hand they that same year offered to Valistaran in marriage after helping him liberate his homeland from the clutches of Thanatanos."

"That's how Valistaran became king and Talohira became free?" Mara whispered. "I was always told he defeated and united the warring Ruumanijan tribes there."

"He did that too. Such an act garnered him legitimacy to rule, and with the blessing of Sangora as a foreign power, Thanatanos eventually had to let it go as an independent country with an autonomous government," Ronin explained. "It wasn't hard to unite the warlords' tribes with the resources at his disposal."

"Why have I never heard these stories? Why are they not found in our libraries? Or taught in the schools of Sangora?" Mara asked.

"Because Valistaran made it illegal to speak of the sadness that brought him to the throne. He even had his own Mindspeakers go from city to city to wipe Liviu and Sanda's sins from the memories of the people. Of course, they couldn't be sure they altered everyone's memories, so many still remembered what had happened," Ronin said. "Very little information about them remained. Mistress Lavinia controlled the Minister of Information, at the time, Kristiana Balana, and forced her to help cleanse our history."

"Okay," Mara said, prompting him to continue. She knew Lavinia held countless secrets, but perhaps, this was the biggest.

"Alongside Minister Balana's invented history, Valistaran instructed the teachers in Talohira to teach that his crown had been handed down from his father before uniting the tribes and warlords of the region," Ronin said.

"But surely the older generation—people in outlying towns..." Mara muttered, trailing off. "This sounds like a conspiracy theory to me."

"What do any of those people know?" Ronin asked. "What do any of the common folk know? They live their lives far from the chaos we know. For all they knew, the stories being taught could be entirely truthful. Not even those in government knew the entire truth, and the rest were too beleaguered to care. They took this new truth as fact, and they taught it to their children. Ask your friend, Aleksander, for he holds in his mind all of these secrets."

Mara wondered for a moment how Ronin knew that Aleksander had been forced to become one of the Secret Keepers of Kurash but considered his apparent alliance with the Supreme One, ruler of Kurash, and said nothing of it.

Ronin glanced to the horizon. The behemoths were even nearer to Zinok, and the countryside blazed in a charred path of destruction behind them.

"So, the Walkers?" Mara asked, perhaps to delay their inevitable fight with the beasts. "I think we got sidetracked talking about Valistaran and the unhappy Daktha family."

"I see that," he said. "The Walkers banded together to avenge the rest of Sangora's men."

"But what was their goal? Sanda and Liviu were both dead. What more did they want to accomplish?" Mara asked.

"They wanted recompense, of course!" Ronin exclaimed. "They themselves wanted a new king on the throne, not a queen appointed by that murderess's own councilors! Do you not believe that they would have been indoctrinated with the same hatred and prejudice as Codruta's predecessor?"

"Is that what *you* want?" Mara asked.

"Much has changed in Walker culture in the years since our original uprising. I am a Lord of the Walkers, and I have tempered their anger as much as I have been able. But still, there are groups that have splintered from our tribe—"

"Extremists," Mara said. Ronin nodded. "Terrorists, like yourself."

Ronin let out an exasperated sigh. "Empress, there are those with even more extreme ideology than my own north."

"The North? Are the Walkers from Terman?"

"Terman? No," Ronin said with a laugh. "Farther north."

Another secret kept hidden from her. The only thing north of Terman was the endless, blackened hellscape of the Deadlands, or so she had been taught.

"What I want is to save my people by ending the threat of Thanatanos and threats to Sangora. This has always been my goal. Please, I beseech you. Do not judge the rest of us by the sins of a few."

"Then I promise not to judge the rest of your people based on *your* actions. The first step to eliminating threats from Thanatanos is not to destroy them, but to fix the relationship between our people," Mara said. "I hope you will accept that."

Ronin did not respond, and Mara said nothing for a long while, contemplating everything he had said. She let out a deep breath and looked toward Zinok.

"I will do what I can for your people," Mara said before turning back to Ronin and grabbing his wrist. "*Our* people—but Ronin, do the right thing."

There was a long pause before Ronin's eyes shifted then the duo was sucked into the dark, swirling shadows of his teleportation magic, continuing their trek across the sunny sky.

Between each teleportation jump, Mara caught distorted glimpses of the world below. Trees, meadows, a vast plain. All on fire. After another hour of travel, they found themselves upon a hill between the twin behemoths and the Faceless siege of Zinok. A perilous place to be, she knew, but also exactly where she was needed.

Rows of rocky, protruding scales lined the creatures' bodies in a flexible shell from snout to the tip of their tails. As one of the beasts lifted its crested head toward the sky, the cracks between the scales on its long neck glowed with the vehement heat of a furnace; smoke billowed from openings along its head and craned neck, followed by a pillar of flame so intense the heat reached Mara and Ronin upon the hilltop.

Mara covered her face to resist the wave of heat as the creatures began to charge on four stocky legs thicker than many of the spires of her palace; they shook the earth and trampled trees as they barreled toward their enemies, smoke and flame flowing from behind their teeth.

"Empress?" Ronin asked, drawing his hooked blades. She both sensed and shared his panic, but she did not flee.

"Go," Mara said. Ronin responded with an expression of concern and confusion. "Be ready if I need your magic, but your swords won't be of any use here."

"And you'll fare any better?!" Ronin exclaimed.

"Go."

Ronin vanished, and the Empress of Blood stood alone without weapon and without word; the beasts closed the distance toward Mara in seconds in their wild stampede.

An inferno of lava erupted from the bellies of the beasts as Mara shot into the sky. The river of molten rock carved through the hilltop where she had been standing moments before until it was a decimated heap of melted earth.

The Empress of Blood reached out with her mind, but could not sense the creature's consciousness, and she swore loudly. She soared around the beast, and as she glanced down its throat through its gaping maw, she brushed the creature's mental presence with her mind.

Its teeth slammed together, and the connection was gone. Perhaps, she thought, the beast's rocky armor provided some kind of shield against mental attacks.

As she circled in the sky above the behemoths, she watched the glow in their bellies and throats dim, and she took her chance. The monster opened its mouth once, and the Empress of Blood dove straight down through smoke and flame as if into the very jaws of hell itself. Darkness surrounded her as the gargantuan mouth closed like a cave collapsing.

Mara lashed out with her knife-tipped wings in an attempt to slow her fall, but they failed to pierce its impervious skin. She swore again as she plummeted down the beast's throat. She exerted all the mental energies she could muster to breach the monster's mind as she caught hold onto a craggy growth before being swallowed whole.

She screamed as the behemoth's superheated breath seared her skin, but she delved deeper into the behemoth's consciousness, finding Thanatan's influence wrapped around the monster's mind and soul. Her mental strength began to falter, and she knew she would not be able to hold the behemoth's mind for long. With a burst of mental energy, she felt Thanatan's grip on the creature snap.

Another scream escaped her throat as the beast stumbled with her still inside. She could feel its disoriented and confused mind still filled with rage and the desire to destroy her and everything in its path. She thrust her own influence where Thanatan's mind had been moments before. Terror filled her soul as she sensed another presence trying to snake his way back into the beast's mind, but she exerted all the mental energy she had left while tapping into the abilities granted to her by the Mind-Prison Cuff.

For two minutes, the equivalent of two years in her Mind-Prison, she battled with Thanatan over mental control of the beast. She felt his power, but in the end, she was able to overpower the behemoth and twisted its mind to the will of a new master.

To the will of an empress.

Mind numbing pain ripped through her skull, and she began to black out; she fell from her perch in the behemoth's throat, and an unearthly glow appeared deep in the belly of the beast. At that moment, she felt Ronin's hands grasp her shoulders, and the next thing she knew, daylight burned her eyes.

"Did it work?" Ronin shouted. Mara did not respond. "Mara?!"

As the second behemoth lumbered toward them, Mara's new servant closed its own jaws around the neck of its former companion, tearing rocky flesh from its throat. As Mara's monster released a river of lava, it tightened its grip. Its massive teeth tore through the other's spinal cord in a spray of ashen, rocky flesh and flaming gore. This caused a chain reaction in the belly of the second beast which caused an erratic and violent explosion of flame and death to rain down on the hills.

The surviving behemoth hesitated for a moment as its companion lay dead and burning. The behemoth turned its massive head and bowed before the Empress of Blood.

"You are mine," she whispered, glancing up at the fiery behemoth, which snorted flame with each breath. "Forever."

"What in the name of Elafris have you done?!" Ronin exclaimed.

With a shaking hand, Mara reached up and touched the beast's massive snout and could feel heat more violent than the sun of Kurash against her flesh. She chuckled, for when the beast wasn't trying to kill her, she realized its snout somehow simultaneously resembled three mythical animals she had read about as a child: a dragon, a crocodile and a hippopotamus. A happy grunt escaped its horrible jaws as if it were pleased to be free of Thanatan's influence.

Both she and her new ally collapsed, much to Ronin's surprise and dismay. For a little over a minute, Mara's body went rigid and convulsed. Ronin tried to hold her steady, but her fist collided with his throat, and he backed off.

"Easy, Empress. Easy!" he said.

Instead of trying to stop her from seizing, he guarded her head from striking the rock behind her. Despite his best efforts, her shoulder struck the boulder. Ronin stayed speechless by

Mara's side until she stopped convulsing; at last, both she and the monster were still.

Mara opened her eyes and jumped as she caught sight of Ronin's face. She glanced around, confused. She felt utter panic as the Lord of the Walkers held up his hands to reassure her.

"Do you remember what just happened?" he asked.

"I—no…"

"Do you know your name?"

"Mara…"

"Do you know your title?" Ronin asked. She didn't answer right away.

"I'm the…" Mara said. She paused for a long while. "…No, I don't—I'm sorry, I…"

"I think you just expended a lot of mental energy to take control of that beast. I believe it was too much for you, and I think you had a seizure or something."

Her face was screwed up out of fear and confusion.

"No, I just fell asleep, I—" Ronin reached for her hand, but she swatted it away and struggled away from him.

"Stay calm, I'm going to get help," Ronin replied. "Empress, you just saved your friends in Zinok! You did it!"

The behemoth groaned and got to its feet. Still disoriented, Mara reached out and patted its snout, and its eyes began to glow. Ronin backed up, unsure of what was happening.

The beast turned and began to devour its dead companion. As it consumed the burning, rocky flesh, bony protuberances jutted out of its back, extending into fingerlike branches.

The behemoth's jaws tore into the carcass of the dead beast, and with each bite, flesh and sinew wrapped around its new wings. When the behemoth had consumed all that remained of its prey, it roared in victory and turned its head to Mara, as if for her approval. She nodded, and it let out a deafening, happy sound.

"Empress, I think—" Ronin said with an amazed pause. "I think it wanted to *honor* you!"

Indeed, the Behemoth's wings looked like massive, rocky versions of Mara's own.

Ronin helped Mara stand; she was confused but calm. The behemoth lowered its neck, and Ronin led Mara onto its snout, up its head, and across its neck. She could feel the creature's joy in serving its empress.

"I think I'll name you… Hippo," Mara said with an amused smile. She laughed to herself.

'Hippo' waited for them to settle on its back before it stood on all four legs, roared, and shot into the sky just as thousands of Faceless swarmed over the hills below them.

# CHAPTER TWENTY-EIGHT
# TEARS AND SCARS

"Are you all seeing this?" Josman shouted.

He waved the others over to the narrow window. The massive creatures looming in the distance had turned on one another, drawing a vast portion of the Faceless horde away.

"Did that one just bite the other one's head off?!" Valis exclaimed.

He cheered as the corpse exploded in a brilliant burst of flame. Rather than standing like grotesque statues like they had been doing for the past few weeks, the Faceless now clambered over one another like hornets in an upset hive.

"I'm not quite sure what's happening, but I think it bodes well for us," Josman said. "Aleksander got your message. Do you think he found someone to save us?"

It had been over a month since the siege of Zinok had begun and several long days since Kamil managed to make contact with Aleksander and his companions through the body of a Faceless.

*"Those monsters were working together before, just like the Faceless,"* Kamil said to their minds.

"What could have caused them to turn on one another?" Valis asked. "Josman's right. Something's going our way!"

*"Powerful Mindspeakers sometimes have the ability to mind control weak minded people—I guess, theoretically, it could work the same way with a giant monster,"* Kamil responded with a shrug.

"Why are they so intent on keeping us trapped in here anyway?" Valis asked. "Why not kill us and end it?"

"Isn't it obvious?" Captain Rayna asked as she approached.

"Maybe not," said Josman with a shrug. He folded his arms and waited for Rayna to speak.

"They know we know the truth about Thanatan. Everything we've been through and everything Kamil told us—if I was in his place, it wouldn't make sense to me to let us live. From a political or military standpoint, that is," Rayna said.

"But then, why not kill us, like the boy asked?" Josman wondered, and then a thought filled his mind, one that he shared with Kamil.

*"He wants us to watch."*

"That's right, and he now has an impenetrable prison," Rayna said.

"Maybe you're right," Josman muttered.

"Perhaps so, but I didn't come in here to be right. I came to bring some rather odd and unforeseen news," Rayna said. "The king has returned."

"The king?" Josman asked, straining his head to see farther through the small window. "So, Aleksander got word to King Verahim, then? He hasn't abandoned us after all?"

"No," Rayna replied. She gestured to Valis and uttered two haunting words. "Your father."

Valis bolted upright, his heart thundering in his chest.

At that moment, a tongue of black flame exploded from the writhing, Faceless mass. The torrent of darkness parted the remaining part of the swarm just enough to allow Valistaran and four other figures to walk through unharmed.

"*Impossible*," Kamil said as he reached out with his mind and sensed the familiar presence of Valistaran Talohir. He covered his mouth with his hands as Josman pressed his eye against the window slit and gasped.

"Why aren't they killing him?" Josman shouted. "Go, Faceless, go!"

"Because Rayna's right, of course. This is our prison. They don't care if someone comes in, they care if we leave," Valis said. He turned to Rayna. "Does my mother know?"

"Who do you think noticed and sent me to fetch you?" Rayna asked with a caring smile. "Come on, kid."

Alia stood just outside Sanctuary's inner gate, the light fabric of her clothes fluttering in the wind. Dark eyes glared out of her chaotic, windswept hair, fixed on one point: the fallen High King of Talohira and his companions approaching the inner keep of Sanctuary.

Valistaran broke his stride and stopped in his tracks as he gazed into the familiar, dark eyes that greeted him. Alia stood more fearsome than any guardian of the gate, and he bent one knee and bowed before her, piercing the earth with his sword. His companions did not kneel but stood behind him in silence.

"This is—" he said, searching for the appropriate word. "Unexpected."

Alia took her eyes off her former husband, and for the first time, she realized the identity of Valistaran's first companion: The Supreme One of Kurash stood before her in a simple traveler's cloak and tunic, leaning on the shaft of a spear. She dropped into a low bow, the custom of her country and people. She did not recognize the Supreme One's other companions.

"Rise, daughter of Kurash," the Supreme One, Kadir, said.

"Please, come in," Alia said in a flustered tone, welcoming the group into Sanctuary as if into her own home back in Tal-Ahosh.

"Thank you," said the third companion, a bespectacled man Alia recognized as Daniel Elafris.

"How did you find us?" Alia asked as she led them into Sanctuary. Lieutenant Marek and two other soldiers closed the gates with a grinding screech.

"Well, you know of my daughter's abilities," Valistaran said, gesturing to one of his hooded companions.

"All too well," Alia said, a look of sorrow in her eyes. "Hello, Valeniya. How are you, my friend?"

"I'm glad you've been safe," Valeniya replied, her eyes vacant and cloudy. "I've been very worried for you."

"Have you been watching me again, Leniya?" Alia asked. Valeniya nodded and hung her head as if embarrassed. Alia smiled and touched the young woman's shoulder. "Thank you for watching over me. I've needed it, you know!"

At that moment, Valis, Rayna, Josman, and Kamil met them at the bottom of a set of stone stairs. Valis and Valistaran locked eyes, and as the fallen king caught the first ever glimpse of his son's face, a tear rolled down his cheek. Alia turned back to Valistaran and shoved a finger into his chest.

"Look who's come home," said Alia; her warm accent wrapped around cold words.

"Alia, I—"

"Don't 'Alia' me. I thought you were dead, Val!" Alia shouted, slamming the side of her fist into his chest.

"Aleksander knew—"

"Oh, *Aleksander* knew you were alive! A fat lot of good that did *me!*" Alia shouted and folded her arms over her chest.

The Supreme One and Daniel Elafris whispered to one another and distanced themselves from the others as if sensing the tension between the members of the fractured Talohir family.

"I'm sorry," Valistaran said. For a long moment, they just looked into one another's eyes. Valis backed away, but Alia reached back and grasped his tunic with a firm hand. He came back with a low groan.

"For what?" Alia asked, raising her eyebrows.

"For putting power before my family."

The words seemed to break through Alia's hard expression, and she screwed up her face as she fought back tears. She shook her head and pounded her fist against his chest twice more, saying nothing.

"Everything I did was to prevent this from happening," Valistaran said, gesturing toward the horde of Faceless beyond the gates. "Finding the Weapon of Ages Past, the camps—"

"I told you to never mention those slave camps again near me," Alia said, her eyes cold. She turned to point to Josman and Kamil and added, "and near *them*, no less! You know they were in your camps, right? That they were your *slaves*? No. How would you? You think people like *them* are what caused this? They're trying to prevent—you know what, Val? I'm sick of these fights every time we see each other. Every single time it's more of the same."

"I know."

He bowed his head, and she felt a wave of empathy wash over her soul; Valistaran said nothing, and Alia wondered if it was remorse or regret that fueled this new, uncharacteristic humility.

"Last time we talked back in Tal-Ahosh, you said you found someone."

"It didn't work out," Valistaran said, the mirthless line of a sad smile crossing his face.

"I'm sorry, Val. You know I always want the best for you," Alia said, stepping toward the fallen king. He expected another fist to the chest, but instead, Alia wrapped her arms around him.

"I know. It was probably for the best," Valistaran said, letting out a deep breath. "By the way, she should be here by now—has Empress Mara not arrived?"

"Mara's coming?" Josman asked, speaking up for the first time. He shared a glance with Kamil. "So, Aleksander got our message to her after all!"

"She's not here," Alia said with a shake of her head. When she broke from the hug, she gestured to Valis, who approached with a slow step.

"When you came by my place that day, I didn't want you to meet your son. I tried to keep him hidden, but I'd like you to meet Valistaran the Second."

"Valis," the young man said with a wave.

Valistaran broke into a wide smile, but his son didn't know how to react other than with a wave and an awkward grin.

"And Valis, this is your half-sister, Valeniya," Alia said. Valis gave another wave, but Valeniya did not respond and seemed to stare straight through him.

"I've gone over this moment so many times since that night in Tal-Ahosh. It is so wonderful for me to meet you," Valistaran said. "There is true evil spreading from Laniras as we speak. I rejoice that you are both alive. Thanatan's minions are welcomed in Thanatanos and are spreading across Sangora as we speak. There is not much time until they reach Talohira as well. I'm not only here to rescue you," Valistaran said, bending his knee before his son.

"What else *are* you here for?" Valis asked.

"To pass the crown to the next king of Talohira. To King Valistaran Talohir the Second."

"King?" Valis repeated, dumbfounded. Alia turned her back on them both, hiding her rage and shook her head in wild protest. "Why?"

"Talohira is without a ruler. In Mara's absence, the people of my country rose up to overthrow the Sangoran government and set up their own king. Others did not believe in that man's claim to power, and they murdered him in the streets. The kingdom is tearing itself apart as we speak. They are without unity and without hope. They need you, Valis," Valistaran said.

"Why not you? You're still alive," said Valis. "Or Mara? Or her?" Valis gestured to Valeniya. In response, Alia grabbed the young man's sleeve and gave a vigorous shake of the head before Valeniya noticed.

"Because I'm not sure how long that fact will remain true. How long have you been cooped up in here hiding from the Faceless? Mara was overthrown by one of her councilors, and Sangora is on the brink of civil war. With a united Talohira, perhaps you could make a difference," Valistaran said. He explained the entire situation in Sangora and Thanatanos to the rest of the group, who listened with rapt attention.

"What about Kurash?" Valis asked. "Why can't they help?"

"There would be geopolitical ramifications beyond your understanding. If we moved on Thanatanos to kill the false god or the usurper queen in Sangora, there are many in either country that would turn on us. A ruler set up by a foreign power will not be seen as legitimate, and there would be bloodshed beyond any this world has ever seen," Kadir explained.

"Empress Mara is in on a similar quest to retake Sangora, but you will not be part of that tale," Valistaran said. "I'll help you where I can, but it's going to be a long road."

"Thank you. But I do have one thing to say. I wouldn't be a Talohir, I'd be a *Shadid* on the throne. Mom and I have both started using her surname again."

Alia smiled, an expression that went unseen by them both. Her rage had dissipated into a hopeful pride for her son.

"A strong name. We'll talk more about this later, but I couldn't risk going any longer without naming you the legitimate king of Talohira," Valistaran said. "However, there's a more pressing matter to attend to. Namely, getting everyone out of here alive. If the Empress and Lord Jakoni aren't here yet, that'll be a bit more difficult…"

Together they made their way up the hill to follow Daniel and the Supreme One toward the central keep of Sanctuary. Alia held back to watch father and son walk together up the hill, and she smiled.

They joined the others around three long tables pushed together in a triangle. Josman, Kamil, and Rayna sat at one table while Kadir, Daniel, and Elafris sat at another. The four Talohirs each took a seat behind the third. A dozen or so of Rayna's defeated looking soldiers clad in full battle gear, including Lieutenant Marek, joined as well.

"I would like to welcome High King Valistaran Talohir and the Supreme one who is called Kadir to this council, and I thank the rest of you for joining me," Rayna said, signaling the unceremonious beginning of the impromptu meeting. "I've stationed one of my soldiers, Pavlina, near the window to alert us just in case the Faceless move in, but I think we have some time to discuss our options."

"Then let us hope she doesn't have to warn us, because there is no way out of here," said Valis, rubbing the back of his neck.

"They got in, so why can't they just help us get out?" asked Lieutenant Marek, gesturing at the newcomers.

"We believe they let us through," Valistaran said. "They're keeping you here as a prison. The fight still appears to be ahead of us. Now, Kamil, I believe you had a message for us?"

Kamil described the vision he had witnessed in as much detail as he could remember. He spoke of the Faceless slaughtering millions and the plumes of flame that consumed everything that was left, as well as the feeling of satisfaction watching it all burn. Daniel Elafris nodded along through the entire tale.

"Your description of the destruction is accurate," Elafris said. "I'm pretty sure you saw the past from one of Thanatan's own memories. Perhaps the destruction of New York City— were you under the impression you were seeing the future?"

"*Yes,*" Kamil replied.

"What you've seen is real. Another source confirmed to me that Thanatan's Faceless destroyed the civilization before our own and plans to do the same thing again," Valistaran said.

"And what source was that?" asked Josman.

"The answer to that question is a bit hard to explain. Some kind of living tree god with magical gateways that saved my life when—look, that doesn't matter now," Valistaran replied.

"What avenues are there to guide us to freedom?" Kadir asked.

"The forward path was designed to be the only way in or out," Rayna explained. "Sanctuary and Zinok were designed to be impenetrable with enough supplies to outlast any siege."

"But not designed against these undying creatures," Kadir said, thinking out loud. He stroked his thin beard, deep in thought.

"I still think Mr. Josman is right," said one of the soldiers behind Rayna, a young man no older than twenty. "Perhaps we should still try a frontal assault."

"I agree. With all your powers to guide us out and our military experience, there's nothing we can't do!" said a second soldier.

"How many soldiers remain in Sanctuary?" asked Valistaran. Kamil scoffed and shook his head.

"These twelve, myself, and eight more who stand guard at the pass, sir. The rest are civilians," Rayna explained.

"Boy, what is your name?" Valistaran asked.

"Danek," replied the young man.

"Danek, do you think twenty soldiers and a handful of sorcerers are powerful enough to take on an entire swarm of Faceless?" Valistaran asked.

"Well, maybe not kill all of them, but—"

"You think they would ever stop pursuing us?" Valistaran asked. "Not until the ends of the Earth."

"Val," Alia said, narrowing her eyebrows. Valistaran backed off, raising his hands.

"What about Kamil's powers?" Valis asked. The room turned to Kamil for an answer. Valeniya stepped away from the table and began to pace the length of the chamber.

*"I was able to take control of some of the Faceless long enough to relay a message to Aleksander,"* Kamil said. *"I can also create mental lures that distract them for a time, but I'm not sure what I could do against so many."*

"If they see any of their number try to flee, they are sure to pursue," Kadir said. He turned to Elafris, who so far had remained silent. "And what say you, he who is called the devil?"

"Oh, would you stop calling me that," Elafris said. "For any of you unfamiliar with what you people call 'magic,' this young man has telepathic abilities. I've never been aware of the full extent of what a telepath can do, but—"

"I'm sorry, but who is this?" asked Danek with a laugh. "I thought I heard you call him Elafris."

Josman exchanged an amused glance with Kamil, for they both knew Daniel Elafris was a normal human that had survived the destruction of his own civilization, but exaggerated tales had led to an entire religion believing him to be the devil himself.

"Elafris," said Valistaran in a matter-of-fact voice.

"The devil?" Danek asked. The other stared at him with deadpan expressions. "Wait, you're serious?"

When the conversation started again, the group argued about how to best free themselves from their prison. The soldier set to watch the window, Pavlina, turned from her post and cleared her throat; the entire room fell silent, and a feeling of dread washed over the room.

"Captain? I think you should see this," Pavlina said, stepping away from the small window.

Rayna stood with such abruptness that her chair toppled to the floor as she hurried away from the table; her soldiers set the chair upright as Rayna pressed her eye to the window slit.

"They're coming!" Rayna shouted.

Josman pressed his face to the narrow window, and sure enough, the swarm was closing in on Zinok.

"There goes our prison theory," he said, and then everyone in the chamber scrambled to fortify the room against the creatures.

Valistaran rushed to the window and pressed his palm against the narrow crack in the stone and unleashed a burst of black flame that extended out of the fortress and into the daylight.

"What are you doing?" Alia asked.

"The captain mentioned there are civilians here, so I'm hoping to draw these things to us instead," Valistaran explained.

The horrible groaning of the Faceless and the dread and hunger that accompanied it permeated the entire keep, but as quickly as it began, it was all over. Pavlina hurried to the window.

"They're pulling back!" she called.

"Don't be so quick to assume that!" Josman shouted. "We didn't do anything to make them give up, so they must have found another way in!"

"There is no other way in," Rayna replied and checked the window herself. To her astonishment, the entire swarm was fleeing from Zinok toward the massive behemoth in the distance. Josman took his turn at the window and gave a hearty chuckle.

"I think that thing might be on our side!" he exclaimed.

"If it's drawing the Faceless away, now might be a good time to go!" Valis replied.

"Valis is right," Rayna said and turned to Lieutenant Marek and Danek. "Fetch the remaining civilian refugees from Sanctuary's saferoom. We're getting out of here! Tell them we will make our way to Laniras if it's safe."

"Yes, captain," said the soldiers. The duo disappeared through the hallway leading to Sanctuary's deepest saferoom housing the displaced citizens.

"It'll take a few minutes for the refugees to get up here. I suggest we scout ahead to make sure this isn't a trap," Rayna said. "The civilians' safety, is of course, of utmost importance."

Alia turned to her son as he, like the others, prepared to set out. It was strange for her to see him with a sword strapped to his waist.

"You okay, kid?" Alia asked, giving the young man a high-five. He smiled in reply.

"I'm fine, mom," Valis said. "You worry too much."

"You don't worry enough!" Alia exclaimed as Josman assisted Rayna in opening the main gateway leading out of the fortress of Sanctuary.

Valis thought for a moment, wondering what it would be like if his mother and father reconciled. He wondered what it would be like to have a complete family, but then he shook the thought from his mind.

Given the identity of his father, a 'normal' life would never be possible, and just because his father had returned, it did not mean his family was now somehow 'whole.' He decided at that moment, his little family of just him and his mother was indeed complete. They were happy, and that was all that he needed.

At that moment, Valistaran pulled himself up to the high opening to help Josman, and together the two men helped the others exit. It was not easy to get in or out of Sanctuary's fortress, and perhaps, Valis thought, that was by design. He watched as Josman took special care in assisting Alia through the opening and caught a glimpse of a faint smile on his mother's lips as their hands touched.

Josman reached down and shouted, "Are you coming, boy? We can leave you here if you like!"

"No, I think I'll join you!" Valis called back with a laugh, reaching up so that Josman could help him out.

The smell of a smoky wildfire filled his nostrils; the sky bled red and yellow as the sun's light filtered through smoke trailing off the behemoths' path of destruction, but no Faceless threatened those within Zinok.

For now.

"Well, despite the oncoming doom, I've always said fires like this do make the most beautiful sunsets…" Josman said, trailing off. Alia smiled.

*"Careful, our resident pessimist wouldn't like you talking like that,"* Kamil said to Josman's mind.

They paused, for they had rarely spoken of Drahomir since he fell against the Faceless, and guilt crept into their hearts.

"Do you think he got away?" Josman asked.

*"He did discover an ability that might allow that,"* Kamil said with a shrug, but his face did not look hopeful.

"Well, I hope he did," Josman said with a deep sigh.

They took a few moments to appreciate the dramatic beauty of the sky before Rayna's calls brought them back to reality.

"My men are bringing a ladder for the refugees," Rayna explained, gesturing to the opening.

"We're more than happy to help any out who can't climb," Josman said. "Despite my bad back."

*"You don't have a bad back,"* Kamil thought with a laugh.

*"Anybody* would have a bad back after sleeping in the dirt as much as we have," Josman said, turning to look at Valistaran with contempt. Kamil shrugged in agreement. "Especially in the slave camp in Talohira."

"You'll be happy to hear that Empress Mara Bartunek has shut down the slave camps in Talohira," Valistaran said, omitting the fact that he had been the one to instate them in the first place.

They both knew he was the reason for their hardships, for the suffering of Mara, Hanna, and the others, and the deaths of many of their friends, but seeing him here made it somehow surreal, as if one man couldn't possibly be responsible for such wickedness. He did not seem to acknowledge or even know about the evil that transpired there.

Did he even care?

When the refugees had all exited Sanctuary, the group made its way into the narrow canyon leading out of Zinok. Josman and Kamil hung back, and Josman pulled Valistaran aside. He brought his fist around, planting it squarely against Valistaran's jaw; the force of the blow knocked Valistaran against the wall, but the fallen king did not retaliate.

"Since you arrived, we've been meaning to talk to you," Josman said, sparing no time to bring up the sore subject. Kamil offered Valistaran a hand, helping him to his feet. He bowed his head, an apologetic gesture, but not one of reverence or respect.

"Mara told me about both of you and the others in the camp. I thank you for being a light to her in that dark place, and I apologize for what had to be done," Valistaran said, massaging his jaw. "Without you, without friends like Hanna Samsa, Shanthah Kalen, the one who calls himself Aleksander, and, I believe, especially without Rehor Toth, the Empress of Blood would have turned out to be much less of an empathetic and caring ruler."

"You're saying Mara would have turned out to be just like you?" Josman asked, folding his arms across his chest.

"Yes," Valistaran said after a moment of silence. Josman was taken aback by the answer, the genuine surprise apparent on the burly man's stern, yet caring face.

"I had reservations when I made Mara queen of Sangora and Talohira. Her nomination came to me from a trusted advisor, although one that I admit, had a hand in orchestrating my downfall," Valistaran said with a chuckle.

"*Is that what you call trust?*" Kamil asked. Valistaran and Kamil helped steady the ladder as the soldiers below helped the refugees to start climbing.

"I could always trust that she knew what she was doing, and that her plans—whatever their outcome—were for a wise purpose," Valistaran said. "And she was almost never wrong."

"*That plan being your demise?*" Kamil asked.

"And look how much better the world is for it," Valistaran said. "I had a vision for a better world. Our world was long ago ravaged by war caused by terrifying technologies and magic. I couldn't let that happen again. My vision, however, didn't turn out to be the best one."

"You're saying your advisor was smarter than you?" Josman asked, helping another elderly refugee escape the darkness of the fortress that could have been their tomb.

"I'm saying Mara is a better person and a better ruler than me," Valistaran said. "But her position is not the only good outcome of my vision."

"*Your son,*" Kamil said. Valistaran nodded.

"If Talohira will give him a chance, my son will prove to be a better ruler of Talohira than I ever was. My hope is for Mara on one throne and Valis on another. My actions, however barbaric you see them, did produce a better future than when I started."

"You claim that everything you did to us, to our friends— people died in there, you know," Josman said. "People I came to love as family never made it out. And why?"

"Because I was trying to stop this! I knew the past was going to come back to haunt us. What are a few lives to save millions? And look out there, Josman!" He thrust his hand toward the window. "*This* is exactly what I was trying to prevent!"

"Oh, well then let's all bow down to the great High King of Talohira!" Josman shouted. He looked at Valistaran with an expression of sadness and a spark of righteous indignation. Great tears welled in the corners of his eyes, and his nostrils flared. His voice cracked as he spoke.

"I stand by my words."

"Yeah? Well, you go and tell that to Hanna. You tell that to Mara! You have *no idea* the horrors they experienced because of *you*! You *will* answer for each and every one of the scars on their backs—for every single one of their tears." Josman was shaking now, trying to hold back his own tears. "You may have *somehow* done your part to bring to pass a better future for all of us, but I will never forgive you for what your slavers did to them. Do you have any idea?! Any at all?!"

"I never sought, or should I say *expected* your forgiveness. But as you say, I attend to atone for each and every one of those tears."

"Empty words aren't enough! They don't excuse anything you did. Do something about it, you disease!" Josman shouted. He grabbed Valistaran by the shoulder and shoved him hard against the wall, forcing him to meet his furious gaze. "And you had better uphold that promise, or I swear I'll kill you myself."

# CHAPTER TWENTY-NINE

# THE EYES OF A FRIEND

The dusty glow of the late autumn sun dipped behind the horizon, golden light giving way to the dark hues of dusk's twilight. Aleksander sat with his back toward the scant campsite, his sword unsheathed. The smooth metal reflected the last rays of sunlight. A fire burned at his back, its long trail of smoke reaching the heavens.

"Come on, you dirtbag…" Aleksander whispered to himself, twisting his blade to reflect in all directions, but as the sun died, so did the glare off his polished steel.

"This is going to get us killed," Vasilica said, warming her wings by the fire.

"Then we won't have to worry," Lavinia said, shrugging her shoulders.

"Technically true," Aleksander said. "Don't you believe in your own plan?"

"I always trust my own plans," Lavinia said. "How do you know my plan isn't just to get us killed?"

"Because you're a survivor," Aleksander said.

He was quiet for a moment as he ignited a fireball in his palm and held it aloft before throwing it into the sky.

"Yeah?" Lavinia asked, a smirk on her face.

"Yeah. And you always play the long game," Aleksander added. Vasilica scoffed, and Lavinia smiled.

"That I do," Lavinia said. "More fire."

Aleksander obeyed without objection, launching a pillar of flame toward the moon. He was bored, and at least throwing flames was something to do.

"We can't be too obvious, or he'll know it's a trap," Rayshel said, her eyes following one flittering ash that was soon lost in the glow of the campfire. Aleksander cast a ball of raging flame into the campfire, and both Rayshel and Vasilica leapt backward to escape the explosion of ash and flame.

And out of the ashes, a dim purple glow heralded the coming of their prey; an arm brandishing a curved blade reached forth from the shifting smoke as the assassin appeared. The assassin's aim was true, and the vicious blade arced toward Aleksander's exposed neck. Just before it met its mark, his cry of pain and surprise filled the night.

Lavinia roared as she dug the bladed tips of her wings deeper into the muscles of his back, forcing him to drop one of his curved daggers. He brandished the other backward and lurched around to hack at Lavinia's wing.

Vasilica's shining blade pierced the man's forearm before he could land the blow. The assassin's entire body seemed to fade out of reality as the deep purple teleportation mist surrounded him. Lavinia did not relent, shoving the blades deeper into his back toward his spine.

The assassin's teleportation magic engulfed them both then sputtered as the man cried out in agony, appearing several feet away, clutching his wounds. Vasilica had failed to remove his hand, but his arm was soaked in blood. He stumbled toward his fallen blade as Lavinia appeared out of the teleportation mist and crashed to the ground, tumbling over rocks and dirt.

Rayshel tackled the assassin before he could reach the blade and brought her fist down, crushing it against the man's exposed throat. He gasped for air behind the broken mask and threw his hands toward her, teleporting her high into the air above, knowing that without wings, she would plummet to the earth.

"Rayshel!" Aleksander shouted, but Lavinia shot into the air and intercepted Rayshel before she struck the earth. Meanwhile, Aleksander grasped the assassin's crimson mask and concentrated all the heat and flame he could on its surface. Before long, it began to glow white hot, and the assassin screamed in pain.

Their foe managed to twist free of Aleksander's onslaught and kicked him in the knee hard enough to knock him backward.

Aleksander's head struck the ground hard as the man crawled away clutching his mask. He began to teleport, but Lavinia yanked him back and threw him on the ground before pressing her metallic boot against his chest. A sputtering cough escaped his throat.

Aleksander limped forward and tried to yank the mask from the assassin's face with no success. Instead, he smashed the pommel of his sword against it, forming a crack along its intricate face. The familiar groans of the Faceless filled the night.

Before Aleksander could land another blow, the assassin managed one last weak burst of teleportation magic, but it was only enough to banish Lavinia and her blade, preventing it from piercing his throat. The weapon appeared several feet away, burying itself into the ground as if thrust there by its master.

"Stop!" the assassin sputtered.

He stumbled to his feet as the chipped and broken portion of the mask fell away, revealing the side of the man's face.

Aleksander gazed into the eyes of a friend.

Drahomir.

"What?!" Aleksander shouted. "No!"

Drahomir gazed back at him, disoriented just as Lavinia smashed her armored elbow into the back of his head. He hit the ground and did not stir.

"What is it?" Rayshel asked.

"I know him—is he—" Aleksander began to say.

The light of the campfire cast an eerie glow across the surroundings, and he stumbled backward in shock.

"Alive? For now," Lavinia said, checking for a pulse.

"We need to get out of here," Rayshel said. "I can sense those Faceless things. They found us."

Aleksander was so focused on the shock of seeing his friend behind the mask that he had almost forgotten the groans of the Faceless coming from the city.

Rayshel and Aleksander finished packing up the camp as Vasilica used her mighty wings to throw earth over the campfire, casting the world into darkness.

"We have what we were here for. I see no reason to stay," Lavinia said, hoisting Drahomir's bleeding, unconscious body over her back. She retrieved her sword and extended her wings.

"Was he a friend?" Rayshel asked, laying a comforting hand on his shoulder.

"I don't know anymore," Aleksander whispered. "I thought so."

Rayshel rubbed his arm with an expression of concern.

Vasilica and Lavinia took flight, carrying their captive away. Aleksander and Rayshel were close behind on foot. They fled through the night until the groans of the Faceless plagued them no more. In time, Laniras faded into the distance behind forests and streams.

"Think we're safe here?" Rayshel asked as they came to the outskirts of a small town.

Aleksander gasped and placed a hand over his mouth as he read a faded sign on the edge of the road that read *Welcome to Cineca.*

"Yeah, until those things spread to every city in Thanatanos," Aleksander said. "And beyond…"

It had been many years since Aleksander had met Mara in this very town, and his heart twisted in his chest, longing for those days spent with her.

"You alright?" Vasilica asked. "You look like you've seen a ghost."

"In a sense," Aleksander said. "I'm fine."

"We're far from safe," Lavinia scoffed. "We're not far from the ruins of Nitra. These hills must be infested with Faceless. I can think of nowhere more dangerous."

Aleksander sighed, wishing they had time to visit Killian and Daniela. But what could he possibly say? Did they even know what had happened to Mara or Pol?

"Mistress Vasilica, Rayshel, how are you doing?" Aleksander asked, trying to push Mara's parents from his thoughts.

Vasilica gave a tired nod, an indication that she was alive, at least. Rayshel flashed a smile, but Aleksander could see the signs of exhaustion setting in.

"The streets look deserted. Makes sense, given what Lavinia mentioned. Let's hope the rest of town is the same way," Vasilica said. "We need to find somewhere for Rayshel to lie down. We all need to rest, but she's exhausted. Scary exhausted, not like us."

"I'm fine," Rayshel said with a dismissive wave of her hand.

"No, you are not," Lavinia said, scolding her friend as she dumped Drahomir's unconscious body onto the ground. Rayshel draped her arm over Lavinia's shoulder, and the Mistress of Dusk supported her on their way into Cineca.

"How's our guest?" Aleksander asked, crouching next to him. "Shouldn't he have woken up by now?"

Lavinia had bound Drahomir's wrists with a line of rope they found at a deserted farm between Laniras and Cineca. While resting there, they had examined the assassin's wounds. Any regular person would have succumbed to the injuries, but some dark magic seemed to be keeping him alive.

Aleksander hefted the assassin over his shoulder.

"Maybe he's dead. He was getting heavy," Lavinia said, heading into town. "And Rayshel is much more pleasant."

They followed the main thoroughfare, seeing only a few townsfolk who scurried away from them while about their business, heads low.

"We're not far from the border with Sangora. These people probably don't like seeing people like us in their town," Vasilica said as Rayshel absentmindedly scratched the incessant itch where one of her wings used to be.

Lavinia tried the doors of several buildings on a winding street off the main path until she found one that was unlocked; she delved into the darkness, and Aleksander followed, lighting a ball of flame in his hand for light.

"No one's here," Lavinia said, checking an old wardrobe.

The home was abandoned except for the roaches that scurried about on the floor away from the light.

"Good," Aleksander said then gestured to the wardrobe. "We can put him in there."

He dropped Drahomir's body inside the wardrobe. He stared at his friend's face through the damaged mask with a look of betrayal.

"Might want to keep the door open. He can teleport, you know," Vasilica reminded the group, propping the door open. Lavinia helped Rayshel into the larger bed in the room, and she was asleep within moments. Vasilica yawned and glanced down at the smaller bed without words then back at Aleksander as if to ask if he wanted it.

"Take it," Aleksander said with a nod. Vasilica smiled and patted Aleksander's knee before settling into the bed.

When Lavinia was sure Vasilica and Rayshel were both asleep, she pulled Aleksander into the small kitchen.

"He was in your slave district," Lavinia said.

"You remember him?" Aleksander asked, taken aback.

"Your district was, shall we say—a little more distinct than the others," Lavinia said with a nod. "But I remember every face I ever saw in the camps. Names, not so much. I was a prisoner there too, you know, serving a punishment I didn't deserve."

"Distinct meaning troublesome?" Aleksander asked. Lavinia gave a curt nod.

"His name is Drahomir, no?" she asked. Aleksander nodded. "I have spoken with Mara at length about him and what he did to her."

"What do you mean?" Aleksander asked, raising an eyebrow.

"You don't know?" Lavinia asked, a look of surprise on her face. She furrowed her brow as if debating her next words.

Aleksander could not tell whether the expression was genuine or feigned, something about the powerful Sangoran that always put him on edge.

"Tell me."

"I'm not sure it's my place," Lavinia replied. "I thought you knew."

Aleksander nodded and turned to exit the kitchen to make sure Drahomir was still confined to the cupboard.

"I can respect that, but if it helps me understand why someone I thought was my friend—"

"Has been killing leaders of Sangora?" Lavinia asked, cutting Aleksander off. "Are the two things mutually exclusive? Can he not be your friend and an assassin?"

"He didn't just try to kill foreign leaders—he tried to kill me as well," Aleksander replied.

"He didn't just try to kill them, Aleksander. He succeeded, and I would appreciate if you understood that."

"Sorry," Aleksander said. "The Mistresses of Dusk he murdered—I thought they weren't your allies. I thought you'd want them gone."

"They weren't my allies, politically or personally, but that doesn't mean I wanted them murdered," Lavinia retorted. "They're still Sangoran."

"Didn't you try to have Valistaran killed?"

"Again, with the *try*," Lavinia said.

"He survived," Aleksander replied. Lavinia scoffed.

"Valistaran the man did, but Valistaran the *king* didn't."

She stood in the entrance to the kitchen with Aleksander looking at Drahomir's boot sticking out of the wardrobe. Lavinia sighed, hung her head, and then looked toward Aleksander.

"He betrayed Mara to save his own life," Lavinia said, arms folded. "Left her behind. It's how she got captured and converted into a Sangoran."

"I thought you said it wasn't your place to tell me this," he said. The revelation felt like a dagger in his heart. "And why wouldn't he tell us?"

"Perhaps it still isn't my place. I'll forgo the details of what transpired, but I think it's important that you know," Lavinia said.

"We thought she was killed that night," Aleksander said. Lavinia nodded.

"Understandable. That night, she began her path to become the Sangoran queen. The path I set her on and kept her on."

Aleksander had never known exactly how Mara had become queen of Talohira and Sangora, and his ears pricked up as the words slipped from Lavinia's mouth. She was being extraordinarily open today; was it a ploy to lower his own defenses? He pushed the thoughts away, hoping to gleam more information about what had happened to Mara two years earlier.

"What do you mean by that?" Aleksander asked.

"Sometime after the mass breakout from the slave camp and the prisons, both of which your troublesome slave district had a hand in orchestrating, might I add, I discovered a new Wingling in a place called the Wingling House."

"I'm afraid I'm unfamiliar with the phrase, but I assume a Wingling is—"

"The first stage of conversion from human to Sangoran, or a naturally born Sangoran developing their wings during puberty," Lavinia said. Aleksander nodded.

"I recognized her immediately. She was one of the few slaves with a fire we couldn't quite extinguish," Lavinia said with a dark chuckle. "The queen of the slaves, I called her."

Her gaze dropped, an expression of shame that Aleksander picked up on, however brief it lasted. "One of Belokej's biggest problems, and one of my greatest successes. I stoked the embers of Mara's hope, and what I got was a wildfire."

"You wanted her to overthrow Belokej. Belokej *and* the camp," Aleksander stated. A grin spread across his face to accompany the realization. "You were guiding her without us knowing it."

"I play the long game," Lavinia said, referring to Aleksander's previous comment. "You recognize that already."

"You didn't believe in the camps," Aleksander said. "Why was that?"

"I was there as a punishment, just as you were," Lavinia said. "And it is the reason I wanted, as you mentioned, to have Valistaran killed."

"What did you do?" Aleksander asked with a smirk, hoping Lavinia's uncharacteristic openness would continue. She scoffed, much to his disappointment.

"A story for another time. By the way, Mara, your friend Hanna, and I shut down what was left of your camp."

Aleksander nodded out of thanks, but neither one of them spoke for a long while until Lavinia smiled.

"What's that for?"

"She loved you, you know."

The comment, which sounded unnatural coming from the usually gruff and intimidating woman struck Aleksander even harder than the revelation of the assassin's identity. He picked his next words with great care.

"I think we can safely say whatever love she had for me is dead now," Aleksander said, unable to meet Lavinia's gaze.

She shrugged, and a long moment passed without either of them speaking until Aleksander glanced over to Lavinia, who had a thin grin across her face. Her usual cynical expression had given way to a soft, knowing one.

"What would you do to help her?" Lavinia asked.

"Anything," replied Aleksander in a near whisper.

"Then consider what you want, Aleksander. I like to think that I know Mara better than almost anyone. I know the beautifully broken girl behind the crown. I see the fire behind her eyes, and I know the true light within the Empress of Blood. But there's one thing I know about her most of all, and I want you to make me a promise, Aleksander. And I want you to make it because I do love her very much."

"What's that?" he asked in a low voice. Lavinia saying the word 'love' was still very unfamiliar to Aleksander's ears.

"Promise me that you'll make sure that she is never, ever alone."

"Mara doesn't need a…" the correct words didn't come to his mind. "She doesn't need a hero or, I don't know, a lover, or a man in her life to be happy. I know that about her too."

"That isn't what I mean, and you know it," Lavinia retorted.

"Then help me understand."

Lavinia began to speak, but they saw Drahomir's boot shift within the closet, and a low groan escaped his makeshift prison. Lavinia strode toward their captive, but Aleksander placed a hand on her shoulder and shook his head.

"No, it should be me," he whispered.

Lavinia nodded in understanding. Aleksander opened the door, and the dim candlelight illuminated Drahomir's mask as he tried to push himself upright.

"Where am I?" he asked in a scared voice. He wiggled backward and looked up to see Aleksander staring down at him. "What is this thing on my face? Aleksander? What the hell?! What's going on?"

Aleksander helped Drahomir to his feet and motioned for him to follow. He led his friend, who hopped with bound legs and hands toward the kitchen where Lavinia waited for them both. Upon seeing Lavinia, Drahomir gasped in horror and turned toward Aleksander, a look of terror in his visible eye.

"What's going on?" he repeated. "How did I get here?"

"Don't play the fool, Drahomir. We brought you here after you tried to kill us," Aleksander said, shoving him into a rickety chair. Drahomir's eyes darted between Aleksander and Lavinia.

"What? No—no, that's not right. I was just with Josman and Kamil—we were trying to get to Zinok, and I was surrounded! What's *she* doing here?!"

"Surrounded?" Lavinia prodded.

"By the Faceless," Drahomir said, glancing around the room before repeating his previous question. "How did I get here?"

"The mask," Aleksander said, turning to Lavinia. "That mask he's wearing. Could it have been controlling him somehow?"

Lavinia spread her fingers across Drahomir's mask, brushing the light burn across his visible cheekbone; he grimaced, and then upon closer inspection, she noticed several scars not caused by Aleksander superheating the mask.

"They're like needle scars," Lavinia muttered, poking each of the wounds. "Like with The Cage…"

"What?" Drahomir asked, wincing as she prodded his bruised and burned flesh.

"Perhaps so he couldn't remove the mask without—oh, dear. Yes, that makes sense," Lavinia whispered. "The Magistrate wears a similar mask. Perhaps it was to allow him to…"

She trailed off and Aleksander finished her sentence. "To control Drahomir?"

"But why?" Drahomir asked.

"Why indeed…" Lavinia said, testing each knife in the kitchen. Most were too dull to achieve her goal, but she found one, a serrated knife that would do the trick.

"What are you going to do with that?" Drahomir exclaimed. Lavinia raised the knife and grabbed the man's shoulder. She chuckled to herself and then sawed through the ropes binding his arms together.

Drahomir cried out in terror as he saw the blood-stained bandages wrapped around his wrist. He looked up at Lavinia and Aleksander for an explanation which they did not provide.

"Something's wrong, you guys," Drahomir said.

"Obviously," Lavinia said in an apathetic tone; Drahomir shook his head.

"No, I mean…" He stumbled backward with a blank look.

Aleksander raced forward to catch him as he stumbled, but then Drahomir raised his head, a dark look of murder in his visible eye. He leapt toward Aleksander as purple teleportation smoke poured from his good hand, but it seemed to sputter like a blocked fountain. Lavinia struck Drahomir in the throat with her elbow, knocking him to the floor. She followed up with a swift kick to the ribs.

"That's for breaking my back!" Lavinia shouted with Sangoran words sprinkled throughout the statement. Aleksander assumed they were Sangoran curse words.

"Is your friend a good actor?" Lavinia asked.

"I wouldn't say so, but I can't say I've ever seen him on stage," Aleksander said.

"I think our theory is right. I think the Magistrate was controlling him somehow," Lavinia whispered. "I have another theory."

"I've got nothing, so let me hear it," Aleksander said.

"As you are well aware, in the slave camp, there was a certain item we used for torture. It was a—"

"A cuff," Aleksander said in a soft voice.

"Yes, the Mind-Prison Cuff. It's an artifact from the civilization of the Deadlands. They developed it to replace prisons. One minute wearing the cuff feels like a year to the wearer."

"I know," Aleksander said, slumping his shoulders.

"I didn't want to bring it up," Lavinia said. "Mara told me what happened, but I wasn't sure if you knew exactly what torture you'd put her through."

"Remember when I said whatever love she had for me was probably dead?" Aleksander asked. "I put that cuff on her wrist for twenty minutes while we were trying to escape."

"If it makes you feel any better, the first time we used it, we didn't know how it worked. We sentenced a man to a full week wearing the cuff…" Lavinia said, trailing off. "Do you know how many minutes are in a week? We sentenced that poor man to over ten thousand years in a prison of his own mind."

"What happened to him?" Aleksander asked, putting his hand over his mouth.

"He went insane, obviously. I felt the obligation to kill him out of mercy. Psychosis and insanity are common results of people wearing that thing. It had a different, very rare impact on Mara's mind. She can go into the cuff's prison-state or dream-state at will, but she's able to plan or study or think during that time, and she's learned to use it to her advantage. Drahomir once wore it. Only for a moment, but I believe it may have fractured his mind in two."

"Is that common?" Aleksander asked.

"It isn't as common as psychosis, but we've seen it a few times. Sometimes, it causes the victim to develop a second personality," Lavinia said. "My theory is that these masks restore a Faceless's humanity or mind, and that Thanatan somehow found your friend and used the mask to 'restore' the second identity to be his dominant one."

"If the Magistrate used Drahomir's second personality to assassinate the Mistresses of Dusk, do you think she could have somehow used him to infect the prison too?" Aleksander asked.

"I was thinking the same thing," Lavinia said. "The Magistrate is the leader of the Pure. He leads them *for* Thanatan in Laniras. She had to be behind the Faceless we saw in Doftaan too. Are you thinking what I'm thinking?"

"That we need to kill the Magistrate if we hope to ever take out Thanatan? Yeah."

"Good. Then you take the first watch, make sure this one doesn't go crazy again. I hope that with the damage the mask sustained, the Magistrate's influence will wear off," Lavinia said.

Without warning, dark smoke exploded from Drahomir's body, and he disappeared once more from the room. Lavinia swore under her breath.

"Well."

"What just happened?!" Aleksander exclaimed.

"What do you think just happened? Take the first watch so he doesn't come back and murder us," she muttered as she stalked into the other room and settled into the bed next to Rayshel. Soon, everyone but Aleksander was sound asleep.

Aleksander waited for nearly an hour, and nothing happened. He sighed and crept out of the home, shutting the door quietly behind him. He'd have to hurry back before the others woke up, but he knew there was one thing he needed to do.

He wandered a path into the center of Cineca, and a feeling of deep nostalgia filled his soul as he looked over the rickety stage where he had first seen Mara, and where he had fallen in love with her voice.

No, where he had fallen in love with *her*.

The town was covered in a blanket of night, but it was all exactly the same as he remembered it. Everywhere he looked brought back more memories, and he slid his hands into his pockets as he strolled through the town. At last, he came to the home of the Bartunek family; he took a deep breath and knocked on the heavy wooden door. No answer.

He pulled the door open and stepped inside. A thick layer of dust covered every surface, and most of the furniture he remembered had been removed. Only the poorly stuffed sofa and a faded rug remained.

He lit a ball of flame in his hand to illuminate the room. No one had lived here in quite some time, and he wondered what had become of Mara's parents. Images of their faces filled his mind, and his heart ached, for he knew that they had no idea their children were both still alive. He hoped, at least.

As Aleksander sat on the uncomfortable sofa, his hand brushed a scratchy blanket hidden by the darkness. He held it in his hands, and he began to sob.

# CHAPTER THIRTY

# THE SUPREME ONE'S HEIR

While Josman, Kamil, and Valistaran helped the last of the refugees and soldiers climb from the entrance, Rayna and the Supreme One led the group through the ruins of the canyon leading to Sanctuary's entranceway. The smell of smoke and hundreds of rotting Faceless corpses haunted the pass; the sights and smells of the carnage caused several in the company to retch and vomit, but Rayna urged the refugees onward, leading them to freedom.

"Supreme One, I'll need you to defend our people should the Faceless return. Valis, come help me lower the second bridge," Rayna said, gesturing to a crevice barely wide enough for a human to step through sideways.

They had to drop the first bridge to prevent the Faceless from swarming into the fortress.

"It shall be done," Kadir replied as Valis eyed the crack in the wall, knowing Rayna intended for him to go through.

"You're sure you don't want him to go through the crack instead?" Valis asked. Rayna did not respond or smile. "No? Alright."

"There will be a fork in the path. You go right, I'll go left, and spin the wheel exactly when I give the signal," Rayna said as they wedged themselves between the craggy entrance and inched down the narrow path.

"What happens if I do it wrong?" Valis asked.

"Nothing. It just won't work. It's not a trap, kid. The original architects just had to make it a secret, because it can only be done once."

He grunted as he pressed forward, his heart beating in his chest.

"I don't like this," Valis said, the claustrophobia setting in.

As he began to panic, the path widened into the fork promised earlier by Rayna. He sighed in relief and reached out for the rocky wall to use as a guide in the darkness, but brushed Rayna's cheek with his fingers. They both yelped in terror, as if each expected the other to be a Faceless hiding in the shadows.

"Where's the wheel?" Valis asked.

"Should be about knee high," Rayna called from her path. Valis lowered himself to his hands and knees, feeling for the wheel to lower the bridge. He let out a happy sound as his fingers brushed a wooden wheel about the size of a dinner plate.

"Got it!" Valis shouted.

"Found mine too," Rayna replied. "I'm going to count from five down to zero. As soon as I say zero, turn your wheel to the right as hard as you can!"

Valis concentrated on the wheel. Each second seemed like an eternity as Rayna began to count down. What if he got this wrong and killed everyone in the pass? Everything would have been for nothing, and—

"ZERO!" Rayna shouted, and Valis turned the wheel to the right with all his strength, resulting in a satisfying click. Nothing else seemed to happen.

"Did it work?" Valis called.

"Yes, good job!" Rayna replied as she began to make her way back to the narrow crack leading to the pass.

"And what exactly did we do?" Valis asked, partially so he could tell where Rayna was in the dark so he wouldn't bump into her again.

"The path outside collapsed to kill some of the Faceless. This is a onetime switch that allows us to reset the path," Rayna replied.

"And I expect it had to be hidden like this so that no one would accidentally find it?" Valis asked. He kept speaking to keep the claustrophobia at bay and not out of curiosity as they pressed themselves through the crags.

"Yes, of course," Rayna said.

She began to speak again, but a feeling of dread filled her heart, causing her to stop. Valis bumped into her again. Neither of them said a word.

"Do you feel it too?" Valis asked in a low whisper.

She must have nodded, for she did not respond with words. They made all haste to reach the pass. A low groan filled their minds; it intensified until it was an incessant growl of hunger and pain.

The Faceless had returned from their diversion.

"Back!" Rayna cried, and the refugees ran back toward the keep, all order lost.

The sound of screams was silenced as the grinding of stone and gears signaled a new bridge extending across the chasm; Rayna and Valis watched in horror as a swarm of Faceless lurched forward, and the segments of the new bridge came together.

A sphere of light brighter than noon's sun illuminated the path, and the incessant groan of the Faceless became a roar. Each person behind Kadir shielded their faces with their hands to avoid being blinded as the Supreme One stood with his hands held aloft before directing the energy within his body in a beam toward their foes. The power of the sun charred flesh and melted bone as it tore through the swarm, silencing their mental groans and roars.

Kadir collapsed to his knees, and the pass faded to darkness. Valis and the other refugees opened their eyes and rejoiced to see that the Supreme One had obliterated the horde ahead of them, the Faceless bodies smoking and charred, melted against the bridge.

"He's done it!" Valis shouted.

He caught sight of Josman, Kamil, and his mother behind him and gave a thumbs-up as Rayna ordered the company to cross once more. Rayna's few remaining soldiers led the way, followed by the mass of refugees.

Alia and Kamil were the first to reach the Supreme One; they helped him to his feet and supported him across the bridge. The exit was close now, and no Faceless were visible from their position in the pass. Freedom was within their grasp, and light beckoned them to safety.

Chaotic darkness pooled at the mouth of the path, swirling around itself until the form of one lone man stepped out of the shadows. The smoke dissipated, leaving the man still and alone. Rayna held her hand aloft, stopping the procession of refugees a little less than a hundred feet from the man's position.

"Who are you?" Rayna shouted then turned to her people as she drew her blade. "Get back!"

The man said nothing, silhouetted against the sun, which was now visible through the mouth of the pass as it dipped below the horizon.

Shadows enveloped the man as he teleported into the midst of the crowd, his twin daggers spilling crimson blood each time he reappeared. Screams went up from the crowd as he appeared next to Captain Rayna, who brought her sword up toward the assassin, but his blade tore through her shoulder before teleporting away. The soldier named Danek cried out as the blade pierced his chest, and the entire group of refugees began to stampede from the pass in a chaotic mob.

"Go!" Valistaran exclaimed, gesturing for Alia, Valis, and Valeniya to flee.

"Maintain order!" Rayna shouted, but her command fell on deaf ears. Eight already lay dead around her, and she could feel blood trickling from the wound in his shoulder. She, along with Valistaran, Josman, Kamil, and Kadir waited for the assassin to reappear as the refugees exited the path out of Zinok.

The sound of swirling shadows filled their ears, and Rayna thrust her graceful blade below her armpit and grinned as steel met flesh. She collapsed with a cry of pain as the assassin's dagger pierced her back, but she felt Kadir's mental presence flow past her as tangibly as the wind, forcing the assassin against the path's craggy wall.

Josman swung his heavy mace with all his might toward the assassin's head. However, the weapon struck the rocky wall where his enemy had been moments before. The assassin crawled away, trying to break free from the Supreme One's mental hold. Josman tried to wrench the damaged, crimson mask from the assassin's face to no avail. He smashed the man on the side of the head, shattering enough of the mask that Josman was able to see part of his friend's mutilated face; it was mutilated with scars and twisted into a gruesome shape, but he still recognized his friend—Drahomir was becoming a Faceless.

"No," Josman whispered, glancing from Drahomir to Rayna and back again. "No, no…"

Drahomir stumbled backward as Kadir thrust his mental presence into the man's mind.

"Go!" Valistaran exclaimed.

Josman and Kamil stood dumbfounded as the rest of the surviving refugees made it out of the canyon. Kadir grasped Drahomir's forehead, and Josman watched his friend scream in pain as both he and the Supreme One were consumed with swirling, dark shadows. A gust of wind passed them by, and both men were gone.

"Kamil," Josman said, turning to his friend.

"*I know,*" Kamil said to Josman's mind, and then, as if in denial, he added, "*Josman. I know what you saw, but I touched that man's mind as soon as his mask was broken, and it wasn't him.*"

"I saw his face, Kamil!" Josman shouted in distress.

"*His mental presence didn't feel like Drahomir. You have to believe me, it isn't him!*" Kamil said, his face contorted in despair.

"I want to," Josman said, shaking his head, "but I think when the Faceless got him—oh, by the gods, Kamil—I thought he was dead. It would have been better for him to have died."

"*That's what they wanted us to believe,*" Kamil said.

Kamil placed a hand on Josman's shoulder as the sunlight touched their skin for the first time in what felt like a lifetime.

He brushed Josman's mind and felt his overwhelming grief, anger, and confusion. As they emerged from the canyon, Kamil couldn't stop the tears from rolling down his cheeks. Josman let out a deep sigh and nodded to his friend in acknowledgment of the pain they shared—a moment of reprieve before the horrendous groans of the Faceless filled their minds once again.

"More of them are coming back," Josman said, unsure if Kamil had felt their presence. "And look!"

He pointed to the distant hills where a burst of shadows dissipated, and Drahomir and the Supreme One appeared.

"*We've got to save him,*" Kamil said.

Josman was unsure if his friend meant he wanted to save Supreme One or Drahomir, but he nodded.

An endless tide of Faceless more numerous than the previous wave flowed like a river of emaciated bodies toward the mouth of the canyon. The refugees and rescuers were cut off from reaching Kadir and the mysterious assassin that, for whatever reason, resembled Drahomir.

"I don't think we're going to get to them, buddy," Josman said, hefting his mace. "Supreme One's on his own."

He watched as Rayna and Marek, both wounded, herded the refugees up the hill, and Valistaran, Alia, and Valis, along with the remaining soldiers stood their ground before the oncoming Faceless. Josman and Kamil took their place between the Talohirs and Rayna's soldiers, and Alia closed Rayna's wound with her healing magic. The captain nodded in thanks.

"Remember when you made that catapult thing to get us out of the slave camp?" Josman asked.

Kamil chuckled and tried to think of another memory with Josman to take their minds off their impending death, but the sight of the Faceless coming toward them was too much.

"*Remember how we felt when we finally got out?*" Kamil asked as he watched the Talohirs speaking with one another as well.

"Let's live to feel that once more," Josman said.

Kamil smiled and turned to the horde as it crashed toward them. Those with weapons drew them and awaited their death.

Valistaran threw up a wall of black flame that charred any Faceless that dared get too close, and Valis fired bolts of electricity through his father's dark magic, felling as many of the creatures as he could strike. Valistaran attempted to encircle the group of refugees with flame, but the Faceless were too quick.

"This is it!" Josman shouted as the monsters closed in.

Rayna decapitated a Faceless just as it sliced out Lieutenant Marek's ankles. She dodged another set of claws but cried out in horror one of the creatures skewered her lieutenant through the throat and tore out his flesh before pressing its disfigured head into the wound, trying in vain to devour his flesh.

Kamil darted forward, casting an explosion of mental energy as far away as he could muster. His ally Pavlina fell as jagged, broken claws raked against her neck and tore chunks from her back, but thousands more of the creatures were still oncoming. Hundreds of the beasts, including the ones that had slain Marek and Pavlina, followed Kamil's lure, but it wasn't enough. He knew he would have died without his powers protecting him.

Josman threw himself in front of one of the creatures as it swiped for Valis; the creature's claws shattered against the man's armored skin and then met its doom as Josman's mace crushed its skull.

Jets of flame erupted all around Valistaran as he tried to hold off the horde, and Kamil hurled explosions of mental energy whenever he was able. The refugees huddled, screaming, and crying, in a terrified mass in the center of their defenders. Kamil mustered the last bit of mental energy he could creating a final mental lure as claws tore at his ankles. The last thing he saw before the mental strain caused him to lose consciousness was the behemoth soaring above them, casting a dark shadow over the mass of refugees.

The refugees screamed, expecting the massive beast to slaughter them, but it trampled the horde under foot with a deafening roar. A lone Sangoran leapt from its back, and the hulking monster opened its massive jaws to release an explosive jet of lava through the swarm.

The Sangoran circled above, releasing bolts of lightning at any that dared near the refugees, but without Kamil's mental lures, the Faceless had surrounded the group on all sides. The earth shook as the behemoth trampled the swarm, crouching next to the group as it bathed the Faceless in molten death.

A dark burst of shadow popped in the center of the group, and where Josman expected to see Drahomir, Lord Ronin Jakoni appeared, grabbed his shirt collar, and vanished, and they reappeared a moment later on the behemoth's back. He disappeared to help others climb aboard.

Josman caught a glimpse of the lone Sangoran's face as she flew by, and he met her with a shout of joy and a round of applause.

"Mara! Yes!" Josman shouted. She passed by him with a wink and a smile before arcing around to let off another round of lightning at the Faceless. "All hail the Empress of Blood!"

"Everyone, onto its back!" Mara called, standing on Hippo's massive head.

Ronin helped the last of the refugees onto the behemoth's back as the Faceless clawed at its feet and began to climb over its legs and tail, much to its dismay.

"Go, Hippo!" Mara shouted, slapping the beast on the back.

She felt Hippo's mental connection affirm her command, and the behemoth stood at its full height before extending its massive wings to take flight.

"Well, if it isn't Josman Faros! I thought I saw you down there!" Mara exclaimed over the sound of wind passing by. An enormous smile crossed her face, and she pulled her friend into a tight hug. "What in the name of Elafris are you doing here, big guy?"

"You have no idea how glad we are to see you, kid," Josman said, his eyes beaming. His expression turned serious, and he pointed to where he had seen the Supreme One fall. "The Supreme One! We have to go back for him! He fell somewhere there with—"

His words faltered, and his mind raced. Had Kadir killed Drahomir? And then another thought entered his mind—had Drahomir killed the Supreme One of Kurash?

Mara scrunched her eyebrows together and willed the behemoth to fly in the direction Josman had indicated. Alia tended to the wounded in a crevice at the base of the creature's massive skull while the rest of the refugees held on for dear life.

"*Mara,*" Kamil's voice filled the mind of the Empress.

It was much easier for her to hear his mental voice than Josman's physical one over the rush of the wind.

*"Kamil, I'm so sorry for everything,"* Mara responded. She felt a wave of empathy flow from Kamil's mind, and she knew there was no animosity between them, and they shared a long hug.

*"There's no time for that. If I die, you need to know the truth. You need to know why it was so important that you rescue us."*

*"What is it?"*

Kamil recalled the images he had seen in his vision while connected to the Magistrate's mind.

*"It's all true,"* Mara thought back. *"And worse than I ever imagined. Thank you, Kamil."*

Hippo the behemoth shot toward the bursts of light and darkness below and kicked at the Faceless still stubborn enough to cling to its legs.

"There he is!" Josman shouted.

Mara nodded and turned to Ronin, who placed a hand on her shoulder, and they disappeared together.

They teleported to intercept the assassin, and Ronin planted his feet against Drahomir's chest as he appeared from the darkness. The assassin struck the ground and threw his hands into the air as Ronin disappeared into a dark purple fog.

He did not reappear.

At first, Mara recognized the man's garb as the assassin that had slain her Mistresses of Dusk, but then she caught a glimpse of the man's face.

"Drahomir?" she exclaimed.

Memories of Drahomir's knife upon the prison tower filled her mind; the feelings of betrayal, loss, and hatred overwhelmed her, and she roared in her fury, blasting him in the stomach with a bolt of white-hot lightning.

Drahomir struck the ground as Mara clambered over to the Supreme One, who lay quite still on the earth. His robes were soaked with crimson.

"Kadir!" she shouted, clutching his robes.

"Behind you!" the Supreme One exclaimed, pushing Mara aside to launch a beam of white light that nearly disintegrated Drahomir as he dodged and attempted to plunge his blade into Mara's back. The behemoth stomped toward Drahomir and loosed a stream of molten lava. The assassin responded by throwing up a portal of dark mist that swallowed up the lava as it erupted toward him.

At that moment, her consciousness brushed Drahomir's; she sensed mental scars and that his mind felt like a door left ajar, and she wondered if Kadir had attempted to break the assassin's mind. But then, she could feel that that wasn't the case, and she realized the truth. Kadir was trying to fuse two broken halves of the man's mind.

"Take them!" Mara roared, and the Behemoth obeyed, fleeing northeast with the refugees. Mara lunged out with her wing-blades, sliding them between Drahomir's ribs. The Empress of Blood reached forth with her mind and sensed the familiar presence of the assassin, confirming her fears.

Drahomir, the man that had caused her such turmoil, was the assassin. He looked at her with cold, vacant eyes through his damaged mask and vanished from the world, her blades coated with his blood.

Mara slammed her wings into the ground, cursing Drahomir's name; it had been over a year since she had done that, and tears rolled down her face as memories flowed back to her mind.

She hurried to the Supreme One's side as he lay dying in the grass. She ripped his tunic open and gasped at the severity of his injuries. Gaping wounds from Drahomir's blade lined his stomach and chest.

"I can save you!" Mara exclaimed in denial. "Hold on!"

"No, my child," Kadir said with a groan.

"No, you aren't going to die," Mara said. "Your people will be without a ruler. They need you!"

"And they will have one!" Kadir exclaimed, wincing. "I must—I must tell you my great secret, Mara Bartunek."

"Live to tell it another day," Mara said.

"I am dying, Mara."

"No, I'm going to save you," Mara replied, the meaning of his words lost on her. She willed Hippo to return to her side.

"Mara, I am a dead man, whether by the wounds in my chest or the cancer in my bones," he said. "No healer, however powerful, can cure what afflicts me."

"What?" Mara said in a low whisper.

She could feel the groans of the Faceless and knew they were close behind, coming to finish their work.

"It is the duty of the Supreme One to appoint his heir—there have been rumors of who this heir would be, but I never told my council my plan… A grave mistake, perhaps, but no matter. That plan is for nothing, now. I thought I would have time to address it, but…I…was…wrong…"

"I will tell them. Tell me the name, and when all is right, I will send an ambassador to bring them word," Mara said.

"Mara…Bartunek…"

"Yes, that's me," Mara said, smiling to try to get Kadir to hold on long enough to say the name. Kadir simply smiled back. "What's the name Kadir?"

"I already have…" Kadir said. The Faceless were nearly upon them now. "It is customary in my land…for the Supreme One to pass on his throne to one to whom he owes his life, or to give his life for his successor…there is no other way, for no other way would give legitimacy. I owe you my throne… You…an Empress taken off her throne by a usurper… You will need… Kurash…together…save Sangora…save Kurash… And save the world… I name you… I name…The Supreme One of Kurash, who is called…Mara Bartunek, Empress of Blood…"

As the Supreme One drew his final breath, he forced a silver key encrusted with an amethyst jewel into Mara's hand.

"No!" Mara shouted, glancing over her shoulder.

She cursed, grasped the Supreme One's dead body by the arms, and shot into the air to meet her behemoth, clutching the key he had given her with all her might.

As she soared through the air, she beheld the path of destruction wrought by the Faceless, and tears rolled down her face. The countryside had fallen; several towns were burning across the countryside near Zinok, their people massacred in the streets.

At that moment of death and loss, Mara understood one fact: she and many of the refugees had escaped the battle with their lives, but Drahomir and the Faceless had won the siege of Zinok.

# CHAPTER THIRTY-ONE

# THE MASTER OF BALGOROD

The one known across Sangora as the Phantom, Shanthah Kalen, Lord of the liberated Balgorod and newly appointed Master of Dusk stood at a balcony overlooking the city. The fires had been extinguished, and a calm silence had settled over the city. He felt Hanna's arms wrap around him from behind.

Since taking the city, Shanthah's forces had converted Florenta's palace on the island between the rivers into their headquarters, but he refrained from calling it a palace. He wasn't a king, and he had no desires to be one.

"You look exhausted, have you slept at all?" Hanna asked, resting her head on Shanthah's shoulder as they overlooked New Balgorod and the distant horizon.

"I don't think I've slept in six months," Shanthah said. "And before that, I had a couple years of good sleep, but before that, I was in a slave camp and didn't sleep for about—"

"You know what I meant," Hanna said. In response, Shanthah collapsed theatrically into Hanna's arms. "I take that as a no. I'm taking you back to bed."

"Oh?" Shanthah said, looking up at her with a wry smile. He straightened up and paused. "Wait."

He resisted her pull on his arm and looked back to the horizon.

"I didn't think that's a sentence you'd ever say no to," Hanna said with a laugh, catching Shanthah's distracted gaze.

A wide smile crossed his face just as a dull orange glow lit the horizon. At first, Hanna wondered if it was the first rays of sunlight peeking up over the horizon, but as she oriented herself to the unfamiliar terrain of Sangora but realized that the light was appearing in the west, not the east.

"What in the socks of Elafris is that?" Shanthah asked.

A gargantuan shape enshrouded in bursts of flame and smoke shot through the sky toward Shanthah's fortress.

"I need to alert…someone," Shanthah said, turning from the balcony with a sense of urgency. However, a burst of shadow and wind erupted before Shanthah and Hanna, rematerializing into the shape of a hooded figure.

"Do not be afraid, Master Shanthah Kalen, I come to announce the arrival of Empress Mara Bartunek," said the figure, before adding, "I am Ronin Jakoni, Lord of the Walkers, and I bid you no ill will or harm."

"I know who you are," Shanthah said with a slight bow of his head. "Which side are you on lately?"

Ronin ignored the comment. Hanna lowered her fists, and Shanthah knew he was safe with her nearby should the Lord of the Walkers choose to go back on his words.

"I also bring news that Zinok and the Sanctuary Keep have fallen, as have many Thannish towns in the region. Thanatan's Pure have slaughtered many across the countryside, and he now controls Laniras."

"What a dumb name for the Faceless," Shanthah said in response. He gestured for Ronin to follow. "This is grave news. I'm glad Mara is safe and coming back—was she able to save them all?"

He offered a high-backed chair to Ronin as Hanna frantically kicked a pile of clothes under the bed. Ronin took no notice, thanked Shanthah, and took the seat.

"I apologize for the pajamas. I don't usually have visitors at this hour," Shanthah said. Hanna huffed and adjusted her loose robe.

"What about King Verahim? What's he doing?" she asked with a scowl. "Let me guess—he's doing nothing."

"He welcomed the usurper with open arms," Ronin replied, gesturing with both hands to emphasize his point.

Shanthah glanced to Hanna for advice or council; she gave him none, lost in thought.

"And what is that thing?" Shanthah asked, changing the subject. He pointed out the window toward the shadowy form making its way toward Balgorod.

"A monster created by Thanatan," Ronin began.

"Are our people here in danger?" Hanna asked.

Ronin shook his head.

"No, no. That beast now answers to the Empress alone," Ronin said. "She is bringing several hundred refugees along with several other honored guests."

"We'll find a place for them," Hanna said. "The castle has plenty of room to house anyone that needs it."

"Honored guests?" Shanthah asked.

"The Empress of Blood and Supreme One of Kurash shall be accompanied by the former High King of Talohira, Valistaran Talohir, and Daniel Elafris, who was once called the devil," Ronin said with a casual air.

"You say that like it's the most normal thing in the world," Shanthah said with a nervous chuckle.

"Are you not now a Master of Dusk? Such a meeting with leaders of this world should become a normal thing to you soon enough," Ronin said. Shanthah shrugged, unconvinced.

"Tell Mara we're happy to welcome her to Balgorod. I'll have someone prepare the council chamber," Shanthah said. He looked to Hanna as if to ask, "Do we have a council chamber?" She nodded.

Ronin thanked his hosts and disappeared in a cloud of whipping shadow, the suddenness of which caused Hanna and Shanthah to jump.

"Well, this is our life now," Shanthah said, hanging his head.

"I wouldn't have it any other way," Hanna said, running her fingers through his hair before planting a sweet kiss on his forehead. "And as fun as a pajama party with a bunch of strangers sounds, we should probably change."

Shanthah had to reach under the bed to retrieve his tunic and trousers, which Hanna had hidden during Ronin's intrusion. When he had one pant leg pulled up to his knee, she cleared her throat to get his attention, and he turned on the spot.

As he did so, Hanna winked and let her silky robe slip from her shoulders. It gathered around her feet, and with a cheesy grin, she twirled before disappearing behind the partition in the corner of the room to change. Shanthah tripped over his trousers, and Hanna's laughter filled the chamber.

He pulled on his tunic, still sitting on the floor as Hanna emerged, now fully clothed in a navy sundress, from behind the barrier. She tucked her auburn hair behind her ear with a loving smile so wide that it made her squint with a scrunched-up nose.

"Yes, I'm pretty sure you're my favorite person," Shanthah said as she helped him to his feet. "And you know, I love when your nose does that. It's very cute."

"Yeah? Well, don't forget who the *real* master of Balgorod is, even if she's cute," Hanna said with a wink.

Shanthah's pure laughter filled their chamber, and she wrapped her arms around him before they shared a kiss.

"I can't deny one word of that sentence."

He wiped joyous tears from the corners of each eye.

"I've missed you," Hanna said, still smiling. "Now come on—let's go find out who the 'someone' is that knows where our council chamber is."

She took his hand and guided him from the chamber. He stopped, a wide smile on his face.

"What's that for?" Hanna asked with a laugh.

"I don't know what I'd do without you," Shanthah said.

"You'd come find me. Isn't that how this goes now?"

She pulled him close once more and locked her lips around his then led him down the corridor.

Half an hour later, they discovered a chamber with a large, circular table in its center, perfect for a meeting of diplomats and kings, however spartan the room appeared.

He had a soldier light the torches in the room and send word to the numerous chefs of Florenta's kitchens to prepare a quick meal for his hungry visitors. Not only for the kings and leaders, but the hungry refugees as well, although they would not be invited to participate at the meeting.

When everything was prepared, Shanthah sat at the far end of the table, Hanna at his right hand.

"And now we wait," Shanthah said, taking a deep breath. Hanna gripped his hand and smiled.

"You've got this," Hanna said.

"You might not know this about me, but—"

"Yes, I do," Hanna said. "I know most things about you, Shan, and it's okay to be nervous."

Shanthah cocked his head, one eyebrow raised. He hadn't ever told her about his dislike for this type of meeting, or his deep fear of public speaking; both were among the many reasons, after all, that he chose his career as a scout before being captured and enslaved by Valistaran.

"I see your powers are growing," Shanthah said with a smile.

"No, I'm not a mind reader now," Hanna said, shaking her head. She hit Shanthah lightly on the shoulder. "You know that. But I *am* a Shanthah-reader. I'm always, always here for you whether you need me or not, and you know that."

"Thank goodness," Shanthah said, gripping Hanna's hand. "In my acceptance speech to become a Mistress of Dusk, I should have thanked Valistaran for bringing us together."

"Master of Dusk." Hanna corrected him with a laugh then planted a kiss on his cheek and squeezed his hand. At that moment, Mistresses of Dusk Raluca and Anca entered the chamber, and both Shanthah and Hanna stood to greet them.

Anca gestured to the table, as if to ask where she should sit. Shanthah responded in an equally nonverbal way, pointing to the seats at his left. Raluca did not share Anca's militaristic coldness; she flashed a smile to Shanthah and Hanna and bowed as she took her seat next to Anca. As the kitchen's chefs began to bring several cases of food and dishes into the chamber, Shanthah, Hanna, and the two other Mistresses of Dusk sat in silence, watching the workers set the table.

"Thank you," Hanna said as a beautiful dish was placed before her; she scowled. Too many forks for a single meal.

Shanthah perked up as he heard footsteps in the hallway. He glanced to Hanna, who smiled and gripped his hand. They stood once more to welcome their guests; a gesture which Raluca and Anca followed.

The Empress of Blood, Mara Bartunek strode into the room clad in majesty, but garbed in shredded clothes, scars, and bruises. Her compatriots looked equally disheveled, and Shanthah bowed before her.

Hanna caught Mara's gaze, and they shared a smile. Everything that had transpired between them appeared to be a thing of the past, and Hanna felt a warm sense of peace fill her heart.

"Welcome back to Balgorod, Empress Mara," Shanthah said, emphasizing the word 'empress' with great joy.

"She looks exhausted," Hanna whispered into Shanthah's ear. "Don't make her control the meeting."

"Thank you, Master Shanthah," Mara replied, taking her desired seat. "Ah, a real meal!"

"And don't worry, the refugees are being fed too," Shanthah said. Mara smiled.

"Thank you."

Valistaran Talohir, former High King of Talohira, stepped into the room next accompanied by Alia, Valis, and Valeniya. Shanthah watched for the Supreme One of Kurash but saw no one that fit his description.

All cares for his whereabouts faded as he caught sight of Josman and Kamil entering the chamber behind Daniel Elafris. He broke out into another smile, and he heard Kamil speak directly to his mind.

"*Surprise!*"

"*I could not be more excited to see you both,*" Shanthah thought, knowing Kamil was reading his mind.

"*Josman says to tell you he's proud of you.*"

"*Oh, stop,*" Shanthah thought in reply, gesturing with a dismissive wave of his hand.

"*Shanthah, you can't fake humility in thoughts,*" Kamil replied, and Shanthah cracked a grin from across the table.

Several other people Shanthah did not recognize shuffled into the room. Liliana and Reka, Hanna's Sangoran allies, entered the room last at Hanna's invitation.

"As Master of Balgorod and Alboras, I welcome you all," Shanthah said after everyone was seated. "Feel free to start eating as soon as you want. I know you're all hungry. And please, don't worry about being treated better than the Zinoki refugees. They are being treated to the same meal in even more comfortable chambers. If anything, they're being treated better than you lot."

A chuckle arose around the table. Hanna was the first to dig into the pile of potatoes, carrots, and meat on her plate, but she perked up as Mara began to speak.

"Thank you, Master Shanthah," Mara said with a slight smile as Shanthah mouthed the word 'mistress.' "It is with great joy that I bring word from Zinok that we were able to rescue many of those that made it there, but I also acknowledge the terrible loss of life that occurred during their trek to safety, and those that abandoned our cause to join Thanatan in Laniras. I pay respect to those that gave their lives to help us escape, and I also acknowledge the death of the Supreme One of Kurash, who is called Kadir."

Whispers and glances escaped those around the table who had not already heard the news, and Shanthah looked to Ronin and said, "Lord Jakoni gave me the impression that the Supreme One was on his way here."

"The Supreme One is here; the One who is called Kadir is dead, but before his death, he named another to take his place," Ronin said. "The Supreme One who is called *Mara*, Empress of Blood."

"No way," Shanthah said.

His eyes darted toward Mara, who stood, a somber look of acknowledgment on her face. The rest of the group looked to Mara for an explanation. She took a deep breath, eyes closed.

"The Supreme One of Kurash named me his successor before his death, it is true," she said, glancing around the room. Josman steadied her as she stumbled and helped her stay standing.

"Then, I think it is appropriate to re-welcome you," Hanna said. "On behalf of the Master of Dusk, I would like to welcome Mara Bartunek, Empress of Blood, Supreme one of Kurash, and rightful Queen of Talohira to the table!"

"Thank you, Hanna," Mara said in a diplomatic tone but allowed a smile to show through. "I'm not sure if I actually hold any of those titles at the moment, but I thank you for your support. This meeting, as formal as it feels, really is a gathering of friends and allies. I'd like it to be, anyway. Please, forget protocol and diplomatic niceties. I want ideas, and I want plans to take back our world. If you have something to say, I ask you, beg you, to share your thoughts."

All eyes in the room turned to Anca as she stood; the general turned Mistress of Dusk commanded respect even amongst those she did not command in battle. Mara settled into her seat as Anca spoke.

"With your blessing, Empress, I would like to explain the situation to those unacquainted with our plight," she said. Mara nodded, and Anca continued. "I believe everyone in this room has some knowledge of the situation, but not the entire picture. First, we all know that Thanatan has returned. He has gathered those Faceless beasts you fought at Zinok to Laniras, and he has named them 'the Pure.' They are now his slaves in Laniras and work so that the people of King Verahim's country no longer need to. They are the blacksmiths, bakers, miners, and laborers of Thanatanos."

"That doesn't sound so bad," said Valis, speaking up for the first time, before hastily adding, "I know, that's the point."

"Yes, quite. The people long ago accepted Thanatan as their god king, and his return is seen as a dream come true to many of them. They see this as a type of salvation, but what they don't realize—"

"The Pure are terrorizing Sangora," Raluca said, cutting Anca off. The general did not seem to mind as Raluca continued. "These Faceless have begun to push into the heart of Sangora, infecting towns and villages all throughout the empire with some kind of virus that raises the dead and transforms them into the Pure."

"Mistress Raluca is correct. We do not know the extent of the carnage or how widespread the virus is, but not even Doftaan is immune. In fact, due to Florenta's poor leadership, it might be the worst off," Anca said.

"I haven't heard any reports of widespread outbreaks in Alboras," Shanthah said.

"Good, but that won't last," Anca said, shaking her head. "I believe that Thanatan is aware of our rebellion here, and he either thinks we're weakened to a point that we are no longer a threat, or on the other hand, he may believe that we've strengthened it to the point that we are able to defend ourselves from their attacks."

"So, either way, we're safe," Shanthah said.

"That isn't the word I'd use," Raluca said, sharing a glance with Anca. "I personally believe that he's preparing an even greater force for us, seeing it as a stronghold of opposition against not only Florenta, but the god king's rule as well."

"But for the time being, we are alive," Mara said.

"Yes, Empress," Anca said with a nod. "King Verahim has done nothing to hinder Thanatan's advances into his kingdom, and it appears he has become a puppet doing the will of Thanatan and his Magistrate."

"I think we all understand the problem," Mara said, nodding. "And what of unrest in Talohira?"

"I think that question is best answered by the deposed king," Anca said, gesturing to Valistaran, who stood.

"After my supposed death, Mara took de facto control over the country, as was her right by law as queen. However, when Florenta's illegal rebellion ousted our beloved empress from her throne in Doftaan, this created a power vacuum in Talohira," Valistaran explained.

"One that was quickly filled," Raluca said with a nod.

"Precisely," Valistaran replied, pacing from his place at the table; he looked out the east facing window, the direction of Talohira. He turned back to the table, eying each of his allies there before speaking again. "I need you all in this room to understand one thing. I do not have any intention of retaking the throne of Talohira for myself."

"Why should we believe that?" Hanna asked.

Many in the room whispered amongst themselves at the abruptness of her comment. Valistaran took notice and raised his hand; the room fell silent once again.

"Because the mistakes I made led us to where we are now," Valistaran said, glancing over at Josman and Kamil. "I know that now, and I admit that, and I expect you to believe me. It personally makes no difference to me if you do; I have no desires of ever taking my place on that accursed throne again, no matter how much I have dreamed of it in the past. Instead, I have other intentions for my homeland."

"You want your son to rule," General Anca said.

"Tell me, oh fallen king, will your people take kindly to another Talohir on the throne? Another Valistaran Talohir, no less?" Ronin asked.

"He is the legitimate king by our laws," Valistaran said. "His rule is right, and he could make true change there, especially if he denounces the failures of his fallen father."

The entire room turned to Valis, who sat in silence.

"Is that what you want?" Mara asked, turning to Valis for the first time. Valis looked straight ahead and let out a slow breath. He said nothing for a long moment before replying.

"No," Valis said with a slight crack in his voice from lack of use. Several others, including Anca, Raluca, and Shanthah began to speak, but Mara raised a hand, and they all fell silent. She gestured to Valis, who spoke again. "I don't want that. I don't want to be a king. But that doesn't change the fact that things are bad there—I grew up in Kurash, not in Talohira. I don't consider myself to be Talohiran, to be honest. My mother taught me both languages, and maybe that's why."

He glanced over to his mother standing behind him. She patted his shoulder and whispered a few words of encouragement into his ear, and he continued.

"I may be the son of the previous king, but I might not be the rightful heir," Valis said.

"You refer to the survival of Empress Mara?" Ronin asked.

"Yes, and no," Valis replied, looking to his father, who simply nodded. A sign of his approval to proceed. "I have a sister. An older sister."

"Then, with you apparently dead, who is the rightful ruler of Talohira?" Shanthah asked of Valistaran.

"All hail the Empress of Blood, rightful queen dowager of Talohira, and the Supreme One of Kurash, who is called Mara Bartunek." Valistaran grinned before continuing. "According to Talohiran law, even in the event of a revolution, a surviving regent or wife thereof still maintains their position."

"I don't know what half of those words mean," Shanthah muttered to Hanna, who giggled.

"But if something should happen to Mara, my sister would become heir to the throne," Valis explained.

"And what do you think, Valeniya?" Mara asked.

Valistaran and Valis shared a furtive glance as Valeniya began to speak.

"I would be a bad queen," Valeniya replied. The council expected her to continue, but she remained silent. An awkward silence followed.

"Neither she nor Valis is known to the general public in Talohira. But changing the order of bloodline rule would still be illegal according to our laws without Mara and my family's express consent," Valistaran said.

"I give mine. Even as Empress of Sangora and Talohira, I will need a regent in Bukaral, as I will not rule from Talohira if I take back my throne from Florenta. Perhaps, Valis, would you be willing to take that rule as one of the rightful heirs? You would be King of Talohira ruling under the Empress of Blood, so you wouldn't be alone in the first years of your rule. And in time, I think it would be wise to give Talohira complete independence."

Valis nodded. "I guess, yes."

"And Valeniya, do you agree to this plan?" Mara asked. Valeniya nodded, and her eyes clouded over with a glassy white sheen.

"One problem that has been worrying me," Mara said, turning to Valistaran. "You 'died' before we were to be married. Do I even have a real claim to the throne?"

It was something she and political dissidents in Sangora had often wondered and one of the most enduring conspiracy theories.

"We did not have a wedding, true," Valistaran said. He trailed off, and Alia placed her hand over her mouth to stifle her laughter and had to turn away from the group.

"We're MARRIED?!" Mara shouted, getting to her feet; her wings extended high over her head. The rest of the contingent rose as well in respect for their queen, but Valistaran stayed seated.

"On paper only! Do you not have reason now to thank me?" Valistaran asked, gesturing out the eastern window. "You spent enough time in the archives and great library of Talohira—I assumed you knew."

"You assumed I…" Mara trailed off, her nostrils flaring. She sat, and the rest of the group did the same. She pressed her eyes shut and went into a short trance for a few seconds before speaking again. "I apologize for my—no, no I don't. I stand by what I said. But you are right; because of our current predicament, I do thank you—dear."

The entire group broke into laughter, and Mara and Valistaran shared a good-humored grin.

"Aleksander's going to be sooo jealous," Hanna whispered into Shanthah's ear; the Master of Dusk laughed, with a slow nod and eyebrows raised high.

"Back to the situation at hand, please," Mara demanded, sending the room back into silence.

"Yes. With the Empress missing, Florenta appointed her own illegitimate Mistresses of Dusk," Anca explained. "My informants tell me that she appointed one councilor to govern Talohira in her stead, but the people revolted. They dragged her into the street and executed her. Her body stayed in the street for an entire week. In that vacuum of power, each of the warlords and slavers of Talohira began to contend for the throne."

Hanna caught Mara's gaze and with a look of concern mouthed the word, "Belokej?"

"To your knowledge, has anyone taken the throne?" Mara asked, her eyes still locked on Hanna.

"Not that I know of, but I have been preoccupied. The warring factions have split the country with the people's support split amongst four warlords as well as a faction who supports the previous government: my most devout followers, who still cling to hope that their queen, Mara Bartunek, is still alive," Valistaran said. "There are conspiracy theorists, of course, that say you are dead or alive but have abandoned your country. It's anarchy on the brink of civil war. Any of you who have been to Talohira knew that it was a safe place to live; the war between Thanatanos threatened both sides, but Talohira was, in the end, always safe."

"Something must be done," Shanthah said, slamming his fist on the table. His mind raced with thoughts of his love for the Alboran and Karpaskan people and knew something must now happen for Talohira. "How has our political system become so fragile?"

"What do you propose, my Master of Dusk?" Mara asked.

The look on her face was genuine; Shanthah was taken aback, not ready to believe that Mara was not the omnipotent, omniscient ruler many in the room believed her to be. They locked eyes, and he saw the girl he had once known in the slave camp, her shimmering blue eyes afire with hope and courage despite the pain life had thrown at her. "Please, share your ideas."

"We can split up into several teams to assess the situation. Let's send one team to Thanatanos, one to Doftaan, and the last to Talohira," Shanthah suggested. "Another to Kurash, too."

"You think one team can stop a civil war?" Anca asked.

"A love story overthrew Florenta in this region," Mara said with a smile, looking between Shanthah and Hanna. "So yes, I do. We can achieve what needs to be done."

"I would like to lead the expedition to Thanatanos," Shanthah said, putting his name forward. He turned to Valis. "It's close enough to the border of Thanatanos that it would be easy for me to coordinate from this stronghold. I think young Mr. Talohir should lead the way into Talohira, and I think it's time for Kurash to meet its new queen, or Supreme One, or whatever."

"And what about Sangora?" asked Raluca. "Is our home not a worthy enough cause to fight for?"

"Mistress Raluca, Sangora is the worthiest of causes, but the team shouldn't include any Sangorans to prevent Florenta from controlling them," Mara said. "With aid from Talohira and Kurash, we can take back our home. And then, with the full force of our people, we may be able to free Thanatanos from the false god's grip."

She sighed, clearly exhausted. Raluca bowed to her empress.

"Or, perhaps, we shall fall as one united," Anca said. A foreboding silence fell over the room.

"Then we shall fall on the side of right," Mara replied.

"Well, we won't have to worry anymore if we do," Shanthah said with a shrug. "Listen, maybe we should decide who is going where."

"A good idea. I would like the following individuals to stand and assemble at the back of the room," Mara said, gazing over everyone in the room, trying to decide the groups. "Shanthah Kalen. Hanna Samsa. Josman Faros. Captain Rayna Kotula. General Anca—and perhaps Ronin Jakoni. He is leaving after this meeting to attend to matters with his own people."

Each named individual made their way to the back of the room, but Hanna hesitated. Mara approached her friend.

"Is everything okay?" Mara asked, her voice hesitant.

"Yes, but—" Hanna said.

"But?"

"With all due respect," Hanna began, "and with all the love I have for Shanthah—"

"No, there is no respect due, Hann," Mara said, shaking her head. She smiled, and Hanna returned the expression.

"Thank you for thinking to put me on Shanthah's team, and I know it's what he wants—and I do want to go with him—"

"But it isn't what you want?" Mara asked. Hanna stared into Mara's eyes for several seconds before breaking eye contact and glancing down at the floor.

"No. It's fine," Hanna said at last.

"No. It isn't," Mara said, her hand on Hanna's shoulder. Hanna looked back up at Mara and sighed.

"I want my friend back," Hanna said.

Her whispered words were far more honest and broken than any Mara had heard recently. She felt tears well up in her eyes, and she wrapped her arms around Hanna. Shanthah looked on and caught Hanna's gaze. He responded with a thumbs-up, knowing exactly what had happened.

"So do I," Mara said, her ruby lips turning upward at the corners. In a louder voice, she announced the second group heading to Talohira, including Valis, Valistaran, Mistress Raluca. Then, at last, she announced the names of those that would accompany her to Kurash, including Alia, Kamil, and Hanna.

This left several people still seated at the table or around it, including Daniel Elafris, and Hanna's allies, Liliana and Reka.

"What shall we do, my Empress?" Liliana asked.

"I have not forgotten you," Mara said. "I have a special request for you both. I wish for you to stay here in Balgorod. Keep Elafris and his secrets safe."

She then said the same in Sangoran for Reka.

"We can do that," Liliana said. Reka nodded.

"You have called me your empress, your queen, the Supreme One, even. Titles I never dreamed I would ever hold," Mara said.

A low chuckle escaped her throat. "I'm just a girl from Cineca who was given the world. But I am a queen without a throne. An empress without an empire. But one thing I do have is a people that I love more than anything. I know what I'm asking of you all risks your lives and may threaten everything we love, but it is for that reason that I ask you now: will you stand with me against Florenta? Will you stand with me against Thanatan himself?"

First, Hanna knelt. Shanthah was next, followed by Ronin, Valistaran, Josman, Kamil, and Alia. Valis took a knee beside his mother, and everyone in the room knelt with bent knee and lowered head, a sign of reverence for a woman who had once been a slave, but now represented so much more.

"Please, rise," Mara said, overcome with emotion.

Then, the Empress of Blood knelt before them. She bent one knee out of reverence and love for those that supported her. Friends. Family. Hope for a free world that she could not bring to pass alone. A single tear rolled down her cheek. For too long, she had felt so very alone. Surrounded, but alone.

Unloved.

Hated.

No more.

# CHAPTER THIRTY-TWO
# TWO MORE SHOULDERS TO HELP HOLD THE WORLD

The grime and blood pooled around Mara's ankles, obscuring the white tile beneath her feet, and each droplet of warm water stung her unbound wounds. She pressed her forehead against the tiled wall beneath the steady stream of water that beat down on her bruised and battered body.

A thousand thoughts rang through her brain. A dull ache had filled her skull since the escape from Zinok, and the soothing warmth of the water was all that seemed to calm her racing mind.

With the exhaustion of recent events catching up to her, she had forced herself to step into the shower.

There was a thump as a thick towel struck the door of the shower chamber, and she heard footsteps leaving the room.

"Hann?" Mara called, guessing the identity of the person who had brought the towel.

"Yeah?" Hanna's voice echoed around the tiled chamber.

"Come back."

"Okay. What's up?"

"I don't know. Do you ever wonder how in the world you got to this point?" Mara asked, her forehead still pressed against the wall, letting water running down her shoulders, wings, and back. She heard Hanna slump against the door of the shower.

"Every single day," Hanna said with a laugh.

Mara smiled and slid down the tiled wall until she was sitting in the pooled water.

"You got an answer? How did it come to us to save the world?" Mara asked.

She hugged her knees against her chest and closed her eyes, letting the water wash over her face; the warmth seemed to wash away her cares just as it washed away the grime from the arduous battles and journeys across Sangora and Thanatanos.

"No, not really fair, is it?" Hanna asked, resting the back of her head against the partition. Steam curled in mesmerizing patterns over the top of the door between them. It was somehow calming, and she watched it, entranced, as Mara spoke.

"Definitely not," Mara said. "It kills me that we couldn't save so many people in Zinok, and it makes me so sad that there are so many unhappy people."

"You're a good person, Mar. Just such a *good* person."

Mara flashed a brief, but grateful smile. "Am I, though? I mean, I've killed more people than I've kissed, and—"

"And nothing. You've done bad things, yes, but you've done so much more good for so many people," Hanna said.

"I don't think it balances out like that." The words slipped from Mara's mouth before she could stop them. "I feel like I finally know who I am, but I feel…trapped."

"What do you mean?"

"I feel stuck between—well, I don't know for sure, but I don't know what else to do," Mara said. "Is that weird? Like being in between the light and the dark, maybe… That ugly dimness that isn't quite bright enough to light the way or warm your skin, but too dark for you to see anything—I feel like that. I feel like it's a part of me, but I don't know what it is."

"Is that a bad thing?" Hanna asked. She listened to the flow of water and understood Mara's silence as a request to keep speaking. "I notice you didn't say you're torn between good or evil. Intentional?"

"Yeah."

"I assume you know where you stand on that front, then."

"I'm starting to."

Hanna cocked her head and considered her next words. "So, the dark and the light," Hanna said. "Do you feel like you have to choose one over the other?"

"I'm not even sure what I mean," Mara replied. "Should I stay in the dark where it's safe or risk being in the light? Or, I don't know, the other way around. It's like—how do I explain this? It's like I have no idea how to keep going."

"Why not both? Walk into the light *and* embrace the dark—find your balance and become who you *want* to be. Who you really are," Hanna said. The words resonated with Mara, as she had said something similar to Aleksander not long ago. "Mara. Why didn't you kill Belokej?"

There was silence for a long moment.

"Because cruelty is weakness," Mara replied in a soft voice.

Hanna nodded. Tears of joy for her friend welled at the corners of her eyes, and she said, "Mara, can I just say—I am so proud of you and so happy to meet who you have become."

Mara wept on the other side of the door, but as she swept her soaked hair from her face, she found herself unable to wipe away the smile.

"Pol always loved all those stories and legends from the Deadlands," she said. "You know, the ones with heroes who go on grand adventures and quests to save the world?"

"I wasn't familiar with any of those stories until I met your brother. He made me look forward to working in the slave camps with him sometimes because he'd tell me about them," Hanna said with a laugh. "Sometimes our workday would end, and he'd say, 'to be continued,' in a dramatic voice, and he'd make me wait until the next time we worked together to tell me the rest."

"Love that kid," Mara said with a smile from her side of the partition. The guilt of a failed sister and protector swelled in her heart as she asked, "Do you know what happened to him after Florenta attacked?"

"Wrong person to ask," Hanna said. "I ended up in Florenta's dungeon, but he wasn't with Shanthah when he and his followers liberated Balgorod, and he hasn't mentioned him at all. I'm sorry, but I haven't seen him. I can ask…"

"I told my Mistresses of Dusk to look out for him during the Peace Summit. I hope one of them or Aleksander found him."

"I'm sure Pol's with one of them, although I'm not sure where Aleksander ended up either," Hanna said, hoping to reassure Mara. "Speaking of which—"

Hanna emphasized those words more than the others, trying to improve her friend's mood. She smiled as she heard Mara's laugh from the other side of the shower door.

"I think you know everything there is to know about the tragic backstory of the Empress of Blood's futile love life," Mara said, hugging her knees as the water continued to beat down on her bruised shoulders. "We talked at the Peace Ball."

"I saw," Hanna said. "I also saw him touch your butt."

Mara burst out laughing.

"That was my idea, all for your benefit," Mara said, still smiling. "We did talk, though. We both agreed that we have a lot to work out. Probably me more than him, but…"

She trailed off.

"It's an oversimplification to say you've been through a lot, so that's okay," Hanna said.

"Thanks," Mara said, splashing the water on the floor with one of her wings. "Oh, and as you know, I'm apparently married."

"Well, like your husband said, only on paper," Hanna said. "But it's no secret that the Empress of Blood is a total knockout." She tapped her fist against the door. Another laugh. "What, is empress-ing that time consuming that you can't find time for a single date?"

"Only when your advisors stage a coup against you," Mara said, rubbing her temples. The headache was getting worse, but her mood and tone were lighter than before.

"That happen to you often?"

"Twice!"

"Well, I'll let your newest Masteress of Dusk know not to try any coups," Hanna replied.

"Masteress?" Mara laughed at the absurdity.

"Shanthah's workshopping new gender norm-shattering titles or something. *Don't* get me started," Hanna said with another laugh. "I shot down Mattress of Dusk."

Mara snorted in laughter, making Hanna giggle in turn, and together, they simply laughed on opposite sides of the partition. Mara fell silent and said nothing for a long moment. The only sound breaking the silence was the soft spray of water on tile.

"You drown in there?" Hanna asked.

"No," Mara said with a laugh then said, trailing off, "I'm just...happy."

"You deserve to be," Hanna replied. No response. "Say it, Mara."

"I deserve it," Mara said at last.

"Deserve what?"

"To be happy."

"Say it all at once," Hanna ordered. Mara was silent for a long moment, listening to the sound of the running water.

"I deserve to be happy."

Hanna smiled from the other side of the door and nodded.

"And that happiness doesn't depend on power or success, or being in a relationship, or anything like that, you know that? But now that you've admitted that to yourself, I have a question for you," Hanna said.

"Oh no."

"Oh yes," Hanna replied. "Do you love yourself? Do you love *Mara*?"

For a long while, the only answer to Hanna's question was the sound of splashing water.

"Sometimes," Mara said at last. "More than I used to."

"What about the rest of the time?"

"I don't know. Sometimes I just don't," Mara answered, absentmindedly splashing the water with her wing. Hanna didn't respond, and Mara knew she was waiting for her to continue. "I don't know, just—sometimes because of things I've done, and I guess because of the things that have happened to me. And I'm just failing at every aspect of my life. I know there are so many people who have it worse than me, but I just…"

She trailed off.

"You don't *only* deserve to be happy. You also deserve to be loved no matter what you've done and no matter what's happened to you," Hanna said. "That might be harder to understand than my earlier gem, but it's true. *So many* people love you, Mar. I know I sure do."

"Yeah?"

"Yeah, no matter what. And you deserve love from yourself most of all," Hanna said. "Because you're amazing, and we all want you to know it, okay?"

"Thank you, Hann," Mara replied. "You're right."

"So?" Hanna asked.

"You're going to make me say it, aren't you?"

"Yup."

"I deserve to be loved," Mara said with a laugh.

"And?"

"And… I love myself," Mara said.

"Do you?"

"I do," Mara said. "Or at least, I'll get there."

"We all will," Hanna replied.

"You are wonderful, Hann."

"Yeah, I know," Hanna said with a cheerful laugh. "Oh, before I forget—Shanthah told me to tell you again that he's sorry for shooting you with that spear-arrow thing. His *exact* words." Not only a single laugh followed, but a string of laughter so intense that Mara began to cough, aggravating her migraine.

"It's a good thing he did, or Florenta would have been able to control everyone in Balgorod," Mara said, splashing happily in the water with both feet. "Shooting a friend is a small price to pay, eh?"

"Getting shot, you mean?" Hanna asked.

She heard Mara stand up on the other side of the shower partition, and the heated water stopped flowing. The door cracked open, and Mara's hand appeared in the opening. Hanna handed her the towel, and the Empress of Blood emerged a moment later wrapped in it, her hair wild, still damp.

Hanna turned to leave to give her friend a bit of privacy but caught sight of the myriad bruises, scars, and wounds that lined Mara's arms, chest, shoulders, legs, and back.

"Mar…" Hanna whispered, absentmindedly reaching out to brush her finger along a mess of scars between Mara's wings.

"Hey, they've made me who I am, and each one is a story to tell." Mara smiled, knowing that Hanna was still eying the faded, yet vivid lines drawn by Belokej's whip. "You still got yours?"

"Every single one." She gestured to her back. "Shanthah says I look like I fought a bear and can therefore defend him."

"I don't believe for a *second* that's what he's looking at when your scars are visible." They both laughed so hard that they cried.

"Oh, you're absolutely right. But my goodness, Mara. You look like you were run over by a stampede of Minotaurs."

"Yeah, well, those are just the ones you can see."

"Ah, yeah. Metaphorical wounds," Hanna said, nodding.

"What?" Mara asked with another laugh as she gazed into the mirror. "No, I meant there's plenty more under the towel. There are definitely metaphorical wounds too, but we won't get into that now, yeah?"

She began to squeeze the water out of her hair onto the floor.

"We'll have plenty of time for that on the way to Kurash," Hanna replied, massaging her wounded arms.

"I hope so. And what in the name of Elafris happened to your arms? Same stampede I got caught in? How have we not talked about this yet?"

"The healers here said I snapped like every single tendon and ligament in my arms, and they said I fractured the bones in over a hundred places."

"An exaggeration? Or—"

"Literally. They said they stopped counting," Hanna replied. "Alia was able to heal them after the other healers set my bones and things. They still ache, and she said I shouldn't do any heavy lifting. She said that if I ever hurt them again, even she might not be able to fix them."

"I have half a mind to stop you from coming with me to Talohira and Kurash," Mara said, a look of concern washing over her face.

"Try and stop me," Hanna said with a wink.

"I wouldn't dare!" Mara said with a laugh. "But what did you do to hurt them so badly?"

"I, uh, used my mind to catch—and vaporize—the prison fortress as it fell on me," Hanna said then added with another wink, "no big deal."

"Exactly why I need you on my side," Mara said, pointing at Hanna's head. "I'm glad we both got out of this whole thing alive."

"We won," Hanna said, grinning. Mara smiled back despite the stabbing pain in her head. "I mean, kind of."

Mara adjusted her towel and wiped the steam from the tall mirror in the corner of the chamber before taking a long look at her collection of scars. She felt a strange feeling of déjà vu and nausea flood over her as she gazed at her reflection. Her mind shot back to a night before she had become the Queen of Talohira, back when her wings had first begun to develop; then, they were just ugly red stumps. She had kicked her favorite black dress into the cupboard in shame, despair.

She had been very, terribly alone. But now?

"I'm happy you're here, Hann. It really means a lot. Thank you," Mara said. She shook her head to rid herself of the headache.

"I'm glad too. I've missed you, miss-ruler-of-the-world-mega-babe," Hanna said.

She turned away as Mara pulled her clothes from where they had been unceremoniously draped across a stone basin.

"I've really missed you too," Mara said as she dressed.

"I know that with you being an empress, a queen, a warrior, and all that, it seems like the whole world is on your shoulders—which, to be honest, it kind of is right now, and I know that. But I hope you know that despite having the body that sculptors modeled their sculptures of the goddesses after, you aren't one. I mean, you aren't all-powerful and that means you don't have to hold up the world all by yourself," Hanna said.

"You're too nice. You always did know how to make me feel better." Mara chuckled and laced up the front of her tunic. She threw her hair over her shoulder and said, "I don't deserve you."

"That's the thing I'm trying to tell you, Mara! You *do* deserve me—and all the people who love you. You deserve to be loved. You deserve to be happy. Remember? Hap-py."

Hanna turned, expecting Mara to be finished dressing by now. She wrapped her bandaged arms around her half-dressed friend, who reciprocated the action with a smile.

"Hanna!" Mara exclaimed, laughing as Hanna planted an exaggerated kiss on her cheek. "Rehor always told me the same thing—you know, that I deserve to be happy."

Thoughts of Rehor flooded her head, but instead of despair, joy filled her heart at the thought of the man.

"Well, it's true, and the world *is* on your shoulders, but here are two more to help hold it up." Hanna pulled away.

"Thank you," Mara said, her eyes glassing over with tears.

"What now?" Hanna asked. "Pants, maybe?"

"Probably a good idea, yes. And a good nap." Mara pulled up her trousers with an embarrassed laugh. "I think I've earned that, eh?"

"I hear you there," Hanna said as they left the shower chamber and entered a long corridor outside.

Mara enjoyed the cold sensation of marble flooring against her bare feet. Together, they laughed and made their way up a spiral staircase toward their bedchambers on the floor above.

Halfway up the stairs, Mara stopped, her breathing heavy. She slumped against the wall and pressed her hands against the sides of her head.

"You okay?" Hanna asked, pausing to hold Mara's arm.

"Yeah. Fine. My head's just been killing me," Mara said.

"Let's get you to bed. I'll see if Alia or her healers can do something for that headache. Time for that nap you so desperately deserve, yeah?"

Mara nodded with a smile, the weight of the world pressing down on her head, and then she sank to her knees. She tried to catch herself, and her hands struck the cold, stone stairs.

The vomiting followed. She looked up at Hanna, who kept hold of her friend's arm. "I'm so sorry," Mara stuttered, appalled.

"Mara!" Hanna exclaimed. "Someone, help!"

Pain shot through her skull. A stabbing, shooting pain that seemed to constrict her very soul. She clutched her head; it was getting worse with every passing minute since leaving the shower, and—

Another bout of nausea, and she heaved all over Hanna's leg and feet then stumbled, mortified, slipping from her friend's grip. She tumbled down a couple stairs and then felt arms around her keeping her still as her wings spasmed. Pain coursed through her shoulder.

She was on her side, now.

How did she get there?

She heard, or perhaps sensed Hippo outside crying in anguish. The sounds of Shanthah's soldiers moving upstairs. The birds outside. Her own breathing. Hanna's cries for help.

All of it. An overwhelming cacophony of deafening pain.

Hanna seemed to melt away as Mara's vision blurred.

"Hanna?"

Mara squeezed her friend's hand, just to make sure she still could. Just to make sure she was still alive. To make sure Hanna was still there. She felt a squeeze back.

She knew what was happening.

She could not stop it.

She had to try. She willed away the pain and nausea, reciting the names of those that loved her just to prove to herself she could still think. That she could still remember.

Hanna…Lavinia…Rehor…Aleksander…

Other names came into her mind.

Shanthah…Josman…Kamil…

Pol…Vasilica…

Valistaran…

…Xanthurias…

She heaved again and tasted bile as a mind-numbing fog began to claim her; she could feel herself succumbing to unconsciousness as her body surrendered to the agony.

Who was screaming?

Oh.

Oh, no.

She could feel hands gripping her wrists.

She was moving, or someone else was moving her.

Overwhelming pain.

And then,

blackness.

# CHAPTER THIRTY-THREE
# DEATH IS NOT YOURS TO TASTE

Aleksander watched his white breath disappear into the cold night air. Only scant leaves were left on the barren trees of the late season, and he wondered when the first flakes of snow would bathe the world in a sheet of white. He ignited a small flame between his fingers to keep warm, for he still had several hours on watch while the others slept.

He was desperately tired, but whenever his eyes shut, his mind turned to Drahomir's apparent betrayal and the unknown fates of his friends. Pol's face came to mind first as the intense guilt of having to leave him behind was still fresh in his heart. He had failed the young man, and he knew it.

Mara. Shanthah and Hanna. Josman and Kamil. He smiled as he thought of them but knew that if he tried to sleep, worry would creep into his mind and dreams, and he risked Drahomir finding them. A grunt and the sound of hooves on cobblestone brought him back to the present from his distracted thoughts.

He extinguished the flame in his palm and pressed himself low against the balcony. It had been hours since the last resident of Cineca had shut themselves indoors out of fear of the patrols of Faceless that had begun to sweep through the town several days ago. The creatures never entered homes, but anyone caught in the streets disappeared. His heart ached for Mara's parents.

He could sense the groans of the Faceless now.

A hulking shadowy form stomped along the cobblestone street, the sound of thick hooves following it—a Minotaur. The massive figure carried something strapped to its back. Provisions, perhaps? Aleksander kept himself low to avoid being seen. Being spotted by a Minotaur loyal to his enemies would lead to a gruesome death indeed.

A horrifying thought crossed his mind, and curiosity told him that he had to get a glimpse of the creature. If Sangorans could become Faceless, could a Minotaur?

As he strained his neck to peer around the corner, a human appeared from the alleyway to follow the Minotaur, and Aleksander heard a voice say something in Thannish, but he couldn't pick up more than a few words. As the two figures disappeared into the darkness of another alleyway, a third, much taller figure appeared from the shadows and made a swift stride into the alley behind its allies.

"Valakor?" Aleksander whispered to himself.

He remembered that there was a Minotaur and a Spirit Warrior in the Court of Thanatan, but he had to remind himself that there were Minotaurs loyal to the enemy as well, and he had seen with his own eyes several Spirit Warriors following Thanatan's throne into Laniras.

Another terrible thought crossed his mind; the mighty warriors of the Court of Thanatan, were of course, members of the Court of *Thanatan*. Did their sneaking indicate that their loyalties had shifted since Thanatan's return, or were they hunting those that did not support the dark god?

He heard the soft thud of an axe which squelched the low groan at the back of Aleksander's mind. At that, Aleksander hurried inside to wake the others. Lavinia and Rayshel were fast asleep beside one another, but Vasilica sat up as he entered.

"Got a minute?" Aleksander asked in the darkness, and Vasilica followed without a word, knowing Aleksander's duty was to keep the others safe.

They closed the door to the balcony, and Vasilica extended her wings to hoist Aleksander into the air. He gestured to the alleyway, and Vasilica glided to the ground level, setting Aleksander down before landing several yards ahead. They snuck into the darkness of the alley toward the Spirit Warrior and his allies, but they were nowhere to be found.

Vasilica raised a confused eyebrow, and Aleksander chose to take a chance, shouting, "Valakor!" in the empty street. Nothing happened for a long moment, and then as if from the depths of the shadows, a looming figure appeared, vicious scythe held aloft. The warrior pointed the edge of the curved blade toward Vasilica, hesitant. In the light of his fireball, Aleksander could see that it, along with Valakor's armor, was coated in dried blood.

"We're on the same side," Aleksander reassured him, raising his hand not holding the ball of flame to indicate that he meant no ill will. Valakor said nothing, his shining armor and blade reflecting the flame in Aleksander's hand.

"Valakor, it's me. Aleksander."

"Forgive my hesitance, young warrior," Valakor said.

His voice had an ethereal quality to it—a deep resonance but a distinct lack of echo. He did not lower the blade.

"I understand, believe me," Aleksander said as the Minotaur Aleksander knew as Bovin and a third warrior appeared, each pointing their own weapons, a massive axe and a sword.

"I am Mistress Vasilica of Empress Mara's court, Regent of Doftaan and Mistress of Dusk," Vasilica said, raising her wings and bowing. The Sangoran sign of respect.

"I am Valakor, formerly of the Court of Thanatan," replied the warrior. He turned to his allies and said, "And my companions are Bovin and Manitrius."

"Formerly?" Aleksander asked after a hesitant pause.

"You wonder of my allegiance," Valakor said.

"You don't wonder ours?" Aleksander replied. "What are you doing here?"

"After Thanatan's return, the three of us disavowed ourselves of his court and went back to the headquarters of the Hidden Flame to find it in ruin," Valakor said.

"And filled with Faceless?" Aleksander asked, nodding.

"We were there not long ago too," Vasilica added. "The Faceless drove us out and we lost the fortress."

"Then you should thank us for going back for this accursed thing," Bovin said with a snort, hefting the pouch on his back to adjust it. "We wouldn't want the Faceless to have access to one of the last remaining Telepillars, would we?"

Aleksander and Vasilica exchanged a relieved, knowing glance.

"Before the fortress was overrun, we used the pillar to see what had become of Doftaan," Vasilica said.

"Then you have ever more reason to thank us, as the pillar was still active when we arrived," Valakor said. "We too used the pillar to see into Sangora and discovered a simple truth: tonight, there is a chance for us to slay Florenta."

"Valakor is right," Manitrius said, seeing the surprised expressions on Aleksander and Vasilica's faces. "We discovered Florenta's main military force in Doftaan moving out."

"Where are they going?" Vasilica and Aleksander asked.

"We believe they are either heading to defend the border of Sangora from attacks from the Pure, or perhaps to quell the rebellion in Karpaska. Several locals told us of a festival to celebrate their new queen. I believe everyone in Doftaan will be forced to attend, despite the current situation there.

"Situation?" Vasilica asked.

"You don't know?" Bovin asked, his voice still loud despite his attempt at a whisper. Manitrius put his hand on the Minotaur's shoulder.

"Much of Sangora is afflicted with a terrible plague, one that turns its host into a Faceless after death," he said. "I am sorry, daughter of Sangora."

Vasilica was silent, and Aleksander could see the worry etched on her face. Manitrius spoke up again.

"The vines," Vasilica whispered. Aleksander nodded.

"A contingent will defend the celebration, which will be held just outside the city," Manitrius said. "The festivities will only happen until sunrise when Florenta will arrive in a procession from her fortress to the festival for her official coronation as Empress of Blood and queen of Talohira."

"Isn't Florenta worried the plague will spread to everyone at the festival?" Aleksander asked.

"Florenta doesn't care about people—she cares about power, and if I had to guess, she's probably denying the plague even exists. If people don't get sick, it'll prove her authority and power," Vasilica said.

"Then perhaps, the contingent is there not for defense, but to prove that point," Valakor said. "Very astute."

"I thank Elafris that they had not discovered a way to use the pillar, or your home in Sangora would already be overrun," Manitrius said.

"I fear that may already be the case," Aleksander said, glancing at Vasilica once more. Valakor lowered his blade and knelt before the duo so that he stood at their same height.

"Explain," he said, his voice chilling and direct.

"The prison tower of Doftaan was infested with vines of some kind, and the prisoners inside, Sangoran and human alike, were all transformed into—" Aleksander said.

"Bloodvine," Valakor said, cutting Aleksander off before turning to Bovin and Manitrius.

"As we feared," Manitrius said. "So that's where the virus is coming from."

"What exactly is the Bloodvine?" Vasilica asked.

"Explain?" Aleksander said, echoing Valakor's earlier request.

"When Florenta overthrew Empress Mara and massacred the delegation there, many of those loyal to the Empress of Blood weren't killed by blade or by the hand of man, no; they died choking on their own blood," Valakor said.

"Explain harder?" Aleksander requested. He shared another worried glance with Vasilica.

"There are two substances derived from the Bloodvine plant. It doesn't spread like a normal vine; it spreads with spores, more like a mushroom, but it can only grow in organic matter and favors human and Sangoran flesh," Manitrius explained, looking Vasilica in the eye. "It spreads out of the dead and can overtake settlements in days. The first substance is derived from these viral spores. It can cause a horrible sickness that manifests after several days, and it is highly contagious. It all makes sense now. Somehow, Thanatan has used these vines to spread the Faceless Plague by mixing the two viruses."

"And the second?" Aleksander asked.

"The second is a toxin from the vine that when mixed with Sangoran blood kills the non-human part of Sangoran physiology," Manitrius explained. "Completely harmless to humans, but—"

"Rayshel," Vasilica whispered. Aleksander nodded.

"Our friend fell victim to the second one," he said. "Speaking of, we have two allies in a safehouse nearby. Would you like to join us?"

He felt strange, as if he were offering the three warriors over for tea rather than refuge from the dark powers at work.

"Any shelter is welcome," Valakor said with a nod before he and his allies followed Aleksander and Vasilica back to their hideout.

"I am sorry for what has happened in Sangora," Manitrius said. "Truly."

Vasilica nodded and pressed her hand over her heart.

"So am I, friend Manitrius."

They came to the door, which Valakor and Bovin both had a hard time fitting through, but they gathered at the bottom floor, and Vasilica went upstairs to wake Rayshel and Lavinia.

"So, what are your plans?" Aleksander asked. "I assume you're not just running around protecting the Telepillar?"

"That's exactly what we're doing," Bovin grunted.

"We don't agree on the best course of action," Valakor explained as the three Sangorans filed down the rickety staircase.

"We should take the fight to the horrible new Night Witch queen," Bovin said.

"I like the bull-man's thinking," Lavinia said in response, emerging from the stairway.

"Bull-man?!" Bovin snorted. "Such disrespect!"

"Then let's not throw out ignorant slurs like Night Witch, shall we?" Lavinia said before stoking Bovin's ego. "Regardless, I agree with the mighty Minotaur. We must bring the fight to Florenta."

"And when Florenta is dead?" Manitrius asked.

"Sangora is free," Rayshel said with a shrug.

"But will it be?" Aleksander asked. "Will killing her solve the problem?"

"She has the Queen's Control. We would literally be freeing the people in Sangora with her dead," Rayshel said.

"I like her thinking," Bovin said, and Lavinia nodded.

"Are we sure she is the only one?" Aleksander asked.

Lavinia was silent for a moment, a strange look of consternation on her face.

"Admittedly, no. Florenta found a way to harness it at the same time as Mara, so perhaps others have as well," she said at last, "but if we take Florenta off Mara's throne, we can fight so that Mara can return."

"Maybe she's given part of that power to her Mistresses of Dusk to help govern Sangora," Aleksander said. Lavinia scoffed.

"If you think Florenta would willingly give anyone else the same power as her, you're a fool," she said. "Logically, yes. She should have a back-up if she is killed so that her house can maintain control over the daughters of Sangora, but realistically, no. I can assure you that she hordes that power for herself."

"A poor military decision," said Valakor.

"Florenta is a poor decision made by an irrelevant king," Lavinia said. "She's powerful and influential, yes, but also flawed in her greed; she's a gluttonous sycophant that cares for nothing but herself while she hordes power, people, and things useful to her. The power of the Queen's Control is no exception. She has what she's always wanted: for others to have to do as she says."

"Then her death would free the Sangoran people to act as they wish, rather than to her whim," Valakor thought out loud.

"But the vacuum left by her death," Manitrius said. "Surely you must all see the political ramifications here."

"No vacuum. Mara *may* be alive. I am alive. Vasilica is alive," Lavinia said. "There is a clear chain of legitimate leadership, should Florenta and her council be removed. Even if Mara is dead, then perhaps Vasilica or I would have legitimate right by Sangoran law to the throne and title of Empress of Blood."

Aleksander, who had been gazing out the window, glanced back over to Lavinia. He said nothing but wondered if this was her true end goal come to the surface at last. She met his gaze and stared back until he looked away.

"Bovin, I relinquish you of your burden," Valakor said, "and I thank you for the strength of your back that has carried it hence."

"You're firing him?" Manitrius asked with a chuckle.

"I've come to agree with my friend," Valakor said, placing a hand on the Minotaur's shoulder. Bovin gave a happy snort and set the teleportation on the floor with a heavy thud.

"Knew you'd come around," he grunted as he pulled the tattered canvas away from the glowing pillar.

"Yes, well, I hope we will not regret this decision."

The pillar emitted a faint red light as if to warn them to stay away from the destination set in its controls. Valakor adjusted the set of gems upon the device's face, and a low hum filled the small home.

"The destination is set," Valakor said.

"What will we find?" Vasilica asked.

"The resolve to do what we must," Lavinia replied, placing her hand on the pillar. The others did the same, but Rayshel hesitated.

"It'll be okay," Aleksander assured her.

"Shouldn't we be more prepared?" she asked. "I don't even have a weapon, and—"

Manitrius unstrapped a sheathed blade from his hip and handed it to Rayshel, who gripped it gingerly before strapping it to the belt around her waist. She nodded, her unsurety obvious. She placed a palm on the pillar, eyes shut. Aleksander brushed her hand with his own as if to reassure her once again.

"We'll make things right," he said. Rayshel nodded.

"This may be the only chance we get to find Florenta alone," Rayshel said to reassure herself. "I know, I know."

She took a deep breath, but before she could release it, bright red light engulfed the abandoned dwelling.

Distant trumpets, fireworks, and cymbals greeted the group as they materialized; soon multiple orchestras filled the night air with stirring melodies.

"Do you think those musicians actually play those instruments, or do you think Florenta has just learned to force them how to do it?" Vasilica asked.

"They're puppets," Lavinia said, confirming Vasilica's question.

"How do you know?" Rayshel asked as Valakor, Manitrius, and Bovin spoke several yards away.

"There is only one *good* orchestra in all of Doftaan. There are thousands of musicians here," Lavinia said. Rayshel laughed.

Aleksander turned and beheld the central palace of Doftaan behind him; gone were the crimson banners of Sangora that he had seen preceding the Peace Summit. The palace, along with every other building in sight, were covered with Florenta's banners, and her symbol, a white fist.

"Ominous," Aleksander muttered, placing his hand on his sword's hilt.

"We don't have much time," Valakor said. He pointed the shaft of his scythe to a far side of the courtyard where a dozen or so Sangorans were preparing a team of stallions and a massive, wheeled platform. Florenta's transport.

"So, what? We just wait here for her to come out?" Rayshel asked.

"I say we give her less room to run," Bovin said.

"I assure you, she can't run," Lavinia said. Vasilica and Rayshel shared another laugh and then turned to the northeast.

"Do you feel it too?" Lavinia asked. Vasilica nodded. "I was afraid of this."

"Her control?" Rayshel asked.

As the words escaped her mouth, Lavinia and Vasilica both took flight; Valakor roared and unleashed a wall of cyan energy just in time to intercept his allies. They struck the wall of energy just as it appeared, and they fell convulsing to the ground.

"What have you done to them?" Rayshel exclaimed. She and Aleksander hurried to their allies as the other trio of warriors readied their weapons.

"They are only stunned," Valakor said. "Restrain them, Bovin—for their own safety."

He turned away from the fallen Sangorans, setting his sights on the Queen's fortress that loomed above them.

Aleksander propped Lavinia's head on her cloak and watched Valakor walk away, seemingly detached from what he had just done, his heart set on one goal only. He passed by the Telepillar, placing his scythe in a strap over his shoulder. He held out his arms, and two short blades like those in Vasilica's armor appeared from beneath his vambraces; he thrust one arm forward and then another, using the blades to scale the outside of the tower.

"We can't all do *that*, you know!" bellowed Bovin from the ground.

He grunted and shook his horned head, gathering the pillar in the tarp and slung it over his shoulder again, looping the strap around his arm. He grunted and stomped toward the wall of the fortress with Manitrius close behind.

"What do we do?" Rayshel asked as Bovin smashed his axe through a high stained-glass window at the base of the tower. He and Manitrius entered the palace and were lost from view.

Lavinia and Vasilica stirred.

"Where'd they go?" Vasilica groaned.

"Are you ok?" Aleksander asked. "The control, is it gone? Valakor told us to restrain you, but if you're good, we'd appreciate your help instead."

"I still feel the order and the pull to assemble with the others, but Valakor must have disrupted it somehow," Lavinia said. "If she issues another order while we're here I'm not sure we could resist." Vasilica nodded with a sigh, confirming Lavinia's feelings.

"We'll be able to help you fight your way through the tower, but Lavinia's right. I don't think we'll be much help in a fight against Florenta herself," Vasilica said.

"As much as I wish I could be the one to put a knife in her heart, I agree," Lavinia said, a tone of bitter regret on the edge of her words. "The risk is less than our potential reward. Florenta dies."

"Then let's do it," Aleksander said. "Let's go take back Mara's throne."

Lavinia smiled. "Yes, lets."

They each stepped over jagged shards of stained glass like spilled jewels of pink, red, and green over the floor. They met no resistance on the first floor as they followed a path of dead guards in Bovin and Manitrius's wake.

They reached their allies as the Minotaur plowed his way through a wall of heavily armed Enforcers, throwing them like dolls against the walls of the corridor. Manitrius's blade was of little use against their thick armor, so he hid behind Bovin's gargantuan form as the Minotaur gored their enemies on his horns and crushed them beneath his massive axe.

Vasilica and Lavinia grabbed Rayshel's shoulders to lift her over the fray, drawing the Enforcers at the back away from the fight. Bovin's skin was covered in needle-like arrows no more than wasp stings to his thick hide, but they began to drive him into a murderous rage.

As Bovin broke through the Enforcers' formation, they changed their stance to surround him and collectively thrust their pike heads into his hard skin, resulting in a bellowing groan that filled the corridor.

Aleksander found his chance to pepper them with fireballs as the Enforcers dug their weapons deeper into the Minotaur's hide, distracting enough of them for Bovin to drive his right horn into the face of his nearest foe. She fell with a gory crack in her armored mask, but her pike stayed imbedded in the Minotaur's side.

"Get to Florenta!" Bovin bellowed as Aleksander unleashed a torrent of flame beneath his foes' legs. Bovin lashed out with one of his hooves, crushing an enemy's knee as she stumbled due to Aleksander's fire.

He grasped the pike in his side but roared in pain as each of the Enforcers released a flurry of needle bolts within his hide. Bovin slumped to his knees, his breathing heavy and forced.

"Go!" Bovin bellowed, decapitating another Enforcer.

His movement was slow as if moving through a deep bog. He fell to his knees as Lavinia's armored footsteps echoed through the corridor. The Mistress of Dusk thrust her silver blade up beneath the gap between her enemy's neck and helm into the woman's spine at the base of her skull. The Enforcer jerked and fell, pulling Lavinia's sword from her hand.

As Aleksander superheated the ground beneath the Enforcers, Lavinia leapt into the air, wrapped her legs around one warrior's head and with one flap of her wings, she snapped the woman's neck between her thighs then flipped over her enemies and summoned her twin vambrace blades and thrust them through the tops of two of her foes' heads. She hit the ground just as her three victims' bodies did.

"Thanks!" Aleksander exclaimed. Lavinia nodded, her breath heavy.

Valakor met them a few moments later as they raced up the stairwell at the end of the corridor, his armor even more bloodied than before.

"Where've you been, then?" Lavinia exclaimed.

"Clearing your path for four floors above!" Valakor replied, smashing the butt of his scythe against the floor.

"You're injured!" Rayshel exclaimed, rushing to Valakor's side, where a faint cyan mist leaked from his damaged armor. "Although, not as bad as Bovin—what can we do?"

Bovin stood through the agony, dropping his axe to the floor amidst the dead around him. As Valakor supported his massive ally, the Minotaur slumped next to the fallen Telepillar, his breathing strained and painful.

"Rest, my friend," Valakor said as Lavinia retrieved her sword from the slain Enforcer's neck.

"I can keep goin'," Bovin grunted through gritted teeth.

"I'm sure you can, big guy, but you've got to stop, or you won't be able to save us in another battle," Rayshel said, stroking his ox-like snout. "Stay still, okay?"

Bovin bellowed in pain as Rayshel tugged a pike bolt from his shoulder; it hadn't managed to bury itself deep through his hide, but she knew those that had been injected into his body would be much more difficult to remove.

"The rest of you, go on. I'll tend to Bovin," Rayshel said. "We'll keep the Teleportation Pillar safe."

"We're going to need all the help we can get," Aleksander objected.

"No. I'm a soldier, but I won't be much use up there, but I can help in my own way. Let me do this," Rayshel said. Aleksander nodded as Valakor hefted the Telepillar upright.

"We'll help barricade the exit to keep you both safe. If you're in any danger, use the pillar. It can get you out of here," Aleksander said.

"It is calibrated to return to its previous location," Valakor said. "Do not let it fall into Florenta's hands."

"But, if you can—I'd appreciate if you didn't leave us behind," Manitrius said with a wink. "Pick us up when the job's done."

Aleksander, Manitrius, and Valakor began to barricade the main entrance with whatever materials they could find. When they were finished, Valakor led the way upstairs.

"Will do," Rayshel said with an affirmative nod. She turned to Bovin, who was still groaning in a puddle of his own dark blood, darkening the already crimson rug.

"Don't hesitate to get out of here if you're overrun," Vasilica said, repeating Valakor's earlier sentiment.

"I know, we won't," Rayshel said. "We'll be safe."

They shared a long hug, and Vasilica clapped her on the shoulder.

"Really, we'll be fine," Rayshel said with a brave smile. Vasilica nodded, a look of pained truth on her face. "Get going!"

"I know you will be. But will we?" she asked.

Their companions hurried up the stairs, but Lavinia remained behind. Rayshel jumped as she felt Lavinia's hand on her shoulder then stood to address her.

"Is everything alright?" Rayshel asked. "You really should get going."

"*Please*, stay safe," Lavinia said, brushing Rayshel's cheek with an armored glove. Before Rayshel could respond, Lavinia planted a deep kiss on her lips. After a moment of joyful hesitation, the Mistress of Dusk pulled away, and with a flap of her wings, she shot up the stairs after the others.

"Well, let's get you patched up," Rayshel said, unable to hide her wide smile. Bovin let out a deep Minotaur chuckle of approval.

As the others made their way up the palace's staircase, Valakor faltered and began to lag behind despite the considerable length of his stride. Manitrius helped steady him.

"Are you okay to keep going?" Aleksander asked, eying the wound. Lavinia landed next to him and said nothing.

"I have much more time before this wound kills me. Time enough to finish our task and escape," Valakor replied. Aleksander nodded, unconvinced.

They made their way up the first staircase with no trouble, finding only slain guards and enforcers in their path. Aleksander couldn't help but wonder how many of these warriors were loyal to Mara but forced to do the bidding of their new queen, a thought that filled him with guilt.

"Listen, Aleksander," Lavinia said, tugging on his sleeve as they walked.

"Yeah?"

"I have to remind you. Vasilica and I will not be able to go into the room with Florenta. She can't know we're here," Lavinia said. "She'll control us, and let's face it, you can't take us."

"I know, we've been through this. Why are you telling me again?" Aleksander asked. Vasilica and Lavinia shared a furtive glance.

"Because that wound on Valakor's side looks worse than he lets on, and we don't have any way to mend it."

Lavinia's words filled Aleksander's mind with dread. With Rayshel incapacitated in the fight for Bovin's life, the two Mistresses of Dusk unable to aid him, and Valakor in unacknowledged mortal danger, the duty to stop the Queen's Control fell to two people: Manitrius and himself.

"We can get you as far as the throne room door, but no farther," Vasilica said. "We'll get back to Rayshel and Bovin and wait for you there."

Aleksander glanced over to Manitrius, sizing him up. He seemed to be a warrior fit for Valakor and Bovin's company, but his sword, however skilled, was ineffective against the enforcers' armor.

They climbed another floor in silence.

"When Valakor said he cleared out four floors, I thought he meant floors like we have back home," Aleksander wheezed as they began another ascent.

"You humans and your short ceilings are so cute," Vasilica said, smiling at Aleksander. Each staircase was easily four times the height of any normal landing back in Thanatanos, and the ceilings just as high.

"Teach me to fly, and I'll be okay with that," Aleksander said.

"Do you see us using *our* wings?" Lavinia asked. "See what we do for you?"

"Thanks," Aleksander said. "Ever so thoughtful."

"Don't forget it."

They kept climbing toward the throne room, passing the floor with the elegant ballroom that had been the sight of the grizzly massacre the night of the doomed Peace Summit Ball.

Aleksander let out a deep breath he had been holding as they approached.

"If we're lucky, Florenta will be abiding by the laws of the coronation, staying in her throne room until she is given the crown," Vasilica said. "Also, does the air seem thicker to you up here? It's getting hard to breathe."

Manitrius and Aleksander exchanged a worried glance.

"Bloodvine?" Aleksander asked without an answer from the others. As they strode around the corner into a hallway leading to the silver and crimson gates of the throne room, they beheld a grisly scene of six guards lying dead and disfigured on the ground.

"This your work, Valakor?" Aleksander asked. Valakor shook his head.

"I never made it up this high."

"This is it," Lavinia said, turning to Aleksander. "Good luck."

Valakor slammed the butt of his scythe against the ground, summoning energy around its vicious blade. He thrust it forward, blasting the throne room doors from their hinges in a cloud of dust.

As they ventured into Florenta's chamber, they came across a dozen or so soldiers defending their queen from violent Bloodvine tendrils which spouted a noxious fog of spores. Upon Mara's throne wearing an opulent crown sat Florenta, a look of utter fear carved into her wide face.

She looked up to see the newcomers and barked an order in Sangoran, diverting eight of her warriors to fend off the trio. Four remained to defend her from the vines.

"A foul act indeed! You brought them here, didn't you?" Florenta shouted in Thannish, spittle flying from her mouth. "I am going to kill you, and then I am going to kill Mara and her pitiful revolution in Balgorod!"

A deep groan filled the chamber.

A realization hit Aleksander; the Faceless weren't just mindless beasts attacking Sangora. They wanted one thing in Sangora: They wanted the Queen's Control.

"Florenta, you need to get out of here now, or we'll be the least of your problems!" Aleksander shouted, knowing they couldn't let her power fall into Thanatan's hands. The gray fog of Bloodvine spores coalesced around Florenta's throne, as if it were an ethereal specter sent to kill her.

A purpose that Aleksander too shared.

Aleksander roared and threw up a wall of searing orange flame, whipping the flow around to ignite the fog. It began to burn, and the groaning in Aleksander's mind intensified to a violent scream. At that moment, he tried to hurl a fallen helmet at the windows to ventilate the room, but he missed his mark.

To his surprise, the windows shattered, and crooked and broken fingers wrapped around the windowsills beneath the smashed windows as the silhouettes of the Faceless pulled themselves up to stand in the moonlight like eerie statues.

"What is this?" Florenta spat. Before Aleksander or the others could answer, another voice filled the chamber. "You brought them to my door?!"

Valakor arced the glowing cyan blade around in the dim light, but it stopped before meeting its target, a shadowy figure that had somehow materialized without Aleksander or Manitrius noticing.

"This, Queen Florenta, is fate's hands in motion."

As the words filled the chamber, the shaft of Valakor's scythe shattered. The broken blade skittered across the floor.

"Go, Aleksander! Finish this!" Manitrius exclaimed, joining Valakor against the new foe. "We'll hold him off!"

As Aleksander rushed toward Florenta, Valakor set his feet against the floor and strained his metallic body forward, but the figure buffeted him with a barrage of shadowy energy, sending him crashing through the throne room floor.

"Bow before your god."

Aleksander could feel his knees bend beneath him; it was not a graceful command of the Queen's Control, but a powerful telekinetic hand that bent his knee by force. He and Manitrius struck the ground on hands and knees as Thanatan turned his attention toward Florenta.

"If you're going to kill me, do so quickly," she said, standing in defiance; Thanatan strode toward her, shaking his cloaked head, his crystal mask and armor beneath the robes reflecting the orange light of Aleksander's flames.

Aleksander groaned as he crawled toward the blade of Valakor's shattered scythe. He felt the hunger of the Faceless looming in the windows, but an unmatchable fear crept into every crevice of his mind; the very presence of Thanatan sent chills down his spine more intense than the feeling of dread that accompanied the Faceless. No, this feeling was doom.

"I apologize, but death is not yours to taste," Thanatan said. "I still require your services."

"You what?" Florenta barked. "Kill him!"

The guards that hadn't yet fallen to the Bloodvine rushed forward, and the Faceless swarmed from their perch on the windowsills, quickly slaughtering each of them in a spray of blood and screams.

Aleksander tried to stand again, but Thanatan's magic still bound him. Thanatan strode toward Florenta, Bloodvine tendrils and the fog trailing behind their master like thorned serpents. More vines that had been hiding within the stone walls broke free, expelling more spores that had been pent up within the brick.

"No wonder Vasilica was having trouble breathing..." Aleksander said to Manitrius.

He fought for control of his limbs, but it was no use. He struggled for a glance at Manitrius, who seemed to be in the same state.

The Faceless stood as sentinels as the vines slowly choked the life out of each of Florenta's guards still clinging to life until she was left alone. The Bloodvine crept up the sides of the throne at Thanatan's command, and the thickest of them plunged a vicious thorn into the base of her skull.

"Why do you not kill *them?*" Florenta shouted, gesturing to Aleksander and Manitrius. She gripped the vine in an attempt to pull it out of her head.

She roared in pain and confusion, throwing herself up out of the throne, but it was no use. The vines restricted her against the back of the seat, choking her until she collapsed.

"Because they are my Ascended, and they shall serve me," the dark god replied.

As Thanatan began to speak once more, a blinding red light filled the chamber, releasing Manitrius and Aleksander from the dark god's magic. The Telepillar emerged from the flash and struck Thanatan in the chest, throwing him across the chamber. Rayshel, Lavinia, and Vasilica hurried to pull the pillar upright and gestured for Aleksander and Manitrius to join them.

"Get out of here!" Aleksander shouted.

In the brief chaos that ensued, Aleksander scooped up Valakor's broken blade and tossed it to Manitrius; the warrior twirled and flung it into Florenta's side, but nothing seemed to change.

Thanatan had regained himself and raced toward Rayshel who stood next to the Telepillar, a look of utter dread etched across her face. As he raised a sword of flame and shadow to cut her down, Lavinia leapt between them and thrust her twin blades through his chest with a cry of rage and a crack of crystal. Before Thanatan could retaliate, Aleksander unleashed a river of flame that engulfed the dark god.

"Hurry!" Rayshel cried as Aleksander found himself once again immobilized by Thanatan's telekinesis.

The flames began to die as Aleksander's strength waned, and in his heart, he knew he was powerless against Thanatan. At that moment, Valakor emerged from the hole in the floor, his armor broken and battered, cyan smoke and energy escaping from each wound in his magical body.

"Go!" he boomed.

Thanatan batted Valakor down with a slash of his blade then telekinetically toppled the glowing pillar on top of him. Valakor reacted by kicking with all his might, striking the pillar just as

Rayshel dove and smacked the controls to activate the magic contained within.

Thanatan spoke, but his voice was garbled as the crimson teleportation magic flowed from the pillar, through his chest, and out his back. His physical form broke apart amidst the crimson glow.

Aleksander shielded his eyes from the light and caught a glance of Florenta, who now seemed to be engulfed in a massive cocoon of whipping Bloodvines.

The Telepillar struck the ground and emitted bolts of crimson light at random. The Faceless and the Bloodvines moved in, sensing their master's peril.

"Bovin, is he—" Aleksander began.

"He's safe! Let's go!" Rayshel shouted.

Manitrius slammed his fist into the gem on the pillar's face over and over, but it sputtered and refused to work.

The Faceless swarmed unrestrained into the chamber. Valakor released a burst of cyan energy from his hands, vaporizing many of the Faceless and carved a line across the floor and up the wall. The tower began to shake under the weight of the Faceless horde, and a portion of it broke away and fell from the rest of the tower.

Hundreds of Faceless fell to their deaths far below, but even more crept through every entrance. Valakor performed the same feat on the other side, collapsing the floor beneath their foes until the Faceless overwhelmed him and pulled him to the ground.

A Bloodvine covered in sharp spines shot toward Lavinia and Rayshel, but Manitrius raised his blade and sliced through it.

He cried out in agony as it whipped around, slicing through his throat and arm with one of the barbs.

Vasilica, Lavinia, and Aleksander held off the Faceless even as the tower collapsed around them. The throne fell through the floor, but the vines kept Florenta suspended above the breach; whether she was dead or alive, they had no idea.

Valakor emerged from the pile of Faceless and struck the gem on the Telepillar, igniting it with the blinding red glow, but the energy sizzled and died away. Aleksander looked up in horror just in time to see a chunk of the tower crush through Valakor's metal chest. The side of the tower crumbled away, and his spirit armor fell into the precipice before he could activate the damaged pillar again.

In the midst of the chaos, a jet of black smoke obscured Aleksander's vision, signaling the arrival of a group of Walkers. He thanked the gods as he caught a glimpse of his rescuers fighting and dying against the Faceless, and then one managed to successfully activate the pillar.

And then their world melted away in a blinding flash of chaotic, crimson light.

# CHAPTER THIRTY-FOUR

# ONE THING AT A TIME

The warm flickering light of a torch and the strange comfort of an unfamiliar bed greeted Mara as her eyes flitted open. She swept the hair from her face by throwing her head to the side, and she groaned in pain as if her brain were bouncing around her skull.

"No…" she muttered, rubbing her temples. "Oww."

The pain threatened to make her vomit, but as she stopped moving, it subsided ever so slightly. It returned whenever she looked into the crack of light between the room's curtains or if she moved too suddenly.

"You're awake!"

She jumped, for she thought she had been alone; she turned her head to see Hanna leaning toward her.

"Hanna…?"

"Hey, Mar. You scared me, girl," Hanna said from the huge, stuffed armchair that seemed out of place in what Mara assumed was a hospital wing of wherever she was… Doftaan? No…

"Where am I?" she asked. She could remember nothing but pain and collapsing. "What happened?"

"One thing at a time," Hanna replied, looking over her shoulder, perhaps for an orderly. After a moment, she spoke again. "You had an aneurysm. The doctors used another word for it, but I've forgotten what that was—it was big and long and medical sounding. Sciencey—"

"You brought me here?" Mara asked. Hanna smiled with tears in her eyes then glanced down as she felt Mara wrap her hand around her thumb. "Thank you."

Hanna took a deep breath. "It was some kind of bleeding in your brain. They thought we were going to lose you, so they opened you up and took a look at all the junk in there. Sorry, that's crass. They did a surgery, and—"

"They opened my brain?!"

"Yeah," Hanna said as she bit her lip, running her hand through her hair. Mara subconsciously did the same and felt that the hair on the side of her head had been shaved. She winced as she brushed the tender skin.

"Do they know what caused it?"

"The leading theory right now is an overuse of mental abilities," Hanna said. She shrugged.

"What about you?" Mara asked.

"I asked about that," Hanna replied. "They don't think I'm in any danger. My body and my brain are genetically designed to handle the stress of my abilities, or something."

"But my powers aren't natural," Mara said, finishing Hanna's thought.

"I always meant to ask you about that," Hanna said.

"The Mind-Prison Cuff broke me. It's hard to explain what happened, but I can go into the Mind-Prison whenever I want to plan or learn, relax, when I can—or whatever I want," Mara said. "I spent *a lot* of time using it to study languages of our world and the Deadlands and I've learned how to give myself abilities and about the science of the Deadlands that originally created our magic."

"That's the coolest thing I've ever heard," Hanna said. "My best friend can beat up anybody else's best friend. So how many languages do you speak, then?"

"Eighty-three, I think, at last count. I mean, I speak them all at different levels, but—"

"You *think*," Hanna said with a laugh. "I love you."

Mara chuckled. "Well, you're now one of very few people who know about it. It looks like that damn cuff isn't done tormenting me yet, though."

"Yeah. It all makes sense. If it wasn't for Alia, they said there was nothing they could have done," Hanna said all at once. "You would have died."

"What would we do without her?" Mara said, closing her sensitive eyes to shield them from the light.

"Well, she tried. Her powers didn't work on some parts of your brain. She said she didn't know why, but it just didn't work. You'll have to heal like us mere mortals. Maybe her powers weren't designed to fix brains. Too complex, that was her theory, anyway. The doctors did what they could, and Alia healed it all up behind them—fixed things in your head as they operated, I guess. You were in there for hours."

"Will I have a scar?"

"Yeah."

"Good."

Hanna clutched Mara's hand with a soft smile. "I'm glad you think that. It looks pretty awesome, to be honest." She laughed. "Alia said it wouldn't have scarred if she wasn't so tired and hadn't used up so much of her power during the operation. She felt so bad that she couldn't fix it all the way, but I told her you'd be thankful for all she did manage to do."

Hanna handed her a small mirror, and Mara spent a long moment examining the bare side of her head where a long scar ran from her temple, past her ear, and down the side of her head. She did not dwell on the scar long, for the rest of her face drew her attention.

The side of her face was horribly swollen and bruised, and she instinctively reached up and brushed it with her fingers, her mouth agape. She caught her own eyes in the mirror, and she felt in her heart that she was gazing into the face of another; the face, the eyes that gazed back at her were filled with pain.

"It's nothing a little make-up won't cover," a nurse said over Hanna's shoulder. Neither woman had seen or heard her enter the room.

"No," Mara said, shaking her head. Pain. She held still. "That won't be necessary—"

She dropped the mirror, although she had sworn that she had a tight grip on it. It clattered to the floor and chipped, but Hanna picked it up like nothing had happened. Her friend smiled and squeezed her hand.

"Impairments in dexterity will be quite normal," the nurse said dispassionately, taking the mirror from Hanna and setting it on Mara's bedside table. She set down a tray of food and several glasses of water. "You're quite lucky your friend found you, really. And lucky to have someone to stay by your side, too. She has hardly left since she brought you here a few days ago. Even used her powers to force the guards away as they tried to remove her. She even brought in that horrible chair too—"

"I've been here that long?" Mara looked to Hanna, who nodded in confirmation.

"I'll be back to check on you in a few moments, please don't go anywhere." The nurse left the room.

"Was that a joke?" Mara asked, coughing. Hanna shrugged.

"She thinks she's funny, but she isn't," Hanna said, rubbing her forehead, eyes closed. Mara knew there had to be more to that story, but she didn't press it.

"Mara…" Hanna said in a soft tone. "I really thought I was going to lose you."

"I'm still here," Mara said, patting Hanna's hand.

"I know. You have no idea how glad I am," Hanna said. She paused, and Mara waited, sensing that she wasn't finished with her thought. "You mean a lot to me."

"You mean a lot to me too," Mara said, offering her friend the biggest smile her swollen face would allow.

"No, I don't think you understand. I never told you this, even in the slave camp, but I wanted to tell you some things." She trailed off and bit her lip. "I know sometimes I can be a bit closed off."

"You?!" Mara laughed. "I'm sorry, I didn't mean to laugh. You are anything but closed off." She gestured to herself, and Hanna let out a chuckle. "You've been completely honest with me since the day I met you. Back in the slave camp, I wouldn't even let Pol tell people where we were from. Do you remember Patrik in our slave district? He was from my hometown, and I wouldn't even let Pol talk to him about it when we met him."

"Thanks, that actually does make me feel better, as odd as that is. Maybe I'm not a lost cause. I mean, you're not either, but…" Hanna said, trailing off with another uncomfortable laugh. She twisted in her chair before saying, "I was engaged to get married before I was taken."

Mara reached out to hold her friend's hand.

"I never knew. Would it help to talk about it?"

"Yeah. I think so. And Shanthah does too, but obviously it's one of the few things I don't want to talk to him about," she said.

"She was my childhood best friend. Viktorija—that was her name. We had three weeks until our wedding. Three weeks. And then, the Talohiran slavers came to Vudapas. They took me, and they made me watch as they killed her and the rest of my family. They didn't even care that they took everyone I loved from me and stamped out an entire future that could have been."

Words caught in her throat, and she buried her face in her hands. Tears welled in Mara's eyes.

"Hann…"

Hanna hugged her knees close to her chest and let out a sigh. She glanced down at Mara's hand and gave it a squeeze. "Two days after that, I was in a whole new world as a slave without Viktorija, without my family—I was so alone. And then, during the worst few days of my entire life, the universe gave me my two best friends. It gave me you and Shanthah."

"Is it weird that I'm thankful for that day?" Mara asked.

"A little," Hanna said with a dark chuckle. She sniffed and wiped her eyes. "I guess what I'm trying to say—what I'm trying to say is that without you, I don't know—I don't think I would have survived that camp. I don't think you understood the difference you made. I'm sorry, you just went through something crazy, and I'm blabbering like a—ah, close, floodgates, close!"

"No, keep going," Mara said. She offered an encouraging smile. "Let it out."

"Okay. Okay. The slave camp was horrible for everyone, obviously. None of us got out of there the same people we were before. But, well, it was worse for us," Hanna said.

"I know," Mara said, knowing exactly what Hanna meant. Her thoughts reached into the darkest, most haunted depths of her memories, and images of the Arcship and the slave camp filled her mind. "There are things the men don't know, and that they won't ever understand even if they did."

"Exactly," Hanna said, brushing the tips of her fingers along the back of Mara's hand. "You know how it was. They punished the others and beat them and starved them and everything, but— they attacked and targeted us differently, you know? So much worse, and—"

"I know," Mara said, squeezing Hanna's hand. "I remember, and I understand."

"Every single time they attacked me, it was you that held me and hugged me and let me know everything would be okay," Hanna said, tears rolling down her cheeks. She sniffed and let out a long breath. "This whole dark, depressing story is just my way of saying thank you. Seriously, thank you. You got me through all of that. I didn't want you to die without telling you."

"We got each other through, Hann. Sometimes I wanted to just fall asleep and not wake up," Mara said. "I am just so *broken*, but you're the one who helped me start to put the broken pieces of me back together, and I love you, friend."

"I regret so much of what happened between us. You have no idea," Hanna said, biting her lip. She began to shake as tears streamed down her face. "I love you too, so much."

"Three, two, one, it's gone," Mara said with a bright smile. "Poof."

"Poof," Hanna said, and then she climbed onto Mara's bed and hugged her with all the love she could muster. "You are the best person I know, and don't you ever, ever forget it."

"Nothing compared to you," Mara replied, patting Hanna's back as her friend cried on her bruised shoulder.

"Well, there's something you need to know about the expeditions you planned," Hanna said, changing the subject.

"I assume that means they didn't set out yet?" Mara asked.

"Good, they weren't sure you'd remember planning them— well, anyway—that's not happening anytime soon," Hanna said. "Looks like all our plans are going to change pretty hard."

She climbed off Mara's bed and sat back in her huge chair.

"They can happen without me," Mara replied.

Hanna sighed, and with a flick of her wrist, telekinetically whipped open the curtain. Light flooded Mara's vision, and she groaned; as she grew more accustomed to the light, although her eyes were still sensitive to it, her jaw fell open in shock. A vast sea of bodies was visible beyond the walls of the city.

"This isn't Doftaan..."

"We're in Balgorod, Karpaska—sorry, Alboras. Forgot Shanthah changed it," Hanna said. "Do you remember?"

Mara shook her head, and Hanna took her hand again.

"Shanthah led a revolution here to overthrow Florenta's forces, and you led survivors from towns the Faceless destroyed here. Josman and Kamil led them to safety. This is, as far as we know, the only place safe from Florenta's control, and you—"

"I think I remember," Mara said. The details were cloudy, but the events were clear. "Are the others—"

"They're okay. For now," Hanna said, pointing out the window. "Gallows humor, sorry. Shanthah's rubbing off on me."

"Good, I like that guy," Mara said, reaching for a glass of water, which Hanna handed to her. When she was done drinking, she said, "So, I assume those are Florenta's forces outside?"

Her mind was racing. They couldn't possibly have enough forces here to repel the armies of Sangora commanded by Florenta. They were her armies, swayed through the magic created by Queen Daktha. For a brief moment, Mara regretted cutting out the Queen's Control but then told herself not to think that way. Hanna took a deep breath and let it out with a contemplative, melodic sigh.

"Yes, Florenta's forces are here."

"But?" Mara asked.

"So are the Magistrate's." Hanna averted her gaze, instead glancing out the window.

"The Faceless?" Mara asked.

"If only. The Faceless and the living, too. There are so many human warriors outside our gates; I don't know how Thanatan was able to influence so many Thans to fight for him, but they…" She trailed off.

"What?"

"They carry King Verahim's banner," Hanna said. "The city is surrounded by Faceless, Verahim's armies, and Sangorans controlled by Florenta. I'm sure there are Sangorans here loyal to her too, but so many out there are probably under her control. No one knows what to do."

"What have we done? What preparations have been made?"

"What else can we do, but pray to whatever gods are up there that our empress awakes and save us?" Hanna said.

"That's sweet, Hann."

"I'm serious." Hanna's eyes were filled with resolve. "Every day, the Alboran people have prayed for you to awake from the death sleep, as they called it." Mara felt a stir of love in her heart, and Hanna continued. "Shanthah's given the order to prepare for battle, and as many as possible are sheltering in the central keep, but it doesn't look good, Mar. We're *heavily* outnumbered."

Mara thought for a moment. "We don't have many options."

"What do you want us to do?" Hanna asked. "I don't want you thinking too hard now, but we—well, we do need you."

Mara was taken aback by the question for a moment; she was used to the people of her court, the Mistresses of Dusk, and her soldiers and generals asking such a question, but not her friends. Despite her injury, despite the usurper on her throne, she was still Empress of Sangora, and her friend was reminding her of that fact.

"Summon Mistresses Raluca and Anca. This will be my war room. I want everything cleared out and a table brought in to direct troops. See if you can't find a giant map of the city and surrounding area, if you can."

"Anything else?"

"Bring Shanthah, for now. I know he'll want to fight alongside 'his' people, but I appreciate and require his voice here. Bring me a specialist on Karpaskan geography, and any military leaders loyal to me." As Hanna nodded along, Mara's nurse reentered the room alongside a nervous looking man. "We'll also need to send word out to Thanatanos."

"But they're already here, and—"

"An ultimatum. If Verahim is too unfit—too much of a coward to call off his men and do what is right, then we have no choice but to remove him from his throne."

"Got it," Hanna said.

She took a deep breath and reviewed the list of Mara's requirements. Mara nodded, and Hanna squeezed her hand.

"I'll be back soon. Don't win the war until I get back," Hanna said, winked then left the chamber. The nurse motioned to the stranger that had entered with her, a man with large circular eyeglasses who fiddled with his hands and didn't look the nurse in the eye as she bowed and left the chamber.

"My name is Daniel," said the man, his sparse eyebrows twitching toward one another.

"I am about to be very busy," replied Mara, trying to fit the man's name and face together. Should she remember him? Her head still felt foggy and trying to remember through the dull ache was difficult.

"You may not remember me, given—" he gestured to the scar on her head. "Daniel Elafris."

"Ah." Mara's mind clicked, and she chuckled to herself, looking straight ahead.

"I asked the kind nurse to, uh, let me know when you were awake. It's very important."

"How can I be of service to the Devil himself?"

Elafris ignored her remark.

"My associate, Lord Ronin Jakoni, do you remember that name? Do you—"

"Yes, I remember Lord Jakoni. Go on."

"Well, a couple years ago, a group landed in the lands your people call the Deadlands. You were there if you recall—"

"Elafris, I haven't forgotten *everything*. If I need clarification, I will ask for it," Mara said. She smiled at a pair of Sangoran men who began to navigate a large table through the door and around her bed. Daniel fidgeted in his seat to avoid being struck.

"My apologies, your nurse was very insistent that—oh, never mind. When that group found me, I was encased in a pod that kept be alive for several hundred years. Three hundred ninety-five to be exact. I awoke to find your world had replaced mine. An associate of mine also was awakened. The last two from a dead world—who you know by the name Thanatan, of course— silly name, not his real one. Did you know, he fashioned it himself—it means death in—"

"In ancient Greek," Mara cut him off with a wry grin. She had been annoyed at his presence until this point, but he piqued her interest in languages. "Kind of. Do you know that it isn't even technically grammatically accurate? It's always baffled me."

"Yes, yes. Although, most of us called him his true name, which I assume has lost all meaning here. Sometimes, I think he named himself after a character from—no, I won't digress with that or by asking how you know ancient Greek. You know, I named my own son after a famous Greek king," Daniel Elafris said. "Although how *do* you know ancient—No, no. Back to business."

Mara rolled her eyes, a feat that pained her, but she felt was nonetheless necessary. She watched the men set up the war room table as a short Sangoran woman entered the room with a large map tucked beneath her arm.

"Well, on that voyage, Lord Jakoni stole something that I tried very hard to keep hidden," Elafris said. Mara nodded absentmindedly, watching the woman unroll the map and pin it down around the edges. "A devastating weapon from my world."

Mara's attention snapped back to the conversation. "The weapon Valistaran sought."

Daniel nodded in grave confirmation. "He hasn't shared the location of the weapon with us—us being, well—Valistaran, me, the Supreme One of Kurash…"

The mention of the Supreme One struck her heart like an icy dagger; she remembered him handing her a silver key, and her heart leapt. Where had it disappeared to? A second memory returned as well; he had made her the Supreme One after his death.

"Okay?" Mara asked, nodding. She could see where the conversation was going.

"He wants to use it to kill Thanatan."

"So? Let him," Mara said, her eyebrows pressed toward one another. "If he has access to this weapon, why not use it?"

"Because it's more powerful than he realizes. Until now, I've been able to reel him in, not control him, but—"

Mara bit her lip.

"You've prevented him from killing us all," Mara said.

"I'm not sure if reason can stop him anymore from doing what he thinks he needs to do. If he sets off that weapon in Laniras, he will level the city, and probably everything around it. There will be *nothing* left. He thinks that he'll be able to..." He trailed off, biting his lip and curling his fist. "No, don't get me started on that. Just know that he wants to activate it, and I think that he might bring it here. Yes, he'd clear out all those Pure out there, but we're within the blast radius. We'd be killed too. We have to find him. I don't want to tell you how to do your job, but I think finding him has to be a top priority. As you know, we've been traveling together, but we haven't had the chance to speak, and, well, he went his own way when we discovered his plan. He went back to his own people north of Sangora earlier than we thought he would."

Daniel was shaking from anger, and Mara felt a twinge of sympathy for the man. Thoughts raced through her mind. How long had the nervous man sitting before her been fighting their foe? What had he been through?

"I'm conflicted. He helped me save a group of refugees, including some of my own personal friends, and guided them here. But I need you to know that Ronin has long been considered an extremist in Sangora, his actions bordering on terrorism."

"Yes, that's in line with his character as I understand him."

"He only wants safety and peace for his people," Mara said. "Over the past few years, I've come to see him not as a terrorist, but a complex, and perhaps misguided, revolutionary."

"I'm no political scientist, but I'm sure there's a similarity between a terrorist and a revolutionary…"

"Yes. Although let me be clear that I don't condone terrorism in any way," Mara said. "But a great man, one of my favorites to read about from your time regarding racial inequalities, which is applicable to my people, said, 'For to be free is not merely to cast off one's chains, but to live in a way that respects and enhances the freedom of others.' Your people saw that man as a terrorist for many, many years, but later considered him a champion in the struggle for humanity."

"Nelson Mandela, ah." Elafris nodded. He sighed. "You know, he also said—he said, 'no one is born hating another person because of…" He faltered as he tried in vain to remember the words.

"…because of the color of his skin, or his background, or his religion. People must learn to hate, and if they can learn to hate, they can be taught to love, for love comes more naturally to the human heart than its opposite," Mara said, finishing the quote.

"Yes, exactly. What goes on in that head of yours?" Elafris muttered. "Well, my point is that we can't fight hate with hate or let Ronin do so."

"Saying that we can't fight hate with hate equates the injustices and suffering that we experience with the prejudices, mistreatment, and violence of those that oppress us. Seeking justice through righteous anger does not mean we are being hateful. It means we love ourselves and our people enough not to stand for intolerance and oppression," Mara said. "I do, however, agree with you. When we overthrow the chains of hate, we must replace them with bonds of love."

"Wow," Elafris said.

He was unable to answer for a few moments.

"Lord Jakoni has only acted to throw off the chains of oppression set by my predecessors, Liviu and Sanda Daktha, Valistaran, and now Florenta. He never tried to overthrow me."

"Does that cloud your judgment on the man?" Elafris asked. Mara watched others file into the room, including Mistresses Anca and Raluca, who bowed to her as they entered then took their seats around the map.

"Perhaps," Mara admitted. "In your life before all of this, did you ever study philosophy?"

"I did, actually, yes. Probably not well enough for the conversation I believe we're about to have, but I was particularly taken by—"

"Focus, Daniel. If we survive this, we can talk about whatever philosophy you want later. You have no idea how much time I've spent in the grand libraries of Talohira and Doftaan—mostly to study languages and the science of magical abilities, but also to justify some of my own past actions and decisions to make myself feel better. Well, in my studies, I came across a couple of concepts—deontological and consequentialist ethical systems. Does that ring a bell?"

"Not really, no. Consequentialism, maybe. Nudge my memory in the right direction," Elafris said.

"Okay. I know I'm oversimplifying this, and I could be getting it wrong, but followers of deontological ethics state that morality and right or wrong is determined by a set of rules. You know, that morality should be based on things like legality, duty, obligation, and the like," Mara explained. "And you said you knew what consequentialism is?"

"Another way to explain morality, I believe," Elafris said.

"Yeah. Instead of rule-based ethics, consequentialists believe that ethics are based in a different type of morality—basically, that a particular action is right *only* if it results in a greater balance of good over evil."

"Okay," Elafris said, trying to follow along.

"When I was studying these concepts, I came across a basic philosophy idea called the 'Trolley Problem'. As I understand it, a trolley is like a carriage that moves without horses, yes?"

"Um, yes, more or less correct. And yes, I know it," Elafris said. "A trolley is coming down the tracks, and for whatever reason, there is a group of people on one path. If they are unable to move, they will die."

"Yes, and if you choose to divert the trolley, it will still kill one person on the other track," Mara finished. "Which is, in the end, the morally right thing to do? If you have the obligation to act, either morally or otherwise—say you're the driver of the trolley—is doing nothing and crushing ten people more or less moral than actively deciding to crush one particular person?"

"Yes, and I think I know where you're going with this," Elafris said, nodding. "You are wondering if the one man on the track is Ronin Jakoni, and the group of other bystanders on the other track are the people of Laniras or Balgorod?"

"That's just a basic example," Mara said. "But let's expand that original problem. Say we have the chance to stop the trolley from crushing the people on either track by throwing something very heavy in front of that magic carriage."

"It's not magic, but—okay, so you're asking if you could introduce a new variable to the problem that would remove the obligation to choose either option and thereby remove the morality question?" Elafris asked.

"Sort of. What if the only 'heavy thing' on board the cart was a very, very fat person? Picture Florenta. Well, maybe that's a bad example, because I'd happily throw her in front of the trolley. No, not Florenta, but someone huge."

"Okay," Elafris said.

"Do you push that one person over the carriage to stop it from crushing everyone else?" Mara asked.

"So, Ronin isn't the person on the second track, he's a person on the trolley that we could throw off to save the others," Elafris said.

"Yes. Does that make it the right choice?" Mara asked.

"No, you're still taking a life," Elafris said. "I mean, that's what a consequentialist would say, right? Because killing someone is upsetting the balance between good and evil? But to a deontologist, it's wrong because the law says so. But is it your duty to do so?"

"You're catching on. Let's take it one step further. What if that fat man you threw over the front of the trolley to stop it from crushing the others was actually the villain who originally put these people in peril? What if he was the one who broke the magic spell driving the cart?"

"Again, that's not how trolleys work, but I understand. Ronin is the villain putting us into the situation where we have to choose who dies. But if we use him, the original villain and throw him in front of the cart before we have to choose..." Elafris trailed off.

"Exactly," Mara said. "He's doing what he thinks is right for his own people. I recognize that. In his mind, he is tipping the balance toward good, even if he has to sacrifice people."

"In the end, life isn't a question of philosophy," Elafris said with a sigh. "It's choices and consequences, often only bad ones. I do understand your conundrum, and I don't envy you."

"You're right. But if we all think we're doing what's right, Thanatan and Florenta included, who really is?" Mara asked.

"Maybe you all are. But what is right for one person isn't always the same for another, and perhaps, you can help your people understand how to tolerate the beliefs of others. Heaven knows that was part of what destroyed my world," Elafris said.

Mara nodded in agreement. "I hope so. What if we could just destroy the trolley?"

"The trolley still being the nuclear weapon?"

"Yes," Mara said. "We could avoid all of these problems. Having to kill Ronin, having to sacrifice the people of Balgorod or Laniras, having to sacrifice ourselves..."

"To play the devil's advocate—" Mara snorted in laughter, cutting him off. "Okay, yes, I see the irony. Pun not intended. For the last time, I'm not the devil. But to play his advocate, if we did destroy the weapon, does that open up the possibility that Thanatan's forces will inevitably overrun Balgorod?"

"That's my fear," Mara replied. "I think I have no good options. I kill Ronin and save hundreds of thousands of people from the Weapon of Ages Past, or I let him live, and kill those same people."

"I'm afraid that you are right," Elafris said. "Well, I think we will soon find out the truth about him." He averted his gaze away from the scar on the side of Mara's head, which he realized he had been staring at for a moment.

"I hope we're wrong about him. I hope he uses the weapon wisely."

"So do I. For all our sakes," Elafris said with a sad sigh as he stood. Mara motioned to the table. "And perhaps, Empress, someone else may be able to take the choice of where to direct the 'magic cart' so you don't have to."

"I don't wish that on anyone," Mara said, motioning to the empty table. "Anyway, please join us."

Elafris obeyed, choosing a seat beside the two Mistresses of Dusk. He began nervously twiddling his thumbs on the map as others began to file into the room to take their seats.

Mara glanced over her shoulder and flashed a wide smile as she watched Hanna, Shanthah, Josman, and Kamil poke their heads into the room. The dread of how to save her people melted away as she caught sight of her friends. Her heart dropped as Aleksander and Pol did not appear. She gestured to the seats nearest to her bed.

"Come in, my friends!" she said in a cheerful voice.

The four other members of her slave district took their seats next to the bed without a word, but she caught Hanna's eye and chuckled as her friend gave her an exaggerated wink.

"Thank you all for coming," said Mara. She gestured for those still standing to sit. Everyone seemed to have assembled. "I apologize for the lack of preparation here on my part, but—" she gestured to the bed. "I have a good excuse."

Laughter filled the chamber.

"I expect, General Anca, that you have been preparing in my stead?" Mara asked.

"Yes, Empress," Anca said, nodding her head.

"I can always count on you for assessments of battle, whether I ask for them or not. I am grateful for your preparation," Mara said. Anca, a woman of few words but a shrewd military mind, nodded again. "I summoned an expert on geography, is that person present?"

The stout Sangoran woman who had carried in the map raised her hand then said in a squeaky voice, "Yes, here, Empress. I am Professor Reitera, a former professor of geography at the University of Doftaan."

"Good. I want you to council with General Anca to properly utilize the terrain and walls of the city to best prepare our troops," Mara said. The two began a low discussion as Mara continued. "Master Shanthah Kalen, do you have an assessment of the number of our troops?"

"Yes, we have—" Hanna nudged him, and he stood. "Sorry, we have some of the regiment here, some three thousand souls. We drove out those in the city loyal to Florenta. Hundreds of other able-bodied volunteers have joined the cause around the city, and I led around a thousand more here from across Alboras. I'd say no more than, oh—two hundred or so are really fighters. A handful of the refugees from Zinok would be able to fight as well."

"A handful being…" Mara said, gesturing with her hand.

"Maybe fifty?" Shanthah said, glancing over at Josman, who nodded with a shaky hand gesture that said, 'more or less.'

"Captain Rayna had very few soldiers left, but those refugees are strong enough to fight, yes," Josman said.

"Is Captain Rayna present?" Mara asked. Josman shook his head. "Josman, would you fetch her? I think she will be vital to this conversation."

"She is with her troops on the wall," Josman said, shaking his head. "I can send a message, if you like."

"No, it sounds like many of our brave spears on the wall are untrained. They will need her there, but we will need to relay her our decisions," Mara said, watching Anca and Professor Reitera place tokens where troops should be moved for the best geographic and strategic placement. She watched Anca place a blue one on the wall: the color for a captain, representing Rayna.

"Have we received any communication from the enemy?" Mara asked. "Threats, ultimatums, anything?"

"Yes, Empress," said Mistress Raluca, speaking for the first time. "A joint communique from the forces of Florenta and Thanatan. It seems, Empress, that they are working together against you."

She shifted in her seat to pull a scroll from her cloak's pocket and began to read the words scrawled upon it.

"Please skip to the demands," Mara said.

"They have only one," Raluca said. "The head and wings of the Empress of Blood."

Mara considered the comment for a moment, all eyes on her.

"I think they'll find my head utterly unuseful at the moment, and I still need it," Mara said with a wry smile, tracing a finger along the scar on the shaved side of her head.

Her comment was met by awkward laughs from her friends sitting nearby, but the others were unsure whether to laugh at the self-deprecating humor. She was silent, contemplative for a moment.

"I think it is no longer a secret that shortly after my rise to the throne of Sangora, I discovered an ability called the Queen's Control, an ability used by my predecessors, Queens Codruta Talohira and Sanda Daktha to control the people of Sangora—I, too, became seduced by that power's influence. I see now the error of my actions. In doing so, I decided to make a change. I cut the Queen's Control from my wings, as, again, many of you may know." She paused for a moment, rubbing her skull.

"However, it seems that Thanatan and Florenta now seek the same accursed power. Florenta discovered a way to imitate it, and my own influence didn't affect her… Until recently."

"Do you have any theories about why that is?" Raluca asked from behind the table.

"I have many theories, but so little time to examine any of them."

"We can send word that the Queen's Control has been destroyed?" suggested Shanthah.

"Or tell them Mara died tonight," suggested Raluca.

"No," Anca said, shaking her hands. "The thought that Mara's control is loosened over Florenta's people may be the only thing preventing an attack. Such a decision would be unwise."

"I agree with Anca," said Mara. "I don't think word of the loss of the Queen's Control or my injury would help our cause. They seek my body, not my death, after all. I destroyed the Queen's Control, but I think they might be able to fix it. How large are the forces against us?"

"Larger than those with us," said Anca. She placed several large tokens on the map, and Mara sighed, knowing what they signified before her most trusted general spoke again. "Several hundred thousand, at our last estimate."

"Is it Thanatan's entire force of Faceless?" Mara asked.

"Hardly," Anca said. "Intelligence suggests that he is creating a force in the ruins of Nitra several million strong."

"Million?" Hanna whispered, concerned. Her heart raced.

"The next problem for us to solve, then," said Mara. "For now: Anca, how do you suggest we combat this overwhelming force?"

"Without a unique advantage, we don't have much chance," Anca explained. "We have a wall around the city and the river surrounding the central fortress. We can more of the citizens to the keep, but we can't sustain them for long. Truly, if the wall falls, so will Balgorod."

"Thanks to intelligence from Valistaran Talohir, we've learned that Thanatan controls his Faceless horde through his Magistrate. He killed the previous Magistrate two years ago, buying us some time, but Thanatan has found another Mindspeaker strong enough to lead his forces," Mara said. "They're after my Queen's Control, perhaps we can use the same idea against him?"

"If Valistaran is correct, killing his Magistrate might scatter the Faceless, but we'll still have to deal with the human and Sangoran threat," General Anca replied. "It's a start, though."

"I'll have my people come up with an estimate of how long we could last," Shanthah suggested. Hanna raised an eyebrow as if to ask, 'what people?' and he said in a lower voice, "I'll find someone…"

"What unique advantages do we have, then?" Mara asked, nodding to Shanthah in acknowledgment.

"Apart from the wall and the river?" Anca asked then glanced at the geographer. "Not much geographically."

"What about magic users?" asked Josman, speaking up for the first time. The entire room turned to him. He took the silence as permission to speak, and Mara smiled. "Those of us that were in the Talohiran slave camps—we've all got magic—there are quite a few of us here." He gestured to his friends.

"You speak truth," said Raluca, nodding. "There are very few magic users left in Thanatanos that were not enslaved by the former king. One advantage over the Thannish forces, then."

"So, would we be of any help?" Josman asked, his large hands held aloft before him as he awaited an answer. Both Anca and Raluca began to speak, but Mara spoke over them.

"Yes." Her councilors did not attempt to change her mind. Perhaps, they were about to say the same. "And I can think of one more unique advantage. Thanatan's beast that now answers to me. That behemoth that stands outside the fortress now." She pointed outside the window, as if they could see. "But Anca, I fear even my Behemoth's power would be more suited to offense, rather than defense, which we sorely need—what do you suggest?"

As Anca explained her strategy to Mara and the other leaders, Hanna, Shanthah, Kamil, and Josman exchanged exhausted glances. It seemed like it had been so long since they'd all been together. They had all come a long way since the camps, and Kamil was the first to voice what they were all thinking, projecting his thoughts into the minds of the other three.

*"Am I crazy to think we were safer back then?"*

# CHAPTER THIRTY-FIVE
# THE SOUL OF THE WALKERS

The crimson light dissipated, and the world faded into darkness. Aleksander wondered for a moment if he had gone blind after the brilliant flash of light but saw the Teleportation Pillar give off a dim glow, letting him know he could still see.

The world was still falling around him. Chunks of the collapsing tower, brought along by the teleportation magic, struck the ground, and crumbled all around him, but after a few moments, everything was silent. His eyes began to adjust to the darkness, and he found himself upon the roof of a spired building resembling a church in the center of a sprawling city.

Much of the rubble had broken through the roof and splintered the main spire. Aleksander glanced around; Valakor and Manitrius were dead, but where were the others? He could see several Walkers scurrying around the Telepillar, perhaps trying to repair it. He crept away while they were distracted.

Rayshel lay unconscious on the ground nearby; blood oozed from a long gash on her head, but she stirred, alive. Aleksander hurried to her side and tried to recall the little medical knowledge he had. He bunched up her cloak and set it underneath her head to elevate the wound, which he thought might be correct. He let out a deep breath and clutched his own forehead then looked at his hand. Blood. Fortunately, he was still conscious, and the wound didn't seem fatal, so he shrugged it off. He'd see to the others' safety first.

"Lavinia…" Rayshel muttered. "Is Lavinia…"

"I don't know yet," Aleksander whispered back. "I'll try to find her. Stay here."

He glanced around but could not locate Lavinia, Vasilica, or Bovin. Hundreds of Sangoran corpses littered the debris around him, but he couldn't tell where the Walkers had brought them or if they even meant to take him and his allies along for the ride.

The landscape was not familiar. He was in a city he had never seen before, one surrounded by a distant forest covered in snow. In a sudden burst of realization, Aleksander clapped his hand over his mouth in realization that the Walkers had unknowingly brought him to their hidden homeland.

Dark black clouds swirled in the sky above, and a cold breeze ran up his spine, heralding an impending storm. The corpses of Florenta's guards and Enforcers were scattered around him.

Many lay with crushed skulls and twisted limbs, and the entire area reeked of fresh blood and death.

"What do you want with the pillar?" Aleksander muttered under his breath, watching the Walkers examine the device as he snuck behind the rubble to spy on them. "How did they know just when to get there...?"

He crept closer and could hear their low voices now.

"Good, my lord," said the first Walker. "Their sacrifice will not be forgotten."

"No, not any time soon, Emil," said another.

He recognized the owner of the voice as Lord Ronin Jakoni. He glanced around for a weapon, as he had lost his in the commotion. He was unable to find one nearby and decided his flames would have to do.

"Everything is set, then. The attack can commence at your word, Lord Jakoni. We have the Teleportation Obelisk and the Weapon of Ages Past. Two thousand stand ready and willing to attack. Their distraction will buy you the time you require, my lord," said Emil.

"Then give the word to assemble, and I will direct the device to send us into the heart of Laniras, and Thanatan will die. Emil, today we kill a god."

Aleksander hesitated. Should he allow Ronin to activate the Weapon of Ages Past inside Laniras? What would happen when they used it? Would the entire city have to die just to stop Thanatan? There had to be another way.

He watched Emil teleport away, leaving Ronin alone and unguarded. If he was going to save Laniras and hundreds of thousands of innocent lives, this was his chance.

He did not hesitate.

A burst of flame exploded from his hands and swept over the Telepillar. Ronin vanished just in time in a jet of black, and the flames passed by, catching some construction scaffolding atop the church ablaze. The swishing sound of Ronin's magic filled Aleksander's ears, and he lashed out with a spiral of flame, unsure where the Lord of the Walkers would reappear. Ronin let out a cry of surprise, and Aleksander whipped around to redirect the stream of white-hot flame toward the source of the noise.

Aleksander screamed as Ronin planted his hooked blades in his side and then yanked them out in the midst of the torrent of golden fire. The flames dissipated, and Ronin staggered backward, his robes ablaze and flesh on the side of his face smoldering.

"What are you doing, Xanthurias?!" Ronin shouted, pressing his palm against his burned face. "Everything is set so that we can end this nightmare!"

"How do you know me by that name?" Aleksander shouted as he pressed his hand into the wound on his side, which was now drenched in blood. He stumbled to his knees, and Ronin brandished his hooked swords but did not disappear again.

"So many will die," said Aleksander. He had lost a lot of blood, and he was already beginning to feel dizzy. "I can't let you do this, Ronin."

"Do you know how many will die at Balgorod if we don't? As we speak, Thanatan's forces assemble to slay the Empress of Blood and the last remnant of our people who oppose Thanatan. Florenta is gone now, and we were both too late to stop Thanatan from claiming the Queen's Control. He can now command all of Sangora and has millions of Pure in Nitra ready to do his bidding. If we strike Laniras, many will die, and I regret that sad truth. But if we do not strike Laniras, multiply those deaths by tens of thousands! What is worse—to lose Laniras or to lose the world?"

"Then why not strike Nitra?" Aleksander asked. He groaned and fell to his knees as Ronin advanced upon him.

"The board is already set, and we now must choose our move," said Ronin. "We will *all* die if we hesitate."

"Then hit Nitra, not Laniras," Aleksander pleaded. "It'll be a crippling blow to his forces, and you'll save innocent lives—"

"We've been through this! Innocents are about to die all across Karpaska—Balgorod will fall unless we act *NOW!* And what is after Karpaska? Doftaan. The rest of Sangora. All of Talohira. Laniras is our sacrifice. Sacrificing all we have to take the king."

Aleksander pent up all the flame in his body he could muster and let them out at once in all directions in an eruption of black flame. He decimated the roof of the church, and the Teleportation Pillar tumbled into the breach with a resounding crash. Severe burns spiderwebbed across Aleksander's body as he tackled Ronin from the roof, still ablaze. He grasped hold of

Ronin's robes as they fell, but moments before they hit the ground, Ronin pulled them into a burst of dark shadow.

"Enough!" Ronin shouted as they rematerialized in the ruined interior of the church.

Aleksander rolled as he hit the ground, smashing hard against a pew. The Telepillar had crushed an intricate altar at the front of the chapel and now lay on its side, pulsating with a dim, crimson glow.

First a dozen and then hundreds of puffs of smoke burst around the desecrated church. Aleksander groaned. He was surrounded with no hope of escape. His burns were healing due to his magical abilities, but he knew he was about to die anyway.

"Xanthurias… You accompanied me and the other Immortals, your father, and Daniel Elafris to the Deadlands more than once. You must remember!" Ronin exclaimed.

Memories of the Deadlands flashed into Aleksander's mind. He could see the great gate that guarded the Weapon of Ages Past, and he remembered that the name carved into his arm was the password to enter the chamber.

"I don't understand," Aleksander said, trying to find an avenue of escape. "You stole the weapon from the Deadlands that Valistaran wanted so badly. We were there. I opened the gate."

"And how did you know how to open the gate?" Ronin prompted, gesturing to Aleksander's arm. Aleksander decided it was best to tell the truth.

"I saw a vision of King Romiton—my own father—carving this name into my arm," Aleksander said. He knew full well that

Aleksander was not his true name and that 'Xanthurias' was dead in more ways than one. Aleksander was his new identity, one that he had to fight for.

"You and your father were not alone that day. You were one of us—one of the Immortals. You, your father Romiton, the Supreme One of Kurash, and Daniel Elafris were all there, even if you don't remember it. I assume you've remembered parts of your past, but not what happened that day?" Ronin asked.

Aleksander did not answer. After the battle of Laniras, a rush of memories had returned to his mind, but many of them had faded like a dream upon awakening. Others came back as strange feelings of déjà vu, and others yet felt like secondhand stories that did not belong to him. They were all his experiences, but other memories had been planted in his brain by the Secret Keepers of Kurash, which further muddied the waters of his broken mind. But at last, he had one more answer: somehow, he had reunited with his father after being captured the first time.

"There's a lot I don't remember," Aleksander whispered.

He could feel himself losing consciousness now. His wounded side prickled and itched, and the world was spinning as Ronin knelt before him.

"We went to the Deadlands to find the Weapon of Ages Past, but also to bring back other technologies to end the war between Talohira and Thanatanos before it expanded to Sangora, Kurash, and my homeland," Ronin explained. "So much for Sangora, eh?"

"And Daniel helped me see why we couldn't bring that technology back—why it had to remain hidden," Aleksander said as he remembered. "It destroyed the world once, and it could do it again."

"The Supreme One and I disagreed. We knew that harnessing the magic found beneath the Deadlands would be the only way to rid our world of Thanatan when he inevitably returned," Ronin said. "One of my Mindspeakers wiped your memories; I wanted him to remove the foolish notions in your mind that our plan was wrong, but I admit, he took more than I had requested, and I do apologize for that. He took less from your father, the Supreme One, and Elafris—you all forgot what transpired that day, but I *never* did. Daniel Elafris went back into his magical hibernation, the Supreme One went back to his throne in the desert, and you were enslaved, but I—*I* kept fighting because I was the only one who knew what needed to be done. I knew this day would come. I knew the Queen's Control would fall into Thanatan's hands."

"I lost my entire *life!*" Aleksander replied, struggling to stand.

"I took away your mind to keep you from stopping me from saving the world! Xanthurias died the day he ran away like a scared child," Ronin said. "And then, a new prince was born, or should I say created. Created only to die at the hands of Mara Bartunek. It's almost poetic, Xanthurias."

"I *was* a scared child!" Aleksander shouted. "I would have gone back, but I had to help Mara save her brother."

"Yes, just like you *had* to save your father and Daniel from *me* in the Deadlands. I would have managed to succeed much earlier if Elafris hadn't sent us all away," Ronin spat.

"But you've been working with us," Aleksander said, igniting a palmful of flame.

"Because I thought my Mindspeaker had cured you of your delusions," Ronin said in exasperation. "Xanthurias, you fool. You cannot stop what we have set in motion, and the world will thank us tomorrow."

Ronin slammed his fist against the gem on the Telepillar, and red energy sparked from the cracks in the stone obelisk as if threatening to explode at any moment. Ronin shouted something in Sangoran, and a few seconds later, several of his followers appeared next to him with the Weapon of Ages Past.

"He isn't just sacrificing the people of Laniras!" Aleksander cried, hoping the Walkers around him would heed his words. "He means to sacrifice you too!"

Emil, Ronin's most loyal follower vanished, but Aleksander readied himself for their attack. Expecting the Walker's trick, Aleksander thrust a fist of flame into the man's chest as he appeared, setting him ablaze. Aleksander reached into the flames, grasped Emil's neck, and twisted.

Ronin drew his hooked blades and raised them to smite Aleksander down, but at that moment, hundreds of Walkers teleported into the ruined chapel, distracting them both. The newcomers turned on the other Walkers, and soon, the chapel was a battlefield.

"What in the name of Elafris?" Ronin roared. Aleksander stumbled backward against the pillar. "What did you do?"

"It wasn't me," Aleksander said, confused.

A silver blade erupted from Ronin's chest. He blinked in disbelief, and then his face twisted in anger and despair.

"You will all *DIE!*" Ronin roared. "You must...believe..."

Lavinia thrust his body down, a tear rolling down her cheek. "Good riddance."

Ronin stared up at her with blank, dead eyes and an expression of disbelief still etched on his face. Aleksander shuddered, unable to help but wonder if Ronin knew more than he was letting on.

"How did you know?" Aleksander asked.

"I know everything," said Lavinia.

"We saw you fighting from up there," said Rayshel. She caught a glimpse of the wound in Aleksander's side and began treating it with the few supplies she had left in her pack. "Oh, good. Your fire-dancer healing powers must have also helped close this wound a bit. Anyway, Lavinia orchestrated the rest."

"But the Walkers—what are they doing?" asked Aleksander.

"Didn't you hear? Lavinia knows everything," Rayshel said with a laugh. "Good thing, too. She had some agents in the Walkers who were able to convince a bunch of the others over the last couple years to join them against Ronin."

"A revolution within a revolution," said Lavinia with a nod. "Never actually met most of them, and maybe that's a story for another day."

"We have no time to waste," Aleksander said. "Ronin said Thanatan and the Faceless are converging on Balgorod."

"Let them," said Lavinia. Rayshel folded her arms in protest. "That's in Florenta's land. Any blow to her rule is—"

"Mara is there," Aleksander said, remembering Florenta's promise to kill him and then Mara and her revolution in Balgorod. He thanked Rayshel as she finished bandaging the wounds on his side.

"Damn it! Of course she is," Lavinia said with a sigh. "That girl can't stay out of trouble."

The conflict between the two factions of Walkers ended as soon as it had begun. Ronin's remaining followers surrendered and were led away.

The victors appeared all around Lavinia, as if awaiting her command. Aleksander hesitated, unsure of what to do. The Telepillar buzzed with life, and thin cracks were spreading down its sides as it hummed.

"I think we should go," said Aleksander. "I think this thing only has one or two more jumps left in it."

"Wait," Rayshel said, her hand on his shoulder.

"I've done my part!" Lavinia called to the darkness. "I've done what you asked! Have I not proven myself honest in denouncing our mother? Have I not paid for her sins?"

Aleksander watched in silence. He had never known Lavinia in the short time they had travelled together to plead or beg to anyone. Several Walkers approached, and they bowed low to her.

"Lavinia, my dear, sweet little sister. You've done more for us than you can ever understand," one of them, a hooded woman, said. The faction's leader, Aleksander assumed.

She removed her hood to reveal a gaunt face haunted by war and loss. Scars from blades and flame spread from cheek and down her neck. One unseeing eye, ghostly and white, followed the gaze of the other, one of dark brown. White hair fell across the other side of her pale white face in an unkempt curtain.

"Zhanna," whispered Lavinia. "I had to kill him, Zhazha. I'm just like mother. Ginka would be so ashamed of me. She'd hate me, but I had to—I promised you I would prove to you that—"

"Oh, sweetheart," Zhanna said, wrapping her arms around Lavinia. "Ginka would tell you that you are nothing like mother. You never were, no matter what I said."

When they pulled apart, Lavina gestured to the others.

"I'd like you to meet my companions, Rayshel Pilu, Mistress Vasilica Radu, and Aleksander Romus."

She gestured to her allies, and the mysterious woman bowed to them each in turn. It was the first time Aleksander had ever heard his new name used with his forgotten, royal surname.

Her companion, a grizzled warrior covered in scars with a braided, forked beard of black flecked with gray leaned on a battle axe like a cane. He eyed the newcomers with the weary eye of a warrior, but he did not speak.

"And my friends—welcome to the homeland of the Walkers, United Baltija. This is my sister, Zhanna Daktha, the true heir to the throne of Queen Sanda Daktha. And this is her husband, Halamir Valdursson."

"Heir?" Rayshel asked. "But—"

"So, this was your goal all along? To dethrone Mara, Lavinia *Daktha?*" Aleksander asked.

"You will *not* call me that name twice," Lavinia replied.

He sighed in relief as he saw Bovin appear, limping, with a group of other Walkers. The Minotaur was covered in thick bandages and moved with a slow limp, but he was alive.

"Hardly," said Zhanna, holding up a hand. "I've never wanted the throne—we both denounced our heritage long ago. Our father was the last king of Sangora, and our family's legacy is as tarnished as his soul. Lavinia has helped me cleanse our nation of those that support him."

"Our mother killed him," said Lavinia. The Walkers are his dark legacy, the spawn of his many mistresses, and perhaps, evidence of the great sin of Sangora—our mother's genocide."

"I still don't understand your end goal," said Aleksander to Lavinia as she approached the Telepillar. She sighed.

"Then I've done a good job. Aleksander, I want to atone for their actions," said Lavinia, looking into Zhanna's bad eye. "How is that not clear? I want to prove that I am not my mother."

"I definitely understand a complicated family," he replied.

Zhanna took her sister's hand. "We will fight with you. I pray to the Goddesses that when the conflict is over, our people can make peace. Halamir, my love, please inform our forces."

Halamir nodded and departed in silence.

Hundreds and thousands of Walkers were already gathering in the street outside the church. Many entered the building using the door, and Aleksander wondered how many of them lacked the ability to teleport. Lavinia thanked her sister with a nod.

"To Balgorod, then," Lavinia said, holding Zhanna's hand. She willed the damaged Telepillar's gem to change direction, and they vanished in an all-consuming flash of red light.

# CHAPTER THIRTY-SIX

# THE BATTLE OF AGES PAST

It had begun to snow. Although fog and drifting flakes of white obscured the enemy forces, the intense hunger and dread that accompanied the Faceless gnawed at every soul in the city.

Death was coming for Balgorod.

Hanna glanced down the high wall, wondering when the creatures would emerge from the foggy unknown; she gripped Shanthah's hand, squeezing it three times. He squeezed back.

They shared no words, only dread.

She thought back to what had been said in the war meeting. If the wall were to fall, they would be overrun in minutes by the sheer number of their foes. Readying herself for the conflict, she let out a deep, icy breath that floated up before fading on the cold air.

Captain Rayna's words were lost on the wind as she gave last minute orders and instructions to her troops. Hanna could see Mara's Mistresses of Dusk, General Anca doing the same farther down along the wall. A sudden, collective lurch of fear and despair washed over the defenders of Balgorod. It could mean only one thing.

"They're moving," Josman said, speaking for the rest of the group.

Hanna was glad to be with her friends; beside her stood Shanthah, Josman, and Kamil, with whom she had endured so much, and Alia and Valis stood a few yards away. Hanna had been so impressed with Alia's courage in volunteering her healing abilities on the wall. She was not a warrior, but she was braver than most. Her abilities would be needed soon enough.

The former High King of Talohira, Valistaran, stood with the Thans he once called his enemies, leading a contingent of other magic users alongside Mistress Raluca. Other warriors, human and Sangoran alike, stood ready for battle, if the word 'warrior' could even be used to describe them. Many were refugees, untrained with a sword, but all the same, courageous enough to volunteer to protect the wall.

Hanna smiled to herself; perhaps she should have spoken up when Mara asked if they had any special advantages. She could recognize one now: heart. The people here had reason to fight, whereas the Pure were mindless, Florenta's Sangorans mind controlled, and the Thans ready to kill their own people.

Hanna's mind shot back to the Battle of Laniras. That battle, now over two years gone, seemed like a distant memory. A different siege in another time. Perhaps the people of Laniras saw the oncoming battle as righteous vengeance for the atrocities committed that fateful day. Of course, Laniras had been armed much better than Balgorod, as were its people today as well. However, the oddest part, Hanna surmised, was that the point of this battle was to protect the very woman who had laid siege to Laniras. Perhaps it was vengeance, after all.

A horn sounded from the distant fog, and Hanna and her friends jumped to attention. Laughter melted away fear as Shanthah began to yell in the general direction of the Faceless swarm. Not only did he yell battle cries in Sangoran, but he shouted obscenities and curses so wild and hilariously vulgar that he soon had the entire wall swearing and mocking Thanatan at the top of their lungs.

Hanna smiled. It was as if someone had lit a torch in a dark room, for the dismal feeling on the wall faded like their breath on the cold air. She threw a fist to the sky and let out one long string of obscenities that even made Shanthah double over in laughter.

"That's the spirit!" Shanthah called to those on the wall, letting out another yell.

Cheers erupted from the crowd, and a rhythmic thudding of spears on stone filled the air echoing Shanthah's yells.

"You call yourself a God, and you're scared of a few swearing peasants on a wall? Come on, then!" he shouted.

As if in response, the host of Thannish soldiers emerged from the fog, and Shanthah let out a slow whistle. The cheering died in an instant.

"Ready!" shouted General Anca, her brown leathery wings extended high above like a banner to her troops; the bowmen on the wall raised their weapons, and those with magic readied whatever skills they possessed. Anca screeched a single word in Sangoran. "Calpai!" *Fire!* An initial volley of arrows filled the sky and arced down toward their targets at her command.

Hanna winced as the arrows met their mark. "This is wrong," she said, shaking her head. "Those are our own people!"

She could tell others on the wall felt the same way, but they each knew their duty and their order: hold the wall above all else. For how long, no one knew. For a moment, Hanna believed that they could hold out against the Thannish forces, but through the fog she beheld the endless tide of Faceless, and she dreaded to admit the truth to herself. Kamil stepped forward, placing his palms on the stone rampart of the wall.

*"There are Thannish citizens here! Hold your attack!"* Kamil's mental voice echoed through the battlefield, and many of the oncoming host hesitated, but it did not slow the advance.

"They don't care," Josman muttered, gripping the handle of his heavy mace. "Even the Thans don't care."

*"I repeat, there are hundreds of Thans here! Hold your attack!"*

A massive boulder struck the wall near Kamil with such force that it broke Kamil's mental concentration, throwing those around him to the ground, dazed. Parts of the wall crumbled where it had been struck.

"What was that?!" cried Josman, readying himself for another. His wait was short. As the Thans advanced, a second boulder shot forth from the fog and raced faster than any arrow straight into the base of the wall, crumbling brick and shaking their world. Several men and women fell to their deaths.

"Catapults?" asked Shanthah. "Or trebuchets like you built in the slave camp, Kamil?"

"No," Hanna said, shaking her head. She lifted her hand and caused a piece of rubble to float before her then launched the stone forward into the crowd. Shanthah understood at once.

"They have Telekinetiks..." he muttered. "Anca! They have Telekinetiks!"

"Yeah, well, so do we!" Hanna screamed at the oncoming horde.

Anca continued to coordinate her forces launching volleys of arrows as three more boulders struck the wall, disrupting her balance. She tripped, her ankle twisting beneath her, causing her to fall through a crack in the wall. At once, Hanna closed her fist and pulled the general toward her, telekinetically pulling her back. Anca remained airborne by flapping her wings to prevent putting too much weight on her injured ankle.

"That we do," Anca said, agreeing with Hanna with a thankful nod. "Be ready, Miss Samsa. We'll need you. All hands, brace yourselves!"

The Faceless swarm, led by Generals Raksil and Kallus and Thanatan's other Spirit Warriors broke through the fog, quickly overtaking their Thannish allies.

"Valistaran!" shouted Anca. "Now!"

The fallen king roared as he launched a stream of black flame straight to the base of the wall. Hanna watched in awe as the flames ignited a deep trench coated with dark fluid, blocking the swarm's advance.

However, the horde of Faceless Sangorans from the infested Doftaani prison emerged from the thick smoke, bypassing the wall. Hundreds of arrows met their mark, felling many of the beasts, but it was no use. Anca sent a contingent of flying Sangoran archers after them, and several magic users with ranged abilities followed.

At that moment, five more boulders shot toward the wall. Hanna cried out as she thrust her hand forward to slow their momentum, but they were too fast; they struck the wall, throwing a dozen soldiers to their deaths.

"Hanna!" Shanthah shouted as he was thrown to the ground. "Take Kamil and find those guys!" She took his hand and he smiled. "You can do this."

She wished the moment he held her close would last forever, for she did not know if she would have another. She ran toward Kamil, hesitant to drop Shanthah's hand. She took one last look and grabbed Kamil's shoulder, knowing he could read her thoughts. He followed close behind without another word.

The duo raced toward one of the few pulley stations used to descend, stepping into the lift as another round of boulders struck the wall. Hanna tried the hoist, but the mechanism clanked and resisted, shaking the cart.

"Jammed!" Hanna exclaimed. "Damn it!"

Kamil began to examine the pulley system's stubborn mechanism. Hanna watched the mute man work, smiling. It reminded her of his brilliant schemes and engineering in the slave camp that had won them their freedom; she hadn't often thought it, but without Kamil, none of them would be free.

Something shook the cart from above, and Kamil acted out of instinct, drawing his blade to slice out one of the ropes. The pulley system shot up, burning the flesh on Kamil's hand. He cried out in pain as the entire world seemed to drop from beneath their feet.

Their screams intertwined as they plummeted downward; Kamil gripped her forearm and the side of the cart to steady them, but it was no use. However, their screams became terrified laughter as Hanna slowed the cart's descent with her powerful mind. The cart struck the ground softer than it would have if Hanna hadn't intervened, but it still threw them both from the wreckage, and they tumbled across the rocky ground. Hanna groaned and helped Kamil to his feet.

*"I'm fine. You alright?"* Kamil's voice filled her mind. Before she could answer, another deeper voice interrupted.

"Couldn't wait for me?" Josman asked, brushing bits of debris from his trousers.

"You—what?! How?" Hanna exclaimed, turning to Kamil, who shrugged.

"We're in this fight together, and I'm not letting you two go alone," the big man said with a scowl. Hanna smiled and drew them both into a tight hug. "I managed to get on the roof of the lift just as you two fell."

"No debate about it then! Let's go," Hanna exclaimed.

The trio set off toward the endless tide of Faceless with a collective glance to the west where the Thannish army had now reached the wall.

Kamil slowed as he focused his mental energy and cast a mental lure far from the battle, drawing many of the swarming creatures away.

"*I can't run and concentrate!*" cried Kamil to their minds, stumbling.

A tide of Faceless turned toward them, both Hanna and Kamil's immense mental presence a tantalizing treat to their undying voracity. Kamil yelped as Josman scooped him up and slung him onto his muscular back.

"Then don't run, just concentrate!"

Josman and Hanna ran with all the speed their feet would allow as Kamil lured hundreds of Faceless away from the battle at the wall. The creatures swarmed over one another in a tide of gray bodies, each craving their prize.

Josman and Hanna screamed at the top of their lungs as they ran, as if it would quicken their flight from the swarm. Hanna cast pebbles and stones into the tide as they ran, punctuating each one with a yell.

The swarm was almost upon them; one Faceless nearly ripped through Hanna's ankle, but it stumbled and fell, its ankle somehow severed.

"They're gaining on us!" Josman roared.

"You think?!" Hanna exclaimed, but before Josman could answer, her toe caught the bottom of a crag, and she struck the ground.

"Hanna!"

"*GO!*" she screamed. Josman hesitated, and both he and Hanna knew his momentary pause gave the Faceless all the time they needed to overtake them. She roared and lashed out with all her might, careful not to tap into her link with Thanatan, however tempting.

Hanna's mental onslaught eviscerated the front row of the creatures; she rent limbs from sockets and flesh from bodies as those behind flailed about as her powerful mind blasted them backward. She roared and brought her foot to the earth, creating a great fissure in the earth between them and the Faceless.

Three massive boulders rocketed toward them, and Hanna screamed as she brought her fist up, creating a shield of mental energy. The energy field reduced the boulders to rubble, and through the chaos, she caught a glimpse of three men crossing the fissure toward them.

Hanna roared once more, stomping her boot into the snow, sending every bit of the crumbled boulders back at the source. Tiny shards and jagged flecks of rock cut through the three Telekinetiks, spraying the white snow with crimson blood.

"Unholy Elafris below!" Josman swore, catching Hanna as she collapsed holding her aching arms.

"I have an idea!" Hanna muttered, her breath was heavy and forced.

"We have to get you back to Balgorod, you've done what we set out to do!" Josman exclaimed.

"No, wait, please." She pulled away from Josman and slapped Kamil on the back of the head, completely unsure if her trick would work. She could not sense Kamil's mind, and tears filled her eyes.

This had to work.

It had to.

Almost there. She could sense Kamil's mind like a faint pulse… She could feel the swarm…

Hanna could feel his breath, for it was her breath. Her thoughts, his. Horror filled her soul, for they were not Kamil's thoughts she was sensing, but Thanatan's, his consciousness ever-present with the swarm.

She wrestled through the mental struggle with the dark god and connected with Kamil's strained mind, adding her own considerable mental energy to that of her friend, all the while keeping Thanatan's mind at bay.

The resulting mental shockwave blasted a crater in the earth, and the intense groaning that accompanied the Faceless, ever more horrible the greater their numbers, was completely silenced. The world seemed still for a brief second as dirt, rock, and confused, emaciated Faceless bodies hung in the air around them before being cast away.

Hanna felt Kamil's mind pulsate again, and a second shockwave ripped through the air far away as their combined powers seemed to break through the walls of possibility and reality. The force of the blast caused the trio to stumble, and they lay motionless for several minutes as the Faceless followed Kamil's powerful mental lure boosted by Hanna's link to Thanatan's Connection to Connection.

No, to *Hanna's* Connection to Creation.

Josman let out a deep breath, and the trio began to laugh, a joyous sound that filled their hearts. Hanna turned her head to see Josman's grimy face covered with a wide smile, his booming laugh filling the silence. Kamil propped himself up, obviously dizzy.

"Maybe we've got a chance yet!" Josman said, getting to his feet.

"*What…was…that….?*" Kamil's thoughts were slow, like one's voice after intense physical exertion. Josman shook his head in amazement.

"Apparently, Hanna's powers plus Kamil's power equals—"

"*BOOM!*" Hanna cried, clapping her hands together. They got to their feet, completely disoriented. The world spun around them, and it took a moment to regain balance.

"Well, if we're feeling this way, I wonder how they're feeling," Josman said, gesturing to the pile of dead Faceless that had been thrown several hundred feet away.

"*Let's not give them time to tell us,*" Kamil thought, and the others agreed. Josman helped them out of the crater.

"By the gods, am I glad you two are on our side," Josman said, clapping his friend on the back. He reached for Hanna as well but pulled his hand back as he caught the look on her face.

Utter horror.

"Hanna?"

She felt the god's presence.

"He's coming!" she shouted, grasping Josman's meaty hand. She took a step on her injured ankle and stumbled. Panic and tears filled her eyes as she shouted once more, "He's coming!"

"Hanna, *who* is coming?" Josman asked, glancing over his shoulder.

The Faceless were still miles away, writhing over one another in the second crater, but he could also see them climbing out, having found no prize there. Kamil stepped forward and patted Josman on the shoulder, pointing. Josman turned and nodded in disbelief.

"Ah."

"What have I done?" Hanna whispered, closing her eyes. "He found us because—"

She could feel invisible arms wrap around her. She began to struggle but then realized it was a familiar, welcome embrace. Tears filled her eyes.

"Hello beautiful!" Shanthah's voice.

Josman and Kamil stood several yards away watching yet another army of men on horseback approaching from the northwest.

"I'm here with you. You're safe," Shanthah said, still invisible.

Hanna said nothing as she sobbed into his invisible neck and pulled him close.

"You were here?"

"The whole time, and I'm not going anywhere."

He did not materialize, but she could feel his warmth. He helped her stand on her injured ankle. "I've got you. What do you need me to do?"

"Stay hidden—might be our only advantage," Hanna muttered as she limped toward their oncoming foes.

She could now see clearly with her physical eyes what her mind had already sensed: Thanatan, the Magistrate, and a contingent of men, Sangorans, and Faceless were visible through the drifting snow.

"And so, we finally meet in person," came Thanatan's voice over the expanse between them. "Oh, how I've waited for this moment, Hanna Samsa."

The god held his hands aloft as if to welcome Hanna into his home. No one replied, the only response to Thanatan's greeting the sound of battle near the wall. He stepped forward, his crystal armor like ice in the drifting snow.

"What are *they* for?" Hanna called, gesturing with a nod of her head at the portion of the army accompanying Thanatan and the Magistrate. "Scared? Scared of one little woman and her friends?!"

"You think too much of yourself."

"Because you *should be!*" Hanna roared, bringing one foot forward and planting it in the earth; she swung her arm around and with an almighty roar, tore the earth asunder before her. Not with the Connection to Creation, but the raw power that belonged to her and Kamil. The earth opened like a great maw, threatening to swallow Thanatan and his army whole.

She screamed as blood dripped from her ears and nose, and she could feel the injuries in her arms tensing and threatening to snap again. The jaws of the earth snapped shut, swallowing hundreds of men, horses, Sangorans, and Faceless alike, including Thanatan and the Magistrate.

Hanna eased her power to a safer level, careful not to injure her arms. She stumbled but felt Shanthah steadying her. Kamil too collapsed to his knees, and Josman caught him and helped him stand.

"You okay, buddy?" Josman asked, concerned. His attention was on his friend, not the mountain that had engulfed Thanatan and his minions.

*"Boosted Hanna's ability again,"* Kamil thought. Using his ability in conjunction with Hanna's had clearly taxed them both to their limit. Hanna was trembling, and Kamil was almost unconscious. *"Maybe I shouldn't have…"*

The clenched jaws of earth, which Josman now realized resembled Hanna's own clenched fist, exploded in a flurry of dust and ash; Thanatan emerged from the fissure as boulders and flame rained down around him, an intimidating site to behold in the blizzard.

He redirected the falling bits of flaming stone toward Hanna, who threw up a shield of earth just in time but failed to summon a mental shield as the wall exploded. The god's onslaught rained down, throwing Hanna, Shanthah, Josman, and Kamil to the ground.

"You can delay me, but to what end? You will die. Your city will fall, and my people will be free from the chaos you bring,"

Thanatan shouted. His crystal armor was scuffed with dirt and ash but seemed to be undamaged.

Hanna knew Thanatan spoke the truth; her energy was nearly spent, and if Shanthah's invisible arms were not supporting her, she would have already collapsed. There had to be something she could do—anything. She reached out and touched Kamil's shoulder, and he peered into her eyes with sadness and defeat. Josman gripped his mace and took a deep breath before sprinting headlong toward the man who styled himself a god.

A flick of a wrist threw Josman into the dirt. At that same moment, a bolt of crimson lightning struck the ground between them and the god, and hundreds of robed figures emerged from the light.

"Josman!" Shanthah exclaimed, still invisible.

He tried to wake his unconscious friend, but he did not stir. Shanthah held his hands aloft, and his friends vanished like himself. He hoped they would be safe enough from the god's fury to regain their strength.

His plan seemed to work, for Thanatan's forces withdrew, confused. For several short minutes, they simply rested in silence, the snow piling on their invisible bodies.

And then, an icy wind picked up, and a massive tube-shaped object materialized, striking the earth and rolling along the bottom of the crater before coming to a stop. The crimson light continued to pour from the unstable Telepillar, casting light that looked like blood on the snow.

Everyone recognized it at once. The Weapon of Ages Past, the Forbidden Weapon, the Death Bringer—the weapon

Valistaran had so badly desired before he was dethroned by Mara—the weapon Ronin Jakoni had stolen. The nuclear bomb from the Deadlands.

Thanatan, the Magistrate, Hanna, Shanthah, and Kamil each bolted toward the weapon surrounded by an army of Walkers. Many of Thanatan's followers rallied behind him as well. Hanna was ready to vaporize any Walker that dared get in her way, unsure of their allegiance.

"Mi nehathaa necavujali, i nehathaa nesinurjašam!" shouted the leader of the Walkers, a woman with a scarred face and silver hair. *We never forgot, and we will never forgive!*

She and a bearded warrior brandishing an axe led the charge; those that could teleport appeared in the midst of Thanatan's forces, while those that could not charged into the fray on foot.

Five figures stood behind the leader of the Walkers, including Mistresses Lavinia and Vasilica, a Minotaur, a Sangoran Hanna didn't recognize, and—

"Aleksander?!" Hanna called.

Indeed, Aleksander stood with flames in hand as the Walkers hacked at bone and sinew with hooked blades, utilizing their teleportation abilities to cut through the enemy forces.

"Hanna! Kamil!" Aleksander replied. "You're alive! What are you doing here?!"

"A reunion can wait!" Lavinia exclaimed, summoning her twin blades from beneath her vambraces.

Thanatan raised a hand, and an entire contingent of Walker soldiers fell dead, their bones twisted in unnatural directions. He thrust his hand forward, but Hanna and Kamil mirrored his action, intertwining their powerful minds. This time, Hanna's powers boosted Kamil's telepathy. With the extra power, Kamil kept Thanatan from disintegrating any more of their forces by binding his mind behind a mental block, rendering Kamil unable to focus on little else.

Thanatan's mind began to overwhelm his own, and he screamed under the strain it took to restrain him. He knew he would not be able to hold the mental block much longer. Thanatan's actions were sluggish, and he stepped toward Hanna and Kamil as if through a deep marsh; each step he took caused Kamil's focus to wane and drove another figurative nail into his mind.

Aleksander, his allies, and the Walkers battled the god's forces with expert skill, but the elite Sangoran warriors controlled by the Queen's Control were their equal in combat, and the Faceless were without number.

Kamil groaned as he failed to hold Thanatan back any longer. The god's blade came down but stopped mere inches from Hanna's neck, stopped by some invisible force. Thanatan hacked again and again, but Shanthah, unseen, parried each blow.

"Where are you?" Thanatan shouted, reaching out with his mind.

Shanthah felt his enemy's mental presence crawl into his consciousness and extinguish his power of invisibility, forcing him to rematerialize. Shanthah looked up in horror and gasped just as the god's blade broke his own before piercing his stomach.

"No!" Hanna screamed in disbelief.

Thanatan pulled the crimsoned blade from Shanthah's flesh, ready to strike once more just as Josman swung his great mace around. The spiked head of the weapon struck the side of Thanatan's head with such ferocity that it threw the god to the snow-covered earth. A surprised look crossed Josman's face for a moment before he realized that Hanna had amplified the speed and strength of his already formidable swing.

Black mist poured from the cracks spiderwebbing across Thanatan's crystal armor. Josman continued his relentless attack, smashing his mace hard against Thanatan's head, neck, and chest again and again, each strike amplified by Hanna's mind.

"Enough!"

A shockwave of mental energy hurled Josman and the others away. They lay dazed in the dirt for a moment, and when they had composed themselves, Thanatan was gone, moving for the Weapon of Ages Past.

Aleksander, Lavinia, Rayshel, Vasilica, and a group of Walkers broke away from the fight at Aleksander's request to defend his fallen friends. Josman had struck his head on a rock; while it didn't pierce his armored skin, it was clear that he had a concussion, and Shanthah's wound was deep.

"Aleksander! Man, is it good to see you!" Shanthah exclaimed. He gestured to the gaping wound in his abdomen. "Before, you know, I bleed out and die. Josman doesn't look too good either. He never really did, but, oh man, this hurts."

"Vasilica, can you get them to safety?" Aleksander asked.

The Mistress of Dusk nodded. She gestured to Rayshel and two other Walkers who helped Shanthah to his feet. Hanna wrapped her arms around him.

"Shan, I don't think we can do this. There's too many of them." Her face turned sad. "Please, please don't die. I can't do this without you."

"I know you can," Shanthah said with a weak smile. At that moment, a horn echoed over the battlefield from Balgorod's central fortress on the island between the rivers. "But the good news is that you aren't alone. That was *Mara's* horn! Before they take me away, I have an idea of how you can beat Thanatan."

Hanna listened closely to Shanthah's instructions, and she grinned. It was a mad plan, but it might just work. Vasilica helped Shanthah to his feet. Lavinia and Rayshel said their goodbyes, pressing their foreheads together before a quick embrace.

"Everything's going to be okay," Hanna said to reassure him.

"I know it is. Thanatan's gonna rue the day he crossed you," Shanthah said. Hanna planted a kiss on his lips and then pulled away.

"Now get going," Hanna said. "We've got this from here."

As Vasilica, Rayshel, and the Walkers vanished with Shanthah and Josman, Mara led a cloud of Sangorans overhead, carving a bloody swath through Thanatan's forces toward Balgorod's main wall, which was now collapsing under the tide of Faceless.

Zhanna Daktha screamed an order to her forces to intercept Thanatan and retrieve the Weapon of Ages Past. The ensuing bloodbath between them and Thanatan's Faceless left a pile of corpses piled around the weapon, but still, the battle continued. Aleksander, Hanna, Kamil, and Lavinia stood helpless as Thanatan himself hewed down many of Zhanna's soldiers.

Several dozen Faceless Sangorans assailed them as well, slicing through throats and carrying soldiers into the air before dropping them to their deaths. Several of Zhanna's brave warriors teleported high into the air to hack at their winged foes, keeping them at bay.

"Shanthah gave me an idea. I don't have time to explain, but Aleksander, when I give you the signal, you throw as much fire as you can into the sky," Hanna said.

"I can do that," Aleksander replied. "What about Zhanna's people?"

"Kamil, I'll need you to boost my powers one more time, can you do that?" Hanna asked. "Send a message to the Walkers to retreat."

*"I can do both of those things."*

"You'll be the fastest of all of us," Hanna said, turning to Lavinia. "As soon as the way is clear, I need you to fly through and get that weapon out of here."

"Vague orders, but if the first part of your plan works, I'll manage," Lavinia said with a nod.

Kamil seemed lost in thought for a moment, his eyes shut tightly. He let out a deep breath.

"You with us, buddy?" Hanna asked.

*"I just contacted Mara to bring her forces back. We'll need all the help we can get."*

"Alright, whatever you and Shanthah have planned—let's do it," Aleksander said, lighting a fistful of flame. Lavinia nodded, her twin vambrace blades at the ready and mighty wings outstretched.

Thanatan had nearly reached his goal. As the four friends sprinted toward the Weapon of Ages Past and the Telepillar, Thanatan held his hands aloft, and by his command, the very ground beneath their feet disintegrated into nothingness. And then, they were falling.

Lavinia shot toward Kamil as they fell, but a piece of rocky debris struck her on the back, and she spiraled downward away from him. Meanwhile, Aleksander tried to rocket himself upward with a burst of flame from his hands. However, he was unable to maintain the stream of fire, and he too found himself falling.

Time stopped.

Aleksander, Lavinia, Kamil, and dozens of Walkers felt themselves suspended in midair surrounded by dust and debris that did not fall. A calm serenity surrounded them, and as he rotated on the spot, Aleksander saw Hanna floating above them with her hands outstretched.

She had managed to once again harness Thanatan's Connection to Creation. Kamil touched her mind, sensing the horror of her necessary mistake, but with their combined power, they were able to levitate to the top of the pit. As soon as Kamil's feet reached the surface, he thrust his mind into Thanatan's consciousness in an attempt to set up another mental block to hold him back.

Meanwhile, the Sangoran forces Mara had gathered landed in the snow around their allies; the beleaguered Walkers and other Sangoran warriors fighting nearby cheered and called out for the Empress, and her very presence seemed to spur them on. With renewed courage and resolve to stand against the darkness, they began to push their enemies back.

Mara approached, still commanding her forces in the Sangoran language with all the air and authority of the warrior-empress that she was. Indeed, she truly looked the part, clad in her finest Sangoran war garb of dark silver, shining gold, and blood-red; her torn, dark cape flowed behind her like a banner of hope. Her face, determined, and unbreakable, was smeared with blood.

She pulled Hanna into a close embrace.

"We got this," Hanna said.

Mara clapped her friend on the shoulder and let out a deep breath. Together, they looked over the horrible carnage within the crater around the Weapon of Ages Past; Zhanna's forces were in full retreat with a brave, doomed few staying behind to stand between Thanatan and the weapon.

"Let's hope you're right," Mara said. Despair filled her heart as she watched her fellow Sangorans dying. "We're running out of time."

"I think you'll like this next part. Just watch," Hanna said.

The snow falling around them obscured their vision, but the battle raged on. Hanna reached out with her mind, focusing on every individual flake of snow. She felt intoxicating serenity overwhelm her mind and could sense the unique patterns of each flake, but she delved ever deeper into their structure. She remembered what she had done to the bricks of her prison, and just as she commanded the dust and earth from the ground to rise, she willed the cellular structure of the snow to change.

In complete harmony with her Connection to Creation, she felt matter rearrange to her whim; soon, the white blizzard became a dark deluge of slick oil that flowed down over the enemy forces like rain. Sensing Hanna's intentions, the Magistrate clutched a Walker by the throat and overpowered her enemy's weaker mind. She forced his power of teleportation to activate, and the two of them vanished from the battlefield.

"*NOW!*" Hanna shouted.

"*Get out!*" Kamil's message echoed through the minds of their allies, and the Walkers made all haste to vanish from the black flood just as Aleksander launched a stream of flame into the sky. Mara joined him, blasting the sky with lightning from her fingers and the tips of her wings.

Aleksander planted his feet and unleashed his full power; black flame whipped around his arms in a pillar of glowing darkness that, together with Mara's lightning, exploded against the rain of oil in a blinding flash of orange and yellow flame that seemed to engulf the world. The winter's sky rained dark hellfire down on the writhing Faceless, whose god exerted all the power he could muster to shield himself and the Weapon of Ages Past from the onslaught.

"Lavinia, Mara, now!" Hanna ordered.

Mara and Lavinia each grabbed one of Hanna's shoulders, and they shot straight into the flames. Hanna screamed and held her hands out, bending the elements to her will. The fiery rain parted as they raced toward the pillar and the weapon.

Five Faceless Sangorans, still ablaze, shot straight toward the trio. Hanna screamed as Mara and Lavinia both spiraled through the air, slicing through four of the creatures' throats and spines with bladed wings. Four mutilated bodies plummeted downward, but the fifth reached out for Mara's throat with bloodied claws. Before it reached her, Hanna mentally grasped both of its arms with her mind and ripped it in half from throat to groin. Mara cheered as the two Sangorans adjusted their hold on Hanna and corrected their flight pattern.

"I hate this!" Hanna screamed.

When the sky stopped raining fiery death on the Faceless horde, Lavinia, Hanna, and Mara dropped down to the carnage around Thanatan from above, blocking him off from his goal.

The god wasted no time, and his crystal sword clashed against Lavinia's twin blades. Hanna focused on Thanatan's limbs to slow him as he lashed out at Mara, who danced around him in a flurry of lightning and bladed wings.

Lavinia managed to wrench Thanatan's blade from his grip, but he brought his fist up against her throat, throwing her into the air. He thrust his other fist into her stomach, crushing her against the ground.

She writhed in breathless agony in the snow, and at that same moment, a horrendous groan filled their minds as a new swarm of Faceless appeared on the ridge overlooking the crater.

Thanatan summoned pillars of stone from the ground to shield himself from Mara's lightning then cast it forward, buffeting Mara's body with bits of rock. She cried out in pain, and Hanna managed to save her from being crushed by larger chunks of stone, flinging the boulders back at Thanatan.

Thanatan vaporized the stones before they hit their mark, and he turned his attention to the new swarm looming above them. Mara groaned and pushed herself up to follow his gaze.

*"May this be the day a false god answers for his sins!"* The mental voice filled each of their minds, one that Mara and Hanna both recognized as the voice of an old friend.

Drahomir was leading the Faceless.

They swarmed down the ridge, and Thanatan released a mental shockwave that vaporized the first row of Drahomir's creatures, only to be overwhelmed by the sheer number claws and gray bodies.

The god's own Faceless minions began tearing Drahomir's forces limb from limb, and Mara lost sight of Drahomir and his crimson mask amongst the chaos. She sprinted toward the Telepillar, reaching it before the others and tapped the cracked gem on its face. She grinned as it thrummed with life, crackling with energy. The obelisk smoked from the cracks along its face, but she slammed her fist against the gem just as Hanna used her powers to fling it in Thanatan's general direction.

"Come to me, *now!*" Mara shouted, seemingly to no one in particular. She screamed in horror as she watched Thanatan's Faceless overwhelm her friends; one of the creatures leapt onto Lavinia's fallen form and began hacking at her stomach. Her shrieks filled the air, but Drahomir tore its throat out with his own jagged claws.

Pain tore through Mara's skull as she used her own powers of telekinesis to force the pillar straight down, and it struck Thanatan in the back. Its magic activated just as it collided with his armor, and with what energy it still had left, it exploded in a flash of brilliant crimson. Mara, Hanna, hundreds of Drahomir's Faceless, and Thanatan vanished, and the crimson light was gone.

Drahomir's Faceless parted, and he knelt next to Lavinia. Without wasting another moment, he grabbed her hand, and they teleported away.

Mara and Hanna reappeared far from Balgorod in a flash of light. Pieces of the Teleportation Pillar were scattered across the ground around them along with fractured pieces of Thanatan's crystal armor. Drahomir's Faceless stood at attention, as if Drahomir had commanded them to answer to Hanna and Mara.

"Mara!" Hanna cried out as she saw Mara clutching her skull in pain.

"I'm okay," Mara said, shaking it off. Hanna gave her a disapproving look, at which Mara laughed. She pointed to the broken crystal armor before them. "Seriously, I'm okay. Is he dead?"

"No," Hanna said, shaking her head.

She pointed to the sky, and Mara turned to follow her gaze. She covered her mouth as she beheld Thanatan's true form free of his crystal spirit armor: a towering, indistinct humanoid form of ash, dust, and darkness flailing above the ruins of Nitra, tearing brick and wood from burned out homes. The debris floated around Thanatan's form as if weightless.

"I think he's building himself a new body," Hanna said, "and I'm way too exhausted to take *that* thing down."

"Is Kamil's mental block still working?" Mara asked.

"Don't think so," Hanna said, shaking her head. "I think he's at full power now."

"Full power but hurt and distracted. If we act fast, we might still win this," Mara said. She adjusted the razor claws on each of her fingers.

"But that means I'm at full power too," Hanna said. "And me and you together? He's got no chance."

"I've got an idea," Mara said after a moment of contemplation.

She was silent as she removed a small pouch from her belt and emptied its contents into her hand, taking extra care as she removed the cloth wrappings from a cuff of tarnished gold. It was marked with scuffs and burns, but Mara treated it with great care, as if it would bite her. For indeed, it once had.

"Is that what I think it is?" Hanna asked. Mara nodded.

"Yup. The Cage," Mara said. "I've carried it with me for a very, very long time."

She had never told Hanna of what had transpired between her and Aleksander, but her friend cocked her head with an empathetic expression as if she knew. Mara's eyes were red with tears, and Hanna shared her anxiety and exhaustion.

"We're almost done, Mar, no matter how this turns out," Hanna said. "We're going to be done soon. Aleksander told me what happened. Twenty years trapped in your mind because of that thing—that's—"

She had no words to finish the sentence, unable to fathom the fate of wearing the prison cuff.

"With our abilities, I think we can use it against Thanatan," Mara said. "I don't think we can overpower him by force, not like *that*."

"If we can, wouldn't he be able to use it on us, too?" Hanna asked, a look of worry etched on her face. "But we can try."

Mara nodded and wrapped the device in the cloth before handing it to her friend, who held it close.

As Hanna looked toward Thanatan, she beheld the Weapon of Ages Past perched precariously upon a crumbling archway leading into a broken home.

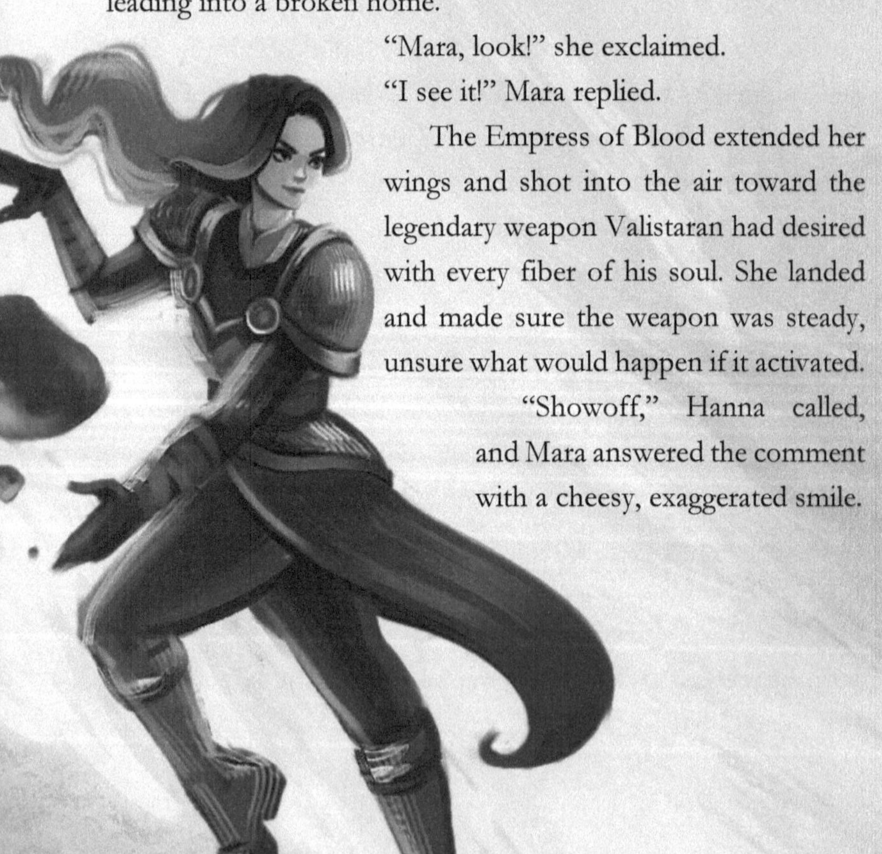

"Mara, look!" she exclaimed.

"I see it!" Mara replied.

The Empress of Blood extended her wings and shot into the air toward the legendary weapon Valistaran had desired with every fiber of his soul. She landed and made sure the weapon was steady, unsure what would happen if it activated.

"Showoff," Hanna called, and Mara answered the comment with a cheesy, exaggerated smile.

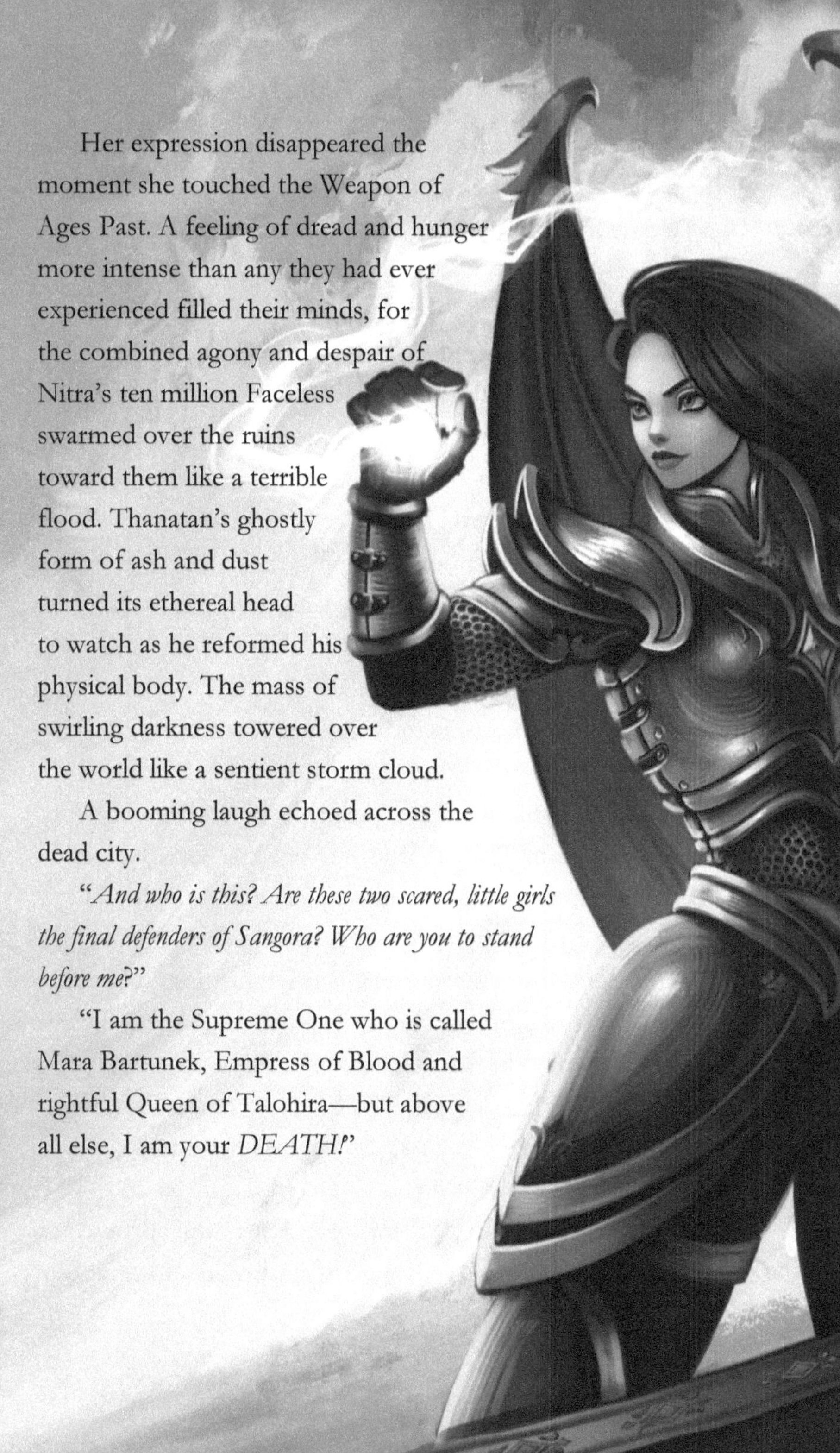

Her expression disappeared the moment she touched the Weapon of Ages Past. A feeling of dread and hunger more intense than any they had ever experienced filled their minds, for the combined agony and despair of Nitra's ten million Faceless swarmed over the ruins toward them like a terrible flood. Thanatan's ghostly form of ash and dust turned its ethereal head to watch as he reformed his physical body. The mass of swirling darkness towered over the world like a sentient storm cloud.

A booming laugh echoed across the dead city.

"*And who is this? Are these two scared, little girls the final defenders of Sangora? Who are you to stand before me?*"

"I am the Supreme One who is called Mara Bartunek, Empress of Blood and rightful Queen of Talohira—but above all else, I am your *DEATH!*"

*"Everything about you, Mara Bartunek, is a lie. From the magic and wings you have stolen to the smile upon your face, you are NOTHING!"*

"We shall see."

Thanatan's disembodied laughter once again filled the world as the Faceless closed in. Mara entered her dream-state, using a few moments to memorize just where each Faceless stood. She snapped back to reality as Hanna's eyes and veins glowed white, and together, they brought swift death to any of the emaciated creatures that dared attempt to reach the Weapon of Ages Past.

Drahomir's own Faceless fought at their side, and Hanna used her mind to summon bits of gravel and stones from beneath the snow, launching them with deadly force into her foes' bodies while Mara flayed them with bladed wings and a web of blinding lightning. They each knew the dreadful truth that it was only a matter of time before they were overrun.

As one Faceless reached for the Weapon of Ages Past, Hanna sent a chunk of brick through its spine, shattering bone and splaying flesh. The monster, broken but alive, lurched at Hanna but fell as Mara's bladed wing ripped through its neck. Ten others rushed in to replace their fallen comrade, and at the same moment, Hanna beheld Thanatan flinging an endless shower of tons of stone and brick toward them through the sky.

"Hanna, look out!" Mara cried as she sent bolts of lightning through the writhing swarm. The Faceless were so numerous that it didn't even matter where she directed her magic.

"Got it!" Hanna replied.

She let out a scream of mental exertion as she uprooted an entire ruined building and hurled it upward to intercept

Thanatan's nearest mountain of earth. Mara cheered as the building and the massive boulder exploded in a shower of debris, crushing thousands of Faceless underneath. Countless others scrambled over the rubble toward their prey, and the dark god's disembodied spirit body loomed above them.

Hanna screamed, holding her left arm, where a bone protruded from her flesh.

"Got my back?" Mara asked, lightning crackling around her hands and wings.

"Always!" Hanna shouted as she whipped up a hurricane of pebbles and jagged debris with her good arm.

The Faceless horde closed in, and the two women struck with all the fury and ferocity of the indomitable souls.

Mara's lightning burned holes through emaciated bodies while Hanna crushed heads and tore their foes asunder, ripping the Faceless limb from limb. Mara continued her onslaught with Hanna at her back, repeatedly thrusting the blades upon her wings through skulls, chests, and throats.

"Can't keep this up forever!" Mara shouted as she raked her steel razor claws against a creature's throat.

"Hold on!" Hanna let out a cry of rage, and with an explosion of mental energy, she disintegrated the flesh and bone of the ring of Faceless nearest to them. Those behind were sent flying and struck the ruins of the city with such force that they crumpled in distorted shapes.

"Hanna, you absolutely wonderful woman!"

Hanna collapsed, and Mara's head began to throb as she too spent the last of her energy defending her tiring friend; claps of thunder shattered the sky as she sent a powerful, spiraling web of lightning into the horde.

As the Faceless overwhelmed them, Hanna beheld Hippo the Behemoth racing toward their position while unleashing a stream of molten lava through the swarm of Faceless. Hanna then understood that it was Hippo that Mara had commanded to come to her before the Telepillar had whisked them away. Hundreds of winged Faceless swarmed him to keep him from reaching his master.

Hanna allowed the Connection to Creation to flood her mind, and she could sense everything around her: the rocks, the Faceless, Mara's breath and heartbeat, the ruins of Nitra, the air itself. She could sense Thanatan's very soul, his being, his essence.

She hurled the Cuff of the Mind-Prison into the sky and willed Thanatan's essence to connect with the magic within the it. His mind wrestled with her own as they twisted together within the cuff's dark magic. The groan of the Faceless was Thanatan's groan as their minds became one, trapped within the cuff's spell.

Would she be trapped forever?

Doubt filled her mind; even if she trapped Thanatan, Mara and her own physical body would surely be overrun by the Faceless. Her mind began to fade as the Cuff's magic distorted her sense of time. Seconds began weeks, and minutes became years, her only companion the dark god's horrible consciousness that threatened to consume her very soul.

What a fool she was.

She surrendered to eternity.

And then she was free, a blinding flash of light illuminating all of existence.

Cold air bit at her skin. She saw her best friend lying unconscious next to her, and she felt the rocky hide of Mara's behemoth, Hippo, as he carried them away. The sensations felt foreign and forgotten to her as all concepts of such things had been ripped from her while trapped with Thanatan inside the cuff's magic, amplified by her own power.

Hanna grasped Mara's hand, now understanding what madness her best friend had been forced to go through because of the Mind-Prison for even longer than she had.

Hippo flapped his massive wings with a mighty bellow and all the might in his form as they shot from the ruins of Nitra.

Blinding pain tore through her ears as the deafening roar of the world being torn asunder with the fury of an exploding sun ruptured her ear drums. The pressure shockwave knocked Hippo, Mara, and Hanna from the sky before the behemoth was able to steady his flight pattern. Hippo roared as he raced away from Nitra.

And then everything was silent.

Hanna stuck her fingers in her ears, frantically trying to hear something, but to no avail. She clapped a hand over her mouth in shock, for she could see blood dripping from Mara's ears as well.

What was happening? Had Mara activated the Weapon of Ages Past?

Had they won?

A blast of smoke and unmatchable heat followed the shockwave. A mushroom shaped cloud of flame and death extended high into the heavens, marking the site where the groans of ten million Faceless were silenced in an instant, and Thanatan's soul was consumed with the very fires of hell itself.

Hanna pulled herself toward Mara and squeezed her friend's limp hand with all the energy she had left, and then she too lost consciousness.

# CHAPTER THIRTY-SEVEN
# THE FESTIVAL OF ASHES

## THREE WEEKS LATER

Continuous explosions of red and green painted the dark canvas of the night sky above Balgorod. Mara and her friends marveled at the beauty in the sky from one of the many balconies in Shanthah's fortress; everyone was content, calm, and most importantly, together for the first time in months. She felt a surge of love and appreciation as the people in the streets below lit off celebratory floating lanterns that drifted around the city, illuminating the light fog and bathing the city in a warm, orange glow.

Hippo the behemoth rocked back and forth below as if dancing; the people had decorated him with glowing lanterns, festive garland, and shimmering silver and crimson ribbons. The natural glow emanating from his throat, chest, and stomach added extra ambience to the street below. Thans and Sangorans alike sang and played Sangoran folk tunes as they danced with Hippo, who shook the earth each time he stomped his legs.

The magnificent fireworks were to announce the start of the year's second Festival of Blood, this time given the theme 'Festival of Ashes'—a fitting theme, Mara thought, for a people who had truly stepped out of the Ashes. However, the lanterns were to celebrate her release from the healing center where she had been recuperating since Thanatan's defeat. The glowing paper lanterns floated up over the city, and to her delight, a couple even landed on the balcony by her and her friends.

During that time of rest and healing, her nurses and healers had regaled her with stories of the miracle that had transpired that day; the Faceless had retreated from the city, fleeing from the brave defenders before the entire city was overrun and slaughtered. It was a welcome update to be sure, but she knew there had to be another explanation.

With each display of fireworks grander than the last, Mara and the others cheered and laughed as they enjoyed each other's company, elation replacing overwhelming fear and dread.

Mara knew the night's joy and celebration had been hard-won. Countless funerals had been held in the past few weeks, drawing a dark mood over the city like a blanket of despair. She had declared Balgorod the temporary capital of Sangora until they could retake Doftaan, which had spread hope and lightened the atmosphere in the city. However, her people truly rejoiced upon hearing the announcement of a Festival of Blood to celebrate the victory over Thanatan as well as the Alboran tribe's liberation from Florenta's Sangora.

Mara scooped up one of the floating lanterns and held it aloft, and the crowd below cheered. Mara couldn't contain her smile watching the pure jubilation in the streets, and as she held the lantern, her eyes glimmered with grateful, joyous tears.

She glanced over at her friends, still smiling. She admired the wonderful people laughing and celebrating with her; not one of them was without scars, but they were happy. Together.

Shanthah and Hanna were huddled under a thick, wool blanket watching the fireworks while Lavinia and Rayshel sat nearby with their backs to the wall, sharing another. Aleksander, Josman, Kamil, Vasilica, Alia, and Valis were laughing and playing some kind of card game around a roaring fire that Aleksander had summoned. Shanthah and Hanna had already been eliminated from the game, and Valistaran and his daughter Valeniya had excused themselves hours ago and hadn't returned.

For the first time in many years, Mara began to sing. The melody that sprang into her head was one she used to sing back in Cineca, but now it had a more profound meaning. She swayed softly under the light of the fireworks as she added her song to the night.

*Nothin' bout you is who I am.*
*I'm stronger now, no thanks to you,*
*But maybe I should thank you though,*
*'cause I learned to fly…*

She wiped the tears of joy and appreciation from her eyes with the back of her hand before settling down next to Shanthah and Hanna with her knees to her side. Shanthah clapped for Mara's song as she settled in.

"Stupid dress." Mara laughed, making sure she wasn't revealing anything as she sat. She smoothed the fabric and let out a contented sigh. She looked up as Lavinia called to her.

"Hey, Marška, you did good out there," Lavinia said, gesturing in the general direction of the battlefield. Mara smiled at her use of the Sangoran diminutive form of her name.

"Thank you, Vinia, but it was definitely a team effort," Mara said. Lavinia responded with a nod and a smile then returned to watching the fireworks with Rayshel.

Mara turned back to Shanthah and Hanna with a wide smile.

"Hi, you two!"

"Are you going to say anything to the adoring masses?" Shanthah asked. "Rumor has it, they're calling for you."

"Oh, and where did this rumor come from?" Mara asked. Shanthah pointed at Hanna, and Mara chuckled. "Yes, I'll go say some words in a few minutes. I'm just so happy right now being with all of you."

Hanna's eyes darted to Mara's mouth as she spoke, trying to read her lips. Kamil had been using his telepathy to transmit whatever he heard into her mind, but he was currently distracted by the game. Alia had been able to heal Mara and Hanna's ears after the explosion in Nitra, but only Mara's hearing had returned. Hanna could still barely hear anything, but she was learning Sangoran sign language. She was good spirited about the whole ordeal, but Mara still felt guilty.

"By the way, I might be obsessed with Hippo," Shanthah said, pointing through the balcony's railings to where the behemoth was dancing with the crowd.

"You and me both," Mara said with another laugh.

Shanthah signed a phrase to Hanna, who burst into a fit of laughter. A moment later, Kamil did the same, and his words and feelings of mirth flitted into Mara and Shanthah's minds.

*"She says to tell you she's laughing because Shanthah used the sign for 'falling in love' with Hippo instead of whatever he actually meant, and that she's, in her own words, totally jealous."*

Shanthah turned to Hanna. "And how do you know that's not what I meant?"

Hanna smiled and planted a kiss on his lips before snuggling in close to watch the fireworks exploding overhead and Hippo, who was covered in lights and other decorations, dancing below.

"You're a smart man," Mara said as Josman roared in victory, apparently crowning himself the victory of their fireside game. They started another round, and this time, Rayshel kissed Lavinia before forcing her to join in.

"What do you mean?" Shanthah asked as an exceptionally awe-inspiring series of fireworks exploded in the heavens.

"You lost that game on purpose after Hanna did so that she'd cuddle you," Mara said in a mockingly accusatory tone.

"Guilty," Shanthah said, kissing Hanna on the forehead. Hanna signed the word for love. "But do you blame me?"

"No, I definitely don't. You're right though, I should say something to the crowd. I'd prefer to fly down, but…" Mara said, trailing off as she gestured to her dress. They laughed, and Hanna whistled as Mara got to her feet, making her way to the balcony's doorway. She retrieved her fur cloak from the unceremonious heap of coats near the door and draped it over her arm. "Wish me luck, everyone!"

Everyone called out encouraging words as the Empress of Blood, their friend, strode from the balcony. As she made her way alone down the corridor, which was decorated as festively as Hippo was outside, she heard quick footsteps coming from the balcony. She turned to see Aleksander hurrying toward her.

"Hi," she said cheerfully, greeting him with a warm smile.

"Hi," Aleksander repeated. "I wanted to see how you were feeling." He tapped the side of his head.

"Oh, that." She touched her scar and let out a deep sigh. "Honestly, it's been rough. The doctors and healers are still worried about me—I had another stroke during the fight with Thanatan right before we killed him, and apparently, I have seizures now, too. I'm okay now—well, no, that's a lie. I'm not okay, not by a long shot, but I'm happy, and I'm alive."

"I'm so sorry," Aleksander said. "I don't know what else to say."

"Nothing else needs to be said." She held his elbow. "They're going to watch me closely. Thank you for caring. It means a lot to me."

"I really haven't been able to get you alone to talk since the battle, and there is just so much I want to say," Aleksander said.

"Lavinia told me everything you went through to try to win me back my throne," Mara said.

"I'm not sure what she told you, but Thanatan killed Florenta, not us," Aleksander said, perplexed.

"I know, but that doesn't change anything. And you helped her against Ronin in United Baltija—who knew such a place even existed?" Mara asked. "She told me that you helped save a lot of people."

"She actually acknowledged my help?" Aleksander asked, walking with Mara down the corridor. Her laughter echoed through the empty halls at the comment.

"Yes, she told me about everything," Mara said at last. "About your adventures in Laniras, Doftaan, and Baltija—about Pol." Aleksander's expression turned sad, and he broke eye contact. "No, not that he didn't come back with you, but that you defended him while you could. It was his choice to stay in Laniras, I think. One that I'll have to live with until I see him again. She also told me about Rayshel, and I think that's the most excited I've ever seen Lavinia about anything."

Aleksander sighed with an awkward grin and shook his head.

"Yeah, about Rayshel—"

"I've seen that look. Hell, I've experienced that look." Mara playfully bumped Aleksander's hip with her own. "Falling for Lavinia's girl?"

"I don't know. I mean, I was, or at least I wanted myself to. But I think things turned out for the best," Aleksander said with a laugh. "Lavinia's terrifying, but I am very happy for them both."

"Beneath that hard prickly shell of hers, she's a sweetheart. And don't you dare tell her I told you that," Mara said. "But that's why we love her. By the way, seems like things turned out pretty well for Josman and Alia too."

"Wait, what?!"

"You couldn't tell?" Mara asked. "You didn't see how close they were sitting or how often she touched his hand?"

Her own hand brushed his.

"I'm clearly oblivious. Speaking of love," Aleksander said with a grin. Mara cocked her head in response. "How's your husband?"

"Oh no, you heard about that?!" Mara exclaimed with a groan as she buried her face in her hands. "Yeah, I need to do something about that. Who told you? It was Shanthah, wasn't it? I'm going to kill him."

She shook her head and took Aleksander's hand. Together, they shared a smile.

"You know, it used to be really strange for me to call you Aleksander, but not anymore. I almost said something so many times back in the slave camp," Mara said.

"But you didn't know if I remembered you?" Aleksander asked. Mara nodded. "Well, you are incredible, so I'm really glad I finally did."

"Me too," she said, swaying with his hand in hers. "Aleks, can I tell you something?"

"Of course," Aleksander replied.

"I loved the glory days of playing in the lake and singing in the concerts in Cineca, but I'm actually grateful we can't go back.

I'll always cherish those memories, of course, but I absolutely love who we've both become. I think we're both pretty great."

"Yeah? Me too," Aleksander said. They shared another smile, one truly full of joy. "But as much as I want them to, I don't think our paths from here on out follow one another."

"I know. That's been on my mind too. Sangora, Kurash, and Talohira all need me, and I think Thanatanos will soon need you, *Prince* Aleksander. We both have so much ahead of us." Mara smiled, her eyes glistening with the sad admission. "But that's okay, because I also know that we'll always find our way back to one other."

"That's right. I love that life seems to keep throwing me back to Mara Bartunek no matter what happens—and aren't you excited to see what's still to come for both of us?" Aleksander asked, smiling. "Maybe someday—"

Without warning, she wrapped her arms around him and kissed him deeply. His heart fluttered as he placed one hand on her cheek and ran the other through her dark hair.

With all the ecstasy of their triumphs and victories, all the pain of her past and hope for the future springing out of the very depths of excruciating betrayal and loss, and the pure joy and exquisite sadness of every hello and every goodbye they had ever and would ever share—with all the passionate euphoria and heart-wrenching despair of one final kiss, not knowing if there would ever be another. A bittersweet surrender to the truth.

With all that she was, she kissed him.

And when it was over, they lingered in a tight embrace for several minutes of silence.

"I have wanted to do that for a very long time," Aleksander finally said with a light chuckle. Mara responded with a smile that reached her eyes.

"I know. About time, right?" Mara said, her eyes full of poignant joy. "I am so sorry about our horrible timing."

Before Aleksander could reply, the sound of rustling winds broke the silence. Aleksander lit a ball of flame in his outstretched hand, illuminating the form of a robed figure as he stepped forth from the shadows.

"*Pol is alive, and he is safe.*" The mental voice filled their minds.

Aleksander stepped forward, and the man lowered his hood. Drahomir, the assassin, clad in his crimson mask and dark robes held his hands aloft to show he meant no harm.

"Drahomir." It was all Aleksander could say. In the light of the fireball, Mara and Aleksander could see Drahomir's deformed face with clarity through the shattered portions of his mask. His transition to Faceless had begun, perhaps slowed by the crimson mask's magic. At that moment, Aleksander realized that must be the reason that Drahomir had not succumbed to his earlier wounds.

"*I checked on him for you,*" Drahomir said. "*I thought it was the least I could do.*"

"It was you that led the Faceless away from Balgorod," Mara said in a moment of sudden realization. "It was you…"

"*It was,*" Drahomir replied. "*Thanatan's focus was on his forces in Nitra and Balgorod, so his hold on the wild Faceless in Doftaan was weak. I led them to the battle and was able to lead many of his own Faceless away. I hope it helped. When the Magistrate disappeared and you killed*

Thanatan, I was able to assume full control as the leader of the Faceless and sent them all away."

"Without you, I think they would have killed us all," Mara said, wishing she could look the man in the eye. However, his eyelid was swollen and seemed to be melting into his cheek.

"She's right. You're a hero," Aleksander said. He knew the words sounded awkward, but they had to be said. Much of Balgorod had been destroyed, but without Drahomir's interference, everything would have been utterly destroyed.

"Hardly. I killed your councilors, which allowed Florenta to take control," Drahomir said, shaking his head. "It was before I even knew I had my powers. The Mind-Prison cuff from the slave camp broke my mind, splitting my personality in two—I guess Thanatan somehow took control of my weaker half and used me to his advantage."

Drahomir's mental presence turned sad, akin to a physical frown.

"Are you okay now?" Aleksander asked.

"Thanatan's dead. His hold on me is broken, and I think my mask is now helping me control my other personality, the assassin, rather than subdue the 'real' me," Drahomir said. "I hope what I've done has earned your forgiveness."

Mara stepped forward and wrapped her arms around the assassin. Drahomir responded, unsure, by reciprocating the gesture.

"Oh, Drahomir. There is nothing to forgive," Mara said. "We're both writing the same story. I remember my transition into a Sangoran and how terrified I was. I can only imagine how you're feeling with this new stage in your own path. Just promise me you'll be a better ruler for your people than I was for mine."

*"But before all of this—I'm so sorry—on the tower—I betrayed you, Mara. It's all my fault,"* Drahomir said, falling to his knees, overcome with grief. *"I betrayed you—after you had been nothing but a friend."*

"And what kind of friend would I be if I didn't see you for who you really are?" Mara asked, placing her hand on the cheek visible through the broken mask. A thought crossed Mara's mind, which became an idea, and then a plan. "Where are the Faceless now?"

*"Far away. Northeast of Krim and the Black Sea in the eastern Deadlands,"* Drahomir said.

"If we could discover the magic behind your mask, you could give your people their identities back too," Mara said. "What do you say?"

*"We would like that very much,"* Drahomir said. *"I need to return to my people, as odd as it is to call them that. But what you said about being a leader to them—I fear that without me, they'll revert to wild beasts. I hope to give them purpose more than slaves and killers. When my mind joined theirs, all I could feel was their sadness and pain. But when you all killed Thanatan, do you know what I heard from them?"*

"What?" Mara and Aleksander both asked at once.

*"I could hear them singing. Their joy was the most beautiful thing I've ever felt. It was like a choir of souls, as cheesy as that sounds. I hope to give them a new life. I came here today with one other goal. I came here to warn you."*

"Warn me?"

*"Florenta is dead, but her councilors are not. My people are very good spies, you know—they told me something horrible that you need to know,"* Drahomir answered. He scratched the back of his neck, anxious to deliver the news. *"They're claiming that Mara Bartunek has returned to Doftaan."*

"I don't understand." Mara furrowed her brow.

*"They've set someone up as you, as an Empress of Blood. A fake. Whoever she is, she's ruling from Doftaan now. They are trying to spin Florenta's death as a victory for Sangora, which obviously it is, but now this Mara is a puppet for Florenta's council. I do not know how she is being received, but I needed to tell you."*

"Thank you, my friend," Mara said. "What do you say, stay and celebrate with us?"

*"No, I really do need to get back, but thank you. I did mingle a little bit in the crowd—I kept my hood on, of course. It was the happiest I've been in a while. Thank you,"* Drahomir said, and with that, he vanished into a purple fog to return to his people, the Faceless.

"Well, we can figure that out together," Aleksander said.

"A problem for another day. I have a lot of those," Mara said, letting out a sigh. She absentmindedly brushed her fingers against the long scar on the shaved side of her head. "Today, we celebrate."

They made their way to the front gates of the fortress, which had been destroyed in the conflict, leaving a gaping hole in the front of the building that let in winter's chill.

"Shanthah's lived here a few weeks, and already he's run it into the ground," Aleksander said. Mara laughed.

She approached the ruined wall with her back to Aleksander, and she smiled, for she could still hear Hippo's happy stomping and the sounds of celebration from thousands of her beloved people.

Mara's backless dress revealed many of the scars that life had given her, and Aleksander eyed them with both sadness and pride, knowing each one had a part in helping his friend become the strong woman, the empress, standing before him.

"I am so insanely proud of you," Aleksander said in a soft voice, shaking his head. Mara turned back to him with an appreciative smile. He picked his next words wisely. "You are so loved. Good luck out there."

The sound of their friends' laughter filled the corridor before they emerged from the shadows of the fortress.

As the others approached, Mara stepped toward Aleksander and took his hands in her own. They said nothing for a long moment until she wrapped her arms around him. When she pulled away, she led him by the hand toward the door, but Aleksander stayed rooted on the same spot. She glanced over her shoulder at him.

"Coming?"

"Yeah, I'm just…" he trailed off.

"Just what?" Mara asked.

"Memorizing this moment," he said as their friends reached them. Mara squeezed his hand. He squeezed back. A mutual understanding. Nothing more needed to be said.

"Me too."

"There you two are!" Shanthah exclaimed upon approach. "We're ready for some celebration in the streets!"

Hanna responded by using her powers to summon the flame from a nearby torch and caused it to explode overhead like a firework.

"Hanna gets it!" Josman exclaimed.

"Josman, Kamil, and I found these," Valis said, handing wine glasses to Mara and Aleksander.

"And more importantly, Hanna, Vasilica and I found *these!*" Alia exclaimed as she held up two bottles of Florenta's finest wine pilfered from the usurper's personal cellar. She handed one bottle to Hanna, and they began pouring the bubbling liquid into each glass.

"Then may I be the first to say 'Ža drogasteju, Maru, i Sangoru'!" Shanthah exclaimed. *For love, for Mara, and Sangora!*

"Your pronunciation is getting really good!" Mara exclaimed, hoping Hanna could read her lips.

Hanna gave a thumbs-up and flashed a cheesy grin before kissing Shanthah on the cheek. She poured an extra full glass for Mara; the liquid nearly spilled over the rim, and Mara laughed.

"Whatever Shanthah said!" Josman exclaimed with a cheer as he and Kamil clanked their glasses.

The rest of the group laughed and raised their glasses in a collective toast to a hard-won victory and the friendship that had survived so much pain and loss.

Mara led the way, keeping hold of Aleksander's hand. The group emerged into the cold where they were met with thunderous applause and cheers from the people of the city. As snow began to drift down over the lights and noise of the celebration, Mara looked out over the crowd of humans and Sangorans brought together in joy and peace.

Despite the crowd of thousands, she turned to speak to Aleksander first.

"Hey, Aleks?" Mara asked, still gripping his hand, hesitant to let go. "Thank you, truly. Part of me will *always* love you."

They shared a lingering look before she dropped his hand, her fingers brushing against his as they slipped away. Aleksander felt his words catch in his throat and simply watched her leave with a loving expression of bittersweet pride.

"Go get 'em, Mar."

That final moment ended, and Aleksander rejoined the rest of their friends, who welcomed him with smiles, open arms, and another glass of wine, which he accepted with a smile.

The expectant masses looked to the Empress of Blood with excitement and hope as she turned one last time to face her friends, taking a moment to appreciate each one of them individually. Hanna winked at her, and Mara smiled back.

She let out a deep breath with absolutely no plan in her mind of what she should say. The words of Shanthah's toast were the only ones that came to her mind, but they were perfect.

With a wide smile for the free people of Sangora, Mara raised her glass, which glittered with the light of the fireworks and floating lanterns around her.

"Ža drogasteju, ža Sangoru, i ža vamu!"

*For love, for Sangora, and for you!*

THE STORY CONTINUES IN:

# SPRING ALWAYS COMES

BOOK THREE OF THE
ASCENSION SAGA

# Sangoran Language Guide

If you're a language nerd like me or Mara, check out my ongoing guide of vocabulary and grammar for the Sangoran language at **bit.ly/theascensionsaga**. Working on Sangoran has become a hobby for me, and I've been so happy to have been able to sprinkle it throughout the book. One day, I hope to have a version of Embers (and Ashes if I'm that ambitious) completely translated into Sangoran.

A link to it can also be found on my Instagram account for the Ascension Saga, **@ascensionsaga.**

# GUIDE/GLOSSARY

**Adess:** One of the seven Sangoran states. (Uh-Dess) Geographically located in today's central Ukraine.

**Akademrajon**: The academic district of Doftaan. Home to the University of Doftaan, thousands of students, and hundreds of professors. (Ahk-uh-dem-rah-yohn)

**Alboras:** The Alborans' name for Karpaska. Also, the name of the Alboran people. (All-bore-us)

**Alboran**: A member of the minority ethnic group in Karpaska, oppressed by the Karpaskans. (All-bore-uhn.)

**Aleksander**: Originally from Thanatanos, Aleksander woke up with no memory other than his name carved into his arm. He was later taken by Talohiran slavers and assigned to Slave District Sixty-Eight. He has the ability to create fire. His identity and parts of his past are revealed during *Ashes*.

**Alia Shadid Talohira**: Ex-wife of Valistaran Talohir and father of Valis. Citizen of Kurash with the ability to heal wounds. (Uh-lee-uh)

**Anandlitin**: The Odauthian name for the Faceless.

**Anca**: Mistress of Dusk over the Isle of Krim and General of all Sangoran armies. (Thannish: Ahnk-uh, Sangoran: Ahnts-uh)

**Antan**: A Talohiran spy in Slave District Sixty-Eight.

**Antanasia**: A Mistress of Dusk and heir of Delia over Terman. (Ahn-tahn-ah-see-uh)

**Apolinarius Bartunek**: Pol's full name. Brother of Mara and messenger of King Verahim. (Uh-pole-in-ahr-ee-oos)

**Arcship**: The colossal Odauthian vessel used to escape Odauthlegur Eyja, later used as a slave ship for Talohira.

**Ascended**: Thanatan's term for anyone gifted with abilities.

**Ascension**: Thanatan's term for someone who has been gifted with abilities on their path to become a god.

**Asiri Valdursdottir**: Sister of Halamir. Escaped on the Arcship.

**Balkar**: Captain of the Guard in Odauthlegur Eyja.

**Balgorod**: Capital city of Karpaska. Built on the former site of Belgrade, Serbia.

**Belokej**: The cruel, head slaver in the Talohiran slave camp. (Bell-oh-kezh)

**Bloodvine**: A vine native to Sangora that spreads with spores and grows in organic matter. Its spores cause a horrible sickness, and the toxin within the vine can destroy Sangoran physiology. The Faceless are able to spread their virus through its spores.

**Borek**: A member of Slave District Sixty-Eight that died in the slave camp.

**Born**: A town in Thanatanos.

**The Boulevards**: A shopping and commercial district in Doftaan.

**Bovin**: A minotaur warrior, former member of the Court of Thanatan.

**Bretislaus**: Brother of King Rastislav. Second prince and de-facto king while his brother was an ineffective ruler.

**Bridge of the Two Princes**: A bridge in Laniras named for Verahim and Xanthurias Romus.

**Bukaral**: Capital city of Talohira. (Boo-kuh-rahl) Located where Bucharest, Romania used to stand.

**Ceveržapath**: A large residential neighborhood in Doftaan – translates to "Northwest" in Sangoran. (Tseh-ver-zhuh-pahth)

**Chiropterans**: The name for Sangorans by the extinct inhabitants of the Deadlands.

**Cineca**: Town in Thanatanos responsible for providing much of the wheat for Laniras. Mara and Pol's hometown. (Sin-i-kuh)

**Codruta Talohir**: Previous queen of Sangora, killed by Shanthah. Married to Valistaran Talohir, mother of Valeniya. (Thannish: Kah-drew-tuh, Sangoran: Tsoh-drew-tuh)

**Constanta**: A Sangoran reporter and messenger in Doftaan. (Thannish: Konstanta, Sangoran: Tson-stahn-tuh)

**Connection to Creation**: Thanatan's ability to mentally rearrange matter. Hanna gained this ability from Thanatan.

**Court of Thanatan**: The elite warriors of Thanatan. Disbanded when much of the court was killed when their ship was lost at sea during the events of *Embers*. Surviving members include Valakor, Bovin, and Manitrius.

**Cuff of the Mind-Prison**: A cuff originating from the Deadlands that traps the wearer in a Mind-Prison. The wearer spends the equivalent of a year trapped in their mind for every minute it is on their wrist. Used as a punishment in the Talohiran slave camp and on the Arcship. (Also called 'The Cage.')

**Čahmadoška**: An upscale neighborhood in Doftaan laid out in a grid pattern. The name translates to "Chessboard" in Sangoran.

Home to several of the Mistresses of Dusk. (Chah-kh [as in loch]-mah-doh-sh-kuh)

**Danek**: A Thannish soldier stationed in Zinok.

**Daniel Elafris**: A man from the Deadlands who survived the events that destroyed his homeland by sealing himself in a life support pod. He helped create genetic abilities and is known as The Devil across Thanatanos, Sangora, and Talohira. Much to his dismay, he is worshipped across Sangora and parts of Talohira. Many people swear, 'by Elafris!'

**Daniela Bartunek**: Mara's mother and inhabitant of Cineca. Married to Killian. (Dahn-yell-uh Bar-toon-ek)

**Daria**: A Sangoran reporter and messenger in Doftaan.

**Dashga**: One of the seven Sangoran states. Covers Eastern Ukraine.

**Deadlands**: The land destroyed by the Faceless Virus and a world-wide war. Much of the known world outside of Thanatanos, Talohira, Sangora, Kurash, and United-Baltija. (Includes today's western Europe, North America, and much of the Middle East and northern Africa.)

**Delia**: One of the Mistresses of Dusk under both Codruta and Mara ruling over Terman. (Del-yuh)

**Diana**: A little girl from the Talohiran slave camp that befriended Mara.

**District Sixty-Eight**: The slave district within the Talohiran slave camp that consisted of Mara, Aleksander, Shanthah, Hanna, Drahomir, Kamil, Josman, Pol, and others. Their main duty was to assist in the construction of a new senate building.

**Doftaan**: The capital of Sangora. Doftaan is the name of the capital city as well as one of the seven Sangoran states. (Sangoran: Dohf-tahn, or Thannish: Dohf-tenn) Geographically covers central and northern Romania.

**Drahomir Zimov**: A member of Slave District Sixty-Eight and the Hidden Flame. Has the ability to teleport and summon others to him using shadowy portals. (Drah-ho-meer)

**Dubovparkh**: A residential neighborhood in southwest Doftaan. Translates to "Oak Park" due to its proximity to a large park of oak trees. (Doo-bohv-par-kh)

**Elafris**: 'The Devil' in Thannish, Sangoran, and Talohiran mythology. See also, Daniel Elafris. (Ell-off-riss)

**Elena**: Mara's handmaiden in Doftaan and caretaker while she was in the Wingling House. (Thannish: Ell-eh-nuh, Sangoran: Yell-eh-nuh)

**Elentinus**: A refugee from Odauthlegur Eyja and friend of Halamir. (Ell-enn-tin-oos)

**Emil**: A Walker. Lord Ronin Jakoni's loyal right-hand and a leader amongst the Walkers. (Yem-eel)

**Empress of Blood**: Mara Bartunek's title as ruler of the Sangoran Empire, including Sangora and Talohira. Blood is considered sacred and pure by Sangorans in contrast with the belief in Thanatanos that it is dirty and evil.

**Enforcers**: Florenta's elite soldiers. They wear heavy armor and wield pikes that can fire needle-like arrows.

**Enrieta**: One of Florenta's Mistresses of Dusk. (Thannish: Enn-ree-ett-uh, Sangoran: Yen-ree-et-uh)

**Eva**: A frail girl and friend of Mara in Cineca.

**Faceless**: The undead creatures from the Deadlands with no faces. Instead, they use mental abilities to track their prey. They cannot eat and feel immense hunger but cannot die from natural causes. They can survive most wounds that would kill a human.

**Feren**: A town in Thanatanos.

**Festival of Blood**: A festival to celebrate a variety of events. Blood is held sacred in Sangora and seen as pure and lifegiving.

**Florenta Karpaska**: Mistress of Dusk over Karpaska under both Codruta and Mara. The usurper queen of Sangora. Her magical ability is that her body is far denser than an average human or Sangoran, making her harder to wound, but she constantly grows in size and is now unable to fly due to her immense weight. Queen after Mara Bartunek is ousted from Doftaan. (Flow-rent-uh Kar-pahs-kuh)

**Garden, the:** A neighborhood in Laniras so named because the buildings were arranged in such a way that they resembled roses on a map, in honor of King Romiton's wife, Rose. Further development has since muddled the design.

**Ginka Daktha**: Sister of Lavinia and Zhanna

**Halamir Valdurrson**: Refugee from Odauthlegur Eyja. Outlives the rest of his friends and family on the Arcship after being trapped in a Mind-Prison for many years. (Hall-uh-meer Vah-door-son)

**Hanna Samsa**: Woman from Thanatanos with telekinesis, the ability to move items with her mind. She also has the ability to tap into the Connection to Creation. (Hah-nuh Sahm-suh, not like the English name, Hannah.)

**Hidden Flame**: Former members of Slave District Sixty-Eight and their allies, including soldiers and diplomats. They fight against Thanatan, Florenta, and others that threaten their home and loved ones. Named by Pol Bartunek and led by Rehor Toth.

**Hippo**: The behemoth created by Thanatan but loyal to Mara.

**Horvath**: A captain in the Thannish army, killed in the Battle of Laniras.

**Ihrin Deleanu**: A Mistress of Dusk under both Codruta and Mara. Ruled over Adess. Killed by the assassin. (Eeh-reen)

**Irma**: Ruta's Alboran grandmother and supporter of the revolution. (Ear-muh)

**Itrus**: A Lieutenant General in the Court of Thanatan.

**Jaromir**: Sixth king of Thanatanos, son of Rastislav. Known as 'Jaromir the Fair.' Father of Romiton.

**Jaromirice**: A small town outside the Gate of Jaromir in Laniras.

**Jempratanrajon**: The imperial district. Home of the Empress of Dusk, Mara Bartunek. Translates to "The Area of the Empress." (Yem-pruh-than rah-yohn) Formerly called Haralevarajon, or "Area of the Queen." (Hah-ruh-lev-uh-rah-yohn.)

**Josman Faros**: A man from Melnik in Thanatanos gifted with armored skin when he has a spike in adrenaline. Member of the Hidden Flame and former slave in Slave District Sixty-Eight. (Jaws-min)

**Kadir**: The Supreme One of Kurash. A Mindspeaker with the ability to absorb and channel sunlight into a deadly beam of flame. (Kuh-deer)

**Kaljacjana**: The southern neighborhood of Doftaan. The western prison infested by the Bloodvine is located here. Translates to "Near the wall." (Kahl-yuh-tsyah-nuh)

**Kallus**: A massive spirit warrior loyal to Thanatan and former member of the Court of Thanatan. A cunning tactician.

**Kamil Ramzi**: A Mindspeaker from Kurash with the ability of telepathy and former slave in Slave District Sixty-Eight. Had his tongue cut out for disrespecting Queen Codruta. (Kuh-meal)

**Karim**: Valis's nickname to hide his identity as the son of Valistaran Talohir. A common name in Kurash. (Kuh-reem)

**Karpaska**: One of the seven Sangoran States. Contains two ethnic groups: the Alborans and the Karpaskans. (Car-pahs-kuh) Located in the present-day Albania, Montenegro, and Serbia.

**Kristiana Balana:** Former Minister of Information in Sangora under the rule of the Dakthas

**Killian Bartunek**: A farmer, Father of Mara and Pol, Husband of Daniela, and inhabitant of Cineca in Thanatanos. Killed by Valistaran during the events of *Embers*. (Kill-ee-uhn)

**Kraluv Mek**: The Thannish king's personal guard. Translates from Thannish as "The Sword of the King."

**Krim**: One of the seven Sangoran states. A highly militarized island in the Black Sea governed by General Anca. Located in present-day Crimea.

**Kurash**: A nation southeast of Talohira across the black Sea, ruled by The Supreme One, Kadir. (Koo-rahsh) Covers modern-day Turkey, Azerbaijan, Armenia, Georgia, and parts Syria, Iran, and Iraq.

**Lacramora**: A Mistress of Dusk from Dashga killed during the events of *Embers*. Was regent of Doftaan for a short time. (Thannish: Lahk-rah-more-uh, Sangoran: Lats-ruh-more-uh)

**Lady**: A title for a noble in Sangora, just under Mistress of Dusk.

**Lakrima**: A section leader and coordinator in Shanthah's revolution. (Lahk-reema)

**Laniras**: Capital city of Thanatanos and home of the King. (Luh-nee-russ) The city is divided into several neighborhoods walled off from one another. Often called 'The City of Walls.' Located on the former site of Prague, Czechia.

**Laniras One**: A cramped, poor neighborhood in eastern Laniras with housing buildings between eight to ten floors high, with three to four homes on each floor. Entire extended families often share one small apartment. Movement is not prohibited out of the neighborhood, but people are seldom able to relocate.

**Laniras Two:** Another neighborhood similar to Laniras One.

**Laniras Three**: An upscale neighborhood in Laniras filled with shops lining long boulevards. Several green parks are scattered throughout the neighborhood.

**Laniras Four**: A neighborhood between the river and the city wall. An upscale neighborhood, although not as nice as Laniras Center.

**Laniras Center**: The most upscale neighborhood in Laniras other than the Star of the King. Wealthy residents live here. There are several markets here open to people from every neighborhood.

**Lavinia Daktha**: A cunning Mistress of Dusk under both Codruta and Mara. Regent of Timishuara. Youngest daughter of Liviu and Sanda Daktha. (Luh-vin-ee-uh)

**Likio**: A town in Karpaska, Sangora.

**Liliana**: One of Hanna's prison guards. Nicknamed 'Lucky.' (Lilly-ahna)

**Liviu Daktha**: Former King of Sangora murdered by his wife, Sanda Daktha. (Liv-yu)

**Lucky**: Prison guard in Doftaan. Liliana's nickname.

**Lukas**: A friend of Mara's in Cineca.

**The Magistrate**: A Faceless woman who wears a crimson mask created by Thanatan that restores her humanity. She has extensive telepathic abilities. There have been two Magistrates.

**Malakurash**: A neighborhood in Doftaan mainly populated by Kurashians. The location of the Kurashian embassy. Translates to "Little Kurash."

**Manitrius**: A former member of the Court of Thanatan and companion of Valakor and Bovin. (Mahn-it-ree-oos)

**Mara Bartunek**: A woman from Cineca in Thanatanos. She was enslaved by Arcship slavers for several years before being brought to the Talohiran slave camp and assigned to Slave District Sixty-Eight. After escaping the camp with her friends, she turned against them for a time after Aleksander unknowingly trapped her in the Mind-Prison, and she was betrayed by Drahomir. She was converted into a Sangoran in the Wingling House and eventually rose up the ranks to Mistress of Dusk, and then Queen of Sangora. After Valistaran's apparent death, she named herself Empress of Blood, ruler of all of Sangora and

Talohira. Through her studies in the grand libraries of Doftaan and Bukaral with the ability to enter the Mind-Prison at will in order to learn, plan, or think, she has given herself multiple magical abilities. These include the ability to create lightning with her hands, telekinesis, telepathy, and she speaks many languages. (Mah-ruh [not Meh-ruh] Bahr-toon-ek.

**Maranparkh**: A beautiful, quaint neighborhood surrounded by a luscious park where Sangorans often go to relax. Translates to "Mara's Park." (Mah-ruhn par-kh)

**Marek**: A human, Thannish Lieutenant stationed in Zinok.

**Mariana Vulpe**: an informant in Sangora loyal to Shanthah's revolution.

**Markus**: A male, Alboran Sangoran assisting in Shanthah's revolution.

**Marška**: The Sangoran diminutive form of "Mara."

**Melnik**: A town in Thanatanos known for their fine dairy products. Josman's hometown.

**Mistress of Dusk**: The ruling council of Sangora. Each Mistress of Dusk governs one of the seven Sangoran states. Each state has their own laws for choosing a new Mistress of Dusk, but they are appointed and approved by the queen. So named in reference to the slur 'Night Witch' as 'Dusk comes before the night.'

**Mind-Prison**: A mental state induced by wearing the Cuff of the Mind-Prison. For every minute the wearer has it on their wrist, they spend a year trapped in their mind. Mara developed the ability to return to the Mind-Prison to learn, study, and plan.

**Mindspeaker**: Someone gifted with telepathy. Their abilities range from reading minds to creating illusions and mind control.

**Nandra**: A Sangoran Lady in Florenta's court.

**Naraka**: The colorful, lively artisan district of Doftaan. Translates from Sangoran as "On the River." (Nah-rock-uh)

**Nedelcu**: A former Mistress of Dusk who ruled over Krim before Anca, killed in the Talohiran slave camp during the events of *Embers*. (Thannish: Ned-ell-ku, Sangoran: Ned-ell-tsu)

**Neklan**: The second king of Thanatanos, son of Nezamysl

**Nezamysl**: The first king of Thanatanos, lived roughly 200 years before the events of the Ascension Saga.

**Night Witch**: An offensive slur used to refer to a Sangoran woman.

**Nitra**: A large city in Thanatanos destroyed by Mara and other candidates for Mistress of Dusk during the events of *Embers*. Now infested by Faceless and center of Thanatan's domain.

**Odauthlegur Eyja**: 'The Immortal Island' – Home of the Odauthians, who fled on the Arcship. The island is also home to Yggdrasil, the World Tree, a sentient tree that protects the island. (Oh-doth-le-ghur Eh-uh)

**Ottokar**: The third king of Thanatanos, son of Neklan. Known as 'Ottokar the Butcher' for committing genocide.

**Pata**: A town in Thanatanos.

**Patrik**: A member of Slave District Sixty-Eight who was reassigned to the mines and never escaped.

**Petar Goncharov**: a slave that was killed rescuing Xanthurias.

**Phantom**: Shanthah's nickname amongst the Alborans.

**Pol Bartunek**: Mara's brother, messenger of King Verahim, and member of the Hidden Flame and former inhabitant of Slave

District Sixty-Eight. Short name of Apolinarius. (Like Pole, not Paul.)

**Paudbramah**: A small residential neighborhood in Doftaan. Translates to "South Gate" due to its proximity to Doftaan's south-western gate. (Puh-ood-bruh-mah, with an aspirated H.)

**Paudzuhoth**: The largest residential neighborhood in Doftaan. Literally translate to "Southeast." (Puh-ood-zoo-hahth)

**Pure**: Thanatan's name for the Faceless.

**Queen's Control**: The Queen of Sangora's ability to control other Sangorans. The ability works by sending signals to organic receivers genetically bred into Sangoran wings, developed by the extinct inhabitants of the Deadlands.

**Raksil**: A spirit warrior and current leader of the new Court of Thanatan.

**Raluca**: Sister of Queen Codruta and Mistress of Dusk under both her sister and Mara ruling over Dashga. (Thannish: Rah-luke-uh, Sangoran: Ruh-lu-tsa)

**Rastislav**: Fifth king of Thanatanos, son of Vladislaus. A largely forgotten king who achieved little during his life. Known as 'Rastislav the Useless.'

**Rayna Kotula**: The Thannish captain of the forces stationed in Zinok. (Ray-nuh Kaht-u-luh)

**Rayshel Pilu**: A Sangoran from Doftaan who lost her wings. Companion of Aleksander, Vasilica, and Lavinia. (Ray-shell)

**Rehor Toth**: A wise, portly man from Thanatanos. Leader of the black market and father figure to Mara while in the slave camp. After their escape, Rehor became a diplomat and later ambassador to Sangora. De facto leader of the Hidden Flame. (Ray-hor Tahth)

**Reka**: One of Hanna's prison guards. (Ray-kuh)

**Ripan**: A city in Karpaska, Sangora.

**Romiton Romus**: The seventh king of Thanatanos, son of Jaromir. His son, Verahim now reigns in his stead after he was killed during the events of *Embers*. (Rahm-it-ahn Roh-muhs)

**Ronin Jakoni**: Lord of the Walkers, an extremist group of wingless Sangoran men. (Thannish: Roh-ninn Juh-koh-nee, Sangoran: Ro-neen Yah-ko-nee)

**Rose Romus**: Queen of Thanatanos, Wife of King Romiton Romus, father of Xanthurias and Verahim. Died of an illness she tried to keep secret from her sons and the rest of the country.

**Ruta Vaal**: An Alboran Sangoran woman loyal to Shanthah's rebellion. Teaches Shanthah the Sangoran language and assists in his revolution. (Root-uh Vahl)

**Sanctuary**: The fortress within Zinok, armed with traps and other defenses.

**Sandor Goncharov:** A slave killed rescuing Xanthurias.

**Sangora**: The country and home of the Sangoran people. There are also thousands of human citizens, but they are often treated as a lower class in several of the seven Sangoran states.

Geographically covers much of southern and eastern Europe, including Romania, Serbia, Albania, Montenegro, and Ukraine.

**Sangoran**: A race of humanoids with leathery wings and heightened senses. Inhabitants of the seven Sangoran states and ruled by the Mistresses of Dusk and the Empress of Blood.

Contrary to popular belief, they do not naturally have sharp claws and fangs, although some do sharpen both.

**Sangoran Empire:** The empire comprising Talohira and Sangora, ruled by the Empress of Blood.

**Sanda Daktha**: former queen of Sangora before Queen Codruta. Committed genocide of a majority of male Sangorans, including King Liviu Daktha. (Sand-uh Dahk-thuh)

**Sapez**: A town in Karpaska, Sangora. (Saw-pez)

**Sevastaan**: A militarized city in Krim. Site of Sangora's highest security prison. (Seh-vahst-ahn, or Thannish: Say-vahst-enn)

**Shanthah Kalen**: A member of the Hidden Flame, former scout of the Kraluv Mek, former inhabitant of Slave District Sixty-Eight. Known as 'the Phantom' to the Alboran people. Has the ability to make himself, and others, to a limited extent, invisible. (Shan-thuh, with a 'th' not a 't' sound.)

**Slave District Sixty-Eight**: The 68th building district of the Talohiran slave camp. Members included Aleksander, Mara, Hanna, Shanthah, Kamil, Josman, Pol, Drahomir, Patrik, Borek, and Antan.

**Sorina**: A Sangoran woman loyal to Shanthah's revolution. (Thannish: So-ree-nuh, Sangoran: Sor-inn-uh)

**Soreana**: Florenta's Mistress of Dusk over Karpaska after she became Queen. (Sore-ee-ah-nuh)

**Spires of Doftaan, the**: A neighborhood in Doftaan covered in tall spires. These spires contain housing, businesses, forges, markets, schools, and more. The towers are mainly made of dark stone and tipped with slender spires or onion-shaped domes.

**Spirit armor**: Suits of armor ranging from six to twelve feet tall used to house the minds and spirits of dead warriors to allow them to keep fighting after death.

**Spirit Warriors**: See 'Spirit Armor.'

**Star of the King, the:** The most elite neighborhood in Laniras housing the royal palace, the headquarters of the Kraluv Mek and Court of Thanatan, as well as the homes of many nobles. The rooves of the neighborhood have a distinct greenish tinge that matches the color of the Thannish flag.

**Supreme One**: The ruler of Kurash. The Supreme one is addressed as "The Supreme One who is Named…"

**Talohira**: Country east of Sangora and Thanatanos on the coast of the Black Sea. Ruled by Valistaran Talohir until his apparent death when it was annexed by Sangora. At the time of *Ashes*, it is in revolt and civil war. (Tall-oh-hee-ruh)

**Tal-Ahosh**: Capital of Kurash – the 'City of the Sun.' (Tall-Ah-Hosh)

**Telekinetik**: Someone with telekinetic abilities able to move objects with their mind.

**Teleportation Pillar** (Telepillar) A pillar created by the extinct inhabitants of the Deadlands. Use of the teleportation pillar eliminated the need to travel vast distances by airplane, car, or train. All but a few were destroyed in the great war that ravaged the land now known as the Deadlands.

**Terman**: The northernmost state of Sangora. (Like 'German') Covers western Ukraine.

**Thanatan**: God of Thanatanos. Has the ability to tap into the Connection to Creation. (Thann-uh-tahn)

**Thanatanos**: The country West of Sangora and Talohira. Exclusively Human citizens. Thanatanos has several major cities, including the capital, Laniras, Vudapas, and Nitra before its destruction. The main population is concentrated in Laniras and Vudapas, with dozens of towns scattered across the country. A Thannish citizen is called a "Than." (Thann-uh-tahn-oss)

**Thannish**: The language of Thanatanos and Talohira, and the way to refer to someone from Thanatanos. (Like 'Spanish')

**Timishuara**: One of the seven Sangoran states. Governed by Mistress Lavinia. (Tim-ee-shua-ruh) Covers Serbia and parts of Romania.

**Turnava**: A town in Thanatanos. (Turn-uh-vah)

**United Baltija**: A large, but sparsely inhabited country surrounding the Baltic Sea north of Sangora. Inhabited by both Sangorans and humans and largely unknown to the rest of the world. Formerly Lithuania, Latvia, Estonia, western Russia, and parts of Southern Finland. (United Ball-tee-uh.)

**Valakor**: A spirit warrior and former leader of the Court of Thanatan. (Val-uh-kohr)

**Valdur**: Father of Halamir and Asiri. (Vall-duur)

**Vah**: A great river in Thanatanos.

**Valeniya Talohir**: Daughter of Valistaran and Codruta. Has the ability to mentally find anyone, no matter where they are. Overuse of her ability has rattled her mind. Valistaran used her ability to find individuals gifted with abilities and threw them into his slave camp. Valeniya is the female variation of the Thannish name 'Valistaran.' (Vuh-len-ee-uh Tal-o-heer)

**Valistaran Talohir**: Former High King of Talohira and Sangora. Formerly married to Alia and Codruta. Father of Valis and Valeniya. Thought to have died during the events of *Embers*, and his country was annexed by Sangora. Made Mara his queen, leading to her rise to Empress of Blood. Has the ability to create dark flame. (Val-ist-air-inn)

**Valistaran Talohir II**: See Valis. Named after his father. Goes back to using only his mother's surname, Shadid, during *Ashes*.

**Valis Talohir-Shadid**: Son of Valistaran and Alia. Has the ability to create lightning with his hands. (Val-iss)

**Vasilica Radu**: Mara's lieutenant and Mistress of Dusk over Doftaan. (Thannish: Vah-sill-i-kah, Sangoran: Vuh-sill-ee-tsuh)

**Verahim Romus**: Eighth King of Thanatanos after his father, Romiton's death. (Verr-i-heem Ro-moos)

**Vinia**: The diminutive form of the name 'Lavinia.'

**Vladislaus**: Fourth king of Thanatanos. Son of Ottokar. Known as 'Vladislaus the Contrite.'

**Vudapas**: A large city on the border of Sangora and Thanatanos ravaged by the Thannish-Talohiran war. (Vuda-pahs) Located where Budapest, Hungary once stood.

**Vydraka**: A neighborhood in Doftaan with many markets north of the river. Translates to "View of the River." (Veed-rah-kuh)

**Walkers**: Sangorans that have severed their wings to avoid being controlled by the Queen's Control. Many Walkers are extremist followers of Ronin Jakoni.

**Weapon of Ages Past**: A nuclear weapon from the Deadlands discovered by the Hidden Flame and Mara's forces. Known as the Death Bringer or Forbidden Weapon.

**Xanthurias Romus**: Prince of Thanatanos and brother of Verahim. Killed by Mara in the Siege of Nitra. (Zan-thur-ee-uhs)

**Yggdrasil**: The World Tree, a sentient Tree that protected Odauthlegur Eyja. (Uug-dra-seel)

**Zinok**: A city in the mountains within the Sanctuary fortress.

**Zvužajecy**: A neighborhood in eastern Doftaan. The prison holding Hanna was located here. Translates to "The Narrows" due to its narrow streets. (Zz-voo-zha-yeh-ts-ee)

**Zhanna Daktha**: Eldest daughter of Liviu and Sanda Daktha. A leader of United Baltija, and sister of Lavinia. (Zhahn-uh Dahk-thuh)

# Dear reader,

From the bottom of my heart, thank you for taking a chance on this world and these characters that I have come to love like very real friends and family. I hope you enjoyed the first two books of the Ascension Saga, which will conclude with *Spring Always Comes*. A prequel, *Her Anthem for Ruin* and a new sequel saga within this world will follow.

Anyone who knows me knows that I hate endings. I cry like a baby whenever a favorite TV show, book, or movie series ends, and so I never intend to stop writing or building this world that I love so much. I will never write the words 'the end' in any of my books.

I would also like to thank all of my writing Instagram friends who have supported me through this adventure.

My biggest thank you obviously goes to my biggest fan (and I'm her biggest fan, too) – my lovely wifey, Shay.

If you happen to work for a streaming service or in movie production, contact me **right this moment** because, well, duh.

Brock Mays

9 781733 816533